The story of Josephine Cox is as extraordinary as anything in her novels. Born in a cotton-mill house in Blackburn, she was one of ten children. Her parents, she says, brought out the worst in each other, and life was full of tragedy and hardship – but not without love and laughter. At the age of sixteen, Josphine met and married 'a caring and wonderful man', and had two sons. When the boys started school, she decided to go to college and eventually gained a place at Cambridge University, though was unable to take this up as it would have meant living away from home. However, she did go into teaching, while at the same time helping to renovate the derelict council house that was their home, coping with the problems caused by her mother's unhappy home life – and writing her first full-length novel. Not surprisingly, she then won the 'Superwoman of Great Britain' Award, for which her family had secretly entered her, and this coincided with the acceptance of her novel for publication.

Josephine gave up teaching in order to write full time. She says 'I love writing, both recreating scenes and characters from my past, together with new storylines which mingle naturally with the old. I could never imagine a single day without writing, and it's been that way since as far back as I can remember.' Many of her previous novels of North Country life are available from Headline and are immensely popular.

'Bestselling author Josphine Cox has penned another winner' *Bookshelf*

'Hailed quite rightly as a gifted writer in the tradition of Catherine Cookson' *Man*

'Guaranteed to tug at th
romantics' *Sunday Post*

Outcast

and

Alley Urchin

and

Vagabonds

Josephine Cox

headline

The right of Josephine Cox to be identified as the Author of
the Work has been asserted by her in accordance with
the Copyright, Designs and Patents Act 1988.

OUTCAST first published in Great Britain in 1991
by HEADLINE BOOK PUBLISHING

ALLEY URCHIN first published in Great Britain in 1991
by HEADLINE BOOK PUBLISHING

VAGABONDS first published in Great Britain in 1992
by HEADLINE BOOK PUBLISHING

First published in this omnibus edition in 2005
by HEADLINE BOOK PUBLISHING

A HEADLINE paperback

10 9 8 7 6 5 4 3 2 1

ISBN 0 7553 2654 7

Typeset in Times by Avon DataSet Ltd,
Bidford-on-Avon, Warwickshire

Printed and bound in Great Britain by
Clays Ltd, St Ives plc

HEADLINE BOOK PUBLISHING
A division of Hodder Headline
338 Euston Road
London NW1 3BH

www.headline.co.uk
www.hodderheadline.com

Outcast

Dedication

Like all mothers everywhere, I have children who instill in me constant feelings of inadequacy, frustration, and helplessness – not to mention anger and utter despair at times! But overriding all of these are the rewarding emotions such as joy, gratitude and shameless, bursting pride in their every achievement.

I thank God for giving my husband Ken and me two wonderful sons, Spencer and Wayne, who I pray will always face with strength and courage whatever obstacles life may put in their way.

This book is also for Elsie May, who befriended and loved me when I lost my own dear mother. Goodbye, Elsie. We'll never forget you, sweetheart.

Foreword

My apologies to those historians who are familiar with convict transporation to Australia in the 1880s. Although I am aware that most of those transported to Western Australia were male, for the purpose of this story I have introduced female convicts, bearing in mind that countless numbers of women were made to suffer the same fate as their male counterparts when being transported to other coasts during earlier days.

Many of these wretches had committed crimes no more offensive than being hungry and ragged. There were many who were branded ruffians and murderers although they were innocent. But in the hearts of each and every one, there was always hope. There must always be hope.

Such hope, and the memories of those who had loved or betrayed her, kept Emma's belief that the day must come when she would seek out those who had loved her, and she would come face to face once again with her betrayers.

Part One

1860

Bad Blood

' —These wretches, who ne're lived, went on in nakedness, and sorely stung by wasps and hornets, which bedew'd their cheeks with blood, that, mixed with tears, dropp'd to their feet . . . '

(Vision of) HELL, Dante

Chapter One

'Emma Grady, you're on the road to damnation! You have it in you to become a woman of the streets. A harlot! And as God is my judge, I will not have such a low creature under my roof!' Here the woman paused and a man's voice intervened, addressing the bowed head of the girl in low and trembling tones.

'Your good aunt sees in you what I have always feared and you will do well to heed her words. I believe the day must surely come when you sink beneath the evil bred in you – unless, by God's hand, you mend your ways. If you do not, you will be banished from this house! Disowned! Struck from our lives as though you never existed!' Caleb Crowther was a man of enormous physique – tall, with large ungainly bones. His movements were slow and methodical and his tone of voice – honed by his duties in the Law Courts – was deliberate and authoritative.

That same unenviable office yielded Caleb Crowther considerable status both within the sizeable community of Blackburn and throughout Lancashire, in whose courtrooms he regularly presided over the trials and tribulations of hapless law-breakers. There was many a petty thief or villain who had been unfortunate enough to have Caleb

Crowther scowl down upon them. One condemning look from those piercing blue eyes was enough to render strong men weak. His features were altogether fearsome, close-together blue eyes above wide high cheekbones, a broad pale expanse of forehead, and a dark tangled mass of beard and whiskers. He could shrink the spirit of a man, but he could not diminish that of Emma Grady, his niece and ward, and such knowledge only served to infuriate him. As he drew himself up to continue his onslaught, a more gentle voice spoke out.

'Please Caleb, don't be too harsh on the child.' This feeble-looking man had risen from his sick-bed and struggled down to the drawing-room where he now defended Emma – this beloved girl who had been raised wrongly believing herself to be his daughter. The truth of her parentage would go with him to the grave – leaving only one other holding the grim shameful secret. 'She's young,' he continued, leaning against the door-jamb for support, 'the lass is only fifteen, and can't help her high spirits.'

'Fifteen or fifty, the devil takes no mind!' thundered Caleb Crowther as he turned to glare at the intruder. Then, upon a sly warning glance from his wife Agnes, he tempered his tone with a little gentleness as he further addressed the other man. 'Thadius, I know how great your affection is for your only child. But, think man! Think to the child's mother, passed on these many years. Have you forgotten the anguish she caused you? Don't you see her bad blood rising in this daughter of hers?' Seeing the other man momentarily falter beneath his cruel words, he stepped forward gesturing for his wife to do the same. When, instinctively, Emma also ventured to assist her papa, Caleb Crowther lifted his hand, and in a forbidding voice told her,

'Stay where you are!' Then, returning his attention to Thadius Grady, he said, 'Agnes will see you safely back to your room.'

The tall dark-haired woman allowed her fragile brother to lean his weight against her arm. Without reassurance or word of comfort, she led him out of the drawing-room and into the spacious wood-panelled hallway. On painful steps, he went with her reluctantly. Their destination was a large room at the rear of the great house, a room from which, even though it was flooded with sunshine on a summer's day such as this, Thadius Grady would never again emerge a fit and healthy man. The lung disease which had struck him down was relentlessly draining away his life.

In the distance, he could still hear the condemning voice of his brother-in-law, Caleb Crowther, and his heart went out to that dear affectionate girl, made to suffer such a biting tongue. It grieved him that he could do nothing to ease her burden. It grieved him deeper still knowing that it was his own misguided weakness and blind trust that had placed both Emma and himself at the mercy of these two pompous devils.

For a long time after her darling papa had gone, Emma stood before her uncle, his torrent of accusations crushing her ears, but never bruising her heart; for she believed, most fervently, that of the two of them, *he* was the sinner. His wickedness was inherent in his dark thoughts, in that relentless voice which spewed them out, and in the way he brought his narrow penetrating eyes to bear on her. She wondered if, in the whole of his being, there had ever been one kind or loving thought, one gentle inclination or a breath of compassion for those less fortunate than himself. She believed not. Yet, Emma pitied him, for she had never seen his serious eyes light up with joy; never heard his laughter – only his condemnation that laughter was frivolous and a sure example of a worthless character; she had never seen him raise his face indulgently to the sun or pause for a moment to enjoy a blossom-scented breeze against his skin; not once had she witnessed his fingers reaching out to touch another person in genuine love or friendship. To her, all of these things were heaven-sent and because she treasured them – because it lifted her own spirits to laugh, to sing and to join hands with another of her own age while they ran freely beneath God's blue sky – she was condemned to stand before him like a sinner, while he poured scorn and damnation down on her head. But he would not make her feel like a sinner. Never! For, she was not, and, even if only her darling papa and her own heart believed that innocence, it was enough.

'You are a disgrace! Your brazen behaviour brings shame to this family, and I will not have it! Do you hear me, Emma Grady? I will *not* have it!' As he continued to glower at her, Emma felt the temptation to protest that she had not meant any harm nor seen any shame in her actions. But it would have been to no avail, for her uncle was not a man to listen nor was he a man who forgave easily. She would be punished, she was sure, just as she had been time and time again just for being young, for daring to laugh out loud and for being so shameful as to talk to those who had the misfortune of being 'born beneath' her. And the crime was all the more wretched if that unfortunate happened to be a boy, for then she was branded a hussy of the worst order!

'Out of my sight!' came the instruction now. 'Go to your room at once. Your aunt and I must consider this latest incident and see what must be done!' That said, he turned from her holding his back stiff and straight. With the slightest curtsy, Emma took her leave from the room, thinking that he must have read her mind when his voice sailed after her, 'You will *not* call in on your papa. Go straight to your room . . . at once!' She might well have disobeyed him and stolen into her papa's room for a forbidden kiss, but, as she hurried down the hall, with her gaze anxiously intent on the narrow corridor, which led to her papa's room, the tall upright figure of Agnes emerged, her boots kicking out the hem of her long taffeta skirt and creating an impressive echo as they tapped the ceramic floor tiles. At once, she swept towards Emma, coming to a halt only when they were face to face.

'You're a great heartache to your papa,' accused the older woman, her hand resting elegantly against her skirt for a moment and her dark eyes riveted to the strong youthful features. 'You'll be the death of him yet – mark my words!' If she expected the girl before her to flinch and cower in the wake of such vicious taunts, Agnes Crowther was disappointed. For when Emma brought her gaze to rest on that overbearing countenance, it was not fear or guilt that was reflected in her warm animated eyes, but strength – the kind of challenging strength which only served to infuriate those who tried to belittle her. She looked a moment longer at that stiff and forbidding figure, at the staunch manly face and the dark hair coiled like a snake above each ear. She noted the two most impressive characteristics of her papa's sour-faced sister: the manner in which she held her head back, as though something distasteful had just presented itself to her, causing her to look down her nose in a most uncomfortable fashion; and her peculiar habit of joining her hands together and pressing them close to her breast as if she were praying.

As Emma momentarily regarded the woman before her, Agnes simultaneously contemplated her. She actively disliked this blatantly defiant child of her own kith and kin, for the girl possessed such a rebellious spirit, was far too imaginative, too talented and too temptingly attractive and there was too much of a blossoming woman in the gentle round curves of her small winsome figure. Those exquisite oviform eyes, which always seemed to be secretly smiling, were a shade too grey, too striking and too bold, and her rich thick hair was too velvety, and abounding with deep, undisciplined waves.

Agnes Crowther found herself mentally comparing the attributes of this wayward girl to those of her own nondescript and friendless daughter, Martha. A tide of jealousy surged within her, and her tongue lashed out all the sharper to disguise her bitter feelings. 'Unless you need to feel the sting of my cane against your knuckles, you will remove that insolent expression from your face this instant.' She trembled to control her voice.

Painfully aware that they were not very far from her papa's room, Emma slowly lowered her gaze. The figure before her gave a long audible shudder, followed by the curt enquiry, 'I take it you have been ordered to your room, while your uncle and I decide on a suitable punishment?' She waited for Emma's nod. Upon its receipt, she issued the impatient instruction, 'You may go. Do *not* leave your room until you are sent for!' Agnes Crowther stood her ground, while her scornful eyes watched the girl move out of sight.

At the top of the staircase Emma turned left, passing

beneath the endless array of impressive portraits depicting Caleb Crowther's ancestors. Each wore the same arrogant smile; each held a stance that spoke of self-importance; and each was encased in elaborate and magnificent golden frames of immense proportion. Emma recalled how, on the day of her arrival in this grand house some twelve long months before, there had been no portraits; only grey spaces on the wall, where they had once hung. Soon afterwards, they had reappeared – no doubt having been purchased back from the person who had secured them against a debt. But, these portraits – re-hung amid great fuss and ceremony – did *not* impress Emma. 'Sour-faced and comical,' she called them. Emma was not unaware of the circumstances under which her papa had brought her to this house for she had overheard the servants discussing it and she was of the same opinion as them – that her papa had been used. Like all of God's creatures he had a weak and vulnerable flaw in his character – his was that he could never see the greed in others. But this just caused Emma to love him even more. She knew deep in her heart that whatever he had done – however disastrous the consequences might be – he had done it for her with the best intentions and fondest love. Before his pained and watchful eyes, she was always careful to make him believe she was happy in this awful house, when, if the truth were to be told, she was far more content out of it. She would go on pretending for as long as necessary, for Emma didn't intend to be the cause of her papa leaving this world a sadder man.

When Agnes Crowther was satisfied that her niece was safely on her way, she resumed her steps. On entering the drawing-room she immediately crossed to the fireplace where, with a short impatient tug on the bell-pull, she summoned a maid. Presently a small round female of about forty years appeared. She was bedecked in dark attire, save for the frilly white cap resting on top of her greying brown hair and a little collar of the same sparkling white, fastened loosely at her neck.

'Yes, ma'am?' spoke the homely little figure, as it bent at the knee and brought its enquiring brown eyes to bear on the lady of the house.

'Miss Grady is confined to her room. She is to be denied all meals until dinner tomorrow evening.' When the eyes looking upon her grew wide with surprise, Agnes Crowther took a small step forward and, with her head high and her hands folded in that familiar pose of prayer, she added in an impatient voice, 'Do I make myself clear?'

'Very well, ma'am.'

'Good! . . . You may go.' She gave an impatient wave of her hand and was obviously pleased to see the figure depart in great haste. She would not have felt so satisfied if she had witnessed the scene which took place below stairs on the housekeeper's return. Mrs Manfred relayed the mistress's instructions, which were at once greeted by a barrage of protest.

'T'aint fair!' declared Amy, the little dark-haired scullery maid who, despite Mrs Manfred's efforts to cultivate her in knowing her place in the hierarchy of a gentleman's house, had never acquired the instinct to keep certain opinions to herself. 'Them two's allus picking on poor Miss Grady.'

'Hey!' remonstrated Cook, a large and squashy, domineering woman, with a rolled halo of iron-grey hair and bright hazel eyes which, at this very moment, were sending warning signals to the pouting Amy. 'You'd do better not to wag that busy little tongue of yours, my girl. If the master should set foot in that door and catch you being disrespectful, you'd be out on the streets and begging fer yer living.' Here, Mrs Manfred intervened.

'Amy, isn't it time you began preparing the vegetables for dinner? . . . Go on, child!' she urged when the girl showed hesitation. The look on the housekeeper's face told the young maid that she'd gone as far as was wise.

'All right . . . I'm going!' she declared indignantly.

When the scullery door was closed, it was Cook who spoke first, saying in hushed tones as she poured herself and Mrs Manfred a small measure of good dark port, 'That one's a cheeky little bugger! But the lass is right all the same. Poor Miss Grady does seem allus to be in their bad books.' Pointing a thumb upwards and rolling her eyes towards the ceiling, she carefully lowered herself into a stout chair. Laying her chubby arms across the pine table-top, she began rolling the glass of port between her hands to warm it. 'The Lord only knows what'll become of Miss Grady when Mr Grady goes.' She shook her head slowly from side to side and, lowering her voice, she leaned forward to face the housekeeper who was now seated at the opposite side of the table. 'They'll have a free hand ter to do as they likes then, won't they, eh?' By the fearful look in her bright wide eyes, and the quick manner in which she threw a great gulp of port into her mouth, it was clear that the thought horrified her.

Not being one to readily participate in gossip below stairs, the housekeeper sat quietly, taking intermittent dainty and careful sips from the port glass, all the while thoughtful, her eyes downcast and with a deeply troubled look in them. She had no liking for the master and mistress.

Indeed, if the truth were to be told, she positively disliked them. It was extremely difficult for her to regard them as her employers, for it was Mr Grady who had taken her on as housekeeper when he had resided in the smart area of Blackburn, up by Corporation Park. Five years she'd been with him and Miss Grady, five satisfying and happy years during which she had been much more than just housekeeper. She'd grown close to Miss Grady, caring for her affectionately because the child had no mother to love her – Mrs Grady having lost her life some years before in scandalous and unfortunate circumstances best forgotten. But what a sweet darling girl Miss Grady was. A little hotheaded and wayward at times, maybe, but that was all part of her charm. For all her obstinacy and exuberance she was a caring creature, gentle of spirit and warm of heart; it grieved Mrs Manfred to see how desperately unhappy the girl had become. The only light in her life was her father – and he was fading fast. Mrs Manfred wondered why it was that the good Lord had seen fit to weaken and cripple such a good man – so much so that, in appointing his sister and her husband as both executors of his affairs and wards to his only child, his judgment had been severely impaired.

'I've allus said what a wrench that must have been fer you to come and bide in this house. One minute living in town, and the next, being fotched ter the countryside of outer Breckleton, at the beck and call of them two.' Here, Cook jerked a thumb upwards again. 'They may *act* proud and superior,' she went on, 'but I'm telling yer, Mrs Manfred, I've said it afore and I'll say it again, if it hadn't been fer Mr Grady and his money, well, them two would be no more than beggars! Y'remember the state o' this place when yer all arrived? I were the only one left ter mek the best of an impossible job. All the silver gone. Money owed everywhere. Y'know, m'dear, fer all ye've been here over a year now, there's *still* things I could tell yer. Things ter shame the pair of 'em!'

'Excuse me. I must go.' Mrs Manfred had no wish to hear yet again how Caleb Crowther was a womanizer and a gambler who had squandered the fortune his father had left him – a fortune built up in the City through sound business sense, for it was not his rector's pittance that had lined Crowther senior's pockets. Nor did she care for another long and detailed account of how Agnes Crowther was a woman of disgracefully extravagant tastes, having a most unhealthy appetite for expensive jewellery and fine parties. She had heard it all before – and it had sickened her.

Thadius Grady had worked ceaselessly to build up his holdings in the cotton mills hereabouts – an ailing heritage he'd received from his father but one which now, thanks to his persistent efforts, was a thriving industry. How unfortunate that the two mills were to be entrusted to the Crowthers.

There was one other viper in this nest, and that was Martha Crowther. She was the same age as Miss Grady, but as different in character from her as chalk from cheese. Mrs Manfred for one would not be sorry to see that spoilt young madam shortly depart for the grand expensive school for ladies somewhere down south. Good riddance to her, that's what *she* said!

'I've been such a fool! Such a blind, stupid fool!' Thadius Grady looked up, his pale eyes glittering with tears. 'I've betrayed her . . . done her a terrible wrong that can't be put right. It's too late . . . too late, don't you see, Mrs Manfred?'

As he struggled to pull himself upright in the bed, the effort proved to be too much and, after a severe bout of coughing, he allowed Mrs Manfred to make him more comfortable. 'I've let her down,' he murmured, as though to himself, 'I've let my darling daughter down!'

'No . . . no.' Mrs Manfred tucked the bedclothes about him for, despite this being a warm summer's day, she could see him visibly shivering. 'You did what you thought was best for the child. You always have.'

'But I've turned it all over to them, don't you see? There was no one else and Mrs Crowther is my sister after all. Half the inheritance would have been hers anyway if only she hadn't angered Father with her choice of husband.' His voice grew quieter, and he continued in a more intimate tone, as though he was afraid they might be overheard, 'There were *other* reasons also why I entrusted my daughter to Caleb Crowther . . . and to his wife.' His voice strengthened, as he pleaded, 'Oh, Mrs Manfred, if only they would show more understanding towards her, more tolerance. Will she be all right when I'm gone? Oh, I fear so!'

Mrs Manfred smiled encouragingly, 'Don't you fret now, Mr Grady,' she told him in a firm voice, 'Your daughter is of strong character and well you know it. She'll be fine . . . just fine.' But however much she wished that to be so, there was little belief of it in her heart and even less conviction in her voice.

A silence followed. Then, suddenly, Thadius Grady let out a great heart-rending sigh, followed by the murmured question, 'What date is it?'

'Why, it's Sunday, August 16th.'

'What year?'

'Bless you, Mr Grady . . . it's the year of our Lord 1860.'

'Almost a year to the day we came to this house . . . you, me and Miss Grady. Oh, dear God! Would that I were strong again!'

There were tears in Mrs Manfred's eyes as she comforted him. 'Ssh now.' She was tempted to say how he *would* be strong again, but it was Sunday and such lies would be tantamount to blasphemy. Instead, she went to a drawer in the dark elaborately-carved sideboard, and took from it a bottle of medicine and a spoon. Returning to the big brass bed, she poured a measure of the brown liquid into the spoon, stood the bottle on the small circular table by the bed, and then eased one hand beneath Thadius Grady's thin bony neck, while with the other, she touched the spoon against the blueness of his lips. 'Come on now,' she coaxed him, 'sip it down.' That done, she crossed to the long casement window where she gently pulled the heavy tapestry curtains part-way together to shut out the bright sunlight. She took a final glance at the now-sleeping figure, before, on tiptoe, she left the room.

A few moments later, Mrs Manfred hurried along the dark corridor which led from Thadius Grady's room, and into the brighter hall. From there she climbed the broad impressive staircase, hurriedly, before peering eyes might see her and sharp tongues find questions to put to her.

Meanwhile, Emma gazed out of the window, her trim figure leaning against the window-frame, her small fingers playing with the curtain-tassle and with a pitifully forlorn expression on her face. Her thoughts wandered: first they were downstairs with her papa, then they were back at their old home in Blackburn town where, from the window of her bedroom she could see the rolling splendour of Corporation Park. How could she ever forget that wonderful day in October 1857, less than three years ago. It was her thirteenth birthday – the very same day on which Corporation Park was opened. What memories! The mayor and other dignitaries dressed up in the regalia of office and thousands of people from all over the borough assembled to see the park opened. After the opening ceremony, they all surged through the arcuated gateways, some of the women wearing clogs and shawls, others dressed in finer fashion and the men sporting an assortment of flat cloth caps and tall black hats. Oh, the excitement of it all!

Emma missed the old house, and her nostalgia was heightened by the fact that, in those early days, her papa had been well – always laughing and ready to play games with her, always enterprising at his work and filled with enthusiasm.

Making a weary little sigh, Emma leaned forward into the window, her attention drawn by the sight of a threshing machine in a nearby field. For a moment she was enthralled by it, her eager gaze following its trail of steam as it got underway. Such things had always held a fascination for Emma, and it was that same curiosity which had caused all the terrible fuss today – innocent though the little adventure had started out.

Now her thoughts came back to her papa and a wave of guilt swept over her. 'Oh, Papa!' she murmured, a tremble in her voice, 'I'm sorry.'

So engrossed in her thoughts was she that, when Mrs Manfred's voice murmured in her ear, 'Will you never learn, Miss Grady!' she gave a start, before realizing who it was, and threw herself into the little woman's arms.

'Did you see him, Manny?' she asked, addressing the woman by a familiar nickname. 'It was *my* fault that he got up from his bed. Oh, Manny, he looks so desperately ill – and I can't go to him! They won't *let* me go to him!' She was crying bitterly now, more from anger than from sorrow.

'I know, child . . . I know.' Mrs Manfred took Emma towards the settle, where she gently eased her away, to hold her at arm's length. 'Oh, child . . . child! What are we going to do with you? What on earth possessed you to go wandering away over the meadows? And then, to hob-nob with the river-people?' She raised her eyebrows sharply and shook her head from side to side as she chastised in a lower voice, 'You know how your Uncle Caleb – yes, and your papa – dislike those people!' She did not explain how Thadius Grady's animosity towards the river-folk had come about, how it had been common talk for some fifteen years back when Emma had been no more than a wee bairn in arms. She hoped Emma would never learn how her mama had taken one of the river-men for a lover, and how the cruel gossip had labelled Mrs Grady a 'loose and shameless woman' who thought so little of her husband and tiny daughter that she could blatantly 'flaunt herself at other men.' It was during one of her illicit visits to her lover's arms that there had been a terrible event which had had such tragic and far-reaching consequences.

'But *why* does he dislike the river-people so much, Manny? Why?'

'It isn't for you, nor me, to ask the reason, my girl. All you need to do is to respect his wishes. It's a good thing for you, my girl, that he thought fit to see this morning's escapade as an impulsive prank!' Mrs Manfred's tone of voice betrayed her absolute disapproval of Emma's behaviour.

'Oh, Manny, are you so shocked? Are you so ashamed of me?' Emma asked. What she had done *must* have been dreadful or Manny wouldn't have chided her like that. She had no business even talking to the river-people knowing how her papa felt towards them. Emma's heart shrank within her. Why was she always so disobedient?

'I have to say I *am* shocked, Miss Grady, though, after knowing you this long while, perhaps I shouldn't be. Oh, but to be found with a young bargee, boldly laughing together on the banks of the canal! You, with your bare legs dangling in the water and he stripped naked to the waist!' Mrs Manfred's expression reflected the utmost despair. 'But worse! Oh, my dear, much, much worse . . . today is the Sabbath! And you straight from church!'

Emma fully realized that it *was* a bad thing she had done, but, at the time, she hadn't seen it like that at all. After the stuffy confines of the church, the sun had struck warm against her face, the breeze had moved the fields of grass so that they looked like a rippling sea of green, and, drawn further and further into nature's splendid beauty, she'd wandered away from the familiar footpath, towards the cool flowing canal, where the colourful barges bobbed about on the water and the sound of laughter emanated from every one. Laughter of the kind she had not heard in such a long while; laughter which infected and brightened her heart with rare happiness; laughter which reminded her of a different world than the one which now held her securely bound and caged. In that special moment, she had felt unfettered; and when she had seen that dark head skimming the surface of the water, something deep within her had cried out to be free also. 'I did it without thinking, Manny,' she said now, although she had given no such explanation to her uncle. She had felt too much anger at how he had embedded his walking-stick in the young bargee's back again and again until the flesh split open and the blood covered his shoulders like a mantle. Emma was convinced that if the men from the barges hadn't heard her screaming and dashed out to pull the young man safely away, Caleb Crowther would have beaten every last breath from his body. The enraged barge-men might have done the very same to Caleb Crowther had it not been for the intervention of the men from the village, together with Caleb Crowther's threat to bring the authorities down on every man-jack of the river-people.

'Have you no idea of the trouble you caused, child? Frightening ordinary god-fearing villagers who answered the alarm that you were missing! You said *nothing*, child! . . . You told *no-one* of your intention to wander away from the path between the church and home!' Mrs Manfred's voice was unusually harsh, but, on seeing Emma's eyes brim with tears and her auburn head fall in despair, she wrapped her two arms around the girl's shoulders and drew her into a loving embrace. 'You're only a child,' she murmured. 'I know you meant no harm and thank the Lord you came to none!' Then, she gave Emma a little shake, saying, 'But soon, you won't be a child. You'll be a woman . . . in a few months, when you're sixteen. When your papa's taken from us, you'll find the need to be more disciplined of yourself, for, there'll be no allowances made. Not any more!' She eased Emma away from her and, still gripping the girl by the shoulders, she levelled an anxious gaze at those sorely troubled eyes. 'Miss Grady . . . do you understand what I'm saying?' she demanded in a serious voice.

'Yes, Manny,' Emma murmured, 'please don't worry about me. When it's time . . . when papa has to leave me at last, I *will* be strong! I promise I will, for his sake. And I really will try so very hard not to give them cause to punish me.' She gave a sideways glance towards the door and, as she did so, she was startled to see the grim face of her aunt. The little cry that escaped Emma's throat alerted Mrs Manfred, who swiftly rose to her feet and took a step forward.

'Oh, Madam! I was just explaining to Miss Grady that she is forbidden all meals until tomorrow evening!' Her voice was somewhat shaky, and beneath Agnes Crowther's dark accusing eyes Mrs Manfred's homely features were suffused in a dark pink flush. 'Excuse me, Ma'am,' she added, 'I will be about my business, if I may.' She hesitated to move, although she was now eager to be gone since she felt most uncomfortable in Agnes Crowther's company.

'Pray do that, Mrs Manfred . . . *without delay*!' Agnes Crowther stood for a moment longer, barring the doorway, with her head held high and tilted back and her hands clasped tight at her breast in that familiar and peculiar posture. Then, she stepped aside and waved Mrs Manfred out of the room, saying in a sour voice, 'Be careful not to abuse your position in this household. One master's choice is not necessarily another's!'

The threat was veiled, but to Emma, who was now on her feet and waiting to be addressed, there was no mistaking its meaning. Manny had come to this house with her and her papa when his health had deteriorated so much that he had felt obliged to accept his sister's seemingly generous offer that he be cared for at Breckleton House. Later, when all legal documents were signed and sealed – transferring all holdings and business interests into the trusteeship of Agnes and Caleb, and affording them a just remuneration for their troubles – a number of conditions were incorporated. One of these was that, on Thadius Grady's demise, his daughter was to be brought up a Christian and afforded every opportunity to be made aware 'in matters of business'. On the occasion of her marriage – or on her twenty-first birthday, whichever came first – Emma was to receive the sum of six thousand pounds. When she reached the age of twenty-five, all remaining assets would be released to her. These presently amounted to the two working mills and the handsome sum of five thousand pounds, which represented working capital together with a sum acquired from the sale of the house in Blackburn. This figure would have been considerably more, but excess cash was rarely accumulated in the course of maintaining the mills – the on-going costs and immediate necessities of production saw to that. It was on heeding his doctor's warning to 'make final preparations', that Thadius Grady had adopted a much more careful and frugal approach to expenditure, his uppermost intention being to leave his beloved Emma duly cared for.

To this end, he had made a further stipulation that Mrs Manfred be retained by his sister Agnes as housekeeper at Breckleton House. Agnes Crowther had made no objection, being well aware of both her own and her daughter's shortcomings in this area. Furthermore, she had a high regard for Mrs Manfred's talents as a housekeeper – even though she took a very dim view of 'the woman's high-handed attitude to her betters!'

Emma's papa had given over to his sister and her husband

absolute authority, and guardianship, with regards to all matters – including that of Emma's upbringing. It was as bearer of such responsibility that Agnes Crowther now addressed the watchful Emma.

'Your uncle and I have discussed the matter of your future and have come to a decision.' Her features moved although it was hard to distinguish whether the movement represented sneer or smile, as she half turned towards the door. 'Your papa will be spared the details, at least until he has recovered from the consequences of your sinful behaviour this day.' That said, she brought down one of her hands to pluck at her skirt, looked down on Emma along the length of her nose and, with a small hissing noise emanating through her small straight teeth, she swung around and departed, leaving the door wide open.

Emma closed the door and returned to her place at the window, where she scanned the surrounding fields reminiscently. It was impossible to see the canal from here because it wound away behind the spinney, and from there it veered out of sight altogether. But, in her mind, she could still see the handsome young barge-man. He was tall and deeply tanned. She hadn't seen him swimming in the water until after she had stripped off her shoes and stockings so that she could feel the cool wet splashes against her bare legs. When he rose to climb out of the water, his naked muscles golden and glistening wet, and his shoulder-length hair, wet and shimmering blue-black like a raven's wing, he looked like a young god. For a startling moment he had taken her breath away. But how quickly he'd made her feel at ease, with his black laughing eyes and infectious smile. He had a low gentle voice, which trembled slightly when he spoke and filled her heart with joy when it was raised in laughter. They had laughed at simple things of beauty and wonder – the squirrel that peeped at them from the spinney and would not be persuaded to come closer; the fish skilfully swimming just below the surface of the water, now and then blowing bubbles at them; and the mallard which played hide and seek in and out of the willow branches that dipped deep into the water.

Emma thought long and hard about the young bargee, and her heart beat faster as it had done when they had sat close together on the warm grass, and a ripple of deep plea-sure surged through her. She prayed he had not been too badly injured by her uncle's vicious attack. She hoped that, one day, they might meet again. Emma recalled his name, Marlow – such an arresting name. Emma knew she would not forget it.

Not far from where Emma gazed out of the window at Breckleton House, the sun beat down on the waters of the canal as it lapped and splashed against the colourful barge. The other barges had long since gone to ferry their cargoes of coal and cotton up and down the Leeds and Liverpool waterways. Presently, the Tanner barge would follow in their wake. But, first of all, there was an unpleasant task to be done.

Inside the cosy living-area of the moored barge, Marlow Tanner winced as the raw salt was rubbed into the open gashes across his back. In his dark eyes there was pain – but it was not simply pain of a physical kind, for the life of a bargee was hard and demanding and a man was used to the pain inflicted on his body. No, Marlow Tanner's pain emanated from his heart. It came from the all-too-brief memory of a young girl with laughing eyes and sun-burnished hair, a girl whose alluring smile had touched something deep within him; a girl who would never be for the likes of him, for she was of a gentler, more privileged stock. His instincts warned him that this girl, whom he knew to be called Emma, would only bring a heap of trouble down on his head; but he could not deny the murmurings of his heart which told him of his love for her. When the cane was brought down on his back, again and again, it was not the impact of it tearing into his bare flesh that hurt him most, but rather the helpless, compassionate look in her tearful eyes. Now, not for the first time since meeting her, Marlow wondered whether he would ever see this exquisite young girl again.

'Still dreamin' o' the lass, are ye?' Sally Tanner was barely past thirty, but, with her thin, wispy fair hair, coarse sun-weathered skin and long-lasting friendship with the beer-jug, she looked some ten years older. Her violet eyes twinkled merrily as she threw back her head, opened her cavernous, almost toothless mouth and gave out a raucous belly-laugh. 'Bugger me if I ain't never seen a lad o' sixteen look so cow-eyed an'smitten!' she roared, leaning forward once again to slap more salt into the wounds.

'*Seventeen* . . . the week after next!' her brother indignantly reminded her. Then he fell into a deep and thoughtful mood. Sal was right. He *was* smitten! It had never been this way with other lasses, for they had not touched him so deep inside; they had never lasted in his heart for more than the passing of a day or a week. The image of this girl, Emma, would not leave him. Nor did he want it to – whatever the consequences.

Chapter Two

'No, Papa!' Emma reeled back from the bed as though she had been slapped in the face. 'Uncle Caleb could *never* take your place. *Never*!' The horror of such a prospect was painfully apparent on her face – the colour had completely drained from it and her eyes, which now stared disbelievingly at her papa, were totally panic-stricken. 'Caleb Crowther! Do you really think I could ever look on him as my p-a-p-a-?' Emma's pretty mouth shaped the final word as though the taste of it on her tongue was bitterness itself.

'Emma, please hear me out.' Thadius Grady was sorely pained to see that tears had sprung to her eyes. His heart ached for her and he knew now that he couldn't tell her what weighed most heavy in his heart. Hour after hour he had lain in this bed, his frail body wasting, but his mind active with thoughts of his darling Emma – thoughts which tormented his every waking moment, as he feverishly wrestled with his conscience. At long last, after all these years, he had found it within himself to forgive Emma's mama, who had been taken from them by her own thoughtless actions and their cruel consequences. He had made his peace with God and he had arranged as best he could that Emma be taken care of when he was gone. He had thought this was enough and had continued to carry the other matter which tormented him so, silently close to his heart, believing this to be for the best. But now, the closer he came to the Lord, the heavier the burden he and Caleb Crowther had kept between them became. Their secret was a part of the past which they had vowed never to divulge to another soul. It had all happened so long ago, yet, at times, when the memories played havoc with him, it seemed like only yesterday.

Only a few moments ago, he had been ready to confess everything to Emma. But his courage had failed him. He couldn't do it. Instead, he reached his tired hand out and wrapped it about Emma's fingers. 'Sit beside me, child,' he murmured. As she did, she leaned forward to stroke his forehead with her free hand.

'I'm sorry, Papa,' she said with a loving smile, 'but I couldn't ever do what you're asking.'

'I know that now,' he replied, his soft eyes searching her face, as though he might find in it the strength to leave her behind in this merciless world, for it took more strength to die than it did to live.

'I know you mean well, Papa, and I love you for it,' she told him, fondly lifting his hand and touching it against her face, 'and I admit that Aunt Agnes and Uncle Caleb are sorely tried by my behaviour at times. They do their best to cope with my wilful ways. But . . . look upon Caleb Crowther as my papa?' She shook her head from side to side. 'I'd as soon live in the workhouse!' There was no smile on her face as she said it, no mischievous twinkle in those serious grey eyes and Thadius now realized, to have made such a comment about an institution which struck dread in folks' hearts, indicated just how strongly Emma felt.

Thadius came as close as he dared to the truth when he told her, 'Caleb will be *like* your papa in that he will control your heritage. He will command your obedience and respect – on *my* explicit wishes, you understand. He will advise and guide you. You must trust his decisions, Emma, for in all truth he has good reason to see you prosper.' He hoped in his heart that Emma would bring out what ever good there was in his brother-in-law. He had to believe that there was some affection in Caleb Crowther towards Emma – such a thing would only be natural after all, would it not? Yet, the man was often unduly harsh and many had been the time of late when Thadius had bitterly regretted having signed over so much power and authority to Caleb Crowther; yet, Thadius had now found it in his heart to forgive Caleb, and he realized that there was no one else to care for Emma, no one with such good reason to hold dear her welfare than his sister's husband. That Caleb meant well and would cause Emma no harm had been Thadius's fervent belief. Now, it was not *quite* so fervent, but he clung to it nevertheless – he must, or his soul would find no eternal rest. 'He isn't a bad man, Emma – nor do I think him totally without compassion. But, please, try not to rile him nor to incur your aunt's wrath, for she sees in you your mama's failings.'

With this he touched upon a great longing in Emma's heart – a deep need to know more about her mama. She had long believed there were things her papa deliberately kept from her. Caleb Crowther's recent remarks intimating that Thadius's wife, Mary, had been a woman of 'bad blood' and that Emma showed signs of having inherited the same blood, had both hurt and intrigued Emma. Now, in a soft, persuasive voice she dared to ask, 'Will you tell me about my mama?' When her papa's response was to gaze on her with saddened eyes, which seemed to look far beyond her, into the distant past, Emma ventured, 'Please, Papa . . . you've told me *nothing* of her. All I know is that her name was Mary . . . she was very beautiful and was lost in some unfortunate accident. Would it pain you so to talk to me about her?' She pleaded with such hope and passion that on seeing it, Thadius was deeply moved.

'Oh, Emma!' There was a depth of anguish in his voice as, lifting his hand to touch her face, he went on, 'Your Uncle Caleb meant nothing by his thoughtless remarks . . . please believe that. There is no "bad blood" in you, my darling. There never could be. You're everything I hold dear, and that couldn't be if you were not the good, loyal creature you are. Your mama . . . well, she was never meant to be tied to one man, and *that* is the only regret I have about her – the only one!'

'You mean, she left you?' Emma was horrified that anyone could leave her papa. 'She left you for another man?'

'No, Emma. Your mama did not leave me. Like you, she was so full of life . . . always searching for some adventure or other. There is nothing "bad" in that. It was just that I was so very different – I was content to live the quiet life. I suppose that, compared to her, I was very serious.' He gave a small laugh. 'Not much fun at all. Also, in the early days, there was very little money, and things were not always easy.'

'You loved her very much, didn't you, Papa?' Emma hated herself for having brought up such a painful subject, but it was so important to her to find out more about her mama.

'I *adored* her!' Thadius Grady ran his outstretched hand

over his face, as though, in so doing, he might be touching his beautiful wife, now so long gone. 'It was a terrible thing, Emma. Your mama was . . . visiting friends, along the canal. Nobody really knows what happened because those who could have told it all made good their escape immediately afterwards. Your mama was caught up in some terrible violence – and she never came home again.' Suddenly it was all too much for Thadius. As though in a frenzy, he grabbed Emma by the shoulders. 'The barge people are little more than wild ruffians, Emma! They're a law unto themselves . . . a bad lot! I want you to promise me that you'll steer clear of them. Will you do that, Emma? For me . . . will you give me your word?'

Emma gave it gladly, for she had never seen her papa so frantic. But, in that same moment she saw something in his eyes she had not seen before: he was keeping something back, she was certain and she was sorely tempted to press him further. But he was deeply distressed and she couldn't bear to see him grieved further. The river-people had taken the woman he loved, and Thadius Grady hated them for it! Emma knew that he was not a man to hate without good reason, and knowing this only served to make the promise he demanded from her all the more profound.

'I've caused you a great deal of anguish as well, haven't I Papa?' Emma wished she was of the same placid, submissive character as her cousin, Martha. *She* was so obedient, so ladylike, and Emma had never known her to do *anything* on impulse. She said as much to her papa now. In answer, he sighed softly and enveloped her face with a look of love. 'Oh, but your cousin will be shrivelled and old before her time, my darling. There is little joy or laughter in her soul.

And you . . . you must *never* wish to be anything other than what you are. You have the very essence of life in you . . . a vitality that shines from your eyes and lights up the space around you!' He paused and squeezed her fingers in his own. 'But try to curb your impulses, just a little, eh? Show your aunt and uncle that you *can* be responsible.'

At this point, the door opened and in bustled the tall commanding figure of Agnes Crowther. Sweeping alongside the huge ornate dresser, she brought herself to the opposite side of the big brass bed where, adopting that familiar and unsettling posture, she raised her brows and, holding her head stiffly, she lowered her eyes to look upon the prostrate figure in the bed. 'You are comfortable, are you not, Thadius?' A great weariness took hold of him and, as he half nodded his head and closed his eyes, she turned her attention to Emma. 'Leave your papa now, child. Let him rest.' Her voice was severe and totally without warmth.

Easing her hand from his, Emma bent forward to place a gentle kiss on her papa's tightly closed lips. 'Don't worry so, Papa,' she murmured in his ear, 'I promise I *will* be good, and I'll stay away from the river-people. I'll *never* let you down again!' It was a promise given in love, written on her heart with honour, and, one which would cost Emma dearly.

Some twenty minutes later, at eight a.m., the entire household was assembled in the dining-room, for daily prayers. This morning, Emma would not be promptly dismissed to her room afterwards, as she had been yesterday, since today was Tuesday and her spell of banishment was over. She had been given permission to attend dinner the evening before, but, not wanting the company of the Crowther

30

family, she had pleaded 'a feeling of nausea' and was consequently excused. She had now been without food for almost forty-eight hours – save for the buttered muffin secretly sent to her yesterday lunchtime by the ever-faithful Mrs Manfred. Thus, it was not surprising when, during a long and frightful passage read from the Bible by Caleb Crowther, Emma's stomach behaved in the most disobedient manner – gurgling and growling with such enthusiasm that it caused the reading of the passage to be temporarily suspended. Caleb Crowther positively glowered at her from beneath dark angry brows.

'Beg your pardon,' she murmured apologetically, whereupon, from the rear of the room where the maids were kneeling in their rustling starched print dresses, came the sound of muffled sniggering. This brought a caustic, shrivelling glance from Agnes Crowther and a look of sheer horror from her offspring, Martha, who, up until now had been sitting with her large brown head most piously bowed, depicting the absolute example of solemn and reverent devoutness. Now, with her prayers so rudely interrupted, she began a series of tutting noises, which only appeared to add to the confusion.

Plunged now into a deep and dour mood, Caleb Crowther declared in sombre voice, 'We shall proceed!' He resumed reading from the great book in trembling and resonant tones. Emma bowed her head and folded her hands obediently, but try as she might, she could not keep her attention on the proceedings. Her heart and her thoughts were down the corridor, in that large sunny room at the rear of the house, where the window lent a lovely view of the curved and spectacular lawns which ran right down to the brook and were interspersed with ancient oak trees and all manner of shrubs and greenery. Emma pictured herself and her papa seated by the window: he propped up in the wicker chair, the high-domed back of which gave support to his wasting limbs; and she perched on the window-seat with her legs tucked beneath her and her great love for her papa spilling over in her excited chatter. How she enjoyed bringing a smile to his face and how wonderful it would be if now and then he would give a small delighted chuckle. Suddenly, Emma found herself praying, confiding in God her innermost fears. 'Please don't let Papa suffer too much,' she asked, 'for he is such a good man.'

Meanwhile, Martha Crowther walked sedately across to the splendid piano which was beside the huge open fire-place, and, with much ceremony, she seated herself on the carved stool of the floral-tapestry seat. She immediately began fussing with the voluminous, cream-coloured, taffeta skirt which rubbed and squeaked as she moved about. Firstly she clutched two handfuls on either side and spread the material out with great deliberation, until it was most admirably draped either side of the stool. Then she began patting and smoothing it, with her ample figure threaten-ing to pop open the seams of her tight-fitting bodice at any moment. When it seemed like she might finally be ready, she paused to bestow a complacent smile on one and all. Though the smile worked her mouth and caused her head to incline slightly, and in so doing highlighting the fact that one of her nostrils was somewhat larger than the other, her small speckley brown eyes remained hard and glittering like pebbles on a beach. As they moved with precision over the sea of heads, they met Emma's warm gaze and, for a brief moment, they were held reluctantly mesmerized until, alerted by the impatient cough of her father, she swung them stiffly away to examine the sheet of music on the piano-stand. She placed her stubby fingers in the correct position on the keyboard, ready to begin the morning hymn. In anticipation of the first note, everyone simultaneously took a deep breath, but were forced to let it out again as Martha Crowther lifted her two hands to ensure that the tight spirals of brown hair, which sat priggishly above each ear, were satisfactorily secure. This was her moment – the moment when the plain, otherwise untalented, daughter of Caleb and Agnes Crowther considered herself to be the star of the stage. As always, she intended to savour every second of it. Unfortunately, she had chosen the wrong occasion to play prima donna, for her papa was not in the mood to be entertained.

'We will forgo the hymn this morning,' he declared, slamming shut his prayer-book. 'Go about your business,' he instructed the servants, who were looking at each other with mouths aghast. As for his wife and daughter, they appeared extremely exasperated: the latter rose from the piano and, pausing only to ask that she may be excused, flounced out of the room with an austere expression on her large, unattractive face. His wife, meanwhile, clapped her hands at the departing servants, with the order to 'serve breakfast at once!' Then she hurriedly followed her daughter out of the room, with not so much as a glance at Emma, who was now on her feet and quite taken aback by the speed of events.

'May I sit with Papa while he has his breakfast?' she asked her uncle, her heart sinking when he abruptly replied, 'You may not! . . . I expect you to be seated at the breakfast table in five minutes. After which, please remain behind!' Emma felt an impending doom, knowing from experience that such an instruction could only mean one thing – she was to be given yet another lecture. But, for the life of her, she could not think what she had done since Sunday to evoke his wrath. On the contrary, she had made every effort to remain inconspicuous for her papa's sake.

In Emma's experience breakfast was always a trying occasion, but today it was unbearable. From the moment Emma entered the room, a heavy, forbidding atmosphere descended over the table. Even the maids, who might normally be seen to occasionally lift up the corners of their mouths in a secret shared smile with Emma, went scurrying about their business with sorry faces and deliberately averted eyes.

Emma was not the slightest bit hungry although, in an effort to keep the peace, she did manage to swallow a mouthful or two of the scrambled eggs and, surprisingly, she enjoyed her cup of tea so much that she indulged in a second one. For the most part, however, she picked at her food, skilfully pushing it about her plate, until it appeared that she had eaten more than she actually had. But her mind was preoccupied with what her uncle had in store for her and, throughout the meal, her attention constantly wandered. At present, it was captured by the monstrous sideboard which spanned almost the length of one wall, its twisted decorative pillars reaching up beyond the picture-rail and supporting numerous small oval- and square-shaped mirrors. On some of its many shelves stood large, black, prancing horses, and in the various arched cubicles all manner of bric-a-brac were displayed: heavily-decorated Chinese vases; assorted small glass containers, and little silver candlesticks. All along the top there were plates of every description; some depicting floral sprays, and others boasting hunting scenes. The accumulated impression was one of clutter and chaos. Emma also contemplated the idea that a small forest must have been sacrificed to provide the wealth of timber from which the huge ornate sideboard was constructed. The same could be said of the table at which the family sat, which was some five feet wide and twice as long, with bulbous legs of enormous dimension.

Emma's gaze went quietly about the room, going from place to place and seeing little there to give her pleasure – apart from the magnificent piano. It was a beautiful object in highly polished walnut, displaying two exquisite candelabras positioned at either end, with a selection of silver-framed photographs between them. This piano had been Emma's salvation since her arrival at Crowther House. She had enjoyed so many hours of pleasure at its keyboard, particularly in the early days when her papa had had the strength to sit close by and watch her play. Strangely enough, her uncle had not thought fit to punish her by forbidding her access to the piano. On the occasions when she had played for the family gathering, Emma had actually witnessed expressions of pleasure on her uncle's face – though *not* on the faces of her cousin and aunt, who remained po-faced throughout and showed little appreciation afterwards.

Emma sneaked a look at them now. As usual, there was little joy on either of their countenances, although, to Emma's left, Martha had a look of absolute bliss on her face as she stuffed great helpings of food into her rather large mouth. So intent was she not to miss a mouthful, that she took her own breath away, causing her odd-sized nostrils to flare open in their frantic gasp for air. When Caleb Crowther impatiently tapped his teaspoon against the side of his cup, Martha lifted her eyes to him. Upon seeing that he was not pleased with her table-manners, she gave a sheepish half-smile, straightened her back and dabbed at her mouth with a napkin. Then she proceeded with her usual irritating habit of picking at the deep pleats of her dress, lifting up great handfuls of her abundant skirt and arranging it about her with painfully laborious deliberation. When her mother let out a tight gasp of irritation, Martha immediately switched her attention to the muffin on her side-plate, collecting it daintily between finger and thumb in preparation for spreading it with butter. Unfortunately, Martha Crowther's thick, clumsy fingers were not designed for dainty behaviour, so when the muffin flicked out of them and somersaulted into the centre of the table, Emma was not at all surprised. Seeing the expressions of exasperation on the faces of her Aunt Agnes and Uncle Caleb, Emma desperately tried to restrain herself from laughing out loud.

'Really, Martha!' Agnes Crowther shook her head in disapproval, her dark green eyes virtually closed into angry slits. However much Emma thought of her aunt as being a sour-faced individual, she could still appreciate that she was a very attractive woman. She had the darkest of hair, drawn back from her high forehead and parted in the middle with exact precision, before being gathered up above each ear, where it was plaited and wound into thick, tight circles which nestled over her perfectly shaped ears – like sleeping snakes, Emma thought, not for the first time. Her dresses were always high at the neck, buttoned from there down to the tight-fitting waist. At the rear was a bustle as large and grand as Emma had ever seen and the skirt, as always, was extravagantly folded in layered pleats, culminating in a beautifully embroidered hem which swept out at the back in an exaggerated train. Her dresses were of the finest taffeta, always exceptionally handsome, yet never glamorous. The one she wore today was burgundy.

As Emma's mind wandered, Agnes Crowther secretly compared her own daughter and her brother's daughter. The former appeared much older than her sixteen years; she was coarse and ungainly, and Agnes Crowther held out little hope that finishing-school would do much to improve her. Her attention then turned to Emma, born a few months after Martha, and already showing the promise of great beauty. Indeed, she was wilful, and she cared little for material things, but even if she were dressed in rags Agnes knew she could command the eye of every man, for she had that elusive beauty which emanated from within and a God-given talent for making the most out of all things. There was a light in those magnificent eyes that shone from a pure and joyous soul – and Agnes Crowther resented her for it.

She glanced at Emma and saw how her longing gaze had sought out the door which would take her from this room, down the corridor and to her papa. She knew how Emma yearned to go to him. She knew also that, long after Thadius had been laid to rest, Emma's love for him would continue to live on. She envied her brother such steadfast devotion. She let her eyes follow the strong, classic lines of Emma's lovely face – the small neat nose, the delicate chin, that laughing full mouth. She noted how her sun-kissed hair fell naturally in deep tumbling waves. Her young figure was perfect – small and dainty, adding to the overall picture of everything a young girl growing to womanhood should be. Agnes Crowther saw all this in Emma, and envied her. She also begrudged the fact that, without her brother's intervention, there would be no finishing-school for Martha, no

Breckleton House or comfortable way of life. She ought to feel grateful but all she felt was deep bitterness, since half of the business left by their father should rightly have been hers. It did not matter that the business was already ailing when Thadius took it on, nor that she herself might never had rescued it in the same way as Thadius had done. The fact remained that she had been cheated of her share, so whatever came her way now was no more than her rightful due.

When, presently, breakfast was over, Emma thought it not a moment too soon. Whatever it was her uncle had to say, it was better said sooner than later. When he dismissed all but her, telling the maids to 'Leave the table . . . You may return when I'm finished,' Emma's stomach felt as if it were going to jump out of her mouth. Yet, despite her inner anxiety, she felt that she was ready to hear whatever it was he had to say. However, even she was not prepared for the news he gave her. Her astonishment was clearly written on her face when it became evident that her uncle's intentions were to put her out to work.

'How do you mean Uncle Caleb?' she enquired as politely as she could. She was not afraid to have to work – indeed, if anything, she welcomed it – but she was anxious to learn exactly what he had in store for her.

'It is, of course, your papa's wish that you be made wise in the matters of business, and as his business has always concerned the cotton mills, as did his father's . . . your grandfather's . . . before him, it is my belief that you will learn much from being involved in the day-to-day running of such a concern.'

'I'm not being sent away to school, then . . . like Martha?' asked Emma, with wide, relieved eyes. She had been dreading such a prospect these past weeks, ever since the dismissal of the woman who had tutored both her and Martha in the rudiments of education – of which embroidery, music and religion and the necessities of keeping house, were given paramount importance. When Martha's finishing-school was chosen, Emma believed it would be only a matter of weeks, once the holidays were over, before she herself would be packed off. She had respectfully raised the matter with her papa, who was under no illusion regarding her reluctance to leave him. But the issue was always side-stepped and Emma had to finally concede that it was her papa's wish for her to be sent away. Such a consideration had been painful for her to accept, but as a dutiful daughter it was not for her to question. At her Uncle Caleb's revelation, she was at first shocked, then delighted, but now she had become apprehensive. Would she have more time for her papa . . . or would she have less?

'May I ask *how* I am to be made knowledgeable in the family business?'

'It surprises me that you ask so politely Emma Grady, for you have shown no such respect in the past.' Emma felt his piercing eyes bearing down on her, seeking as always to shrivel her spirit. But she stood straight and proud, her gaze defiantly meeting his. As he continued to look down on her, Caleb Crowther's thoughts were abruptly transported back over the years, to Emma's exquisite and beautiful mother, Mary, who had bewitched him beyond belief, and whose fiery, magnificent character was so painfully evident in this young girl who so often dared to challenge him. But she would not get the better of him – not this side of Hell she wouldn't. A pang of regret touched his bitter heart. If only he had been blessed with a son. If he had had a son to carry on his name, he might well have altered the course of things, the consequences be damned. As it was, despite his efforts to escape them, he had been shouldered with certain responsibilities towards this girl and Thadius which he would rather not have had thrust upon him. However, these same responsibilities had afforded him salvation from the debtor's prison and, because of Thadius Grady's impending departure from this world, had bestowed upon him a fortune and a great deal of power. That much, at least, he liked.

'Uncle Caleb?' Emma felt the need to catch his attention, for he appeared to be so deep in thought it seemed he had forgotten she was there.

'Hhm? . . . yes!' He cleared his throat and, taken by surprise at the sound of Emma's voice invading his secret thoughts, he cast down his gaze for a brief moment to quickly compose himself. 'Leave me now. All will be explained in good time once your papa has been acquainted with my intentions.' He straightened both his arms outwards, before placing one behind his back and dipping the long sinewy fingers of the other into the pocket of his waistcoat to draw out a silver watch. As he did so, something else came out with it and tumbled to the floor. It was the tiniest, most delicate, finely chiselled lady's pocket time-piece, enriched by the most intricate figuring. With a furtive movement, Caleb Crowther bent to scoop it up, but not before Emma had seen it. She was furious, for she knew the watch to be a precious gift from her own papa to her mama. It was a thing he had always treasured and she could not let the matter pass.

'That pocket-watch doesn't belong to *you*!' she accused, stepping forward a pace. 'It belongs to Papa!'

'The devil you say!' The self-indulgent smile had disappeared from Caleb Crowther's bearded features, and had been replaced by a look as evil as any Emma had ever seen. But she was not intimidated by him, and where lesser mortals might have fled, she stood her ground and repeated the accusation, this time with more vehemence.

'It's my *Papa's* watch, I tell you,' she confronted him boldly as he began trembling from head to toe.

'Go to your room!' he insisted, his voice now hardly more than a whisper. But Emma made no move until, the next moment, Mrs Manfred appeared at the door. Her original intention had been to enquire when the master intended to allow the maids in for the purpose of cleaning away the breakfast things, but when she sensed the impending terrible scene, her enquiry was of a very different nature. She had heard Caleb Crowther order Emma to her room and had witnessed with horror how Emma displayed no such intention. Quickly now, she stepped forward in a bold attempt to diffuse the situation.

'Excuse me, sir . . . shall *I* escort Miss Grady to her room?' Her anxious eyes swept with relief as he threw out his arms in a gesture of helplessness, telling her in an impatient voice, 'Please do so; and quickly, or I will not be responsible for my actions.' He then swung round to face the fireplace. Meanwhile Mrs Manfred swiftly came to Emma's side where, casting a sideways warning look at her, she pleaded, 'Please Miss Grady.' Emma's heart fell like a stone inside her as she thought, I've done it again. However she did not regret having spoken up about the pocket-watch, but rather that the entire incident would be reported to her papa in a way that would put her in the wrong.

41

As Emma followed Mrs Manfred from the room, Caleb Crowther's angry voice called after them, 'See that she stays in her room until I send for her.' He did not look up, but remained poised with one foot planted on the brass fender, one hand clutching the mantelpiece above, and the weight of his body bent tautly over the fireplace.

It was now two o'clock. Emma had spent over four hours pacing the blue-patterned carpet in her room, asking herself again and again why it was that, without fail, she always managed to get on the wrong side of her Uncle Caleb. Then she would defend her actions by reminding herself that it was not entirely her fault. It was *he* who was the thief, not she; it was *he* who instilled in her the need to be ever on her guard; and it was *he* who saw wickedness in every innocent thing she did.

At ten minutes past two, Mrs Manfred came to fetch her. 'Oh, Miss Grady!' she chided. 'When will you ever learn to curb that impetuous tongue of yours? Lunch is finished and you are to go without . . . *again*.' She made a clicking noise with her tongue and shook her head, a sad expression on her loving face. 'Here,' she said in a soft voice, sneaking her fingers into the pocket of her dark dress and taking from it a white lace handkerchief. Thrusting it into Emma's hand, she explained how it contained one of Cook's gingerbreads. 'Oh, but there's no time to eat it now, child!' she cautioned, as Emma began to unwrap it. 'Master is back from dispensing harsh justice with his own kind in the courts, so now, no doubt, he seeks to do the same with you.' At this, Mrs Manfred drew herself up sharply, as she suddenly thought of what the sweep had said when he'd come to clean the chimneys. It seemed the whole of Blackburn was deep in talk of how this very morning Caleb Crowther, along with other Justices of the Peace, must have been in a mood more foul than usual. A harmless rascal had been brought before them, whose misfortune it was to be crippled, and whose greater misfortune it was to have been apprehended in the act of unlawfully acquiring a loaf of bread from a baker's basket, during the process of which the portly baker suffered a slight seizure. The Court took a very serious view of the whole business and, as a result, the offender was sentenced to transportation on a convict-ship to the other side of the world.

'Quickly child!' Mrs Manfred was quite suddenly overcome with a deep sense of urgency and panic. 'Don't keep him waiting. You'll only make matters worse.' Seeing Emma start towards her, she turned about and hurried out of the room, adding, 'They're all in your papa's room. You're to join them there.' She gave no answer when Emma demanded to know why they should congregate in her papa's sick-room, 'disturbing him so.'

When Emma was ushered into the downstairs room, it was to find not only her papa – who appeared to be somewhat uncomfortable in the dome-backed chair, supported in a half-sitting position by the use of several feather bolsters – but also her Uncle Caleb, her Aunt Agnes and a small nervous man with a mop of sandy-coloured hair and eyes of almost the same hue. Emma knew him at once to be Mr Gregory Denton, manager at one of the two mills owned by the family. Her papa had a great deal of respect for Mr Denton, for he was an amiable and forthright character, a good son to his elderly, cantankerous mother and a first-rate mill-manager. His sense of fairness, his business acumen, and his utter devotion to his work, went without question. Even Caleb Crowther had been obliged to recognize the worthiness of Gregory Denton – talents made even more remarkable because of his age, which was not yet twenty-eight.

'Come in . . . Come in, child!' Agnes Crowther dislodged one of her hands from the other – thus abandoning her customary posture of prayer – and waving her left hand in a dismissive gesture to Mrs Manfred, she instructed her, 'Be good enough to close the door behind you on your way out.' However, she appeared somewhat exasperated when her husband in turn addressed her.

'You will not be required either, thank you, Agnes. I'm quite certain your brother and I can conclude whatever business is at hand without you. Would you be so kind as to escort Mr Denton to the drawing-room, where I'll join him later.' He glanced at the inconspicuous little fellow, telling him, 'I shall be obliged if you would wait a while longer. There is a further matter to be discussed which you will possibly need to be made aware of at some point.'

'Of course, Mr Crowther, sir . . . I shall be pleased to wait.' Pausing only to respectfully acknowledge the man he came to see, he wished Thadius Grady well, adding, 'It's been an excellent month, sir . . . I hope the figures cheered you.'

'They did indeed, Gregory. I'm most grateful for your constant loyalty . . . as I know is Mr Crowther here.' Thadius Grady's weakened voice betrayed his sapping health as he abandoned his effort to lift his hand to point at his brother-in-law.

'Indeed. Indeed,' rejoined Caleb Crowther, growing impatient and whereupon, both his wife and their visitor left the room.

'Now then, Thadius.' Satisfied that the door was securely closed, Caleb Crowther shifted his piercing gaze from it to the gentler face of his brother-in-law, as he continued, 'To the business of . . . your daughter.' For the briefest of moments, he seemed almost embarrassed and to Emma, whose eyes were fixed intently upon him, his hesitation on referring to her as her papa's daughter seemed strange. Yet, she gave it little thought, for in truth, she considered her uncle to be altogether a curious man.

The next moment Emma found herself the centre of attention and concern on her face must have betrayed itself because her papa immediately attempted to put her at ease. 'Emma . . . there is nothing for you to be afraid of,' he assured her. But Emma sensed little conviction in his voice. What she did sense, however, was that her papa was slipping away from her. She took a step forward and would have come to his side were it not for his telling her at that point, 'Be still, child, and listen to what your Uncle Caleb has suggested. When you have given me your views on what he has to say . . . then, I will gladly give you mine. I know no more of your uncle's plans for you than you do, as I prefer we are told them at one and the same time.'

Although Emma was prepared for the worst, what Caleb Crowther had to say still came as a shock to her. It appeared that her uncle and aunt did not consider her worthy enough to be given the same opportunities as Martha. In Caleb Crowther's words, 'To send Emma to school would be a futile and expensive gesture, for, in no time at all, she will have found a way to bring shame and scandal down on our heads.' He also explained how much more embarrassing such a thing would be for *him*, being 'an upholder of the Law, and consequently a very eminent figure, expected at all times to set an example.' What he proposed instead was that Emma should be sent to work in the Wharf Mill, where she would no doubt be of some use in a clerical position, assisting the manager, Mr Denton, and 'where she might learn discipline and respect.'

If the plans for her future had come as a shock to Emma, they appeared to have left her papa totally horrified. All the time his brother-in-law had been talking, Thadius Grady had made no comment. But, Emma had noticed how grim his expression had become and how his eyes had darkened with anger. She was sure this anger must have been caused by her behaviour and she had let him down so badly. She was mortified when he looked directly into her shamed face and, in a trembling voice, instructed her, 'Leave us, Emma.' Then, seeing her hesitate, he raised his voice, 'At once!' Even when he was taken by a fit of coughing and she started to approach him, he waved his hand in a dismissive gesture and ordered, 'Go!' Reluctantly, Emma left the room. She sat dejectedly on the stairs outside, her head in her hands and her heart an unbearable weight within her.

It was here that Mrs Manfred found her. 'Aw, child . . . don't take on so,' she said, not really aware of what had taken place in Thadius Grady's room. She comforted Emma and would have led her away, but all of a sudden, there was a burst of activity. First, Caleb Crowther emerged from the room and swept past Emma and Mrs Manfred with a black and furious expression on his face. Within minutes of him disappearing into the drawing-room, Gregory Denton rushed out from it, cap in hand and looking eager to depart. Seeing this, Emma broke away from Mrs Manfred's consoling embrace, to return to her papa.

Shaking her head in exasperation, Mrs Manfred quickly

closed the front door behind Mr Denton, after which she rushed after Emma, her intention being to ensure that all was well.

Emma was shocked to find her papa in a state of great anxiety. In his hand was the tiny watch that she had seen earlier in Caleb Crowther's pocket. Emma made no mention of that particular fact, but, somehow, she guessed her papa already knew, for, when she was settled on her knees before him, he told her in an urgent voice, 'This watch is *yours* . . . it was your mama's before you and now it's yours. I recently entrusted it to Caleb, in order that he would get it inscribed. I feared it lost. No matter . . . I have it now.' He paused a moment, before gazing down on her with great tenderness.

'Emma.'

'Yes, Papa?'

'Come closer . . . I have something very precious to give into your keeping.' He took the watch out of its case and held it up between his finger and thumb. 'Read the inscription, child,' he urged, placing it in her hands, with the back of it facing her. Inscribed at the top, in gilded lettering, were the words: *For Mary, Christmas, 1840.* Beneath that was a new inscription reading, *To Emma, 1860.*

'Oh, Papa!' She could hardly believe her eyes.

'Open the back,' he now told her. 'Press the button at the base.' As she did this, she saw, nestled into the tiny cavity, a lock of hair, still golden as the brightest ray of sunshine and so small that the softest breath of wind might blow it away forever. 'You see that, Emma? . . . That's a part of your mama. Her hair was so lovely.' He smiled at the memory and Emma thought the smile almost ethereal. He continued, 'Golden, it was, like a summer's day. You have a touch of it in your hair, Emma, now and then when the light plays tricks with it, and you have the same deep, undisciplined curls.'

Emma continued to gaze on that tiny piece of her mama . . . of *herself* . . . and all kinds of emotions took hold of her. 'Am I to keep this, Papa?' she asked, thinking that she had never been given anything more precious.

'I hope you will, Emma,' came the reply, 'because, small as it is, it holds a precious memory of a day shortly after we were married. It was a beautiful day in the month of June, and everything was smelling sweet and fresh after a week of rain.' After a long, thoughtful pause, he continued, 'I pray you will find a love of your own one day, child, for love is a wonderful thing . . . though it can often bring its own heartache.' The years rolled away in his mind and the tears brimmed in his eyes. Mary had been his only love, yet she had brought him so much pain with the joy. It hurt him to recall how, even when Emma was only a few months old, her mama had felt compelled to seek the company of other men. It was the flaw in her nature and a sad thing.

'Enough, Papa.' Emma could see he was emotionally exhausted. 'You must rest.'

'You'll take care of the watch, Emma? You'll cherish it?'

'Of course, Papa . . . always.'

'Good.' Taking a deep sigh, he touched her hand with his own. 'Fetch Mrs Manfred to me. I must speak with her.' No sooner had the words left his lips, than Mrs Manfred stepped forward. 'Forgive me, sir,' she said, her voice subdued by the emotional scene she had just witnessed, 'I came to see if you and Miss Grady were all right.'

'*I* will be safe from harm's reach, when the Good Lord sees fit to call me,' he murmured, obviously relieved at her presence, 'but Miss Grady must be protected.' He began to grow agitated. 'I must see Holford, before it is altogether too late!'

'Mr Holford? The solicitor, sir?'

'Yes, yes. Send Thomas on a fast horse! *Quickly* . . . he must be fetched at once!'

'What is it, Papa?' Emma asked, when Mrs Manfred had departed with haste. '*Why* must I be protected? From what?'

'From *them*!' Emma could hardly hear his whisper. 'I've given too much into their keeping . . . too trusting. Have to make amends.'

'Please don't fret yourself, Papa.' Emma wasn't really listening, as she was too troubled by his cadaverous appearance and his erratic breathing. Suddenly, she sensed someone behind her. On turning, she saw that it was Caleb Crowther and, standing beside him, white-faced and fidgeting, was Mrs Manfred. 'Oh, Manny . . . did you do as Papa asked? He seems so agitated!'

Before Mrs Manfred could reply, Caleb Crowther stepped forward. 'No, she did not!' he said. 'It was just as well that I discovered her errand, for it would only serve to aggravate your papa's health even further. Whatever business he wishes to discuss with Mr Holford must wait, at least until he is stronger.'

Emma was obliged to agree with him. 'Quickly, Manny. Help me get him into bed,' she pleaded, beginning to link her arm beneath that of her papa's.

'Of course!' rejoined Caleb Crowther, as Mrs Manfred hurried to help. 'You two see to that, while I summon Mrs

49

Crowther.' At this, without any further regard for their efforts, he went swiftly from the room.

Only once in those desperate few moments did Thadius Grady open his eyes, and that was to beg of Mrs Manfred, 'I *must* speak with Holford! My daughter's future depends on it!'

'We have to appease him, Manny,' Emma told her. 'For whatever reason, you must send Thomas to fetch Mr Holford straightaway.'

Mrs Manfred went at once, careful to avoid crossing Caleb Crowther's path. Within a few minutes, Thomas had departed on one of the hunting horses. 'I'll have the fellow back here in no time at all!' he had assured the concerned housekeeper. 'Mrs Crowther's sendin' me in the same direction . . . I'm ter tell the doctor to make his way along.'

In the meantime, Agnes Crowther despatched Emma from the sick-room. 'The doctor will be here shortly,' she told the protesting Emma. 'You're only disturbing your papa by being here.' Instructed to 'run and fetch Mrs Manfred. Tell her to bring more blankets and fresh hot tea,' Emma went at once. But wild horses would not have torn her away had she known that never again was she to see her papa alive!

The next half an hour was one of the worst nightmares Emma would ever suffer in her eventful life. Time and again she begged to be allowed in to see her papa so that she could comfort him and give him strength. She knew that he was in pain for, every once in a while, he would cry out. Then he would call out her name in a fitful voice – wanting her, needing her.

'Let me go to him!' she pleaded to Agnes Crowther. 'I must be with him.'

'No, child! . . . you'll do more harm than good!' retorted her aunt.

At one moment, the grim face of Caleb Crowther appeared from the door of the sick-room. 'Be sensible, Emma Grady! Your papa needs to be kept calm until the doctor arrives,' he remonstrated, shutting the door in her face and turning the key from the inside. At this, Emma made such a commotion by throwing herself at the door and crying out for her papa, that Agnes Crowther, who was always nearby, grasped her by the arm and dragged her upstairs.

'You're hysterical!' she snapped, 'and better in your room, until the doctor has gone!' That said, she locked the door and hurried away, leaving Emma banging her fist on the door and pleading to be allowed down.

'I promise I'll be still and quiet,' she cried, 'only, don't keep us apart. Please! Don't keep me from him!' She was fearful for her papa. Some deep instinct warned her that she should be with him, for he was helpless and needed her now more than ever.

Emma's cries echoed throughout the house. The servants heard her and cried with her; Mrs Manfred silently cursed all the devils that had delivered Emma and her papa into the clutches of people such as these; even Agnes Crowther was made nervous by the pitiful cries coming from Emma's room. However, they made no impact at all on Caleb Crowther, as he stared down on Thadius Grady.

'Caleb . . . please.' Thadius knew that he was sinking fast. 'Bring her to me, I beg you!' Emma's desperate cries were tearing him apart. 'Have you no heart, man?' he pleaded. If only his limbs had an ounce of strength in them, he would crawl from this bed and go to his darling child. But, God help him, he was as helpless as a new-born babe!

'No, Thadius!' Caleb Crowther's face was a picture of dark and evil cunning as his eyes bore into the poor sick man before him, whose only dying prayer was that he could hold his beloved child close once more and make amends before he left this world. 'I can't let you talk to Emma, for I'm of the mind that you want to confess to her who her real papa is.' He shook his head slowly, as Thadius protested that this was not the case. Even when Thadius began to cry like a child, there was not an ounce of compassion in Caleb Crowther's body. 'Nor can I allow you to talk to Holford. Have you the intention to change your will, Thadius? Do you regret the terms already laid down?' The sneering smile on his face was terrifying to witness, and Mrs Manfred, who had been stocking a supply of blankets in the large walk-in cupboard and was, as yet, unseen, was so horror-struck that she began to tremble uncontrollably and retreated deeper into the safety of the cupboard.

The next moment there came a flurry of movement from outside, and a low drone of conversation which grew louder as the sound of footsteps came ever nearer. Thadius, his voice now weakened to a whisper, began calling, 'Emma! Emma!' He would have dragged himself from the bed, with every ounce of strength left in him, but, although his mind was strong, his poor wasted limbs were not.

From her hiding-place within the cupboard, Mrs Manfred heard Thadius Grady's desperate cries, and her heart bled. When he suddenly grew silent and an eerie quietness ensued, she feared the worst. Her feet felt as though they were pinned to the floor; her legs were like water; and her heart was beating so fast within her breast that she thought Caleb Crowther must surely hear it. Gradually she crept to the door and dared to peep round. What she saw was the body of Thadius Grady hanging lifeless across the bed and Caleb Crowther standing over it, a pillow still clutched in his hands so tightly that the knuckles on his fists were sharp and white.

Quickly, Caleb Crowther swung the lifeless form of Thadius Grady back into the bed, placing the pillow beneath his head and arranging him in a natural position. Then, with an equally swift movement, he went to the door and unlocked it, only just having time to get to the window before the door opened and Agnes Crowther entered with the doctor, who at once hurried to the bed.

From his position at the window, Caleb Crowther followed the doctor's movements, a contrived look of deep concern on his face. When the doctor turned to declare, 'I'm afraid I was too late. We can do nothing for Thadius now,' the look of concern deepened, and, passing his hand wearily over his face, he gave a painful groan, 'Poor Thadius, but at least his sufferings are over now.' When, out of the corner of his eye he saw Mrs Manfred emerging from the cupboard and hurrying out of the room, a suspicious look crossed his face. But he could not be sure of what she had seen . . . he would never be sure.

It was into this sombre scene that Mr Holford, the solicitor, came, but he quickly realized what had happened and left the room. Caleb Crowther followed him into the hallway, where he answered the solicitor's immediate question with regret, 'No, I'm afraid I know nothing of why Mr Grady should want to speak to you.' He secured an appointment at which time Thadius Grady's legal arrangements would be confirmed. Then, with a show of compassion for that same departed soul, he bade Mr Holford good day.

When Agnes Crowther made her way upstairs to break the news to Emma, Mrs Manfred found a quiet place to consider what had taken place. She could not be certain of what had happened. Already, she was trying to wipe from her mind all memory of what she had seen. After all, it was possible that Thadius Grady had passed away naturally as he tried, in his fevered state, to see Emma. It was possible that Caleb Crowther had simply recovered the pillow from the floor where it had fallen. It was also possible that she had too vivid and dangerous an imagination. Yes, all of these things *were* possible, but she was not convinced! All the same, she resolved that she would put everything that had transpired out of her mind. To *know* something was often a burden; but to *suspect* something was usually dangerous! She was just a housekeeper, after all. But she had a particular love of Mr Grady and young Miss Grady. Yet, what was she to do without proof of her suspicions? She would have given *anything* not to have been in that room – but she *had* been there, God help her! And, even if she was wrong in her suspicions regarding the death of Thadius Grady, she knew she was not wrong about the evil nature of Caleb Crowther: a man with no compassion; a man who had deliberately denied his own brother-in-law his last dying wish of the comfort of his daughter by his side; a man who had cruelly kept Miss Grady from her dying papa. What sort of creature could hear a father and daughter crying out for each other yet wilfully keep them from one another's arms? The composition of such a man was beyond comprehension. However, of one thing she was certain. He was a man with the power to completely discredit any accusation a mere housekeeper might bring against him! But what of the comment she had heard regarding Emma's real papa? No, it *was* her imagination! It had to be!

Later, when Mrs Manfred found a desperate need to confide her thoughts to Cook, they were greeted with scorn and given short shrift.

'I've never heard such foolishness from a growed woman! It's a dangerous thing to let your imagination run riot, and you'd do best to put such dreadful thoughts from your mind!'

Mrs Manfred reluctantly agreed. She immediately reproached herself for having broken her self-imposed rule of not indulging in gossip below stairs.

Emma was devastated! All through the service when the rector spoke in respectful and glowing terms of 'the good man, Thadius Grady', she gazed at that long wooden box beneath the altar. There, within its cold and silent darkness, lay her darling papa – denied in his last moments the words she would have uttered to him. Oh, there was so much she had wanted to tell him! She would have held his frail familiar hand in her own, and murmured of her deep and grateful love. She would have told him of her heartfelt intention to become the daughter she suspected he had always wanted – not wild or wilful, not bold and adventurous, but more sedate and ladylike. She would have given her word that, with all her heart, she would try always to be a sophisticated and genteel young lady, who, one day, would marry a man much like her own papa. She would be a good, respectful wife to that man, and a fine mama to the children she bore him. All of these things, Emma would have said. Instead, her papa had died without hearing any of them. So, she said them now in her heart, strengthening also her promise to steer clear of the river-people. But, even as she made this silent resolve, the dark, laughing image of Marlow taunted her memory and touched her heart.

Outside, in the churchyard, with the sun beating down on her bowed head, Emma waited until the last mourner had moved away. Then, hardly able to see for the tears burning and swimming in her eyes, she went on her knees. 'I love you so, Papa,' she whispered into the ground, 'I pray you know how much I'll miss you, my darling.' In her heart, there was such great sorrow that it felt like a physical weight pulling her down – down, into that place where her papa was sleeping his final sleep. But mingled with this pain there was a strange, inexplicable feeling of another loss besides that of her papa. Although Emma was aware of this, she did not realize its implications: this other loss was that of her youth, her girlhood, all the lightness and irrespon-sibility of laughter and innocence. But there was also something else. In the fullness of time, her joy of life would return and the laughter would once again light up her eyes, but this other feeling – so deeply etched into her very being – was destined to stay with her forever. Emma knew that no passing of years nor easing of grief could ever ease it, for, never would she forget how Caleb Crowther had so vindictively kept her from the one person she loved, thus denying him the touch of her hand in his last moments. It *was* vindictive! It was inhuman. Thadius Grady had always taught Emma to forgive and for his sake she would try – but not yet, for she truly believed it would be the hardest thing she would ever be called on to do.

Emma had been unkindly forced into womanhood by her suffering, and this now betrayed itself in the shadows of her lovely but sad face. These shadows carried away her youth and brought in its place the strong, resolute lines of womanhood. Not once during the service inside the church nor in the churchyard outside, had Emma moved her eyes to look upon Caleb Crowther. Thus she had not witnessed the terrible bitterness on his face as he stared at where her papa lay; she did not hear the secretly whispered words, 'Mary was mine, Thadius . . . she was *always* mine!' If only Emma had been aware of the black hatred eating at Caleb Crowther's heart at that moment, she might have been better prepared for the terrible injustice he would one day inflict upon her.

Chapter Three

'Poor Mr Grady would turn over in his grave at the way they treat Miss Grady.' Gladys, the parlourmaid, joined Mrs Manfred at the casement window. From there they watched the dog-cart carry the master and young Emma out of sight. 'T'were a different kettle o' fish a week ago, when Martha Crowther left fer that fancy school!' declared the maid, in a scornful tone. 'Tis a great pity the solicitor didn't get here in time, don't yer think, Mrs Manfred? For I can't help thinkin' as Miss Grady's papa had begun ter see through the master an' that wife of his!'

For a moment, it seemed as though Mrs Manfred might engage in small conversation with the chubby, likeable maid, but, thinking it unwise to endorse such comments with a reply, Mrs Manfred instead gave a weary sigh and pointed out to the young woman that there was 'still much work to be done.' With this, the maid shrugged her shoulders, realizing she'd already said too much, and hurried about her business.

Mrs Manfred lingered for a moment longer at the window, her eyes fixed on the upward spiral of dust that marked the progress of the dog-cart along the sandy lanes, which, because of the lack of rain these past weeks –

almost the whole of September – were unusually dry underfoot. Presently, she turned away, her thoughts with Emma
on her first day as clerk at the Wharf Mill. She hoped it
would not be too bad, for, in spite of Emma's deepening
maturity resulting from the painful loss of her beloved
papa, she was nevertheless untutored in the ways of the
world. But, Mrs Manfred was not altogether despairing, for
Emma had always had a deep and precious gift for accepting most things with a wisdom way beyond her years.
Somehow, she was always ready to make the best of things,
however daunting they might seem to another, and these
traumatic past four weeks had only served to strengthen this
precious quality in her. Mrs Manfred's thoughts reflected
briefly on the dreadful thing which Caleb Crowther had done
in keeping father and daughter apart at a time when they
had needed each other more than ever before in their lives.
She had convinced herself that Caleb Crowther must have
thought it for the best, but it was still a terrible thing; it had
swept Emma's childhood away seemingly overnight, taking
with it a tender innocence and a certain softness from her
eyes, which once had seemed to smile all the time.

Still, Mrs Manfred was most confident that Emma would
not let this business of working in the mill get her down.
Indeed, if she knew Emma, and she did better than most,
the lass would seek to do well – if only for her papa's sake.

Certainly, as Caleb Crowther urged the horse onwards,
out of Breckleton and into Blackburn via Preston New
Road, Emma's thoughts were of a similar nature. After her
initial reservations regarding her clerical assignment to
Mr Gregory Denton, Emma had begun to look upon it as
a test, and she vowed to herself she would show Caleb
Crowther that she was her papa's child – made of the same

stirling quality! It would take more than being incarcerated in one of the Grady mills to break *her* spirit.

There was no lasting envy in Emma's heart towards her cousin, Martha, who, only a week ago, had also departed to begin a new adventure. But how very different Martha's departure had been from her own, she mused with a wry smile. Such fuss and ceremony! From the moment the pampered creature was risen from her bed to the moment she clambered into that fine, luggage-laden carriage – when her doting mama had thrust into the grasping gloved hands yet *more* refreshments for the journey – Martha Crowther had utilized a whole range of emotions. She had panicked, whimpered, wept, and indulged in every manner of tantrum!

Martha's departing words to Emma had merely been an attempt to raise herself above her cousin, with a cut to the heart. 'Of course, Emma,' she had started, mimicking her mama by peering down the length of her nose at Emma, 'you would gain *nothing* by going to a school for young ladies, having shown yourself to be at times unruly and vulgar. Oh dear me, no! But, I'm quite certain you will do well at the mill. Papa is an excellent judge of your limitations. Such work should suit you eminently.' With that, she allowed her mama to kiss her lightly on the cheek, but had seemed somewhat depleted when her papa merely gave her a curt instruction to 'attend well to your studies.' She had then swept out to embark upon her journey, which was some two hundred miles long and taking her to a grand school situated in the heart of Bedfordshire.

Now, here am I embarking on mine, thought Emma, with a strange feeling of satisfaction for, if the truth were told, she would not wish to change places with Martha – not for all of Queen Victoria's crown jewels!

These past weeks had been a hard and painful experience. She had known for a long time that her papa was desperately ill and had tried so hard to prepare herself for his leaving her on her own. Yet, when it happened she was *not* prepared; the manner of his death was such that now she missed him even more. And it was all the fault of the man seated beside her now – his very nearness caused her flesh to creep. Once or twice since Caleb Crowther had climbed into the dog-cart and taken up the reins, Emma had sent a caustic glance in his direction, thinking all the time what a foul and sorry creature he was. His sober and serious expression gave nothing away; the tails of his long black coat were ceremoniously laid out behind him – like the mantle of a devil, thought Emma bitterly; his stomach protruded grotesquely over his lap; his back was as straight and rigid as the look upon his stern, forbidding face; and perched on top of his mass of brown and iron-grey hair was that tall, upright hat which he was so seldom seen without.

'I would rather have found my own way to the mill,' Emma ventured. 'It would be no problem, because papa took me there many times.' She had made the same observation on the previous evening when Caleb Crowther had told her of his intention to 'See you get there, on your first day.' The resentment at his accompanying her was easily evident in her voice as she raised the issue again. So Emma was not surprised when he turned his head sharply to glower down at her. Then, giving only a grunt to signify that he had heard her, he returned his full attention to the road ahead. 'Giddyup!' his voice boomed down on the bay mare, as he slapped the reins in the air until they made a cracking sound which spurred the animal on at an even faster trot. It was not often that Caleb Crowther took it upon himself to drive the dog-cart into town, but on the odd occasion when he did, it was to be both heavy-handed in his management of it, and to present a fearsome spectacle to the less law-abiding citizens, who at some point along the journey would recognize him as Caleb Crowther – a tyrant who infused his sweating horse with terror, just as he did the miscreants upon whom he legally dispensed justice. He was not a liked man, nor was he respected – only despised and feared.

'Thomas has instructions to bring you in future. I have far more pressing matters which demand my time!' spoke Caleb Crowther now. 'As for you . . . Mr Denton has instructions to keep you plied with work and kept busy for the four hours you will be there each day; with the exception of Saturday, when no doubt your aunt will instruct you in duties of a more domestic nature. Later, of course, you will be called upon to put in a very much longer day.'

Emma thought this idea must please him intensely, for he now turned his head slightly to bestow on her a stiff little smile. But she paid him no attention. The prospect of work was not one that worried her. True, the mill was a daunting place in which to be confined – as she had witnessed on the numerous occasions she had been in there with her papa. She had seen for herself how dark and grimy conditions there were. But she had also seen how, despite this, the work-hands applied themselves wholeheartedly to the task in hand. And that is exactly what *I* shall do, Emma told herself now, certain that her papa would be proud of her resolve. Then she softly began humming a tune, as she assiduously observed the bustling activity all around, which increased significantly the nearer they came to Blackburn town centre.

At this early hour of eight a.m., there was much coming and going in every direction. The muffin-man was busy pushing his wicker-trolley along, his cloth cap perched precariously over his forehead, his step a lively one, and his lips pursed together in the whistling of a jolly melody. The brewery-waggon ambled along across the street, loaded with hefty wooden barrels brimful of draught beer. As usual, the big black shires harnessed up front were magnificent in their polished brass and leather harness, with their long tails neatly plaited, and their manes gathered in rows of intricate decorated braids. So delighted was Emma by this scene, that she raised her hand in a friendly wave as the waggon rolled past them in the opposite direction.

'Mornin' to you,' called one of the two men from the drivers' bench, both of whom were dressed in dark coats and trim little bowlers, with light-coloured breeches tucked into their black knee-length boots. These boots were polished to such a deep mirror finish that they gave the impression of being shiny wet. Emma thought the whole ensemble to be a proud and dignified one – albeit for the purpose of carting ale!

As they passed the grander houses of Preston New Road, the ladies emerged in twos and threes. Some were dressed in flouncy crinoline style, while others favoured the newest bustle line; but all were bedecked in extravagant bonnets, and all were unquestionably elegant and resplendent. It amused Emma to see how her Uncle Caleb's countenance suddenly changed at the sight of all this female finery. At once, he was wearing the sickliest of smiles, and doffing his hat in exaggerated gentlemanly gestures – only to scowl and curse, in characteristic fashion, when a four-horse carriage immediately behind began showing signs of impatience at his dawdling.

Emma grew more and more engrossed in the hustle and bustle as their route carried them farther away from the open countryside and wide roads, into the heart of industrial Blackburn town, with its narrow cobbled streets of tightly packed back-to-back houses, overlooked by towering and monstrous mill chimneys – themselves alive as they pumped out long creeping trails of choking black smoke. On a day such as this – when the earth was parched and devoid of a breeze which might cool it or lift the billowing smoke higher into the air – the dark swirling clouds could only cling to the roofs and chimneys like a thick acrid blanket enveloping all beneath, and shutting out the brilliant sunlight from above. But, to the vast majority of Blackburn folk it was a natural and accepted thing which was as much a part of their daily lives as breathing itself. The cotton mills were the life-line of almost every man and his family, whether they were mill-workers, mill-owners, river-people, or others who benefited from this industry. They tolerated the smoke and the shrill scream of the mill whistle calling them from their beds at some ungodly hour, for cotton was the thread by which their very existence hung. It gave them work; it gave them a means by which they could raise their families in dignity; and, above all, it gave them a sense of pride and achievement.

Cotton mills were going up at an unprecedented rate all over Lancashire, but, here in Blackburn the programme of mill construction was staggering. Emma had inherited her papa's own pride in these great towering monstrosities, and she knew all their names – Bank Top Mill, Victoria Mill,

Infirmary Mill – and, oh, so many more! Cotton was big business, keeping the town a hive of bustling activity. No hard-working mill-hand ever grew rich by it as his wages were too meagre; but, for the man with money to invest, the opportunities grew by the day. The Leeds to Liverpool Canal was a main artery from the Liverpool Docks to the various mills. Along this route the fuel and raw cotton which kept the mills alive was brought, thus affording a living to the many bargees who, with their families, dwelt in their colourful floating homes and spent most of their lives travelling to and fro with their cargoes. This consisted mainly of raw cotton, unloaded from the ships which carried it across the ocean from America.

Even Caleb Crowther's brooding mood, and her own feeling of bitterness towards him, couldn't quell Emma's enthusiasm as they clip-clopped towards the wharf. Oh, it brought back so many pleasant memories! Over Salford, along Railway Road, and into Eanam itself they went. Then, marked by tall cylindrical chimneys reaching high into the sky, the mill came into sight. It was a huge building of some several storeys high, with each level lined with dozens upon dozens of long narrow windows. Soon, they were passing through the oppressive big iron gates of Wharf Mill.

As they came into view of the open warehouse doors, Emma could see a group of cloth-capped men gathered just inside, exchanging conversation – which was evidently causing a great deal of fist-waving, finger-wagging and head-shaking. It all seemed very intense. Suddenly, one of the men caught sight of Caleb Crowther approaching, whereupon there was a flurry of activity and the group dispersed immediately – all except for one hump-backed little fellow, who came towards them at an urgent pace.

'What the devil's going on here?' Caleb Crowther demanded as he brought the horse and vehicle to a halt. He clambered down as the hump-backed fellow caught hold of the horse's halter. 'Why aren't those men at their work, eh? . . . What the hell do they think I pay them wages for, eh? . . . eh?' His neck stretched forward and his voice grew shriller.

The nervous explanation was offered that it was an accident the men had converged on that particular spot at that particular minute – being 'all good souls, an' grand workers doin' a regular job.' But that, 'findin' theirselves face to face, had stood a while to voice their fears o' the terrible unrest as seems ter be grippin' America – afeared fer their jobs an' their families, if owt should come a tumble wi' the shippin' in of our cotton from there.'

'Be that as it may . . . I don't give a damn for their reasons!' exploded Caleb Crowther. 'If I suspect it happening again, on *my* time, you can rest assured they'll all be out of work – and it won't be because of what's happening in America! Do I make myself clear, yardhand?'

As the little hump-backed fellow nodded most fervently, Caleb Crowther made a mental note to bring the matter to Gregory Denton's attention. But at the same time, he grudgingly admitted to himself that if there *were* any truth in what the papers would have them believe – that there really was the rumble of unease in America, between the North and the cotton-growing areas in the South – then, by God, there would indeed be cause for concern!

'See to it that Miss Grady is brought along to the office,' he now instructed the little man, 'then busy yourself, man . . . *busy yourself*. I don't hold with a man being a minute idle!' Then, leaving Emma in the care of this fellow, he strode away in the direction of the stairs which led up to the office where, at that very moment, Gregory Denton was nervously pacing the floor in anticipation of Caleb Crowther's arrival. The whole place seemed so much darker when *his* shadow fell upon the step.

'Hello, yardhand.' Emma fondly addressed the hump-backed fellow who would answer to no other name; indeed, most folk had forgotten what his real name was. Now, as he extended a helping hand, Emma leaned upon it, to swing herself to the ground. 'Are you keeping well?' She had a special affection for this poor deformed creature both because of his deep loyalty to her papa and because, in spite of his cumbersome affliction, he never grumbled or complained, but was always ready with a cheerful grin. He wasn't capable of putting in a heavy day's work but was invaluable in keeping the place free of clutter, booking loads in and out and generally making himself available wher-ever and whenever he was needed.

'Oh, I'm well, Miss Grady . . . very well . . . yes, indeed,' he replied in a jolly manner, but his face suddenly became crestfallen as he commented, 'I was so sorry about your papa . . . we all were. Thadius Grady were a good man, that 'e were!' When Emma gave an encouraging smile, but made no comment, he went on in an excited voice, 'I'm telled as ye'll be keepin' the books here? Oh, that's grand . . . keep your mind occupied, so it will, eh? Oh, we're glad ter have yer with us, Miss Grady . . . yes, indeed, very glad.'

As Emma started towards the office with the little fellow chatting alongside her, she did not see the tall, handsome young man, stripped to the waist, carrying bundles of raw cotton from his barge to the warehouse.

But, although Emma had not seen Marlow Tanner, he had seen her and he was overcome by what he saw. Emma looked beautiful in her best cornflower-blue dress with its pretty white fluted collar and scalloped hem, from beneath which peeped the toes of her dainty ankle-boots. Her rich chestnut hair hung loose down her back, framing her magnificent face perfectly. Yes, he had seen Emma – and was now smitten even more by her. But he had seen Caleb Crowther also, and in his heart he felt a deep conflict of emotions. He would never hesitate to go through Hell's fire for this lovely lass; but for the man, he felt only bitterness and disgust.

As he paused to watch Emma disappear into the interior of the mill, Marlow Tanner presented a splendid and formidable sight, with his lithe, muscular form upright and taut and his two strong fists clenched tight at his sides. His heart was torn in two.

''Ave yer gone on bloody strike or what?' The voice of Sal Tanner rang out across the yard to call her brother's attention. Her heart was deeply troubled for Marlow, whom she loved with the fierce protective instincts of a mother. Since the death of both their parents some fifteen years before – in a manner which had never been fully revealed – she had been to Marlow mother, father, sister and friend. In all truth, Sal revered only one thing above him, and that was her precious jug of ale. For, while Marlow had her to rely on, she could only fill the empty void in her life by losing herself in the comforting dregs of that cherished jug.

As Marlow made his way back, Sal Tanner murmured to him, 'Don't ever look above yer station, darlin', else ye'll surely fotch a heap o' pain down on yerself!'

Her mind was drawn back over the years to the time when

she was just a child, and Marlow was barely two years old. Their name was *not* Tanner then, but Royston; circumstances had forced them to change it. There had been the most dreadful scandal – the truth of which she had never learned, because, as was always the case when a boat-family was threatened, the others would close ranks to the outside world and closely guard their own. All she had learned over the years was that her dah had been seeing some fancy-born lady. There had been talk of it all up and down the river. So, when he began making plans to leave his wife and two youngsters, one of the bargees made it his business to warn the wife.

Sal Tanner remembered that very night like it was only yesterday. The awful way her mammy had looked when she left to follow her husband along the towpath. The fear within her when neither her mammy nor dah returned. Then, the following morning, both she and Marlow were snatched by the river-folk and hidden away for many a long month. It was then that their names were changed from Royston to Tanner. It was years later before Sal discovered why it was that her mammy and dah had never come back. It was rumoured that Eve Royston had found her husband Bill with his fancy lady, and, with the help of loyal friends, had murdered them both. Soon after she was hanged. Sal never did learn more than that, and, she was so disheartened and ashamed that she had no desire to learn any more. Her only thought then, as now, was to protect Marlow from the truth. Now, here he was, burning with the very same fever that got his dah murdered and his mammy hanged.

Her troubled violet eyes watched Marlow's downcast expression, and, for a moment, she made no move. Sal

Tanner was a familiar sight hereabouts, with her long calico skirt flowing about her dark heavy clogs, her brown crocheted shawl flung haphazardly over her shoulders, and that unmistakable chequered cloth cap tilted at a jaunty angle on her wispy fair hair. She could generally be heard roaring with laughter long before one might catch sight of her, and straightaway one could picture her with two sturdy hands spread-eagled, one over each hip, head thrown back and mouth wide open, revealing more gaps than teeth.

Today, however, Sal Tanner was in an unusually quiet mood. She was afraid – afraid for both Marlow and for herself. She knew Marlow was in love – had known that since the day he'd been carried through the door, flayed and bleeding. Her instincts had told her then that her young, reckless brother had become a man. Her deeper instincts now told her that it was a blessing the Lord had seen fit to give Marlow a strong broad back and an iron will together with the stoutest heart, for, God help them both, she could sense a dark and troublesome time ahead. It was most frightening how history had a nasty habit of repeating itself.

'Bloody fancy folk,' Sal Tanner snorted, at the same time grabbing a small flask of gin from within the folds of her skirt. 'Ye'd best keep yer soddin' distance from me an' mine!' she grumbled, taking a long gulp from the flask and glowering after Emma's disappearing form. However, Sal had to grudgingly admit to herself that this particular young girl was maybe not so fancy as some she'd come across. In fact, the smile she gave that little hump-backed bugger was a genuine, warm one, and there was nothing posh nor dandy about the lass's voice. 'If anything, she seemed a deal outta place aside o' that sour-faced whiskered feller as fotched 'er 'ere,' Sal told the empty air, grunting and then helping herself to another mouthful of the fiery liquid. 'But I'll keep me bloody eyes peeled all the same, 'acause me bones tell me there's trouble brewing . . . Gawd 'elp us all!'

Brimming with an equal measure of gin and foreboding, Sal Tanner sought out one of the loaders from the ware-house, a brash, brawny fellow by the name of William. 'What d'yer know o' that there lass?' she demanded to know. 'That pretty little thing as come 'ere with the whiskered bugger!' When William explained how the lass was none other than Miss Grady, the daughter of the late Thadius Grady, whose own dah came up from poor and common stock, to make himself known and respected amongst the workers, Sal Tanner threw back her head and roared with laughter. 'There!' she cried with delight. 'I *knew* it! . . . I bloody well knew it! That lass . . . the one yer call Emma . . . she don't come fro' no more fancy folk than *I* do!'

'That's as mebbe,' William told her, 'but, thanks to her dah, she'll come into a tidy little fortune one o' these fine days.' Here, he pursed his lips and clicked in serious manner, 'That is if she ain't cheated out of it by that conniving uncle of 'ers.'

'Oh?' Sal Tanner was intrigued. 'Got 'erself an enemy or two, 'as she?' There was no shifting Sal Tanner until she knew all there was to know about the lass who'd struck deep into Marlow's heart. As Emma's story unfolded, the barge-woman found herself sympathizing with this Emma. 'Poor little sod!' she exclaimed, taking another swig from the flask. 'Livin' in a big 'ouse an' belonging to fancy folk . . . well, it don't keep the troubles off yer back, do it, eh? Not if ye've med an enemy or two, it don't!' And, suspecting what a terrible misfit Emma was in Caleb Crowther's house, William had to agree.

'Aw, but you an' me ain't plagued wi' no such troubles, are we, Sal darlin',' he laughed, giving her a puff of his pipe and a knowing wink. He and Sal had an understanding . . .

'Why, yer randy bugger!' roared Sal Tanner, slapping him heartily on his shoulder and feigning a look of surprise. 'There ain't no 'olding yer, once yer teks a fancy!' Quickly now, she looked about and seeing there was nobody watching, she grabbed his arm. 'Come on then,' she laughed, tugging him round the back of the stacked bales, 'but it'll cost yer a wad o' that there baccy!' And, with both of them laughing, he carelessly knocked out his pipe and flung his arm about her.

'By! Yer a rum 'un, Sal Tanner,' he said, 'but I ain't complaining.'

'Bless me, if I've never seen that ledger so correct and neat! What an astonishing young lady you are, Miss Grady . . . if I may say so,' remarked Gregory Denton, collecting up the sheaf of invoices and scrutinizing the leather-bound ledger which lay open on Emma's desk. He had always suspected the daughter of Thadius Grady was a bright, intelligent lass – in spite of the stories that flew around town of her foolhardy escapades. Mind you, who could blame her? She was young and healthy with a particular thirst for life which, by its very nature, must drive her to seek a taste of adventure, away from the scrutiny of that dreadful Crowther lot. What a great pity the lass's papa had been taken. It was a sure fact that he was sorely missed here at the mill. That being the case, how much harder it must be for young Miss Grady, now securely in the clutches of her uncle, who was renowned for his lack of compassion!

Gregory Denton's admiration for Emma was two-fold. For all the heartache she must be suffering, the lass bore it well; indeed, when he compared Emma to other members of her sex, including his own ever-complaining, elderly mater, Emma was a female apart. Furthermore, she was exceptionally lovely, and had stirred in him long-forgotten cravings which he had accepted would never be satisfied. Like a fool, he had thrown away his few early opportunities. Now, he had only one great passion left, and that was his work. This mill was his pride, his joy . . . and his only reason for living! It was also his means of escape from a woman who believed that to be given a son was to be given absolute control over his very soul. Oh, what regrets he had! And how much deeper they seemed now that he was privileged to have such a delight as Emma Grady gracing his office. More than once in these past few hours he had averted his eyes from her because of the havoc she wreaked within him. Yet, to secretly gaze upon her was a deep, satisfying pleasure which he found impossible to deny himself. And, after all, he told himself, was it not so that a cat might look upon a queen?

Emma had sensed his eyes on her, but had paid no attention. Mr Denton was a pleasant enough fellow, and she had no wish to embarrass him in any way. Now, she looked up as he replaced the invoices on top of the ledger. 'I'm glad you're pleased with my work, Mr Denton,' she smiled. But, in all truth, she believed she had earned his praise, for she had checked and re-checked every detail on those invoices, before meticulously entering them on to the page. Now, she was ready to make a start on the warehouse dockets – starting with the one directly in front of her with the name 'Tanner' on top. 'If you'll just set me an example,' she asked.

Gregory Denton was so caught up in Emma's enthusiasm that he made a suggestion quite out of character. 'The ledgers can wait a while, Miss Grady,' he told her, 'and, if you've a mind, I'd like to take you on a tour of the mill . . . so you can see for yourself what procedure is followed.'

Emma had already toyed with the idea of asking this very favour, once her clerical duties were done. 'Oh, I'd like that, Mr Denton,' she said, quickly climbing from the stool in case he should change his mind.

Just over an hour later, with only ten minutes to spare before midday, at which time Thomas was due to collect her, Emma followed Mr Denton down the stairs and into the warehouse. 'Thank you for taking me round,' she told him, greatly impressed by what she had seen. On visits with her papa, the farthest she'd been allowed to go was the office enclosure. But today she'd seen virtually the whole process the raw cotton had to go through. She had seen the loose bales thrown into a machine that tore any knots or lumps from the cotton; then she was taken to the cardroom where it was combed; after this she saw how the twisted rovings were spun on machines which were some twelve feet wide and two hundred feet long. The cotton was then washed, bleached, dried, beaten, folded and pressed, before being considered suitably finished and ready for use. In the loom-weaving shed, Emma had wondered how the mill-hands could stand the relentless noise, day after day, without going totally deaf.

They were now on the lowest level, where the bales of

raw cotton, after being unloaded from the barges, were stored ceiling-high before samples were taken to ascertain the different grades and quality.

'Do you think you'll enjoy your work here, Miss Grady?' Gregory Denton ventured, feeling pleased with himself.

When Emma assured him that she'd had an exciting morning and was looking forward to learning all there was to know about the business, his face beamed with joy. 'Oh, that's grand!' he declared, feverishly nodding his head and rubbing his two hands together in a nervous fashion. 'That's right grand!'

By the look on his face as he leaned towards her, Emma could see he had a great deal more to say. But, at that moment there came a loud and frantic cry from the mouth of the warehouse, where the bales were brought in from the barges. This was immediately followed by a series of alarming noises and the unmistakable smell of fire. Emma was taken aback by the swift change in Gregory Denton as, grasping her arm, he propelled her at running pace towards the side exit. 'Take yourself out of here! Quick as you can!' he ordered, sending her the last few steps with a thrust of his arm. He then hurried towards the black smoke which was already billowing up to the ceiling and blocking out the light of day. By now there were men coming from all quarters and rushing to the scene. Emma's ears rang with the noise and her nostrils were overwhelmed by the smell of burning as the blanket of thick black smoke continued to grow. When the cry went up that someone was hurt, it took her only a moment to decide to try and help. Quickly now, she changed direction and hurried after Gregory Denton, her long skirt lifted high, and her throat burning from the dry smoke.

'You'd best stay clear, miss,' came the suggestion from one of the men who had been hurrying past, and grabbing her arm, he would have escorted her out of there.

'No! . . . If someone's hurt, I can help!' Emma cried, shrugging him off and hastening her steps.

Emma was determined to be of use, and what she saw when she reached the scene only strengthened her resolve. The fire had got a hold amongst the newly off-loaded bales, and was in danger of rapidly spreading right into the heart of the warehouse. Darting about and doing the work of ten men, Gregory Denton had swiftly organized an army of workers who, on his orders, were tearing down the great bale-stacks nearest the fire and throwing them outside, where other men quickly doused them with water bucketed from the canal. Over by the far gantry, near the area which the men were clearing in order to stop the fire spreading, a lone man was making frantic efforts to reach two people trapped beneath. He had bravely spurned all offers of help, insisting that the other men get the bales outside 'or we'll *all* end up burning.'

Ignoring all warnings, Emma made straight for this solitary figure. It was only as she drew closer that she recognized the handsome features, the shoulder-length black hair, and that fine strong physique, the back and shoulders of which were interlaced with a complex lattice of scars. Her heart gave a skip as she spoke his name, 'Marlow!' For a brief moment she hesitated as she stared at the young bargee who, because of her, had been cruelly whipped, and who, no doubt, would never want to set eyes on her again. She felt ashamed and deeply pained. How could she *dare* face him? In that moment she would have turned back, had it not been for the fact that people were hurt and every other pair of hands but her own was frantically working to beat the fire.

In a moment, Emma was by Marlow Tanner's side, down on her knees, scrabbling to reach the injured woman, who was by now almost free from the weight that pinned her down. When, totally astonished by her presence, Marlow called out Emma's name, she turned her head to glance up at him. In that all-too-brief moment when their eyes met, Emma's heart was aroused by such unfamiliar yet exhilarating emotions, that they left her visibly trembling. As his dark, passionate gaze absorbed her face with love and admiration, Emma's sparkling grey eyes reflected her wonder at these turbulent and exquisite feelings which possessed her. There was a blossoming of some deep, inner awareness within her, unlike anything she had ever known before. But with it came a murmuring fear, and the echo of a promise she had made.

Tearing away her gaze, she and Marlow set about the task in hand with renewed zest. When the two injured people were finally recovered, it was all too apparent that the man was beyond help.

'It's William!' cried Marlow. 'Poor bugger . . . there's nothing we can do for him, I'm afeared.' He straightened himself up, his bare flesh glistening with sweat in the fiery light, and his expression clearly reflecting his anger that a good man should die in such a way. 'Christ!' he moaned, wiping the back of his hand over his face, 'What the hell happened here?' Quickly he came to Emma's side, where she was cradling the unconscious woman in her arms.

'Is she . . . dead?' Emma asked softly.

Bending to collect the prostrate form into his arms, Marlow saw that it was his sister, Sal. His heart sinking deeply within him, he gave no answer to Emma's question, other than to instruct her in a gruff voice, 'Quickly! Away from here!' As he spoke, two men rushed in to carry away the body of William.

They made their way outside, where the scene was one of great confusion. Weary, red-faced men were frantically dashing about in their efforts to contain the still-raging fire, which, thanks to the quick thinking of Gregory Denton, had not spread to cause the major catastrophe that could have ensued.

As they came to rest in a quieter place by the canal bank, Emma watched as, with great tenderness, Marlow Tanner laid his sister on the ground. At once, she began moaning. Quickly, Emma got to her knees and, taking the limp form into her arms, she told Marlow, 'Get Thomas . . . hurry! We must get her to the infirmary.' Whereupon, Sal Tanner stiffened and began struggling in Emma's arms.

'Jesus, Mary an' Joseph!' she called out, reaching up to grab Marlow as he stooped towards her. 'The buggers are after killin' me!' When Marlow laughed out loud and hugged her, she threw him off, shouting, 'I ain't goin' ter no bloody infirmary . . . so yer can piss off, the lot on yer!' But when she made an effort to get to her feet, she promptly fell back with a cry of pain.

'You'll do as you're told for once, Sal Tanner!' Marlow told her, raising her skirt up to her knee and seeing her already swollen, twisted leg. 'Looks to me like your leg's busted.'

Emma was surprised to find herself smiling at Sal Tanner's outspoken manner. What was more, she'd taken an instant liking to her. 'You ought to go to the infirmary,' she said, 'Thomas will get you there in no time at all.'

'He bloody *won't*, yer know!' came the swift retort, after which she gave Marlow an accusing glare. 'An' as fer you, yer bugger! . . . Yer oughta be ashamed tryin' ter put yer sister in such a place!'

'Yes, she *is* my sister,' Marlow explained to Emma, having seen the puzzled look on her face, 'so, you can imagine what a cross I have to bear, can't you, eh?'

'William!' Sal Tanner's concern suddenly shifted from herself to that of the man she'd been with. 'What about William?' When Marlow told her, in the gentlest way he could, that William had been beyond saving, she fell back in Emma's arms making a sign of the cross and saying in a quiet voice, 'Get me 'ome, lad. I'll mend all right, wi'out goin' to no infirmary.' When he hesitated, she turned to Emma, 'I'd be done fer sure, if I was shut up in a place like that. You'll 'elp me, won't yer, lass, eh?' When she began crying, Emma held her close, her only concern being for this poor, distressed woman.

'Of course I'll help you,' she promised, 'don't fret your-self . . . we'll get you to your own bed.'

The Tanner barge was moored close by, so Marlow gently lifted his sister into his arms, while Emma caught hold of her hand and held it comfortingly, half-walking, half-running, as she tried to keep up with Marlow's long strides. He was deeply aware of Emma as she brushed against him, and at that moment Marlow knew he would never love any other woman – not for as long as he lived. As for Emma, just being close to him gave her a wonderful feeling of belonging – one that she had not experienced since her papa had died.

As the horses thundered by, drawing the fire engine behind them, Marlow and Emma were forced to one side.

'They'll have it safe now,' he told Emma, and as their eyes met, they shared an intimate smile which made Emma's heart somersault. But, his eyes grew serious as he told her, 'I'll have to set Sal's leg . . . it won't be a pleasant thing to see. Do you still want to help?'

Emma was undeterred. 'Of course I want to help,' she said. Then she ventured, 'Is there no one else but you and your sister?' When Marlow replied that no, there was just the two of them, Emma boldly asked after their parents. However, she soon wished that she had not mentioned it when she saw Marlow's face grow serious, and in a darker mood he told her, 'No, we've no parents, me and Sal . . . we were *robbed* of 'em, some many years back!'

In the ensuing silence, Emma felt awkward and angry with herself. Sal Tanner, meanwhile, was totally shocked when she heard Marlow's reply to Emma's questions, for there was so much bitterness in his voice, that it seemed as though he knew something of the terrible way in which both their parents had been taken. Their father murdered and their mother hanged.

Indeed, Marlow was deeply troubled by certain things which he had recently discovered regarding what had taken place in the past. But his fine features betrayed little of his worries as he continued on his way – with his sister in his arms, Emma by his side, and an overwhelming love in his heart for both of them.

Emma was also troubled, for she knew that in going to Marlow Tanner's barge she was going against both her papa's wish and Caleb Crowther's instructions. She didn't feel that she was breaking her promise by helping an injured person, but she knew she was in grave danger of doing so through the irrepressible feelings she had for the man beside her. She could never betray her beloved papa, so she determined that she would give her help, as one human being to another, but after that, she must never see either of the Tanners again.

On seeing Emma disappear along the wharf in the company of the Tanners, and seeing how contented she appeared to be, Gregory Denton was overcome with jealousy. Without thinking too deeply of the possible consequences of his actions, he quickly searched for Thomas amongst the men who were busy helping to clear up the mess. On finding him, he instructed him to make haste and report to Caleb Crowther.

'Tell him we've lost one man – the fellow as started it, I reckon! Make sure he knows how quickly we got the fire under control. But, tell him as there's another matter he should know about. The matter of his ward, Miss Grady, being enticed away by river-folk . . . not fit company at all for a young lady of Miss Grady's standing, as I'm sure Mr Crowther will agree.' In this unusually vindictive mood, Gregory Denton might well have given the name of these river-folk. But he was no fool! Marlow Tanner and his sister were that rare breed of worker who could always be relied on, and he didn't want to be deprived of their services. Added to which, the men who worked here wouldn't take too kindly to having one of their mates put out of work on account of what *he* said. No, thought Gregory Denton, it would be enough to have Marlow Tanner realize that Miss Grady was a young woman he must steer clear of. Yes, that would suffice.

'Go on!' he instructed Thomas. 'Tell Mr Crowther exactly as I've told you.' Then, with a feeling of satisfaction, he watched the dog-cart move out of sight at an urgent speed. And, even though he astonished himself with his own boldness, Gregory Denton was thinking that one day he might even ask for Miss Grady's hand in marriage!

Emma had watched with admiration as Marlow firstly straightened Sal Tanner's leg, and then skilfully strapped it between two stout canes. During this painful operation, Emma had comforted the woman. She had talked to her, bathed her other wounds, mopped the sweat from her face and, at both Marlow's and Sal's insistence, had kept her topped up with a good measure of gin.

'Yer a good lass, Emma Grady,' Sal kept telling her. 'Yer don't belong ter them there Crowther toffs. Oh! . . . I've 'eard all about the buggers, full o' their own importance an' lording it o'er other creatures. An' that bearded divil . . . well! That's *Justice* Crowther, ain't it? Now *there's* a laugh, eh? What fair justice has *that* bugger ever given out? None at all, that's what! Oh, aye . . . that slimy sod's well known, by name an' bloody nature!' Peering at Emma, she added, 'Ain't that right, Emma Grady? . . . Ain't every word I say the very truth?' She waited for an answer, as though she was willing Emma to give the right one – or be damned along with the rest of the Crowther brood.

Emma, however, would not be drawn into Sal Tanner's little game, although, deep inside her, she knew every word Sal spoke to be the very same as those emblazoned on her own heart. 'Why don't you rest, Sal?' she suggested tactfully, 'You've been through a lot today.' She leaned forward and drew up the blanket from the bottom of the bunk, where Sal had contemptuously flung it. 'You need to keep warm,' she chastised, 'and you might get better that much quicker if you did as you were told.'

'Be buggered!' Sal Tanner retorted. 'You're nowt but a snotty-nosed kid an' I ain't being ordered about by no lass young enough to be me bloody daughter!' She began snorting and cursing and searching for her flask of gin. 'Sod off!' she told Emma. 'Go on, piss off back ter them fancy buggers yer live with.' Taking the blanket in both hands, she flung it to the floor. 'I ain't no bloody babby!' she grumbled, folding her arms and lapsing into a fit of sulks.

'Is that right?' demanded Emma, equally determined, 'Then stop *behaving* like one!' With that, she collected up the blanket and flung it over the stiff, angry figure, 'And you're not likely to get your own way by throwing insults at *me* Sal Tanner . . . because I've been insulted by pastmasters at it! So you'll have to think again, won't you, eh?' Emma's eyes were twinkling as they met the other woman's defiant yet curious expression.

'Well, I'm buggered!' Sal Tanner roared, throwing herself back into the pillow and cackling with glee. 'Yer a little she-cat, ain't yer? A little she-cat wi' claws!' Then, calling out to the galley, where Marlow was brewing up a jug of tea, 'What the bloody 'ell 'ave yer fotched under our roof, Marlow, lad?' she chuckled, 'A right little madam, I'm thinking!' At the same time she affectionately slapped the back of Emma's hand, as the two of them laughed together.

'A right little *angel*,' corrected Marlow, as he squeezed his broad shoulders in through the narrow doorway. 'And one that's got the better of *your* temper, I see,' he laughed. Setting down three pots of tea on the little dresser, he cautioned both women, 'Be careful, it's piping hot.'

Emma helped Sal Tanner to a more comfortable, semi-upright position, and after carefully placing a pot of tea in her hands, she picked up another one for herself and proceeded to sip it. All the while, Marlow's eyes followed her every move, his love for her emanating from them for all the world to see.

Being so close that she could feel the warmth of Marlow's breath against her face, it took all of Emma's will-power to stop herself from looking up at him. Knowing her eyes betrayed the love she felt for him, she merely nodded and gave the slightest murmur, 'It *is* hot.' In the short silence that followed – when all that could be heard was Sal Tanner noisily slurping her tea, the loud ticking of a large round clock which took up the whole of the polished wooden panel above the tiny dresser, and the gentle slapping of the water against the sides of the barge – Emma experienced a welcomed feeling of happiness and belonging here in this homely barge.

It was the first time Emma had ever been inside a barge, and it had been a great surprise. Not for a moment had she expected to see such a cosy and exceptionally pretty home as this. All the walls and ceiling were made of highly-polished panels. In the living-quarters the walls were decorated with lovely brass artefacts – plates, old bellows and the like; from the ceiling hung three oil-lamps of brass and wood, each sparkling and meticulously kept; there were two tiny dressers, both made of walnut and display-ing small china ornaments – which, according to Sal, were 'put away when we're on the move'; as were the china plates which were propped up on shelves beneath each porthole; the horse-hair chairs were free-standing, but the dressers were securely fixed to the floorboards. There was also a small cast-iron fire, and the narrow galley which was well-stocked and spotless. In one of the two bedrooms there was a tiny dresser with a tall cupboard beside it, and a deep narrow bunk beneath a porthole. Emma had been astonished that everything a person might need could be provided in such a limited space.

All the time Emma had been attending to Sal Tanner, she had encouraged her to talk at great length about the barge.

'She's been in the Tanner family fer a good few years now . . . ever since me mammy an' dah were wed. It's named Eve . . . after me mammy, d'yer see?' Judging by Sal's moist eyes when she spoke of the barge, and by the proud look on her face, Emma could see that the barge was greatly loved. Not only did she see this in Sal's face, but she could feel it all around her. There was a special kind of goodness and love in this little home, which she would have given everything for!

Emma's mind was overrun by a multitude of thoughts – of her papa, of what they had both been denied at his last moments, and now, of this young man sitting so close to her that all she had to do was reach out her hand and he would surely take it. Suddenly she felt afraid, and as the tears sprang to her eyes, warm and stinging, she told Marlow, 'I must go . . . Thomas will be concerned about my disappearance.' But it wasn't Thomas she was thinking of so much as the possibility that, in his anxiety, Gregory Denton might have alerted Caleb Crowther. A quick glance at the clock told her that over an hour had passed since she had made her way here with Marlow and Sal.

Quickly, Emma got to her feet, before astonishing Sal Tanner by leaning down to kiss her warmly on the forehead. 'Remember,' she told her, 'you do as you're told.' Then, deliberately averting her eyes from Marlow, she edged her way towards the door, through the living-area, and up the small flight of steps to the deck. Once there, she glanced along the wharf, feeling less anxious when she saw that it was unusually quiet, save for two little lads in floppy caps and knee-length breeches who were scrambling up a stack of coal and occasionally skimming the smaller pieces on the water. Up to mischief while everybody else is giving help and clearing away the mess at the warehouse, she thought with amusement.

'Must you go, Emma?' She turned, startled, as Marlow climbed out to stand beside her. As her gaze settled on his face, her heart felt suffocated. He looked so handsome and was staring at her now with such intensity and passion. Soon after they had come into the barge, Marlow had grabbed a grey chequered shirt, quickly shrugging himself into it and rolling the long sleeves up to the elbows. He had been too preoccupied with Sal to waste time doing up the many small buttons down its front. Now, as he stood tall and upright before her, Emma was conscious of the breeze which playfully tugged at his shirt, occasionally whipping it backwards to display his sunburned and muscular chest. Emma was immediately reminded of the vicious scars that Caleb Crowther had etched into Marlow's back. She had made no mention of the incident, believing it to be one that was best forgotten. But, as it now reared its ugly head in her mind she suddenly became fearful. Thus, when Marlow suggested that if she really had to leave, he would walk her back to the Wharf Mill, Emma felt frantic.

'No, I don't want that!' she told him. 'Please . . . your sister needs you just now.'

'More than *you* need me, Emma?' he asked in a soft voice, which was little more than a whisper, and penetrating her trembling soul with his loving gaze.

Deliberately now, and with every ounce of strength she could muster, Emma looked him in the eye, and in a quiet, controlled voice said, 'I'm glad that your sister wasn't hurt more badly, and I'm pleased to have been of help. But . . . believe me, Marlow, I *must* go!' Lowering her eyes, she tried to turn from him, only to find her way barred as Marlow placed himself before her. In a minute he had one hand on her shoulder, and, with the other, he gently touched her chin, tilting her face to look up at him. For a long cherished moment, he held her like that, his dark eyes burning into her and his fingers tenderly caressing her face.

Emma was mesmerized. Try as she might, she couldn't tear her gaze away from his; and though every instinct told her to run from this place, she was unable to move. 'I do love him so,' she thought, 'and I don't want to go. I would wish for nothing else but that I could stay by his side.' As he lowered his face so that it almost touched hers, Emma's heart melted; and when he murmured, 'I love you Emma,' a wonderful tide of emotion surged through her. She offered no resistance when, suddenly, he grabbed her in his arms and kissed her with such longing that he took her breath away. In that exquisite moment, their passionate and intimate embrace warned Emma that, because of the way the river-people had taken her mama and ruined her papa's life and because of the promise she herself had given her papa, there could be no future for her and Marlow. Emma also knew that any relationship which might have grown between them would be dangerous for Marlow – the scars on his back were a caution that must be heeded. So many things were against them, against their love, and Emma's instincts urged her that she and Marlow could ignore these only at their own peril!

As Emma wrenched herself from his embrace, Marlow made no move to restrain her because he already feared he'd gone too far. Instead, he reminded himself that Emma was of a different kind to the lasses he was used to. She had been brought up accustomed to the finer things in life, and was used to folk who might seek her affection in a more restrained fashion. He had also seen that, in spite of her outburst with Sal, Emma was quiet and deep-thinking, and might be overwhelmed by his forward display of emotion. Having her so close, yet still so far away from him, gave him a feeling of desperation. He wanted her so much. He meant to have her. But even now, when he was no more than a heartbeat away, Marlow Tanner sensed the barrier between them. For the first time in his life, he felt unsure and afraid.

Hating every step that took her further away from him, Emma hurried along the quayside. On reaching the corner before she turned off towards the mill, she paused to look back, and, seeing that Marlow had gone, her heart sank within her. For a brief moment she was tempted to go back, and, as she stood there watching the spot where he had stood, an overwhelming sensation of warmth and joy came over her – just as she had felt on the two memorable occasions when she had found herself in Marlow's company. However, Emma painfully realized that both times had been overshadowed by suffering and tragedy. The first meeting had culminated in the agonizing beating inflicted on Marlow by Caleb Crowther, as well as the distress she had unwittingly caused her dying papa through her foolhardy behaviour. Now, at their second encounter, a man had been killed and Sal Tanner badly hurt. For a moment, these thoughts haunted Emma and she prayed this was not some terrible omen for the future. 'No matter,' she murmured, still gazing towards the barge, 'for our paths won't likely cross again. They must not, Marlow Tanner. And I hope you can see that just as clearly as I can!' But even as she muttered these words aloud, her heart was disobediently murmuring something to the contrary, and filling her with trepidation.

Emma was so engrossed in her tortured thoughts of Marlow Tanner that she did not hear the stamp of swift and angry footsteps drawing ever closer to her. When a hand fell upon her shoulder and roughly swung her round, she gave out a cry of fright, her alarmed eyes coming to rest on the furious face of Caleb Crowther.

'Well?' he said, in a voice which warned Emma to be most careful. When she hesitated, he dug his fingers deeper into her shoulder. 'I'm given to understand that you've been with the river-people. What I want to know . . . right now . . . is who are these people? What are their names? Take me to them this instant.' His eyes grew even darker as they glared at her.

'You've been misinformed, Uncle Caleb,' replied Emma in a remarkably controlled voice, considering the turmoil within her. 'There was so much chaos and confusion when the fire started, that Mr Denton urged me to get out quickly. I would have made my way straight home but . . . I couldn't find Thomas.' Thomas was standing slightly behind Caleb Crowther, to his left. Emma glanced at him and gave up two small prayers – one that Thomas would not betray her, and the other asking forgiveness for the blatant lie she had just told.

At that instant, something happened which struck the fear of God in Emma's heart, and for a brief moment she was convinced it was her just punishment for the sin she had just committed. For, loud and clear, Sal Tanner's voice sailed the length of the wharf. 'Sod an' bugger it Marlow! 'Ow the 'ell am I supposed to get better if yer keeps depriving me o' me bloody booze! Best medicine in the world is a swig of booze, yer silly arse!'

At once, Caleb Crowther stretched his neck to see where the voice might be coming from. Thomas also glanced along the wharf, a fearful expression in his nervous eyes. As for Emma, she crossed her fingers behind her back and kept her serious gaze constantly on her uncle's face. For a long, nerve-wracking moment, it seemed as though Caleb Crowther would stride off to investigate. When he looked back into Emma's calm and seemingly innocent face, there was still the germ of suspicion lurking in his fiery eyes. Without taking either his hand or his probing gaze from Emma, he said in a quiet voice, 'Thomas . . . is what Miss Grady says the truth? Were you not at your station waiting to speed her home the minute her duties were done?' Still, he kept his eyes securely fixed on Emma.

Emma felt Thomas's gaze on her, but she dared not look at him. All she could do was to hope desperately that he would give credence to her lie. For, Thomas had indeed been ready and eager to take her away the minute Gregory Denton had thrust her towards that side door.

'T'ain't Miss Grady's fault at all,' replied Thomas, and Emma had to stop herself from visibly showing her heartfelt relief. 'When that fire started, I saw Miss Grady making her way towards me . . . but I could see the way of things right enough, Mr Crowther, sir. If it hadn't been every man

91

to the helm . . . so to speak, well, the whole place could a' been engulfed, don't yer see? I called out to Miss Grady to get right away from there!'

'And that's what I did, Uncle Caleb,' Emma intervened with a wide, innocent look. 'I've been wandering up and down the wharf . . . staying out of harm's way, that's all.'

Now Caleb Crowther let go of Emma and swung himself about to address Thomas. 'Why didn't you tell me that before, you bloody fool?' he demanded.

''Cause yer never asked me, Mr Crowther, sir,' replied Thomas, looking suitably sheepish.

Caleb Crowther gave out a groan, together with the instruction. 'Get Miss Grady home this instant. Then come back here. There's damage to be assessed and a certain fellow to be spoken to.' As he strode away, neither Thomas nor Emma had any doubts as to who that 'certain fellow' was.

'Poor Mr Denton,' said Emma with a little smile, hurrying alongside Thomas as they made their way back to the carriage. 'As if he hasn't had enough trouble for one day.'

To which Thomas gave a noisy snigger. 'Oh, he'll be all right, Miss Grady. They do say as how Gregory Denton can handle any occasion *most admirably*!' The last two words were greatly exaggerated, causing Emma to lightly reprimand him.

'All the same,' she said, 'I shouldn't think he's yet had to deal with such an occasion as Mr Crowther in full sail.' In all truth, Emma hoped poor Mr Denton wouldn't be subjected to too much condemnation on her account. She was certain that Mr Denton would be unable to get a word in against the fury of her uncle's explosive temper; which was just as well since he had after all seen her going off with the Tanners – and there was not the slightest doubt in her mind that it was *he* who had alerted her uncle.

As they left the wharf, the dry acrid smell of charred cotton bales followed them – clinging to their clothes, stinging their throats, and causing Emma to be gripped by a severe coughing spasm.

'Lord love us!' exclaimed Thomas, expertly manoeuvring the horse and carriage in and out of the numerous highly-stacked piles of merchandise, and skilfully avoiding the dockers who were by now filtering back from the fire to their posts, ready to work that much harder in order to catch up on their duties. 'It's to be hoped you ain't goin' down wi' some'at nasty. By! That Mrs Manfred would 'ave me swinging fro' the end of a rope if you've tekken badly on *my* account!' It was well-known that Mrs Manfred considered Miss Grady almost as her own lass. Look at the way she'd almost thrown a fit just now when it was reported that Miss Grady was suspected of going off with the river-folk. But then, Thomas didn't blame Mrs Manfred, because Miss Grady was a grand little lass, that she was. What's more, he hadn't minded saving her with a lie just now – though it would cost him a prayer or two come Sunday! But then he was sure the Lord would understand, and he said as much to Mrs Manfred on their return, adding with fervent belief, 'I'm sure if the Good Lord were faced wi' Caleb Crowther on the one side, an' Miss Grady on the other, himself would a done the very same thing!'

'Away with you!' Mrs Manfred had told him, with feigned horror, 'You'll not ease your conscience *that* way.' However, before he skulked away, she brought back the smile to his face by adding, 'All the same, Thomas lad . . .

there are times when we're called on to go against our teaching, in order to see justice done!'

As Thomas made his way to the stables, Emma found herself being unceremoniously ushered into the house. 'I watched from the window for you, Miss Grady,' Mrs Manfred explained, 'I wanted to come out and stop you, before you were confronted by Mrs Crowther.' As they drew nearer to the front door, she lowered her voice, saying, 'She's in the drawing-room, waiting for an explanation. You just tell her what you told Mr Crowther . . . you did *not* go near the river-folk!' Here, she gave Emma a suspicious look. 'You can tell *me* the real story later!'

It was six p.m. when Emma answered the knock on her bedroom door, to find Mrs Manfred standing there. Her audience with Agnes Crowther had been brief and, much to Emma's surprise, less of an ordeal than she had anticipated. Her aunt appeared to have other things on her mind, not least of which appeared to be a letter that she continuously played with throughout her questioning of Emma. She appeared to Emma to be extremely agitated and unusually nervous and Emma mentioned this now, to Mrs Manfred. 'She hardly seemed to mind a word I said, Manny,' Emma concluded.

'Aye, well . . . she and the master had a deal of words over that letter . . . the pair of 'em got so worked up, we could hear the heated exchange all over the house!' explained Mrs Manfred in a hushed tone. 'And well they might be worked up!' she went on, drawing Emma away from the bedroom door, fearing that they might be overheard. Now, in an even more subdued tone, she told Emma how the letter appeared to have been sent by the headmistress of 'that posh establishment' to which Martha Crowther had been despatched with such fuss some weeks ago. 'A right to-do, there is, Miss Grady,' continued Mrs Manfred, her hand on Emma's arm as she constantly watched the door. As she continued, Emma was horrified to hear how Martha had caused such trouble at the school that the headmistress had insisted on seeing both of her parents straightaway. There was even a possibility that she might be expelled!

'Expelled? . . . *Martha Crowther*?' Emma could hardly believe her ears.

'There is every chance that such a thing could happen,' said Mrs Manfred, afterwards shaking her head and drawing her lips into a tight little pucker.

'I'm not surprised Uncle Caleb was in a worse mood than usual,' exclaimed Emma, 'and that certainly explains why I was sent so swiftly from the drawing-room, earlier.'

'Hhm! For all her airs and graces . . . and for all that she never once passes an opportunity to slap you down . . . Mrs Crowther's precious daughter is not the blameless little soul she would have her be! From what I was able to gather, the peevish and spiteful side to Miss Crowther's nature has been given full rein since leaving this house. Apparently, she's caused a deal of mischief, and upset a number of the other girls at the school . . . also, there's a question of something going missing, which Miss Crowther insists has been stolen by a certain individual.'

All the while Mrs Manfred was relating her story, Emma's eyes were popping from her head. She just couldn't believe it. Martha Crowther – that arrogant and thoroughly spoiled girl, who could never do anything wrong! Well, it seemed now as though her true colours were flying at long last! Trying desperately hard not to laugh, Emma thought how *dreadful* the scandal hereabouts would be if the only child of Caleb Crowther, the Justice, and his wife Agnes, the proud peacock, was sent home in disgrace from the posh school? Oh, the very idea! Emma swung away from the homely housekeeper and, throwing herself on to the bed, collapsed into a fit of laughter, burying her head in the pillow to smother the sound.

'You stop that at once!' ordered Mrs Manfred, striding to the bed and shaking Emma by the shoulder. 'This is a very serious matter, I'll have you know . . . not one to be taken lightly by any standards.' Mrs Manfred had very firm principles regarding a young lady's behaviour, and, at the moment, neither Martha Crowther's, nor Emma's in making so light of the matter, was an example of good upbringing.

'Oh, I'm sorry, Manny,' said Emma in a contrite voice, as she leaned on one elbow and raised her mischievously smiling eyes. 'I shouldn't laugh, I know. It's a disgraceful thing for Martha to cause such mischief and bring shame on the Crowther name . . . but . . . well . . .' Then, in spite of her best efforts to contain herself, Emma's serious expression began to crumble, her eyes grew increasingly merry and she evaporated into a convulsion of giggling. 'Oh, Manny!' she cried, looking directly into the other woman's disapproving scowl, 'Can't you just see the funny side of it?' Whereupon, she fell against Mrs Manfred and hugged her fiercely. In a minute, Mrs Manfred was also chuckling.

'You're a naughty one!' she reprimanded Emma, 'But you're right. I can just see Mrs Crowther's expression when she opened that letter!' Still holding Emma fast, she too shook with laughter.

When they eventually composed themselves, the discussion turned to the other incident of the day — involving Emma and the river-folk. Mrs Manfred related to Emma how the letter had arrived not long before Thomas had brought the message from Gregory Denton. 'In fact, the two of them were still loudly arguing over it,' she explained, 'when the news came, that not only had there been a fire, but that you had been seen going away in the company of the river-folk!'

As she listened to what had taken place, Emma could easily see how such a series of events might send Caleb Crowther into an explosive mood. Suddenly, she felt sorry for Gregory Denton, who had no doubt borne the brunt of that temper. In all truth, Emma thought, he had probably acted in what he thought were her best interests. She made up her mind straightaway to make amends with the poor fellow at the first opportunity.

'And *did* you go off with the river-folk?' demanded Mrs Manfred now, a tremor of fear in her voice.

For a long moment, Emma gave no answer. Instead, her thoughts had wandered back to the wharf, to that colourful, welcoming, Tanner barge, and to Marlow Tanner himself. Whenever she thought of him, that same warm glow and wonderful feeling of contentment came into her heart. She was both afraid and possessive of the thoughts which now suffused her mind — that special way in which his dark, lustrous eyes murmured to her in the warmth of his smile; the way her foolish heart trembled when he spoke to her in that soft, caressing voice. But, most of all, Emma was held forever in his embrace, with the tender strength of his kiss still burning on her mouth, and that passionate look of longing in his eyes doing unexplainable things to her aching heart. All of these emotions were alien to Emma. They frightened her. But, for all that, she could not help but cherish them.

'I *will* have the truth, child!' Mrs Manfred interrupted Emma's thoughts. She had watched Emma closely, and was filled with apprehension when she saw Emma's face light up as she became lost in her thoughts. Her treasured memories of Marlow Tanner were clearly reflected on her lovely features as she raised her soft grey eyes to Mrs Manfred. In answer to the older woman's question, she replied simply, 'I love him, Manny.'

'No, no, child! You *don't* love him . . . What can you even know of love? With you a child not yet sixteen?' The desperation betrayed itself in her voice, as she lifted her two hands and tenderly placed one on each of Emma's small shoulders.

'You're right, Manny darling,' Emma conceded, her heart moved by the stricken look on the older woman's face. 'I don't know anything about love . . . or how it should feel. All I do know is that, whenever I think of him, every corner of my being lights up, and I want nothing more than to spend my whole life by his side!' Emma held nothing back now, as she poured her heart out to the only real friend she had. She whispered of her love and her fears . . . of the way Marlow beckoned to her and how she could see in him all of her dreams. And now, with her eyes downcast and her heart heavy, Emma told Mrs Manfred of the fervent promise she had given to her papa, and how it weighed on her shoulders 'like the end of the world.'

All the time Emma had been talking, Mrs Manfred had softly wept. If she had thought Emma to be still a child, she was sorely wrong. If she had believed Emma could know nothing of love, then she herself knew even less. If she had convinced herself that, in having lost first her mama, then her darling papa, and consequently having been placed at the mercy of the Crowthers, Emma had been dealt all the cruelties that life could deal her, then she was indeed an old fool. For, Mrs Manfred had never seen a person so in love, and so tormented because of it, as her darling Emma was now. Because she regarded Emma almost as her own flesh and blood, she must advise her for the best: and that meant persuading Emma to put the young bargee out of her mind and out of her heart.

Having confided her most secret thoughts to Mrs Manfred, Emma now looked up and, seeing the still-wet tears on that much-loved face, she was deeply touched. 'Oh, Manny,' she murmured, bringing her fingers to brush against the older woman's face, 'don't fret yourself. I can be strong, you know that. Papa told me how he felt about the river-folk . . . and *why*. He asked me to give him my word that they would find no place in my life, and I freely gave it.' Emma's firm, clear gaze met the sorry eyes that looked into hers, and in an unfaltering voice she went on, 'Papa was a fine man, with a deep sense of justice. If he had not believed it to be for the best, he would never have asked it of me. I trust his judgment in all things and I *must* keep my word!' In her heart, Emma prayed to God that he might help her.

'Aw, child . . . much as I loved your papa, I have to say that he had no right to ask such a thing of you,' said Mrs Manfred with a sigh.

'He had every right!' declared Emma, and, to all intents and purposes, she considered the discussion to be at an end. However, in spite of herself, somewhere deep inside her,

Emma had much sympathy with Mrs Manfred's senti-
ment. Furthermore, her curiosity concerning the past was
now aroused; what had happened between her mama and
the river-people? 'Bad blood' Caleb Crowther had said of
her mama, and, though she had later been given an explanation for this by her papa, there was still a murmuring of
unease in Emma's soul. How had her mama *really* come
to die? *Why* was Caleb Crowther so bitter towards Mary
Grady? And why had she herself been kept in the dark, only
to be told of it by her papa as he lay on his death bed? Emma
despised herself for raising questions which, by their very
nature, must cast doubt on her own papa's word. Quickly,
she pushed the entire matter to the darker recesses of her
mind. But not before she was filled with the earnest hope
that, one day at some time in the distant future, she might
know the full truth of what had happened all those years
ago.

It was nearing dusk when Marlow Tanner accompanied the
little man to the place where his faithful old cob-horse was
tethered. Both men were silent, both deep in thought – one
wondering whether he had been wise to pay a rare visit to
these parts; the other, curiously considering a guarded
remark made some time before by Gabe Drury, concerning Marlow's own dah.

 'Gabe . . . you take care now,' Marlow told the little man
as he climbed on to the bare back of the cob. As Gabe Drury
looked down, to find Marlow's dark eyes intent upon him,
there was a long heavy silence, interrupted only by the slapping of the canal water against the moored barges. It was
Marlow who spoke first, and what he asked only served to
agitate the little fellow, 'Can you tell me *anything* . . .

anything at all, about the fellow you saw making good his escape that day?'

'No! . . . I've told you before, Marlow,' already Gabe Drury was hurriedly spurring his horse on, 'I saw nowt but a pair of legs just running, that's all! I were sleeping off a boozy night . . . found mesel' spread-eagled in the hedge, an' when I heard all the commotion, I just looked up . . . saw *nowt*, except for a pair o' legs. I can't tell you more than that!' With a wary look about him, he urged the horse on its way, but not before glancing over his shoulder to warn Marlow, 'Leave the past be, lad. It's done an' there's nowt to change it. Take good care of your sister, and God bless the pair of you.'

As he went into the gathering darkness, Gabe Drury thought himself a fool. What in God's name had ever made him mention seeing anybody on that terrible day when Sal and Marlow's dah was murdered, together with his fancy piece? All these years he'd kept to the backwaters, out of harm's way, but when Marlow had recently sought him out – the subject of his parents being his motive – the lad had somehow managed to persuade him to reveal how he'd seen a fellow running from that place. Now, Marlow wouldn't let it be! All the same, Gabe Drury hoped that tonight he'd laid that particular ghost to rest once and for all.

As he reflected on events, Gabe Drury thought what a pity it was that he had been brought back to this area by the news of Sal Tanner's accident, for he was very fond of her and her brother. But, he wouldn't be so bold as to make his way here again – not for *any* reason! Because, even though nigh on sixteen years had passed since the murders, Gabe Drury had suffered many a nightmare ever since. Try as he might, he couldn't forget that fancy fellow who had rushed past him, with the dark crimson stain of blood on his hands. As he fled past, the man had turned to see him lying there. In that moment, Gabe Drury was horrified to recognize the gentleman as being one who was seen to be an upright and prominent member of the community; and who was well-known hereabouts; one who would never in a million years be thought capable of committing such a heinous crime as that which was later discovered. At the moment his frantic stare plucked out Gabe Drury's half-hidden form, he seemed like a thing possessed! When those mad, savage eyes scoured his face, Gabe Drury found a strength he never knew he had. Like the wind he had fled from there – and he'd been running ever since, knowing in his heart that if a certain evil fellow ever caught him, he'd be dead for sure! Wild horses wouldn't have dragged him back to these parts, only for the long-lasting friendship he had enjoyed for many years with Sal and Marlow's dad, Bill Royston, and consequently his affection for the two young 'uns. Added to which was Gabe Drury's shame at being such a fearful coward that he daren't speak up when their mother, Eve Royston, was hanged for the murders. He had come to despise himself for being no better than that fancy fellow. After all, wasn't the blood of Eve Royston on *his* hands . . . just as surely as if he'd hanged her himself?

With a grim face, Marlow watched horse and rider out of sight. Gabe Drury knew more than he was letting on. He was frightened, Marlow was sure of it! Well, he would be patient, and for as long as it took; if he came to one dead-end, there'd be other roads he could take. But, for now, he was driven by an even greater tide of emotion – his abiding love for Emma Grady, and the burning desire to take her as his wife. It wouldn't be easy, he knew that. But then, nothing really worthwhile ever was!

Chapter Four

'There's a war brewing in America, I tell you!' The portly fellow tipped the brandy glass to his lips and drained it dry. Then, taking a chunky cigar from his top pocket, he placed it between his teeth and began biting on it. 'It won't be long now before Lincoln's elected to office, and, with the republicans so intent on this anti-slavery policy, there'll be fur flying in no time. You mark my words, there'll be war on the other side of the Atlantic!'

'I hope to God you're wrong, Harrison!' declared a small, square-looking fellow seated in the deep, leather armchair by the fire, his weasel-features bathed by the heat from the flames, and his eyes most anxious as they swept the eight figures seated around the room. 'Each of us here has all our money sunk in the Lancashire cotton industry. *Should* there be a war in America . . . and the issue is the slaves who pick the cotton which runs our mills . . . it could mean catastrophe for Lancashire. And for every one of us here!' The thought appeared to horrify him because he was suddenly on his feet and pacing anxiously up and down.

'You're exaggerating!' protested one man.

'It's a fact though,' said another, 'it was *May* when

Lincoln was nominated for the presidency – six months ago! And just look how the southern states have put up every obstacle to keep him from coming to office. There *is* strong feeling. There bloody well is! If you ask me, it's a situation which needs to be watched most carefully!'

'You're panicking, the lot of you!' intervened a bald-headed man. 'I'm telling you, there'll be no war. The cotton will be shipped in just as regularly as it's ever been and the mills of Lancashire will continue to thrive, just as they are now.' With that said, he leaned back in his chair, embracing one and all with a smug expression.

'Gentlemen.' All eyes turned to look at Caleb Crowther. So far, he had made no contribution to the debate which, since the men's departure from the dinner table to the sanctuary of the library, had become somewhat heated. Now, however, he strode to the centre of the room where he tactfully waited to ensure that he held their absolute attention. When satisfied, he continued in a sombre tone, 'The very reason you were all invited here tonight, was to discuss this matter. Of late, there has been too much talk of what's happening in America and it's time to put an end to it!' Here his vivid eyes pausing, he oppressively scrutinized each of his guests in turn, and each was visibly affected. 'Isn't it enough that the *Blackburn Standard* puts out such articles that have our very mill-hands stopping their work to air their views and spread even *more* unrest? It's up to *us* . . . the owners . . . to set an example! If we show ourselves to be affected by unfounded gossip and troublesome rumours, then how the devil are we to expect any different from the fools we employ?' Though his expression was one of fury, his voice was remarkably calm. 'I say there will be no war in America. The slaves will pick the cotton as they always have, and the people of Lancashire will go on processing it in our mills. There is no place here for scaremongers!' Now, his accusing glare sought out the portly fellow who was chewing on his cigar in a nervous manner.

For a long, silent moment, Caleb Crowther and the man called Harrison, continued to glower at each other. Until, taking the cigar from his mouth and lowering his eyes, Harrison asked, 'You're saying we have nothing to worry about then . . . in your opinion?'

When Caleb Crowther firmly replied, 'Nothing. Nothing at all,' a wave of sighs filled the air and at once the atmosphere became calmer.

'Crowther runs more mills than any of us here,' said one, 'and if he's not concerned, then I'm buggered if I don't go along with him!'

'Well, I tell you . . . I was seriously considering looking to India for my cotton supply . . . but I reckon Crowther's right,' agreed another. 'The ships will keep fetching their cargoes from America, just as they always have. The North and South will have their domestic squabbles . . . as we all do. But I'm convinced it'll come to nothing serious.'

With this, they all agreed unanimously, and there followed another round of brandy and cigars, and an otherwise congenial evening. It was not until some time after midnight that the men joined the women in the drawing-room. Shortly afterwards, the guests departed from Breckleton House to make their homeward journeys – their various horses and carriages making an impressive sight as they slowly made their way down the lamplit drive.

* * *

The next day was Saturday, and, much to Emma's dismay, Caleb Crowther's mood was little better than on the previous night. All through breakfast he could be heard muttering under his breath, 'Damned fools!', and occasionally he would lift his eyes from the food before him to glare at one and all who had the misfortune to be seated around the same table.

Emma carefully kept her gaze averted. She had no wish for her day to be tainted by his thunderous mood since today was the one day she considered to be truly her own. She felt extremely anxious, because as a rule on a Saturday, she was given permission to go off on her usual errand without being accompanied, but it would be just like her uncle to vent his spite on her by maliciously forbidding such a thing. Thus Emma was on her best behaviour, and, when breakfast was finished, she crossed her fingers behind her back before asking, 'Uncle, please may I be excused . . . I don't want to miss the tram.' In that desperately long moment when he held her gaze, his mouth set tight and his manner unyielding, Emma was sure her request was about to be denied. But then, with a grunt and a dismissive wave of his hand, he told her, 'Go, if you must.' And she did, pausing only to excuse herself from Agnes Crowther, who seemed not to care whether Emma went or stayed. It had been like this ever since the disgraceful business of Martha, which had finally been resolved with her remaining at the school. All the same, Emma reasoned, the suspicions that Martha had stolen from herself in order to implicate an innocent person, had left a smear on her character which might never go away. It was a hard and bitter pill for the Crowthers to swallow, and their relationship was greatly strained because of it.

It was a fine October day, made even warmer for Emma by the fact that in just one week's time she would be sixteen years old. She was so excited! As she left the house, waved off by the ever-vigilant Mrs Manfred, Emma's heart felt curiously light and her step was decidedly jaunty. How she loved her Saturdays! Oh, she didn't mind her work in the company of Gregory Denton, for he was a nice enough fellow, and had readily accepted part of the blame for the nasty incident with Caleb Crowther regarding the river-people. To Emma's surprise, there were even times when, not only did she find herself enjoying a good deal of laughter with him, but she also had come to be very fond of him. Indeed, on the odd occasion, he seemed almost like a brother to her.

'Good morning, Miss Grady.' The tram-conductor held out his hand to ensure that Emma was safely aboard. 'Off to the churchyard, is it?' he asked, glancing down at the small bunch of snow-white chrysanthemums in her hand. Like most people hereabouts, he knew of Emma and her circumstances. She was a grand lass, he thought, smiling at her, but immediately correcting himself, for she wasn't a lass any more. Indeed she was a woman – a good-looking and most desirable woman. He'd noticed the change in her these past weeks when, every Saturday as regular as clock-work, she'd board this tram for the trip into Blackburn. She always got off at the church where her papa, Thadius Grady, lay. She always had a ready smile for folks, and never once made them feel that she was not exactly the same as them. Why, Emma Grady might be any one of the workers who filed into the mill every morning, so straight-forward and natural was she. Her papa had been the very same, God rest his soul.

As always, Emma asked after the conductor's wife and three bairns whom she had come to know through his incessant and cheery chatter. All the way to the church gates she was told, in the greatest detail, of how well or how poorly they all were. As she alighted from the tram, Emma gave the fellow a friendly wave which he gladly returned, as did a number of elderly passengers.

As Emma entered the churchyard the uniquely sharp, fresh after-smell of newly-cut grass filled the air. 'This is a lovely place, Papa,' Emma murmured, as she checked the water in the container and, seeing enough there, arranged the flowers inside. Then, dropping down to her knees, she began to absent-mindedly play with the coloured marble stones in the well beneath the black headpiece. This was simply inscribed with the words:

Thadius Grady
1820-1860
Rest in Peace

It had taken Emma a long, heartbreaking time to come to terms with the fact that here, in the dark silent ground, lay that darling man who had been by her side for as long as she could remember. He had always been there, unceasingly reliable, and loving her, strong and true – like a mighty tree that could never be hewn, and which even time itself could make no impression on. Now, Emma had come to accept that no one was immortal. When God called you to his side, there was no use protesting. During his long illness, Thadius had answered Emma's heartfelt question when she insisted on knowing why the Lord was taking her beloved papa. Emma could recall the moment as though it was only a heartbeat ago, when, cupping her small tearful face in his hands, he had told her, 'I expect he's short of angels.' Emma had softly cried at his words. She cried now, but the tears were tempered with a smile, 'I wonder if the good Lord made you an angel, after all,' she said, fondly touching his name upon the headstone, her silent thoughts indulged in times long gone.

Some moments later, Emma went into the Church of the Sacred Heart where she lit two candles – one for each of her parents. Afterwards, she knelt before the altar and gave up a heartfelt prayer. 'Keep them both safe in Heaven, dear Lord,' she asked, 'and let them find again the love they have for each other. Tell them not to worry about me because, with your help, I'll be just fine.' She betrayed nothing of the ache in her heart and of her great need for the young bargee, who filled her every waking thought. All the same, Emma was convinced that the good Lord probably knew already; and she couldn't help thinking that if this *was* the case, then *why* had he brought her and Marlow together in the first place? Surely he must have seen the heartache that would follow? Then, she recalled how her papa would often tell her that if the Lord did anything, it was not without reason. 'Forgive me, Lord,' she murmured now, as she quietly closed the vast panelled doors, 'but I hope you know what you're doing!'

The next stop was Corporation Park, a place of great beauty, with a myriad of narrow footpaths and secluded places where a person could sit and lose themselves for as long as they liked. Emma loved this park, for it took her back to the days of her childhood when she and her papa enjoyed many a happy time together exploring the meandering walkways and feeding the ducks in the lake. Every

Saturday, Emma still always found a space in her drawstring purse to secrete a small bag of crumbs for that very purpose.

But first of all, Emma felt the urge to visit what had always been her favourite place in the park. This was the very highest point, where the gun turrets from the Crimean War were on display. Emma took the route along the main broad walkway, which would lead her there, via the tall glass-domed conservatories which housed all manner of beautiful plants. As she hurried along the rhododendron-lined walkways, where every now and then the long swaying tentacles of the many weeping willows dipped and played in the breeze, a soothing sense of peace and love came into Emma's heart. Now, rather than grieve for her losses, she gave thanks that at least she still had Manny – her very dear friend and confidante. And here she was, young and healthy, with her whole life ahead of her. Only once did a shadow cross Emma's heart – when she let herself think how empty life might be without Marlow Tanner by her side.

Climbing the last few steps, Emma realized just how long ago it had been since she had come this far. There they still were – the great long-barrelled guns from the Crimean War. Emma was not surprised to see people already strolling about. To her left there was a tall, willowy man with a flat cap and heavy boots, and by his side, a weary-looking woman. The woman was carrying a large hessian bag and wearing a long dark frock, covered with a grey shawl. This she pulled tight about her against the breeze, which cut like a knife across the hill-top. Since taking up her clerical duties at the mill, Emma had become aware of many things she hadn't known before, such as the fact that many unemployed and hard-up families were forced to find out-of-the-way hiding holes in the park, where they made themselves a shelter in which to sleep. She wondered whether that was the plight of this sorry-looking pair. If it was, she thought, they had such a proud and independent look about their faces, that it made her heart go out to them.

In the distance, Emma could hear the laughter of children and, stretching her neck as she approached the gun-barrels, she could vaguely distinguish five figures approaching. Smiling at the sight of the two smaller figures running and jumping ahead in the same way she herself had once done, Emma pulled herself up on to the cold, hard gun-barrel, all the while puffing and panting from the long upward climb. Once she was settled comfortably in a secure position on the slippery metal barrel, Emma straightened up to take in the view. It was a magnificent and awesome sight to behold. From here, she could see over almost the whole of Blackburn town, with its sea of graceful church spires, and, standing tall beside these, as many mill chimneys – the former sending prayers to Heaven, and the latter sending up black rancid smoke, which day after day settled over the houses to become an intricate part of the landscape. Yet, for all that, Emma saw a curious magic in Blackburn town, particularly on a busy day when it was filled with the hustle and bustle of horses and carts, bent, shawled figures, and flat-capped little men, all answering the summons of the mill siren, and all either hurrying to, or from, their weaving and spinning machines. How they talked and laughed, Emma thought, as though they hadn't a care in the world. They would exchange friendly greetings as they hurried towards those great formidable mills, as though they were on their way to make a fortune – their indomitable spirits belying the fact that their wages did little more than feed and clothe them, and maintain a distance between themselves and the workhouse.

From the better houses the clerks and the other more important business folk would emerge and, like her own papa, Emma remembered nostalgically, they presented a very different spectacle – all sporting handsome tail-coats, together with those familiar tall hats of black and sombre appearance and some carrying canes. Then, at a later hour still, the ladies would step out in their pretty flowered bonnets and rich taffeta skirts. And, constantly, making their own particular music over the jutting cobbles, the clip-clop of horses' hooves could be heard up and down the street as they pulled along the merchants' flat-waggons, brewers' drays and carriages of all manner and style – all going about their business and all most exciting to Emma.

Today was market day, and from her vantage point, Emma imagined she could see the grey flapping canopies which covered the stalls and hear the urgent and colourful shouts of waremongers. As she sat there, perched on the gun-barrel with the breeze numbing her face and pinching her ears, Emma gazed across Blackburn town and told herself that, in the whole of her life, she would never want to be anywhere else but here.

When the family of five strolled by, Emma thought what a lovely sight they made. There was papa, impressively dressed in a dark suit, with a white silk scarf around his neck, and on his head a most expensive looking tall hat. He had long side whiskers and a friendly smile, which he directed at Emma. His wife was also extremely well turned-out in a fine green velvet outfit, with a large sweeping bustle. The two older children, both boys, were smartly dressed in short, dark breeches, grey cloth caps and little fitted jackets. Emma could see by the way they constantly broke free from their parents to run and hide, that they were probably quite a handful. Holding onto the woman's hand was a little girl of about three years old; a pretty chubby-cheeked child with a serious face and regal step. As the family sauntered away, they reminded Emma of the Royal Family. The little girl in particular looked just like that picture in the paper of Queen Victoria's youngest child, Princess Beatrice.

Smiling to herself, Emma got down from her perched position, rubbing her hands against the cold and thinking it was time she started making her way back down. She would head for the lake and the ducks and spend a while there.

Emma was surprised to find herself the only one down at the lake. But then, she reminded herself, she was much earlier today on account of wanting to get away before Caleb Crowther might change his mind. Coming to where the railings finished and the grassy bank sloped gently down to the lake's edge, Emma stepped forward until the tips of her boots were almost touching the water. Then, throwing the crumbs as far out as she could, she watched with pleasure as the ducks sped forward, loudly quacking and nudging each other in order to be the first to grab them. Emma reflected on how peaceful it was here, and how soothing for a person's turbulent thoughts.

Not far away, there was another who was of a similar mind to Emma. After seeing to his sister's comfort that morning, Marlow Tanner had walked the mile or so which took him to Corporation Park. He felt a great need for peace and quiet, away from the incessant banter of Sal – who he thought must be the worst creature on God's earth when struck down and made virtually immobile – so that he might reflect on things. It was in Sal's nature to be obstinate and demanding, he knew, but never more so than since the accident. And, above all else, she insisted on constantly reminding him that there was only one thing to be got from giving your heart above your station – and that was grief. 'More grief than you could ever imagine!' she'd warned over and over. This morning, however, she had finally got under his skin. If he hadn't got away he might well have been tempted to dunk her in the canal, for he knew only too well the wisdom of her words.

'Come here Jake!' he called now, as the panting dog strained hard on its lead, 'Ease up there!' But the dog did not like the rules which dictated that he must at all times be kept on a lead. He was hot and thirsty – and his eye had caught sight of the wide, shimmering lake, alive with noisy fluttering ducks.

Meanwhile, Emma was so captivated by the comical antics of the water fowl that she was totally unaware of the dog presently bounding up behind her – the great bull-mastiff had slipped his lead and was now full of mischief. The first she knew of it was when, with a great energetic bound, the dog launched itself towards the lake. The only obstacle between the dog and the water was Emma. With a thud the bull-mastiff careered into her shoulder sending her reeling off balance, and with a cry she flung out both hands, one into mid-air and the other to clutch hold of the railings. The dog landed heavily in the lake, sending both water and ducks in every direction – the ensuing noise rising like a crescendo into the hitherto still and quiet air. As the ducks fled, flapping their wings and sending up a volley of noise, Emma also yelled as she hung suspended by one hand from the railings, her feet and skirt-hem in the water, and her arm aching so much that any minute she was afraid she might let go. Emma was frantic as she believed the water here was considerably deep.

Suddenly, the dog's owner came rushing round the corner. 'Jake!' he was shouting, 'Get back here!' – every word accompanied by a threatening shake of the dog's lead. Emma saw him before he saw her, and when she realized who it was she began calling, 'Help! . . . Please help!' Whereupon, seeing her through the railings, he flung down the lead and raced towards the lake's edge where he immediately plunged into the water, sinking up to his knees as he waded to where Emma was hanging by her fingertips. Within a minute he had her by the waist and the next moment she was in his arms, being gently carried to the bank. When Emma saw that the water was not as deep and dangerous as she'd feared, and in fact came no higher than Marlow's knees, she looked into his concerned eyes with a smile. The smile quickly became a grin and then she began laughing. She felt such a fool as she realized what a comical spectacle she must have presented, and, what a comical sight the two of them must look now – with Marlow's dog yapping at their heels in a delighted frenzy, and the ducks quacking their disapproval from a safe distance.

When Marlow stumbled on to the bank, where he fell over with Emma still in his arms, they were both gripped by fits of laughter; and when the dog bounded from the water to shake itself vigorously, and in so doing drenched the pair of them, Marlow and Emma laughed even louder and clung to each other beneath the deluge of water that showered down.

It was at that moment that two other regular visitors to the park entered this uproarious scene. One was a shawled lady of some fifty years of age, slow of footstep and with slightly stooped shoulders beneath a sour, wizened face. The other was a small homely-looking fellow with sandy coloured hair, and was none other than Gregory Denton. The disagreeable woman with her arm linked in his was Doreen Denton, his fearsome, widowed mother.

Gregory Denton was somewhat embarrassed to witness such untoward frolicking, although, for a brief moment, he envied the couple their obvious joy in each other. Coughing and quickening his step, he averted his gaze and began to change direction.

'Really! Upon my soul!' Doreen Denton gripped her son's arm as she forced him to a halt so that she might observe the scene more closely. 'Disgraceful!' she declared with a fierce scowl. 'I shall have words with the park attendant, you can be sure of that!' she told her acutely embarrassed son. 'What in Heaven's name is that young lady doing in the company of a ruffian like him? She looks to come from a decent family . . . while the fellow, well! He seems no better than a bargee!' She hoped to catch their attention with her loud tutting noises, so that she could give them both a piece of her mind.

Something in what his mother had said made Gregory Denton look back at the couple. On looking closer, he was horrified to see that they were no other than Miss Grady and Marlow Tanner! For a long, unbearable moment he refused to believe what was painfully obvious. Then, as the truth sank in, a black, suffocating jealousy arose in Gregory Denton's heart. He found himself unable to tear his wide, disbelieving eyes away from where Marlow had raised himself up on one elbow and, his laughter now replaced by a serious expression, was gazing down on Emma intensely. On seeing the way in which Marlow was looking at her, Emma also grew quiet. This shared moment of silence between them was spellbinding and, as Marlow's passionate gaze mingled with the wonder in Emma's soft eyes, it became one that they would both treasure forever. In her heart, Emma was afraid. Every corner of her body was trembling as she experienced sensations of excitement such as she had never known. She sensed that Marlow was going to kiss her, but still she made no move, for she was held helplessly in the same magic spell as Marlow. Now, as he lowered his head towards her, Emma's heart jumped and her hand reached up towards his face. When his mouth covered her open lips and his body leaned into hers, Emma thought there could never be anything more wonderful in the whole of her life.

Meanwhile, as Emma found herself moved by great joy and love as she lay in Marlow's arms, witnessing this scene Gregory Denton was immersed in the darkest, most crucifying mood, which swallowed his reasoning and suffocated the kindliness of his nature. As he quickly turned his stricken eyes away and led his mother from that place, a malicious plan of action was already forming in his affected mind. Once before he'd warned Caleb Crowther of Emma's involvement with the river-people, but because of his concern for Emma he had not followed it through when confronted by her furious uncle. Now, however, he would have no such reservations. For the first time in his uneventful life, Gregory Denton intended to put himself first – and bugger the consequences!

'No!' Emma's eyes were anxious as she looked into Marlow's surprised face. Whatever was she thinking of, to roll about in the grass and to conduct herself in a way that, to certain eyes, was no better than if she were a harlot! As she scrambled to her feet, Emma was both ashamed and frightened – ashamed of her own behaviour and, remembering how his back still carried the scars of another incident, desperately afraid for Marlow. Instinctively, she looked all about her, praying that no one had seen them. When she saw only two figures – a man and a woman in the distance – she gave a little prayer of thanks. Then she swung herself away from Marlow – who was still on his knees and looking up at her with a quizzical gaze – and, pausing only to call out in a troubled voice 'Please! Stay away from me!' she clutched the cumbersome folds of her skirt in her hands, and, ignoring the wet discomfort of her boots, ran as though the devil himself was chasing her! With every step she took, Marlow's voice was in her ears, 'Emma! I love you. Wait . . . please wait!' But she paid no heed, only quickening her steps even more. In her trembling heart she prayed for forgiveness and help: forgiveness of the Lord for those feelings she had experienced in Marlow Tanner's arms when she'd craved much more than the feel of his mouth against hers, and when every instinct in her body had been that of a woman; and forgiveness for having so easily betrayed the promise given to her papa. Emma could feel herself slipping away from all she had been taught, and it frightened her. In her heart, even while she was running from him, Marlow Tanner made her feel warm and intoxicated, and he filled her with such a joy that it took all of her will-power to stop herself from turning round and going to fling herself into his arms. Emma doubted whether she would ever be able to get him out of her heart, especially when she didn't want to! Yet, she knew she must, and so she asked the Lord for the strength to do so. She also asked that Marlow might find the strength to put her out of his heart; for Emma knew that if she loved Marlow Tanner, it was no less than he loved her. And, for both of them, it was an impossible love – a love which, although born in Heaven, could carry them both to Hell!

Chapter Five

Monday, 17th October 1860 was a fierce kind of day. It was a day of bitter cold winds and driving rain; a day when the sky stayed dark from morning till night and even the dogs took shelter. It was also a day which heralded a chain of events destined to bring about Emma's worst nightmare.

On the late evening of this particular day, two men stepped from a hansom cab in a back street of London town. Both were well-dressed and authoritative in their bearing. They had both been drinking and were full of high spirits, and had come to this area of Spitalfields to indulge their baser nature. The one who went by the name of Bartholomew Mysen was a man of law; he was tall and willowy with clean-shaven features. The other was a large, loose-limbed fellow, with dark hairy features and formidable blue eyes. He was also a man of the legal profession, who had a reputation for being a man of little mercy. His name – Caleb Crowther.

'Come on, Crowther . . . the night's almost spent!' reprimanded the tall, willowy man as his companion delayed in giving instructions to the cab-driver – these being that he should return for them on the morrow before the break of day.

'Have you got that?' Caleb Crowther demanded. When the fellow touched his cap and assured him that he certainly had, the fare was put into his palm and he was dismissed.

The two men immediately went into a large, red-bricked, seedy establishment. By their confident manner, it was obvious that this was not the first time they had frequented such a place. Inside, the subdued lighting made the surroundings appear gloomy. The grimy walls and threadbare carpets were effectively camouflaged by the deep, dark shadows and the plentiful, long frilled curtains.

In the distance the sounds of laughter, music and frolicking could be heard. Then, the air was cut silent by the sudden cessation of music. Presently, there came a man's voice announcing the evening's programme of entertainment, which was greeted by an uproar of shouting, clapping and stamping of feet.

'Looks like yer just in time, guv,' said the man at the desk, presenting a comical sight with his bald, shiny head, full face of whiskers and wide, spectacular, pink dickie-bow, 'I reckon they're about to start.' When neither Caleb Crowther nor his companion showed even the slightest appreciation of his comments, he gave a snigger, then a shrug of his shoulders, and when Caleb Crowther dipped into his waistcoat to spill a number of coins on to the counter, he grabbed them up and pointed to the double doors ahead. 'Yer knows yer way, guv!' he sneered, already preparing to sink back into his chair, and continue with his solitary game of cards.

On the other side of the double doors was a narrow walkway, beyond which was the heart of the club. There, numerous chairs, tables and people – mostly men – were squashed into the vast space. At the far end was a grand old stage, adorned with rich, red velvet curtains, and which was lit up by the footlights hidden in the recess along the front. Remaining in the dark private walkway, the two men watched and waited. On seeing them there, the portly proprietor made his way towards them, with the semblance of a smile on his face and one hand fidgeting about in his pocket, as if preparing to count the money which these two eminent figures represented.

The next moment, a great wave of shouting and cheering erupted as the music started up again and the dancers tapped their way on to the stage.

'Now, *there's* a sight to set your pulses racing, Crowther!' murmured Bartholomew, running the tip of his tongue over his lips and gently nudging his companion.

Caleb Crowther gave no answer but continued to move his narrow eyes along the line of chorus girls. When the proprietor made his presence known, by stating 'Young an' fresh . . . *all* of 'em,' the two men nodded, all the while observing the scantily clad girls who were thrilling and exciting the audience with their provocative body movements and beckoning smiles.

Without either shifting his gaze or uttering a word, Caleb Crowther raised his cane and pointed it towards the far right of the stage. When, in a low cunning voice, the proprietor murmured in his ear, 'The redhead? . . . you mean the tall redhead?' he merely nodded, lowered his cane and gave a soft laugh as he turned to his companion saying, 'Come on, damn your eyes . . . there's a game waiting.'

'The little baggage third along,' the willowy fellow told the proprietor with a drunken giggle. 'The little blonde. Do you see the one?' he asked.

'I see,' confirmed the proprietor, with a knowing look

from one man to the other, asking, 'I take it you want their company *after* the game?'

'Of course *after* the game!' Caleb Crowther intervened, 'Use your common sense, man!'

'Of course, yes, indeed!' came the hurried response, 'I'll see to it.' He held out one hand, and, when the tall, willowy fellow dropped a guinea into it, he bent his head forward, saying in a patronizing manner, 'Off you go then . . . room eight. You know where it is.'

In room eight the evening was spent in a serious mood, with a number of straight-faced, dedicated men seated round a table, each one with a fist full of cards and a wallet bulging with money – most of which rapidly found its way into the centre of the table, until the mound of bank bills there represented a small fortune.

As the night went on and the pile of money grew, each man furtively watched the others, wallets were emptied and flung down in anger, and the atmosphere became unbearably tense. Of all the devastated faces, there was none more so than Caleb Crowther's. Having lost more than most, and seeing no way to make restitution, he was obliged to bow out of the game, after which he sat in a dark corner downing glass after glass of whisky. Finally, in the small hours, when the game was eventually over and the players departed, he struggled to his feet, hardly able to walk across the room to where his companion, Bartholomew, was gleefully counting his handsome winnings.

'Leave it!' he said, in a slurred voice, 'get the women!'

'They'll be along, Crowther . . . any minute now,' assured his companion, 'and you surely don't expect me to leave this money just lying about?' The very thought caused him to glance at Caleb Crowther with horror. He finished stuffing the bank notes into his coat pockets before reverently folding the coat and laying it over the back of a chair some safe distance away. 'You know how light-fingered these trollops are!' he reprimanded, 'Pluck the gold from your teeth, they would!'

Apart from the large oval table in the centre of the floor, and the chairs around it, there were five other items of furniture in the room – an ornate wash-stand containing a jug and bowl, a tall, ungainly clothes cupboard, a short, broad chest of drawers, and two narrow iron-framed beds, one either end of the room. As the girls were ushered into the room by the proprietor, Bartholomew grabbed the small blonde one and hurried her away to the farthest bed, the pair of them laughing and stumbling as they went, eagerly shedding their clothes along the way.

For a long moment, the tall red-haired girl stayed by the door, her round green eyes intent on Caleb Crowther's features. On seeing his unsteady gait and the manner in which he began to look her up and down, she asked cheekily, 'D'yer think yer can manage me, Toff? . . . Yer look to me as though it's all yer can do to stay awake!'

'You think so, do you?' murmured Caleb Crowther, a strange look on his face as he gestured for her to go to the bed. As he followed, the cries of pleasure coming from the other side of the room caused them both to look. The two figures thrashing away there were already naked, both in a frenzy of excitement, and both totally oblivious to the presence of anyone else. Like their gyrating bodies, their anguished and fevered groans rose and fell one into the other, the sight and sound of which enthused Caleb Crowther into hurrying toward the other bed where the red-haired girl stood waiting.

With his eyes looking directly into hers and without uttering a word, he lifted his hands and began fumbling at her clothes, firstly loosening the straps at her shoulders, then tugging at the tiny pearl buttons at her breast. The drink he had swallowed that evening made him more clumsy than usual, and when, after unsuccessfully attempting to undo the buttons, she began to softly laugh at him, he became agitated and the look in his eyes darkened with fury. With a low, rumbling growl, he clutched his fingers over the bodice of her dress and, leaning all his weight forward, he ripped the garment from top to bottom, afterwards wrenching it from her back and slinging it across the room. The girl was not shocked, nor was she afraid, for she had been subjected to such rough handling before. It was not in her nature to question such men – only to assure herself that they were here to make love, *not* to hurt or maim.

Now, when Caleb Crowther pushed her back on to the bed, she lay there impassively, looking up at him as he made hard and laborious work of undressing himself – all the while muttering and cursing – until, with a smile still on her lips, she stood up to help. Presently, they faced each other in their nakedness, all barriers between them gone, and in their eyes the look of hunger – his for the taste of her body, and hers for whatever money he might later see fit to leave her.

At first, as his fingers explored every inch of her body – touching first her ravishing red hair, then travelling from her neck to her nipples, where the light touch of his fingers lingered a moment before reaching down to where her thighs were warm and moist – there was a gentleness in his approach, almost a reverence. But then, when she also reached out to stroke and caress that most sensitive part of his body, he began to shiver and grow excited. Suddenly, he had his arms around her and was pulling her to him, moaning in ecstasy as her warm naked body merged with his. In a moment they were on the bed and he was bearing down on her with bull-strength.

It was then that Caleb Crowther was rendered useless by the drink he had consumed and, in spite of his repeated attempts, it became obvious to both himself and the girl that he was unable to satisfy either of them. With a contemptuous expression, she pushed him away from her, saying with a laugh, 'I'm buggered if you ain't the very first let-down I've ever had!' The effect that her cruel taunt had on Caleb Crowther was immediate. With a cry of 'Bloody whore!' he flung out a hand to grasp the back of her head, his fingers intertwined in her hair and his nails digging into her scalp. Even before she could cry out, he had formed his other hand into a fist, and with a cry of 'Trollop!' he swung it into her face with such force that he sent her reeling across the room towards the fireplace, where the coal was still glowing. As she fell against it, her arm was flung sideways to touch the searing-hot bars of the basket. With a cry of pain she snatched it away and, clambering to her knees, she looked up at Caleb Crowther with venom in her eyes. 'You bastard, you!' she uttered through clenched teeth, at the same time raising her hand to where the blood was gushing from her nose and from the deep gash along her cheekbone made by his ring.

'Get out!' came the instruction, 'before I forget altogether that I'm a gentleman!' He scooped up the torn dress and, with an angry flick of the wrist, sent it through the air towards her. Without delay, she collected the garment, held it over her nakedness and swiftly left the room.

Unaware that the two occupants of the other bed had ceased their activities to watch his treatment of the girl, Caleb Crowther stumbled to the table, from where he collected the last remaining bottle of booze. Then, throwing his grotesque and naked form on to the bed, he downed every last dreg of the fiery liquid. Soon after, he fell into a deep, restless stupor, every now and then flailing the air with his arms and constantly calling out two names – first Mary, then Emma. Only once did the name Thadius touch his lips, after which he was seized by a fit of uncontrollable trembling.

For a long while afterwards, Caleb Crowther's companion lay quite still on the other bed, his eyes narrow and wary as he studied Caleb Crowther's sleeping form. 'You really are a bastard, Crowther,' he murmured, giving a low laugh, 'but you'll get your come-uppance if you're not very careful.'

'What's that you say, darlin'?' came the sleepy voice beside him, 'Want some more do yer, duckie?' Whereupon he told her with a friendly laugh that she had worn him out. Then, throwing Caleb Crowther a scornful look, he flung his arm about the girl next to him, and the pair of them fell into an exhausted sleep.

With the dawn came a summons from the proprietor that the hansom cab was waiting outside. In no time at all, Caleb Crowther and his companion were out of their beds; washed in the warm water brought by their host and poured into the wash-stand, and were hurriedly on their way downstairs before the coming day might rise to light up the skies and expose them for the dregs they were.

At the door, Caleb Crowther felt the urge to glance back, and there he saw the tall, slender red-headed girl watching his every move. While he had slept, she had paced the floor, her swollen face a mass of pain, and in her heart the fervent desire to see the devil who'd done it fester in Hell! Pure hatred was in her eyes now as she glared at Caleb Crowther. Seeing the loathing she harboured for him, Caleb Crowther thought it thoroughly amusing. With a gentle laugh, he reached into the top pocket of his waistcoat, from where he withdrew a silver coin which he spun in her direction. 'For services rendered,' he told her with a cunning smile, which became a laugh when she plucked the coin from the threadbare carpet and threw it back at his feet.

'Your money's tainted darlin',' she said scornfully, 'like *you*! . . . And just as bloody useless!' At the last words, the smile slithered from Caleb Crowther's face. Ignoring the coin at his feet, he swung away and went smartly through the double doors to where the cab was waiting.

'Cor! Gerra bloody move on, mate!' urged the driver, 'The old horse is bleeding-well agitated . . . an' I'm bloody frozen!' He pulled his cape tighter about him and began blowing into his gloved hands, at the same time giving instructions to the handsome bay horse to 'be patient, yer old mare! Be patient!'

Once inside the cab, Caleb Crowther settled back into the buttoned leather seats, as Bartholomew gave the driver directions. '14 Bedford Square,' he called out, adding at Caleb Crowther's request, 'then on to King's Cross Station.'

Before the driver could urge the horse forward, three men appeared as if out of thin air; in fact they had been waiting for quite some time in a second carriage further down the street, and had observed the proceedings with particular interest. When one of the three dark-suited men took hold of the horse's reins, saying to the astonished driver, 'Just sit tight. None of this is your business, grandad!' he did exactly as he was told, for this was an area where crooks and villains thrived in every dark corner. Behind him, the driver could hear a scuffle and shouts of protest from the occupants of his cab, but he wisely kept his eyes looking directly ahead; even when he heard a heavy thud as the tall, willowy fellow was pulled from the cab to the pavement, he did not avert them. The other two dark-suited men had by now climbed into the cab, and placed themselves one either side of Caleb Crowther. When he began thrashing his arms about and threatening to call for assistance, the larger of the two men grabbed his arm, wrenching it behind his back until he cried out. The second man, finding it amusing, said in a mocking voice, 'Really Jack . . . you mustn't *hurt* Mr Crowther.' Then, throwing Caleb Crowther a menacing look, he continued, 'Not *yet* anyway. You know the boss likes folk to be given every opportunity to settle their debts. Now . . . if they don't *care* to settle their debts, well . . . they *deserve* to be hurt, don't they?' He prodded a sharp stiff finger into Caleb Crowther's fleshy stomach. 'It's well-known that Victor Sorensen has a kind heart. Wouldn't you agree?' he asked quietly, his eyes never leaving his victim's fearful face.

'Yes! Yes . . . you tell your boss I have every intention of settling my debts.' With this, Caleb Crowther drew up his shoulders in a futile attempt to regain his dignity. Then, looking from one of his assailants to the other, he told them in a more controlled voice, 'I've never let Mr Sorensen down, he knows that. It's just that, well, I have to step care- fully with my brother-in-law not long gone. But, I have it all in hand . . . in fact, I have a meeting with the bank official this very week.'

'Is that so?' remarked the fellow seated on Caleb Crowther's right. 'Mr Sorensen heard about the responsibilities you inherited. Cash, too, we understand?'

'No! . . . no cash. Just two mills, and they're like a dead weight round my neck! I'd sell them tomorrow if I could.'

'Well now, the boss don't care which way you get the money. Just get it, Crowther – or there'll be more of a dead weight round your neck than the mills! Get my meaning, do you?' When Caleb Crowther nodded, he continued, 'You've got one week from today.' He prodded Caleb's stomach again, this time more viciously. 'Remember that, Crowther. One week!' Then he made a short sharp movement of his head, whereupon the other man released Caleb Crowther, before throwing open the cab door and stepping out into the road. His colleague did the same on the pavement side, after which he held the door open and, peering into the club doorway, where Bartholomew Mysen had retreated, he beckoned him forward. 'You were going somewhere, I believe,' he said in a smarmy voice, as the man came out of the shadows to climb with haste back into the cab . . . but, not before the dark-suited man had slipped a roll of notes into his fist and given him a knowing wink.

The journey was completed in silence. Only when Bartholomew was delivered to Bedford Square and was about to close the door behind him, did he warn Caleb Crowther, 'You don't mix with their sort, Crowther . . . not if you've got any sense. You're a bloody fool! For too long you've been sailing close to the wind. I'm telling you for your own good . . . get them off your back, man! Whatever it takes to free yourself of them, *do* it!' With that, he slammed the door shut and called up to the driver, 'Get him to King's Cross Station,' at the same time reaching up to hand him a generous fare. As he watched the cab pull away, he clicked his teeth and shook his head. 'You're a fool, Crowther,' he murmured, thinking how glad he was that it wasn't he who had fallen foul of the likes of Victor Sorensen, for he did not know of a man more evil than that one. This abominable fellow ran his own empire underground; every sordid and corrupt organization was under his control; yet he was so cunning a fiend that nothing could be traced back to him. He preyed on men like Caleb Crowther – weak, indulgent men, who took women and played the gambling dens as though their lives depended on it. Well, now it *did*, and the possible consequences made Bartholomew Mysen shiver in his shoes. He fingered the notes in his pocket, and reflected on his part in betraying Caleb Crowther. But he had few regrets, for, if he had refused, it was likely he would not have lived to see another day. Besides which, he had come to know the dark side of Caleb Crowther's character, and was repulsed by it.

The very same sentiments were ravaging Caleb Crowther's thoughts as the train carried him back to Blackburn. What he had told Sorensen's men was the truth. He had every intention of selling the mills, but his hands were tied, and the bank already held them as security against recent loans. He had little hope that his meeting on Friday would bring the results he wanted, for, on the last occasion, the bank had warned him that he was getting in over his head. That left only the trust fund which Thadius had left in his charge for Emma. It was this which played on his mind for the remainder of the journey, and the manner in which he might safely cheat her of it! His thoughts might have been less feverish if he had known how events in his absence had already presented such a possibility.

'I hate these damned meetings!' exploded Caleb Crowther, as he got up from the fireside chair to storm across the drawing-room towards the window. 'Little bloody men . . . with little ideas!'

'But it's *those* men who keep things going in your absence!' Agnes Crowther pointed out in a respectful tone, being still somewhat peeved that her husband had stayed over so long in London. 'Thadius was always insistent on these meetings, as you know. He thought them very necessary.'

At this point he might have made a caustic comment, but his glance was drawn through the casement window to where Emma was running from the house. At the sight of her, he became darkly silent, as all kinds of thoughts crossed his conniving mind.

Unaware that both Caleb Crowther's thoughts and his eyes were on her, Emma kept running. After the deluge of rain yesterday, the sun on her face was warm and the birds could be seen nestling in the tree tops. Today was one of those rare autumn days which held a semblance of spring, and now, as the daylight began to fade, Emma felt her heart lighter and closer to the past than she had for a long time. At this hour, when her duties at the mill were done and she had talked long and deep with Mrs Manfred, her thoughts invariably turned to the happy times she'd had with her papa.

Now, with Marlow's dear love alive in her heart and with thoughts of him in her mind, Emma made towards the bottom of the hill, where, gathering up the folds of her skirt, she ran and ran until her chest became a tight band squeezing the life from her. Yet, with the effervescence of youth – and feeling the need to put as much space between herself and the Crowthers as possible – she kept on running, stumbling and scrambling ever upwards over the grassy slope which fronted the house.

Only when Emma had reached the very top of the hill did she stop to look back. She felt exhilarated and as free as the wind, which, up here, was strong enough to blow her about. Oh! The taste of freedom – it was wonderful! Here, she could touch the sky and vie with nature; here, there were no rules or regulations, no Caleb or Agnes Crowther to scowl at her and make her miserable; here, there was only her, the breeze, God's lovely creations and her own thoughts. Feeling inspired, Emma loosened her auburn hair from its confining ribbons so that it tumbled about her shoulders and spilled down her back to touch her waist. Then, she began running like the wind, flinging out her arms to the heavens as she laughed aloud. Exhausted, she sank to the grass where she lay prostrate, blissfully out of breath and staring up at the sky to follow the light curling clouds as they were shifted first this way, then that, by the heightening breeze.

After a while, those deeper, more serious thoughts which were never far away, reared up to darken Emma's mood. Drawing herself up into a sitting position, she fumbled about in the folds of her skirt until her fingers located the deep narrow pocket there. Dipping into it, she brought out the silver watch, so slim and small between her fingers and thumb, and so surprisingly warm to the touch that she could almost imagine it was only in this moment that her papa had entrusted it to her. Holding it to her ear, she thought how like a heartbeat was its rhythmic tick. Tenderly, she sprang open the rear to gaze at that minute lock of hair which lay curled up inside. Not daring to take it out for fear that the wind might snatch it away, she cupped the watch in one hand while with the other she lightly stroked her fingertip against the soft golden hair. Emma had hoped that by so doing, she might somehow feel closer to her mama. But she did not. Nor was she comforted, for a great tide of sadness washed over her and, feeling disillusioned, she closed the watch and returned it to the safety of her pocket. Wherever she went, Emma always carried the tiny watch, because, little though it was, it was all she had of her past.

Falling back into the long, waving stalks of grass, Emma closed her eyes and surrendered herself to a feeling of peace and nostalgia. In the eerie silence high up on this pinnacle, where nothing but the wind and birds disturbed the air and where little else mattered, Emma felt a curious sense of contentment. However, when pleasant recollec-. tions of Marlow began invading her thoughts, she deliberately shut them from her mind, rising quickly into a sitting position, as though in doing so she would be better able to defend herself against those things which were forbidden and dangerous.

Her gaze drawn downwards, Emma couldn't help but admire the house which, like it or not, was her home. It was said that Breckleton House had been in the Crowther family for many generations. Flanked either end by huge turreted edifices and decorated with spacious bay windows – which were arched at the top and framed by exquisitely carved mullions – it had the quaint appearance of a small castle. The main entrance was also arched, but it was of a grander, more imposing dimension, seeming more like the entrance to a church. The roof was tall and graceful, its elegant lines accentuated by the inclusion of numerous high-reaching, fluted chimneypots. Immediately behind, the majestic trees formed a natural and fitting backdrop.

Not for the first time, Emma wondered how truly indebted Caleb Crowther was to her papa, for if her papa had not been so generous, he would most certainly not be so well endowed. This grand dwelling would by now surely be in the possession of some other fortunate person. Her papa had never revealed the full extent of his assistance to her uncle, for such matters of finance were always considered to be the business of gentlemen, with no place in such affairs for women-folk. But Emma was no fool, and since her employment as clerk to Gregory Denton, she had learned much more of her papa's generosity to the Crowthers when, on the odd occasion, she had walked in on conversations between the warehousemen. Also, Gregory Denton himself was never averse to singing her papa's praises, often to the detriment of the Crowthers. However, of late he had been in an unusually sullen mood – since the weekend in fact. These past two days he had been going about with a dark, angry expression on his face, asking occasionally whether her uncle was sure to be back for the arranged meeting on Tuesday evening. She had told him she didn't know, and that was the truth. Caleb Crowther came and went, sometimes to attend his duties at the Quarter Sessions and sometimes to other affairs in the city of London. Whatever the reason for his absence though, Emma was thankful for it, and the longer the duration, the more she liked it. Thinking about it now, though, Emma was most curious as to why Mr Denton should be so eager to see Caleb Crowther, for she knew he had no particular liking for him.

As though summoned by her thoughts, Gregory Denton was even now stepping down from the carriage which had drawn up at the front door. Emma leaned forward and peered down, her hand over her eyes to shield them from the sun. Yes, it was Gregory Denton right enough and with him was a gentleman Emma recognized as Mr Wordsworth, the manager of the other Grady mill on Cicely Top. Emma watched as the two men disappeared through the front door while the driver went to the rear of the house for some of Cook's cherry cake. Then, drawing her shawl tight about her small frame, Emma leaned back into the grass, bending a long, ripe stalk towards her and chewing on its end. 'Come for a meeting, I expect,' she murmured to herself. 'Well, sooner them than me.' Feeling safe and secure hidden there in the curve of the earth, she closed her eyes. A gentle smile appeared on her attractive mouth as she recalled the antics of Sal Tanner; but, suddenly, Emma felt deeply sorry that so many things were against the friendship the two of them might have enjoyed. Sighing, she regretted how sad it was that because of her age and because of adverse circumstances, she was not in charge of her own destiny. Ah, but one day, she thought, maybe, one day. Yet, had Emma known how the evening would develop, her thoughts would not have been charged with such ambitious hope.

'So!' Caleb Crowther stood up from his desk, flung his two fists behind his back and locked them into one. 'We'll consider that to be the end of it for today.' He looked long and pointedly at the short, stocky fellow in the chequered waistcoat, before saying to him, 'Just one thing. Wordsworth . . . you're too eager on stockpiling raw material. Not necessary. Not necessary at all.'

'But . . . what with these rumours concerning the American shipments, I thought . . .'

'I'm not interested in such rumours . . . nor in what you think,' returned Caleb Crowther with a definite warning in his voice. 'Run off some of that stock, man. It's dead money, I tell you!' When the man nodded and scribbled something in his ledger, Caleb Crowther smiled with satisfaction. He then gave the same instruction to Gregory Denton, who had also increased his stock of raw material, in view of the accelerating and worrying developments in America. Now, with all due reports meticulously made, Caleb Crowther called the meeting to an end.

'Mr Crowther, sir . . . could I beg a few more minutes of your time?' asked Gregory Denton, feeling somewhat nervous, but determined to convey the unpleasant details of what he had seen with his own eyes that very Saturday in Corporation Park. 'It is *most* important,' he quickly added, on seeing Caleb Crowther's hesitation. 'A . . . personal matter . . . not regarding myself, you understand.' He glanced sideways to where Mr Wordsworth was paying sharp attention to this intriguing little development.

'You be off, Wordsworth,' instructed Caleb Crowther now. 'Thomas can take Denton home shortly.'

'Oh, there's no need for that,' assured the fellow, his curiosity heightened, 'I'll wait in the carriage. No trouble at all.' And, before anyone could raise an objection, he quickly departed from the room.

'Now then, Denton, what's on your mind?' demanded Caleb Crowther, returning to seat himself behind the desk, while leaving the other man standing. 'Be quick with it, man. My time's precious!' If the truth were to be told, he was still suffering the effects of his trip to London. He kept his eyes fixed on Gregory Denton's pink features as, first in a nervous tone, then gradually growing in confidence, Gregory Denton relayed the whole sorry episode – his voice quivering with anxiety when he relayed how 'The fellow had Miss Grady in a disgustingly bold embrace . . . the two of them rolling about and laughing quite shamelessly!' That said, a heavy and frightening silence settled over the room, during which Gregory Denton fidgeted in a most agitated manner while Caleb Crowther sat deathly still, his head bent forward and his fingers tapping out a frantic rhythm on the desk-top.

'I'm convinced that Miss Grady played a *lesser* part in the dreadful incident!' Gregory Denton added lamely. He was very much afraid that he may well have gone too far in confiding the whole business and, suddenly, his only concern was that he should not be the cause of Miss Grady being cruelly punished. Oh Lord, he thought in a panic, if only I'd kept my mouth shut! He hated the jealousy which had driven him to do such a terrible thing! 'Mr Crowther,' he ventured again, 'I wouldn't want you to come down too hard on Miss Grady. After all, she is very young, and easily taken advantage of.' His voice was trembling, and, seeing how dark Caleb Crowther's countenance was, he would have given anything to turn the clock back.

Caleb Crowther was not unaware of the fellow's anxious state. Indeed, he thought any minute Denton would start blubbering like a baby. His first instincts on learning of his ward's latest and very serious misdemeanour was to administer the gravest punishment without delay – both to his wilful ward *and* to the bastard who had dared to encourage her! But now, confronted by this fellow Denton, whose motive was undeniably that of painful jealousy, a plan was already being devised in the back of his mind. One which just might get him off the hook, and rid him of Emma Grady into the bargain. For she was a constant reminder of things he would rather forget!

'Denton, my man . . . tell me . . .' As Caleb Crowther stood up to come round the desk, a cunning smile on his face and his two arms outstretched, the sight so terrified Gregory Denton that he took an involuntary step backwards. When the two sizeable fists fell on his shoulders in a fearsome grip, and those startling eyes drilled into his with the most evil smile, he began visibly trembling. 'Relax my dear fellow,' urged Caleb Crowther now. 'Just tell me the truth. Have you a deal of affection for my ward, Miss Grady?' When Gregory Denton's mouth opened and closed without uttering a sound, he went on, 'Do you *love* her, you fool? . . . *Desire* her, eh? Do you?'

Gregory Denton was so taken aback that he found himself gaping open-mouthed into the other fellow's smiling face. What's he playing at? he thought. What trick is the devil up to?

'Come on, man!' Caleb Crowther told him in growing impatience. 'Any blind beggar can see you're sorely struck by the girl. Isn't that so?' he insisted, both his eyes and fists holding the victim fast.

Acutely aware of the warm breath which stank of stale booze fanning against his face, Gregory Denton's words came out in a rush. 'Well . . . I must admit I do find Miss Grady . . . most attractive!' There! It was said. And, because of the effort it had taken, he felt weak all over.

'Ah!' The word fell from Caleb Crowther's lips with a smile. Patting both his hands several times against the younger fellow's shoulders he said it again – this time actually laughing out loud as he moved away. 'You and I have a deal to talk over,' he said, seating himself behind the desk and gesturing for Gregory Denton to occupy the seat before it. With that done and each man eyeing the other, he went on to question Gregory Denton at great length on issues concerning his domestic arrangements, his relationship with his old mater, and whether it was she who had discouraged him from ever taking a wife. In answer to the first question, Gregory Denton spoke with great pride of how he and his mother still resided in the smart little house on Montague Street, explaining how it had been in their family for some years now.

'It's a well-dressed, cosy little dwelling, though I say so myself,' he emphasized, not being able to resist puffing out his wiry chest just a little. 'I've spent a lot of time and effort on that little house in Montague Street,' he said.

He was a little more coy when coming to the business of his never having taken a wife, but it was *not* because of his demanding parent, he was quick to point out. 'Oh no . . . indeed no!' He felt most hurt by such a suggestion. 'Although I must be truthful and say that she is never the easiest person to get on with. In fact, she can be quite a demon at times!' he admitted, 'But, you see I've never met the right woman whom I might take as a wife.'

'But you are attracted to Miss Grady, are you not?' insisted Caleb Crowther.

'Tell lies and you'll make the Virgin Mary blush!' remonstrated the young man now, becoming bolder by the minute. 'Yes! Yes! I *am* very attracted to Miss Grady.' Then, made fearful by his own words, he swiftly added, 'Begging your pardon, sir!'

'Fine!' smiled Caleb Crowther, ignoring his employee's apology and leaning across the desk towards him. 'That's all I wanted to hear. Now then, Denton . . . how would you feel if I said I thought you to be a man worthy of my ward?' The younger man gave no reply, for he was so dumb-struck that all he could do was to prickle involuntarily from head to toe and continue staring in disbelief. Thoroughly enjoying the situation, Caleb Crowther went on, 'Miss Grady will be sixteen years of age in a few days time. She'll be a woman, with a woman's needs.' Here, he paused to let the meaning sink in. 'We neither of us want her messing about with these lowly river-people.' Now, at the thought, his eyes grew darker. 'Scum! That's what they are . . . scum!' he murmured, seeming to be lost in a deep, distant mood.

'No, no, Mr Crowther, that would never do,' agreed Gregory Denton, 'Miss Grady is a fine and lovely creature, and she must be protected from such folk. Why! . . . Isn't that the very reason I spoke out this evening!' He began to feel pleased with himself.

'We're in agreement then!' Caleb Crowther was back in command. 'Tell me, Denton . . . what *is* your financial state? Do you have any money in addition to what you earn from me?'

'No, sir.'

'Then you would not refuse the sum of one thousand pounds if it were offered to you?'

'*A thousand pounds*, Mr Crowther? Why should anyone offer *me* such a grand sum?'

Caleb Crowther sat slowly back in his chair, his hard eyes fixed on Gregory Denton's astonished features, and a half smile on his mouth. For a long time – too long for Gregory

Denton's comfort – he stayed thus, tapping his fingertips on the arm of the chair and eyeing the younger man with such intensity that Gregory Denton had to force himself to remain in his seat.

At length, the silence was brought to an abrupt end when Caleb Crowther sprang up from his chair to unlock a drawer in the desk. Taking from it a sheaf of documents, he began browsing through, until at length he snatched one out and put it face down before him. He explained to his patient employee, 'I have here a most vital piece of paper, and it concerns Miss Grady.' Pausing, he subjected the younger man to a most severe look. 'I rely on your word, Denton, because you have proved yourself to be a most truthworthy man. I want your word now, indeed, I *demand* it! Your bond that what I'm about to confide in you will never be repeated. *Never*, you understand. *Not even to Miss Grady herself.*'

'You have my word.'

'Excellent! Of course my ward is familiar with the general terms of her late father's will. But, it would be in bad taste, and most distressing, for you ever to discuss it with her. You *do* accept that?'

'Of course, of course! I do understand, Mr Crowther, sir. And I have given you my word,' declared Gregory Denton with a serious nod of his head.

Satisfied, Caleb Crowther continued, 'Thadius Grady provided well for Miss Grady, bequeathing her the very sum I have just mentioned . . . one thousand pounds . . . to be paid over to her husband in the event of her marriage.' He watched as realization spread over Gregory Denton's face, amused to see a dark red blush suffuse the younger man's cheeks as he added, 'I can see that you understand my meaning.' Still smiling, he asked, 'So, Mr Denton, what is your answer?'

'My answer? Please, Mr Crowther, sir, am I to believe that you are . . . you are offering Miss Grady's hand to me, in *marriage*!' He dared not believe his own ears. He was convinced that he was imagining things. But, he was not, and in the next few minutes, no time was lost by Caleb Crowther in securing a short legal statement and a number of signatures from the trembling hand of the fortunate young man.

'These will ensure that, on the very day you are joined in wedlock to my ward, you will receive the sum due, as I've said . . . one thousand pounds.' His tone grew more serious, as did the look he now bestowed upon the fellow before him, as he continued, 'Mark me well though, Denton. If you're foolish and spendthrift enough to go through this legacy in a short time . . . you had better not come crying to me, for you'll not get one more farthing out of me! There'll be nothing more until my ward reaches her twenty-fifth year. You had better understand that from the outset.' When he was assured that 'no such thought would ever cross my mind', he shook the hand of Gregory Denton, who was, unknowingly, his saviour. Then, bidding him farewell, he said, 'Say nothing of this to anyone. *I* will inform the necessary people, after which you will be summoned to finalize the finer details . . . a date for the ceremony and so on.' As an afterthought he added, 'I'm placing a great responsibility in your hands, Denton. A great and precious responsibility, for I am exceedingly fond of Miss Grady, as you no doubt already know.' Gregory Denton did *not* know, but he nevertheless gave an agreeable smile. The only thing he *did* know at that moment in time was that everything he'd dared to dream had come true! Momentarily, he wondered how Miss Grady might feel towards him, for of that he was unsure; yet he dared to hope she might nurture the same affection for him as he did for her.

Meanwhile, from her vantage point, Emma watched as the two men emerged from the house. Already, dusk was creeping over everything like a shroud, and the breeze had grown sharp and bitterly cold. Yet, Emma made no move. It fascinated her to see these two men together. It also aggravated her to witness the clear arrogance of one compared to the gentler nature of the other. Even from this distance, and in the gathering twilight, Emma thought how very easy it was to distinguish master from servant – the former being a large, ungainly yet formidable figure, seeming to avoid any physical contact whatsoever with the latter, who in turn appeared to bow and scrape in a totally subservient manner. It sorely irked Emma to see how Gregory Denton grovelled before her uncle, for she truly believed that, of the two men, Caleb Crowther was the lesser man.

As the carriage pulled away, Gregory Denton was still in a daze, his face warmly flushed as he marvelled at his unbelievable luck.

'By! . . . you look like the cat who got the cream, Denton!' observed Mr Wordsworth, with a laugh. 'Some'at *I* should know, is it?' he asked, hopefully. When there was no answer, his colleague seemingly completely unaware of his presence, he prodded him roughly, saying in a firmer voice, 'I say, Denton . . . what went on atwixt you and the big man, eh? Some'at *I* should be told, is it? Is it, eh?'

'No! No, indeed, Mr Wordsworth!' Gregory Denton assured him, in a greatly alarmed voice. 'Nothing at all that might concern you. It was . . . a personal matter, and one which Mr Crowther would prefer to be kept quiet . . . at least, for now,' he added with a secret smile. Oh, how excited he felt; so elated and exhilarated that he wanted to shout out from the roof-tops. But, he was also afraid: he felt as though he was walking on eggshells and at any minute the ground would give way beneath him. Mr Crowther had given instructions that he was to say *nothing* of his impending marriage to Miss Grady, and, he would not! For, even now he felt it to be such a delicate and unbelievable thing that he was mortally afraid it would crumble at the very first opportunity – and he dared not risk that! Whatever he was told to do, he would do it gladly; and, if keeping his mouth shut for the moment ensured that Miss Grady would soon be his very own, it was a small price to pay for such an honourable and wonderful thing. He admonished himself for dwelling too much on his forthcoming marriage, since the very idea made him tremble so violently that he felt positively ill. The prospect of telling his mother had the same effect!

Going back into his study, Caleb Crowther threw himself into the chair and stared down at the documents spread out across the desk. Picking up one in particular, which he had surreptitiously slipped between two others, he congratulated himself at having so cunningly concealed the *real* figure of Emma's inheritance – not one thousand pounds, as he had led that fool Denton to believe, but *six* thousand! The larger part was now *his*, and only a much smaller share would accompany Emma Grady to her marriage-bed.

Now, chuckling quietly to himself, he scanned the short statement which he had written in his own hand, and which the naïve and trusting young man had promptly signed. He experienced a deep satisfaction and a welcomed rush of relief, as he read:

> I, Gregory Denton, having been accepted by Caleb Crowther as being suitable to join with his ward, Emma Grady, in wedlock, have been fully acquainted with the details of her inheritance. It agreed that, on the day of our marriage, the entire sum due – being £1,000 – will be entrusted to me, on Miss Grady's behalf, thereby complying with the terms of Thadius Grady's last will and testament.

When the younger man's signature had been added after his own, Caleb Crowther had held his breath. He had to admit a great deal of surprise when Gregory Denton's signature was so readily given, since this young fellow was, as a rule, very astute in matters of business. But then he was in love, was he not? And, Caleb Crowther knew only too well – from one particularly painful experience long ago – just how cruelly blinding and all-consuming fierce love can be!

Taking up his pen, he carefully added a loop to the bottom of the one following the pound sign, thereby making the figure read six thousand pounds. Then, putting the pen down, he leaned back in his chair and smiled a knowing smile. 'My thanks to you, Denton,' he murmured, 'though you're more kinds of a fool than I took you for! *This* is my insurance.' Collecting the papers together, he returned them to the drawer, afterwards locking it and slipping the key into his waistcoat pocket. There! Now it only remained for him to make arrangements to draw the money from the fund, and the rest would be child's play. It occurred to him that the sooner the wedding, the better. So, with this in mind, he went in search of his wife, finding her in the drawing-room, busy with her embroidery.

'Mr Denton was a long time going,' she remarked in a stiff voice, her eyes intent on the circle of tapestry, and her nimble fingers seeming to move with increased agitation at his sudden intrusion.

'Could you put down your work?' he asked, lifting apart the tails of his coat as he made a great fuss in seating himself opposite her. 'There are matters you will need to know, concerning both Gregory Denton and Emma.' At once she lowered her hands and lifted her gaze attentively. Seeing her ready, Caleb Crowther launched into a long and detailed explanation of his prolonged meeting with Gregory Denton; concealing, however, the matter of his own fraud and concluding with the words, 'So you see, my dear, there is much to be organized, as it would suit all purposes to have the thing over and done with as soon as possible. Already she appears to have taken an unhealthy liking to this unsavoury river-person. There must be a stop put to that . . . at once!'

As the news had begun to unfold, Agnes Crowther was visibly astonished that her husband had matched Emma with such a mouse as Gregory Denton – a fellow with pitifully small means of support, and who was socially inferior to themselves. Yet, she did not interrupt. since she thought Caleb to be a shrewd man and an excellent judge of char-acter. He would not have agreed to this betrothal lightly, or without good reason; of that she was certain. Then of course, there was this dreadful business of Emma's fasci-nation with the river-people. Indeed, it was of great concern to her. Just think of the awful scandal which could erupt if this wild and wilful girl persisted in these disgraceful encounters! It was all too much for her – what with that shameful experience concerning Martha and her school!

'I can see that she *must* be married off as soon as it can be arranged,' she said now, with a great sigh of relief, 'but why Gregory Denton? Surely there must be someone more suitable, more *socially* acceptable?'

'Who else has expressed a desire to marry Emma?' he replied, before going on to answer his own question. 'No one, but the fellow concerned. Who else can bring her down a peg or two, and let her see the folly of taking for granted our fine big house and way of life?' Again, he quickly gave the answer. 'Only a modest man like Gregory Denton, with a modest manner of living, and the kind of simple virtues that might just teach her to be more thankful!' He made no mention of the main reason for his decision – that of embezzling Emma out of her inheritance.

'You're right, of course!' agreed Agnes Crowther, now caught up in the rush of events. 'There is much to be done, and I shall start at once.' After her initial surprise, she was positively enthusiastic. Emma Grady had been pampered for too long; and, perhaps she might even fit in better with a simple working-man's family. Yes, of course she would! But suddenly, it occurred to her that Emma would not be going to him empty-handed. 'Is the trust fund to be handed over?' she asked quietly, not particularly liking the idea, but knowing it was unavoidable.

'But of course, my dear!' Caleb Crowther appeared suitably horrified that she should even question such a thing. All the same, it would not do for his wife to dwell too much on this particular issue, so, putting on his most

151

authoritative and judicial voice, he told her, 'I don't want you bothering your female head over such matters . . . nor discussing them with anyone, anyone at all! Your brother entrusted me to carry out his wishes, and I will do just that. As far as you are concerned, my dear, let that be an end to it. You may rest assured, it is all in hand.' When he was promptly informed that she was more than delighted to leave such matters in his capable hands, and that it was not her business to discuss such delicate and private issues as finance with a single person, he was much relieved. 'Be so kind as to fetch Emma to me straightaway,' he instructed.

Putting down her work, Agnes hurried from the room. At long last, she thought jubilantly, we'll be rid of the wretched girl, and the responsibility that goes with her! The trust endowed in her by Emma's papa, her own brother, touched her conscience only briefly.

High up on the hill, Emma had watched the carriage disappear out of sight, and now as the pinching cold began to make her teeth chatter and the light of day was swallowed into a greying sky, she thought about making her way back down. But she was loathe to do so, for up here, surrounded by so much beauty and precious freedom, she was answerable to no one.

'Miss Grady!' The call came from down below and was carried by the breeze to where Emma was already on her feet. Looking down towards the house, she could see the familiar figure of Mrs Manfred waving her arms and shouting, 'Come down from there, come down!'

Waving in response, Emma was warmed by that familiar little figure, and, cupping her hands about her mouth, she shouted, 'All right, Manny . . . all right!' At once, she began to scramble down the slope with the same exuberance with which she had climbed it, laughingly slipping, sliding and tumbling until at length she came to the bottom, where Mrs Manfred was waiting with a look of frustration on her face.

'Just look at you!' she told Emma between a series of tutting noises. 'Covered in grass and bracken and looking less like a well brought-up young lady than I've ever seen!' She carried on tutting while she proceeded to brush Emma's dishevelled skirt most vigorously. Presently, looking Emma up and down, she seemed satisfied. Then, patting Emma's long auburn hair into a semblance of tidiness down her back and beginning to tut again, she asked, 'Where's your ribbon, child?' When Emma replied that it must have been lost on the way, she gave a great noisy sigh. 'Well, you do look more presentable now,' she said, 'so the ribbon won't matter.'

'Oh, Manny . . . why all the fuss?' Emma wanted to know. She was both intrigued and amused at Mrs Manfred's concern over her appearance. 'I'll go straight in, have a wash and change my clothes . . . will *that* satisfy you?' she laughed, throwing her arms about her good friend in a fearsome hug.

'*Listen* to me, Miss Grady.' She disentangled herself from Emma's arms, her voice falling to a more serious tone, as she cautioned, 'You're wanted. You're to go to the drawing-room right away.'

'What for? Who wants to see me?' Emma was puzzled and, racking her brains to find a reason why she should be summoned to the drawing-rom, her heart nearly stopped when she remembered a certain incident. But no! How could anyone know of what happened between her and Marlow in the park on Saturday? Calm yourself, Emma Grady, she told herself. Whatever it is, it *can't* be that, it's not possible! All the same, though, she couldn't stop her heart from beating fearfully.

'It's the master who wants to see you,' explained Mrs Manfred. 'Oh, child . . . what have you been up to now?'

She looked so distressed that Emma's heart went out to her. 'Now Manny, don't look so worried, darling. It'll be all right, you'll see,' she assured her, leaning forward to kiss the older woman's face. 'I don't *think* I've done anything so bad.' She lifted her hands to catch the strands of hair which had strayed over her shoulders; flicking them backwards, she then ran her hands over the top of her head and afterwards patted the bunched-up pleats of her voluminous skirt. 'Come on, Manny,' she said, starting forward, 'into the lion's den I go. Wish me luck!' Emma truly felt as though she *was* about to do battle, and the flippancy of her words belied that knot of fear inside her, which would not go away.

As she was soon to learn, Emma had every right to feel afraid. For what seemed to be a lifetime, she was made to stand before Caleb Crowther while he relayed a graphic account of what had taken place in Corporation Park between herself and 'this river-person by the name of Marlow Tanner.' When he had accused her of the incident itself, Emma had been mortified, but when he actually spoke out Marlow's name, her trembling heart fell like a dead weight inside her.

'Please, Uncle Caleb . . . it really *wasn't* what it might have seemed,' she began, only to be silenced when, coming to stand so close to her that she thought for a minute he intended to strike her, he said in a harsh voice, 'It is *exactly* what it seemed! I've told you before, Emma Grady . . . you have it in you to be a harlot! The lowest woman on the streets!'

'Am I to be punished then?' Emma was desolate at the prospect of being confined to her room yet again. But, more than that, she was afraid for Marlow. 'Please believe me, if anyone is to blame, it is me, *not* Marlow Tanner,' she pleaded.

'Do you think you don't deserve to be punished?' demanded Caleb Crowther. 'Do you think this river-trash should be allowed to get away with what he's done?' He paused, staring at Emma with deliberation, and waiting for her answer. When her eyes challenged his, he went on, 'I had a mind to flay the skin off his back, then to hand him over to the authorities . . . with a recommendation that he be shipped off to Australia on the next sailing!'

'You *can't*!' The thought was too much for Emma. 'He's innocent, I tell you. He did nothing to be treated so. Please, Uncle Caleb, leave him be, for none of it was his fault. His sister was crippled in the fire . . . she has no one but him.'

'Be quiet, damn you! Listen to what I have to say.' He was no fool. It was plain to him that she was in love with this Tanner fellow. Fate did seem to be handing him a most useful and rewarding set of cards. 'Arrangements have been made for your future. Should you see the sense in these arrangements, and go into them wholeheartedly with both your aunt's and my blessing, then you have my word that not only will you escape punishment but this fellow also will be let off with only a warning. But, a *severe* warning, on account of the nature of the incident. Of course, I can't allow him to continue in my employment!' he added.

Emma was puzzled. She was not in the least surprised

that Caleb Crowther should terminate Marlow's employment at the Grady mill. But that would be of little consequence, she was sure, since there were other mills which would be only too pleased to employ someone of Marlow Tanner's hard-working breed. But why? *Why* would he be let off so lightly, when for just laughing with her on a previous occasion, the skin had been sliced from his shoulders? And what were these 'arrangements' to which her uncle referred? She dared to question him now on this subject. His immediate answer was to walk away and, with irritating slowness, to seat himself in the chair behind his desk – from where he continued to regard her with a quizzical and cunning expression. At length he said, 'You should thank Gregory Denton, for pleading with me on your behalf.'

'*Mr Denton*?' Emma could hardly believe her ears. Since when did Caleb Crowther listen to the likes of Gregory Denton? There was something strange here, thought Emma, but, for the life of her, she couldn't think what. 'Why? Why should he do such a thing?' she asked now.

'Because the fool thinks the world of you!' came the retort. 'Because he does not want to see you punished. Because he has asked for your hand in marriage. And I have agreed!' He grew increasingly irritated.

Emma was riveted to the spot. *Marriage*! She had been promised in marriage to Gregory Denton! For a moment, Emma couldn't fully comprehend the significance of her uncle's words; but when she did, they froze her heart and paralysed her tongue. She had been naïve enough to believe that she was not to be punished; when, in actual fact her uncle was exacting the very greatest punishment he had it in his power to do. He was ridding himself of her, and she was not in a position to defy him. Oh, she could make things difficult, by being obstinate and unwilling to see things his way; she could irritate and frustrate him. But that would only bring the full weight of his wrath down on both her and Marlow. Emma didn't care what *she* might endure, but the thought of Marlow being beaten and hounded was more than she could bear. Furthermore, she had no doubts about what Caleb Crowther threatened. If it became his intention to see Marlow Tanner transported to Australia as a convict, there would be no power on this earth to stop him. So, when he now put the question to her, 'You find Gregory Denton to be an amiable young fellow, do you not?' she answered truthfully that yes, she found him to be so.

'And you think him also a conscientious and industrious person, who would look upon marriage as a serious and pleasant state . . . where he would execute the duties of a husband to the very best of his ability?'

'I believe so.' Emma also believed that no matter what *she* thought, said or did, the outcome would be the same. If the price for Marlow's safety was to be her own freedom, then it was a small enough price to pay, for she had never really known freedom since coming to this house. And, in all truth, Emma wondered whether life with Gregory Denton might not actually be preferable to life here, beneath the iron rule of Caleb Crowther.

'Good!' Caleb Crowther got to his feet. 'I find the arrangement altogether satisfactory. As from today, you will no longer attend your clerical duties. It would not appear proper. Your aunt will speak with you in due course, and Gregory Denton will shortly begin calling on you.' Making a dismissive gesture, he added, 'You may go!'

Emma did not need to be told twice, and hurriedly departed, her heart heavy with despair, and lightened only by her deep, abiding love for Marlow.

As she closed the door behind her, a small four-leaf clover fluttered from her shoulder. Stooping down to collect it into her hand, she marvelled at its simple beauty and striking deep green colour. As she gazed at it, she recalled Marlow's laughing words when he had plucked a four-leaf clover from the canal bank the very first time they had met. 'God's little secrets, these are,' he'd told her, 'meant to be lucky, too.' Smiling quietly, Emma closed her fingers around it, murmuring as she departed the room, 'Perhaps you'll bring me luck one day?'

Upstairs in the privacy of her bedroom, Emma folded the four-leaf clover into the case of the silver watch. As she did so, she could never have known how truly prophetic were her words.

Chapter Six

It was New Year's Eve, the last day of 1860, and for many it was a time of rejoicing; but, as she prepared herself for the celebrations which even now were underway downstairs, Emma could find no real joy in her own heart. As the orchestral music filtered up the stairs to fill her room with its haunting melodies, Emma was moved and, as was her way, she tried to look on the bright side of things – realizing that, following her marriage on 14th January, she could turn her back on this house and on the Crowthers for ever! The thought cheered her so much that she found herself humming in tune to the music and gently swaying from side to side.

'Keep still, child!' ordered Mrs Manfred, who was growing more agitated by the minute. 'I'm blessed if I've ever come across such unruly hair as yours, in all my born days!' When Emma immediately sat still, saying 'Sorry, Manny', she continued her efforts to pin the wild auburn hair into a cluster on the crown of Emma's head. 'It's no use!' she declared after another frustrating moment. 'These pins are too delicate . . . I shall have to fetch a few of my own. Just you sit still!' she told Emma, before hurrying from the room. 'I'll not be a minute.'

No sooner had the amiable housekeeper departed the room, than there came a knock on the door and a quiet voice asking, 'Can I come in, Miss Grady?'

'Please don't,' Emma replied, turning on the dresser stool to look towards the half-closed door. 'I'm not ready yet, Mr Denton.'

'Will you be long then?' he asked, but before Emma could say anything, there came another voice, assuring the timid young man hovering at Emma's door, 'She'll be *twice* as long if you don't let me by, so I can finish her hair!' Much as she had tried to dislike Gregory Denton for taking away her darling Emma, Mrs Manfred found that she could not – although she would *never* take to the idea of Emma being wed so young. And not if she lived to be a hundred could she ever forgive Caleb Crowther for ridding himself of the girl in such a way. She still had her suspicions regarding the manner in which Emma's papa had departed this world, and now this whole hurried and unexpected business of Emma's betrothal to Gregory Denton had only increased her suspicions. Mrs Manfred had worked hard at convincing herself that her suspicions were groundless and were rooted in her dislike for the Crowthers. But that cold uneasy feeling remained with her. Caleb Crowther was a bad, heartless fiend, of that she had no doubts whatsoever, and his wife was little better. Right from the moment Emma told her the news and then wept on her shoulder, the belief that Caleb Crowther had first helped Thadius Grady meet his maker and then sacrificed young Emma to an ill-suited marriage – all in the name of greed – haunted her.

'I'm very sorry, Mrs Manfred,' muttered Gregory Denton, turning an uncomfortable shade of pink and stepping quickly away to hasten towards the stairway, 'only . . . I'm so looking forward to seeing her,' he explained.

'Of course you are,' Mrs Manfred declared with a warm smile. 'Be patient, young man. Miss Grady won't keep you waiting much longer, I promise.' When he gave a small nervous laugh and thanked her, she went into Emma's room, closed the door behind her and remarked to Emma, 'He's a nice enough fellow, I'm sure.'

Emma's response was a quiet smile and a thoughtful look. During the next few moments, as her hair was pulled this way and that, pinned up then loosened, and finally arranged such that the centre portion was pinned up with the outer curls falling naturally about her face, Emma resigned herself to take just one day at a time. That way she felt more able to face what lay ahead and more determined to try and make the very best of it. However, there was one particular event which was to take place on the morrow which she was positively dreading; she was due to meet, for the very first time, Gregory Denton's old mother, a woman who, according to talk below stairs, was a 'cantankerous and bloody-minded old tyrant!'

'Manny,' she asked now, looking into the mirror and anxiously gazing at the older woman, 'will it be just *awful*, meeting the infamous Mrs Denton?'

'Awful . . . nothing!' retorted Mrs Manfred, who in spite of her efforts to put Emma at ease with regard to the girl's forthcoming trial, suffered no illusions where the elderly woman was concerned; for, if there was anybody more spiteful and more demanding than that old bully, then Mrs Manfred had not heard of her. There were only two things that mattered to Gregory Denton's aged mother – her own comfort and the absolute attention and obedience of her only offspring. Her domineering nature

161

regarding the latter was well known, and it would not be easy for Emma to successfully fit into this strange and rigid set-up; nor would it be without a certain degree of pain and determination. But, Mrs Manfred was confident that Emma, who had known enough pain to help her cope, would prove a good match for that determined old woman. Mrs Manfred concealed a little smile, for she truly believed that, if this possessive parent meant to break Emma's will, she must expect to see sparks fly.

'I do so want us to get on,' Emma said, getting down from her seat and walking the few steps to the full-length mirror where she looked at her reflection, her expression still troubled by the thought of leaving one tyrant behind only possibly to be faced with another.

'Don't dwell on it, child,' remonstrated Mrs Manfred, coming to stand by Emma's left side. 'If she *does* start her old games, then you just stand up to her . . . like you often do with me!' she laughed. 'The old bugger'll soon learn to respect you.'

Emma was so astonished to hear Mrs Manfred using a swear word that she promptly forgot about the troublesome subject which had prompted such colourful language.

'There!' declared Mrs Manfred. 'For the first time in my life the old sod's got me swearing!' Whereupon Emma began chuckling, and soon they were both convulsed in laughter and holding on to each other when Emma pointed out, 'If she has that effect on *you*, Manny, whatever might become of *me*?'

Two weeks before the New Year's Eve ball, Caleb Crowther had ordered his wife Agnes to accompany Emma into Manchester where they were to purchase a gown which 'will show how the girl has matured into a woman.' Emma suspected his intention was to show all who might have quietly thought her still a child, too young to be married, that she was in fact a woman, more mature than they had realized and ready for marriage. Finding a suitable gown had not been easy, since Emma was so slim and petite and the adult gowns so heavy and overwhelming. After Agnes Crowther had impatiently rejected several rather loud and fussy articles, a particular gown in a warmly attractive shade of burgundy was brought out. The skirt was not full and flouncy, but long and flowing, with a silky look; the hem was deeply scalloped and edged with fine black braiding; and the waist was tiny, and at the back was the merest suggestion of a bustle. When Emma slipped it on and came out for inspection, Agnes Crowther was visibly taken aback; for there before her stood not a young girl, but an incredibly beautiful woman, possessed of poise and graciousness.

Now, as Emma came down the stairs, every admiring pair of eyes were turned in her direction. Agnes Crowther's gaze was also drawn to her. As she followed Emma's every step, her narrowed eyes swept from the top of Emma's lovely hair, which shone the colour of polished chestnuts, to the straight delicate lines of her bare shoulders, which were enhanced by the small unfussy dropped sleeves. She looked the whole length of Emma's tiny and exquisitely formed figure, her young breasts rising from beneath the gown, and her small feet dressed in black button-over shoes to match the pretty frilled bag at her wrist. Agnes Crowther suffered such terrible pangs of envy as she gazed at her niece's beautiful face, with that perfectly generous mouth and those deep grey smiling eyes, and saw the natural and elegant way in which she moved. She saw Emma's papa's – her own brother's – qualities so evident in Emma's own proud, handsome features, and was so affected that she hurriedly averted her eyes, turning her head away and moving to where she need not gaze on her brother's child any longer. Instead, she looked at her own daughter, Martha, and tried, with extreme difficulty, not to draw comparisons.

'Oh, Emma!' Gregory Denton felt as though he had waited a lifetime, and all of that lifetime had been lived only for this moment, with Emma as the focal point of his every dream. As he took her hand and threaded it through his arm, there wasn't a prouder man alive on God's earth. 'You're the loveliest creature I've ever seen,' he murmured, leading a path through the dancers and into the centre of the floor where they might find a space. Having done so, he stopped and turned to face her, 'I do love you so,' he whispered above the music.

'I know you do,' Emma whispered back. It would have given her a lot of pleasure to be able to say 'And I love you,' but she could not, as there would be no truth in such a statement. However, she was fond of him, and gazing into his sincere eyes, which now looked on her with such warmth and shining adulation, Emma was deeply moved. 'You're such a good man, Gregory,' she told him with an affectionate half-smile. 'I pray I won't disappoint you. I do so want to make you a good wife.'

For a long, lingering moment, Gregory Denton continued to gaze at her, his eyes feasting on her gentle beauty and his face saturated with pleasure at her words. At length, he said quietly, 'Any man would be more than proud to have you for his wife, Emma. I know how lucky I am. And, if

you don't love me now the way I love you, I feel you will
. . . in time.' He stepped closer to murmur in her ear, 'I know
it in my heart. You *will* come to feel as I do.'

But Emma thought not. She had already given her heart
to Marlow Tanner. It had been given freely, and for ever.
It did not matter that she may never see him again, for she
was powerless in her love for him. His tall, strong image
and those dark, brooding eyes, which simultaneously
tortured and pleased her, were always in her heart and
more alive with every life's beat – and, Emma knew,
would remain with her for the rest of her life.

Telling herself that she mustn't think of him, not here,
not now, Emma took to the floor with her partner and, for
the remainder of the evening, she danced and smiled, she
listened attentively to the meaningless chatter of others, and
she gave to one and all the appearance of a young woman
looking forward to her imminent marriage. She fooled
everyone but those who knew better. She did not fool
Caleb Crowther, who spent most of the evening huddled
in a quiet corner with other industrialists, whose intense
conversations covered everything from the rebellious attitude of the common worker to the persistent rumours
regarding the unrest in North America.

Neither did Emma's forced gaiety fool Agnes Crowther
and her daughter, Martha, who commented, 'How clever
of Papa to hand over the burden of Emma to that peculiar
little man. By all accounts he has a nasty and overbearing
mother . . . who, no doubt, will curb Emma Grady's wilful
ways at the first opportunity!'

'Really, Martha, that's a very strong and condemning attitude, if I may say so.' The speaker was a large, well-built
fellow with quiet brown eyes, a military-type moustache

and thick mop of hair – all of the same shade of brown. His skin was of an even deeper shade and, because of his seafaring interests, was leathery in texture. He and Martha had met when, during her recent holiday, she had accompanied her mother into Lancaster to purchase shoes and accessories for the New Year's Eve ball. With their shopping finished, they had begun to make their way across the busy main thoroughfare, when, through her own foolishness, Martha was almost trampled underfoot by a coach and four. It was the quick thinking of Silas Trent which had saved her. Afterwards, finding certain things in common, they had struck up a friendship which had later deepened into a manner of courtship. Both Caleb and Agnes Crowther heartily approved of the relationship. Agnes believed him to be a stabilizing influence on her daughter, and, at the age of twenty-four years, he made both a commanding and kindly figure. Also, in spite of Martha's many faults and plain appearance, he was obviously extremely fond of her. Caleb Crowther's reasons were two-fold and very different from those of his wife: one stemmed from the recent and shameful business regarding Martha's deceitful behaviour at her school; but much more importantly were his enquiries which revealed that Silas Trent was the only son of Marcus Trent – founder and sole owner of the highly lucrative Trent Shipping Line out of London and Liverpool. The Trent fleet of ships was most impressive, and from the execution of his duties as Justice of the Peace, Caleb Crowther recalled that, not only did the Trent fleet sail various other cargoes across the Atlantic, but these ships were the foremost carriers of convicts to Australia. The company was a proud and successful one. Therefore, never being one to miss an opportunity, Caleb Crowther was seen to actively encourage the relationship between Martha and the young man Silas Trent. Yet, he was most careful not to confuse the character of this accomplished young man with that of the timid and subservient Gregory Denton: the latter was easily cheated, but Silas Trent was no fool, and had strong opinions of his own which he would express without hesitation.

'Martha . . . don't you think it would be proper to introduce me to your cousin?' Silas Trent's disapproval of Martha's spiteful remarks concerning Emma sharpened the tone of his voice. 'I should like to be allowed to form my own opinion of the young lady in question.' The smile on his face belied the frown in his voice. His smile deepened on seeing Martha pout in that familiar manner which he had become accustomed to – a bad habit which he intended to break at the first opportunity.

Agnes Crowther also had noticed her daughter's immature and sulky attitude, and at once she had stepped from Martha's side and was graciously assuring Silas Trent that 'Of course you must meet Emma.' She did not want this eligible young man to be left with the impression that Martha was churlish in her attitude towards Emma, nor that she possessed a spiteful side to her nature. Quickly now, she made her way around the perimeter of the dance floor to where Emma was seated, waiting for Gregory to return with her glass of sarsaparilla.

From her place in the hallway, where she watched to see that all was going well, Mrs Manfred saw Agnes Crowther collect Emma from her chair. She saw how the woman ignored Emma's protests that Gregory would wonder about her disappearance, and she saw the two of them returning to where Martha waited with her rather large but good-natured young man. When Emma was introduced to Silas Trent and he, gallantly taking her hand to his lips, smiled down at her, it warmed Mrs Manfred's heart to witness the stony and petulant features of Martha Crowther as she looked on reluctantly and with some disgust. But it also hurt the dear woman to realize how this selfish and undeserving girl had secured for herself a strong and wealthy man, while her own lovely Emma had been fobbed off with second best as usual. Oh, it wasn't that Mrs Manfred had not come to like Gregory Denton, for she had, yes indeed. But, to her mind, Emma's going from the Crowthers to that old Denton woman, was akin to falling from the pan into the fire. She only prayed she might be proved to be wrong. But, somehow, she doubted it.

As Emma looked up into Silas Trent's kindly smiling eyes, something in their genuine honesty made her heart warm to him. She liked him instantly and she considered Martha to be very fortunate in having gained his affection. 'Martha's told me about you, Mr Trent,' she said with a smile, when in all truth she should have said that Martha had never stopped bragging about him and cruelly comparing him to poor, harmless Gregory. 'I'm very pleased to meet you at last.'

'And I you, Emma . . . if I may call you that?' When she gave a half-smile and nodded, he ventured, 'I wonder whether your intended might object to me dancing with you?'

For a moment Emma was quite taken aback. She could feel Martha's eyes glaring at her, daring her to accept. And she was not unaware of Agnes Crowther, standing rigidly, with her hands joined and pointing to Heaven. Probably praying to God that I'll fall through the floorboards and out of sight, mused Emma, with the desire to laugh aloud. She was also aware that Silas Trent still had hold of her hand and was waiting for her answer.

'Thank you, Mr Trent,' she said, 'I'd love to dance . . . I'm sure Gregory won't mind.' As he swept her on to the dance floor, Emma couldn't resist glancing back. As she expected, there stood Martha in her severe grey dress – which was adorned with a huge, unsightly bustle and frilled with broad white ribbon – with such a dark and furious scowl on her face that would surely be enough to curdle the cream! And there beside her, looking regal and splendid in a cream-coloured, extravagantly designed, voluminous gown, was Agnes Crowther, her familiar posture of prayer even more fiercely disciplined and her lips drawn in with such severity that her mouth had become a thin, taut line and the muscles in her neck stood out like tramlines.

'Now I can see where Martha gets her fits of petulance from,' remarked Silas Trent as he began with much enthusiasm, the steps of a foxtrot. 'Looks like I've got my work cut out when I take her for my wife,' he laughed. It was an easy, infectious laugh which enthused Emma to reply light-heartedly, 'I think I'd rather you than me, Mr Trent.' To which, and to the fury of the two Crowther women watching, they both burst out laughing.

In a quieter mood, Emma asked him, 'You love her very much, don't you?'

'I'm afraid so,' he replied, 'but I'm not blinded to her faults. But then we *all* have faults, do we not?' To which Emma replied that there was nothing surer.

When the dance was over and each about to return to their respective partners, Emma thanked him. 'Not at all!' he replied with a sweeping smile, 'I can't think when I've had so much fun!' But suddenly, the smile disappeared from his face and in its place was a tender concern. 'Emma . . . I know enough of your background to suspect that there may come a day when you need someone to turn to. I hope such a day never does come. But, if it does, I want you to consider me as a friend. Will you do that?'

For the second time since meeting him, Emma was deeply surprised by this man. But, there was something about him – an honesty, a compassion and truth – that prompted her without hesitation to say 'Yes. To have you as a friend would be a fine thing.'

'Good!' he said, smiling down on her and slowly nodding his head back and forth. As she watched him striding back to the sulking Martha, Emma believed that the day when she had to run to him for help would never come. But Emma could not know that in the hard years to come, there would be occasions when Silas Trent proved to be both a friend and an invaluable tower of strength to her.

When the last guest had gone and Gregory had reluctantly said goodnight, Emma went to her room, took off her clothes, slipped into a nightgown and, after brushing out her long rich hair, climbed gratefully into bed. Yet, in spite of her tiredness, she felt strangely restless. There was something uniquely sad about seeing out the old year, she thought, and for her, it wasn't just a farewell to 1860, but to her life as she had come to know it. Soon, she would leave this house. She would be a wife and, one day, she must also mother Gregory Denton's children. For the moment the prospect was too daunting to dwell on at any length – especially when, in her deepest heart, Emma had prayed that it could be Marlow who was about to make her his wife, and Marlow's children whom she might bring into the world. But, however much she found herself wishing it, she knew that this could never be. She was wise enough to accept that.

'If you have any influence up there with the angels, Papa,' she murmured into the darkness, 'will you ask them to send a little good fortune down here? Help me to be a good wife to Gregory and see that his mother might grow fond of me?' Then, with all kinds of unsettling images and thoughts in her mind, Emma fell into a restless sleep.

The short sleep was feverish and fitful. In the early hours, Emma woke suddenly from her nightmares with a cry of alarm. Realizing that she was safely alone in her room and that the clawing monsters had remained behind in the realms of her frantic dream, she relaxed against the cold brass bars of the bed-head. With a grateful sigh, she brought up her hands to wipe from her face the sweat which stood out in small wet beads, clinging to her skin like early morning dew. Then, stretching out her arms and locking her slender fingers together behind her neck, she leaned back again and closed her eyes. 'You'd best shake your feathers, Emma Grady!' she reproached herself. 'Dreaming isn't for the likes of you!'

She found herself thinking of Martha, who at least had been given some say in choosing her man. The thought of Martha brought a wry little smile to Emma's face, and as she imagined her cousin with a brood of children she couldn't help herself from laughing out loud. She wondered for a fleeting moment whether, given the choice, she would prefer to swap places with her cousin Martha. The thought terrified Emma! No! She was who she was – Emma Grady, daughter of Thadius and Mary. She had some wonderful memories and she had Manny. If her lot now was not everything she might have wished for, then there were many more worse off than her.

In the face of such reasoning, Emma chided herself and decided that she must be grateful for every mercy, small or otherwise. After all, Gregory Denton was a good man, and he loved her. But, try as she might to console herself with this, Emma's heart could not wholly accept it, for the image living there was not of Gregory. Nor was that deep well of love she felt, meant for him. And, even though her memories of her beloved Marlow warmed her heart and gave her immeasurable pleasure, she yearned for more: she longed for those dark eyes to gaze on her and for those strong arms to hold her close. Emma knew she could never be truly happy without Marlow; she could never forget him. But she could – she must – learn to live without him.

Getting up from the bed, Emma crossed over to the window where she opened wide the curtains and looked out at the sky. Soon, the sun would rise and a new day begin. A new year, and, for her, the start of a whole new life. What would it be like, she wondered, with that deep anxiety which would not leave her.

Emma went across to the small circular table where she lit the oil lamp. Then, glancing at the small brass clock on the mantelpiece which told her it was almost five a.m., she realized that the day had already begun for her because it would be futile to return to her bed and try to sleep. There was no more sleep in her, not now. She grabbed a shawl from the back of the stand-chair, which she flung about her shoulders before going out of the room and down the stairs to the kitchen. Seeing that the fire had been well stacked the previous evening and was still giving out a cheery glow, Emma half filled the big blackened kettle with water and wedged it on top of the coals. When she thought it must be warmed, she took a cloth from the bar which fronted the big oven, and, wrapping it firmly round the kettle handle, she lifted it from the fire.

Quickly, she returned to her room, where she tipped the warm water into the large ceramic bowl on top of her dresser. Then, putting the kettle down in the cold fire-place, she opened the top drawer of the dresser and withdrew from it a face flannel and clean towel. From the second drawer, she collected a freshly laundered set of under-clothes. After stripping off her nightgown, Emma took the soap from its stand beside the bowl and washed herself thoroughly all over. That done, she quickly dressed, brushed her hair into its ribbons, wrapped the long, fringed shawl about her, gathered up her small dark boots into one hand and went on tiptoe back down to the kitchen. There, she put on her boots, and going into Cook's larder she helped herself to a cup of milk, a muffin and a portion of Cook's special fruit jam. After heartily enjoying her early break-fast, she took the cup and plate to the sink, washed them under the tap and dried them, before returning them to the big pine dresser. Then, going to the great black fire-range, she scooped up a measure of coke from the brass scuttle and got the fire going more cheerfully. That done, she pulled up Cook's favourite deep, horse-hair armchair and curled up into it.

It was on the stroke of six a.m. that Cook came bumbling into her kitchen, a dumpy vision of clean, starched white-ness with her sleeves already rolled up ready to tackle the day ahead. 'Well, I never!' she called out, seeing Emma fast asleep in the chair, her face warmed to a fetching pink by the glow from the fire, 'the little rascal!'

Of a sudden, Emma was wide awake, giving her apologies and assuring Cook, 'I haven't interfered with anything, except I had a muffin and a drop of milk from the larder.'

'I should hope you ain't interfered with anything, young lady!' remonstrated Cook. 'You'd best take yerself off while I gets the breakfast underway. I can't be doing with you under me feet, and that's a fact!' She then began ranting about 'folks as wander around instead o' sleeping quiet in their beds.'

Thinking it best not to antagonize Cook any further, Emma decided she'd better either return to her room or go for a walk in the early morning air. She decided to go for a walk.

'And don't you go far, Miss Grady!' Cook shouted after her. 'Ye'll likely catch yer death o' cold out there. And breakfast'll be served within the hour!'

'Don't worry,' Emma told her. 'I won't go far.'

Once outside Emma drew her shawl more tightly about her. Cook was right, it *was* cold; but she was not deterred for, if anything, the cold morning air gave her a feeling of well-being. She stood for a while taking in deep revitalizing breaths, before exhaling slowly and watching with curious delight as her breath curled and danced in the still, crisp air.

As she began walking down the path which would take her across the meadow, round by the spinney and on to the banks of the canal, Emma was cheerily greeted by old Benjamin – the same ancient and bewhiskered old fellow who had been delivering the milk in his churns every morning since she and her papa had first come to this house. Seeing him reminded Emma of what Gregory had told her – that it was about this hour of the morning when the barges began their way along the canal towards Liverpool Docks, where they would be bright and early for their first cotton cargo of the day. It always amused Emma to see how much old Benjamin resembled his faithful horse, who was also ancient and bewhiskered. As it passed her by, the flat waggon rumbled and swayed, making its own kind of music. 'Good morning, Benjamin,' she replied with a bright smile, thinking it wouldn't be long before the other tradesmen were coming up the path, when the day would snowball into the busy pattern of life that went on, come what may.

There was always plenty of comings and goings to and from Breckleton House. And the day always started when most folks were still in bed. It crossed Emma's mind to compare how different life here must be from that of the residents along Montague Street in Blackburn town. Well, she reminded herself, she would know soon enough. And in just a short time she would also be brought face to face with the one they called 'the old tyrant'.

Reaching the canal bank, Emma recalled the last time she had found her way here and her heart ached. Such an innocent little adventure, she thought with both regret and pleasure, yet one which had inflamed Caleb Crowther enough to launch a spiteful and wicked attack on Marlow Tanner. Sitting for a while on the stump of a felled tree, Emma's attention was caught by the unmistakable snorting of a horse and that soft swishing of water which only a barge on the move could make. Gregory was right, she thought, the canal is already coming alive. Of a sudden, the big piebald cob was in sight, his neck straining hard as he towed the barge around the curve towards the spinney. Emma recognized the horse at once as belonging to the Tanner barge. Her every instinct told her to hurry away from that place as fast as she could; but her heart persuaded her to stay and watch as horse and barge went slowly by. Being some way back from the canal, and being partly hidden by the shrubbery, Emma thought she would not be easily seen.

Whether it was the bite of the morning air so near the water or whether it was the nearness of Marlow, Emma didn't know, but she found herself trembling more the closer the barge came. So much so that suddenly she was afraid. She must go! She must not stay here to torment herself so! Emma could not control the emotions which raged through her; emotions which brought with them their own kind of pain. Already she was on her feet, but even as she began to turn away, she saw Marlow standing tall and straight at the tiller, his dark, magnificent eyes stretching ahead to scour the water. What great delight the sight of him brought to Emma. Joy and a searing tide of love surged through her. Yet, she knew she must hurry away, for this love was not to be, and it could bring nothing but heartache for both of them. But she lingered too long . . .

'Emma!' He had seen her, and like the wind his anguished cry sailed the water towards her. But Emma did not look back. Instead, she ran faster and more blindly, until in her haste she was slipping and tumbling over the bracken beneath her feet – her heart racing with both fear and excitement, and the overhanging branches catching her face and hair as she fought her way through the spinney.

In her determination to flee, Emma did not see the deep rabbit-hole ahead. When she ran headlong into it the heel of her boot caught fast, throwing her to the ground and knocking the breath out of her. She had heard Marlow pursuing her, and now, when he came upon her, Emma was frantic. 'Go away!' she told him. 'Please, leave me be.' For a moment he stood quite still as she began struggling to her feet. But then, with a cry of 'You can't send me away from you, Emma', he came forward to catch her in his arms. As he rained kisses on her face and mouth, all of Emma's resolves melted away. She clung to him, kissing him back, and wanting him so much that it hurt.

'You love me! Tell me you love me, Emma!' he demanded, half laughing, half afraid as he pulled her to him and covered her mouth with such fierce demanding kisses that left her weak and vulnerable in his arms. Her response was every bit as passionate and eager as his own, until, somewhere in the distance, the sound of Sal Tanner's voice could be heard shouting, 'Marlow! Yer a bloody fool! That lass means nothin' but grief an' all kind o' trouble. I'm warnin' yer. If yer don't come back this very minute, I'm leavin' . . . I'm washin' me 'ands o' yer. D'yer 'ear me, Marlow Tanner?'

Marlow paid no heed, except to hold Emma even tighter and kiss her harder. But for Emma, Sal Tanner's warning was enough.

'Go back!' she told Marlow, snatching herself away, 'Your sister's right. I *will* bring you only grief.'

'Emma, do you love me? That's all I need to know,' he asked in a soft voice, holding her by the shoulders, his fiery dark eyes gazing pleadingly into hers. 'Just say you love me, and nothing else in the world matters.'

Emma gave her answer, though it stuck in her throat. 'No, I *don't* love you. I'm to be married in two weeks time, you must know that.'

'Aye, I *do*! You're to be wed to Gregory Denton, or so they say. But you can't love the fellow . . . not when you love *me* Emma, and you do love me, I know it. Don't try to hide that from me, Emma. Don't deny what we feel for each other.'

'You're wrong, Marlow. I do love Gregory, very much,' Emma lied. 'Caleb Crowther warned you away, didn't he?'

'He did.'

'Then do as he says. You must stay away, or you'll ruin us both.'

'Do you really want me to stay away?' Marlow asked now, his grip on her relaxing and his eyes filled with pain and disbelief. When, in a firm, quiet voice, Emma assured him that yes, that was what she wanted and he must forget her, he took away his hands, saying, in soft anger, 'There will *never* come the day when I forget you, Emma Grady. Nor when I stop loving you! But I'll not go against your word, don't fear!' Then he turned from her and disappeared into the spinney.

'That day will never come for me either, Marlow,' whispered Emma, as she watched him go, the tears running freely down her face, 'but it's for the best, believe me. Please believe me.' She cared not for what might happen to her, but Emma knew in her heart that should she go against Caleb Crowther's wishes, he would move heaven and earth to have Marlow transported to Australia as a convict. She sensed it, and was terrified by it.

* * *

'Fools, the lot of them!' Caleb Crowther folded the newspaper into a tight rod before flinging it down on the table in disgust. 'They haven't got the slightest idea. Not the *slightest* idea!' He snatched up his napkin and viciously wiped each corner of his mouth. Of a sudden, he grabbed the newspaper again, opened it out and spread it before him. Then, peering down at it, he told his wife, 'I shall make it my business to have words with the editor about this.' He prodded his finger over and over again at the offending article, and Agnes Crowther became so curious that she leaned over the breakfast table in order to see more clearly. What she saw was a large cartoon, over which was a bold black caption which read, 'WHO ARE THE SLAVES?'

The cartoon showed a prosperous and surly-faced fellow standing on a barrel in the centre of the picture, his arms flung wide open – his left hand pointing to a family of dark slaves in the American South, and his right one pointing to a Lancashire cotton mill family. The former appeared to be well fed and clothed, with the child in its mother's arms positively chubby ; while the Lancashire family were shabbily dressed and painfully undernourished. The man in the middle was drawing a comparison and concluding that of the two, it was the Lancashire cotton mill worker's family who seemed more subdued by slavery than did their dark-skinned counterparts.

'I pay my workers good money, and if they've got no more self-control than to breed like rabbits, then they deserve to starve!'

Seeing the look of utter disgust on his face, Emma wondered whether there was even one ounce of compassion in Caleb Crowther's bitter heart. It was no wonder that of all the men previously employed by Thadius Grady, not one of them either liked or respected her uncle. That much she had learned during her time working alongside Gregory Denton, and it had come as no surprise to Emma. Indeed, she would have been surprised had it been otherwise.

'Emma, go along and get yourself ready. Mr Denton is due to collect you within the hour, is he not?'

'Yes, Aunt.' Emma excused herself from the breakfast table and was almost out of the room when Agnes Crowther instructed her, 'As Mrs Manfred is to accompany you, I would like a word with her first. Of course, I myself would be taking you,' here she made a small grimace and moved about in the chair, 'but I really haven't been feeling too well. Still, it is only a courtesy meeting between yourself and Mr Denton's mother. A necessary and dutiful one, however ... since you will be moving in with her, in her own home. Yes indeed. Send Mrs Manfred to me straight away. I'll be in the drawing-room.' She turned her head to where Caleb Crowther was still brooding, his eyes scouring the page before him. 'That is all right, isn't it dear?' she asked.

'Yes! Yes!' He did not look up, but he waved his hand with some impatience. 'Do as you think best. I intend to leave all this woman's business to you. As for myself, I must attend the courts at Manchester.' With that he pushed the newspaper aside and straightened his neck to peer at Emma, who was still waiting at the door. 'Be off with you, girl!' he told her. 'You have your instructions from your aunt. Inform the Manfred woman that she's wanted in the drawing-room.'

As he rose from his chair Emma nodded and, grateful to depart from their company, she excused herself again, and closed the door behind her. As she approached the stairs,

Amy came rushing along, her cap askew and a look of apprehension on her face. In one hand she carried a dustpan and brush, in the other a large wooden tray.

'Oh, Miss Grady!' she cried. 'I shall get the full length of the mistress's tongue an' no mistake. I 'ad a bad night . . . a real bad un! An' I can't seem to catch up with me work no how!'

'Are you on your way to clear the breakfast table?' Emma asked, noticing how dishevelled Amy appeared and seeing that she was in such a state of agitation that she would probably end up by breaking every cup and plate on the table. When the frightened maid nodded in response, Emma continued in a kindly voice, at the same time putting a hand on the girl's shoulder to turn her back in the direction from which she had just come, 'Mrs Crowther is on her way to the drawing-room, and Mr Crowther is about to depart for the Manchester Assizes, so there's no need for you to panic. How about if you go and straighten your cap and calm yourself down? Mrs Crowther would not be too pleased to see you like this, now would she?'

'Ooh, you're right, Miss Grady,' the girl agreed, as she hurried away in the direction of the kitchen, 'an' she's been in such a sour mood lately. Oh, but Mrs Manfred will give me what for an' all, when she claps eyes on me!' said the little maid, shaking her head from side to side and growing more agitated by the minute. When Emma assured her that she herself was on her way to see Mrs Manfred to tell her to go immediately to the mistress in the drawing-room, the girl gave a great noisy sigh of relief. 'I'll be away an' tidy meself up, Miss Grady,' she said. 'Mek meself more presentable afore I come to do the breakfast things . . . oh, but I did 'ave a bad night, I'm telling yer . . . a *tirrible* night!'

181

Then she scurried away, all the while muttering to herself, 'Be quick, Amy, be quick!'

Emma watched until the figure had gone from her sight. Amy's not much younger than me, she thought, and already she's learned to be afraid. Why! She's dictated to by more people than I am! The thought was a sobering one – as was the belief that the little maid was a true survivor and would come to no real harm. Emma hoped the very same could be applied to herself, because, in spite of her determined spirit, she could not rid herself of the feeling that there may well be rough times ahead.

Just over an hour later, Emma and Mrs Manfred emerged from the house. The older woman was dressed in a navy straw boater, dark dress and fitted calf-length coat which left the full hem of her skirt peeking out, while Emma looked lovely in a royal-blue full length coat over a paler blue dress. Her hair was brushed up and covered by a small plain bonnet of the same deep blue as her coat. She carried a black drawstring purse and wore black, small-heeled shoes with a cross-over bar at the ankle.

'How pretty you look, Miss Grady,' Mrs Manfred declared on first seeing her.

'By! Mrs Denton won't be able to resist you, Emma!' Gregory Denton remarked as he ushered both ladies into the carriage. Hiring this conveyance had set him right back on his savings, but he didn't begrudge it, for he intended to do everything in style to impress Emma, knowing, however, that his mother would never approve of such extravagance.

When the little party was safely aboard and comfortable, he gave the driver instructions to 'make for Montague

Street, if you please.' Then he settled back in his seat opposite the two women. He gave Mrs Manfred a small nervous smile, and he looked at Emma, his face blushing a dark shade of pink at her very closeness, with the fawning eyes of a man either in great pain or extreme love – or both!

The carriage went from Breckleton to Blackburn by way of Preston New Road. The journey was not too long, only some four miles in all and, the main road being pleasantly free of traffic, it hardly seemed even that distance. Emma found herself under close and embarrassing scrutiny all the way. She could feel Gregory's eyes on her, and she knew that his adoring gaze had not left her face for an instant. Now and then, to reassure both Gregory and herself, she looked up to warmly smile at him. But this only seemed to make matters worse as, bit by bit, he edged forward in his seat, until, by the time they turned into the steep and cobbled Montague Street, he was clinging so precariously to the very edge of his seat that when the carriage swung in from Preston New Road, he slithered to the floor. For a long, excruciatingly embarrassing moment Gregory Denton seemed perfectly surprised to find himself on his knees before Mrs Manfred, with his right hand actually clutching the top of her leg.

When, completely taken aback, Mrs Manfred declared, 'Mr Denton! Do get up!' Emma was struck by the absurdity of it all and, in spite of her every effort not to, she collapsed into a fit of helpless laughter.

'Oh, Mrs Manfred, I do apologize!' Gregory Denton was mortified. But, for Emma, the whole incident was delightful. Somehow in laughing at poor Gregory, and in seeing the shocked, indignant expression on Mrs Manfred's face, she felt less nervous of the encounter she herself was about to endure. Surely the woman who gave birth to such a gentle and apologetic creature as Gregory couldn't possibly be the awful creature that people claimed she was. This thought gave Emma a great deal of comfort.

The carriage was brought to a halt and the passengers disembarked. Emma and Mrs Manfred waited while Gregory paid the driver and asked him to return to collect the ladies upon the hour.

Oh, Lord! thought Emma, as she stood before the gate, her gaze taking in how regimental and neat the small front garden was and how sparklingly bright the lace curtains were. There was no going back now!

In a moment, Gregory had inserted his key into the front door lock. Pushing the door open to reveal a long narrow corridor with an open stairway at the end and two doors along the right wall, he shepherded Emma and Mrs Manfred inside. He then closed the door, plunging them all into semi-darkness, since the only incoming light was through the half-circle of stained glass above the door.

Still Emma was determined not to feel too apprehensive and was succeeding in keeping herself calm until, with the best intentions in the world, Gregory said in a low, trembling voice into her ear, 'Emma, don't be nervous. And, please . . . do be careful not to upset her, because she can be *very* touchy.' Whereupon Emma's brave resolve instantly crumbled, leaving her so apprehensive that she was annoyed to discover herself actually trembling.

'It's cold in here, isn't it?' she asked, looking from one to the other for reassurance.

'You're right, dear,' Mrs Manfred quickly agreed, 'it is a bit chilly to the bones.'

'Yes, well . . . Mother can't abide it being too warm,'

explained Gregory, propelling them towards the first door on the right, 'she says it meks a body soft to be too warm,' he finished lamely. Now, turning the brass door knob, he inched open the door saying, 'If you'll just mek yourself comfortable in here, I'll bring a pot of tea. Then, I'd best go upstairs and see whether she's ready to receive visitors.'

'Upstairs?' asked Emma with some surprise.

'Is your mother ill?' rejoined Mrs Manfred, feeling decidedly uncomfortable and wondering how in God's name would Emma fare in this house.

'Oh no! No, indeed, she's not *ill*,' replied Gregory, with a forced laugh, 'just a little off colour, I dare say. There are days when she doesn't set foot downstairs, you see, but, she's not ill, or bed ridden. Oh no!' He seemed most anxious that Emma especially should believe that. 'It's just, well . . . the old ones do have their funny little whims and fancies, don't they!'

Mrs Manfred merely nodded, thinking to herself how one of Mrs Denton's 'whims and fancies' was no doubt the pleasure she got from being waited on hand and foot by a doting son!

'It's all right, Gregory,' Emma felt the need to reassure him, for she could see how desperate he was that all should go well on this first meeting between his mother and his prospective wife. 'Mrs Manfred and I would love a cup of tea. Then you go and talk to your mother, like you said.' She cast an appealing glance in Mrs Manfred's direction, 'That's all right isn't it, Manny? We'll be content supping our tea until Mrs Denton's ready to receive us.' When back came the grudging reply 'Yes, of course,' Gregory was visibly relieved, and a moment later had gone to put on the kettle. Emma would have much preferred to busy herself in making the tea, but she thought the offer might offend Gregory.

It was fifteen minutes later when Emma and Mrs Manfred were ushered up the enclosed and darkened stairs. On reaching the landing, Emma was reminded by the anxious Gregory, 'Remember, Emma, you mustn't be nervous. Her bark really is worse than her bite, you know.' The look on his face, and the pleading tone of his voice was enough to make Emma want to turn round and flee. But, bracing herself, she stiffened her back, brushed down her dress, patted her bonnet and, in a deliberate voice told him, 'I'm quite ready, Gregory, and not a bit nervous.' Oh, if only that were true, she thought, making sure that Mrs Manfred was not far behind as they all trooped alongside the polished carved ballustrade towards the main front room.

If Emma had been expecting to be confronted by some sort of ogre when she entered that bedroom, then she was *not* disappointed! The very first thing that struck her was the size of the room which was surprisingly large and, judging by its dimensions, must span the entire width of the house. Situated at the front and facing east, it was well positioned to enjoy the best of the early morning sunshine. To Emma, the room was in stark contrast to what she had already seen of the rest of the house, which was unpleasantly cramped and gloomy. But, even though the sun brightened it up, the huge and oppressive articles of furniture cast their own dark shadows, sadly negating the effect of the light coming through the wide bay windows.

To Emma's right, and taking up a greater part of the green distempered wall, was a long cumbersome chest of drawers, made in dark wood and some three feet deep from front to back. It contained six drawers, each with two enormous wooden knobs at either end. On top of the dresser was a solitary wooden-framed photograph of a man, woman and young boy standing between them. The humble-featured man had a long drooping moustache and his fair colouring was echoed in the face of the boy. The woman had a sour, impatient expression on her face and, by the way in which she thrust herself in front of the other two, she totally dominated the picture. Emma could see that the small boy was Gregory, and she assumed that the man and woman were his parents. He was later to confirm this and to tell Emma how the whole experience of having that picture taken had been not only a long, laborious and frightening procedure, but that it had cost his father no less than three days' takings in his butcher's shop. He remembered quite clearly though, how his parents had argued the issue, but, as always, his father had given in to his mother's insistence, and, ever since, the picture had pride of place on that dresser.

Along the wall to the left was a tall, broad wardrobe in the same dark wood and design as the dresser, and beside it stood an iron-legged washstand, the lower shelf of which was packed from end to end with all manner of toiletries. The centre of the floor was covered by a large, patterned rag-peg carpet, with the highly polished floorboards visible around the edges. To one side of the window was a small rush-seated stand-chair which held a bulbous circular snuff-tin and a brass candle-holder containing a half-used candle. Directly beneath the window was the largest bed Emma had ever seen. Made of brass, it was most decorative. It had two corner-posts at either end; halfway down each of these was a large petalled flower in fine beaten brass, each one touching another to form a garland right across. On the top of each post was a tall, ceramic, floral acorn, each one polished to a brilliant shine. The bedcover was of the same rag-peg design as the carpet which Emma now stood on, and, sitting bolt upright beneath it, with her back stiff, yet slightly stooped, was Doreen Denton – the formidable sight of whom turned Emma's stomach over in a series of somersaults. Physically, she was small and, with her pretty lace-coloured nightgown, tiny frilled white cap and large green-speckled eyes, at a distance she might have appeared to be no more than a child.

In truth, her presence was overpowering. Emma could feel her influence from every corner of the room. Then, when those large, all-seeing eyes came to rest their probing gaze on her, Emma wished herself a thousand miles away.

'Here!' The voice was thin yet charged with such authority that one dared not disobey. 'Don't stand dithering there! Come *here*.'

When the voice pierced the air, it also seemed to pierce something in Gregory Denton, for he was now fidgeting uncomfortably and nervously winding his hands together. 'Emma . . . she just wants to see you more closely,' he said softly, beginning to step forward, 'it's all right.'

'You were not asked to speak, Gregory!' came the sharp retort from the bed. 'Nor were you asked to stay. Kindly leave! And you can take that other woman with you.'

'But this is Mrs Manfred, Mother . . . the lady sent by Emma's aunt, to speak on her behalf,' he spluttered.

'Take her with you, I said. If she's here to speak on Miss Grady's behalf, then there's no need, is there, for the young lady herself is here? She can speak on her own behalf. And, if this . . . Mrs Manfred is here to speak on behalf of Miss Grady's *aunt*, then I don't want to hear. If Mrs Crowther has something to say, or to ask, then she must come here and speak on her *own* behalf!' With this, she swung her eyes round to Mrs Manfred, asking, 'Unless of course the woman's struck down badly! Is that the case?' When Mrs Manfred gave the somewhat impatient and indignant answer that, yes, Mrs Crowther had been poorly on getting from her bed that very morning, there was a painfully long silence before, with a sharp clap of her hands, the older woman told her, 'I can't say as I altogether believe such a convenient excuse, but, very well . . . Take yourself downstairs with Gregory, and I'll let you know whether to come back up.' Before Mrs Manfred could voice the protest which was already registering on her face, Gregory Denton had moved forward to assure her quietly, 'It's best we do as she says. Emma's all right, Mrs Manfred. Please . . . let them get to know each other.'

When the door had closed behind them, Emma thought she hadn't felt so alone since her papa had been taken from her – except, of course, when she had forced herself to tell Marlow that they had no future together.

'Now then,' the voice piped up, 'fetch yourself closer.'

Emma was moved by the urge to take off her bonnet, and quickly doing so, she came forward to stand beside the bed. She was aware of her fingers nervously twisting the bonnet in her hands, and she could see the old lady watching with irritation; but, for the life of her, she couldn't keep still! Then, in a sharp angry voice, came the instruction to 'Put that blessed thing down!' But when Emma felt the bonnet being wrenched from her hand and flung on to the bed, her fighting spirit came to the fore. Bad-tempered old thing! she thought. I won't let you get the better of me, because I intend to start as I mean to go on. Reaching forward, she retrieved the bonnet, held it perfectly still in her hands, and, looking directly into that sour, wizened face, she said in a firm voice, 'I'm pleased to meet you, Mrs Denton.'

After curiously regarding Emma for a long time, the older woman's expression grew darker. 'I can't say I'm pleased to meet *you!*' She began looking Emma up and down, noting the blue outfit, of a kind not worn or afforded by the likes of folk round these quarters. She saw how Emma's rich auburn hair shone in the sunlight, and searching those strong and defiant eyes she saw how beautiful Emma was. Now she was even more suspicious than she had been when Gregory had first told her the news. Gregory, *her* Gregory, her unattractive son, whom she loathed to share with another woman. *Any* woman! Yet, there was something strange here. Something not quite right that she hadn't fathomed out. Now, she bluntly asked the questions which had presented themselves to her.

'What do *you* want with my lad? You, a young woman from a far better background, whose uncle is a man of the Law, and who should know better than to think you could fit in with the likes of us? What do you want with my Gregory, eh? Is there some'at *wrong* with you, that you're not telling?' Of a sudden, she was bolt upright in the bed, her eyes enormous and her hands thrown up in alarm. 'That's it!' she said with astonishment. 'You're with child! I'm right, aren't I, eh? You're with another man's child and the Justice thinks to rid himself of you . . . palm you on to my Gregory!' Her voice had risen with every word, until she was shrieking at the top of her voice. Before Emma could assure her that such suspicions were totally unfounded, the door had burst open to admit both Gregory and Mrs Manfred.

'What's all the shouting?' Gregory demanded, 'We could hear you downstairs!' One look at the woman in the bed told him she was indulging in one of her tantrums, and coming to put a protective arm about Emma's shoulders, he led her away towards the door and Mrs Manfred. When, in a high-pitched and hysterical voice, his mother told him, 'You're being *used*, you bloody fool! The girl's with child! Ask her! Go on! Let her deny it if she can!' He was stopped in his tracks. Bringing his gaze to Emma, he saw her smile and shake her head. It was enough.

'Emma is a good and lovely creature,' he told the agitated woman, 'I love her, and I'm deeply grateful that she's agreed to be my wife.'

'You're being *used*, I tell you!' insisted Doreen Denton, struggling to get from the bed. 'You'll not fetch her into *this* house, I say!'

Emma felt Gregory's hands fall from her shoulders. She watched as he slowly turned, went to the bed, and looking directly into his mother's eyes told her in a tone of voice which neither Doreen Denton nor Emma had heard him use before, 'Emma and I are to be wed in a fortnight's time, and I shall be bringing her here to live with me. But, only for as long as it takes for us to buy our own home. That's now my intention, and that's the way of things . . . whether you approve, or whether you don't.' When he had finished speaking, the silence in the room was painful to Emma. She might have stepped forward to diffuse the situation, but was stopped when Mrs Manfred's hand gripped her arm. Seeing the fire in Gregory's face, and having heard how lovingly and fiercely he had defended her, something warm stirred within her.

But Emma had also seen the venom in old Mrs Denton's

eyes as the old woman had stared across the room at her. There had been such loathing in her voice hitherto, that when she now spoke in a completely different tone, Emma was totally shocked.

'It seems I've been too harsh on you, Miss Grady . . . Emma. If my son loves you enough to fight for you in such a way that I never would have believed, then you must be everything he says you are.' Now, she switched her attention to Mrs Manfred, who also was puzzled and surprised by this sudden change of attitude. 'Mrs . . . Manfred, isn't it?' When there came a nod of confirmation, she went on, 'Thank you for having the courtesy to come along. You can go back to Mrs Crowther and tell her that I am in full approval of the marriage between Miss Grady and my son. She will be made welcome in his house.'

'Oh, thank you, Mother!' Gregory bent to kiss the wizened cheek. 'Emma *is* everything I say. You'll see. You'll come to love her as I do.' He was greatly relieved to see the old woman's change of heart, and he believed above all else that his mother *would* come to bless the day when Emma came to live under this roof as his own darling wife. God had been good to him, and he would strive to be as loving and dutiful a husband, as he had always been a son.

Emma also was glad of Mrs Denton's change of heart. It had been so sudden and unexpected that it had at first worried her. But then she reasoned that the old woman must be prone to such swift changes of mood, for Gregory seemed to have accepted it and of course, he knew his mother better than *she* did. No doubt, in time she would get used to old Mrs Denton's ways – though, in all truth, she had not taken to her, and would never go out of her way to keep close company with the old woman.

As they climbed aboard the carriage for the journey back to Breckleton House, Emma began to think she was fortunate in finding such a champion as Gregory, who was kind and thoughtful in every way. And though there were many things she would change if given the chance, Emma was gradually coming to accept the deep and generous affection Gregory Denton had for her. She would make him as good a wife as she knew how – working at it that much harder because she knew she could never love him in the way she loved Marlow Tanner. Emma consoled herself with the belief that, because of her marriage to Gregory, Marlow would be safe. I *am* doing the right thing, she thought. But the deeper she thought, the more curious she became about the old feud between her papa and the river-people. There was something sinister about it, Emma knew – something ominous that rose like a phantom between her and Marlow. In marrying Gregory and removing Marlow from Caleb Crowther's antagonism, Emma trusted that this phantom would no longer haunt either her or Marlow. The thought gave her a small feeling of contentment.

Too trusting! Mrs Manfred thought, as she gave Emma a quiet sideways glance on their way back to Breckleton House. You're too trusting, Emma, my girl! But, you'll be all right, child . . . because I'll never be far away.

Upstairs in the house on Montague Street, old Mrs Denton watched from the window as Gregory said goodbye to his darling Emma and her companion. She ached with bitterness when she saw the look on his face, so filled with love. She recalled the way he had stood up to her, defending that Grady creature with the ferocity of a tigress defending its cubs. She recollected his words which were etched on her heart: 'I shall be bringing her here to live . . . But, only for as long as it takes for us to buy our own home!' But she had cleverly put paid to *that* idea by her devious little display. It had been a damned hard thing to do, but she was determined. Nobody would ever take her son away from under this roof. There wasn't a soul alive who she would ever allow to part her from her darling Gregory – not even Emma Grady!

As Gregory waved the carriage out of sight, Doreen Denton murmured venomously through clenched teeth, 'So, Gregory, you think I'll come to love her, do you? *Never!* Not while there's a breath left in this old body of mine! Oh, but I'll do what needs to be done, to keep *you* here, where you belong.' She hurriedly climbed back into bed, contriving to look suitably exhausted for when her devoted son mounted the stairs to fetch her some refreshment.

There was something else niggling her also. She'd seen this Emma Grady before, she was sure of it. But where? Where? It would come to her – one of these days it would come to her.

Chapter Seven

'Lord love an' save us, Marlow Tanner, will yer never go to bed?' Sal Tanner squeezed her way through the narrow doorway which led from her sleeping cabin into the living area. She had been suffering a restless night herself, but for very different reasons than those of her brother. Firstly, the sound of his footsteps pacing up and down with increasing agitation, had prevented her from falling easily into a slumber; then, when she had eventually managed to close her eyes, the wind had picked up into a mad frenzy – shifting and thrashing the barge about until she gave up all attempts at getting a good night's sleep. 'It's like the bloody divil's 'aving a party underneath us!' she complained with a shake of her tousled head.

'Aw, Sal . . . I'm sorry if I've upset your night's sleep,' Marlow apologized, coming to put his arms about her and leading her to the narrow seat which was fixed round the corner beside the small black stove. 'Sit yourself down here, and I'll fetch you a hot drink.' He was wonderfully patient as she laboriously made her way on slow faltering footsteps, for, since her accident, neither her leg nor her nerves had fully recovered. Still, she was in finer form than the week before, and Marlow knew she'd be in even better form as the weeks went by. Smiling to himself at her merry abuse of him now, Marlow eased her on to the seat. Then, going to the small bench beneath the porthole, he lifted the hinged lid and withdrew from it a thick grey blanket, which he wrapped tightly around his sister's ample form. Next he stoked up the stove with the small coke pieces from the nearby scuttle, and, seeing that the fire was going well, he went into the galley to fetch a small pan of water. By the time he had gone back into the galley and returned with two sizeable mugs, into which he'd spilled a good helping of tea, sugar and milk, the water was boiling. In another moment he was seated beside his sister, each of them warming their hands around the hot, comforting mugs, with their faithful dog, Jake, stretched out at their feet, indignant at having been disturbed from his night's sleep.

Pretending to sip the scalding-hot liquid, Sal gave her brother a crafty but concerned sideways look. God above, she thought, how tortured he looks. In all the time since their parents had been tragically taken from them, Sal could not remember ever seeing Marlow so badly troubled. And, oh she loved him so much that to see it now tore her apart. So deeply affected by his heartache was she, that Sal had to swallow several times in order to melt that great hard lump which was stuck hard in her throat, preventing the words she wanted to say from coming out. Even when she did manage to speak, the tears which were threatening to fall, trembled in her voice, 'Aw lad, will yer stop punishing yerself?' she asked, 'Can yer not see what it's doing to yer?'

At once, suddenly aware that Sal had been closely watching him, and anxious not to be questioned on matters too painful to discuss, Marlow's expression changed. When he turned his eyes to her, they were smiling, and the answer he gave was not the one he truly felt in his heart. 'The only thing wrong with me is a sister who will insist on reading the darkest things into the smallest upset!' he told her in a chastising voice.

'Oh, I see.' Sal Tanner knew that she'd subtly been told to mind her own business, however gently it had been put. 'Keep me long nose out? That's what yer telling me, ain't it, yer bugger?' she laughed, although the laugh lacked merriment. 'All right fella-me-lad, I'll not mek matters worse by harping on at yer,' she conceded, unable to stop herself from adding, 'Aw but lad, it'll do yer no good to keep baying fer the moon, yer do know that, don't yer?' She waited for an answer, her troubled eyes never leaving his face.

'Don't worry, Sal.' Marlow put down his mug on the small round hearth, and giving a deep inner sigh, patted the back of his sister's hand, saying with a brighter smile, 'I may be *wanting* the moon . . . but I'd be a bloody fool to think I could ever *have* it! I know that, sweetheart. And it's only a matter of coming to terms with it.' With this, he put his arm around her and drew her near to him. They stayed like this for a while, Marlow concerned that he was causing his sister to fret about him, and Sal, although comforted by his embrace, was still disturbed because she had never seen her brother in such a quiet, distant mood. Yet, she knew Marlow to be an honourable and sensible man and it was these very qualities which she counted on now. For, however much he loved Emma Grady and longed for her to be his, Sal Tanner knew that Marlow would never pursue her once she had made her marriage vows to another man. And that day couldn't come quickly enough for Sal Tanner, because there was never more heartache caused than when two men craved the same woman, and she wanted only one.

In her heart, Sal gave thanks that Emma Grady had made her choice and promised herself to the Denton fellow; for Marlow was fooling himself in hoping that the likes of her would ever give her favours to a bargee. Indeed, Gregory Denton was not as high up as the Crowthers, but neither was he as low down as the mill-hands and bargees who worked beneath him. He evidently had both the seal of approval of Caleb Crowther and the devotion of Emma Grady. The thing was settled, and, as far as Sal Tanner was concerned, it had been settled the right way – though she would never be so callous as to declare such a thing out loud in Marlow's presence. But, in time he would come to see this for himself, she hoped. Until then, she must guard her tongue.

Of a sudden, Marlow stood up, saying in a cheerful voice, 'It's Saturday tomorrow. I've to ferry a cargo of fowl from Liverpool to Lancaster, so, what say if I take you round the market afterwards . . . I need a new stout pair of boots, and you can choose that curtain material you've been going on about these past weeks.' It was a deliberate ploy to change the subject, and also to compensate for his sister having been laid up in this cramped barge for such a long time, with little else to occupy her mind but *his* business.

'That'll be right grand!' Sal Tanner was at once enthused by the idea. 'Over four years them curtains 'ave been at them there winders . . . an' if I wash the buggers just once more, they'll end up in tatters!' Now, she was on her feet, tugging at the worn floral curtains and addressing Jake, who peered up with only half-awake, droopy eyes. 'Blue 'uns, I think,' she said, 'bright blue 'uns, wi'out flowers on.' She made her way back to the cabin, muttering to herself, and, just before disappearing through the narrow doorway, she turned to tell the bemused Marlow, 'Nothin' wi' *green* on! We don't want to upset the little folk. Well . . . unless there's some right grand material there, an' nothin' else ter choose from, eh? But if it's got any green in it at all . . . we must ask permission from the little people first. Oh, yes!' Even after she was out of sight, Marlow could hear his sister's voice, low and reverent, and he knew she was talking to the 'little people' – asking them whether she might be allowed to choose a material which had a *little* green in it.

Later, as he stood at the window in his own berth, from where he gazed out across the water, Marlow found himself smiling at Sal's fervent belief that the colour green was most precious to the 'little people', and that anyone using it, wearing it or keeping it without their permission, would be horribly punished. It was a peculiar belief of Sal's which went as far back as Marlow could remember. But Sal had always been that bit different from anybody else he'd ever known; eccentric some folks called her. Whatever her little quirks and fancies though, she had a heart of gold and she was all the family he had, and if anybody was ever to cause her harm, he'd tear them limb from limb!

Marlow was a man of deep loyalties and great passion. And now, as he watched the wind churning up the waters outside, he felt his own heart churning over and over with his memories of Emma. Sal was right, he thought, he might just as well be crying for the moon. He had heard from her own lips her declaration of love for Gregory Denton. Yet, Marlow would have laid down his life in the belief that it was he whom she really loved. Had he really been fooling himself when he'd seen that same look in her eyes that was in his own? When his mouth had covered hers and she had trembled in his arms, was he so wrong in feeling their hearts beat as one? Could a man be so misled and blinded by his own love that he should imagine such a thing? Dear God! How could he tell? What else could he be guided by if his own instincts proved him wrong? The more Marlow tortured himself for an answer, the more he realized that only Emma herself could confirm or deny what he felt in his heart; only she could raise or dash his hopes. But Emma had told him that she loved the man who would soon be her husband; she had begged him to leave her be; and Marlow knew that, however much it grieved him, he had to respect her wish. Nothing good ever came of a man forcing himself on a woman – particularly a woman so soon to be wed. Oh, but it was a hard thing to do! And even harder for Marlow was the thought of remaining in these parts once Emma had become Mrs Gregory Denton.

Of a sudden, Marlow thought he and Sal might sell off the barge and go to America – the land of opportunity they called it. But then he considered how Sal would react to such a proposition, and his hopes were dashed. Sal did not possess such a spirit of adventure as he. She was a home-loving soul who wanted no more than a fire with which to warm her outside, and a bottle of booze to warm her inside. They were both born and bred river-folk, but, whereas he would now be tempted to sail the seven seas, Sal would never leave the shores of old England, not for all the treasure in the world. Marlow knew this, and though it might curtail the boundaries of his own existence, he loved her nonetheless. He was bound by his love for the sister who had selflessly raised him. He was also bound, and even more deeply, by his hopeless love for Emma. He could no more suppress the love he felt for her than he could graciously accept her rejection of him – however much he might wish otherwise.

'I wish you were coming with me, Manny.' Emma lifted the hem of her wedding gown and, seeing that Mrs Manfred had gathered together her sewing paraphernalia, stepped down from the stool, at once beginning to feverishly strip the ivory silk gown from her body as though its very touch was unbearable to her skin.

'Stuff and nonsense, Miss Grady!' declared Mrs Manfred, easing her aching back into the chair and frowning as Emma carelessly flung the expensive wedding gown over the bed. 'Don't be so rough with that dress!' she chided, at the same time dropping her sewing basket to the floor and adding in a weary tone, 'Twice they've had the blessed thing back, and *still* they can't get it to sit right on you, child! I did tell Mrs Crowther that it would save time and money to let *me* make the alterations in the first place.' She blew out her cheeks in exasperation, 'And here we are . . . the very evening afore your wedding, and it's all rush and push!' She scraped the straying locks from her face and seemed to visibly sag.

'That gown will *never* feel right,' Emma interrupted. Then, having put on her nightgown, she came to sit cross-legged at the older woman's feet. 'It isn't the dress, Manny . . . it's *me*!' she said in a quiet, forlorn voice.

'Come here, child,' said Mrs Manfred, holding out her arms as Emma gratefully leaned into them. 'Tell me what's playing so heavy on your mind. This past week you've seemed to be miles away.'

'I sometimes wish I *was* miles away,' replied Emma, feeling cheered by Mrs Manfred's comforting presence, but

201

growing more and more dismayed by the fact that from tomorrow, when she left this house as Gregory Denton's wife, these long intimate talks with this darling woman could never again be taken for granted. 'Oh, Manny!' she said now, her eyes sorrowful as they looked up to that kindly face, 'I shall miss you so very much.'

'Away with you, Miss Grady!' came the retort, 'You'll be that busy as Mrs Denton . . . what with being a wife and running a house, together with making new friends and afore long, looking forward to being with child.' Here, she smiled warmly and gave Emma an extra tight hug. 'Well . . . there'll be little time left for missing anybody, I can tell you!' She became nostalgic as she thought of times long gone, of a husband she had lost, of the children she never had, and her eyes grew misty. 'Be happy, child,' she said softly, stroking the girl's hair, 'you must try to be happy.'

Emma wondered about Mrs Manfred's past, for it was something the dear lady had always been reluctant to discuss. Yet, seeing how deeply affected she seemed, Emma felt obliged to ask, 'Were *you* happy, Manny . . . with your husband? Were you very much in love on the day of your wedding?'

'Bless you, of course not!' came the surprised reply. 'It was a rare thing for a lass to be in love with the man she married. Often, she had little say in who it was to be . . . very much the same as you. Circumstances prevailed and convenience was more important than whether or not the two loved each other. Oh, but, I can tell you Miss Grady that you do grow to love a man over the years.' With this she paused and gazed into Emma's uplifted eyes with deliberation. When she spoke again, her voice was soft but serious. 'Tomorrow you'll stand in God's church and you'll be asked to give yourself to the man who stands beside you. When you make your vows, it can't be just your voice that speaks . . . it must also come from the heart. There will only be room in your heart for one man – and that man *must* be your husband. From the moment you give those vows, you give yourself also, *all* of yourself, mind and body, to Gregory Denton.' Cupping Emma's small troubled face between the palms of her hands, she asked meaningfully, 'You do know what I'm saying, child, don't you?'

Emma was left in no doubt as to what Mrs Manfred was saying. What she was telling her was that she must put Marlow Tanner out of her heart for ever! She was stressing the purity of the marriage vows Emma was shortly to take, and the total commitment they demanded. Mrs Manfred was warning Emma, but Emma could also sense the older woman's fear. Yet, she need not be afraid, thought Emma, for hadn't she herself gone over it all again and again these past weeks? Hadn't she tormented herself and questioned the rapid sequence of events which were taking her along at such frightening speed that she could hardly catch her breath? Didn't she know how serious, and demanding, and final were the vows which she would utter in that church tomorrow, before God and before Gregory? And wasn't she all too painfully aware of how, in that moment, she would be called on to ban all thoughts of Marlow Tanner from her mind? Never again must she think of him; never again must she indulge herself in her memories of that splendid, radiant smile which lit up her heart as nothing else could; never again must she close her eyes and listen to the soft murmur of his voice which caused her heart to tremble so. Those dark, laughing eyes and the feel of his strong arms about her . . . that wonderful, exquisite sensation when his mouth had covered her own in a kiss which had spread its pleasure throughout every corner of her being. These things would all be forbidden her. In their place would be Gregory, a kind and gentle man who, Emma knew, loved her perhaps in a way she would never deserve. But she would *try* with all her heart.

Emma said as much now to Mrs Manfred, before asking in a shy, quiet voice, 'How am I to behave . . . as his wife, Manny?' So acutely embarrassed was Emma by her own question, that she withdrew her gaze from the older woman's face and rested it on the floor.

Mrs Manfred's answer was given with great love, and tempered by an awareness of Emma's innocence in such matters. 'Behave as he wants you to. Behave sensibly and don't be afraid, for I'm sure Gregory won't hurt you, child. When he speaks softly to you, just listen quietly and know that he loves you. When you see his nakedness and he takes you in his arms, comfort yourself with the fact that he will be gentle . . . for Gregory Denton seems to be a tender-hearted fellow. And when he makes love to you, think on pleasant things . . . fill your heart with gladness, and it won't seem as terrible as you anticipate.'

Without lifting her face, which by now was suffused with a burning pinkness, Emma murmured her thanks, adding, 'I'll try to remember everything you've told me, Manny.' But, in her heart, she was still terrified of the ordeal to come. Unable to stop herself, she contemplated the fact that, if it was Marlow's bed she was going to, the prospect would not seem anywhere near as harrowing!

The day of Emma's wedding might have been a day in the middle of summer rather than January, for it was warm and filled with sunshine. The little church was packed as Emma came up the aisle to the resounding music of the organ. Everyone agreed that, in her lovely silk ivory gown, with a simple spray of yellow rosebuds in her hands, she was the most beautiful bride they had ever seen. On this splendid occasion, her rich, burnished hair was swept into clutches of ringlets either side of her head, secured by delicate mother-of-pearl combs.

As she knelt before the altar, Emma turned to look into Gregory's face. What she saw were the proud eyes of a man who adored her, and she felt ashamed that, on first waking that very morning, her thoughts had been drawn not to Gregory, but to Marlow Tanner. For his part, what Gregory saw as he looked deep into Emma's magnificent grey eyes, was a host of emotions which greatly moved him. He saw her fear, and prayed that it was not fear of him; he saw trust and compassion; he believed he saw the glimmer of love – but it seemed a sad kind of love, for there was pain in Emma's eyes, not joy. There was kindness also, and such strength that it made him tremble inside. Yet, in spite of all this and of the all-consuming love he felt for Emma, Gregory Denton was afraid. From the first moment Emma had been promised to him, he had been afraid – afraid he might lose her. Now, even while he heard her speak the marriage vows, he was mortally afraid that she might never love him in the way he loved her. He was afraid of the change she would find in her way of life, and he knew it would be difficult for Emma to adjust. Yet, for all his fears, Gregory Denton had hope – hope for their future together, and hope for Emma's lasting affection.

In the celebrations which followed, Breckleton House

echoed to the sound of music and dancing. Throughout the evening, a wide variety of guests mingled in and out of the rooms; some were business acquaintances of Caleb Crowther, dressed in dark formal wear; others belonged to Agnes Crowther's social circle, and were serious-faced and full of meaningless talk; and there were those known only to Martha and her intended, colourful in dress and loud of voice, and all of whom constantly pecked Emma on the face and forgot her name!

Emma was pleased to spend a few quiet moments in the company of Silas Trent, who took the opportunity to remind her, 'Don't forget, Emma. If ever you need a friend . . .' Whereupon she thanked him once more and assured him that she would not forget, but that, 'I am now in the hands of a good man, and doubt that I'll ever need to take you up on your kind offer.'

Three times Emma made a gentle approach to old Mrs Denton, and three times she was made to feel so uncomfortable that she tactfully gave up the effort.

It was some way past nine p.m. when Emma saw Caleb Crowther leading Gregory into the study. Ten minutes later they both emerged, seeming pleased with themselves and crossing the room in opposite directions – the older man to rejoin his cronies, and the younger to firstly join his mother, and then to hurriedly make his way towards Emma. Emma, meanwhile, had observed how stony-faced her mother-in-law appeared during the few exchanged words with her attentive son.

When Gregory told Emma, 'Please make your goodbyes, Emma, for it's time we left,' Emma's heart sank. This was the moment she had been dreading – when they must depart for that little house on Montague Street where the presence of old Mrs Denton brooded in every dark corner. Emma lost count of the number of times Gregory had apologized for the fact that 'I had it in mind to take you to Scarborough for a week, but, what with my duties at work and Mother being in such delicate health, well . . . I know you understand, Emma.' Emma understood all right. She understood that, on this occasion, at least, she was not of paramount importance in her new husband's life – first came his work, then came his elderly mother and *then* came his wife. Emma understood and, for the first time, she saw the imperfections in Gregory's love for her. Yet, she weighed that up against the imperfections in her love for him, and believed that it was *she*, not he, who had need to apologize.

When the word was given that the newly-weds were about to leave, well-wishers came from all sides.

'Good fortune,' said one.

'May you be blessed with many children,' said another.

'I don't suppose we shall have occasion to see each other often,' remarked Martha, with her arm linked boldly in that of Silas Trent's, and a cunning look on her face.

'Quite!' rejoined Agnes Crowther, whose hands were stiffly joined and pointed to Paradise.

The sentiments of Emma's aunt and cousin were echoed by Caleb Crowther's remark, 'Emma is a married woman now, and all responsibility for her has gone from this house.' Then, addressing himself not to Emma, but to her husband, he continued, 'Thomas has instructions to deliver your wife's belongings to your house first thing in the morning. I believe Mrs Manfred has the matter in hand.' Giving a sly look and lowering his voice, he surreptitiously patted Gregory Denton's jacket above his waistcoat pocket. 'You have the most important item right there. Be frugal with it Denton . . . for it was hard earned!' When Gregory nodded and made the observation, 'I know how careful Thadius Grady was, and I shall be equally careful with what he has entrusted to me, Mr Crowther, sir,' Emma knew at once that they were discussing the marriage fund left by her papa, and which she suspected, like her, must now be the responsibility of her husband. The knowledge that she was no longer under the jurisdiction of Caleb Crowther gave her a curious feeling of satisfaction and a sense of freedom – but the latter was cruelly curtailed when Gregory remarked, 'Come along, Emma. It's been a long, exhausting day for Mother, and she's ready for her bed.'

Before Emma climbed into the carriage, she clung to Mrs Manfred, who on impulse had thrown her arms around her. 'Oh, Manny!' she murmured, in a quiet voice unheard by anyone else, 'Pray for me, eh?'

When the older woman held her at arm's length to say in an equally soft voice, 'Emma Grady, your strength is in yourself! I'll just pray that you use it well,' there were tears in her eyes, and in Emma's also.

'You will come and see me, won't you, Manny?' Emma felt the need for that reassurance.

'You see if I don't!' came the retort in a choking voice. 'You just see if I don't!'

When a third voice interrupted, saying, 'Of course you'll be welcome at my house, Mrs . . . Manfred. But please don't forget that it is *my* house, and that your own duties as far as Emma's concerned, are at an end. She is, after all, answerable to my son now,' both Mrs Manfred and Emma abruptly looked up at the carriage where old Mrs Denton was leaning forward on the edge of her seat. The conniving smile on her face was not pleasant, and nor was her voice as she instructed Emma, 'It's time we went, young lady! Afore the cold gets into my poor old bones.'

The big mantelpiece clock struck eleven, and Emma wondered who was more loath to climb the dark narrow stairway to bed. Certainly the thought gave her little comfort, and neither Gregory nor old Mrs Denton seemed prepared to make a move.

On returning to the house on Montague Street, the elderly woman had made a great fuss about folks wasting good money on fancies and fripperies, but then, 'folks such as the Crowthers are partial to showing off and making fine displays!' With that said, she had taken off her cloak and bonnet, which she promptly handed to Emma with the curt instruction, 'Put the bonnet carefully on to the peg. And make sure that you drape my cloak *inside out* . . . it keeps the dust from settling on the outer material.' From the hallway, where she took care to do exactly as she was told for fear of alienating old Mrs Denton any further, Emma could hear the conversation now taking place in the back parlour. First she heard Gregory's voice pointing out to his mother how late the hour was, and did she not think it was time he helped her up to her bed? Then came the surly reply that it was not for *him* to say when she should go to her bed! And, what was more, she should like him to prepare her a hot drink, which 'might well help me to sleep all the better, and keep me unawares of what's going on in the dark under my own roof!'

Hurrying back down the passage and into the parlour, Emma pleaded with Gregory, who was already on his way into the adjoining scullery, 'Let *me* do it, Gregory . . .

please?' Of a sudden she would have done *anything* to escape the scathing eyes which constantly sought her out, and, if the truth be told, she resented Gregory being used in such a way.

'Why, thank you, Emma.' Gregory was obviously delighted, 'Come on then, I'll show you how Mother likes her drink made up.'

'You'll do no such thing!' Old Mrs Denton had grabbed her walking-stick from its resting place beside the fire-range, and was hitting it on the floor with increasing agitation. 'I want nobody else messing with my drink . . . nor my food, neither! You see to it, Gregory,' she said in an authoritative voice, 'same as you've *always* done. Or I shall simply go without!'

'But I'd *enjoy* preparing your drink, Mrs Denton,' Emma intervened, her sympathy for Gregory tempered by his obvious inability to stand up to this spoilt and vindictive old sourpuss.

At Emma's protest, old Mrs Denton gave out a gasp, then followed a choking cough. Quickly recovering, she fixed Emma with narrowed eyes, and in a low voice said, 'When I speak to Gregory, I expect *him* to reply. You being his wife does not give you the right to interrupt a conversation between mother and son.' Pausing, she glanced from Emma to Gregory, who seemed to be about to defend Emma. Seeing this, she immediately bestowed on Emma a begrudging half-smile, saying in a more friendly manner, 'You are young and you have a lot to learn about your duties as a wife. The first thing you need to learn is that your husband's word is law. Please remember that.' She began struggling to her feet, and, in a pitiful voice, pleaded with Gregory, 'See me to my bed, son. I feel faint after a most tiring day.

I don't want a drink now, because if I ever tried to swallow it, I think I might be ill.'

As Gregory lit a new candle from the sideboard, cupped his hand beneath his mother's elbow, and led her from the room, neither of them looked back at Emma, who had seated herself on the horse-hair stand-chair by the scullery door. She sat with her head dejectedly bent forward, her thoughts in turmoil. When, a moment later, she heard Gregory's footsteps hurrying down the stairs towards her, she put her head in her hands and shut her eyes tight. 'Oh, Manny!' she whispered, 'I pray I'll remember everything you told me.'

So many things rushed through Emma's mind as Gregory led her by candle-light, so tenderly, up the stairs and into the bedroom which was to be theirs. It was a good deal smaller than old Mrs Denton's, and was situated directly at the top of the stairs. From its long, narrow windows, the flag-stoned yard could be seen and the mill chimneys stretching out beyond. The furniture was of the same dark wood and practical design as the rest of the furniture throughout the house. Beneath the window stood a sturdy squat chest of drawers with a dark-framed mirror standing on top of it, together with two glass containers and a small crucifix on a stand. Either side of this chest of drawers was a rush-seated chair. Fitted into the alcove on one side of the floral-tiled fireplace was a deep, handsome wardrobe with shiny brass handles. In the other alcove was a smaller, more dainty wardrobe of exactly the same pattern, but with a fancy scalloped pelmet above.

As they entered the room, Emma caught sight of the bed itself. Her first impression was that it was immense. Indeed, standing close to it, she found that it almost reached up to her chest. For Emma, the tall, panelled ends resembled the confines of a coffin – this image being reinforced by the raised laurel leaves and sprigs of lilies carved in every deep, dark panel. The eiderdown was clearly woven from home-made patchwork, with each piece in the most ghastly of colours. The thought crossed Emma's mind whether old Mrs Denton had deliberately chosen such a cover in the hope that it would make Emma as sick as she herself professed to be! If Emma had been brought into this bedroom under different circumstances, she might have seen the funny side of it. But, as it was, the forbidding atmosphere of the room and that hideous eiderdown, only served to make her feel even more nervous than she already was.

As though sensing her fear, Gregory put the candle-stick down on to the chest of drawers, then, touching her shoulder lightly, smiled at her with gentleness. Bending to kiss her softly on the forehead, he murmured, 'Emma! Emma!' all the while letting his hand slide slowly down her back. 'If only you knew how long and how often I've dared to dream of this night.' For a moment longer he gazed into her eyes and, in spite of the knot of fear inside her, Emma could feel the warmth of his love spilling from his gaze to wrap softly about her, and her heart was filled with gratitude when he said in a quiet voice, 'I'll leave you alone a while, Emma . . . I'm going downstairs to make sure the house is secured.' Emma had seen for herself just how meticulously Gregory had bolted all the doors and checked the windows downstairs and knew that, being the good and considerate person he was, he was giving her the oppor-tunity to undress away from his eyes. In a quiet voice, she thanked him.

By the time Gregory returned to the bedroom, Emma had

taken off her dress, petticoats and undergarments and having laid them over one of the chairs, she had taken the white cotton nightgown from the valise, which Thomas had brought to the house the previous day. Then, with every limb shivering – more from fear than cold – she had climbed into that great bed and slithered down into its icy interior as far as she possibly could. When Gregory came into the room, holding another candlestick, only Emma's frightened eyes could be seen, peering apprehensively from the bed into the shadows where he stood.

The sight seemed to amuse him as, giving a soft laugh, he said affectionately, 'What a child you do seem, Emma.' But Emma wondered how he could make so light of the situation when to her it was a most traumatic and nerve-wracking experience.

Gregory sensed Emma's nervousness as she shyly watched him, and the smile slid from his face to be replaced by a deeply serious expression. His eyes, which still held Emma's fearful gaze, seemed to darken until, in the candle-light, they appeared almost black.

For Emma the tension was unbearable as he continued to gaze at her in that most unsettling manner. He blew out the candle in his hand and placed it beside the still-lighted one on the chest of drawers. Making no effort to blow this one out, he proceeded to undress with slow and fumbling movements. Emma was completely mesmerized by the gradual unveiling of Gregory's body, and was unable to avert her eyes despite her deeper instincts which told her to. Witnessing Gregory's awkwardness, she was comforted by the realization that he too was nervous about the ordeal which awaited them.

Silhouetted in the candle-light with the shadows moving

all about him, Gregory stood for a moment in his nakedness. Still Emma could not avert her eyes; she noticed how slim he was; how narrow and well-proportioned his shoulders were – almost like a woman's, she thought with surprise. But when he turned slightly to round the foot of the bed and approach her, Emma saw how naïve she had been! Quickly, and with all of her fears cruelly returned, she looked away. But the image of this man exposed in a way she had never known, would not leave her. As he slid into the bed beside her, Emma was still afraid and trembling; but she also shivered with a murmuring of excitement which surprised her.

As his warm nakedness touched her, Emma tried hard not to cry out. When he murmured softly in her ear, 'I do love you so, Emma,' she began to melt inside. And when he began kissing her hair, then her neck, and roving his hand towards her breast, Emma tried desperately to recall Manny's words, 'When he makes love to you, Emma, think on pleasant things.' Emma tried to do this now. She thought about flowers and little creatures, about sunny days and rippling brooks; and, as her thoughts dwelt on these things, they conjured up memories of other, happier days in the past when she laughed out loud and felt joy in her heart.

Before Emma could deny it, there he was – Marlow! With his dark, handsome features and laughing eyes he looked just as he had on their first meeting when he had been stripped to the waist, resembling a bronzed god. She could hear his voice, murmuring softly of love. But, no, it wasn't *his* voice! It was that of her husband. They weren't Marlow's gentle fingers which caressed her breast – they were Gregory's. The kisses being rained on her face and body were indeed gentle and loving, but they weren't fired with a passion intense enough to light her own. They weren't fervent or teasing enough. They didn't demand that which, deep within her, was waiting to be stirred. The voice whispering in her ear wasn't evocative and trembling, nor was it filled with that excitement and animation which would lift her out of herself. The body which pushed against hers didn't awaken that within her which cried out to be released and fulfilled. In that instant of realization, Emma hid something precious deep within her that she knew she could never share with Gregory; she could share it with only one man . . .

'I won't hurt you, Emma,' murmured Gregory's voice in her ear, 'but you must help me . . . please.' It was with a small shock that Emma realized that this was *his* first time also. Of a sudden, she was confused and more afraid than ever. The only thing she could do was to remember Mrs Manfred's words, and to do as she was asked. She felt him lift his body over hers, and she lay passively as, with a gentle touch, he parted her legs and roved the tips of his fingers over her inner thighs, and she waited tremulously while he positioned himself above her. Then, as he began to lower his body, he murmured over and over how lovely she was, until, his voice breaking with excitement and the beads of sweat dropping from his face on to Emma, he thrust himself into her again and again with mounting frenzy. His heady cries were rapid and filled first with anguish, then with mounting rapture. Emma cried also – but not from joy, nor pleasure. Her tears were quiet, bitter tears, and her feelings were only of disappointment and pain.

With a small, suffocated climactic scream, he gripped his arms so tightly about her that she could hardly breathe, and, like a pent-up dam, he burst inside her, all the while whimpering and moaning and telling her he loved her. But there was no such response from Emma, for she felt no love for him in her heavy heart. She felt nothing but sharp, searing pain and disillusionment. Whatever warm feelings she had begun to have for this man who was her husband, had been driven away in terror, like a small, frightened creature who feared for its life and who nothing on God's earth could ever persuade to come out into the open again. Emma would fulfil her wifely duties, as was her station, but beyond that, God help her, there was nothing more she could ever give.

As the dawn broke, the clouds burst open, spilling out a deluge of rain to splatter the pavements and drive against the windows with a vengeance. For a long time, Emma lay awake listening to the rain's patter as it fell on the roof, playing merry music on the tiles. One of her favourite feelings was lying in bed, cozy and warm, while outside the rain poured down and washed the windows, and then ran speeding into the overflowing gutters. She had always derived great comfort out of knowing that while outside the world became cold and drenched, she was warm and safe within. But that had been in the days when she had her papa and Manny close by, when there had been happiness in her heart and a sense of adventure in her soul. Now, there were only long, endless days stretching before her, when she must learn the ways and duties of a wife and, whatever illusions had been shattered on her wedding night, to please her husband and to bear his children.

In the half-light, a smile crept across Emma's mouth as she thought of the idea of children. No doubt carrying and giving birth to a child would be as degrading and painful as the conception of it. Oh, but at the end of it all there would be a reward in the form of a tiny and wonderful babe, warm and real, with a heart which would love her as its mama. That much at least she could look forward to; and she would, for it was a joyous and natural thing to want a child in your arms – a new-born child of your own flesh and blood whose life was so intimately bound up with your own. Emma wondered now whether that life was already starting deep inside her body. If it was, she would welcome it, but, she prayed to the Lord that if he saw fit to bless her with a child, he would never let her use it in the same way Gregory's mother used him.

Emma now turned her head to glance at Gregory, whose tousled hair touched her shoulder; and, looking at that boyish face, she thought how much kinder life might have been to him also. For, she could not be all he might have desired in a wife – any more than his domineering mother could be all he might have been blessed with for a parent. Still, she thought, there isn't a single soul in this world who doesn't have a cross of some sort to bear, and, as long as the good Lord sees fit to bless us with the strength to carry it, there's little else we can ask for. With that small comfort in her heart, and warm thoughts of motherhood, Emma went gently back to sleep.

If Emma was determined to rid herself of the memory of her first unhappy night under this roof, there was another who preferred to dwell on it, and to let the memory fester until it ate at her very reasoning. In that dark hour when Doreen Denton had lain in her bed listening to her son's cries of ecstasy as he had taken his new virgin wife to himself, there had fused in her heart a wickedness and a

217

deeper hatred of Emma than even she could have envisaged. Doreen Denton wanted her son's wife out of this house now more than ever; so much so that in her fevered mind little else mattered. Emma Grady was an intruder. She would *always* be an intruder, and, like all intruders she must be routed at the first opportunity.

As a rule, Sunday in the Denton household followed a hard and fast routine which had not varied for nigh on thirty-five years – since Gregory Denton's father had brought his new bride to the house on Montague Street. On the stroke of eight a.m., when the sound of church bells resounded over the length and breadth of Blackburn town, the worshippers would tumble from their houses, answering the summons of the Lord with the same automatic response with which they answered the summons of the mill whistle. One of the first doors to open was always that of the Denton house, when, looking respectably sober and devout, the family would follow the well-trod path up the hill and into the church. In earlier years, there had been only Doreen Denton and her husband; then along came Gregory, making the number up to three. After Mr Denton's demise, the number had reverted back to two. Doreen Denton had never once trod that particular path alone, and she had grown used to having a man by her side. Now the number had become three again, but it gave her no comfort, and she would have no part of it. So, for the first time in many years, the church bells rang out and the door of the Denton household remained firmly shut.

'Fetch me my rosary, and I shall talk to the Lord in my own way,' came the command from the bedroom, whereupon Gregory hurried about, fussing until she was left to 'talk to the Lord' in privacy, with the door firmly shut and both Gregory and Emma left in no doubt as to how dreadfully ill she felt.

For Emma, the day began as a long and tedious ordeal, with old Mrs Denton constantly banging the floor with her walking-stick, and Gregory fetching and carrying until Emma thought he would fall down from sheer exhaustion. Emma also kept herself busy. She took up the coconut matting and the big rag-peg carpet from the hearth, taking them out into the backyard where she beat the dust from them. Then, after cleaning the oilcloth floors, she polished the furniture, washed the breakfast things brought down from Mrs Denton's room, and cleaned and tidied the upstairs room which was hers and Gregory's. With that done, she then collected the kindling wood from the cellar, and watched most carefully as Gregory stuffed newspaper and wood into the fire-grate before lighting it with a match and quickly forming a pyramid over it with the smaller pieces of coke taken from the scuttle. As he worked, he took great care to explain the procedure in meticulous detail to the attendant Emma. For her part, she was surprised to find herself somewhat ignorant of such matters; she had seen the scullery maid make a fire often enough, and thought it an easy thing to do. Certainly, she would make it her own foremost task from now on.

'There'll be little need for *you* ever to make the fire, Emma,' Gregory told her as he held a sheet of newspaper over the open fire-grate to create a pulling draught up the chimney. When the small brown scorch which appeared in the centre began to spread right over the page, he swiftly drew it away and crumpled it into the coal-scuttle.

'But I won't mind at all,' replied Emma, who would be

219

thankful for *any* little job that might keep her from under Doreen Denton's feet.

But before Gregory could comment any further, another voice interrupted, 'The fire is *Gregory's* job! I'll thank you not to interfere with the smooth running of this household, Emma Grady. With a little help from Tilly Watson next door, we've managed admirably these many years, and I see no call to bring about a change now.'

Emma bit her tongue though she was sorely tempted to make a scathing comment as Doreen Denton made her way slowly across the room, her white frilly cap pulled low on her wrinkled brow, her full dark skirt squeaking and swishing as she went, and her brass-capped walking-stick making a soft thudding sound against the floor.

Quietly incensed by what he suspected was a deliberate mistake on his mother's part in addressing Emma with the surname of Grady and not with the name he had given her, Gregory said in an unusually firm voice, 'There *has* been a change brought about in this house recently though, Mother. You referred to Emma just now as Emma *Grady*. You remember . . . she is Emma *Denton* now, *Mrs* Denton, like yourself.' His words pierced the air like daggers, and each one seemed to make the uneasy silence beneath that much more intense.

Sensing that there was more fire to Gregory's character than she'd previously thought, Emma watched as the older woman sat stiff and stooped in the chair, her eyes staring hard into the crackling flames of the fire, her mouth a tight, thin gash in the angry redness of her face, and her jaw muscles working in a fury. She straightened herself up, the thin gnarled fingers of her right hand gripping the handle of her walking-stick so tightly that the blood had completely drained from them, and the other fist resting on her lap, clenching and unclenching like the muscles of her jaw bone.

Despite her pretence at making Emma welcome here, Gregory's words had unleashed her acute dislike of what she considered to be the cuckoo in her nest. When she spoke, it was with a viciousness which shocked Emma to her roots. If she had any hopes at all about this woman coming to accept her in this house, they were utterly dashed with these words, which were spoken to Gregory, but so obviously intended for Emma. 'Don't you dare speak to me of our good name! The good and respectable name of Denton . . . a name which I have been proud to carry these many years. A name given to me by a man of upright and faultless character, and who I prayed you might one day live up to!' Not for a moment did she remove her cold, condemning stare from Gregory's face, and, because of the desolate look which was wrought on it by the onslaught of her words, all of Emma's sympathy rose towards that poor, cowardly fellow who was her husband. But it was not finished yet, as old Mrs Denton poured scorn upon scorn – belittling his efforts as a son, and condemning his new status as a husband. Finally, exhausted by her own tirade, she gave out a cry, let her cane fall to the floor, and, dropping her head between her hands, she began sobbing as though her heart would break, muttering through her crocodile tears, 'You don't want me any more, do you? I'm old and weary . . . and you're tired of me. She'll be the same, I know. She'll want rid of me soon . . . out of my own house.'

Never having come across such a situation before, Emma was at a loss as to what to do. Gregory came to her and, putting his arms around her shoulders, murmured, 'Emma, will you busy yourself in the front parlour while I talk to her. Don't worry.'

At that same moment, old Mrs Denton looked up to see why her doting son had not come to put his arms about her like he'd always done before. When she saw that instead his arms were wrapped around Emma and the two of them appeared to be about to depart the room, she was incensed. Getting to her feet, she shouted, 'I heard you! Last night, I heard the pair of you . . . like animals! Filthy animals!'

The outburst shocked and shamed Emma. But it was the last straw for Gregory, who almost flung Emma to one side as he burst from her to confront his mother. 'That's enough!' he told her. 'You've gone too far!'

'Too far, eh? It's *you* that's gone too far. Fool that you are, you don't know what you've taken on.' Now her tone became less severe as she cajoled. 'Oh, son . . . think what you've done. We're not moneyed folk, and while you might keep two of us on a manager's wage, you'll never keep three. And what if she gets with child?'

To her astonishment, Gregory was not fooled by her change of manner, nor was he placated. 'If Emma gets with child, we'll manage well enough, for she didn't come to this house a beggar!' Here, he thrust his hand inside the jacket pocket of his best Sunday suit, and drawing out the long bulky package given to him by Caleb Crowther, he brandished it under her nose. 'Emma brought a handsome sum to this household . . . more money than you or I have ever seen! I thought you might accept Emma with more grace, but I see you never will! But, thanks to Emma's money, we can make our own plans . . . for we're neither of us welcome under *this* roof, that's clear enough!'

For a long time afterwards, Emma thought that something in Doreen Denton's face should have warned her and Gregory of what was to follow. But, when it happened, it came so quickly that they were both taken completely unaware.

On her son's defiant words, Doreen Denton reached herself up to meet his face and, fixing him steadily beneath a terrifying look, she said, 'So! Your trollop came here with her fancy money, did she? Well, we can do without *her*, and we can bloody well do without her money!' In a swift movement which belied the stiffness of her bones, she thrust out her arm and grasping the package from Gregory's fingers, she flung it into the farthest reaches of the fire where, in a matter of seconds, it was engulfed by the flames.

As both Emma and Gregory surged forward with the intention of grabbing the poker with which to salvage the blackened package, Doreen Denton pushed herself in front of the fire, grappling with Gregory as he fought desperately to remove her. When, with a triumphant look, she shouted, 'You're too late!' Emma saw that it was true, and her heart sank within her.

In that same moment, Doreen Denton's cry of victory became a cry of terror as the fringe of her shawl was caught by the flames and the back of her hair began smouldering. In a panic, she began screaming and thrashing at herself, and the more she panicked, the harder it was for Gregory and Emma to snatch the burning shawl from her and to stamp it out on the floor. Quickly, Emma threw off her own shawl and smothered it over Doreen Denton's hair and shoulders, and though she had been saved from serious burns by the swift action of her son and Emma, it was plain that the old lady was badly shocked and in a state of hysteria.

Outside, Thomas was about to knock on the door when he heard the dreadful commotion. Finding the door unlocked, as it always was during the day, he rushed inside to find Gregory stooping over the chair in which sat his mother, her face a ghastly colour and every inch of her trembling. 'It's all right, Mother,' he was telling her, one arm holding her tight and the other raised to his forehead as he wiped his hand backwards and forwards across it in a state of great agitation. Emma meanwhile had rushed to the scullery, where she was hurriedly filling the saucepan with water – her first thought being that a hot, strong brew of tea might help to calm Doreen Denton's shattered nerves.

No sooner had Thomas poked his head round the parlour door to ask Emma, 'Is everything all right, Mrs Denton? . . . I've fetched your belongings,' than Gregory had pounced on him, saying, 'Stay with my wife and mother. There's been an accident . . . I'm going for the doctor!'

As Gregory sped away up the passage towards the front door, Thomas returned to the room, where his eyes were immediately drawn to the bent, shivering figure hunched in the chair; he was terrified by her low, whimpering cries and the wide stare which wandered round the room looking at nothing in particular. 'Lord above!' he exclaimed in a quiet voice, 'What's happened, Mrs Denton?'

Having neither the time nor the inclination to stop and explain, Emma swiftly recruited Thomas to watch over the pan of water while she gave whatever comfort she could to Doreen Denton.

In no time at all, Gregory returned with Doctor Harrison, whose home was situated just over the Preston New Road in one of the big houses. Within a matter of minutes, he had examined old Mrs Denton, pronouncing, 'She's a very fortunate woman indeed. And it's due to your quick action that she's not badly hurt.' Sweeping his small, bright eyes from one to the other, he added for Emma's benefit, 'Take heart, Mrs Denton. All I can say is that your mother-in-law can thank her lucky stars that she was not alone in the house when it happened.' This led Emma to suspect that Gregory had not told the full tale, for had she been alone in the house, there would have been no argument, and consequently no accident! Pride and shame kept her from mentioning the money. As Gregory's wife, it was not for her to draw attention to such private and domestic matters, and she instinctively felt he would not thank her for doing so.

As Emma watched the doctor and Gregory assist the badly shocked patient up the stairs, she found herself trembling also. What had taken place in this house today was something she wouldn't forget in a hurry. But, in spite of the awful things that had been said, and regardless of how spiteful old Mrs Denton had proved to be, Emma couldn't help but feel some compassion towards her, for her son was all she'd got and she felt herself being replaced by someone else in his affections. But the money! Oh, what a tragic thing to have happened, because, without that, she and Gregory were really trapped here. Still, Emma wouldn't lose hope; they'd have to stay until the old lady had recovered, she knew that, but perhaps later they could find a house to rent.

Before he left, Thomas cheered Emma up with the news that Mrs Manfred intended calling on her Monday week. 'After you've had time to find your feet, so to speak,' he added with a forlorn look, thinking that, as far as he could see, she had been knocked right *off* her feet.

Shortly after the doctor had gone, with instructions for

Emma to 'Just keep her quiet and follow the procedure I've written down for your husband. She's not injured at all . . . but she is in a deep state of shock. I'll be back first thing tomorrow,' Gregory sat with his head in his hands, staring at the floor and saying again and again, 'God forgive me, Emma. I could have caused her terrible injuries . . . even . . .' His voice broke and dropping his head lower, he began quietly crying. Watching him, Emma wondered who was in a deeper state of shock – Gregory or his mother!

Coming to kneel before him, Emma said comfortingly, 'You can't blame yourself, Gregory. She *will* be all right . . . didn't the doctor tell you so?' When he nodded his head and reached out to take her hand in his, Emma realized that fate had thrown her into a situation where, of the three of them, *she* must be the strongest.

If it was a day of revelations for Emma, it was also a day of reckoning, for, on this day, Doreen Denton took to her bed and was never again seen out of it alive – except on one occasion, which was to have far-reaching and disastrous consequences.

Chapter Eight

'Oh yes, Manny, I'm more content than I ever was at Breckleton House.' Emma leaned over to place the wooden tray on to the sidetable. Lifting the china teapot, she poured tea into one of the pretty floral cups, and then handed it by the saucer to Mrs Manfred, who graciously accepted both milk and sugar together with a root biscuit from the small plate. Emma collected her own cup and saucer, before seating herself on the opposite side of the fire, directly facing the familiar little figure, who so often visited on her time off to keep Emma company.

'I have to be honest,' Mrs Manfred said, 'I never believed in all my born days that you'd fit comfortably into this household.' As she spoke, she examined the delicate bone china tea service, thinking how even Mrs Crowther had no finer.

Emma considered the other woman's words and she recognized some truth in them, for hadn't she herself believed the very same at first? And if she were to be honest, wasn't there *still* a semblance of truth in Manny's observation? Her reply, however, betrayed none of these inner thoughts as she said, 'I count my blessings, Manny. I have a comfortable home, and a good husband.'

Emma might have added 'loving' husband, but somehow she couldn't bring herself to say it; not because it wasn't true, for it *was* – Gregory positively doted on her – but because Emma's idea of love was not the same as Gregory's. He smothered her with his affections, and what took place in the bedroom at night gave her no pleasure; indeed, without exception, it was a humiliating and painful ordeal for her, and she thanked God that, though it was always frenzied, it was over very quickly.

'It does my old heart good to know that you're content and looking much stronger since your illness.'

'Oh, you mustn't worry about me, Manny. I'm a survivor, you know that!' Emma said with a small laugh. Then she added more seriously, 'I don't miss the Crowthers, *ever*. But I do miss having you around all the time.' There had been many occasions since she had come to Montague Street – particularly during the two endless weeks when she had been confined to her bed because of a vicious chill – when Emma had sorely needed a shoulder to cry on, usually because of old Mrs Denton's spiteful tongue and constant condemnation of her. All of this had come to a head when the old woman had flung the breakfast tray, which Emma had fastidiously prepared, across the room with the warning, 'If you ever dare to step one foot in my room again, I'll not be responsible for my actions!' Emma had wondered at the time what form the threat would come in: would she throw herself out of the window, or cut her wrist on a teacup, or perhaps make a dive for Emma's throat. In the ensuing weeks, Emma became convinced that she meant the latter!

Even Gregory could not persuade his bedridden mother to be more amiable towards Emma. So, at an extra cost of one shilling and sixpence a week, he assigned Tilly Watson to attend his mother under Emma's instruction. Since the young woman from next door had been employed for the previous two years to carry out the more menial tasks in the Denton household, the arrangement was a simple one. Tilly Watson was a bright young thing whom Emma had grown quite fond of, and her year-old son, Joey, had become the highlight of Emma's day. However, Emma knew virtually nothing about Tilly's husband, for he worked long hours as a weaver and according to both Gregory *and* Tilly, he had a very quick temper. Emma had not made his acquaintance, nor did she particularly want to.

Emma asked after Cook and other members of the Crowther household, with the notable exception of the Crowthers themselves. But Mrs Manfred couldn't resist telling how Martha had suddenly turned up on the doorstep just two days before, 'in a dreadful state, and calling Mr Trent all the names under the sun!'

Emma was astonished. 'But they've only been married four months!' she said. However, she was not surprised when Mrs Manfred explained how Martha was still spoilt and selfish.

'Being married hasn't altered her one jot. I'll tell you what, though . . . she's met her match in that husband of hers, for he seems untouched by her sulky manner.'

'A good thing too, if you ask me,' declared Emma, thinking what a handful Martha was, and sure that her cousin would never grow up. 'But what made her come running home from Liverpool, Manny?'

Mrs Manfred gave a low snort of disgust and, leaning forward, she lowered her eyes, saying, 'She's with child.' Straightening herself up and adopting a thoroughly disdainful look, she added, 'It's only just been confirmed. When the news was given her, it seems that her husband had a sailing commitment which he had to honour and which would take him away for the better part of two months. Well, of course, he was delighted at Mrs Trent's news – she didn't deny that to Mrs Crowther – and he spared no expense in ensuring her comfort and well-being till his return. But she would settle for nothing less than his abandoning his contractual obligation and staying with her. Well, of course, since his father's demise, Mr Trent has a great responsibility on his shoulders, as Mr Crowther pointed out to Mrs Trent with a deal of impatience.' Mrs Manfred leaned forward once again to look Emma in the eye and say more intimately, 'In fact, he told her in no uncertain terms that she was a married woman now, and neither he nor her mama would be seen to be interfering in private affairs of matrimony. Well, he as much as showed her the door . . . "Your place is in your own home, waiting for your husband, and looking forward to the arrival of your child," he told her. And, I do believe that if it hadn't been for his own imminent departure on a tour of the Assizes, and Mrs Crowther's fawning attitude to her daughter, Mrs Trent would straightaway have been sent packing!'

'And what of Silas Trent?' asked Emma. 'Had he already set sail for foreign parts?'

'Well, no. Just as Mr Crowther was ready to depart, Mrs Trent's husband turned up. There was a private discussion in the study, after which I was informed that Mrs Trent would be staying at Breckleton House for the duration of her husband's absence. Oh, Mr Trent was very attentive towards her, and was seen to kiss her goodbye before he left.' Here, Mrs Manfred clicked and tutted disapprovingly. 'A blind man could see how he worships the ground she walks on. Oh, but she is a mardy and sulky madam. Lord only knows what kind of parent she'll be for the coming child!' Mrs Manfred suddenly realized how she had let her tongue run away with her. On seeing Emma's crestfallen face, she put her cup and saucer down on the table, saying in a forlorn voice, 'Oh, child, forgive me for prattling on so.' She reached forward to pat Emma's hand, asking in a low voice, 'Have you still no sign of being with child?'

Deliberately lightening her expression into a smile, Emma shook her head. 'Afraid not, Manny,' she replied, cleverly disguising her growing disappointment that, in spite of almost five months of marriage and Gregory's insatiable sexual appetite, she had not yet conceived a child. She dreamt longingly of holding her own new-born babe in her arms, but as the months passed and there was still no sign, she had begun to feel less and less of a woman. She also knew that, despite his assurances to the contrary, Gregory had come to believe that she might be lacking in some way. In fact, once Emma had recovered from her illness, he had arranged for all their bedroom furniture to be taken up the flight of stairs to the large attic bedroom. Emma was in no doubt as to his reasons why: he obviously felt as keenly distressed as she did at the thought of old Mrs Denton lying awake at night, listening to every word and noise they made. She was glad to have moved to the upper bedroom, but it disillusioned her to see how Gregory had already started stripping their old room, with the intention of turning it into a nursery.

'Now, you mustn't fret, child.' Mrs Manfred was not fooled by Emma's disarming smile. She thought to herself that, while the Martha Crowthers of this world could never live up to motherhood, Emma was of such a warm, loving nature that she would cherish a child and bring fulfilment to them both. 'It'll happen . . . in its own good time, it *will* happen, you mark my words.'

'I know, Manny, murmured Emma, 'I know.' After which, a silence ensued as they each sat staring deep into the fire's dancing flames.

Looking around the room, Mrs Manfred couldn't help thinking what a remarkable difference Emma's delightful and bright presence had made to his house, and to this room in particular. On that very first occasion when they had made their courtesy call to meet old Mrs Denton, there had been a most forbidding and unwelcome atmosphere in this very room. Yet now, it positively glowed with warmth . . . reflecting Emma's enchanting personality, thought Mrs Manfred. But then, maybe it was not very different after all and perhaps it was just the fact that she was close to Emma herself, that brought such comfort and delight to Mrs Manfred.

The room itself had not changed physically. The walls were still a murky cream colour and the curtains the same flock-tapestry ones. The furniture was in exactly the same place – a low, polished wood sideboard spanned the length of one wall; there was a small circular table in the far corner, which was covered with a lace cloth that draped down to the brown patterned carpet, and on which was a silver five-stem candelabra that had been a wedding present to Gregory's parents; two deep, black, horse-hair armchairs sat either side of the fireplace, and a small, square side-table stood beside the larger of the two chairs. Standing pride of place in the centre of the room was a huge round table, covered in a frilled green-cord tablecloth and surrounded by four long-back chairs finished in rich tapestry. Both the quality of the oak furniture and the ornaments dotted about gave a feeling of decayed grandeur – almost like the old lady herself, mused Mrs Manfred.

'Coo-ee!' The call came from the front door and immediately following it came the slim, beshawled figure of a young woman, with painfully thin features, bright blue eyes, and a chubby child in her arms. The child's thick fair hair was identical in texture to the woman's and, like hers, was short and curly about his face. The child was bare-headed, while she had on a small white cap with a gathered and frilly brim which flopped on to her neck and forehead. 'It's only me,' she said, coming into the room, 'only Tilly.' Then, catching sight of Emma's visitor who was by now a familiar figure to Tilly, she added, 'Oh, hello Mrs Manfred, I'd no idea you were here.' At once, she pulled out a chair from the table and fell wearily into it, lowering the child on to the floor where, for a while, he stood on unsteady legs, clinging to her skirt. 'I ain't stopped all day,' she said, looking first at Mrs Manfred, then at Emma. 'I woke up with the urge to clean the house from top to bottom, once the man had gone off to work.' She leaned back in the chair and laughed out loud, 'It was the very same when I was carrying Joey here,' she explained. 'I'd like to bet a tanner that there's another on the way.' She opened her shawl and patted her stomach. 'I can tell. I feel different in here.'

Emma was not in the mood to discuss whether Tilly was or wasn't likely to be with child. So instead she asked, 'Would you like a cup of tea, Tilly?'

'No thank you, luv. Seeing as how it's nearly time for the duchess's tray,' she replied, pulling a face and jerking a thumb up towards the ceiling. 'I'd best set about giving her a wash first eh? Y'know what a pain she can be if I'm late making a start.' Giving a loud shiver, she exclaimed, 'By! It's that nippy in the air this morning . . . you wouldn't think we were well into June.'

Emma was always conscientiously aware of her duties regarding old Mrs Denton and even now the big old kettle was happily spitting out its bubbling contents on to the burning coals. In no time at all, Emma had removed the kettle to the kitchen where she mixed both hot and cold water into a large bowl; then making sure it was comfortable to the touch, she collected soap and flannel from a drawer in the small pine dresser. She put these into a drawstring bag which she threaded over her wrist. Then, taking care to avoid the area where the child was playing, she went through the parlour and up the stairs. At the top of the stairs, she put the bowl and toiletries against the wall on the landing. As she turned to descend the stairs, her eyes glanced towards the closed door of Mrs Denton's room. She paused for a moment, wondering whether the old lady was asleep or awake and whether, just once more, she might go into the room and make a determined effort to befriend her. It was something which Emma often thought about, for she couldn't easily accept things as they were. When she tentatively made her way forward along the landing, she was abruptly stopped in her tracks by the loud shriek which came from the room.

'Go away! I don't want you anywhere near me, Emma Grady! I know that's you skulking about out there.'

Feeling both angry and belittled, Emma hurried down to the scullery, deliberately averting her gaze from the two watching women who must have heard old Mrs Denton's cry. Having quickly refilled the kettle, Emma brought it back into the parlour and wedged it firmly on

234

to the coals in the fire. Then, thankful for the discreet silence, she gave her full attention to the child, who eagerly clambered into her arms when she reached down to enfold him.

'Right, then,' said Tilly, getting to her feet, 'I'd best get on with it eh? Fresh towel in her chest-drawer as usual, is there luv?' she asked. Upon Emma's affirmative nod, she said, 'Y'know, you don't *have* to take the bowl upstairs, luv. Though I expect you like to feel you're doing your bit for the old duchess, eh? . . . in spite of her surly ways.' She knew Emma would have preferred to look after the old biddy herself, but that Doreen Denton would have none of it, oh dear me no! Still, it earned Tilly an extra one and sixpence a week, so she didn't want to complain.

Long after both Tilly Watson and Mrs Manfred had departed, Emma sat ruminating on the way of things. She had meant what she'd said to Mrs Manfred – she *was* more content than she'd been for a very long time. It wasn't a hard thing to be, she mused, once you had the commonsense to accept that the things you *really* want in life are not always the ones you get. There was much that Emma would have chosen to be different; but choice was a luxury reserved only for a few. So, she had come to terms with her disappointments; she had learned how to push disturbing thoughts of Marlow to the back of her mind; and she had hardened her heart to the callous attitude of old Mrs Denton. Emma had also resigned herself to the frequent and insensitive night-time advances of a man she could never love and who, in the light of day, was gentle and selfless. It was almost as though the grasping, thoughtless man who climbed on top of her at night was someone totally different from the man who tenderly pecked her on the cheek when he left for work and seemed to live only for the hour when he came home to her again. Emma wondered whether all men were like that. It was all a revelation to her, and not a very pleasant one at that.

'That was wholesome, Emma.' Gregory Denton picked up his napkin and dabbed at each side of his mouth. 'I do believe you make the best rabbit pie in the whole of Lancashire.' Stretching up, he patted the flat of his hands on his stomach, gave a groan of satisfaction and, pushing back his chair, got to his feet. In a moment he had rounded the table to where Emma had already started clearing away the plates and, coming up behind her, he placed his hands on her shoulders. Then, bending his head into her neck, he kissed it with the utmost tenderness. 'Never a day passes,' he murmured, 'that I don't know how lucky a man I am.'

He then spent a few minutes standing with his back to the fire, contentedly smoking his clay pipe but seeming to Emma restless in his manner. As a rule, once he had eaten his fill of the meal she prepared so well – thanks to the guidance of Mrs Manfred over these past months – he would chatter incessantly about many things: what could have been if only her money had not been so wantonly destroyed; the price all three of them were now paying for it; and how, in spite of it all, he supposed they were content enough. Then he would go on at great length about his fervent desire for a child and of how, when the child *did* arrive, as surely it must, then please God that it be a son. He also talked with great pride about his work, exaggerating the praises bestowed on him by Caleb Crowther when the figures showed a good return and making small of any condemnation that might have come his way from the same source.

On this Friday night, however, he was unusually quiet and Emma sensed that something was wrong. So, after Gregory had brought down his mother's tray and Emma had finished the washing-up, she sat herself in the armchair facing him across the fireplace. Taking up her sewing, she glanced at him and, seeing that he was leaning forward in his chair with his head dropped in his hands and his eyes trance-like as they gazed at the glowing coals, she asked quietly, 'Are you ill, Gregory?'

At once, his full attention was on her. 'No, of course I'm not ill, Emma.'

'But there *is* something wrong, isn't there?' Emma was sure of it.

'No, no . . . nothing at all for you to worry your lovely head about.' He made no mention of the rumours which had assailed him from two sides these past days. On the one hand there was talk concerning Emma's own uncle, Caleb Crowther, who, or so it was said, was deep in debt to the bank and the two Grady mills had been used as collateral against that debt. Then there was talk that both Arkwright's Mill and two of the smaller ones along the wharf had gone on drastic short-time due to a glut on the market. In addition to all that, the unrest in America had accelerated beyond all their fears. Like many whose livelihood depended entirely on the cotton industry, Gregory Denton sensed an avalanche developing over his head and what struck the fear of God into him was the knowledge that he was powerless to prevent it.

Being unable to draw her husband into any kind of conversation, Emma concentrated on her sewing. She was not ignorant of the way things were going in the industry, for as the child of Thadius Grady she had grown up to understand its fluctuating moods. Nor was she blind to the newspaper articles that followed developments in certain areas of America and which indirectly controlled the well-being of Lancastrian folk. Abraham Lincoln had assumed office some three months ago, in March. A month previous to that, the Southern Confederacy had been constituted, and, only six weeks ago, in the month of April, Fort Sumpter was captured by the Confederates. Emma had read every report with the realization that a civil war between the North and South of America was no longer a threat – it was a reality. But, even now, many believed it would have few repercussions, if any, in Lancashire itself.

Emma had persisted in looking on the bright side, for she knew only too well how Gregory had been building a healthy stockpile of raw cotton despite Caleb Crowther's belief that such a measure was unnecessary. Emma sensed that matters of work and security greatly troubled Gregory. She also knew that whatever she might say, he would derive no comfort from her words, for he was the sort of man who saw every problem as being one which he alone could solve. Although Emma admired him for this, she would have preferred it if he could at least talk these matters over with her and respect her opinion. But he could not. His paramount intention was to protect Emma at all costs from troublesome responsibilities, the consequence of which was only to make Emma feel that *she* was the most troublesome of his responsibilities.

Later, after Gregory had said goodnight to his mother before going to their own bedroom, he lost no time in climbing into bed beside her and Emma discovered that, while his appetite for conversation had waned, the same could not be said of his lustful appetite for her body. She had grown used to the precise manner in which he satisfied himself, for it never varied. Nor did it awake any response in her. If anything, it had become a tiresome and uncomfortable experience which left her feeling only relief when it was over. In absolute silence, he would lean himself up on one elbow, with his face nudging hers and his hand feverishly pulling up her nightgown. When it was up about her waist and his hand had found her thighs, he would begin to frantically explore that which he most coveted. Then, making a low, smothered cry, he would hoist his naked body above hers and, roughly prising open her legs and thrusting himself into her, he would make no more than six feverish strokes, all the while smothering her face with his mouth, before collapsing with a groan on top of her. Emma often thought that she got more pleasure from washing up the dishes!

'Things are going from bad to worse, Marlow lad. What shall we do?' Sal Tanner had been gazing at the ripples in the water made by the small stones which Marlow occasionally skimmed across its surface. Shifting herself about on the big upturned crate which they both now shared on the wharf, and trying to capture his downcast, thoughtful gaze with her round, violet eyes, she repeated, 'Marlow, lad . . . I said things are going from bad to worse!'

'I know, Sal,' he murmured, keeping his troubled gaze on the water, 'I know.' He leaned down to throw into the water the small handful of pebbles which he'd scraped into a pile with the edge of his boot. Then, stretching his back, he ran his hands through his long dark locks which had fallen about his face on stooping. 'It's a sorry state of affairs, Sal,' he said, dropping one hand to affectionately stroke the dog which was sitting to attention by his side. 'Yet there's folk much worse off than we are, and that's a fact.' Sighing noisily, he got to his feet and began walking along the wharf to where the barge was moored. The dog trotted close to his heels and Sal hurried along by his side trying to keep up with his long, determined strides, and the more she hurried, the more prominent the limp she'd sustained from her accident became.

'Folks worse off than us!' she snorted. 'Well, if that's so, where are they?' she demanded. 'You tell me that!'

As she shook her fist in the air, Marlow wrapped his fingers around it and brought them both to a halt. When he looked down at her with serious eyes which seemed even darker than usual because of his anger, Sal wished she'd learn to keep her mouth shut.

'I don't *need* to tell you, Sal,' he told her, 'you know well enough. You've seen them . . . in the soup queues. And you've seen the boarded-up houses where folks have been thrown out because they can't pay the rent. We at least have some work, and we have a roof over our heads.' Releasing her hand, he turned from the direction in which they had been going. 'I'll be back before dark,' he said in a quiet voice, and with a click of his fingers he signalled for the dog to follow him as he departed at an impatient pace.

'Where yer going?' shouted Sal, following him a short way, but slowing down as the distance between them grew even wider. 'T'ain't my bloody fault if 'Merica goes to war! T'ain't my fault if folks is hungry! I have ter count us bloody pennies an' all, y'know, since the work's dried up. Marlow! Come back here, yer bugger!' But he had already gone from her sight. Crashing her two fists against her sides, she hung her head low and headed home, muttering, 'Yer a windbag, Sal Tanner . . . a bloody windbag!'

An hour later, Marlow had climbed to the highest point in Corporation Park where, seated on the turret of a Crimean War gun – the very spot to which Emma had been drawn when deeply troubled – his eyes scoured everything below. The long winding shape of Montague Street was just visible and it was here that his gaze lingered for a seemingly endless time. Emma lived down that street, he knew. He didn't know which house it was, but it was no secret among the mill-hands at Grady's that Gregory Denton resided in the better-class part of Montague Street. 'Oh, Emma,' he whispered now, his heart simultaneously heavy and joyous by the memory of her and by the feel of her name on his lips. 'Emma, Emma,' he repeated, pulling his brown cord jacket tighter about him and thrusting his hands into his pockets out of reach of the biting October air. Though the wanton wind whistled frantically across the hill top, screeching gleefully as it sliced into everything vulnerable, Marlow hardly felt it as he was warmed by tender thoughts of Emma. Yes, she was wed to another, but he still loved her. Yes, she had told him that he had no part in her life now and never would have, but there wasn't a single waking moment when he didn't crave her with every fibre of his being. A man might have many women; he might know tender loving times with each of those women, and he might profess to love them. But in every man's life, there is just one very special woman who reaches so deep inside him that she becomes a living part of his very existence; just one woman with whom he could spend the rest of his life and never regret a single heartbeat of it. For Marlow, that woman was Emma. That was the simple truth and the knowledge that she belonged to another only made his love that more tragic.

So much had happened in the nine months since Emma's marriage. It was said that, despite old Mrs Denton's impossible character, Emma was happy enough. He was glad of that, but he was also devastated that Emma had not found it in her heart to return the love he felt for her. So often of late, with Emma growing ever distant, the thought of a new life in foreign parts had become more prominent. Now, in these hard times – when American ports were blockaded and cotton shipments stopped, and when the industry was grinding to a halt and hundreds of thousands were struggling to survive because of it – Marlow consoled himself with the knowledge that at least one of the Grady mills was still working; the one managed by Emma's husband. He thanked God that she was secure, yet, in the same breath, he prayed that relief might come to others who were not so fortunate.

After a while, the wind subsided and the air grew colder. Dusk began gathering and still Marlow made no move, until even the dog at his feet grew weary. When he felt the dog's warm nose nuzzling into his hand, he looked down to see how miserable his four-legged friend was. Reaching down to laughingly rough-up the flat, smooth coat which felt cold to the touch, he said, 'Aw, sorry, old thing,' at once getting to his feet and fishing out the leather lead from his jacket pocket. 'Let's away home, eh? See what Sal's conjured up for tea.'

'I don't *want* tea!' Gregory Denton pushed away his plate, got to his feet and stormed from the table to stand facing the fire, his two hands resting on the mantelpiece and the fiercest look on his face Emma had ever seen there. 'Don't question everything I say!' he told her in a harsh voice. 'When I say I want no bloody tea, I mean exactly that!'

Thinking her best course of action was to clear the table and depart to the scullery, Emma lost no time in doing just that. For the rest of the evening she busied herself doing this and that, while Gregory silently brooded. He brooded late into the night; he brooded as they climbed the stairs to bed; and when they lay side by side in the darkened room, he remained lost in a deep dark mood, until, with a mumbled 'Goodnight, Emma', he turned away from her. But, even then he would not sleep and for a long time afterwards he turned and fidgeted, more restless and disturbed than Emma had ever known him. From her very first meeting with him, when she was a child by her papa's side, Emma had known how devoted he was to his work. It was only now, however, seeing him in such despair at possibly losing it, that she realized how passionately obsessed he was with the means of his livelihood. All of his tireless efforts, all his enthusiasm and that particular fierce pride which only a man could feel towards his work, Gregory Denton had channelled into his responsibility and duties at the Grady Mill. He had carved himself a coveted place in the running of things. He was highly respected and answerable to only one earthly authority above him; and, having achieved such esteem, he was now fearful of having it all snatched away. Every day he saw it happening up and down Lancashire as the stranglehold which America had on an entire industry many miles from its battlefields, was squeezed tighter and tighter until the cries of hunger and deprivation were beginning to be heard from every corner.

Emma was also conscious of the dreadful consequences

the cotton starvation could reap on the people of Lancashire and in Blackburn particularly because of its concentrated investment in this industry. She wondered where it would all end. Yet, although the signs were alarming, Emma convinced herself that reason would prevail and things were never as bad as they might seem. She did her best to persuade Gregory of this, but for her pains she was dismissed with the comment, 'You're only just seventeen, Emma. What can you possibly know of such manly matters!' At which point he would grow even more agitated, and she wisely withdrew.

Some four weeks later, in the month of November 1861, Emma's peace of mind was further disrupted. It was on a Thursday evening, after Gregory had brought down his mother's dinner tray. 'God!' he shouted, crashing the tray down on to the table and bringing Emma hurrying from the scullery. 'Will that bloody woman *never* let up?'

'Your *mother*?' Emma couldn't hide her astonishment at hearing Gregory refer to old Mrs Denton in that way. As a rule, he went out of his way to defend her.

'It's this article in the *Standard*,' he said, collecting the folded newspaper from the tray. 'I knew I shouldn't have let her see it, but she can be fiercely demanding when she has a mind!' He opened out the newspaper at a certain page and peered at it, a deep frown etching itself into his brow as he did so.

Emma knew at once which article her husband was referring to, for she had also been disturbed by it. It reported on how the newly elected Mayor of Blackburn, Mr R.H. Hutchinson, had anticipated that great distress and trouble would manifest itself in the coming winter. To this end, it had been agreed that the sum of two hundred pounds would be set aside for distribution to the growing number of needy by the clergy and ministers of the town. But, meanwhile, a meeting of the textile manufacturers had resulted in the drastic step of closing down even more establishments, the consequence of which was to throw an even greater number of operatives into the ever-increasing ranks of the unemployed. Not a man was safe in his work and though Emma's heart bled for those families already living in fear, she also felt desperately concerned for her husband. Gregory Denton was a changed man. Whereas he had once gone to work of a morning with a spring in his step and a warm kiss for Emma, he now left without a word of farewell and with his face gravely serious. His stooped figure went down the street as though he was approaching the hangman rather than his place of work.

In all of this, Emma had to admit a sneaking admiration for the way in which Caleb Crowther had managed to keep the Wharf Mill functioning when so many others were going under. Time and time again, Mrs Manfred had assured Emma of her uncle's grim determination to keep open that particular avenue of income. 'I can tell you this, Emma,' she said, 'he's so determined not to lose that revenue, that at times . . . well, he seems like a desperate man.' She had shaken her head, adding, 'Almost as though he's driven by the same fear as drives the lesser mortals like us. Still and all, whatever his reasons for fighting like a madman against closing down the Wharf Mill, if he's looking after his own interests then it must follow that he's looking after yours, eh?' Emma had replied how she realized that one day her papa's concerns would be passed on to her and she was aware in these hard times what an uphill struggle it must be to keep the looms turning, but, her greatest concern at the moment was for Gregory's sanity, in the light of his ever-changing moods.

On the last Monday in November, when she had seen Gregory out as usual and Tilly Watson had returned home after attending to old Mrs Denton, Emma had an early-morning visitor.

'Manny!' she cried on opening the door, 'what a lovely surprise!'

'Hello, child,' said Mrs Manfred, placing a swift kiss on Emma's face. 'Mrs Crowther asked that I fetch a few urgent articles from the shops, on account of her having invited a number of ladies to a social gathering this afternoon . . . where they might discuss matters which mean absolutely nothing to anyone at all!' Emma smiled, for it was clear that Mrs Manfred's opinion of the Crowthers was still as low as it had ever been. 'I took the opportunity to leave the tram early, so I could call in on you.' With that said, she expertly gathered her skirt into her hands just enough to lift the hem above the step of the door, and then swept past Emma and down the passage. By the time Emma reached the parlour, the homely little woman was already seated and warming herself by the cheery fire. As Emma came into the room, she was asked in a quiet tone to, 'Come and sit near me, child.'

'Are you all right, Manny?' asked Emma, being somewhat perturbed by the serious expression which greeted her. 'Is everything all right at the Crowthers?' Of a sudden, and in spite of the way she had been treated by Martha Crowther in the past, Emma was fearful that something terrible might have happened regarding Martha's pregnancy. When she was assured that both Martha and her mama enjoyed an excellent state of health, Emma asked, 'Then what's troubling you, Manny?' As she spoke, she seated herself in the armchair directly facing the older woman and not for a moment did her worried eyes leave Mrs Manfred's face.

'I'm afraid it's bad news.' She reached out a hand as though to touch Emma in comfort, but the distance between them was too great and instead her hand lay fidgeting in her lap, screwing and unscrewing the taffeta folds in great agitation. 'Yesterday evening, Mr Crowther met with a number of other manufacturers at Breckleton House. Twice I was instructed to personally take in refreshments. On the first occasion the intense discussions fell to a hush on my entry.' She screwed her mouth into a tight pucker, as though making an effort to stifle those words which might tumble from it.

'Manny . . . please!' Emma had already sensed that Caleb Crowther's meeting might indirectly affect her, otherwise, why was Mrs Manfred so concerned to inform her of it?

'When I went in the second time, the discussion had reached the pitch of a heated argument, and I was hardly noticed at all. Oh, look child, I overheard a statement made by Mr Crowther.'

'What was it, Manny?'

'The Wharf Mill. He's closing it down, and he intends to inform Gregory of his intentions this very day.' There, it was said! But she felt no better for being the bearer of such unwelcome news.

For a while, Emma was struck silent, her thoughts churning over and over in a flurry. He's closing it down, she told herself, yet hadn't she seen it coming? It *had* to come because, the way things were, there was no alternative. Gregory had seen it coming also and now, this very day, his worst nightmare would be realized.

'He'll take it badly, won't he child? Although, by all accounts and thanks to your papa's foresight regarding yourself, you'll fare better than most. He must think on that.'

Emma was aware that Caleb Crowther had made sure it was common knowledge how he had handed over 'a sizeable dowry' on the marriage of his ward. Old Mrs Denton's disposal of it was known only in this house and Emma preferred it to stay that way.

'He'll be devastated by the closure, Manny,' she replied, 'and I'm at a loss to know how I can help him over it.'

They sat in deep thought: Mrs Manfred secretly even more disturbed by Caleb Crowther's crippling debts to the bank, which, although common knowledge below stairs, Mrs Crowther was totally and blissfully ignorant about; and Emma thinking how shattered Gregory would be on hearing Caleb Crowther's plans.

'Oh, Manny, do you think I should go to him?' she asked now, feeling the greatest sympathy for him. 'Do you think I ought to be there when he's told?' The thought of being in the same room as her uncle made Emma's stomach turn. But she would be there if it might help Gregory.

'No. You mustn't even think of it, Emma!' declared the older woman, with a hint of compassion in her voice. 'It will be enough for him to cope with, child, without *you* being there to witness it all.' Rising from her chair, she went to where Emma sat quite still and unsure as to what to do next. 'Just be here when he gets home. He'll tell you in his own good time,' she advised, and Emma knew she was right.

After she had seen her dear, concerned friend out of the house, Emma closed the door and made her way down the passage. As she reached the parlour door, she heard a loud insistent knocking from upstairs and old Mrs Denton's voice calling out, 'Who's that? Who've you been entertaining in my son's absence, you little baggage!' When the knocking grew even louder, seeming to bounce off the walls and shake the house, Emma pressed her hands to her ears and went into the scullery where the noise was not so terrible. For what seemed like ages, she leaned against the cold windowpane, staring out into the flagstoned yard and wondering what kind of mood her husband might be in when he came home that night.

At half-past six the meal of steak pudding and roast potatoes was ready. The kettle was boiling on the range and the table was laid. In its centre was a lighted candle which, together with the glow from the fire, made a warm, cozy atmosphere ready to lift the night chill from Gregory's bones, while Emma waited to lift the spirit in his heart.

By half-past eight, the meal was ruined, the kettle almost dry and the candle-light flickering dangerously low. Several times, Emma had gone out into the cold night but there was no sign of Gregory. When old Mrs Denton began her persistent knocking and demanding her dinner at the top reaches of her voice, Emma took the remainder of the Sunday pork-roast from beneath the mesh cover in the larder and slicing four helpings of it, she made a plate of sandwiches and a pot of tea. These she put on a tray, then, feeling both frustrated and angry, she threw caution to the wind and climbed the stairs to her mother-in-law's room – every step taken to the increasing volume of that witch-like shriek, which first demanded the whereabouts of its meal, then launched into a vicious attack on both the son who neglected her and Emma Grady who was 'a trollop in fancy clothes.'

When, undaunted, Emma flung open the bedroom door, never once bringing her eyes to gaze on the source of that harsh, abusive voice, she was subjected to the vilest verbal attack she could ever have imagined, which finished with the demand, 'GET OUT OF MY ROOM!' A series of strangled cries followed which, to anyone else might suggest that the old lady was breathing her last, but which only told Emma that the crafty article was using every means at her disposal to rid herself of her unwelcome intruder. Emma acted as swiftly as possible, for she had no intention of staying in this room for one minute longer than was necessary. After placing the tray on the chair beside the bed, she went quickly from the room, breathing a sigh of relief as she closed the door behind her – just as the heavy brass bed-knob came hurtling through the air, to thud into the door with such force that it split the upper panel from top to bottom.

Downstairs, in the long silence which ensued, Emma thought that old Mrs Denton must be tucking into the sandwiches. 'You old bugger!' she said under her breath, feeling both indignant and amused at the old lady's artfulness. Only once did Emma suspect that the silence might be ominous, but then she reminded herself of such games previously played by old Mrs Denton for her son's punishment. 'God doesn't want you yet,' Emma told her through the ceiling, 'You're too much of a handful!'

The mantelpiece clock struck nine and there was still no sign of Gregory. When, of a sudden, the knocking and abusive shouts began emanating from upstairs once again,

Emma thought she'd go mad! Frantic, she threw her cloak about her shoulders and ran next door to Tilly Watson's house.

'Well o' course I'll come and keep an eye on the old 'un,' Tilly said on Emma's request. 'The bairn's not got a wink of sleep in him, an' my old fellow's gone off to one of them blessed meetings in the Thwaites pub near the Wharf.' On learning that Emma intended to go out in search of her husband who had been given bad news concerning his own livelihood, she added, 'I'll bet my last farthing that you'll find him in the pub along the Wharf an' all!' She added one more thing as Emma went on her way; it was a warning. 'You watch yourself down that Wharf at this time of night, luv. There's all manner of curious creatures roaming the streets in the dark hours!' That said, she gave a loud shiver, pulled the bairn into her shawl, wrapped the shawl tighter about her slim figure and disappeared into the Denton household, slamming the door shut with such panic that the sound echoed after Emma as she hurried away down Montague Street. Another sound rent the quiet evening also. It was the same banshee wail which had haunted Emma all day. 'Who's that? Who's banging the door? Answer me, you harlot!' rang out the offensive tones of Emma's mother-in-law.

Not certain whether Gregory might come home via Preston New Road or King Street, Emma made the decision to walk up King Street, along by Ainsworth Street and onto Eanam Wharf that way. If her uncle's news had hit him harder than even she imagined, Emma believed it might just be possible that he *had* sought refuge in a public house. Such a thing would be quite contradictory to Gregory's nature, Emma knew, but he had changed so much of late and had become so unpredictable that Emma thought Tilly Watson might just be right. At least, it was something to bear in mind.

Going straight to the Grady Mill along the Wharf, Emma noticed that there were no lights on at all – save for the cheery red glow from the night-watchman's brazier. 'Ow do, miss,' he called out, rubbing his hands together over the fire, before doffing his cap as Emma drew nearer. 'By! yer a brave 'un to be out on such a cold night, lass,' he said through a large, toothless mouth. Then, on seeing that Emma was not the usual type of female to be seen loitering in the shadows along the Wharf, he added in a more serious voice, 'T'ain't a safe place round these parts after dark, lass. Yon pubs won't be long afore they turn out, then there'll be drunks and ruffians stalking about. Best be off 'ome, miss . . . where it's safe.'

Emma thanked him for his concern, assuring him that she had no intention of staying out longer than was necessary. As she talked with the old fellow, she took off her mittens and warmed her frozen hands. 'But I'm looking for my husband,' she explained, while replacing her warmed mittens, fastening her bonnet tighter and drawing the cloak more snugly round her shoulders. 'You might know him . . . his name is Mr Gregory Denton, and he's the manager of this mill.' She inclined her head towards the big iron gates behind him.

'Oh aye!' came the reply, 'I knows Mr Denton right enough. But I ain't seen 'im, miss.' Here, he frowned hard and, rubbing his gloved fingers behind his ear as though scratching away a bothersome irritation, he went on, 'That's a shame about the closure, eh? . . . A right bloody shame! D'yer know, miss, there were folks as could a sworn by Mr

Crowther keepin' it open. But, like I telled 'em . . . when times is bad, we *all* on us get dragged into it! It don't matter if yer a rich powerful fella, or a broken down-and-out, 'cause if yer can't sell the goods, yer gets no brass. And if yer gets no brass . . . well, like I say, the world stops turnin' an' we're *all* on us affected.' He fell silent, slowly shaking his head from side to side and dropping it lower and lower until Emma could no longer see his face.

'Goodnight,' she said, hurrying away and wondering where to look next. The old night-watchman gave no reply, but shook his head all the more.

Coming out on to Penny Street, Emma paused beneath the gas lamp on the corner. She reached into the neck of her dress and withdrew the tiny, delicate watch that had been given to her by her papa. Then, holding it carefully between her finger and thumb, she raised it to the flickering light to see that the time was half-past nine. The public house which Tilly had referred to was further along Penny Street and so Emma immediately began making her way there.

'Hello, darlin' . . . looking for company are you?' The voice came out of one of the darkened doorways, causing Emma to hurriedly look away and quicken her footsteps towards the bright windows of the public house, where the accordian music wafted into the night air and the merry sound of singing voices promised a safer haven.

Not daring to set foot in such a place, Emma stood on tiptoe in order to look through the windows. Her vision was impaired by the frosted pattern on the glass and the large words which read 'Public Bar' on the first window and 'Snug' on the second. Peering through a small corner below, where there was an area of clear glass, Emma's view was still frustrated by the thick smoke screen and the wall of bodies inside. 'Where are you, Gregory?' she muttered through frozen lips, pressing her nose harder against the windowpane. Suddenly a cackle of laughter erupted from within and as Emma peered through the haze in search of her husband, the unmistakable figure of Sal Tanner rose before her. The next moment, the laughing figure was hoisted on to one of the tables by a bevy of reaching, grasping hands. The music took on a more urgent note and the hands all began clapping as Sal Tanner executed a frenzied dance -- showing her pink, grinning gums at one end and her pink, dimpled thighs at the other. The whole spectacle was that much more comical because of Sal's pronounced limp, which had the effect of throwing her off balance in a most peculiar yet rhythmic manner.

Dropping from her tiptoes, Emma moved away from the window to lean back against the wall, the cold air seeming to have penetrated every inch of her body. She knew the time must by now be approaching ten o'clock and some deeper instinct made her suspect that Gregory might have come to harm. 'He would *never* stay out till this hour without telling me where he was,' she muttered to herself, a part of her feeling desperate enough to go into the public house where she could at least satisfy herself as to whether or not he was there. Yet, there was an even greater urge within her to run from that place, and to get home safely. Before Emma could decide what to do for the best, the decision was abruptly taken out of her hands.

'Bloody hell! Look at this, lads! We've got the buggers queuing up at the door for us, eh?' If the voice was gruff, its owner was even more so. The burly, unshaven fellow all but fell out of the pub doorway on to the spying Emma who, on hearing the loud and drunken revellers emerge, had tried to wedge herself behind the large concrete mullion which surrounded the entrance. Unfortunately, she was quickly spotted by this burly fellow who, though he appeared to have the weight and size of an elephant, possessed the small beady eyes of a shrew. As his hand pounced on her shoulder and drew her out, Emma vehemently protested. At the sound of her voice, another of the group lurched forward to look at her. Emma was shocked to see who it was. 'Gregory!' she cried, shaking herself free from the big fellow's grasp and rushing forward. Her first sensation at seeing him was utter relief; her first thought was to get him home as quickly as possible. To this end, she began looking up and down the street for a carriage. 'I've been searching everywhere for you!' she told him, preparing to take his arm. As she smiled up at him, he stared down at her, a drunken frown on his face.

'See that, fellas?' shouted another of the group. 'His little wifey's come ter find 'im!' There followed tumultuous laughter and taunts of 'Aw! Did thi mammy lose yer, eh? The little woman wants ter tuck 'im in his little bed!'

'Shut it, you fools!' Not only were the men taken aback by Gregory Denton's acid tone, but so was Emma! Now he turned on her, and as he bent to deliver his instructions, the stench of booze on his breath was so powerful that it turned her stomach. 'Get off home!' he told her. 'I don't want you here . . . I don't need you to come looking for me like I was a bloody kid!' He gave a cruel laugh, saying, 'Oh, but happen you look on me as a kid, because you ain't got any of your *own*, eh?' His voice fell to a whisper, so low that only Emma could hear it and so vicious that it made her heart tremble. 'Oh, but it ain't been for want of trying. Oh no! But you see . . . I'm no good as a man, am I? If I

255

was, then you'd have been with child *months* ago! I ain't got the ability to make a bairn. And I ain't got the ability to keep my work. I'm no good either way. I'm useless, d'you see?' He lifted his hands to her shoulders and, to the delight of his cronies, he began shaking her.

'Stop it!' Emma was mortified by his words. But now she was even more determined to get him home, because to leave him in such a drunken state with such low company, was more abhorrent to her than was his verbal attack, which in her heart she knew was the drink talking. Emma had been horrified to discover that the very sentiments which had been going through her mind regarding their childless state, had been torturing her husband even more. He had been thinking it was due to his inadequacies as a man, while Emma had been equally convinced that it was her fault.

'Are yer coming with us, or are yer running off home like a good little lad?' Once again, the other men fell into uproarious laughter, whereupon Gregory shook Emma all the harder. 'I've told you,' he said, 'I don't need you following me, making me look even less of a bloody man! Take yourself off home.' That said, he turned to fall in with the others as they made their way along Penny Street to the next ale-house, all stumbling about in the same witless but merry state – all except one, for Gregory Denton was a bitter and sorry man, who saw the drink not as a friend, but as a means of forgetting his own shortcomings.

'I'm not going home without you!' Emma called out, pursuing them down the street. 'I won't!' Somehow, she felt responsible for him. Maybe it was because of the guilt she always carried for not being able to love him in the way a woman *should* love her husband.

Hearing Emma's cry, Gregory Denton came to a halt, turned sharply and, encouraged by the other revellers, came hurrying back towards her on fast, angry footsteps. At first, Emma was delighted because she thought he had decided to accompany her home after all. But on seeing how swiftly he came towards her and, as he drew nearer, realizing the thunderous expression on his usually kindly face, she halted in her tracks. As he came to within arms reach of her and the street lamp bathed his face in its trembling yellow glow, Emma was actually frightened to see the fury on Gregory's features. 'Will you not be bloody told!' he snapped, at the same time bringing the flat of his hand hard against her head with such a spiteful swing that it sent her reeling towards the wall. 'Now! Perhaps you'll do as I say!' he told her through clenched teeth and whereupon, hardly glancing back at her, he rejoined the others to quickly disappear down Penny Street, into Eanam and out of sight.

Dazed from the force of the blow to her head and desperately trying to stem the flow of blood from her nose, Emma leaned on the wall for support. Her thoughts were in turmoil and her heart was in shock. She would never have believed it possible that drink could change a man so much. Yet, as she recalled Gregory's every word, his every mood over these past weeks, Emma realized that it wasn't simply the drink that had changed him, it was fear, and, because she herself had known that same destructive emotion, she could perhaps understand at least a little of what he was going through. But whether she could *forgive* him for his treatment of her this night was something else. For now, however, she must make her way back to Montague Street, and leave Gregory to come home when he was ready.

Emma dabbed the blood-stained handkerchief to her face and seeing that the flow of blood had stopped, she found a corner in the cotton square with which she scrubbed her face clean. She then straightened the bonnet which had been knocked askew and, with her head throbbing painfully, she emerged on to the kerb from where she cast her gaze up and down the street. 'I must find a carriage,' she thought, beginning to walk along the narrow pavement. Feeling as ill as she did, Emma was sure she could not make the long trek back to Montague Street on foot. Furthermore, the night was pitch-dark and dismal, and Emma was mindful of the danger she could be in at this hour of the night and in this particular area. As she walked along, only once did her thoughts stray to forbidden territory, and that was when she felt briefly tempted to turn the corner into Eanam Wharf, where she suspected Marlow's barge might be moored. Quickly, and with a rush of guilt, she dismissed these thoughts, but, in doing so, she felt only sadness in her heart.

As Emma came towards the top of Penny Street, she was relieved to see a number of carriages crossing Ainsworth Street and beyond that the street lamps seemed brighter. But she was still a long way off yet and here, between one public house and the next, it was uncomfortably dark. Alarmed, she quickened her footsteps, at the same time becoming aware of the resounding tap-tap of her boot-heels, which rent the night air with a disturbing echo.

Emma was so intent on escaping the dark area of Penny Street that she did not hear the footsteps which crept stealthily up behind her. The moment they were on her, it was too late! Emma felt herself being swung round and even as she opened her mouth to scream, a hand was clapped roughly over her face, smothering the sound and striking a greater fear into Emma's heart than she had ever known before. She was propelled harshly against the wall and in the brief glimpse she caught of her attacker's face as he thrust her away from the glow of the gas lamp, Emma was horrified to see that it was the same unshaven burly fellow who had been in Gregory's company earlier and who had got such satisfaction out of the humiliation she'd been made to suffer.

'Oh what a little beauty you are!' he murmured in a low trembling voice as he pinned her against the wall with one hand, keeping her mouth covered with the other and bending his coarse face to brush against her neck. The more Emma struggled, the more excited he became by it and the harder she pummelled at him with her small clenched fists, the more it amused him. ''E's a fool, your man,' he muttered in a drunken breath, 'but if 'e don't want yer . . . I do!' Now, using the brute strength of his enormous body to pin her fast against the wall, he raised the hand which had been holding her and, with spiteful force, ripped the bonnet from her head and threw it contemptuously away, afterwards grabbing at the coil of hair so beautifully curled into the nape of Emma's slender neck. When her hair came tumbling freely about her shoulders, he began stroking it and frenziedly thrusting himself against her body, all the while moaning and clutching at her clothes as if he were about to tear every shred from her back. 'I won't hurt yer,' he murmured, wiping his open mouth up and down her neck until Emma feared she would die or lose her senses and be even more at his mercy. As it was, the hand across her face desperately impaired her breathing and she was growing weaker by the second. She had to get free. She *must* get free!

But how? Oh, dear God, how?

The moment came when, in his feverish excitement, the burly fellow relaxed his hold on her in order to take down his trousers. Though he still had her pinned fast with his chest and shoulders, Emma saw her chance and she took it. Summoning every remaining ounce of strength within her, she quickly twisted away, at the same time sinking her teeth into his shoulder. When with a growl he grabbed at her, a swift and furious struggle followed, during which his nails scored deep and bloody grooves down her neck and as she fled with her heart in her mouth, he whipped the cloak from her back before pursuing her relentlessly along the shadowy lamp-lit streets and across towards Eanam Wharf. Whatever Emma's misgivings about contacting Marlow, she had no choice now but to seek his help, for her assailant appeared to have been sobered by a more driving appetite, and his determined strides as he came after her were both longer and faster than her own.

'Dear God, help me!' she prayed, as, racked by pain and feeling her strength ebbing, her steps began to falter. As she rounded the corner into Eanam Wharf and saw the lights from two lone barges along the water, Emma's heart almost collapsed with relief. 'Marlow! Marlow!' she shouted repeatedly, fearful that he might not hear her cry. By now, her heart was pounding and feeling like a lead weight inside her. Her legs felt like rubber beneath her and the cold had bitten so deeply in through her dress, that every inch of her body was numb.

When there was no rush of help from either of the barges, Emma grew frantic, stumbling towards them, calling out Marlow's name and tears streaming down her face, blinding her.

Emma could hear her pursuer coming ever closer, until, in a minute he was on her and the two of them struggling dangerously close to the water's edge.

'Yer bloody wildcat!' the burly fellow shouted as he caught hold of her. 'But that's 'ow I likes my women!' he chuckled. When Emma bit him hard on the hand, his triumphant cry turned to cries of pain and anger. 'Sod yer eyes!' he yelled, slapping her about the face and shoulders. 'Ye'll not get the best o' me!'

In that moment when she began to lose consciousness, feeling that on this night she would surely die, Emma heard a dog frantically barking. She saw a running figure launch itself through the air towards her attacker and when the burly fellow saw it too, Emma felt herself being thrown aside as the two became locked in combat. When she lost her footing and the icy-cold water sucked her into its dark, quiet embrace, the last words on Emma's lips were a desperate prayer.

'Oh, Emma! Emma sweetheart . . . thank God!' Marlow's voice reached Emma through a haze, where, for a long, strangely peaceful time, she had felt as though she was floating – neither asleep nor awake, and not wanting to be either. Only when he slid his arms about her body and pressed her close to him, did she realize that the nightmare was over. She was alive! She was safe in the arms of the man she loved. For just a fleeting moment, nothing else mattered, and the rush of overwhelming happiness to her heart was more than Emma could bear.

'Marlow,' she murmured, the tears rolling down her face but her great love for him alive and burning bright in her eyes. But, suddenly, as everything became clear again in Emma's mind, the pain returned to her eyes. 'I must get home!' she told him, stiffening in his arms and drawing away.

When he spoke, Marlow's voice had also changed. It was not the soft endearing tone it had been; it was now quiet and sad, yet still filled with love and aching to utter those words which were so deeply etched on his heart. Instead, however, he chided her gently, 'What in God's name were you doing wandering about the Wharf this time of night?'

Softly, and not without some shame, Emma explained how Gregory had not come home and how she'd gone in search of him. She then described the sequence of events which followed.

'I heard that Crowther was having to close down,' replied Marlow in a serious voice, 'I can't say anybody's all that surprised, what with the way things are.' Here, he sat up stiff and straight as he went on angrily, 'All the same, that's no excuse for Denton to take it out on you! I ought to lift the bloody head from his shoulders!' He punched one clenched fist into the open palm of his other hand, 'You could have been killed because of him!'

'No, Marlow,' Emma could see he was so agitated that he was ready then and there to search out her husband. 'It's as much my fault as his. Just let me get home.' She began to draw herself up in the bunk, but the effort was great and seemed to charge her every limb with agony.

'Easy does it,' Marlow said, 'you've had too much of a rough and tumble to start gadding about afore you're properly rested.' Gently, he cupped his hands on her shoulders in order to ease her back against the pillow. It was when his rough, warm hands touched her bare flesh that Emma realized with horror that she was naked. Marlow was quick to see the alarm in her eyes as she tugged the over-blanket up, until all that could be seen above it were her two startled grey eyes.

'I'm sorry, Emma,' he said, his gaze growing darker the longer it fed on her beauty, 'you fell into the canal . . . though I don't suppose you remember.' Emma did. 'When I fished you out, you put the fear of God in me. Oh, Emma!' He paused, as though remembering it was too terrible. 'I thought you were drowned, Emma. God help me! There was nobody else to strip away your wet things. Sal's on one of her jaunts and won't likely be back till daylight.'

Still clutching the over-blanket beneath her chin, Emma self-consciously lowered her eyes from the dark intensity of his gaze, because, despite her desire to get away from here as quickly as possible, the warmth and unashamed passion in those troubled eyes together with the mere near-ness of Marlow and the way every part of her being trembled at the wonderful intimacy of this moment, created a fearful struggle inside Emma, so that she secretly prayed that this precious moment could go on forever. There was so much she wanted to say to him, so many heartfelt words she would have liked to confide to him. But something even stronger, an ingrained sense of right and wrong prevented her. Instead, she asked, 'And the man who chased me?'

At this, Marlow leaned backwards to rest his weight on the palms of his hands and, laughing aloud, he told her, 'The bigger they are, the more cowardly. Me and my old friend here,' he dropped a hand to stroke the dog's head, 'we saw the bugger off. One crunching blow from me, and a bite up the rear end from "fangs" here . . . well, he went up that Wharf like something demented!'

Picturing the whole scene, Emma burst into laughter. 'I'm glad!' she said. Then, more seriously, 'Oh, but Marlow, there can never be a way for me to thank you enough!'

'I just thank God I was there,' replied Marlow, rising from the edge of the bunk. 'Your clothes should be dry by now. I'll get them. But it's two o'clock of a morning, and I must insist on seeing you safely to your door.' His expression became more serious, as he added in a quieter voice, 'There are things I need to say to your husband as well.' When Emma pleaded with him to leave Gregory to her, he merely looked deeply into her uplifted eyes, saying, 'We shall see!'

When he returned with her clothes over his arm, the sight of Emma lying with her slender shoulders now exposed and her long chestnut tresses falling gently over them, caused such a storm in Marlow that he was moved to hitherto unknown depths of emotion. 'Oh, Emma! My darling Emma!' he murmured. Without taking his eyes off her, he draped the clothes over a chair and coming to kneel beside the bunk, he told her with tenderness, 'You said just now that there could never be a way for you to thank me. There *is*, Emma. One way.'

'Don't Marlow.' Emma was afraid of the feelings he was creating in her, disturbing, glorious feelings which took her breath away. Involuntarily, she reached out her hand from beneath the bedclothes and, when he grasped it tight within both of his fists, she made no move to withdraw it. In fact, she thought there had never been anyone in her life as dear to her as Marlow. Not even her papa, for that was a very different kind of love.

'I'm making arrangements to leave England,' he said quietly. 'I've talked it over long and deep with Sal. She won't come with me, so I'll send for her just as soon as ever I can. But you, Emma! Oh, you *must* come with me! Please, Emma . . . say you will?' The fear that she would refuse dulled the light in his eyes and the tension within him betrayed itself in the fierceness of his grip on Emma's small fist.

For a long, agonizing moment, the silence between them was unbearable. Emma desperately wanted to go with him. Indeed, she craved for nothing else and the thought of him leaving these shores and that she might never see him again, filled her lonely heart with dread. How she longed to cry out, 'Oh, yes, Marlow! Take me with you!' But she thought of her husband and the distress he was already suffering; she reached deep inside herself, down through the years, over every moral lesson she had learned from good people – from her papa, from Manny – and in her heart she could find only one answer. When she gave it, it broke her spirit to see how Marlow's head bowed low, and in a crushed voice he said, 'How will I live without you, Emma?'

'In the same way I must live without you,' she murmured, raising her hand to his dark, tousled head.

'No!' he exclaimed, clasping his hands about her shoulders, 'I won't *let* you refuse me!' With a small, stifled cry, he had her in his arms, kissing her hair, the deep scratches along her neck, all the while murmuring his love and creating chaos in Emma's overburdened heart.

'Don't Marlow . . . don't!' she cried, grabbing the blanket around her and struggling from the bunk. 'It's no good, you *know* that!' She was now crying as she fumbled helplessly with her clothes.

'I love you, Emma,' he said, coming to stand before her and, with his fingers, raising her face to look up at him. What

he saw in her eyes tore him in two. 'Come with me, sweetheart,' he said again, his magnificent dark eyes willing her
to say yes. 'Please . . . come with me.'

Emma became still, her gentle sobbing filling the air and
seeming to bring it alive all about them, like the softest heartbeat. She spoke not a word, not even when his hands began
to gently stroke her hair. Instead, she lifted her arms and
entwined them around his neck, letting the blanket slither
to the floor, showing him what was really in her heart and
how very much he meant to her.

As he bent towards her, his mouth eager to taste hers and
his hands following the curves of her nakedness, Emma was
helpless to resist the urges of her heart. As he gathered her
up into his arms and laid her tenderly on the bed, such a
wave of warm and wonderful emotions raged through
Emma that she was left trembling from head to toe. When,
in a moment, Marlow was stripped naked, she thought she
had never seen anything so beautiful as his strong, magnificent body; the upper part was broad and warmed by the
sun and his entire physique was sculptured to manly perfec-
tion by the laborious means of his livelihood. Yet, though
he was muscular and of splendid appearance, Emma sensed
a great tenderness and beauty of heart about Marlow
Tanner. She also sensed his enveloping love and need for
her, as strong and compelling as hers was for him.

'I love you in such a way that there are no words to tell
it,' Marlow told her now in the softest murmur, as he knelt
by the bed and gazed into her eyes.

Emma was so choked with emotion that she was unable
to say anything, although her answer was there in her
heart. Instead, she reached out her fingers to touch his
shoulder and when he came to lay beside her, the whole

of her being shuddered with pleasure at the warm shock of his nakedness. He began kissing her in such a way that made her cry out. His soft, moist lips took the taut nipple of her breast into his mouth, sending shockwaves into every corner of her body. Now he was seeking out those sensual areas of pleasure which Gregory had never found, and Emma was transported into rapturous and burning emotions, the like of which she had never known.

Marlow had lived and loved many times, as all healthy young bargees did. But with Emma it was different. She was that someone special; the one he had searched for; the only woman he would ever truly love. Yet, even now as he held her in his arms as intimately as any man might hold a woman, he knew that it was to be short-lived. How could he have this woman? How could he keep her for ever? His heart cried out and as he took Emma's soft yielding body into his, his desire was such that he craved not just her body, but her heart and soul as well. Dear God in Heaven, *must* he let her go? How could he bring himself to part from her, for she meant more to him than his own life.

In Marlow's arms, Emma found Paradise. Time and time again, she gave herself to him and together they blossomed with the beauty and pleasure which neither had found in any other's arms. Like two enchanted dancers, they clung to each other and moved and weaved in and around each other's bodies, finding ultimate pleasure and exquisite pain in the ecstasy which bound them together and which neither wanted to ever end.

But the beauty and wonder which held them fast was not merely physical. It was beyond that, for their very souls were merged. And when, at last, she lay quiet and exhausted in her lover's strong, protecting arms, Emma thought she had never felt so much at peace in the whole of her life. When Marlow found her softly crying, he laughed kindly, saying, 'Have I made you so unhappy, my darling?'

Emma wiped her eyes and smiled up at him. 'I love you so very much,' she said softly. It was a painful thing to say, for soon she would have to go – back to her life and her husband. Never again would she know such precious moments as she had experienced on this night. This had been their farewell, for she could not expect him to stay and neither could she go with him. Soon, Marlow would be far away and she may never see him again. This was her night – hers and Marlow's – and they must be forever thankful that it had given them a memory to last a lifetime. May God forgive them both.

Yet for all those guilty feelings which now plagued Emma, one persistent question tore at her heart: how could something as beautiful as she and Marlow shared be so terribly wrong?

Chapter Nine

Emma was pregnant! Night and day she had tormented herself with the knowledge that the child growing inside her had not been conceived in wedlock with her husband, but in a night of shame with Marlow Tanner. Yet, despite being beside herself with fear, Emma would not have missed a single exhilarating moment in Marlow's strong and loving arms. She had loved him ever since their very first meeting and throughout the endless time in between, he had never been far from her mind or her heart. During that last wonderful meeting, they had shared such tenderness, such harmony of body and spirit, such deep need for each other and such glorious love, that Emma knew she would never in the whole of her life experience its like again.

Now, on this cold February morning, Emma crept out from beside Gregory's sleeping form. Going across the room on tiptoe, she collected her slippers, took up the long fringed shawl from across the back of the chair and, wrapping it about her small, shivering shoulders, she grasped her long chestnut hair in one hand, drew it from beneath the shawl, and flicked it back so that it fell freely and magnificently down her back. As she silently left the room, which was already being penetrated by the growing daylight,

269

Emma took care not to make any noise, for she had no wish to disturb either her husband or her mother-in-law – at least not yet. She felt the need for a moment or two on her own before the house was properly awake.

Downstairs, Emma put on her slippers and quickly opened the curtains, but the light was not yet sufficient to brighten the parlour, so she took a match from the tray on the sideboard, struck it alight and put the flickering flame to the candlewick. Lifting the brass candle-holder and moving towards the fireplace, she placed it up on the mantelpiece. Then, she set about emptying the dead ashes from the grate and making a small fire. When she saw it crackling cheerfully, she filled the kettle and wedged it into the coals. Already, the day ahead seemed that much brighter, for Emma thought there was nothing more peaceful than sitting in a quiet room, watching the spitting, dancing flames of a coalfire and sipping a cup of tea held snugly between one's hands. Times like this were becoming increasingly rare. On the odd occasion when she was fortunate enough to steal such precious moments for herself, Emma would use them to the full, contemplating what the future might hold.

Having prepared her cup with a small helping of tea, Emma placed it in the hearth and, while the kettle boiled, she wandered to the sideboard where she peered into the mirror, looking at herself intently, once again astonished at how she had changed in the year since coming to live in this house as Gregory's wife. The small elfin structure of her face had not changed, for her cheekbones were still high and prominent, her forehead still wide and her mouth set full and rich above a firm rounded chin. Her thick chestnut hair fell, as always, from a centre parting into a rich wavy pattern which spilled over her shoulders and way down her back; but now, it was very much longer. None of these features had changed too much – although they were perhaps more pronounced and more mature. But her eyes! Those magnificent grey eyes – which, in moments of stress or pensive mood, were streaked with black, making them darker and more mysterious – had changed above all her other features. In their peaceful beauty, they appeared even more brilliant as her emotions were cleverly hidden beneath. In anger, the emotions would surface, striking astonishment in the beholder; the greyness would darken to ebony and their beauty seem fathomless. Through her eyes, Emma saw and felt everything. They were the filter of her soul, the mirror of all she suffered and, at the height of their splendour, they had the power to hold a person mesmerized. Yet, they had also become secretly scared and at times, the light in them would grow dim as Emma's deepest emotions and most-treasured memories surfaced.

'Oh, Emma Denton!' she now reproached the image in the mirror. 'You had your time with Marlow . . . you both clutched at what small happiness you could and it was a memory to cherish for ever. But now . . . oh, now Emma, your secret will find a way out. In a short time, your condition will surely become evident to all and Gregory will know that the child couldn't possibly be his!' The thought made her tremble. Gregory was no fool. Even before she had become pregnant by Marlow, her husband's urges to take her to himself in their marital bed had greatly diminished. Since being deprived of work, he seemed at times to be so altered in personality that he frightened her. Emma was now haunted by how he would react when he knew that the wife, who seemed destined not to bear *his* child, was pregnant by another man.

Emma shivered loudly as she turned her attention to brewing the tea. There was no escaping the fact that Gregory would know soon and, in all truth, she would rather confess the whole thing than wait for the horror of it to suddenly dawn on him. But how could she tell him? Dear God above, she thought fearfully, how can I bring myself to tell him such a thing! Yet, however daunting the prospect seemed, Emma told herself that she had no alternative. Of late, the child had begun to move inside her and, though it warmed her heart to feel Marlow's flesh and blood mingling with her own, it also struck the fear of God in her!

'Why the hell didn't you wake me?' It was eight a.m. when Gregory rushed into the parlour, his braces dangling over his hips, and his chin bristling with sandy-coloured hair-stubble. 'I must be on that quarry site bright and early if I'm to make a good impression.' Quickly he dashed about, dressing, shaving, washing and rushing down the eggs and bacon which Emma had prepared. 'Get me a shilling or two from the jar,' he told Emma between mouthfuls. 'There's the tram fare . . . and, like as not I'll need something for a bite to eat, because if I get work I'll start right away.' Emma was pleased to see him so enthusiastic. It was said that the work in the quarries was hard and demanding, but it was the only prospect which had come up these past weeks. As she took two silver shillings from the earthenware jar in the cupboard, Emma gave thanks that they were still better off than most folk. With the small amount of money carefully put by when Gregory was in work, together with the proceeds from her various bits of jewellery, they were not yet in danger of starving.

Emma often asked herself what she would do if circumstances *were* ever to become that desperate. Two things she knew for certain: she would *never* go cap in hand to the Crowthers – nor would Gregory ever allow such a thing – neither would she ever pawn the little watch entrusted to her by her papa. Indeed, as though to put it out of the way of temptation altogether, Emma had slit a tiny pocket in the inner collar of one of her best boots. She had wedged the delicate watch inside and there it had remained. So small and inconspicuous was it, that its presence went undetected even when she wore the boots to church on Sundays. In fact, if Emma didn't now and again take a private peep at it, she might never even know it was there.

At the door, Gregory snatched his coat from its hook, shrugged himself impatiently into it and, without even a backward glance at Emma, he said, 'I pray to God he finds me a man's work on this day!' As she closed the door after him and the freezing February morning, Emma prayed also. 'If he gets work,' she murmured, 'he'll get his purpose back, and life might become that much easier.' She daren't also ask the Lord for an easy way to tell Gregory of the child. Not now, for she remembered Mrs Manfred's teaching that, if she dared to ask for too much, she might end up with nothing.

Quickly, before old Mrs Denton started banging her stick on the floor and shaking the ceiling, Emma cleared away the breakfast things and refilled the kettle. While the water was heating, she tiptoed back upstairs and brought down her undergarments, petticoat and a full-skirted soft green dress of serviceable cotton, which had a high white collar, fluted hem and bib front. She also brought her dark stockings and lace-up black shoes with small square heels. When the water was boiled, she filled the bowl from the scullery, stripped herself naked and, in the warm glow from the fireplace, she washed from top to toe. It alarmed Emma to see how evident the rise of her abdomen was becoming and, there and then, she decided that come what may, she must confess all to Gregory within the next few days – placing herself and her unborn child at his mercy. It was not a pleasant thought and, having decided on the only course of action left open to her, she put it deliberately out of her mind.

No sooner was Emma washed, dressed and ready to face another day, than the rhythmic, insistent banging began, accompanied by the loud harsh voice of old Mrs Denton. Emma was thankful when, as though summoned, Tilly Watson called through the letter-box just as the mantelpiece clock struck half-past eight.

'By!' she exclaimed as Emma let her in. 'It's bloody freezing! I've left the lad in bed a while, 'cause he was deep in the land of slumber and it seemed a pity to disturb him.' Inclining her head sideways, she cocked a cheeky grin towards the source of the increasing volume of noise coming from above. The sight of the small brass candelabra swinging to the tune of old Mrs Denton's stick upon the floor, set her off in a peal of laughter. 'Old sod!' she cried above the racket. 'She's got more strength than all the rest of us put together.'

Emma also couldn't help but laugh. 'That's true,' she agreed, 'and I believe she'll be the death of us too . . . if we let her.'

'It'll be the death of me!' wailed Agnes Crowther, one hand

gripping the frilly lace handkerchief with which she dabbed at her puffy eyes and the other clutching her daughter's arm, as though without the support of it she might fall in a faint at her husband's feet.

'Nonsense, woman!' Caleb Crowther cried, impatiently shunting his clenched fist back and forth along the mantel-piece. Clearly made more agitated by his wife's reaction to what he had just told her, he stared hard at his daughter, Martha, saying in a clipped tone, 'Leave us! Leave the room!'

'I'd rather stay with Mama, if you don't mind,' came the pertinent reply, 'it's all come as such a shock to her.'

'I told you to leave!' Caleb Crowther thundered, looking impatiently at his wife when she began shaking and crying anew. 'As a matter of fact, Martha, please take your son and return to your *own* home! I understand your husband is due back any day. *He* is your concern – not us! I'll thank you to remember that this is *my* house. You have been made welcome here many times since your marriage. Not once, when your husband has seen fit to sail the seven seas, have you been turned away by either myself or your mama.' Here, his expression darkened and, coming forward a pace or two, he looked her straight in the eye, 'Now . . . I'm asking you to leave. Please do so, at once!'

One look at her papa's twitching features warned Martha Crowther to do exactly as she was instructed. Removing her hard round eyes from his face, she gave a kindlier look to her mama, kissed her on the forehead and said, 'If you need me, please send Thomas and I'll be here straight-away.'

'She won't need you,' Caleb Crowther interrupted and when, without further argument, Martha flounced from the room, he gave a small, unpleasant smile. Then, taking his wife by the arm, he led her to a nearby chair where, with small ceremony, he sat her in it. 'The plain fact is, my dear, we must preserve what funds we still have. I'm sure you . . . like myself . . . have no wish to leave Breckleton House. But unless we budget very carefully, there may well be no alternative.'

'Oh, dear me!' Agnes Crowther wrapped the fine lace handkerchief round the tip of her nose and blew delicately into it. 'How will I ever manage without a housekeeper? And with only one maid?' She found the prospect horrifying.

'Come now, woman.' He began to grow impatient at her whining. 'You'll still have Cook, and with a maid to see to all the menial tasks, it won't really be that bad!'

'But the housekeeper. Oh, I just wouldn't know where to start.' It seemed there was no consoling her. 'I know the mills are closed, Caleb, and perhaps I have been a little too extravagant at times, but I *will* try. I really will!'

'You'll do more than try, my dear,' he told her with a surly look. 'In fact, you won't get a *farthing* from me before I've seen for myself exactly where it is going.'

'Is all this frugality really necessary? Aren't you panicking just a little?' Uppermost in her mind were the cruel, humiliating things people would say.

But, Caleb Crowther was not prepared to discuss the matter any further. He could have pointed out that the bank had foreclosed on the mills. He could have explained how even Breckleton House itself might be in danger if they did not immediately, and drastically, cut down on expenditure. And, not by any stretch of the imagination, could he see the financial returns from his judicial office as being sufficient to keep either a full stable or a full staff – certainly not if he was to continue enjoying life's other little pleasures. Things were desperate! *He* was desperate! And, though in one or two low moments he had briefly thought about how he had squandered Thadius Grady's legacy to Emma, Caleb Crowther's pity and regret was reserved only for his own fate. It was *his* well-being that was ever paramount in his mind – not Emma's, not even his own wife's. It was his own escape from the walls of deprivation which were closing in on him, more and more, that concerned him most.

Even in the midst of his selfishness and greed and his determined fight for survival, Caleb Crowther knew that the day of reckoning with Emma would come eventually, for, even though he hated to admit it, the woman had spirit. She was still young, but she had a strong character. The day would come when she would expect him to hand over that which Thadius had left to her. If he remembered rightly, that particular day of reckoning would come on her twenty-fifth birthday.

Here, Caleb Crowther chuckled. 'Hhm,' he told himself, 'by that time every penny due her will be long gone.' And, he thought, with the grace of either God or the devil, so would she! Who knows what dreadful *accident* might befall a young woman before she reaches her twenty-fifth birthday.

The thought gave him a great deal of pleasure as he turned it over and over in his mind. The more he dwelt on it, the more his evil smile deepened, until, feeling benevolent towards his weeping wife, he said, 'If it will help, you may keep Martha here with you for a further week or so while I'm away about my legal duties. She can perhaps give you a hand about the place, once Mrs Manfred and the upstairs maid have departed.' If he thought that might cheer her he was mistaken, for his wife suddenly got to her feet and in a sullen mood she told him, '*You'll* be all right! Staying in the best inns and being waited on hand and foot! Really, Caleb, you have no idea how difficult it will be here without Mrs Manfred!'

'Then you must learn to cope, my dear,' came the stiff reply, 'for I intend to terminate her employment this very evening.' Turning his back on her, he instructed curtly, 'Be so kind as to send her in on your way out.'

'But where will you *go*, Manny?' Emma called from the scullery. She was horrified at her old friend's bad news. It had hardly occurred to her that the present hard times, which had befallen so many of Lancashire's working population, could ever seriously affect those who seemed too high up for the present tide of need to lap about their ankles. Even in the face of Mrs Manfred's news this evening, Emma was convinced that her dismissal had less to do with any financial hardship on Caleb Crowther's part and more to do with his dislike of her. He had never made any secret of that dislike and, when Emma put it to her now, Mrs Manfred made it quite clear that the feeling between her and Caleb Crowther was mutual.

'He's not a good man,' she told Emma, pausing for a while as her mind was beset by images which would not go away. Images of Emma's papa, lying in his sick-bed and crying out to hold his beloved child. Images of the way in which he had departed this world – with his cries suddenly stifled and Caleb Crowther standing over the bed with the most evil look on his face that she had ever witnessed. 'No, he was never a good man and it may be that he has good reason to hate me.' Dropping her voice to a whisper, she added, 'or, even to *fear* me!'

'What was that, Manny?' Emma came rushing in from the scullery with a tray of sandwiches and a pot of tea. She had not quite heard that last remark and half expected it to be repeated. When it was not, she put the tray down on the sideboard and passed her visitor a freshly brewed, and much welcomed, cup of tea. 'Help yourself to sandwiches, Manny,' she said, the concern she felt at the older woman's predicament still evident in her voice. 'Oh, Manny, if only I could have you here . . . to stay with us.' But Emma knew only too well that neither Gregory nor his mother would ever condone such a thing.

'Not at all, child!' Mrs Manfred was at once alerted to Emma's distress. 'I have my plans already made,' she said with a kindly smile, 'and Mr Crowther gave me four weeks' severance pay. If you ask me, the owners are also finding this depression most uncomfortable . . . though they'll allus have a guinea or two tucked away, no doubt. Even Mr Trent has had to sell off a number of his ships. Apparently, he's been hit bad, what with the blockades on American ports. It's the transportation of convicts to Australia that keeps his business from floundering, so they say. It's all a sorry state of affairs, and no mistake! But I have a lot to be grateful for, child, when I think of the soup queues, the bulging pawnshops and the faces of starvation and misery I've seen.'

'Oh I know, Manny, I know.' Emma had also witnessed these things. 'But where will you go? Oh Manny, I couldn't bear it if I never saw you again!' Through all the bad times, Manny had been like a rock of support to Emma and the thought that she might be gone from her for good was too painful for Emma to contemplate.

'I shall travel down south, to Luton,' she told Emma. 'You remember, I have an older sister there?' When Emma nodded, vaguely recalling Mrs Manfred's mention of such a relative, the older woman continued, 'But I shan't stay, oh no! We're very fond of each other, d'you see . . . but we've never been the sort to live in each other's pockets. No, I shall likely stay a week or two, then I'll make my way back to settle in these parts. There's allus plenty of work for women who don't mind a bit of skivvying and I've done enough of that in my time. Happen I'll secure a position in one of the bigger places along Preston New Road or up by the park. We shall see.' While she had been talking, Mrs Manfred had grown increasingly aware of how pale and troubled Emma looked. Somehow, she wasn't convinced that it was altogether her own predicament that was at issue here. She ventured to ask, 'There's something else on your mind, child, isn't there?'

Ever since Mrs Manfred had arrived, Emma had been deeply tempted to confide in her the secret she was carrying. In fact, although Emma was as certain as she could be that she was with child, she knew very little of these things and would have welcomed Mrs Manfred's advice. But, when she had seen that she wasn't the only one with problems, she hadn't the heart to pour out her troubles. 'What makes you ask that?' she queried her caring friend now.

'Oh, child, I've known you since you were this high.' She lifted her hand to signify a height no more than three feet. 'D'you think I don't know when there's something preying on your mind?' She brought her hand up to pat Emma's knee and with her soft, devoted eyes bathing

Emma's face, she coaxed, 'You'll have to tell me, y'know, because I won't go until you do.' When Emma made no reply and just dropped her eyes to the floor, Mrs Manfred said nothing. Instead, she let her gaze wander over Emma's countenance more closely. She saw the pinched white face full of anxiety; she saw how Emma's hitherto small breasts appeared somewhat fuller beneath the bib of her dress; she noticed that Emma's waist was not as reed-thin as it had been and there was a gentle rise beginning to show below it, which perhaps only a woman might perceive. Yet if, as Mrs Manfred suspected, Emma was at long last with child, why should it make her so unhappy? She could have sworn it was what Emma wanted. All the same, she mustn't force matters, because no good ever came of such a thing. If Emma wanted her to know, she'd confide in her in her own good time. What she did say, however, as she patted Emma's hand more vigorously, was, 'If you'd rather I didn't pry, then of course I won't. But, there's an old adage that a troubled shared is a trouble halved. And if you need me, I'll never be that far away from you.' Her voice was soft and her homely face a great comfort to Emma, who lifted her eyes to meet her old friend's anxious gaze as she went on, 'I mean it. Whatever it is that worries you so, well, it can't really be so bad now, can it, eh?'

For a long time there was such a deep, undisturbed silence between them that Mrs Manfred suspected Emma might not have heard a word she'd said. Presently, she got up from the chair. 'I'll just take the tray out for you,' she told Emma, thinking it might be best to potter about and give Emma a few quiet moments to herself. But she was worried, very worried, and did not really want to abandon Emma in such a strange, quiet mood.

281

'No, Manny! Please . . . sit down.' Emma had made up her mind. She would tell Manny everything, for who else could she turn to?

Without a word, the older woman resumed her seat and, before her resolve disappeared, Emma told her everything. She explained how things between her and Gregory had gone from bad to worse since he'd lost his work. She spoke of her deep abiding love for Marlow and of how she had kept a great distance between them, remaining as dutiful and loyal to her husband as any wife could be. She told of how he'd grown cold and distant, blaming himself for their childless state and for the loss of his livelihood, and of how he had turned to drink in his most depressed moments. She explained the impossibility of ever creating a relationship with his mother who 'hates me beyond reason, Manny.' And, finally, with the tears by now falling helplessly down her face, Emma gave an account of the night when Gregory hadn't come home. She held nothing back and, in a whisper, she finished, 'I'm sure I'm with child, Manny. Not Gregory's child . . . but Marlow's.'

'Lord above!' Mrs Manfred was shocked at the series of events just related to her, but even as the seriousness of the situation dawned on her, her only thoughts were for Emma. The very idea of condemnation never even entered her mind. 'Does Gregory suspect?' was her first question.

'I don't think so, Manny . . . not yet.' But Emma knew it was only a matter of time.

'And Marlow?'

Emma wiped the tears from her face with the back of her hand, her voice firm and determined as she replied, 'Marlow doesn't know. And he never will. He's gone.'

'Gone where?'

'Sailed away to foreign parts.' Now, fully composed and feeling better having confided her secret worries to another person, Emma continued, 'Gregory has to be told the truth, Manny. You see, when he discovers that I'm with child he'll *know* it isn't his. For a long time now ... since befo Marlow and I ... well, you see, Manny ... Gregory didn ... he ...' Emma couldn't go on.

'All right, child. It's all right. I understand.' Mrs Manfred leaned forward and lifting both of Emma's small hands into her own, she quietly agreed. 'You're right. There is no other way as far as I can see, but to put yourself and the unborn child at your husband's mercy. Oh, but Gregory's a good kind man, even in spite of his present distress. You told me earlier that he'd gone off to look for work in the quarries. Well, he's not back yet, is he?' she said optimistically, glancing up at the clock and pointing out to Emma that, as it was already well into the day and he hadn't returned, that might just mean that he'd been successful. 'You'll see. Come tea-time, he'll breeze in through that door with a smile on his face and secure work at last!' She prayed it was so, for it would take a special man to accept not only that his wife had sought refuge in another man's arms, but that she was also carrying that man's child; and he wouldn't even be able to get the satisfaction of leathering the fellow concerned, because by now he was in a far-off country.

In her heart, Emma wasn't convinced by Mrs Manfred's words, though she knew that the darling woman meant well. And, even though she had already decided that Gregory would have to be told, it wasn't a prospect she was looking forward to. Mrs Manfred didn't know how wrong she was about Gregory. Oh yes, he *had* been a 'good and kind man', but that was so long ago now that Emma could barely remember it. These days he was morose and silent. He was unloving and bitter, for he had lost all that he revered most: he had lost his work, his dignity and, above all, his belief in himself as a man – and it was that in particular which made Emma most fearful of his reaction to her confession. Just thinking how she might even *begin* to tell him left Emma trembling, so much so that she said now, 'Perhaps it might be better if I'd done as Marlow wanted, and gone with him!'

'Never!' The mere suggestion of compounding what she believed to be a sin of the worst kind, was unthinkable to a woman of Mrs Manfred's strict moral beliefs and, much as she adored Emma, she was convinced that there was only *one* course of action. 'How can you even think of such a thing, child?' she demanded. 'What you two did was wrong enough, without seeking to make matters worse!'

There was little left to say; it was now just a matter of confessing to Gregory. At Emma's request, Mrs Manfred agreed to stay over for one night. 'But this is purely between you and your husband, and, of course, he must agree to my staying. There's an early train out on the morrow and, once matters are resolved between you and Gregory, I'll be on my way.' Her fondness for Emma shone in her small brown eyes, as she assured her, 'I'm only staying just so you know I'm near. Beyond that, it's really no business of anyone's but yours and Gregory's.' She did not want to intrude in their private affairs, but, when Emma had asked her to delay her departure until the morrow, how could she refuse her?

'Thank you, Manny.' Emma was grateful all the same. What she had to do wouldn't be such a lonely thing with Manny so close by. 'I can't make your sleeping arrangements too comfortable, though,' she apologized, 'because the back bedroom still hasn't got a bed in it. I think there's a small spare bed in the loft, so perhaps when Gregory comes in . . .'

'You'll neither of you put yourself out for me!' interrupted Mrs Manfred. 'I'll be quite cozy snuggled up in this here armchair, afront of a small cheery fire.' As Emma began to protest, she put up a halting hand. 'That's settled!' she said. 'I've put up with far worse in my time!' When Emma smiled, she smiled back and soon they were both laughing. To Emma, it felt wonderful. Thank God for friends such as Manny.

At five p.m. Tilly Watson came round to see old Mrs Denton, leaving Emma and her visitor to enjoy her little lad's antics. First of all she took up a tray prepared by Emma and then she carried up the bowl and toiletries with which to wash the old woman. 'I've never known such fuss in all me born days!' she cried in exasperation when, finally, she brought down the soiled linen. 'She gets more and more cantankerous! It took me ten full minutes to get her to use that blessed bedpan. She's more of a baby than that little fellow there!'

'I don't know what she'd do without you, Tilly,' Emma said affectionately, 'she doesn't deserve you.'

'Aye, well, I get paid for me troubles,' came the twinkling reminder, 'though if your fellow don't get work soon, happen even *that* won't go on, eh?'

Emma smiled, saying, 'Well, she won't let anybody else within an inch of her, Tilly, so I don't know what would happen in that event.' All the same, thought Emma, Tilly wasn't far from the truth.

On her way out, Tilly remarked in an intimate manner,

'Between you and me, that old fox has a big tin box underneath her bed, and she screams blue murder if I even touch it with me toe. I wouldn't mind betting it's stuffed full o' banknotes!' Whereupon they all laughed, but none of them would have been surprised to discover that Tilly was right! Mrs Manfred believed it to be of small consequence, since Emma was secure financially because of her marriage settlement and Emma gave her no reason to think otherwise. Emma wondered whether Gregory suspected old Mrs Denton might be hiding a sizeable nest-egg. Still, they were not desperate yet and whatever old Mrs Denton had or didn't have, she considered to be none of her business.

On the stroke of six, Gregory burst in through the door, his face brighter than Emma had seen it in a long time and he actually rushed forward to grab her by the waist and swing her round. 'They took me on!' he shouted jubilantly. 'The buggers took me on!'

'Oh, Gregory!' Emma was overjoyed at his good news. 'That's wonderful!' The thought that perhaps her ordeal might not prove to be as fearful as she'd anticipated, fleetingly crossed her mind. Oh, but there was time enough for that later, when he had washed and eaten and they were in the privacy of their bedroom. Somehow, the knowledge that Mrs Manfred would be downstairs made Emma feel much braver and this seemed the perfect moment to raise that particular matter. 'Gregory,' she said, adjusting her dress which, in his exuberance, Gregory had made uncomfortably tight across her middle, 'Manny's come to visit.'

'Oh, goodness!' He followed Emma's smiling eyes to where Mrs Manfred sat. 'Forgive me,' he said, going towards her, 'I didn't even see you there.' Mrs Manfred told him that her employment with the Crowthers had been terminated, and he offered his sympathy. 'Oh, I'm really sorry to hear that, Mrs Manfred,' he said, with such polite and genuine concern that Mrs Manfred wondered how Emma could possibly describe him as a changed man. In fact, when Emma explained how she had invited Manny to stay the night and delay her departure until the morning, he made no objection whatsoever. 'There's a narrow bed up in the loft,' he said, 'I'll bring it down and set it together in the back bedroom before I go out.'

'Before you go out?' Emma was already on her way to collect his meal from the oven, when his words pulled her up short.

'It's grand, Emma,' he said, seeming to her more like his old self than he'd been for a long time. 'Look at that! He pointed first to the clay on his boots, then to the clay beneath his fingernails. 'I've got work again! Work! I can hold my head up alongside *any* man, at long last. I feel proud . . . proud to be fetching home a wage!'

'But you're surely not going out without a hot meal inside you?'

'My stomach's that excited, it would just churn over at the sight of any food. No! I shall get myself washed and changed, give the old 'un the good news, get that narrow bed down . . . then I'm off to spread a bit of cheer and hope in the alehouse. I've been drowning my sorrows far too long, Emma, now, I've some celebrating to do!'

In less than an hour, he was gone. He didn't kiss Emma goodbye in the manner of old, before hard times had come on them; neither did he walk out with a surly face and without a word, as he had done of late. Instead, he smiled, waved his hand and, before he turned away from Emma at the door, leaned forward to murmur in her ear, 'It seems our luck is changing, eh? Happen other things will fall into place as well. We shall see . . . we shall see. Expect me home afore eleven.' Emma was left in no doubt as to what he meant, though, before such intimate relationships could be resumed, he must be made aware of the situation. If there was any kind of a choice, Emma would have taken it, but there was not, and the issue must be faced head on. It was the only way.

'I'm surprised he'd choose to go off drinking,' remarked Mrs Manfred with concern in her voice. 'I never took him to be a drinking man . . . though I can understand how he turned to it in his worst hours. Still an' all, I should have thought he'd want to celebrate his good news here, in his own home, with you.'

Before Emma could voice her own concern and as though she had heard Mrs Manfred's words, another voice pierced the air as that dreaded rhythmic knocking began to shake the ceiling. 'If my lad's gotten a taste for the drinking, Emma Grady, it's on account of *you* . . . you'll pay for your sins, you'll see! The Lord punishes the wicked in his own way!'

Being used to such abuse, Emma paid no attention, but Mrs Manfred was appalled. 'For two pins I'd go up there and give her a piece of my mind! she declared, her face uplifted and her eyes glittering. 'You let her get away with too much, my girl!'

Seeing her old friend seething with indignation and listening to that voice from above still screaming out its vile abuse, Emma couldn't help seeing the humorous side of things. 'Oh, Manny!' she laughed. 'Do you really think I dare let the two of you at each other's throats? Like as not, you'd have the whole street out!' Whereupon, the stiffness in her old friend's face melted away and the homely features began crinkling into a smile. It only took Emma to begin gently giggling and the two of them collapsed into fits of laughter.

'Oh, ssh, child!' came the broken warning, as Mrs Manfred composed herself. 'Or she'll be down them blessed stairs and laying that stick of hers about both our shoulders!'

Smothering the laughter which insisted on bubbling up inside her at the comical image presented by Mrs Manfred's words, Emma promptly offered to brew up a fresh pot of tea. Then she asked, 'Perhaps you'll cast an expert eye over my sewing, Manny, and tell me where I'm going wrong?' Emma despaired of ever being truly able to master the art. In fact, since her marriage to Gregory, Emma had had many regrets regarding her limited experience in domestic matters, for every new task she had to learn seemed like a milestone which, without Mrs Manfred's constant help, she would never achieve.

'Of course, child. It'll be grand, eh? You and me aside o' the fire and spending a cozy evening together,' came the smiling remark. 'I can't think of anything more lovely.' And Emma agreed – unless it was an evening spent in Marlow's adoring arms!

When eleven o'clock came and went, Mrs Manfred made the announcement that, try as she might, 'I just can't stay awake another minute.' Emma lit her a candle and led the way upstairs to the back bedroom. 'Sleep tight, Manny,' she said, lighting the dresser-candle from her own and feeling the bed sheets to ensure they were not damp to the touch.

At the door, she turned to receive a peck on the cheek and the warning, 'I don't know if it is wise to tell Gregory the way of things . . . not at such a late hour and when he's only just returned from a public bar.'

The very same thought had occurred to Emma. 'Don't worry, Manny,' she said with a wry smile, 'bad news can always wait. At least till morning.' After which she went quietly back downstairs, tidied away the crockery, washed up, put a little more coke on the fire and settled down in the chair to wait.

When the clock struck midnight and still there was no sign of Gregory, Emma told herself she might just as well go upstairs to bed. 'Like as not he's gone off to some fellow's house, till the early hours,' she murmured into the half-darkness. Anyway, she decided, there was nothing to be gained by staying down in the parlour. So, placing the mesh guard in front of the fire, she took up the candlestick from the sideboard, clutched a handful of skirt to lift up the hem of her dress and slowly, all the while listening for footsteps at the door, she mounted the stairs.

Judging by the loud and rhythmic breathing sounds as she passed first Mrs Manfred's room, then old Mrs Denton's, it seemed they were both deep in slumber. As she closed her own bedroom door behind her, there was a strange and eerie moment when Emma felt utterly alone in the world. So real did it seem that, for a while, she felt panic-stricken and began trembling. But, reminding herself that this upper room was always chilly, Emma shrugged her shoulders, put the candle down on the stool and started to undress.

Of a sudden, there was a scuffling and rattling at the front door, with the sound of Gregory's voice rising muffled through the letter-box. 'Open the door, yer buggers. I've lost my key!'

Quickly, Emma flung her shawl about her shoulders and was halfway down the first short flight of stairs when the sound of the front door being flung open to crash loudly against the passage wall rocked the house. 'The buggers were in my pocket all the time!' came Gregory's jubilant shout and it sounded even stranger from drink than Emma could ever remember.

'Who's that? Gregory! Where's my son?' Emma winced as old Mrs Denton's angry voice sailed through the house.

'It's all right,' she called out, 'it's nothing to worry about. Go back to sleep.'

'Who are *you* to tell *me* what to do, you little trollop!' came the indignant retort. 'Where's Gregory? Gregory!' she called even more loudly.

As Emma carried on down the stairs and along the landing, the back bedroom door opened and a tumbled grey head peered out. 'Is everything all right, child?' asked Mrs Manfred.

'Yes, it's only Gregory . . . thought he'd lost his front door key,' replied Emma in a whisper. 'Goodnight, Manny. You'd best get back to sleep if you want to be up bright and early,' she reminded her.

'All right, lass. Goodnight, God bless.' As she disappeared back into her room, Mrs Manfred's thoughts were troubled. She'd had no idea what Emma had to put up with, and, although it went against everything in her upbringing, she half wished that Marlow *had* taken Emma with him. There was a bad situation here. But, deep down, Mrs Manfred believed that Emma would cope. She'll make the best of a bad job, she told herself, the lass always does.

From the top of the stairs, Emma peered down, holding the candle out at arm's length. 'Are you all right, Gregory?' she asked in a loud whisper.

'Course I'm all right, sweetheart,' he began stumbling up the stairs. 'Never felt better in all my life! There were two other fellows tekken on at the quarries today. By! We've done some bloody celebrating!'

'I can see that.' Emma hated to see a man so affected by drink. 'Be quiet as you come up. You've wakened your mother.' She wondered how in God's name he'd be fit to go to work the following day. It was likely he'd end up losing the job which was the very cause for his celebration.

'Don't you worry about the old bugger!' came the retort, as he fell up the last few steps. 'I'll have a word with her.' As he mounted the top tread and came on to the landing, he grabbed hold of Emma to stop himself from reeling backwards down the stairs. 'I think I'm drunk,' he chuckled, his breath fanning out over Emma's face and turning her stomach. 'Hey, look at you, you little vixen!' he said with delight, on seeing that Emma had removed her dress and beneath the shawl her shoulders were bare. 'Oho! Waiting for me, were you?' he asked, roving his hand over her upper arm and leaning forward as though he might kiss her. 'You be a good girl and get the bed warm, eh?' he said with a sly wink. 'I'll just look in on the old 'un . . . see she gets off to sleep, eh?'

Without a word, Emma turned to leave him groping along the landing towards old Mrs Denton's room. The touch of his hand on her naked skin had seemed somehow revolting to her. She would go to bed, feign sleep and hope to God that her drunken husband would be so exhausted by the time he got into bed, that the idea so evidently uppermost in his mind would come to nothing!

Lying in the dark, Emma heard every sound Gregory made, his movements so exaggerated and clumsy that they drove all tiredness from her, replacing it with such nervous panic that her heart seemed to be turning somersaults of its own accord. As he lumbered into the room, it became apparent to Emma that since that glorious night spent in Marlow's arms, when the child now moving inside her was created, no other being but herself had cast eyes on her nakedness. Somehow, despite the fact that she had a husband, it seemed right to Emma that this was so. The thought of Gregory ogling her and exploring her body with his own caused such turmoil within her. Yet, she was his wife and, as such, must be prepared to yield to his demands.

'Awake are you, my beauty?' came the slurred voice into the half-darkness. 'Waiting for me, are you, you little vixen?' Emma gave no indication that she was still awake. She made no move, nor uttered even the slightest sound. Instead, she lay quite still, her eyes tightly shut and a little prayer in her heart that Gregory would be so exhausted from his evening of revelry that he would fall fast asleep the minute he tumbled into bed beside her. For what seemed a lifetime, Emma could hear him falling about and chuckling, as time and time again he made the effort to undress. 'Buggered if I ain't too drunk to stand up!' he kept saying, as he crashed first on to the bed, then on to the floor. Emma could hear him hopping about on one leg and when, curious in spite of herself, she opened one eye, it was to catch a glimpse of him in the long wardrobe mirror with one leg bent in the air, his hand making desperate grabs to yank the trousers from it, and all the while performing a comical tap dance, which looked all the more fascinating in the eerie flickering candle-light. 'Told me off, she did!' he now complained to Emma's back. 'My old mater! Said I was drunk and should be ashamed!' Suddenly his trousers were jubilantly snatched into the air, followed by his belt and braces, shirt and undergarments. 'I told her straight, Emma! I told the old bugger I'd give her cause to be proud of me. Oh aye! You wait till I present you with a grand-son, I told her! Me an' my little woman – we'll do it this very night. I've got work, and I feel it in my blood that, between us, we'll make a grandson for her tonight!'

When he slid into bed beside her, his hands coveting her neck, her shoulders, her hair, Emma felt herself shrink from him. When the warm nakedness of his body pressed itself into her back and his face leaned forward to touch her own, Emma thought she would die. God help her, but she couldn't let him invade her body! Not now, with Marlow's seed warm within her; not *ever*, her heart growing cold as his fingers began pulling up her nightgown. 'Come on, Emma,' he coaxed in a whisper which seemed to have suddenly sobered by his desperate need of her. 'It's been so very long . . . I'm sorry. Oh, but I want you now. I need you so badly that I can hardly breathe!' Feeling her resistance, his demands grew more urgent and when he roughly gripped her thigh in order to swing her round towards him, he quickly sensed the stiffening of her body. 'Stop that!' he growled, his tone marbled with both astonishment and anger. 'Your husband has need of you and by God, he'll have you!' He spat the words in her ear, at the same time beginning to straddle her crouched body. In that split second, Emma looked up and, seeing his naked body towering above her, she made a desperate scramble to get out from beneath him.

'What the hell's the matter with you?' Gregory lashed out with his right arm, intending to pin Emma to the bed. But she would not be held! In the ensuing frantic struggle, she managed to escape his clutches, but not before he had ripped the nightgown from her back. From the far side of the room where she had run to escape his searching eyes, Emma stood transfixed, ashamed that both Manny and old Mrs Denton must by now be listening to every word which passed from this room. As Gregory came towards her in slow, deliberate steps, holding the candle flame out at arm's length and a look of terrible confusion on his face, Emma averted her eyes. He stopped within only two or three paces of her. She felt his colourless eyes scrutinizing every inch of her nakedness. She heard the gasp of incredulity which, to Emma's trembling heart, seemed to infuse the very air with terror.

When the cry came, it was like a roar of thunder, yet it was transfused with the threat of tears. 'Christ Almighty! *You're with child, Emma*!' Now, he was on her, so close that the heat from the candle flame seared into her skin as he held it near her face. When he asked her, in a suspicious voice, 'Is it mine? . . . can it be?' and she lowered her gaze to the floor, he had his answer. 'Whose bastard is it, then, eh?' He was shaking her to and fro, not caring that each time her head was banged hard against the wall. '*Whose* bastard, I asked?' The shock of his discovery showed on his twisted face as, flinging her away from him with contempt, he went on drunken, unsteady legs to the dresser, put down the candle and began frenziedly pulling on his clothes as though his very life depended on it. 'You think you'll not tell me who it was, do you?' he scorned. 'Well, you'll do better than that, because you'll bloody well *take* me to the swine! He'll not touch another man's wife again, I'll be bound. And, as for you, you *are* a trollop! A harlot . . . just as my mother warned me!' In Gregory Denton's eyes there was no worse sin to be committed than that which Emma had committed against him! Having put on his shirt and trousers, he grabbed Emma's pile of clothes and, flinging them at her, yelled, 'Get dressed!'

Never having seen any man in such a fury – not even Caleb Crowther – and feeling all the more intimidated because it was Gregory, her own husband, Emma was mortified. But, even so, she did not wish to leave this room on a fool's errand. She frantically scrambled for her best course of action. Should she put on her clothes and make some futile trek into the streets with him, where the cold night air might temper his fury and give her the opportunity to reason with him? Or would her best move be to dress, but to go no further than the downstairs parlour, where she might have the chance to explain and talk more calmly. Or might she fare better by refusing to budge from this room until he had listened to what she had to say. Oh, but dear God, what *could* she say, other than to confirm what his instincts told him already – that the child was not his, but another man's and that that man was the bargee, Marlow Tanner. No! That was the one thing she would never reveal. Whatever else she might confess to, Emma would not betray or defile the exquisite memories of that night, of Marlow's fathomless, undying love for her and of her own for him. She would hold close those wonderful memories and treasure them in her heart for always – whatever the consequences!

'There's no point in discussing anything, until you can listen *calmly* to what I must tell you.' Emma's voice was quiet and controlled, belying the tightening knot in her stomach and the uncomfortable fluttering of her heart.

The sound of her voice cutting the air with such dignity seemed only to infuriate Gregory Denton further. 'I will not tell you again,' he said through clenched teeth as he bent to lace up his boots. 'What! . . . I've half a mind to flay you alive here and now. Get dressed and cover up your sins! Or, so help me, I'll do it for you!'

When, in defiance, Emma made no move other than to take the shawl from a nearby chair and wrap it about her shivering body, he seemed like a man demented. 'So you're *proud* of your sins, are you? Proud that you're nothing but a cheap trollop, eh?' He rushed towards her, his work boots making a peculiar sound across the floor and his face pinched with rage and filled with loathing as it thrust itself into Emma's. '*Proud* is it?' he demanded, gripping hold of Emma and propelling her violently towards the door. 'Well, then . . . why not show the whole world, eh?'

Unable to fight his manic strength, Emma felt herself being pulled across the room and through the door. Out on the landing she was dragged from one bedroom door to the other as he yelled at the top of his voice. 'We've a harlot here, who's *proud* of it! Come and see, why don't you?' Whereupon the back bedroom door was opened wide and through it emerged the homely figure of Mrs Manfred. Attired only in the long white nightgown taken earlier from her portmanteau and with her hair, which was usually rolled neatly up, hanging just as tidily about her shoulders, she had a look of both consternation and disgust on her round, honest face.

'Take hold of yourself, Mr Denton!' she told him, coming forward to place the lighted candle on the landing windowsill, her eyes as hard and condemning as her voice. 'If Mrs Denton has little to be proud of, then *you* have even less! Take your hands off her this instant!'

'No, Manny . . . go back to your bed, please!' pleaded Emma, for she had seen the rising anger in her old friend's face and she knew of old that Manny's sharp tongue would get her into deep trouble. 'I'm all right, believe me.' She was not afraid of Gregory now. Ashamed yes and also regretful that she had not found the courage to face the whole issue many weeks before when she'd first suspected her condition. But she now felt indignant that Gregory should humiliate her so in front of others, for if he had been half a man, he would have found the courage to discuss the situation more rationally. Instead, he had chosen to use it as a means to belittle her even further and to subsequently demonstrate his total lack of compassion and tolerance. In this illuminating moment, Emma saw Gregory for what he really was and she did not like what she saw. She herself had a great deal to answer for, that was true enough; she had no reason to be 'proud', as he had claimed – but then, neither had he! No! Emma wasn't ashamed, nor was she afraid. She was angry! Angry enough to turn on him now, first with her fists, then with her teeth, sinking them into his arm, and finally with her feet, when he attempted to knock her off balance against the balustrade.

'You little cow!' he screamed as the blood trickled down his arm.

'Leave her be, I tell you . . . leave her be!' Now Mrs Manfred dashed to help and all hell was let loose.

Of a sudden, old Mrs Denton's door flung open, revealing a face as dark as thunder and eyes alive with hatred. Standing there, silhouetted in the glow from the candle on her dresser, she made a fearsome sight. Over her cream cotton nightgown a fringed brown shawl was flung, crocheted by her own hands when they had been more nimble. Enormous in size, it reached down to touch her bare, gnarled feet and to tangle itself in the crooked walking-stick upon which she now leaned so heavily. Her nightcap was at a peculiar angle, covering one ear, and her surprisingly long grey hair protruded from beneath in wild tangled clusters before falling about her stiff bony shoulders in such disarray that it gave her a witch-like appearance. Her eyes were slitted and venomous as they took in the scene before her. 'I *knew* it!' she hissed, letting her weight slump on to the door-jamb as she viciously thrashed the air with her stick. 'I know what you've been up to, Emma Grady! My son might only just have found out, but I've known all along what you are! Who gave you the right to fetch your cheap, loud-mouthed friends into this house? Who, eh . . . tell me that!' But her voice fell on deaf ears, only adding to the noise and confusion as the struggle between the two figures – one intending to harm Emma while the other tried to save her – grew even more frantic.

Meanwhile, outside, Tilly Watson was terrified that there was a murder being committed. 'For God's sake, open this door!' she yelled through the letter-box. 'Else I swear I'll fetch a constable!' When there was no acknowledgment and the shouting grew even more fierce, her husband pushed her aside and, peering through the letter-box, he was so alarmed to see Gregory frantically struggling with the two women, that, giving no further warning, he ran like the wind to seek out an officer of the law, telling his wife as he went, 'There's madness goin' on in there, Tilly. Stay well away till the constable comes!' As he ran, it crossed his mind that, unless he acted swiftly, some poor unfortunate would go hurtling down those stairs and end up with a broken back. He thought again on what he'd seen and judging by the way that aggressive older woman was grappling with Mr Denton, his instincts told him it would likely be his neighbour who came off worst! As for young Mrs Denton, well, she seemed more *against* her husband than *with* him! By God, it was a right do!

Tugged and torn between the two equally determined forces, Emma was also terrified that someone would be badly hurt. On the one hand Mrs Manfred was like a tigress protecting her cub, while on the other, Gregory was beside himself with inconsolable fury, made all the more terrible by drink. It was when Gregory lashed out with the intent of stripping the shawl from Emma's otherwise-naked body that the inevitable happened. At the very moment when the enraged Mrs Manfred struck out to prevent his arm from grasping the shawl, Emma twisted from the vice-like grip of his other fist, which had seized her and pinned her fast to him. Without Emma's body to hold him balanced against the older woman's feverish attack, he stumbled backwards and, with a cry which struck a chill deep in Emma's exhausted heart, he hurtled down the steep, narrow stairs, to land crumpled and misshapen at the bottom.

For what seemed a lifetime, not a sound could be heard: not the slightest movement disturbed the eerie silence. Until a few moments later, the odd shuffling of old Mrs Denton's bare feet penetrated the unnatural quietness as she slowly took herself from her bedroom door to the balustrade. From there, she stared down at the tragic figure which was barely visible in the shadowy passage below. At once the silence was broken with her low pitiful sobbing, which, to Emma's shocked spirit, was terrible to hear. Amidst it all, Emma ran swiftly down the stairs to where Gregory lay unmoving. Bending close to him, she began murmuring his name and looking into his face. When his wide, shocked eyes stared back at her unseeing, Emma's hand flew up to stifle the cry in her throat and, her heart torn with anguish, she turned to look at Mrs Manfred who seemed frozen to the spot. In a broken voice she said in a loud whisper, 'Oh, Manny! . . . he's dead. Gregory's dead!' Whereupon Mrs Manfred visibly sagged and seemed close to collapse.

'Murderers! It were you . . . the *both* of you! You killed him . . . pushed him down the stairs! Murderers! Old Mrs Denton fell forward across the balustrade, her eyes going from Mrs Manfred to Emma and her voice at such a pitch that, within minutes, there wasn't a soul along Montague Street who hadn't been roused from their beds. On and on she went, growing more and more hysterical. When the sound of the constable's whistle outside rose above her shrieking, she went into a spasm, her every limb shaking so violently that the stick in her hand played a sinister tune against the balustrade and her grief-stricken wails became like the sound of muted laughter.

Suddenly, the door was burst open. The constable stretched out his arms in order to keep the crowd back. What he heard behind him was Tilly Watson's husband telling one and all 'The buggers 'ave done for him! We saw it! . . . me an' Tilly, we saw the poor sod struggling for his life!' What the constable saw by the flickering light of the candle which brightly burned on the landing windowsill, was Emma kneeling ashen-faced and terror-struck beside the still figure of her husband. Above her, on the landing, was the figure of Mrs Manfred, flattened back against the wall, on the verge of collapse, her eyes closed and, clutched tightly in her hand, a torn remnant of Gregory Denton's shirt sleeve. Some further way along the landing, old Mrs Denton was slumped over the balustrade like a rag-doll, her eyes fixed on the still and twisted figure of her precious son. Over and over in a small shocked voice she accused Emma, 'You killed my lad! The both of you . . . you murdered him.' And, going by what he had been told by those who had seen the fracas through the letter-box, together with what his own eyes told him now, the constable's first instincts were to totally agree with what that frail old woman was saying. However, when he moved down the passageway and saw Emma's tragic eyes looking up at him, he could find nothing there to convince him that she had a wicked heart. Still, he had a duty to perform, where instincts and feelings did very little to influence the outcome.

When the constable took hold of Emma's arm, saying in a kindly but firm voice, 'Come along now. Let's get you decently dressed,' Emma felt numb, but not from the biting cold which took her breath away and made the pores on her skin stand out; she was numbed by all that had taken place and by the tragedy which she had witnessed with her own eyes. Emma prayed that it was all some terrible nightmare from which she would soon wake up; but deep in her heart she knew it was not.

Some time later, when the house on Montague Street had seen more visitors and officialdom in a few hours than it had seen in many years, an uneasy quietness descended upon it. The constable had secured all the details of what was construed to have taken place. Tilly Watson and her husband gave their excited and colourful account; old Mrs Denton gave her version in the greatest detail, laying the blame with renewed vigour on Mrs Manfred and Emma. Now, after she had helped Emma to dress in her best clothes and boots before delivering her, along with Mrs Manfred, to the waiting officers, Tilly Watson had only old Mrs Denton to contend with.

'My lad . . . they murdered my poor lad!' was all the old woman could murmur from the depths of her bed – her voice, like her shocked heart, growing weaker with every breath.

'That'll be for the Judge to decide,' Tilly Watson reminded her. Although, if the truth were to be told, she thought, there was little hope that the Judge's verdict would be any different to that of old Mrs Denton's because, much as she liked Emma and Mrs Manfred, there was a powerful case against them – including what she herself had seen with her very own eyes. However, if the question was put to her, she would have to say that, in her opinion, it was *not* Emma's hand that actually pushed Mr Denton, but that of Mrs Manfred.

Of a sudden, Tilly was struck by the unearthly quiet in the room and, looking down on old Mrs Denton's grey, silent features and wide-open eyes, she was riveted to the spot. 'Lord, love us!' she said in a thick whisper, making the sign of the cross several times on herself. 'Looks like the old bugger's followed her lad!' Quickly, she examined the old woman more closely and seeing that she had indeed left this world, a crafty look came over Tilly's face. Turning her head stealthily from side to side to ensure there was no one else present in the room, she gingerly picked up the old woman's wrist between her finger and thumb and lifted the arm which had been hanging from the bed towards the floor. Laying it over the eiderdown in reverent fashion, she looked about the room once more. Then, stooping so that she might easily stretch her hand under the bed, she began feverishly rummaging about.

'Got it!' Tilly gave out a little cry of triumph as her groping fingers clutched the square cold box. In her excitement, she was almost flat on the floor, both arms reaching beneath the bed to secure the hard metal object.

Tilly Watson's guilty heart was beating furiously as she eased her reward towards her, but it almost stopped completely when old Mrs Denton's arm slid from the eiderdown, to come tumbling on to her thieving neck like a tap from the devil! 'Jesus, Mary and Joseph!' Tilly screamed at the top of her voice, scrambling to her feet and grasping the cash box to her chest, just as the two officials from below came crashing into the room.

'You gave us the fright of our lives,' said one.

'What's up?' demanded the other, taking out his notebook and pencil.

Tilly had to think quickly. Gave *them* a fright, she told herself, t'weren't *nothing* to what that old sod did to me! With swift and dexterous hands, she pulled her shawl over the cash box, saying with a feigned look of regret, 'The old lady's gone, I'm afeared. Sudden like it was . . . gave me a real turn, I'm telling you!' She hurried out of the room before they had the opportunity to detain her. 'I'd best away and get help for the laying-out of the body, afore the bones begin to stiffen.'

Thankful that she had been allowed to leave the house straightaway, Tilly didn't stop until she'd safely closed her own front door behind her. 'I'm sorry for thieving your valuables, old Ma Denton,' she murmured, 'but you'll not be wanting 'em where you've gone and me an' mine have more need of this 'ere box!' Of a sudden, a startling thought entered her head. With both the old lady and her son gone, the cash box would next go to Emma. But not if Emma were never to come home again, she thought wickedly. Not if she was hanged for murder! A cunning and avaricious look washed over Tilly Watson's hitherto homely face. 'I'm sorry, Emma,' she whispered into the night, 'but, now I come to think on it more clearly, I swear it was *your* hand that sent poor Mr Denton to his maker. Oh yes, I saw what I saw and I'm duty bound to explain it in the very manner in which it all happened!' Whereupon, she crept into the darkened front parlour, making sure she did not disturb her husband in the back room, hid her treasure and hurried back to have quiet words with the officials next door. She must be quite sure they'd got her story right. There was time enough for the old one to be properly laid out – that was none too urgent. But what she had to tell the officials, well now, the sooner that was done, the better!

Part Two

June 1862

Hearts of Stone

Beset me with trials
Or test my heart
And make my spirit lowly,
But I will grow stronger
Wherever the wind may blow me.
J.C.

Chapter Ten

'You get yer bloody 'ands off my arse, ye randy sod! Else I'll 'ave the law on yer!' From somewhere beneath the street grime and layers of holey clothing, Sal Tanner's weather-worn and wrinkled face expressed indignation at being so crudely manhandled. Her booted feet lashed out at the officer who had come up from behind the marauding trouble-makers, to thrust her out of harm's way.

'Now then old Sal,' he told her firmly, 'if you're locked up again, they'll likely seal up the door for good and all!' He took her by the scruff of her neck and as he propelled her from the black heart of the mob, his voice was kindly but threatening. 'Be off with you, Sal Tanner. Afore I'm tempted to run you in along with the rest of them!'

'Go on then, why don't yer?' she demanded, fighting and struggling in his determined grip.

'Because I know you're not here to cause real trouble, you old bugger! D'you think I don't know that you're just here to take advantage, whilst folks is looking the other way? Do as I say, and be off . . . else I'll turn you in for the pick-pocket you fancy yourself to be, you silly old bugger!'

'I ain't pickin' *anybody's* pockets!' Sal was defiant, though she knew well enough now that she'd been tumbled.

When he contemptuously threw her to the kerbside, saying with a laugh, 'And as for being "randy", well now, that *might* be the case. But if I wanted to touch anybody's arse, Sal Tanner, it wouldn't be yours, I can tell you! I'd be a bloody fool to risk catching the pox from the likes o' you, wouldn't I, eh?' Sal knew when to leave well enough alone. As the constable turned to assist his fellow officers in trying to bring the ensuing crisis under control, Sal ambled away to where she might find better pickings – thinking there could well be a free gill o' beer going begging at one or other of the alehouses round the market square, never mind that the last time she'd gone into such a place for a gill and a card game, the result had been to reduce her to living like a beggar and sleeping in the cobbled alleys. 'Sod 'em all!' she muttered now, as she scurried away into the descending darkness, jingling the few coppers she'd swiped from a few back pockets. ''Appen I can catch another game, where I might win back me barge an' all me belongings! 'Cause if I *don't*, our Marlow'll likely skin me alive when 'e finds out what tricks I've been up to while 'e's across the seas!'

The scene which Sal Tanner had left behind was a bad one. Feelings of despair amongst a minority of the unemployed had erupted in a mutinous revolt. The cause of it had been the arrest and consequent imprisonment of a number of unfortunates who had been caught poaching. Following the harsh results of the hearing, an angry demonstration had ensued, which moved down King Street, causing much damage to property. From there, many of the marauders marched on to Pleasington Hall, smashing the windows, while others proceeded to the Town Hall and caused further aggravation. A meeting of magistrates was eventually called, the Riot Act read and special constables sworn in. In addition, a troop of soldiers was brought from Preston to quell what at first appeared to be the brewing of a long and bloody siege. As it turned out, hostilities quickly ceased and peace was sensibly restored. For many nights afterwards, however, talk of the commotion filled the alehouses and parlours, as ordinary, law-abiding folk condemned such behaviour, although they were themselves desperate for food and warmth, and still despairing of ever finding work. The community of Blackburn was shaken to its roots, and those in authority took a dim and serious view of what had taken place.

Caleb Crowther was more condemning than most. His opinion of the working-class was that they should all be either flogged to within an inch of their lives or hanged from the tallest gibbet! When, at a late hour on this particular night, after peace had been restored, he emerged from Blackburn Railway Station in search of a carriage to take him home, it did not improve his irritation and fatigue after a long journey from London, to find a ragged and drunken tramp besieging him for 'a copper or two for a poor unfortunate, if yer please?' Being in a sourer mood than usual, he cracked his walking-cane about the shoulders of the ragged creature. 'Out of my way!' he snarled. 'Unless you want to feel the weight of the *law* on your shoulders into the bargain!'

Locating a carriage, he climbed smartly into it – leaving Sal Tanner raising a bottle to his departure. 'May the divil keep yer company, yer miserable old bugger!' she called after him, taking a hefty swig of the colourless spirit and heartily chortling as she set off drunkenly to the back alleys which were her home. 'May the divil tek all yer fancy bloody folk, an' drown the lot of 'em!' she told a passing constable, tripping away at a faster pace when he paused to eye her more closely. From a safe distance she turned to inform him, 'The buggers are allus up to some'at! Allus whispering an' causing trouble fer some poor sod or other! Drown 'em all!' Shouting defiantly as the constable began making his way towards her, she repeated, 'Drown 'em all, I say!' Then, as he came too close for comfort, she tossed her head and ran off, stumbling and laughing as her legs gave way beneath her.

The constable watched her out of sight. Then, smiling to himself, he went on his way. 'Poor old bugger,' he said with sympathy. Everyone knew the story of how Sal Tanner had come to ruin since her brother had sailed away. She was a familiar sight, haunting the streets of Blackburn like a lost soul. Ah well, perhaps one of these days her brother would make his way back; there was nobody else who could handle Sal Tanner – and nobody else who could save her!

Meanwhile, in the carriage, with only the clip-clop of the horses' hooves to disturb his thoughts, Caleb Crowther reflected on the reason for his journey to London. Bartholomew Mysen was not an easy man to do business with. He had become stiff-necked and unapproachable since his appointment to Circuit Judge. At this point in his thoughts, Caleb Crowther smiled to himself as he softly murmured, 'If you don't want your sins to find you out, then you should be more careful, Mysen.' It pleased him to have succeeded in the errand which had taken him so urgently to seek out his colleague of old. As he himself was not to sit in judgment at the trial of Emma Grady as was, then who better to be acquainted with the necessary facts than the man in whose hands her future would lie? Facts which might also affect the future of the learned Judge himself! Facts which told of past indiscretions in the brothel houses and gambling dens. Facts which, if made public, could topple a fellow from the pinnacle of his career in the time it took to wink an eye! Indeed, there might well be repercussions for others who also shared those indiscretions, but, somehow, Caleb Crowther's instincts had been correct when they told him that Bartholomew Mysen would do anything rather than risk losing his own income and new-found status in society.

As to the facts regarding Emma Grady and her accomplice . . . well now, wasn't there more than enough evidence to show how they had deliberately murdered that poor young man? Wasn't it obvious how Emma Grady herself was the ringleader? And didn't the pair of them show such evil and cunning that warranted nothing less than to be publicly hanged! The fact that Emma Grady was with child and as such could not be hanged was no great stumbling-block, as had been painstakingly pointed out to the reluctant Bartholomew Mysen by his unwelcome visitor. By the time her trial came to court and the sentence called upon, Emma Grady would have delivered her brat into the world. There were institutions enough to see to such a burden on society.

Caleb Crowther's paramount objective was to ensure that Emma Grady be swiftly despatched from the face of the earth. That would conveniently rid him of his three greatest problems: his need to explain to her what had become of her legacy; his own nagging conscience; and his innate and desperate fear that, should she live, Emma might well discover certain things about the past which should be left forever buried, out of harm's way! Then, there was Mrs Manfred, whose loyalties were steadfastly with Emma and her papa, and the very same woman who had seen more than she had revealed of Thadius Grady's death and of his own unholy part in it! He'd never been really sure how much she had actually seen, but had suffered tormenting nightmares that she must surely have witnessed something! However, he was now satisfied that both of them would be dealt with forthwith and would no longer represent any kind of threat to him. Persuading his legal colleague had not been easy, but, when it came right down to it, a fellow must look out for his own survival. There was no doubt that when Emma Grady and her companion were brought before the Courts in two days' time, they would each get their just rewards. It mattered not that they were probably innocent of all charges against them, only that here was a prime opportunity to be rid of them once and for all!

Only once did Caleb Crowther's thoughts touch on a much deeper issue. No one alive, apart from himself, knew that Emma was *his* daughter! His and Mary Grady's, got during an illicit affair behind Thadius's back. Oh, if only that was the *single* dark secret from the past, he thought now. If only that was all, he might rest easier in his sleep!

'Emma Denton, you have been found guilty of a serious crime. Whilst in the company of another, you behaved in such a way that contributed to the death of your own husband.' Judge Mysen's voice echoed across the courtroom like the strokes of a hammer on Emma's heart. Only now, after what seemed an eternity in these Lancaster assizes, did she raise her eyes to look into the face of Judge Mysen. She had told the truth of what happened on that fateful night some months previously, but her words had fallen on unbelieving ears; to them the more sensational accounts of others had seemed more credible. With every word now spoken, Emma could see the gallows looming up before her and her trembling heart was overwhelmed with fear. However, she was determined not to betray her terror; she would not let her spirit become cowardly at this late hour. Her love for Marlow and her cherished memories of him had been a great source of comfort and strength to her throughout. Her regrets were many, but, if she had the power to change anything, it would be only one thing; for her deepest regret was the injustice which would now be inflicted on the innocent inside her. Her heart ached when she thought of how that helpless little being, who was conceived in such joy and love, would be taken along with her to the gallows and there its beating heart would be stilled with her own. But Emma was prepared, and when the moment came, she would offer up a special prayer for her and Marlow's defenceless unborn child.

Although Emma gazed steadfastly at Judge Mysen's serious face, her thoughts were far away, constantly churning and always concerned for others rather than for herself. As he gave out his declaration, Bartholomew Mysen found himself deeply moved by Emma's calm strength and by the tragic innocence in those sad eyes which looked at him with such disarming directness. In his deliberations he was cruelly torn between the fate of this young woman who was so close to being a mother, and his own future, which rested on the sentences he passed here this day. He was not unaware of those who had sat in the gallery throughout this trial, in particular the man he had come to so despise; a man who, with other members of his family, had followed every detail with the utmost interest. Now, as he spoke, he could feel Caleb Crowther's eyes feasting on him, urging him to deliver the ultimate penalty on the two women who stood before him. 'Hang them!' he had been warned, 'Or face the consequences!'

Bartholomew Mysen was under no illusions regarding the treacherous character of the man with whom he had once foolishly haunted the fleshpots of London. Yet, how could he live with his own conscience if he was to send Emma Denton to the gallows? The older woman, in his eyes, had been more damned by the evidence put before him and he believed, in all truth, that she was indeed the guilty party. He, like others, was not entirely convinced that the younger woman's intentions had been truly malicious. Indeed, he himself had been half persuaded that initially, it was *she* who was being attacked. However, the verdict had been returned and he was now called upon to pass sentence. In a final effort to calm the dictates of his own conscience, as well as appeasing the demands of Caleb Crowther, he made his decision. There was one other option still open to him, which, though coming to a close, had not yet outlived its usefulness. In his eyes, it was as good as a sentence to the gallows. In latter years, such harsh sentences had been reserved mostly for males, but, as in cases such as this, there were always exceptions.

While her fate was being decided, Emma remained calm. In her heart, she softly asked that the Lord look upon his children with mercy and that dear Mrs Manfred, who had become so ill and pale, should be spared.

'And so, Emma Denton,' Judge Mysen's stern voice infiltrated Emma's thoughts once more, 'in view of these things, and taking into account both your tender years and advanced state of pregnancy, this court will show a measure of mercy.' Emma's heart was suddenly filled with hope, yet, not daring to anticipate her freedom, she held her breath and waited. But her hopes were not to be realized and, as the voice continued to reverberate around the court-room, she had to grip the rail before her desperately tight, or all of her strength and resolve might have fled, and the black tide which ebbed about her senses would swallow her up.

'It is therefore ordered and adjudged by this court that you, Emma Denton, of the parish of Blackburn in Lancashire, be transported upon the seas, to such place as Her Majesty Queen Victoria, by the advice of Her Privy Council, shall think fit to direct and appoint, for the term of no less than ten years.'

Emma was devastated! She was *not* to be set free. She had escaped the gallows, yes, but only to be discharged from the beloved land of her birth and sent over some vast, terrifying ocean, to the edge of the world! All this time she had kept her strength, she had made herself hope against hope that justice would be done by both her and her unborn child. She had prayed as never before and she had tried so very hard not to be afraid. Yet, now, she *was* afraid! More than that, she was terrified, in awe of the unknown and in despair of what might become of her and the little one.

Of a sudden, Emma's fears were further charged as the court reacted to the sentence passed upon her, some people being in full agreement with it, and others – Caleb Crowther in particular – loudly condemning it to be a 'travesty of justice!' and 'too lenient by far!' Then, the court became quiet once again as they all awaited the sentence about to be imposed on the other defendant. When it was duly passed in echoing sombre tones, Emma's heart collapsed within her and she gave out a cry of anguish. If she had thought her own punishment to be harsh, then Mrs

Manfred's must have come straight from Hell. Dear God above, it *couldn't* be! Her darling innocent Manny was to be committed to the gallows! Manny was to be hanged! The words echoed over and over in Emma's distorted and desperate thoughts. 'No, it can't be!' she heard her own voice cry out. She saw the shock and disbelief on her dear friend's face and when, suddenly, the child within her grew so agitated that the pains shot through her body like many knives, Emma felt her strength ebb away. She saw the peering eyes of strangers on her as the room spun into itself, until the darkness swamped her senses and she sank silently to the ground.

Chapter Eleven

The laughter echoed from bow to stern of the coal-barge as wily Sal Tanner merrily hoisted up her ragged skirt and danced a jig on the spot. 'While their eyeballs is glued ter them there gallows,' she told one and all, 'we'll lighten their pockets an' be away, afore the buggers know what's hit 'em!' Her words were greeted by rapturous applause and raucous laughter, followed by a burst of accordian music and a great deal of ale-supping. After which the women got to their feet and entertained their menfolk with a tap of heels and vulgar show of legs.

'By! They're a motley crew and no mistake!' The barge-man stretched his neck from his place at the tiller and, casting his merry eyes over the live cargo which had made itself comfortable in amongst the mounds of black, shining coal, he laughed out loud, saying to the round, jolly woman by his side, 'I must a' been all kinds of a fool to give in to that lot, eh?'

'Away with yer, our Jack!' declared his wife, playfully nudging him in the ribs. 'They might look like the worst villains abroad, but they're harmless enough. Yer did right in giving them a ride ter Lancaster, 'cause they're no different from anybody else when it comes to attending a

319

hanging.' She nudged him again and laughed out loud. 'But there's many a one as'll find their purses gone when this lot departs the scene!' Whereupon, the two of them laughed all the louder and shook their heads as they began tapping their own feet to the rhythm of the melody coming up from the hold.

Outside in the square, the gibbet was being put in place, and though the event was not scheduled to happen until early the following day, the crowds were already beginning to gather and jostle one another for the most advantageous position.

From her cramped and tiny cell, which was shared by others who awaited transportation, Emma could hear the outer hammering noises which told her that Mrs Manfred's time was growing ever nearer. She felt strange and disloyal that there was no sadness in her heart; no anger, no bitterness and no prayer for Mrs Manfred. She felt nothing but a cold, numb emptiness within her. And, in these past long hours, when she had lost all sense of time, Emma had come to realize that even the child inside her was still and silent.

When she and Mrs Manfred had first been incarcerated some long, endless weeks before, Emma had made several pleas that both her own and Mrs Manfred's plight should be brought to her uncle, Caleb Crowther's, personal attention. When the reply came back that Caleb Crowther and his family no longer considered Emma Denton to be in any way related to them, nor did they intend to intervene on behalf of either of the two unfortunates who had so callously caused the untimely death of another, Emma's heart had bled more for the child and Mrs Manfred than for herself.

Now, there was nothing. She wasn't even fearful of the unknown journey which awaited her and, may God forgive her, she also appeared to be losing her faith. Her comforting belief in the good Lord had sustained her throughout, but now, because some deep, awful instinct told her that the small, helpless life within her was fast fading, so too was her faith. Emma had always possessed both the strength and compassion to forgive her enemies, but, if that tiny life created by her and Marlow was to be cruelly wasted, then how could she find it in her heart to forgive such a thing?

Now, Emma's thoughts were overturned as the other prisoners began to make a racket at the approach of a particularly formidable female warden. 'Watch out, 'ere it comes!' said one in a loud whisper. 'Aye,' rejoined another, ''appen the bugger's come ter march us *all* ter the gallows!'

'Enough of that, you lot!' rapped the officer as she thrust the great key into the lock. 'Back away from the door, I tell you . . . unless you want swilling down like the pigs you are!' As a second warden, a great hulk of a man, stood by with a bucket of ice-cold water, the first one beckoned to Emma, calling out her surname and instructing, 'Get out here. There's someone wants to see you!'

Astonished that she should be the one singled out, Emma threaded her way forward through those around her. When, harshly, she was pulled through the door to face the warden, it was to be told, 'Your partner in crime has been given permission to say her goodbyes.' She reached out a stiff arm and propelled Emma along the corridor, adding, 'If it was up to *me*, she'd not have her way, I can tell you. But this new governor's not yet had time to toughen up. He's too gullible by half, but he'll learn soon enough if I know anything!' Emma hoped not, for in a place such as this it surely wasn't a bad thing for the governor to show a measure of compassion. As for herself, some little corner of her being had lighted up with the thought that she was being taken to see her beloved friend. Maybe God was listening after all.

When the door to the cell was opened and Emma saw that dear, familiar face watching for her to appear, she was unable to put one foot before the other. Even when Mrs Manfred called out her name she stood rooted to the spot. Of a sudden, she felt engulfed by such pain and emotion that all she could do was to gaze at the older woman, tears tumbling down her face and her arms reaching out towards her.

'Oh, my darling child!' Suddenly they were in each other's embrace, clinging tightly to each other, and so filled with emotion that neither could speak. Presently, Emma felt herself being gently held out at arm's length, while Mrs Manfred gazed at her with great concern. 'Oh, child, look at you,' she murmured, the shock at seeing Emma so emaciated evident on her face. 'Why, you're nothing but skin and bone!'

'I'm fine, Manny,' Emma protested, not having seen the sorry spectacle she now presented and caring even less. 'But *you*, oh, Manny, I'm so afraid for you. And it's all my fault . . . if only I hadn't asked you to stay that night.' Emma thought that if she was given the grace to live a lifetime, she could never forgive herself for what Mrs Manfred must be going through.

'You must not blame yourself, my darling, for you have brought me nothing but joy in all the time I've known you.' When Emma looked up to see those generous, round eyes looking so softly at her, she was amazed at the peace and beauty there. There were tears also, but they were not self-pitying tears, nor were they tears of anger or bitterness. As those bright, friendly eyes roved over her, Emma felt ashamed.

'I'm not afraid, child,' Mrs Manfred said tenderly, thinking how if she *was* afraid, then it was for Emma and not for herself, because in all honesty she had come to accept the blame for Mr Denton's death. She looked long and softly at Emma's ragged countenance and her old heart was moved by it. Though heavy with child, Emma was painfully thin – her cheekbones jutting out from that small, pixie face and those expressive grey eyes deep and large with the pain she had endured. The dress on her back was nothing like the fine gown she had been wearing when they had escorted her from Montague Street; it had been replaced by a plain, ill-fitting brown dress with scooped neck, loose sleeves and limp skirt which was torn and dishevelled at the hem. Oh, there was nothing so despicable as those who took advantage of their authority to strip away anything of value which was the property of those left helplessly in their charge. However, the boots which peeped from beneath were Emma's own, which unknown to anyone but Emma, still carried her mama's tiny and precious watch secreted within the ankle-lining. But the biggest shock of all was seeing how Emma's long, magnificent chestnut hair had been savaged from her head, the remnants of which were left at various jagged and unruly lengths.

When Emma was asked, 'Will you pray with me, child?' she had to ask herself how could she possibly do such a thing when, in her heart, she had already begun to reject the very idea that there was a God. As a child and throughout her youth, Emma had been taught to love, respect and fear that special, magnanimous idol who watched over all those lesser creatures below. Now, when His help and mercy was sorely needed, where was He? How could she pray to a God who would let the child die within her and who would allow the innocent life of Mrs Manfred to be taken also?

'Please, child.' The older woman had sensed the struggle going on in Emma's mind and meant to resolve it in the right way. 'I need you to pray with me.'

As they knelt down together, to join their voices in quiet prayer, Emma felt her spirit returning and her heart growing stronger. Once more, a kind of comfort crept in to give her hope and when, as she embraced Manny in a final farewell, she was astonished to feel the child within her surge and struggle, Emma asked forgiveness for the doubts which had torn her in two.

Emma listened attentively as Mrs Manfred quietly advised her, 'When you get to those far-off shores, don't be afraid. Be careful not to antagonize those who hold the key to your freedom. Work hard, keep your mind busy and the years will swiftly pass. When the day comes that your life is returned to you, use it well. Cherish it, and never forget the things you were taught. Will you promise me that, child?' she asked now and, before she was returned to her own cell, Emma gave the promise with all her heart. It grieved her to learn how even Manny's only relative, her sister in Luton, had turned her back when she had been most needed. But Emma was greatly moved by the courage Mrs Manfred had shown in the shadow of the gallows. Both touched and shamed by it, she had cried, 'I'll never forget you,' as she wept in Mrs Manfred's comforting arms. Nor would she. For Manny had come to be a part of her that she would carry forever.

In the silent early hours of the morning, Emma got up from her crouched position on the floor to tiptoe over towards the metal grill which sliced the growing daylight into grotesque shadows on the wall. Through the window she could hear the soft thud of hurrying footsteps outside, yet she could see nothing, for the window was too high.

''Ere, climb aback o' me, darlin'.' The whisper bathed Emma's ear, and the touch of a hand on her shoulder was a gentle one. Emma recognized the girl as Nelly, a cockney waif not much younger than herself. Since being made an orphan by tuberculosis which had taken most of her family, she had wandered from her East London beginnings to tramp the length and breadth of England in search of a better life. Circumstances had driven her to stealing, which in turn had landed her with the same fate as Emma. Together they were banished from the shores of their beloved and familiar homeland, to set sail under guard for some distant and unknown destination. Yet both were strong of heart and they had found a small measure of consolation in each other.

Emma had liked Nelly on first sight. She smiled warmly as she looked on that rather large and coarse face, the features of which seemed peculiarly exaggerated – the nose was too spread across, the chin jutted out a shade too much and the dark eyes were so round and large that they seemed almost bulbous as they stared fondly at Emma. Yet, for all this, there was an aura of such warmth and compassion about her as appeared almost beautiful, and to Emma, Nelly had become a shining example of great fortitude. In turn, with her stalwart and quiet strength of character,

Emma gave Nelly a great deal of hope and comfort. In the short time since they had been thrown together, these two young women had forged a friendship which, in the years to follow, would help them to face many terrible adversities.

'Bless you, Nelly, I can't use you in that way.' Emma smiled affectionately at Nelly's suggestion. When Emma considered how undernourished and weak Nelly was, and she so heavy with child, the very idea of doing what Nelly instructed was unthinkable. Yet, it was a wonderful gesture and Emma was deeply grateful. She gazed fondly at those large ungainly features, noticing how the girl's blue dress was so tattered that she had been allowed to keep it; even the plain brown shoes on her feet had lost their laces somewhere along the way; and the dingy brown scarf knotted at her throat was riddled with tiny round holes, as though the moths or lice had found it to be a tasteful feast.

When, with a plea in her voice, Nelly protested, 'It's all right, Emma, you'll be light as a feather and I've a broad enough back to lift you up to the window,' Emma reached out a hand to stroke the girl's untidy brown hair and gently laughed when it sprang back up again as if it had a mind of its own.

'Happen there are things going on outside that window that neither of us ought to see,' she told her quietly, whereupon one of the louder, bolder women nearby, offered her own opinion.

'That's right enough, young 'un,' she said, 'gallows ain't a pretty sight – not for us to see an' even worse for them as is set upon it! Keep yer head down an' thank yer lucky stars it ain't you as is walking up them wooden stairs this morning!' Suddenly there was a loud, excited roar from some way off. 'They've seen their first sight of her!' the woman called out. 'The crowd's on their feet!' At this, every other prisoner in the cell got to their feet, a look of fearful anticipation on each one's face and an ear cocked so as not to miss a sound.

Making the sign of the cross, Emma sank to the ground where she sat small and still against the cold damp wall, a fervent prayer issuing from her lips in a whisper. 'Forgive me Lord, if I've doubted you, but Manny is so good, and her punishment shamefully unjust. Please, Lord, help her now and take her innocent soul to your arms.' Emma pictured her beloved friend in the smallest, most familiar detail. She recalled being comforted by that darling woman; she remembered her unceasing kindness and her steadfast love; she thought about the wise and wonderful words which dear Mrs Manfred had often spoken to her; and her heart ached with both regret and bitterness at the way in which the life of such a wonderful woman had to end.

'I'm afeared, Emma, gal,' said Nelly, coming to sit beside her, 'afeared that the buggers can string a body up so easily!'

'You mustn't be afraid, Nelly,' Emma told her, reaching out an arm and drawing the trembling girl towards her. 'Manny isn't afraid, and we must learn from her example.' However, when the crowd outside fell ominously silent, Emma also began to tremble; and when a great, tumultuous roar erupted, followed by loud, hearty clapping, she clung to the other girl for reassurance with the same desperate fear as that frightened creature clung to her. Manny's ordeal is over, thought Emma, while mine is only just beginning. Suddenly, the child inside her grew restless, thrashing and protesting at being so long incarcerated. 'Be patient, little one,' Emma reassured it, but thinking how she felt equally desperate. The idea of attempting to escape had crossed her mind more than once, but Emma knew the futility of that because, even if the officers' vigilance was relaxed somewhere along the way, she was so heavy with child that before she'd gone half a dozen steps, they'd be on her. Furthermore, it was likely she'd be severely flogged and further restricted for her pains. Yet it filled Emma with despair to think how her unborn child would simply be swapping one prison for another.

After a day of acute discomfort and cold, when the prisoners were roughly disturbed several times for one reason or another, Emma found herself being roused from a restless sleep in the still-dark early hours.

'Come on you lot! The waggon's arrived!' yelled the voice of an officer, as he threw open the cell door. 'File out one at a time, and don't get clever, 'cause we're ready for any o' your tricks!' He waved his cat-o'-nine-tails in the air, his face suffused with pleasure at the thought of laying it across some of their backs.

Emma followed the others, shuffling out with Nelly ever close by her side. Already made uncomfortable with her every bone aching from the cramp and cold, Emma prayed that the child inside her might be still for a while, for it seemed unusually agitated and the spasms of pain in her abdomen had become increasingly difficult to bear without crying out. Emma's anxiety must have shown on her face because, in the lowest and most urgent whisper, Nelly's voice sounded in her ear, 'Hold on, darlin' – it ain't the right time yet.'

But however desperately Emma tried to contain the upheaval taking place inside her, nature dictated that the child was ready to be born. Outside by the main gate, as Emma and Nelly were pushed towards the cage-topped waggon where a number of prisoners, whose journey had begun some time before, were already squashed inside, Emma felt her ankle being roughly grasped and shackled to Nelly by means of a heavy iron. It was as they were then propelled forward that Emma was racked with such a searing pain that it brought her to the cobbled ground and, try as she might, she could not find the strength to pull herself up again.

'On your feet!' With the officer's cry came the sting of leather across Emma's unprotected shoulders.

'Leave her be – *please*. Don't be so bleedin' heartless!' pleaded Nelly as he raised his arm again. 'She's giving birth, can't you see that?' Whereupon there came a volley of protest from the rest of the prisoners. After safely and swiftly securing the others inside the waggon, the older of the two officers stepped forward to look down on Emma's small, writhing figure. 'You!' he addressed Nelly, who was still held fast to Emma by the shackles on their ankles. 'Do you know what to do?'

'Yes!' lied Nelly, anxious that she and Emma should not be separated.

'Get on with it, then! We've a long way to go and a ship to board! A few minutes, that's all – then you'll both be flung in the waggon to do the best you can along the journey!'

Some twenty minutes later, the still-dark air was rent with Nelly's jubilant cry of 'It's a girl!' A cheer promptly went up from those in the waggon. 'Oh, Emma! She's beautiful!' Nelly said, as she followed the procedure which she'd seen her own mother follow after giving birth to a lusty-lunged boy. That babe had yelled the minute it appeared and Nelly was concerned when Emma's newborn made neither sound nor movement.

Numb with cold and weakened by loss of blood, Emma held out her arms to take the child which Nelly had wrapped in a piece of muslin torn from her own petticoat. When she saw the rich dark hair that was the very same as Marlow's, a warm happiness spread though Emma's heart and, holding the small bundle close to her breast, she cried bitter-sweet tears and gave thanks that the child had been delivered. 'Oh Nelly, she's got the look of Marlow.' Emma was half-laughing, half-crying as she ran her finger along the small, still face. But, suddenly, her deeper instincts were aroused as she realized how still the child was and that it had not yet cried out.

'Come on! We've lingered too long! In the waggon with you!' The officer had come to the end of his patience.

But Emma took no notice of his gruff instruction. Instead she asked the other girl in a fearful tone, 'Why isn't she moving, Nelly? Why won't she cry?' When, leaning forward, Nelly examined the child and, seeing the worst, murmured, 'I'm sorry, Emma. It was too much of an ordeal for the little 'un,' Emma's heart froze inside her. 'No!' she protested, hugging the small bundle tighter and pushing Nelly away, 'Leave me be! My baby's all right, I tell you!' Fearing that the shock would be too much for Emma in the face of what she had already endured, Nelly looked appealingly at the waiting officer, shaking her head and drawing his attention to the child in Emma's arms.

'No, I tell you!' Emma had caught the look which passed between them and she clung desperately to the defenceless infant that was hers and Marlow's, all the while fighting off the weakness which threatened to rob her of her senses.

'In the waggon, the pair of you! The brat's dead as ever I've seen. Leave it!' ordered the officer, the compassion which Nelly had hoped to see never materializing.

Afraid that he might snatch the child from her arms, Emma began struggling to get up and when Nelly gave a helping hand, she took it gratefully. Yet, neither were prepared when the officer lost patience altogether, raised his leg, put his booted foot square on Emma's back and sent her sprawling towards the waggon, with Nelly stumbling also and the child rolling from Emma's arms across the cobbles and into the gutter, where it came to rest, silent and still.

Struggling to get to her feet, yet not having the strength left in her, Emma's frantic cries echoed into the darkness. Quickly, Nelly half-pushed, half-carried her into the waggon, both of them urged on by the prisoners there who, despite their renowned hardness of heart, were deeply moved by Emma's plight. But, being streetwise and familiar with the rudiments of self-survival, each and every one knew, as did Nelly, that the sooner Emma was whisked away from that poor lifeless little creature, the sooner she would mend.

Of a sudden, the cage doors were slammed shut and bolted. Both officers clambered up next to the driver, one of them cracking a horse-whip into the air above the geldings and causing them to jerk forward. 'Move away, man!' he instructed the driver. 'Move away!'

Behind him, the prisoners fell quiet, Nelly softly cried and Emma's haunted eyes remained transfixed on the spot where that tragic little bundle lay, until, like her, it became engulfed by the darkness.

As the waggon trundled away, only Nelly saw the shadow as it appeared beneath the solitary gas-lamp at the prison gates. The stooped, beshawled figure came out of nowhere, creeping along on unsteady legs made even more unsteady by the small limp which caused it to dip in a peculiar manner. At its heels was a great, thick-set and fearsome-looking dog that ran ahead and began sniffing Emma's blood which still bathed the child. The shawled figure called out to the dog and hurried to the spot where it began pawing the ground. Then, as the waggon lurched its way round the bend in the cobbled road, the pair were lost to sight – but not before Nelly heard a sound to make her ears prick. There was no mistaking that thin, distant wail which only a newborn could make – that demanding, persistent cry which seemed to tell the world, 'I was warm and now I'm cold. I was safe and now I'm afraid.'

Of a sudden, Emma was stirring, for she had also heard something. 'My baby!' she cried, pulling herself round so that she could see behind. But the streets were dark and strange and she saw nothing to console her.

As she gazed at Emma's weak and sorry countenance, Nelly was afraid that her new-found friend would be taken from her all too soon. 'No, Emma,' she said in a comforting voice, 'Your baby is gone. You must think of yourself now, darlin'.' She made no mention of what she'd heard, nor did she give Emma the smallest hope that her daughter might be alive. To do such a thing would only make the hard years to come that much longer and more difficult to bear. It was better for Emma to go on thinking the child had gone forever, because what she didn't know couldn't cause her any pain.

Emma felt herself raised to a sitting position as Nelly's

strong arms cradled her close. But Emma could not be consoled and, despite her strong character and normally resilient nature, in her aching heart she cared not whether she lived or died.

'Well, I'm buggered! What we got 'ere then, Jake, eh?' Sal Tanner peered down through bloodshot eyes acquired from a night of revelry following the occasion of a hanging; and bending closer to see what it was that the dog was frantically licking, she suddenly sprang back, startled by the piercing cry which even took the dog unawares. 'It's a young 'un!' she cried, kicking the excited animal aside and stooping nearer to take another look. 'It bloody well is, Jake,' she said in an astonished voice, 'it *is* a young 'un!' She looked furtively about, sensing it might be a trap of some kind – a temptation put there as an excuse to clap her in irons. When she saw nothing to alarm her, she bent to pick the infant up, saying in a softer tone, 'Who d'yer belong to, eh? What in God's name are yer doing lying in the street in the cold, eh?' As she drew the muslin cloth round the tiny thrashing child, her foot kicked the boot which Emma had lost in her struggles and the tiny bright silver watch that had been secreted there spilled out, its dainty facets sparkling in the light from the street lamp.

'What's this, eh?' Holding the child securely in one arm, Sal reached down with the other and picked up the watch. 'Well, I'm buggered!' she cackled. 'It's a time-piece – an' worth a bob or two, I'll be bound!' Turning it over and over in her fingers, she was surprised when the back sprang open to reveal something tucked inside. At once, she crossed to the street lamp and, standing in the yellow stuttering light, she juggled with the bundle in her arms so that she could dip a finger and thumb into the small cavity of the watch. When its contents were laid reverently in the palm of her hand, she was at once struck by the four-leaf clover, so lovingly put there by Emma and now shining a brighter green in the garish circle of light from above. 'By! See that?' Sal asked the dog, who was busy sniffing and licking at the child's muslin shawl. 'D'yer see how bright an' green it shines, eh? Now that's a sure sign if ever I saw one.' She now looked from the clover to the fretful child and back again. ''Tis the *little people* as belongs this bairn! Oho! . . . I 'ad half a mind ter leave the wretched bundle where I found it, for I don't know what to do wi' no infant, do I, eh? What do ol' Sal Tanner know of fotching up an infant, eh?' She gazed once again at the rich green colour of the four-leaf clover and then, with round, fascinated eyes, she examined the dark hair and pleasing face of Emma and Marlow's child, indeed her own kith and kin if only she'd known it. 'Yer a pretty little thing an' all,' she said in a gentle voice, 'but what sort are yer, eh?' Here she peeked into the muslin shawl. 'A lass! It's a little lass,' she told the dog, 'sent to me by the little people, to watch o'er.' Raising her face to the dark sky above, she said more loudly, 'I'll do me duty, yer can depend on that. Ol' Sal won't let yer down.' As she reverently returned the clover to its place, the tiny lock of hair which had been with it was taken by a small gust of wind. Sal paid it no mind, for she was concerned only that the infant and the clover were safe. 'C'mon, Jake,' she told the dog, 'this little lass is 'ungry. There ain't nothing in *my* withered old tits ter satisfy it . . . so we'll mek our way back ter Blackburn and Derwent Street. Hildy Barker's not long lost a young 'un, and there'll 'appen be enough milk there ter keep this bundle thrivin' eh? That's if it can keep breathin' long enough to mek the journey back!'

Sal Tanner made a strange but agreeable sight as she moved away up the street, her small limp causing her now and then to give a little skip, the child still crying in her arms, the great bull-mastiff lolloping along beside her, and she holding a long, detailed conversation with the 'little people'. But, strange sight though it was, how it would have gladdened Emma's heart to have seen it.

Chapter Twelve

On the fourth day of January 1863, Emma was disembarked, along with some two hundred and fifty other prisoners, at the mouth of the Swan River in the port of Fremantle, Western Australia – some thousands of miles and vast oceans between her and her beloved homeland. It was the first time the prisoners had set foot on land since boarding the ship in England; during the short stopover in Singapore they had been confined below decks. Now, the sun was so brilliant it was blinding, and the heat so intense that it sapped what little strength they had left. But, after the dark, cramped conditions they had endured the air smelled fresh and sweet and the big, open landscape gave a strange sense of freedom.

The long and arduous sea voyage was over. For Emma, it had been a terrifying experience, every detail of which would remain with her forever – from that first moment when she had seen the towering ship rising out of the murky waters in Langston Harbour, England, to this equally daunting moment as they were filed out like cattle, creating a dishevelled spectacle for those curious few who had come to watch, those whose duty it was to contain them and the privileged few who were given first choice of convict labour.

'Keep your fingers crossed that we'll be kept together,' Emma now told the girl by her side. For as long as she lived, Emma would never forget what a true and steadfast friend Nelly had been. During those first few weeks of their journey, when Emma had lain close to death's door, Nelly had never been far away. Emma remembered another who had also shown kindness and concern when she had been at her lowest ebb. She had been both embarrassed and relieved to find the voyage was being made in Silas Trent's vessel, and he was on board. He had persuaded the captain to allow Emma the company and support of her friend, Nelly, when she needed it most; and when Emma was eventually discharged from the sick-bay, he kept a constant eye on their well-being, though he was more careful not to show undue favouritism lest it should alienate Emma and her friend from the other prisoners.

The daily routine was the same for all. The cooks were usually the very first prisoners to show themselves, usually at the early hour of five-thirty. While they were up-top preparing the first rations of the day, the prisoners below deck would stow away their hammocks before washing. Then came the surgeon's sick round, followed by the issue of the daily ration of water and biscuits. At eight a.m. breakfast was served, usually consisting of a basin of gruel, a mug of cocoa and a few ounces of biscuits; at noon, dinner comprised of soup, salt beef or pork and a further helping of biscuits; at about five-thirty p.m., half a pint of tea and four ounces of biscuit were provided for supper. Each prisoner was allowed three quarts of water daily. There were religious services and assembly of school if needed. At eight o'clock the prisoners were sent back down below to the forward of the bulkhead, where space was severely limited and the air rank and stale. Prisoners' berths were ranged in two continuous rows, above and below, against the hull, with a walkway down the centre.

For Emma this was the worst time of all. The air was stifling with so many bodies crammed in such a confined space, and there was the constant, dreadful fear that any minute they would all suffocate for want of air. Yet, if the night brought its nightmares, so too did the long, trying hours of the day. Security was formidable, with hatchways enclosed by stout iron bars and barricades across the entire width of the ship on deck, behind the main mast. A guard of grim-faced soldiers with guns ready remained wary night and day; loaded cannons were aimed forward, with other equally fearsome weapons kept close by. A sight to sober not only the prisoners, but all present on the voyage.

Severe punishments were inflicted for various crimes on board. Emma remembered one in particular with great horror, when a woman prisoner – known to be a 'seasoned lag' by many of the others – was caught stealing another prisoner's ration. For her troubles, she was dragged away screaming, to be incarcerated in what was referred to as the 'Black Box', which was a dark and narrow cell erected under the forecastle. She was kept there for eight days, after which she emerged a broken, nervous wreck.

'They're coming, gal!' Emma was alerted back to the present situation by Nelly's loud whisper and, looking up, she saw two grim-faced men approaching, with an armed soldier either side and the figure of Silas Trent to their left. Some short way behind them was another group of people – one of which was a surly-faced woman of authoritative bearing.

As Emma kept her eyes on the approaching party, they

drew to a halt at the beginning of the line of prisoners, with quiet consultations taking place between the soldier in charge and various members of the civilian group. Much pointing and nodding of heads followed, before the one in charge was approached by Silas Trent.

Having taken off his hat some minutes earlier, he now smartly replaced it as, concluding his furtive discussion with the soldier in charge – during which Emma could have sworn she saw money changing hands between himself and the soldier – he now beckoned to two men to accompany himself and the man in charge. Together, all four came down the line at a fast, purposeful pace, coming to a halt directly opposite Emma. So shaken by it was Nelly, that she took an involuntary step backward, until Emma looked encouragingly at her, so that with a shameful face, she came back into line to stand shoulder to shoulder with Emma.

'Emma Denton?' the soldier in charge addressed her, continuing when she answered affirmatively, 'Your services have been assigned. Mr Trent here will explain the formalities and due procedure, after which you'll report to the authorities at the dock exit.'

When Emma appeared unsure as to what all this meant, Silas Trent smiled at her, saying in a reassuring voice, 'You've been assigned well, Emma . . . to assist at the trading post. They're good people and you won't be ill-treated.'

'And Nelly?' Emma was concerned that Nelly should be equally 'well assigned'.

After a moment's hesitation, Silas Trent gave the soldier in charge a sly look. 'I'm sure there's work enough at the trading post for both of them, wouldn't you say?' he asked, surreptitiously fingering his coat above the pocket where his wallet was kept.

'All right by me,' agreed the soldier, immediately casting his eyes towards the other two men – the older of whom was near fifty, round and jolly looking, while the younger one, with his blue eyes and unruly fair hair seemed to Emma to be of a decidedly arrogant disposition.

Both men nodded in agreement, the older one knowing he would be paid well – and anyway *two* healthy young girls would take the weight of the more laborious tasks off his back, what with his wife having fallen to bad health lately – and the other, Foster Thomas – Roland Thomas's son – in favour of having two healthy young girls about but for very different reasons! Life had become somewhat tedious of late and handsome girls the like of that one called Emma Denton were few and far between.

As Emma was led away, she gave thanks for people such as her friend, Nelly, and the caring Silas Trent, who had promised not to discuss her fate with Martha. Yet, even with what would appear to be a fair start in this strange and awesome new land, she wondered what might become of her. Through her mind raged distorted and painful images of all that had gone before, the loss of all those who were most precious – first Marlow, then Mrs Manfred, and finally hers and Marlow's precious little daughter.

No matter how desperately Emma tried to put these unbearable memories behind her, she could not. How could she ever forget that wonderful night when she and Marlow had lain in each other's arms? How could she not dream of his laughing black eyes, whose cherished gaze echoed the love in her own heart? Where was Marlow now, she thought. Where was he? And the babe? Oh, dear God, how often had she thought of that dear little creature, whose colouring was so like Marlow's and whose delicate life was so mercilessly denied?

Emma thought the world to be a cold, cruel place. Who could blame her, she wondered, for keeping those treasured memories alive if it meant her heart was warmed and revived? Of a sudden, she recalled Mrs Manfred's last words to her: 'When you get to those far-off shores, Emma, don't be afraid. Be careful not to antagonize those who would hold the key to your freedom. Work hard, keep your mind busy and the years will swiftly pass. When the day comes that your life is returned to you, use it well, Emma. Cherish it, and never forget the things you were taught. Will you promise me that, Emma?'

Under her breath, Emma murmured, 'I promise, Manny . . . with all my heart.' And as she gave this final promise to her dear friend, she made another one to herself. Her day of freedom *would* come and when it did, she would make every endeavour to return to the land of her birth. For there, she had old scores to settle, and an undying love to salvage. If only the Lord would keep her safe until then.

'I'm buggered if we ain't landed on us feet!' came Nelly's excited whisper. 'We've been placed well, and we've got each other. Oh, Emma gal! I reckon we're gonna be all right after all!'

As Emma smiled at her and took her hand to squeeze it in a gesture of friendship, she made the comment, 'We *will* be all right, Nelly. Take heart. Something tells me the good Lord will watch out for us after all.'

Alley Urchin

Dedication

For all their steadfast love and support, my thoughts go out to my two lovely sisters, Winifred and Anita.

Life hasn't been easy for them, but they can always find a smile, bless their hearts.

Not forgetting my seven brothers, Sonny, Joseph, Bernard, Richard, Billy, Harry and Alec. They could never be described as angels, but our late, lovely Mam would have been as proud of them all as I am. (Keep the meat an 'tater pies hot, lads!)

Foreword

The research for this book took me to Australia and Singapore, where I travelled many miles and talked to countless numbers of people. As a result, not only did my research prove to be fruitful, but became a labour of great joy. Everyone went out of their way to help, advise, and 'dig up' relevant documentation and information which have proved invaluable.

My husband, Ken, and I spent many long hours browsing through material under the artificial lights of libraries, and in museums and archives. We also traipsed many miles on foot in the tiring heat of Australia, a magnificent land. We saw wonderful buildings which were built by the convicts themselves in the Port of Fremantle, the most striking (and ironic) in my opinion being the prison which was to house them. One particular building which will live forever in my nightmares is the formidable Victorian-style lunatic asylum. This has, fortunately, been preserved as an arts centre and museum. But a one-time padded cell is kept almost exactly as it was, when the inmate might be dragged, screaming, into its dark and grim interior.

To stand inside that cell, to see the narrow iron bed and the high beamed walls, with the only light coming in through a tiny barred window, is to feel real terror. It was the most unnerving experience of my life. The atmosphere seems to have been absorbed into the very fibre of the walls – to touch those walls is to feel the presence of those wretched souls.

When, quite shaken, I emerged from that dank and dismal place, it was to be told by the curator, 'If the poor convicts weren't insane when they locked them in . . . they certainly were when they let them out!' (I, for one, was not about to argue with that.)

Below are mentioned a few of the many people who went out of their way to help in my search for the human story of what might have taken place there so many years ago. Australia is a vast and beautiful land, whose people rightly feel a great sense of pride in it. But picture the unfortunates who are wrenched from home and family, then taken on a long harrowing journey across the oceans to the other side of the world, nto knowing whether they might ever again find freedom, or be returned to the bosom of their family. What paradise for them?

Lorraine Stevenson (Archives), Town Hall, Fremantle WA
Sunita A. Thillainath (Librarian), Fremantle WA
Mary faith Holloway (Custodian), Prison Museum, Fremantle WA
Ralph of Ralph's Cafe, Fremantle WA
Gloria McLeod, Daglish WA
The Port Authority Officials, Fremantle WA
Chamber of Commerce Officials, Fremantle WA
The old Darwin fella in the Cafe – Good on yer, mate!

My love and thanks to Ken who, as ever, gave me constant support and was a wonderful companion.

Part One

Australia 1870

Ambitious Dreams

When night moves in
To hide the sun,
When enemies rally
And your strength is done,
When your weary heart
Longs to be free
Think of me, beloved,
Think of me.

J.C.

Chapter One

'If it takes a lifetime and if I am driven to follow you to every dark corner of the earth, I mean to have you. And I *will*. Mark my words, Emma . . . for you'll find no escape!' Though delivered in barely a whisper, the words struck deep into Emma's heart. The half-smiling, taunting mouth was so close to her face that she could feel the warm breath fanning her skin. 'You *will* learn to love me, Emma, I promise you.' The voice was trembling with passion and, as before, it was charged with a deal of arrogance. There was something else besides. Some deep, dark obsession, something akin to desperation. Or insanity.

'*Love* you!' Emma's stout heart was fearful, yet her grey eyes glinted like hardened steel as they bore defiantly into the leering face above her. Even though she would have denied it to the world, Emma could not deny to herself that she *was* afraid. Ever since that fateful day some seven years before when, along with other like wretches she had stumbled from the convict ship, Emma's every instinct had been disturbed by the covetous manner in which Foster Thomas had brought his gaze to rest on her.

As always, Emma put on a brave front. Drawing her trim form upright and squaring her small, straight shoulders, she told him, 'I could *never* love you, Foster

3

Thomas. Never! The only emotion you raise in me is one of disgust.' Yes, of repugnance and loathing too, thought Emma, being painfully aware of his close proximity as he stood his ground, determined that she should not pass. She saw him as everything vile in a man. Oh, it was true that he had about him the compelling quality that might easily turn a woman's head. He was a fine figure of a man – tall and lean, with wayward sun-bleached hair atop a bronzed handsome face. There was a certain attraction in the coarseness of his manner, yet when the occasion suited him, he carried an air of elegance and devastating charm. But those eyes: only the eyes betrayed the truth of his nature. Small they were, and calculating; murky-blue in colour as the ocean, yet more deep and dangerous, and ever watchful, like the quick, darting glance of a lizard.

For what seemed an age, he made no move. Instead, his smile grew more devious, then, raising his hand, he made as if to stroke Emma's long chestnut hair. But, being somewhat startled by a sudden intrusion, he angrily lowered his arm and swung round to face the intruder. 'You!' he snapped, glowering hard at the homely young woman silhouetted in the barn doorway. 'Haven't you got work to do?'

'Course I 'ave!' came the chirpy reply, as the irrepressible Nelly strode into the barn, quickly dropping the wooden bucket from her arm to the floor. 'Yer surely don't think I've been sitting on me arse all morning, d'yer?' Then, before he could lay the yard-broom across her shoulders, as she knew he would, she added quickly, 'Old Mr Thomas sent me ter fetch yer. He said yer was ter come straight away, on account of it being most urgent.' She manipulated her plain, kindly features into an expression of alarm. 'The poor old thing were having a real fit about some'at,' she said, nodding her head so frantically that her frilly cap tumbled into the dust at her feet. By the time she bent to retrieve it, Foster Thomas was gone, after first asking, 'You say my father wants me right now . . . this very minute?' To which she replied with suitable anxiety, 'Ooh yes, Mr Thomas, sir. This *very* minute!'

'You little wretch,' laughed Emma, as she and Nelly watched him stride away, both knowing full well that he was being sent on a fool's errand. That rascal Nelly, thought Emma, as she lovingly put an arm about her friend's shoulders; she knew every trick in the book. Brought up in the East End of London, she was a Cockney through and through. Since an early age, Nelly had been forced by circumstances to fend for herself, and she was a past master at it. It wasn't the first time she had made a timely intervention on Emma's behalf. Though Emma knew only too well that Nelly could take care of herself, she was constantly afraid that, one of these days, Foster Thomas might take it into his head to get rid of Nelly once and for all.

Emma knew it would be an easy thing, because all that was necessary was for the Governor to receive a formal complaint against the prisoner Nelly, and she would be punished, assigned elsewhere, or both. So far, Emma had stalled such a move by appealing to *old* Mr Thomas, Foster's father, who was after all the employer to whom both she and Nelly had been entrusted since being brought to these shores. With his wife in ailing health, Mr Thomas senior had been thankful for the labour supplied by the two female convicts, and was never too mean to say so – both to them, and in his regular reports to the Governor.

Emma respected and liked him. He was a hard-working and shrewd man of business, having built up his trading post from selling the few items he brought with him when he first arrived in Western Australia as an early settler many years before. He was a good man, and his wife a good woman. Emma thought they deserved a better son than Foster Thomas.

'Oh, Nelly . . . I wish you'd be more careful.' Emma hoped this little episode wouldn't bring trouble down on their heads. 'You know what a vicious temper he has, yet you will keep going out of your way to infuriate him.' Much as she understood Nelly's unselfish motive and her first instinct was to thank her, Emma thought that better purpose would be served by showing her disapproval: 'I'm quite capable of looking after myself, you know.'

'Yer bleedin' well ain't!' came the indignant retort. 'I saw him . . . with his filthy paws all over yer. What! The bugger's lucky I didn't clap him on the back o' the neck wi' a shovel!' Her angry brown eyes twinkled at the thought. 'Randy bleeder,' she went on, at the same time retrieving her wooden bucket and leading the way to the inner recesses of the big barn, where she proceeded to gather up the numerous eggs which had been laid here and there. When Emma pointed out that Foster Thomas was *her* problem and said, 'He's sure to cause trouble for you, when he finds you sent him on a wild goose chase,' Nelly was quick to assure the concerned Emma. 'Old Mr Thomas'll cover up fer me. He's done it afore.'

Exasperated, Emma shook her head, rolled her lovely grey eyes heavenward and laughed out loud.

'What *will* I do with you, Nelly?' she chuckled. Where-upon, Nelly laughed heartily, 'Send me back ter England.' She added with some gusto, 'The sun don't cook yer brains there, and there's more bleeding pockets ter pick.'

Quickly now their laughter subsided, when a shadow came between them and, looking up, they saw the large, ungainly figure of Mr Thomas. His face was unusually stern and, as he stood unmoving with his two large hands spread one over each hip, Emma saw the frustration in his dark, round eyes which were usually kind and smiling.

For a long, awkward moment, no one spoke. Feeling uncomfortable beneath his accusing glare, Nelly cast her eyes downward. Emma however met his gaze with an equally forthright one, until, seeing that there was no immediate explanation forthcoming and that, as always, he was hopelessly outnumbered two to one, Roland Thomas took his hands from his hips, plunged them deep into his pockets and allowed the whisper of a smile to creep over his craggy, kindly features.

'What a pair of baggages you are,' he said good-humouredly. Then, to Nelly, who had raised her merry brown eyes to smile at him, 'You've got that bloody son of mine running round in circles . . . me as well!' Of a sudden the smile slipped from his face and his voice held a warning: 'You're playing with fire, though. Be careful, Nelly, because though I say it as shouldn't . . . that son of mine is a bad lot!' His eyes were now on Emma, as though willing her to convince Nelly that she was putting herself in danger, 'Be warned. Don't antagonise him.'

'But he were pestering Emma again!' protested

Nelly, afterwards falling quiet when Roland Thomas stepped forward, his concerned eyes never leaving Emma's face.

'Don't worry about me, Mr Thomas,' Emma promptly assured him, 'I can look after myself.'

'Look here, Emma' – his voice was quiet now, and on his face a look of anxiety as he told her – 'I'm no fool and I'm not blind.' His gaze lingered on her face for a moment. 'Stay out of his way as best you can. Keep a good distance between you.' Having said that, he turned away to leave them to their duties.

It was a moment before both Emma and Nelly recovered from the seriousness of the warning they had just been given. The first to speak was Nelly who said, in little more than a whisper, 'Well, I'm buggered! I ain't never seen old Mr Thomas so harsh.'

Neither had Emma, and her every instinct had been aroused. Was there something going on that neither she nor Nelly was aware of? An idea wormed itself into her troubled mind, and swiftly, Emma thrust it out. No. Surely to God, it couldn't be that Mr Thomas was about to turn over the business to his son! No, he would *never* do that . . . would he? Oh, it was true that Violet Thomas's health had gone steadily downhill these past months, and it had been a source of much anxiety to her husband. But knowing his great passion for the trading business he had nurtured all these years, Emma couldn't believe that Mr Thomas was about to let go of the reins. And certainly not to his son Foster . . . who had never shown an ounce of interest in the business; except, of course, in the money it provided him with, to waste on grog and gambling. Yet there was something . . . definitely something: she was sure of it.

'I'd best get these eggs inside . . . afore the buggers are cooked!' Nelly remarked, at the same time slapping Emma heartily on the back as she passed. 'Roll on three o'clock, Emma . . . and we can put our feet up, eh?' Then, turning just once before she went from the shadows of the barn into the baking heat outside, she added, 'The buggers don't worry me, dearie, and they shouldn't worry you.' Emma smiled to herself. She admired Nelly for her fearlessness, yet she also saw it as being foolhardy. When the two of them had been exiled from their homeland, Nelly's sentence had been less severe than her own. Now, seven years on, their roles were reversed and, while Emma had earned her ticket-of-leave through good conduct, Nelly's rebellious attitude had put back the day of her freedom even further. Yet even though she was her own worst enemy, Nelly was a warm, loyal and steadfast friend, whom Emma loved like a sister. And, though the Governor had told Emma that her ticket-of-leave gave her at least the freedom to choose her own employer and place of work, Emma remained alongside Nelly in the Thomas trading post. While her friend was forced to stay, then so would she. Emma shook her head and chuckled softly, 'The way she's going on though . . . we'll both be old and grey before we get the chance to make our way in the world.' Afterwards she sighed, and turning her attention to the task in hand, at the same time subconsciously noted that the stock of small oil lamps would need replenishing.

Emma loved her work here, and she took a great pride in all of her duties. Mr Thomas himself had remarked on more than one occasion, 'You're a born trader, Emma . . . you've got a real knack for it.'

Emma was grateful that she had been assigned to the trading post, for she did feel so much at home, serving the customers, making up the orders and keeping the books for Mr Thomas. It wasn't so very different from being a clerk at her father's cotton mill in Lancashire. Sometimes, when the sun had beaten down mercilessly all day and the stream of customers continued from early morning to closing, when Emma's feet ached and her back felt as stiff and uncomfortable as the ladder she might have to run up and down a dozen times a day, Emma was glad to crawl back to the small room she and Nelly shared, at the back of the stables. It was a hard life, with each day as demanding as the one before. But Emma poured herself heart and soul into her work. Mr Thomas was a good employer and lately, he had been shifting a good deal of the more confidential duties on to Emma's shoulders, so that, besides keeping the stock-book up to date, she was often responsible for the accounts ledger, and even for cashing up and securing the takings.

One particular evening, Emma had overheard a raging row between Mr Thomas and his son Foster who, she knew, bitterly resented his father's increasing dependency on her. Afterwards, she had respectfully pointed out to Mr Thomas, 'I don't want to be the cause of bad blood between you and your son.' His immediate reply was to inform her of two things. Firstly, that he was obliged to spend as much time as possible with Mrs Thomas, who 'is a delicate and refined creature who unfortunately does not enjoy good health', and secondly, 'if she had been able to bear me another son . . . or even a daughter of *your* calibre, I might be fortunate enough to lean on them.

As it is, Emma . . . I have a worthless son who thinks it more natural to take rather than to give.' Here, the weariness melted from his craggy features, and in its place was a great tenderness. 'Then, I have you, Emma. And though the hand of fate was so cruel as to condemn you to this land a convict . . . I can only bless my *own* fate, for having deigned that you should be assigned to me.' On this last word, he had turned away before Emma could see how deeply he had been affected by the vehement row with his son, and the added burden that Emma might decide to seek employment elsewhere, which, having earned her ticket-of-leave, she had every right to do. Some time later, her heart filled with compassion at this good man's dilemma, Emma made it her business to explain to him that she would not desert him. He spoke not a word, but touched her gently on the shoulder and when he turned away, it was with a brighter, more contented light in his dark eyes.

Thinking about it all, Emma later reflected on her assurance to him, which amounted to a promise. She thought also about her determination not to desert Nelly. As she dwelt on it more deeply, it became apparent that she was enveloped in a prison other than the one to which Her Majesty's Government had despatched her. It was a prison within a prison, made by her own hand, and one which by its very nature would thwart her plans towards absolute freedom and her eventual return to England. This above all else burned fiercely in Emma's heart. She knew with every breath in her body that her day *would* come. That wonderful exhilarating moment when she would embark on the ship which was destined to carry her over the oceans to the other side of the world. To England! To the 'friends' who had cheated and betrayed her. And, with God's help, to Marlow Tanner . . . the man whose child she had borne and tragically lost. The man she had loved then, and whom she had loved every waking moment since. Oh yes, that day would surely come. Until then, she must count the hours and be frugal with every penny she earned. Above all, she must thank God for the love and devotion of a dear, dear friend, and count herself fortunate to have the confidence, loyalty and trust of another. She wouldn't let them down. Not even in the face of a no-good like Foster Thomas.

Some two hours later, Emma had completed the laborious task of taking account of all stock, both in the general store and in the huge outer barn, which doubled as a warehouse. Afterwards, when coming back into the small office at the rear of the store, she put the heavy ledger on to the bureau and commented to Mr Thomas, 'That consignment of goods from England is overdue. Another twenty-four hours and we'll likely be sold out of candles, boots and general harness. And another thing, Mr Thomas . . .' Emma quickly finished her final entries into the 'Urgent' page of the ledger, before emerging through the office doorway and into the store. There she assured herself that Mr Thomas was attentive to what she was about to say. Then, taking off her dusty pinnie, she replaced it with a freshly laundered one from beneath the counter and continued, 'I do wish you would think about what I said some time back . . . about taking up a lease on one of the more substantial warehouses on Cliff Street. That old barn isn't secure, as well you know it, Mr Thomas, and there's a lot of money tied up in the goods stored there.'

'Oh, Emma!' Mr Thomas raised his finger and thumb to tickle his mutton-chop whiskers absent-mindedly; it was a peculiar habit of his whenever he seemed slightly amused. 'Do you think we're about to be robbed?' He chuckled aloud and, bending his back, he grasped the corners of a box of carbolic soaps with his two hands. He swung the box upwards, before bringing it down in a flurry of dust, on to a shelf he had just cleared. 'Or mebbe you've got a notion that some rascal creeping about at night has the intention of putting a match to it, eh?' He chuckled again. 'You're a little scaremonger, that's what you are,' he declared with a broad and confident smile.

Emma was not amused. Nor would she be dissuaded from pointing out the errors of continuing to store valuable goods and equipment in such an insecure and vulnerable place. 'There *are* "rascals" enough who might well put a match to anything, if it suited their purpose!' she reminded him. 'You know as well as I do that there are certain unsavoury characters in Fremantle who wouldn't think twice about razing that barn to the ground, after helping themselves to a good deal first.' When Emma saw that, at last, she had his serious attention, she went on quietly, 'Oh, Mr Thomas . . . I'm not saying as they would, but you've seen the strangers about of late . . . diggers and bushmen . . . some new to the area, and some looking even rougher than the worst convicts sent to break stones on the road. Wouldn't it make sense to house your more valuable goods at least, in a small secure lock-up on Cliff Street?'

Pausing a moment longer in his work of setting out the blocks of soap in a fetching grey display, Mr Thomas played one lip over the other, biting first at the top, then at the bottom, while he quietly pondered Emma's suggestion. Wasn't she right after all, when the goods were hard come by, and cost a fortune to ship out from England? Then, once out on the high seas they were at the mercy of every wild storm and natural disaster that a ship might encounter on its long voyage. She was right! Emma was right. Some of the stuff . . . shovels, pickaxes, and good working tools were going out as fast as he could get them in. There had been guarded murmurs about little pockets of gold being found here and there, and that was no doubt the explanation. All the same, merchandise was an increasingly valuable commodity hereabouts, and a person could never be too careful.

'You do see why I'm so concerned?' asked Emma, her shrewd business instinct telling her exactly the thoughts going through her employer's mind. 'I can arrange it . . . if you'll trust me to do the job right,' she offered, knowing only too well that his mind was lately taken up with his wife's unfortunate illness. Emma felt sorry for Mrs Thomas, who had never gone out of her way to make friends, was a very private person and, unlike Mr Thomas, kept both Emma and Nelly at a distance. The only person who enjoyed her confidence, other than Mr Thomas himself, was the blacksmith's spinster daughter, Rita Hughes. Rita pampered her every whim and saw to her every need, for the small weekly payment of a few shillings. Emma suspected that Nelly was right in her observation that 'Rita Hughes has one eye on Mrs Thomas . . . and the other

14

firmly fixed on *Foster* Thomas'! Adding, to Emma's disapproval, 'Though if yer ask me, she's well past it and gone sour.' When Emma protested that that was a cruel thing to say, Nelly was quick to point out, 'Huh! T'would be even *more* cruel if he took a fancy to her! What . . . a fella the likes o' Foster Thomas would mek her life a bleedin' misery.' Emma had to agree.

Emma was convinced that poor Mrs Thomas had withdrawn into herself on account of her husband and son forever being at loggerheads. At one time she had doted on her only son. Now he showed little interest in his mother, and she showed none in him. All the same, Emma suspected that her heart was quietly breaking.

'I tell you what' – Mr Thomas's voice cut into Emma's thoughts – 'leave it with me, Emma. I'll bear in mind what you've said.' Beyond that he would not be drawn. Except to promise that the shop takings would not in future be kept upstairs in his room for up to a week at a time, as had become the habit of late. Emma did not agree with his belief that such large sums of money must always be to hand. 'The captains of the pearl-luggers want always to be in and out in a hurry, and, if I'm to keep up with the competition to buy the best pearl-shell in, then I need to have cash to hand at any given minute.' It worried Emma. But this was his trading post, not hers, and she mustn't forget her place.

Neither Emma nor Mr Thomas could have known how tragically Emma's fears were about to be realised, before the hands of the clock had turned full circle!

'Sat'day's my favourite day!' exclaimed Nelly, leaning over the ceramic rose-patterned bowl which was rested atop a cane-bottomed chair. 'Once we've reported to the authorities we'll have the rest o' the day . . . and all tomorrer afore we're back in the shafts.' She gave a loud 'Whoopee!', punched her fist in the air for the sheer joy of it and, scooping her two hands deep into the bowl, she splashed the water on to her face, neck and ears. 'I fancy a fella!' she chuckled through a mouth full of water while peeping at Emma out of one cheeky brown eye.

'Away with you!' laughed Emma, who was patiently waiting for her turn with the bowl. 'If you intend walking along the jetty with me, you'd best curb your urges for a "fella". The way you're going on, my girl, you'll be marched to the top of the hill, where you'll be clapped in irons and thrown in a prison cell, so every poor "fella" will be safe from your clutches.' When, mockingly holding her wrists together and limping as though shackled, Nelly started towards her, at the same time making an eerie wailing sound, Emma grabbed up a towel, held it out before her and, amidst much laughter, launched herself at Nelly. In a minute the two of them were rolling about the floor helpless with laughter. Then a kick from Emma's leg sent the cane-bottomed chair into such a violent swaying fit that the water in the bowl slopped first over one side, then the other. Convulsed by new fits of giggling, Nelly and Emma made to grab the chair, causing it to overbalance completely as the bowl shot forward to empty its entire contents, drenching them both. 'Bleedin' Nora!' shouted Nelly, scrambling to her feet and proceeding to shake herself like a dog. 'I'm bloody soaked!'

Subdued by the initial shock, Emma got to her knees and looked up at Nelly, all the while coughing and spluttering, her long chestnut hair hanging limp and bedraggled over her shoulders. When she saw Nelly's outrage and witnessed her frantically shaking her long skirt while at the same time swearing and cursing enough to frighten hardened criminals, Emma thought of her own ludicrous position and an old saying sprang to mind – 'Oh dear God, the gift to gi' us, to see ourselves as others see us.' In a minute she had fallen back to the ground and was laughing out loud.

'Yer silly cow!' yelled Nelly, throwing the damp flannel at her. 'I only wanted a cat-lick . . . not a bleedin' *bath*!' Whereupon she too began roaring with laughter. It was quite some time before they had regained their composure sufficiently to clean up and refill the bowl with fresh water for Emma's wash. Unlike Nelly, Emma preferred to strip down to her camisoles for a thorough scrubbing and, having rolled about the floor, then been doused with dirty water, Emma took longer than usual at her daily ritual.

Some time later the two of them emerged from the stables. Having discarded her grey work-frock with its over-pinnie, Emma looked delightful in a plain blue dress with a small bustle on the skirt and crisp white frills about the cuffs and neck. Her thick chestnut hair was well brushed and drawn into a shining, most fetching coil at the nape of her neck. Her face was bright and lovely and her strong grey eyes brimmed with the steadfast confidence that set her apart from others.

Nelly, however, did not present such a striking picture. Oh, it was true that her thin brown hair had also been brushed with vigour. But, being under closer scrutiny of the prison authorities, and on more than one occasion having earned the punishment that dictated her locks be shorn, her hair did not enjoy the length that might cause it to lie smoothly against her head. Instead, it stood up and out in little wispy bunches which gave her the odd appearance of having just received a fright. Not being one for dainty things and 'feminine fripperies', Nelly was therefore proud of her heavy buttoned boots which came up to her calf. At one time, when Emma had pointed out that there was no need to wear such clumsy, uncomfortable things in the heat of the summer sun, Nelly had been adamant that she would wear nothing else. 'I'd wear an even *longer* pair if I could get me hands on 'em,' she retorted; 'I ain't having no bloody snakes nor spiders running up *my* legs!' However, she did gratefully accept a brown calico dress which had, until recently, been Emma's best one. It was of the very same style that Emma was wearing now, except the frills at the cuffs and neck were black instead of white. Also, Nelly was some inches taller than Emma, therefore the ankles of her boots were visible to the world, even though Emma had twice let the dress hem down for her. But, all in all, she was presentable and, as she put her arm through the crook of Nelly's elbow, Emma cared not who might look down on her friend. The prospect never worried Nelly either!

'Mind you're not on the streets after the curfew bell!' the duty officer warned, simultaneously noting down their intention to stroll along to Arthur's Head. As they hurried away, he took his eyes from the book and fixed his suspicious gaze at Nelly's retreating figure. 'I wouldn't mind betting a week's grog that *you*'ll be in trouble before long, girlie . . . it's about that time,' he chuckled, shaking his head and leaning back in his chair

18

to take a long choking draw from his clay pipe; he was soon engulfed in great billowing clouds of smoke.

Following the old tramway route, Nelly and Emma sauntered along at a leisurely pace . . . down Henderson Street, along Essex Street and down towards the bay. 'This is the time of day I love best,' said Emma, shielding her eyes with the back of her hand as she looked upwards to where the seagulls soared above them. In spite of the fact that she was imprisoned in this vast, sparsely-inhabited island of Australia, Emma could not help but be deeply drawn towards its primitive beauty. There was an awesome savagery about it that struck at the heart and inspired the mind. It was a land of turquoise seas and vivid blue skies which merged together on the horizon, creating a sense of greatness and eternity. No mere human eye could ever hope fully to comprehend the vastness of it all, for in every direction the sky stretched, never ending and seeming to engulf those insignificant specks below, who both feared and marvelled at its majesty. Immediately inland from Fremantle to Perth, the landscape was sandy and gently undulating, relieved here and there by weird and wonderful trees, patches of shrub and rapidly growing signs of denser civilisation, with a number of the original timber and bark-roofed buildings being constantly replaced by the more permanent brick and stone buildings. There were also a number of splendid examples of architecture, such as the round-house and other buildings constructed by the convicts. The lunatic asylum, the road-traffic bridge and their own prison were such landmarks.

There were creatures here such as Emma had never seen before – kangaroos, brilliantly coloured birds, and even camels brought in from the desert countries. Most were friendly, but there were those which were not, such as certain snakes and spiders. Also a number of the dark-skinned natives whose resentment of the white man's intrusion on their shores was not entirely appeased. And everywhere the nostrils were assailed by the fresh pungent smell of the sea, so marked as to be almost a taste on the tongue.

Intent on appearing friendly towards a group of aborigines, two of whom were dressed in their traditional kangaroo-skin boukas – the other, a young male, wearing European trousers – Emma was startled by Nelly's jubilant cry as her attention was drawn in another direction. 'Look at that . . . the buggers are naked!' Whereupon she gripped Emma by the arm and propelled her in the direction of Bathers Bay. 'They're *naked*, I tell yer . . . bare as the day they were born. We've got to get a closer look, gal!' she told Emma in an excited voice, her brown eyes laughing, mischievously. 'It's been a while since I saw a fella in all his prime an' glory!'

Sure enough, Nelly was right. As Emma stared in the direction in which Nelly was rushing her at great speed, she too saw the group of swimmers in Bathers Bay. There must have been upwards of ten men, all shouting and frolicking one with the other, and all stark naked!

'Nelly!' Emma forced them both to a halt. 'We can't go down there. *You* can't go down there.' She saw the defiance in Nelly's eyes that told her the temptation was much too great to resist, and to hell with the consequences. Yet Emma was equally adamant that they would about-turn and make off in the opposite direction. 'Don't be a fool, Nelly,' she told her. 'You were warned that if you were brought before the Governor just *once* more, you'd be thrown in the lockup.' By this time the men had seen them, and had grown even more excited and rowdy. 'Come on, girlies . . . take a look, we don't mind,' one of them yelled, clambering from the water and brazenly displaying himself. Whereupon the others laughed encouragement that they 'needn't be shy.'

In a minute, Emma had succeeded in dragging the reluctant Nelly away and out of sight of the bathers. 'Cor, bugger me, gal,' protested Nelly, 'it wouldn't have hurt to watch from a safe distance.' Emma made no comment. Instead, she hurried towards South Bay. Once there, she sat down in the sand, with Nelly sitting cross-legged beside her, irritatedly clutching up fists full of sand and throwing it into the air, where the light breeze caught it and deposited it back into their laps.

After a while, when Nelly's attention was taken with the lapping of the water against the sand, Emma lay back, settled herself comfortably and closed her eyes. Of a sudden she was back in England, and her heart was gladdened by warm, if painful, memories. The image of Marlow filled her being and she was standing beside him on the colourful barge which had been his home. Oh, how plainly she could see him: that strong lithe body so often stretched to breaking point in his labours at the docks. In her mind's eye, Emma ran her fingers through his thick dark hair. She lovingly returned the smile from those black passionate eyes which had always seemed to see right into her very soul. Now his arms were about her. His warm tantalising mouth brushed her hair, her ears and, in one exquisite moment, he was kissing her with such ardour that made her tremble. With a shock, Emma sat up to find that, even in the heat of the evening sun, she was shivering violently. Both Nelly and she had been disturbed by an intruder.

When that intruder stepped forward, it was with a feeling of disgust that Emma recognised the tall handsome figure of Foster Thomas. He was not alone. Quickly, Emma got to her feet. 'What do you want?' she demanded, at the same time shaking the sand from her skirt and casting her angry grey eyes over his two rough-looking companions. One was tall, painfully thin and had an old jagged scar from eye to ear; the other was of medium height, stocky with a dark surly expression. Both had thick bushy beards, both wore flat wide-brimmed hats and chequered shirts, with dark serviceable trousers. 'Swag men,' thought Emma, as she met their arrogant stares unflinchingly.

Foster Thomas twisted his mouth into a crooked smile. 'Me and the blokes . . . we reckoned you and Nelly might be glad of a little company,' he said with a low laugh, at the same time reaching out to rest his hand on her shoulder. As he leaned forward with the intention of encircling Emma's tiny waist with his arm, the smell of stale booze on his breath was nauseating. His deep blue eyes were little more than slits as they bored down on her, betraying his lecherous intentions and instantly putting Emma on her guard. 'You're drunk!' She spat the words out vehemently, at the same time twisting away from him with such speed and agility that she caused him to lose his balance. When the two bushmen thought it so amusing that they began sniggering and pointing to Foster Thomas as he struggled to remain upright, the smile slipped from his face and was replaced with a particularly determined and vicious expression. 'You little bastard!' he snarled, lurching forward to grasp at Emma's swiftly departing figure.

In her indignation and urgency to get away, Emma lost sight of Nelly. Pausing to look back, she was horrified to see that her hapless friend had made no move to follow her, but instead was shamelessly taking delight in having all three men dance attendance on her. Foster Thomas, in particular, was handling Nelly with a deal of intimacy, which was greatly intensified when he saw that Emma was hurriedly making her way back towards them.

'What in God's name are you thinking of?' Emma demanded of Nelly, whom she thought seemed to be as intoxicated as the men when she began blushing and giggling at Foster Thomas's over-amorous advances.

'*This* girlie knows how to be grateful for a man's attentions,' he sniggered, holding Nelly closer and winking knowingly at the other men, who appeared to be thoroughly enjoying themselves.

'That's right,' rejoined the stocky fellow, sidling up to Emma and running his tongue round his dry lips. 'Like a dog going for a chop,' thought Emma as he stood, legs astride in front of her. 'Now then me beauty . . . how about you showing me what *you're* made of, eh?' In a minute he would have had her fast in his grip, but in that same instant Emma had swung her arm out sideways and, before he realised her intention, had brought her fist across his ear with a resounding thud. As he staggered back, his hand clapped to his throbbing ear and a string of foul language issuing from his mouth, the second man ran forward to lock his two arms about Emma and swing her bodily into the air.

'She's got spirit, has this one!' he laughed. 'She'll do fer me!' No sooner were the words out of his mouth than Foster Thomas had landed his fist in it. 'Take your filthy bloody paws off her!' he yelled, as the fellow released Emma and, confronting his assailant with a furious expression, he invited in a low growl, 'So! *That's* the way, is it? . . . C'mon then, me bucko . . . let's have it out!'

In a minute the two of them were locked in combat, the one pounding his bunched fist time and time again into the other's stomach, and the other with his finger-tips digging into his opponent's fleshy eyeballs with every intention of gouging out his very eyes. The third fellow, having miraculously recovered, was hopping up and down, screaming encouragement, first to one, then the other. Nelly did the same.

Never one to miss an opportunity, Emma lost no time in grabbing hold of Nelly who, by the degree of resistance she put up, would much have preferred to stay and watch the fight than run away with what she considered to be the cause of it. 'Ye slapped him good, Emma!' she cried, jubilantly lashing the air with her fists. 'Fetched him a right bleedin' clap aside o' the ear, y'did.' She was beside herself with excitement, and though Emma made every effort to remain above it all, she could only sustain her indignation as far as the old cemetery, when she paused, breathless, against some unfortunate soul's headstone. 'Oh, Nelly, Nelly!' she said, the smile already creeping into her eyes and lifting the corners of her mouth. 'I'm supposed to be the sensible one, who keeps you on the straight and narrow.' The smile broke into a small laugh.

'And you *do*,' Nelly assured her, pausing to catch her

breath from the fast and furious pace with which Emma had propelled her from the fracas on the beach. 'It's just a bloody shame that being kept on the "straight and narrer" don't allow fer a bit o' fun! Just now and then . . . I might like ter throw caution ter the wind and join forces wi' the devil.' When Emma rightfully reminded her that in encouraging a grog-sodden lout like Foster Thomas she was doing just that, Nelly retorted, 'Handsome devil, though, eh?' And in her twinkling brown eyes was a deep thinking expression which Emma had not seen before.

Nelly's remark both astonished and disturbed Emma very deeply. But she made no comment, other than to say it must be coming up to curfew time and they should be on their way.

No sooner had Emma made the observation than the curfew bell rang out, warning all bonded persons that they must be off the street. Emma hoped she and Nelly would not be challenged by an officer because, while she herself was able to show her ticket-of-leave, Nelly was already under suspicion, and being caught out even one minute after curfew could well cost her dear. As the two of them hurried towards Thomas's store, Emma led the way round the back streets, fearful that at any minute an officer would come upon them. Every now and then there would ring out the challenge, 'Bond or free?' as others, less artful, were stopped in the busier streets adjacent. Only when Emma had manoeuvred Nelly on to the porch of the store did she breathe a sigh of relief.

'You really do play fast and loose with the law, don't you?' came the thin, tired voice from a wicker chair in the far corner where the trellis was much higher. Mrs

25

Thomas was very rarely persuaded to come and sit out of an evening, but, when she did, it was on three conditions: it had to be past curfew 'when the criminals amongst us are safely out of the way'; it had to be almost twilight so she could sit in the shadows; and, her high-backed wicker chair had to be positioned securely in that particular corner where the trellis was highest, so the shadows would be that much deeper. Now, when her voice piped out on the sultry evening air, Emma gave a start . . . her heart still beating fast from the fear that she and Nelly would be stopped after curfew.

'Oh, Mrs Thomas!' she gasped, putting her hand to her heart. 'You gave me a fright.'

'And you gave *me* a right turn an' all!' joined in Nelly, whose face had gone an odd shade of parchment.

'Well now, I am sorry,' laughed Mrs Thomas, and Emma likened the sound of her laughter to the soft tinkling of the water in the Leeds and Liverpool Canal back home; that gentle, delightful sound that was made with the smooth passage of a laden barge as it gently churned up the water beneath. But then, *everything* was 'gentle' about poor Mrs Thomas. She was a tiny pathetic creature now, sitting in that high-backed chair like a duchess of old, or a china doll who was much too frail and exquisite to play with. Emma thought that Violet Thomas must have been a very beautiful lady when she was young, for she had finely sculptured bones and long delicate fingers. Her hair, though snow-white now, was still rich and thick with deep attractive natural curls, which even the scraped-back and severe hairstyle could not disguise. Her eyes were large and soft, as blue in colour as the sky, but they were filled with sorrow, always heavy with pain, and something akin to tragedy perhaps, a kind of deep inner suffering almost as though, even when the finely etched wrinkles on the face were lifted in a smile, the eyes remained haunted.

'Are you all right out here on your own?' questioned Emma, not liking the idea of leaving her seated here alone. 'Where's Mr Thomas?' she added with concern, at the same time coming closer to assure herself that the thin little figure was encased in a blanket, for there wasn't enough fat on Mrs Thomas's bones to keep her warm . . . sunshine or not. She needn't have worried though because, as always, Mr Thomas or Rita Hughes had taken good care of the lady's needs. There was a rug carefully draped about her legs, and a soft shawl wrapped about her small shoulders.

'Please . . . go to your beds.' The long, fine fingers waved into the air in a gesture of dismissal. 'Mr Thomas will be here presently, and I would rather you didn't fuss.' Her voice was sharper now, and the words came in short, tired little bursts. Emma sensed that, as always appeared to be the way, she and Nelly were not wanted by Mrs Thomas. That invisible barrier, which she so cleverly created, had been drawn up between them. They were being sent on their way and, not for the first time, Emma suspected that it was because they were convicts. Although Violet Thomas had never made or intimated the slightest complaint of such a nature regarding the two assignees who worked about the house and shop and who resided in the room behind the stables, her strong condemnation of 'the criminal element thrust among us' was well known. Emma therefore went out of her way not to antagonise her employer's wife, and she implored Nelly to do the same.

Emma would have liked to have been on closer terms with Mrs Thomas, because she knew her to be a lady, and she also felt something of the other woman's deep desire to go home to England 'to live out my days under a cloudy sky and to sup afternoon tea in a more genteel atmosphere'. Many times she had been heard pleading her cause to her husband and, as many times, Mr Thomas had been heard to promise, 'Soon, Violet, soon . . . When we've made our fortunes, for I'm sure you don't wish to starve under a cloudy sky, do you now, eh?' His wife never gave an answer, nor did she make any response within his hearing. Instead, they seemed to converse less, to drift further apart, and to execute a strange verbal dance whereby each might broach a subject close to their hearts; he of his store and business, she of England and her desire to return. Then the other would nod, smile and make meaning-less noises, after which a great painful silence would envelop them, as they each retreated into their own precious dreams. Emma thought it sad that they could not find it in their hearts to share the *same* dream. However, she sympathised with Mrs Thomas's obses-sion to return to England, because Emma herself had been possessed of that same obsession ever since being so cruelly and unjustly taken from her old homeland. Yet she had never once allowed this obses-sion to become so deeply rooted that it ravaged her entirely, as was the case with Mrs Thomas. Emma had deliberately thrown herself into her work, always striv-ing towards that ultimate freedom which she knew must one day be hers. In so occupying her mind and thoughts, she had deliberately suppressed her heart's desire, always aware that it was futile to dwell on it too deeply in the early years. Now though, with seven years of her sentence behind her, the realisation of once more being in charge of her own destiny was in sight.

Day and night, Emma's thoughts had begun to dwell on her freedom. Her heart would tremble at the prospect and her spirit was charged with such great anticipation and excitement that there were times when she could hardly contain herself. At these times, and often in the dark small hours when she was unable to sleep, she would get up from her bed to pace back and forth across the room like a caged creature. After a while, when the desperate emotions retreated and other, more tender, emotions flooded her heart, she would go to the window and gaze out across the moonlit sky. Then tears would flow unheeded down her face. Thoughts of home would storm her senses, pulling her first this way, then that, until she could hardly bear it. 'Oh, dear God,' she would murmur, 'will it ever come right for me again?' She longed for Marlow's arms about her, but even if in three years' time by some fortune or miracle there was the money and freedom to return to England, how would she find him? And, if she *did* find him, would he still love her? After all, she had deliberately spurned him in favour of another man even though, unbeknown to Marlow, it was for his own protection. Then there was the fact that she was a convict, charged and marked with a terrible crime. Oh, and what of the child she had borne him, and which was lost to them both? How could any man forgive her? The torture never ended for Emma. But she prayed that it would one day, otherwise there was no reason to go on.

'Emma!' The voice cut sharply across Emma's turbulent thoughts. 'Mrs Thomas has a mind to sit out a while longer. You and Nelly get off to bed.' Mr Thomas had returned from inside and he was quickly aware that his wife was becoming agitated by the presence of the two young women. 'Off you go,' he urged as Emma bade his wife a good night. 'Go on . . . go on. I'll see to her when she's ready to go back upstairs.'

'Miserable old bugger, that Mrs Thomas,' remarked Nelly, pulling off her clothes and getting quickly into her own narrow wooden bed. 'Anybody'd think we'd got the bleedin' plague . . . the way she starts panicking every time we get within arm's length of her!' She was greatly peeved and Emma's reply that 'we must make allowances for her' made no difference to Nelly's mood. 'Well, *I* ain't mekkin' no allowances for the old sod,' she retorted, blowing out the candle which was on the cupboard by her bed. 'It were *her* sort as pushed me into crime when I were a kid. Look down on yer, they do. Won't give yer no work, in case yer cut their throats at the first opportunity!' Then her mood quickly changed, she told Emma to 'sleep tight . . . mind the bed-bugs don't bite', and was soon fast asleep, the gentle rhythm of her soft snoring seeming a comfortable and homely sound to Emma as she lay in her own bed.

There was no sleep in Emma just yet, only a strange sense of quiet. Sometimes, she wished she could be more like Nelly, because nothing worried her for very long. She had no driving ambitions, no real grudges to bear, and no one person in her heart who could tear it apart. Here Emma checked herself. How did she know whether Nelly secretly loved anybody in particular? What about the way she enjoyed Foster Thomas's attentions today, and what of the remark she made about him being 'a handsome devil'? The very possibility that Nelly might be quietly attracted to that man filled Emma with dread. Indeed, it was too horrible to contemplate, for Emma truly believed that such a man as Foster Thomas would take the greatest delight in destroying someone as devoted and vulnerable as Nelly. Emma prayed that, if Nelly really did feel a certain attraction towards him, she would never let it be known to him, or he would likely take her to the depths and *leave* her there.

With this disturbing thought in mind and with the intention of warning Nelly the very next morning, Emma leaned over in her bed to blow out her candle. She closed her eyes and forced her mind to more pleasant dreams. Of a sudden Emma realised how tiredness had crept up on her. She was ready for sleep.

'Emma, wake up . . . *please* wake up!'

'What is it, Nelly?' Emma was not yet fully awake, but pushing back the coarse grey blanket from her face, she lifted her head and screwed up her heavy eyes to look on Nelly's frightened face. 'Have you had a nightmare?' she asked, not being sufficiently awake to be certain it wasn't she who was suffering the nightmare.

'No, no!' Nelly continued to poke and shake Emma until at last Emma was sitting up against the pillow, her eyes almost blinded by the light from Nelly's candle, which was presently thrust only an inch or so from her face. 'There's some'at going on over the store . . . noises there were!' She was obviously in a fearful state.

'Noises?' Quickly now, Emma got up from her bed and began dressing. 'What *sort* of noises?' she asked, suddenly wide awake.

'Funny noises . . . like scraping and thumping . . . and' – here Nelly hesitated, looking at Emma through the candlelight with big frightened eyes – 'I could'a sworn I heard somebody scream.'

Emma paused as she pulled on her boots, and glancing up towards Nelly, she said in a serious voice, 'You stay here. I'll take a look.'

'You bloody *won't*, y'know!' came Nelly's indignant retort. 'Not without me, you won't. *I* ain't staying here on me own!'

'All right then. But put out the candle. There's no sense in broadcasting what we're up to, is there? Besides . . . if you've been imagining these "noises" and such, and we're caught creeping about in the dark, we'll look a right pair of idiots and no mistake.' A quick glance told her that Nelly was barefooted and wore only her dress over her nightgown.

'I *ain't* imagining it, Emma. I heard strange voices . . . I just *know* there's some'at funny going on!'

'All right, Nelly. We'll take a look, if it'll put your mind at rest. But mind you keep quiet. Promise? Or I will leave you here!' Emma was under no illusions that, given just cause, Nelly could make herself heard from one end of Australia to the other. On securing Nelly's firm assurance that she would creep behind 'as quiet as a church-mouse', Emma patted her gratefully on the shoulder. 'Good girl,' she told her, taking the brass candlestick from Nelly's trembling hand, and after blowing out the light, she placed it down on the bedside cupboard. They didn't need a light to show them the way, for they had trodden it often enough. In any case, there wasn't much in this room to fall over, there being only one cumbersome wooden wardrobe, a tall chest of drawers, two narrow wooden beds, each with a little side-cupboard, and a small oblong rag-peg rug between the beds. Emma had thought it a grim little room when she had first seen it, with its one tiny window overlooking the dirt yard between the stables and the store. The Thomases lived in the four large rooms above the store, and the windows of the big bedroom looked down over the stables. Many a time, Emma had noticed Mrs Thomas seated by her bedroom window, gazing out at the skyline with a look in her eyes that was almost desperate, and her heart bled for the poor creature. She had often thought that if *she* were in Mrs Thomas's position, nothing on earth would prevent her from going home! But then she was reminded of two things. Firstly, Mrs Thomas was in very poor health, and secondly, perhaps even more important, it was obvious that despite their deep differences on the matter of which country was now home, she loved her husband and would never contemplate leaving without him. It really was a sorry state of affairs, and one which seemed irreconcilable.

Opening the door with some caution, Emma peered into the darkness. Surely Nelly must be wrong? She could hear no 'noises' of the kind described. Indeed, everything appeared perfectly normal for the early hours. The two grey work horses were quiet in the stable and the only sign of life in the sultry heat beneath

33

the moonlight was a lone furry creature who scurried by their feet. 'Jesus!' Nelly cried in a loud whisper. 'What the devil were that?' When Emma told her to be quiet while she listened, Nelly murmured, 'Sorry,' at once taking up a better grip on Emma's shawl and shuffling closer behind. 'P'raps I never heard nothing after all,' she loudly whispered in Emma's ear, 'p'raps I were imagining things . . . like yer said, Emma.'

'Ssh!' Emma had come to a stop against the end of the stable wall, pausing for a moment before crossing the open yard. 'Look there, Nelly,' she murmured softly, at the same time raising her arm to point upwards towards the Thomases' bedroom, 'see that?'

'Cor, bugger me, gal!' gasped Nelly. 'The light's on! They *never* leave the light burning . . . on account o' Mrs Thomas can't sleep when there's a light burning. There! Y'see, Emma . . . I told yer there was some'at going on, didn't I, eh? I told yer!' She was silenced by Emma's hand being pressed hard over her mouth, after which the two of them crept stealthily towards the back of the store. There was a loose wall board some three feet off the ground, which Emma had often stressed should be made more secure, but which was never on the list of Mr Thomas's priorities. Emma was thankful for his neglect of it, as she now eased it aside then carefully clambered in, helping the reluctant Nelly in behind her. 'Bleedin' hell!' Nelly whispered, regaining her balance and straightening her skirt to her bare ankles. 'What the devil d'yer reckon we're getting usselves into, Emma gal? I don't mind a fight . . . not bad wi' me fists, I can tell yer. But I like to see the enemy coming a mile away.'

'Nelly, be quiet!' Emma was afraid that if there were

intruders in the store, like as not Nelly's gabbling would put them on their guard, and the blighters would come at them in the dark like bats out of hell. 'Not another word,' she instructed, standing still as a statue and straining her ears for the slightest sound. There! There it was, muffled, yes . . . but unmistakably a man's voice, and raised in anger. Emma felt Nelly stiffen behind her and for a moment she was afraid of her calling out. But Nelly remained silent as Emma concentrated in an effort to distinguish the voice. She couldn't make out what was being said, but two things she was certain of: that voice did not belong either to old Mr Thomas *or* his son Foster, and, it was *not* a friendly voice! Strange, thought Emma, it couldn't be a business caller, not at this unearthly hour. Why, it must be two in the morning! The doctor then? Was it possible that Mrs Thomas had been taken badly and the doctor had been called out to her? Yes, that was possible. Yes! That was it, Emma was certain. But then she reminded herself, if it had been the doctor, then they would surely have heard his pony and trap, for old Dr Shaw liked the folks to know when he went about his business, especially when he was brought from his bed. No! They would have heard him slapping at the reins and driving like a fiend. Emma had come through the back store, round by the office, and was now almost at the foot of the stairs that led up to the Thomases' living quarters. If not either of the Thomas men, and not the doctor . . . who then? Her heart was beating against her ribs like a caged bird trying to get out. In the dark with Nelly pressed close behind and God only knew what was up in front, Emma felt suffocated. The heat was oppressive and the beads of sweat which stood out along her back began to break into tiny rivulets, which trickled irritatingly behind her shoulders. What should she do? Should she creep out again, and raise the alarm? No, she couldn't risk it, because the minute he knew he'd been tumbled, the intruder would either be away like sheet lightning, or, even worse, in his desperation, he might harm the Thomases. Emma couldn't risk such a thing.

Her mind was working frantically. Emma felt her way towards the rack which held the shotguns. She knew every inch of this store like the back of her hand, but she never thought such knowledge would prove so very useful. In a matter of minutes, she had the shotgun and ammunition in her grasp. In another minute, she had the gun loaded and ready. When Nelly indicated that she also wanted a gun, Emma thought better of it. 'No,' she whispered, 'one of us who can't shoot straight is more than enough. You stay down here.' When Nelly vigorously shook her head, Emma saw the futility of such a suggestion. 'All right . . . but stay close, and keep a sharp eye out. We've no idea who it is up there . . . it could be a friendly visitor, but somehow I don't think so.' By the fearful look on her face neither did Nelly.

As they inched their way up the stairs, Emma thought they would never reach the top, so long and painstaking was the journey. Only once did they pause, and that was when there came a small cry, followed by Mr Thomas's voice. Again, because the bedroom was situated at the far end of the landing and the door was obviously closed, it was not easy to distinguish what was being said. But it was plain to Emma that the cry they had heard was that of a woman, and Mr Thomas's voice had seemed to carry a tone of desperation. She was never more sure of anything, but that the Thomases were under threat with, no doubt, their son lying in a drunken stupor somewhere. Emma also believed that there was no immediate help other than herself and Nelly. Clutching her small hands tightly about the shotgun, Emma went stealthily on, her heart in her throat, and a prayer on her lips that she wouldn't have to shoot anybody! The thought of such a possibility made her tremble and her throat was as dry as a dirt-track road.

With every step they took along the darkened landing, Emma was in dread that she or Nelly might bring their weight to bear on one of the loose creaky boards hereabouts. At last, they were at the door and, pressing her ear to it, Emma listened. The conversation coming through the chinks in the ill-fitting door was enough to confirm her suspicions. First came the stranger's voice, which Emma felt sure she had heard somewhere before, and it was threatening.

'My patience is fast running out, Thomas! You've had time enough, I reckon. There is money stashed away here . . . I'm sure of it! But you've hidden it well, I'll grant yer that.' Then there came the sound of a scuffle. 'I mean it, Thomas . . . I'll break her bloody neck!'

'Leave her be, you bastard!' Mr Thomas cried out brokenly. 'Leave her be. I'll show you where the takings are.'

Emma chose this moment to throw open wide the door and to confront the intruder. 'Let go of her!' she yelled, thrusting herself into the room and quickly taking stock of the situation. She was right. The tall thin fellow with the scar, who now quickly took his hands from round Mrs Thomas's throat, was the same bushman who had been with Foster Thomas down on the beach that day. As he raised his arms in the face of the shotgun, Emma was puzzled by the arrogant smile which seemed to turn the whole of his features downwards. It took only a split second to see that, though relatively unharmed, both Mr and Mrs Thomas were in a state of shock. Mrs Thomas was bound hand and foot in a chair to Emma's right, and Mr Thomas the same, but nearer to the window. The astonishment at Emma's sudden intrusion was evident on both their faces and, even as Emma opened her mouth to issue the instruction, 'Untie them, Nelly,' she saw the astonishment slip from Mr Thomas's face, and in its place came another, more desperate expression.

Emma saw his neck stiffen and his head reach forward. She saw his mouth open and, even as his first word of warning split the air, Emma understood. But it was too late! The very last thing Emma heard before it seemed like the world fell in on her, was Mr Thomas yelling, 'Watch out!' and Nelly's broken scream as she came running towards her. Then the gun was snatched from Emma's hands and a shot rang out. The last that Emma saw before her senses slipped from her was the tall bushman's evil smile as he lowered his arms, and the sight of Mrs Thomas's wide-open terrified eyes before they snapped shut, and her grey head fell sideways to loll against her shoulder like that of a rag doll.

As Emma was sucked deep into the black yawning chasm which engulfed her, her mind began to play tricks, and she saw another limp and lifeless body. It was the body of a young man who had idolised her, but whose love she had not been able to return. It was the body of her husband on the day of his tragic death. The sight of it had made her cry out then. It made her cry out now. But it wasn't his name that fell from her lips as she slipped, unconscious, to the floor. It was another name: the name of Marlow, the man she had lost forever. The man she could never forget.

Chapter Two

'Tell me she ain't gonna die, Dr Shaw.' Nelly's brown eyes swam with bright tears as she leapt up to meet the grim-faced doctor. 'Please . . . I couldn't bear it if Emma were to die!' Of a sudden she had her face bent to her hands and was sobbing. 'She won't die, will she?' she kept saying over and over and even Mr Thomas, who had also been anxiously waiting for the doctor to return from Emma's bedside, had to lift his hand surreptitiously to his face, where he quickly wiped away a tear. When he raised his dark eyes to study the doctor's face, as though he might see the light of hope in it, his own suffering was plainly written in the folds of his aged features and in the weary stoop of his thickly set shoulders. It was there also in the anguish of his voice as he spoke to the doctor. 'What of Emma?' he asked, and he thought how cruel it would be if the Lord saw fit to take Emma's life. The whole town was still buzzing with the story of how Emma had bravely confronted the robbers in an effort to save her employers, in spite of the obvious danger to herself. Why even the Governor had been so filled with admiration at her loyalty to the Thomases that he had passionately pursued an absolute pardon for her. Unfortunately the recommendation had been rejected on the grounds that, if Emma had not been carrying the shotgun, Mrs Thomas might still be alive.

In the four days following the incident, neither hide nor hair had been seen of Foster Thomas. His distraught father had sent out messengers far and wide, seeking to inform his son of the fatal, if accidental, shooting of Violet Thomas, and that she would be laid to rest in the churchyard on the morrow. So far, the whereabouts of Foster Thomas remained a mystery. With the passing of the days old Mr Thomas had suffered a whole range of emotions. First, there was the grief for his departed wife, and the cutting knowledge that her body would be put to rest in a land which she considered to be alien to her. He had knelt beside her in the tiny chapel, asking her forgiveness time and time again. He had paced the floorboards till all hours of the morning and there were times when he had a mind to put an end to it all and join her. Then he was swamped with guilt and the awful knowledge that, because of his reluctance to hand over the takings, his wife had been put through an ordeal which resulted in not only the loss of her life but perhaps Emma's as well. In the beginning he had felt a desperate need to have his only son by his side; he was anxious, for the sake of his wife's memory in particular, to heal the rift between himself and Foster. In spite of his every instinct, Roland Thomas was prepared to give his son fresh opportunities to prove himself for, of a sudden, he felt the weight of every one of his fifty-nine years. He had thought it was time to relinquish some of the burden on to the only other person who carried the family name. Was it not true that Foster was his own flesh and blood, after all? And wouldn't it have gladdened Violet's weary heart to see father and son working together?

Oh, it would! Dear Lord, how he yearned to be able to put the clock back! He could have been more compassionate, more sympathetic to his wife's unhappiness. He might even have been more tolerant towards his son.

But when the days passed and there was no word from his son, Roland Thomas began to realise that he would be the only family to grieve at Violet Thomas's grave. They had a son, yes . . . but he neither knew his parents, nor cared for them. The need to be reconciled with such a son became less and less in Roland Thomas's grieving heart. Instead, he began to believe that he would not care if he never saw him again. Turning from those who were past all hope, he brought his attention to Emma. Dear, loyal, hard-working Emma, who gave everything and asked for little in return, and he prayed to the Lord that she should live, both for her own sake and for his sake, because a plan had begun to take root in Roland Thomas's mind. A plan to preserve all that he held dear. A plan which he intended putting to Emma as soon as she was fully recovered. And she *must* recover, she must, for everything depended on it.

Now, both he and Nelly anxiously awaited the doctor's verdict. When it came, there was a sigh of relief, for what Dr Shaw told them was this: 'She's mending . . . at long last Emma has turned the corner.' He went on to warn them of her poorly state all the same. 'She isn't fully recovered by a long chalk, and she'll sleep twenty out of twenty-four hours . . . sleep that she badly needs.' He stressed that, even though Emma's condition had shown significant improvement, 'The blow on her head very nearly fractured her skull.

43

There'll be times when she appears lucid . . . and times when she'll be delirious. You, Nelly, must tend her as constantly and carefully as you have been doing. See that she takes the broth, and keep her comfortable.' With that, and the curt issuing of a few more instructions, he was gone.

'See to her, child,' Mr Thomas urged the anxious Nelly. He had accompanied Dr Shaw to the top of the stairs and now he had come into the bedroom where Emma lay; the very same bed from which he and his wife had been viciously dragged so few nights ago, but what now seemed the span of a lifetime. Nelly had already taken up position in the cane rocking-chair which was pulled up close to the bed. Her brown eyes, that normally were alive with mischief, were sore and red from the tears she had shed for Emma, her one and only real friend in the whole wide world. Many were the times these past years when Nelly had thanked God for Emma's stalwart love and friendship, and she never tired of telling Emma how, if she could choose a sister, it would be no one else but Emma. These last few days had been a nightmare, because every minute that passed, night and day, it seemed that Emma would breathe her last and be taken from them. The thought was so terrible to poor Nelly that she had gone without food or sleep, and she had found herself praying to the very same God who, for so long, she had cursed for her ill fortune. The strain of it all showed on Nelly's homely face, in her unkempt brown hair and in the way she rarely took her anxious gaze from Emma's pale, still features. It showed in the manner of her constant fidgeting, and it betrayed itself in the small bony fingers which were, even now, wrapped about Emma's seemingly lifeless hand as it lay frail and unmoving on the chequered quilt cover. 'Oh, Mr Thomas, sir,' she murmured now, raising her sorry eyes to look on his face, 'I know the doctor said she was mending but . . . well, she looks so ill and she ain't opened her eyes, not once.'

Nelly's brown eyes followed Roland Thomas as he strode further into the room. When he came to rest just an arm's reach from Emma, he stood with one hand across the back of Nelly's chair, his large coarse fingers tightly clasping the top. He gave no answer to Nelly, nor did he betray the slightest inclination of his thoughts as, for what seemed an age, he stared down on Emma's prostrate figure. His serious gaze roved over the finely structured lines of her lovely face and, every now and then, a small shuddering sigh formed deep within his chest, before softly escaping through partly opened lips. Then, with his head bowed and a dark, grim expression on his face such as Nelly had not seen before, he turned away. At the door he stopped, and in soft, halting tones, he told the watching Nelly, 'I'll never forget how Emma put her own life at risk to help me and mine. *Never! Nor your* part in it, child.' His heartfelt words caused Nelly to look away. Not for the first time, she was plagued with a sense of guilt. Should she tell him that, on the night his wife died and the culprits were making good their getaway, there were *three* figures fleeing across the yard? She had kept quiet about it until now because, when she went to the window to shout for help, the moon had gone behind the clouds and there were dark moving shadows. But, in that fleeting moment before the three scoundrels scurried away, Nelly thought she recognised the third man. She wasn't sure and she would never swear to it. That was why she had kept it to herself when the officers questioned her. Besides which, how could she say in Mr Thomas's hearing, and with the body of his poor wife not yet cold, that the man she saw running away was to her mind Foster Thomas, his own son! It was a terrible thing, and one which Nelly wanted no part in. It had been a shock and she hoped with all her heart that she was wrong. Not least of all because, in spite of Emma's warning, or maybe because of it, she had fallen hopelessly in love with Mr Thomas's handsome, wayward son, and somehow, Nelly knew that Emma was right in all she said . . . Foster Thomas was a bad lot. He was capable of all manner of grief. But then hearts are unpredictable things, and love even more so.

At five o'clock, Rita Hughes helped Mr Thomas to close up the store, then, after preparing a tray for Nelly and some broth for Emma, she bade him good day and made her way down the road to the blacksmith's house. Hers was a figure which was easily recognised, being stiffly upright, reed-thin and always dressed in a long dark skirt and cloak, with a small-brimmed bonnet of black, tied beneath the chin with an unusually extravagant bow. Should even one wisp of black hair stray from beneath, it was quickly wedged back into place by small square fingers encased in fine white gloves. She was an odd, almost eccentric figure as she trod the well-worn path from Thomas's store to the blacksmith's house, occasionally deigning to smile woodenly at anyone she passed. More often than not, they would see her coming and find some reason to look the other way, for no one was quite sure how to treat the blacksmith's daughter who, those less Christian of folk claimed, was 'a little bit strange'. There was nothing to substantiate such an observation because Rita Hughes was of a responsible age . . . twenty-nine years. She was most polite to one and all, she was hard-working and helpful and she went to church regularly. She was adored by her parents, being an only child, and there was no more good or dutiful daughter than she. However, though her tight and plain features were easy to look upon, there was one physical characteristic in particular which might account for people's discomfort whenever she paid them close attention. Her eyes, while being of a most fetching hazel colour, were somewhat unnerving to the onlooker, because the right one had within its rich brown colouring a deep marbling of vivid blue, which appeared like a splash across it. This, in turn, created the impression that she was half-blind, which of course she was not.

But there was one who was glad to see Rita Hughes approaching. Quickly, as she swung her way into the front yard through the small gate, Foster Thomas briefly stepped from the shadows of the forge, before she might turn away towards the house without seeing him. When his movement caught her eye, the whole of her face was transformed by a smile which, although it could never be described as beautiful, was close to being pretty. 'Foster!' Seeing the anxious look on his face, she quickly glanced about to ensure that there was no one watching, then, in a hurry, she was inside the darkened forge and being pressed against the wall. 'What are you doing . . . hiding in here like a criminal?' she wanted to know.

'Never mind that, girlie,' he said gruffly. 'Tell me . . . is it right that my mother's been killed . . . shot? And that Emma might die?' He appeared frantic as he waited for her answer. His hair was dishevelled, his face unshaven and his dark jacket and trousers besmirched with dust, as if he had been living rough, or ridden horseback for some considerable distance. Or both.

Quickly, Rita Hughes explained all that had happened. She told how his father had sent people out to look for him and yes, his mother was to be buried the next day, and Emma was only just pulling back from the brink of death. But she was past the worst . . . the doctor had said so.

'Thank God,' he muttered. But then, on seeing her puzzled expression, he quickly added, 'Oh, but my mother! Who could do such a terrible thing? And what of my father . . . how is he taking it . . . badly, I expect?' When she confirmed that it was so, and that his own absence had made it all the more painful for his father, Foster Thomas's reaction was immediate and seemingly sincere. 'I must go to him. But first I'll need to clean up.' He explained how he had been on a business trip of sorts and he hadn't expected to be away so long.

Rita Hughes knew better. She suspected that he had been on a drinking binge, and that he didn't want to evoke his father's anger by turning up in such a disgusting state. What he really wanted though was a good woman to bring him to heel and to show him the Christian way. She saw *herself* as that woman, and one day quite soon, she would convince him of it also.

'Stay here,' she told him. 'Give me a while and I'll

48

bring what you need.' Then she smiled warmly at him, gently moving away a blond lock of hair that had fallen over his forehead. 'You can always rely on me, Foster.' For a moment it seemed as though he might kiss her. But then he pushed her from him. 'Be as quick as you can,' he said, trying not to show how unpleasant it was to be looked at in such a way by those odd and penetrating eyes.

It was half-past ten, some three hours and more since Nelly had heard the raised voices from the back store-room below, and she was relieved that Foster had returned. Even now, she refused to let herself dwell on, or believe, what played on her mind. It hadn't been Foster. He might visit the grog-shops with such men, but he would never be a party to robbing his own parents, she was sure of it. But no, she wasn't sure of it! Yet she would put it out of her mind, for nothing good would come of dwelling on such a thing.

'You go and stretch your legs, child. I'll sit with Emma awhile.' Mr Thomas had come into the room, and Nelly hadn't even heard him, she was that tired. But she declined his suggestion, for she had no intention of moving one step away from Emma's bed until there was some sign of what the doctor had promised. 'No, Mr Thomas, sir,' she said, wedging her narrow frame deeper into the chair as though afraid he might pluck her from it, 'I ain't going nowhere . . . not till I know Emma's all right.'

As he turned away, a weary little smile appeared across Roland Thomas's features. 'All right . . . all right. Nobody's going to make you leave her if you don't want to,' he assured Nelly. 'Foster's taken my make-shift bed in the stores . . . there's no sleep in me at all this night. I've too much on my mind for sleep.' Here he paused and it was obvious that he was dwelling on the sorry fact that the following day his wife would be laid to rest. 'We've a hard day tomorrow, I'm thinking, child,' he murmured, adding as he left the room, 'should you need me, I'll be in the sitting-room next door.'

Nelly thanked him and nodded her appreciation, then she dropped her thoughtful gaze to the floor as he closed the door behind him. Neither Roland Thomas nor Nelly saw how Emma gently stirred, how her grey eyes flickered open for the briefest moment before closing again to seem as they were before. Yet behind Emma's quiet and still expression, a host of gyrating shadows was beginning to emerge and a confusion of hazy images which were too distant for her to recognise. For the moment all was dark and silent, save for the twisting spirals that moved this way, then that, gradually floating closer and closer until the shadows became people, and the people became faces . . . faces she thought she knew, plus those of strangers whose touch she feared. Now, they merged to become one, and again they split asunder to become a multitude. She was afraid yet she was desperate to know who they were. But no! Don't come nearer: she cried out . . . 'Don't touch me!'

Emma had to fight them, or they would kill her, she knew! But listen. There was a voice, a familiar Cockney voice, kind and loving, which made her feel warm and unafraid. 'Ssh, darling,' it said, 'there ain't nobody gonna touch yer while *I'm* aside o' yer.' For a while her heart stopped its fearful trembling. But then she saw him. Her husband, Gregory Denton, with his body in a grotesque and twisted heap at the foot of the stairs. He was dead! And there above them was his aged mother. 'Murderer!' she screamed, her face alive with hatred. 'Emma Grady . . . you're a murderer!' Hands reached out to take Emma, to punish her. Oh, but where was Marlow? Would he not come to help her in her hour of need? Dear God above, would *no one* come to help her, and oh . . . her baby, her baby! 'Don't take my baby!' She was on her knees, pleading with them, but they wouldn't listen. 'Marlow, where are you? They mean to take our baby. No, No . . . please. DON'T TAKE MY BABY! Dear God, DON'T LET THEM TAKE MY BABY!' Frantically, she shook her head from side to side and, thrashing the air with her arms, she fought them off. Yet still they advanced, on their faces were looks of revenge as their outstretched hands threatened to grasp the tiny girl-child from her breast. 'Marlow, help me!' she cried as the child was torn from her and flung into the gutter. Her desperate cries echoed in the blackness, but there was no one to hear them.

In her terrible anguish, Emma was forced to relive the horrors which had plagued her since the loss of her adored father, Thadius Grady; the awful events which led to her being accused of murder now rose into her subconscious with such stark realism that they struck terror into her very soul. As she fought and struggled against those who would separate her forever from the man she loved and from their newborn, Emma was unaware that her cries were just as painful to another who loved her dearly.

As Nelly fled to the sitting-room to fetch Mr Thomas,

she could hardly talk for the sobs which racked her. 'Oh, Mr Thomas . . . come quick! It's Emma.' Then, unable to stand still even one moment longer, she ran back to the bedroom, with Mr Thomas hard on her heels.

'She's delirious.' Roland Thomas took one look at Emma's face, and when he saw the horror stamped upon it, his heart turned over. 'Quick, child,' he told the frantic Nelly, 'get the doctor!' The minute Nelly had gone to do his bidding, he set about preparing a bowl of water and collecting together a flannel, towel, and then placing them on the bedside cupboard. Next, he rolled up his sleeves and pulled the chair as close to Emma as possible. Quickly, he plunged the flannel into the water and squeezed it gently, before applying it to Emma's forehead. 'Easy does it, girlie,' he murmured, 'the doctor's on his way.' Until the doctor arrived, he tenderly wiped away the rivers of perspiration from Emma's face and upper body, all the while murmuring encouragement and soft assurances. 'You'll be all right, Emma . . . I reckon you'll pull through, just like the doc said.' He hoped so, yes indeed, he certainly hoped so, for they had things to discuss, he and Emma. Important things which would affect *both* their futures.

When Dr Shaw arrived, he sent them all from Emma's bedside but they went no further than the doorway. Here Nelly and Roland Thomas stood, silently watching the doctor's every move as he carefully soothed and eventually sedated Emma. When, on stealthy footsteps, Foster Thomas came up behind them, it was to say in a strangely subdued voice, 'She'll be fine, I reckon. Emma's made of strong stuff . . . she won't buckle under so easily. She'll be fine, I'm telling you.'

His words were echoed by the doctor, who assured them, 'She's out of the crisis now . . . you'll see her grow stronger by the day.' His report to the authorities would read the same, he said, for there was no doubt that Emma would be up and about within the week, 'But, of course, I shall recommend that she be given leave from her duties for at least as long again.' A decision which was heartily endorsed by Roland Thomas, who was in no hurry to see Emma back at her work.

But there was something else bothering him, something that he should have seen long ago perhaps. It was the look in his son's eyes when he had come to see how ill Emma was, within the very first few minutes of his return. Even before he had asked after his own mother, he had gone to the bedroom where Rita Hughes had told him Emma lay. He had not made his presence known to Nelly. Instead, he had remained by the door, and from there had gazed towards the bed, his mouth set taut and his knuckles white as he clenched and unclenched his fist against the doorpost. He had not spoken a word, but remained there for a few moments before descending the stairs to discuss with his father all that had happened. Not once had he made any mention of Emma. But Roland Thomas had become curious about his son's obvious affection for her, and he wondered whether he might have misjudged him after all, for any man who could feel genuine affection towards a woman like Emma could surely not be all bad?

Yet he was not convinced, because in his own heart,

he suspected that the son he and Violet had produced had more badness than goodness in him. It was a terrible thing for him to contemplate, but his every instinct warned him that it was, sadly, the truth. It was because of his instincts, therefore, that he decided to press on with the proposition he intended putting to Emma when she was well enough. Indeed, he believed there might now be more urgency to finalise his plan than he had at first realised, because, although there had been many times when he had wished his son would wed and settle down, it horrified him to think he could have designs on Emma. Women of Emma's admirable calibre were few and far between. She would be sorely wasted on the likes of his son, for it seemed that everything that one touched, he managed to drag down to his own level. So, if he had his way, Roland Thomas would persuade Emma towards greater things. She had it in her to make her mark on this land, he knew, and the thought excited him. All the same though, he did feel a small pang of guilt and there was just the slightest doubt in his mind as to whether he was judging his son too harshly. Time would tell, he thought, time will always tell.

Roland Thomas was right. Time did tell; but the tale it told was both grim and shameful.

'I'll stay by Emma awhile, child. You go and lay your head down in a proper bed.' It was midnight and Roland Thomas intended to turn in for the night. Foster had made himself scarce – probably gambling or supping grog with the ruffians who wandered hereabouts, he thought. Now that Emma appeared to be resting easier, the tiredness had crept up on him. In a few hours, there was a most unpleasant and heart-breaking duty to perform. He would need his strength for that.

'No, thank you, Mr Thomas, sir. I feel better when I'm near Emma.' Nelly could hear the weariness in his voice as he bade her goodnight, and it was there in the slump of his shoulders as he left the room. 'He'll sleep well tonight,' she told Emma, 'and he'll need all the sleep he can get, 'cause the ordeal ain't over fer the poor old sod yet.'

For the next half-hour Nelly continued to chatter, even though she knew well enough that Emma was in a deep sleep and heard nothing of her snippets of gossip. All the same, she told how folks had come to the store with their best wishes for Emma. She revealed how Rita Hughes had helped Mr Thomas in the store and 'been a real blessing in disguise'. Then she went on in great detail about how Foster Thomas had come home after four days, 'full o' cock-eyed excuses as to where he'd been all that time', and what was more, she had been excused from the routine of daily reporting to the authorities . . . ''cause the buggers know I won't be far from where my Emma is!' she laughed. After a while, a great weariness fell over Nelly. Her tongue grew heavy and her eyelids felt like lead weights against her eyeballs until every limb in her body ached for sleep. Then, unable to fight it any longer, she glanced at Emma's still and quiet form. With a sigh, she lay back her head and let the wave of welcome sleep wash over her. In a matter of minutes, she was out to the world and gently snoring.

When Foster Thomas came softly up the stairs he had but one thought in his mind, and that was Emma.

The big round clock above the landing window struck one in the morning as he felt his way along the bannister in the pitch black. He dared not carry a lamp for fear he might be seen and, as he'd put away a jar or two of best grog in the company of those who were considered to be undesirable in the best social circles, he might be shown the way back down the stairs – worse still, his old father might take it into his head to show him all the way to the front door! Here he gave a small laugh, lost his balance and clung to the bannister as though his very life depended on it. Why was it, he asked himself, that Emma insisted on fending him off, when all the while she was as hot for him as he was for her? The little baggage . . . teasing him like that, when she knew full well that they were meant for each other.

Quietly now, he eased the door open just wide enough to admit his long lean body into the room. The room was in darkness, save for the shaft of moonlight coming in through the window where the curtains were not quite pulled together. In this soft yellow light, which showed the burned-down candle and which fell on Emma's pale and lovely features, he was guided towards the bed where she lay. All the while, the sound of Nelly's gentle snoring pulsated through the room, raising in him the comforting knowledge that, at long last, he and Emma were alone. And oh, he had such a longing in his loins for her . . . such a desperate need for her that he couldn't stop himself from trembling. Emma was *his*! Fight it she might, but there was no escaping the outcome. She was his, and though he could have taken her by force if he cared to, he had not, for there were any amount of women he could have in that way, but they meant nothing to him.

Emma was special, and he would never rest until she came to his bed of her own accord. Oh, but in spite of her little games, she would! Yes indeed she would.

When, in a moment, he touched his fingertips to her temple, Emma made no movement at all. When he stroked the silkiness of her rich chestnut hair, she gently stirred. Afraid that she might cry out, he took away his hand from her forehead and, for a while, he stood very still, his arms loose by his sides and his blue eyes, made all the more murky by the drink he'd consumed, raked her face until they knew every finely chiselled line and curve. How greedily he devoured that creamy forehead with its heart-shaped hairline and high, perfectly shaped dark brows; even now, though they were tightly closed, Foster Thomas could imagine Emma's startlingly beautiful steel-grey eyes at their most magnificent . . . this being, to his warped mind, when she looked on him with the utmost contempt. Oh, but he wasn't disturbed by it for he had convinced himself that it was all a show, a ploy to drive him crazy with desire. And it had worked! By God, it had worked because, as he gazed on her now, savouring her beauty to the full, there came over him an insatiable and feverish desire to draw back the bedcovers and to gaze upon the sleeping Emma in all her naked loveliness. The more he thought of it, the more urgent became the yearning, until the breath quickened in his throat and his pulse raced with excitement. He had never seen Emma unclothed. Not once had he feasted his eyes on her nakedness. Now the urge was too strong to resist; he *must* see her, for nothing else would satisfy him this night. And, if he were to slide in beside her, who was there to stop him? Certainly not his father, who was sleeping the sleep of the dead, downstairs; nor Nelly, who was also deeply exhausted. As for Emma . . . even if she had a mind to, she was in no position to object.

By now, every sense and nerve-ending in Foster Thomas's body was tingling at the prospect of taking Emma's nakedness to himself. There was a torment within him which pulled him two ways: he had vowed never to take Emma without her full and eager cooperation, but, having her lying before him now, so warm and vulnerable, and with the raw passion racing through his body when the need in him was as proud and obvious as ever it could be in a man, his resolve not to invade Emma's beauty without her wanting it as much as he himself did was weakening – already he had lost control.

As he reached out, with trepidation, to pluck the bedclothes from her, the palms of his hands were sweating and his every limb trembled uncontrollably. Gently now, and all the while holding his breath for fear of being discovered, he slid back the clothes which hid Emma from him. He had suspected that she might not be wearing a nightgown; not when the heat of the day was such that men were forced to cease their labours or fry in the merciless sun. In the dead of night that same heat was so oppressive and suffocating that even when lying still in bed, a body was bathed in sweat.

Emma was *not* wearing a nightgown, having come through a feverish crisis when it would have clung to her like a second skin. The doctor had given instructions that Emma be covered up to the chin by the bedclothes, and occasionally flannelled down with fresh water to reduce her soaring temperature. Nelly had allowed no one else close to Emma and not once had she failed in her duty to carry out the doctor's instructions. So, when Foster Thomas drew back the bedclothes, the sight of Emma's slender body caused him to gasp out loud. If he had thought her face the most beautiful he had ever seen, then how much more magnificent was her body!

Riveted to the spot and almost afraid of what his astonished eyes beheld, Foster Thomas scored every detail into his lecherous mind. His eyes narrowed and his desire for Emma was greatly intensified as he let his gaze wander over her nakedness. Even when she softly stirred and turned her head deeper into the pillow, he was so mesmerised that he could not drag his gaze away, nor could he move, although his instincts warned him that Nelly could wake at any minute. Greedily, his eyes took in all that he could of Emma, this adorable creature whom he had vowed to have for his own. He gazed at the long, thick hair which was fanned out over the pillow, its vibrant autumn hues a stark contrast against the starched white pillowcase. He stared long at that lovely face, with its large wonderful eyes and those high aristocratic cheekbones, the perfect full mouth and that chin which, though completing the exquisite oval shape of Emma's face, was strong and determined, as was her character. Oh, what sensual delights invaded him as he roved his narrow opaque blue eyes over Emma's youthful, thrusting breasts, so small and perfect with proud inviting nipples standing warm and dark against the creamy whiteness of her breasts. He thought her waist was small but not tiny and the curves of her thighs deliciously inviting, and how impatient he was to tangle himself between those exquisite legs. *Too* impatient, he chided himself, because already he was aching with such excitement and anticipation that in a minute it would be too late! Quickly he stripped off his clothes to stand naked and desperate for a taste of Emma's loveliness.

When with great care, or he would surely give the game away, he inched himself on to the bed, Emma was trembling from being uncovered for so long. She stirred, raising her arm above her head, and softly moaned. In a minute he was on her, covering her nakedness with his own and murmuring tender words against the warmth of her neck. With one arm stroking her hair and the weight taken by his elbow, he reached his other arm down to ease open her legs. When, this time, Emma became agitated, twisting her body this way then that and calling out the name 'Marlow', he stayed still, not daring to move for fear she had alerted the others. For what seemed a lifetime, he remained frozen against her, tormented by the touch of his body on hers, but terrified that he might be discovered. But no, Nelly was still deep in the sleep of exhaustion, her rhythmic snores breathing into the darkness like the beating of his own heart. As he waited a moment longer, listening for any sound from the stores below or perhaps a footstep on the stairs, he wondered who was this 'Marlow' whom Emma had called out to. How soft and loving her voice had been, almost a caress of his name. He would not forget the name either: as Foster Thomas emblazoned Marlow's name on to his memory, a terrible hatred crept into his black heart.

The tender feelings which had smothered him were now tempered with a fury that, even in her subconscious, Emma should cry out some other man's name! But this 'Marlow' wasn't here, coveting Emma's nakedness, while *he* was! For the moment, at least, he was pacified, and in that moment when his whole being flooded with his need for Emma's heart and soul, he placed his mouth over hers, and gently probed himself towards her. Then with such a tide of ecstasy rushing through him that he thought his heart would burst, he thrust his way deep into Emma, his great excitement causing him to cry out.

Emma cried out also, but it was a strangled and terrified cry of the kind made by a nightmare which caused her to thrash out at those who would hurt her. In her ill and confused mind, she knew only that she must escape; she must flee from the pain and horror which hounded her, and which had already pushed her over the line between nightmare and reality. When it seemed that in her anguish Emma might betray him, she was cruelly silenced by her assailant's clenched fist. Being so intent on satisfying the cravings of his own body, Foster Thomas cared not for his unconscious victim's helplessness, for, in the throes of his madness, he was frantic to gratify only the base primitive instincts which drove him. Gripping Emma into him again and again, he smothered her with his vile body and kissed her nakedness, all the while telling her how she was *his* now . . . and could never belong to any other.

Of a sudden, there came another scream as Nelly woke to the horror of what was happening. Almost at once, there was a rush of footsteps into the room and the darkness was penetrated by the light which Roland Thomas carried high before him. With a cry of 'You filthy bastard!' he sprang forward, dropping the lantern to the floor and clawing at his son's bare flesh, his nails digging so deep into it that the blood spurted out like a crimson shower to fall in spattered drops along his back and shoulders. With the might of a demon, he yanked him from the bed and from Emma, who was as still and white as death.

'Oh God! Emma, will yer forgive me, will yer ever forgive me, darlin'?' Nelly had recovered the lamp which, in his rage, Roland Thomas had dropped to the floor and she had placed it on the bedside cupboard. Having drawn up the bedclothes over Emma's violated body, she was cradling her dear friend's head to her bosom and sobbing as though her heart would break. 'Will yer ever forgive me, darlin' Emma,' she cried over and over, 'for I'll never be able ter forgive meself!'

It was a night that no one there would ever forget. For although he was an older and slower man, Roland Thomas's fury and disgust knew no bounds as he thrashed his son unmercifully. First throwing him down the stairs, he took a bull-whip from the stores and, without heed of his cowardly son's cries for mercy, he brought it down again and again across his bare back and shoulders, the tip of it lashing over his face and neck and cutting so deep that he would carry the scars for the rest of his miserable life. Afterwards Roland Thomas flung Foster out on to the porch, with his clothes and belongings in a heap beside him. 'You're a no-good bastard!' he told his son in a voice that still trembled with rage. 'Your own mother's to be buried this day, and you bring nothing but shame on our heads. Let the devil take you, Foster Thomas, because *I* want nothing more to do with you! *Never* set foot near me again . . . stay out of my sight. You're no son of mine. From this day on, I have *no* son!' He watched the crumpled figure begin to stir on the porch, and he knew that his words had been heard. It was enough.

In the darkness, Roland Thomas's terrible words had also been heard by many of the startled neighbours, who had been roused from their beds by the worst upheaval they had ever been witness to. No one knew what dreadful reason could have provoked such an amiable and mild-mannered man as Roland Thomas, the well-liked and respected trader, to cast his own son from his house, and to issue such strong and awful words that made them tremble. Yes, it was true that Foster Thomas was not the man his father was . . . nor the man his father might have wished him to be, for he was both weak and wasteful. It was also true that the confrontation between them had been a long time brewing. But, so terrible and final, and on the very day in which poor Mrs Thomas was to be laid to her rest? It didn't bear thinking about. All the same, they were intrigued to know what awful thing had triggered off Roland Thomas's fury. But, as the trader stormed back into his store, and the son spat in the dust behind him with a look of deep hatred on his bleeding face, something told them that they might never know the truth of what had happened that night, for the old one was too proud to disclose it, and the other too cowardly.

Chapter Three

It was a wonderful balmy day, with the sun playing hide-and-seek amongst the clouds, and the gentle breezes blowing in off the sea to cool the land and bring with them the promise of rain.

Four whole weeks had passed and January had given way to February since the awful night when father had disowned his only son, and that son had fled the area without trace, almost as though he had disappeared from the face of the earth. At first light after the violation of Emma, when Roland Thomas had come down to the porch, there had been no sign of the perpetrator. When the funeral procession had taken Mrs Thomas along the High Street to the churchyard, there had been no sign of her son: not during the service, nor at the graveside afterwards. There was much talk of it for many days following, with people curious to know what had taken place. They declared their sympathies to the grieving husband and he, in turn, quietly thanked them. They expressed their horror and regret at what had transpired between him and his only son, and he nodded gratefully, but made no comment. They fidgeted nervously with their black neck-ties and meticulously adjusted their prim little bonnets; then, feeling somewhat perplexed and frustrated, they went on their way. Roland Thomas was a private man, they knew, and they respected him for it. All the same, that son of his must have committed an evil deed for such a man as the trader to be so unforgiving! But now, with his wife gone, his son gone, and two female convicts residing on the premises, the circumstances at the Thomas store left much to be desired. There was talk that he intended taking on a young lad to help him in the store, and what with the upright and prim Rita Hughes having taken on the role as housekeeper there, they supposed it was respectable enough. What was more, Roland Thomas, a strong, fine figure of a man at fifty-nine years old, was not past taking himself a new wife, no indeed! Who could be more suitable than the blacksmith's daughter, they wondered.

Emma could hardly believe her ears. '*Marry* you!' she exclaimed, an expression of incredulity on her face as she looked at Roland Thomas through astonished grey eyes. 'Do you know what you're saying, Mr Thomas?' Surely she had misheard, Emma thought. Only ten minutes before, she had been busily attending to her duties in the store, feeling grateful to be back at her work, and exchanging pleasantries with the customers. Now, here she was, summoned to the upstairs sitting-room and seated on the stiff horsehair couch opposite Mr Thomas, who was perched somewhat precariously on the edge of a tall ladder-back chair, his homely face wreathed with anxiety as he waited for her answer. But he dared not wait, for he saw the answer written plainly all over Emma's countenance, so, taking his courage into his hands, he leaned forward in the chair to fix her all the more with his dark, troubled gaze. 'Think on it,

Emma,' he urged, 'don't reject me out of hand . . . not until I've been through the advantages of such a union between the two of us.'

He then went on to explain how he had thought long and hard about the proposition, and how after each painstaking deliberation he had come to the very same conclusion. 'It can only benefit both of us, Emma . . . for my part, there are two main considerations. The first is that, when my time comes and I'm called to take place alongside my Violet, that no-good son o' mine won't be able to get his hands on this 'ere business! The second gives me even greater pleasure: not only will the business come into *your* capable and deserving hands, Emma – the good Lord knows how hard you've worked to make it flourish these past seven years – but I reckon with your energy and clever business head, you'll take the Thomas name far higher than I ever could! You've got youth on your side, girlie . . . and that special inner drive to succeed. Oh, and there's so much more opportunity now, to expand and prosper in *all* directions; you must see that . . . Why, you yourself pointed out the openings in the pearl-shell trade, and we've got the profits to prove it! And look how you've badgered me about the benefits to be got from coastal trade. You can do it, Emma . . . with me alongside you, and our name over that doorway . . . we can branch out in whatever direction you like!'

As he talked, his dark eyes alive with enthusiasm, Emma was caught up in his mood of excitement. He was right. All he was saying made a good deal of sense, her every instinct told her so. With overland transport difficulties and more settlers arriving all the time, there was a fortune to be made from taking the goods by sea, investing in good, sturdy seagoing vessels and building up a thriving trade along the coast. The openings were there, and the benefits would be most handsome, she knew. What a challenge that would be! What an exciting and demanding challenge! But on her own it would prove to be a very difficult, if not impossible, task, because of the stigma of being a convict and because she was a woman, women being denied a place in the man's world of business. Yet Emma knew that she *could* do it, given the opportunity. Mr Thomas was right. She'd work her fingers to the bone and raise the Thomas Trading Business to such a height that its reputation and importance would be carried from one end of Australia to the other and, in time, across the oceans to England and the rest of the world! There was no doubt in Emma's mind that one day this vast land of Australia would be a great and important country, when it would play an even more important part in international trading. Indeed, it was already beginning to happen, and all the signs were there that Australia was coming into its own. The convict ships had stopped coming some two years ago; there was now partial self-government, and only recently a privately-owned telegraph link with Perth had been installed. Already plans were underway to construct a network of over-land telegraph lines which would link not only major cities and ports, but countries far and wide. Railways were also being constructed. It was an exciting time, Emma realised, a time of innovation, growth and expansion of a kind unparalleled before. Oh! What she would give to be a real part of it!

But could she betray herself by agreeing to marry a man old enough to be her father? Could she live such a lie, when there would never be any other man in her heart but Marlow Tanner? No, she thought not.

Once more, Emma prepared to give Roland Thomas his answer. And once again, sensing that she was about to turn him down, he bade her wait a moment longer. 'Hear me out, Emma,' he pleaded. And she did, waiting most attentively, while he outlined how, on the very day of their marriage, he would sign an official contract stating that, from that day forwards, Emma was his full partner, and that, on the day of his demise *everything* he owned, lock, stock and barrel, would become her property, and hers alone, to do with as she wished, because he knew in his heart that he could not leave his affairs in better hands than hers.

Emma could have pointed out that he had a son, and that son must surely be included in any such agreement. But she said nothing, for she knew that, as far as Roland Thomas was concerned, he had no son, and that even to mention his name would infuriate and antagonise her employer. Besides which, the very name of that creature on her lips would taste so foul that she would feel tainted ever after! Only now, after weeks of agonising, had she made herself put that terrible night behind her, when he had invaded her body while she lay ill and helpless.

For a long time afterwards, she was unsure as to where the boundaries of her nightmares ended, and where they had become stark, horrifying reality. When Nelly revealed the awful truth, in as gentle a manner as possible, Emma had felt physically sick, but more than that, she had felt dirty and degraded. There had been murder in her heart, such bitterness that coloured her every sleeping and waking thought, until she could see no pleasure in anything. All those things she loved were as nothing to her. The delightful things of nature and God's creation . . . the turquoise ocean, the brightly coloured birds and even the daily tasks of the work she pleasured in, meant nothing. She had grown morose and withdrawn for a time, and was not moved by Nelly's pleas, nor by her love and stalwart friendship, so vile and unclean did she feel.

After a while though, some deeper instincts within her persuaded Emma that it was not *she* who was vile and unclean, it was the monster who had forced himself on her. So, with Nelly's unswerving determination to show Emma her own worth, each day had grown a little easier to accept. Also, the fact that only she, Mr Thomas and Nelly knew of the deed Foster had committed against her that night lessened Emma's shame.

In spite of Emma's Christian upbringing she could not find it in her heart ever to forgive Roland Thomas's son. So now when the older man spoke of his revulsion for the 'dog he had sired', and explained how he would never know a moment's peace if everything he had worked for should come to a sorry end in the grasping hands of such a no-good, Emma understood. And she was glad that it was so.

'There's something else, Emma,' Mr Thomas told her now. 'If you and I were married, the authorities would declare you a *free* woman! Oh, think of it, Emma . . . you would be free, in command, and one day you'd inherit everything! You'd have freedom, money, and power! Say yes, Emma! You *must* say yes!' His voice was trembling and he reached out to lay his hand over Emma's small, work-worn fingers. 'You and me, Emma . . . not man and wife in the true sense, for

70

I suspect your heart belongs to this "Marlow" you cried for when you were close to death, and . . . I would never want another woman after my Violet. No! *Partners*, Emma! Business partners, and an agreement that would be good for both of us. Say yes, Emma. *Please!*'

But Emma could not say yes so easily. Yet in the face of such a strong and sensible argument, neither could she now say no without first giving it a deal more thought.

Roland Thomas sensed her slight hesitation, and his hopes were raised. 'All right, Emma,' he conceded, 'I won't ask for your answer right away. But . . . I beg you not to keep me waiting too long for your decision.'

'I won't,' she promised. There the matter was laid to rest for the time being.

'E's asked yer ter marry 'im, ain't he, gal?' Nelly and Emma had finished their long day's work and were presently making for the beach, where they might sit awhile and discuss matters close to their hearts. 'I *knew* it!' exclaimed Nelly with big, round eyes, her voice breaking into a giggle. 'I saw it comin' a bleedin' mile away, ever since he asked yer up ter the parlour the day afore yesterday.' Here she gave a little skip and playfully nudged the smiling Emma. 'G'orn!' she laughed. 'He *did*, didn't he, eh? What a dark horse you are, Emma gal!' Of a sudden, she grabbed Emma by the arm and pulled her to a halt. 'Hey, bugger me!' she said, as the full consequences struck her. 'T'ain't such a bad idea at that, is it, eh? When the old bugger pops orf . . . well, you'll come into everything, won't yer? Cor, just think of it, Emma darlin' . . . the Thomas Trading Business'll be yours, and yer won't be a convict no more either. Why! Yer could even go back ter

England!' At this Nelly began trembling as she cast her mind back to that fateful dark morning when they were taken from the cell in an English gaol and bundled into a rickety cage atop a flat-waggon.

Emma was also remembering. 'Yes, Nelly,' she said in a strangely quiet voice, 'it could be the means of me going back to England . . . if I wanted to. 'And oh, yes, she *did* want to! It was that one thought above all others that had kept her going these past years. Back to England! How her heart rose at the prospect! But nothing was ever as black and white as it looked. To her mind, there were two alternatives offered to her. One, she could refuse Mr Thomas's generous offer, and that would mean serving out her sentence, after which it could take many long and laborious years before she accrued enough money to take her back to England – there was always the possibility that her plans to return might never be realised, and that was too much to bear. On the other hand, if she were to accept the offer of marriage, there must surely come a day, as Mr Thomas had forecast and as Nelly had rightfully pointed out, when she would be a woman of significance hereabouts, a woman of property and prosperity, with the means to go wherever in the world she chose.

There were two desperate needs inside Emma, two deep and driving ambitions that would not let her be. She had so many ideas and plans with regard to exploiting the numerous business opportunities which beckoned those with the determination and courage to go after them. However, she was also driven by the desire to go back to her homeland, where she had many enemies to root out and scores to settle.

Above all, she would never rest until she had found Marlow, for there was much to explain, and forgiveness to be sought.

'Oh, Emma . . . if yer do marry Mr Thomas, yer won't go back ter England and leave me, will yer? Don't do that ter me, Emma darlin' . . . 'cause what would I do without yer, eh?' There were tears in Nelly's voice as she looked at Emma with fearful brown eyes. 'Yer wouldn't desert yer old friend, would yer?' she asked, and Emma's heart went out to her. 'I ain't going another step till yer tell me yer won't clear off ter England and leave me!' Nelly vowed, putting on a brave front, yet betraying her nervousness by the manner in which she had drawn her long skirt up and was twisting it round and round her fingers.

'Come on,' Emma smiled at her reassuringly and, taking hold of Nelly's arm, she started walking at a smarter pace until they covered the entire length of the tunnel, which had been cut through the limestone cliffs by a whaling company, for speedier access from the landing beach to the warehouses inland.

Emerging from the relative gloom of the tunnel and coming out on to the sandy beach, Emma sat down on a small boulder and patted another alongside. 'Come and sit beside me, Nelly,' she said. When Nelly had done so, she brought her quiet grey eyes to rest on her friend's anxious face, saying, 'I haven't told you before, about Mr Thomas's offer, because I haven't yet made up my mind. When he first asked me my instinct was to say no right off. And, I'm still of the same mind. So you see, Nelly . . . you're working yourself up into a state for nothing.'

'But you'd be *daft* not to say yes, gal!' exclaimed

73

Nelly, somewhat surprised. She would have said yes the minute he asked her!

'Maybe, Nelly. But I don't know that it would be right, to take him up on his kind offer . . . when I would be getting much more than I deserve, and taking more out of the relationship than I could ever give back. Here,' she paused a while before telling Nelly, 'there's a deal of thinking to be done, but . . . I mean to give him an answer this very night. And whatever my decision is, Nelly, I could *not* go back to England and leave you behind. What! I wouldn't have a minute's peace, wondering what trouble you were busy getting yourself into!' When she softly laughed, the smile returned to Nelly's downcast face and soon the two young women were in a better frame of mind.

It was gone eight o'clock when Nelly and Emma began their gentle stroll back along the High Street. When Emma made clear her intention of stopping awhile on King's Square, as she wanted to 'go into St John's Church and talk things over with the Almighty', Nelly's reaction was immediate. 'Yer can if yer like, Emma darlin', she retorted with a vigorous shake of her brown head, 'but I ain't comin' in! It's bad enough being made to go by the authorities . . . but I ain't bloody *volunteering*!' By now they were outside St John's Church, and Nelly found a shady spot in which to wait. 'Me an' the good Lord don't see eye ter eye at the minute, gal,' she laughed, 'on account of I keep finding meself up ter me neck in trouble . . . and he seems ter have no control over me whatsoever! I do believe he's washed his hands of me!'

'You can't blame God . . . or anybody else for that matter,' Emma was quick to tell her. 'The trouble

you've landed yourself in has been your *own* doing!'
Here she turned at the church doorway and added in a
quieter voice, 'If only you didn't want to keep fighting
with the authorities, Nelly . . . and if you could curb
that wicked little streak in you, that always wants to
chase after the kind of fellas who bring nothing but
trouble.' Here she gave a great sigh as she let her
concerned grey eyes linger a moment longer on that
rebellious but homely figure that had thrown itself
haphazardly at the foot of a gum tree. The sight of
Nelly's defiant, upturned face sent a pang of affection
through Emma. 'You're incorrigible, Nelly,' she
smiled, shaking her head. 'But look . . . it's been a
good while since you've been in trouble, hasn't it, eh?
So maybe you and the Lord *are* on speaking terms,
after all?' She hoped Nelly might change her mind and
step into the church with her, but no.

'Then I'd best stay where I am, and not push me
luck, Emma, gal!' came the chirpy reply. After which,
Nelly set up whistling her tavern song, and Emma left
her to it.

Inside the church, Emma knelt at the altar, closed
her eyes and offered up a prayer. She made a special
mention for Nelly, and asked that her impetuous
nature didn't get her into any deeper water. Then,
feeling ashamed and guilty at bringing such a terrible
thing into God's house, she spoke of the awful deed
committed against her by Roland Thomas's estranged
son. She asked for forgiveness because of the bitterness
in her heart towards him and, above all else, Emma
prayed for guidance on Roland Thomas's proposition.
She reminded the Lord about her love for Marlow
Tanner, and of her need to take revenge on Caleb

75

Crowther, the trusted uncle who had betrayed her.

When Emma came to the subject of her lost baby, her heart was too full for prayer and the tears ran down her face as, in her mind's eye, she saw again that small, precious life which had been safe in her arms for such a desperately short time. The tiny face of her newborn daughter was as fresh in her mind now, more than seven years on, as it had been when she had given birth to it, there in an English cobbled street outside the gaol. It was deeply painful for Emma to know that her beloved daughter was no more.

Emma stayed a moment longer, neither thinking too deeply nor praying. It was enough that she had unburdened her heart, and so in these few precious moments, she just knelt in the peace and serenity. She let it flood into her heart and, as the moments passed, she felt a new kind of strength within her. She had made up her mind. Roland Thomas would have his answer that very day, and Emma would abide by it, come what may. First though, there was much to be said between them; things of the past which must be revealed.

'I don't want to know, Emma. You're a good woman, I can tell, or I wouldn't be asking you to be my wife.' Roland Thomas was seated on the horsehair couch and, when he spoke, Emma turned round from the window to look at him with her strong eyes and an unusually severe look on her face. 'I *mean* it, Emma,' he urged, 'you don't have to tell me anything!'

Emma's gaze lingered on his face for a moment longer, before she turned away to look out of the window once more. Her gaze was vague and distant and her voice painfully quiet as she told him, 'There can be no agreement between us . . . until you know all there is to know about me.' She waited, her back to him, shoulders taut, and an air of defiance in her countenance. When, in reluctant tones, Emma was told, 'Very well . . . if you feel that strongly,' she returned to sit on one of the four ladder-back chairs which surrounded the circular table.

Pulling herself in closer to the table, Emma clenched her fists together on the green corded tablecloth and, after a moment spent composing herself for what she knew would be a painful ordeal, she began to unfold the story that had eventually brought her here in shackles. A story of deceit, betrayal and brutality. A story of love, of lost dear ones, and of heartbreak. A story that, though it seemed already to have spanned a lifetime and had its origins so many thousands of miles away across the oceans, was not yet over. Might not be over for another lifetime to come!

Quietly, and with great regard for the turmoil which he suspected was raging within Emma as she revealed the roots of her nightmare, Roland Thomas paid close attention to her every word.

Emma spared nothing. She told of her heartbreak when her darling papa had died. She explained how he had innocently appointed his brother-in-law, Caleb Crowther, to be trustee of his mills and fortune, and gave the same man complete and irrevocable guardianship over his beloved daughter, Emma. Yet no sooner had his bones been laid to rest, than Emma's uncle, Caleb Crowther, saw fit, first of all, to put her out to work . . . while his own spoilt and petulant daughter, Martha Crowther, was sent to a fashionable school for young ladies, her place there being bought and paid for by the money which Emma's father had left in trust for *her*. Then, when it suited his purpose, and in spite of the fact that Emma had fallen hopelessly in love with a young bargee by the name of Marlow Tanner who loved her in return, Crowther married her off to Gregory Denton, a manager at one of her father's mills. It was a disastrous match for Emma: Gregory was impossibly possessive and wrongly suspicious of her every move, and his jealous old mother detested Emma so much that she confined herself to bed and from there she created enough malicious mischief to make Emma's life a misery. All this time, only Emma's old nanny kept her sane and remained a true and stalwart friend.

'If I had thought that things were so bad they couldn't possibly get worse . . . I was miserably wrong,' Emma went on. 'With the Civil War in America, the shipments of cotton to Britain were strangled to a halt. People starved in their millions, and mills all around were shutting down at an alarming rate.' Here the memories became too vivid in Emma's mind and, for a long moment, she paused to reflect until, in a gentle voice, Roland Thomas persuaded her, 'Go on, Emma.'

In faltering tones, Emma told how her husband had gone to pieces after he lost his job. She told how she had searched for him when he was most troubled, and how she had met him leaving a public house in the company of others as drunk as himself . . . she revealed how he had struck and humiliated her in front of them; then later, how she had to flee for her very life when one of those same men relentlessly pursued her. When it seemed as though she were lost, Marlow

Tanner had been there to save her. 'It was the beginning of the end,' Emma murmured, feeling shamed at the memory of herself in Marlow's loving arms, yet at the same time feeling warmed by that precious recollection.

Soon after, Emma explained, she was horrified to discover that she was expecting Marlow's child. Her only friend, her nanny from childhood, Mrs Manfred, persuaded Emma that her husband must be told the truth and, to give Emma moral support, she stayed over on the night Emma decided to make her confession. 'It was a nightmare. Gregory came home in the early hours . . . he was more drunk than I'd ever seen him.' Emma described how he had discovered her pregnancy after violently stripping off her clothes. 'He went completely crazy!' A struggle followed and Mrs Manfred came to Emma's help; during the confusion, Emma's husband lost his balance and crashed down the stairs. His neck was broken in the fall. Old Mrs Denton accused both Emma and Mrs Manfred of plotting to murder her son, and they were arrested. The outcome was that Mrs Manfred was hanged, and Emma sentenced to ten years and transported.

'And the child?' Roland Thomas had a great impulse to go and comfort Emma, who had been devastated by the cruel demise of her dear, gentle friend, Mrs Manfred. But he dared not, for fear that Emma would surely reject him. 'What became of your child, Emma?' he asked gently. Then, he was moved to a deeper compassion when Emma went on in faltering tones. She described how, in the dark, early hours of a grim morning as she was being loaded into the waggon along with other prisoners, the child would be contained no longer. 'I gave birth to Marlow's daughter right there, in the street, with only dearest Nelly for strength and comfort. The child never drew breath . . . She wasn't given the chance!' Emma was up on her feet now, the memory of it all causing her to pace the floor in agitation. 'She was snatched from my arms and left in the gutter, like so much dirt!'

'Can you be *sure* she wasn't alive?' Roland Thomas had unwittingly voiced the tiny hope which had burned in Emma's heart ever since that day. But no! How many times had she questioned Nelly over and over about it? What had Nelly seen when Emma passed out? Was there even the *slightest* chance that the newborn was still alive, as the waggon moved away? Could she be certain? Oh, the questions she had asked . . . and each one a fervent prayer. But always the answer was the same: 'No.' Nelly was adamant, 'Don't torture yerself, gal . . . the bairn were dead.' Gradually, the light of hope was dimmed in Emma's weary heart. But not extinguished. Never completely extinguished.

'The chances of the infant having survived are desperately slim . . . almost non-existent,' she replied now, 'and I have made myself accept it, or be driven crazy.'

Roland Thomas nodded. 'And Marlow . . . what became of Marlow Tanner, the man you loved?'

'The man I will *always* love,' Emma corrected. 'And it's only fair that you know it, Mr Thomas,' she told him, the edge returning to her voice. Then she saw him nod and heard his reply, 'I'm aware of it, Emma, and it matters not to any agreement we might make.' Emma answered his question and the words pulled on her heart like heavy weights. 'I sent him away. I *had* to . . .

for his own good! If I hadn't, then Caleb Crowther would have made it his business to hound him, and to bring him forward on some fabricated charge that would have meant transportation . . . or even the gallows.'

'This uncle of yours . . . this "Caleb Crowther" . . . he had that kind of power?'

'He did . . . and has, as far as I know. He was a Justice of the Peace, and moved amongst the most influential and powerful people.'

'Was it he who arranged your own transportation, Emma?'

'I don't know,' replied Emma thoughtfully. But such a possibility had long troubled her. And if he were guilty of that, then what else did he have a hand in? What of Mrs Manfred's hanging? What of her own inheritance? And why had none of the Crowther family come to her aid when she had sent out messages from her cell, *begging* for their help? Yet they had not replied . . . not once, and she had no other family to turn to. Oh yes, these were matters which had sat long and uncomfortably on Emma's mind. One day she would learn the answers. She must.

'Now that you know all of my background, do you still want me to enter into a marriage agreement with you, Mr Thomas?' she asked of him now.

His answer was immediate. 'Now . . . more than ever!' he told her with an assuring smile, 'Just name the day, and I'll be a proud and fortunate man to have such a woman alongside me. After hearing your story, Emma, I reckon you're more of a victim than a criminal. All I ask of you now is to name the day . . . and your fortunes can't help but take a turn for the better.' He was on his feet, as though the occasion warranted it, and when Emma looked at his broad, craggy face, then smiled at him with gratitude shining in her warm grey eyes, he appeared unusually self-conscious. Lowering his dark gaze to the peg-rug where he seemed intent on studying the reds and browns of the ragged tufts there, he said quietly, 'I'll never ask more of you, Emma, than you already give.' He made no move to lift his gaze, lest it linger too long on hers. 'You have my word on it,' he told her.

'I know that,' Emma assured him, 'and I thank you for it.'

Of a sudden, Roland Thomas raised his eyes before stepping forward, saying with a more serious expression and in a sterner voice, 'There are *other* matters though, which do give me cause for concern. I've given you my word on a particular issue, Emma . . . now, I must ask you to do the same for me.'

'Oh?' Emma was intrigued yet, at the same time a deal of anxiety had crept into her heart for fear that she might not be able to give her word on whatever was troubling him. Emma was now deeply committed to their agreement, because it would indeed open doors for her that might otherwise stay forever closed. 'What is it, Mr Thomas?' she asked, her concerned eyes searching his large, loose features as though she might find her answer there.

'First of all I reckon you could forget the *Mr* Thomas . . . and begin calling me by my name, Roland. It doesn't seem right for a woman to be calling her intended by his surname. Most of all though, Emma . . . I want you to promise that you'll not be itching to make for England the minute you slip the shackles of a convict. Oh, I wouldn't blame you, girlie! Not after what the devils back there have put you through! What! . . . I'd do the very same myself. But y'see, Emma, the whole idea of this partnership between us is to deny that waster son of mine any access to my money or business, and for you and me to work side by side in building it up to the kind of business that I've always dreamed of, ever since first setting foot here. Oh, I know it's a grand concern now, and I'm right proud o' what I've achieved . . . but I feel in my bones that where I've stopped, Emma . . . *you* are only just beginning. I want to be a part in it, Emma, afore I'm put to rest alongside my Violet.' The darkness in his eyes grew almost black as he drew in a deep and trembling breath, and when he spoke again, Emma was struck by the pain and bitterness in his voice. 'Take the name of Thomas to the very top. Take it where the likes o' Foster Thomas can never get their grubby paws on it . . . and, while it grows and prospers, I hope the one I've disowned sees it happen and rues the day he set his hand against his own flesh and blood! Do that for me, Emma, and above all else . . . do it for yourself.' He now seemed to shrink before Emma's eyes, as, lifting his hand and drawing it wearily across his brow, he went over and sank into the same chair in which his wife had been cruelly tormented on that fateful night. Of a sudden, he leaned forward, dropped his head into the palms of his hands and began quietly sobbing, his broad shoulders shaking with emotion, and occasionally gently moaned the name 'Violet' with heartrending broken voice. To Emma, who was torn between going to comfort him and leaving the room, it was a sad and humbling sight.

83

'I let her down badly,' he said now, keeping his face buried from Emma's sight. 'I should have taken her home . . . that was her only wish, and . . . I let her down. I'll never forgive myself. Never!'

'Never is a long time,' Emma said softly, 'and I'm sure Mrs Thomas understood your reasons for not going back to England. What you did here . . . the work you *both* put into this fine business, you did it for her, and for your son. She knew that, and I'm sure she understood well enough.' There was no answer and little response from Roland Thomas, and Emma expected none. Instead he nodded his head and kept his body bent forward in the chair.

'As for *me* wanting to seek out the answers I crave, well, I've waited a long time and I can wait a little longer. You're right . . . there's so much more to be done here, so many opportunities that mustn't be missed. Things are beginning to happen, and we have to be ready. Don't concern yourself about me turning my back on you after you've given me such a wonderful opportunity to prove myself. I won't desert you, I promise, and between us, we'll show the competitors as clean a pair of heels as they've seen in a long time. We *both* have our reasons for seeing the growth of the Thomas Trading Company. When the time is right for me to take leave and trace my path back to those who heartlessly forged it, nothing would give me greater pleasure than to go back, not as a young innocent upon whom stronger men would prey, but as an accomplished business woman . . . a woman of property and consequence, a woman who is more than capable of bringing her enemies to account!' There was a hardness in Emma's heart as she spoke, and it was betrayed in

the icy edge to her voice. '*That* will be worth waiting
for!'

And so it was agreed. For three years or more,
Emma would dedicate herself to matters of business.
After that, if she deemed the time to be right, she
would take leave and sail for England, to attend to
issues that were personal and close to her heart. The
wedding date was set for the month of March, some
eight weeks hence, in the year of our Lord, 1870.

'Married now, eh! Well . . . all the luck in the world ter
yer, Emma darlin'!' Nelly raised her merry brown eyes
to where Emma stood with her back to the cell door,
and, in a voice that was somewhat subdued by her grim
surroundings, said, 'Oh, I'm sorry, gal! I *know* I
shouldn't have got to fighting with that Rita
Hughes . . . but the bastard said some'at as put me
back up.' Here she gave a small laugh. 'If yer ask me,
she's bleedin' lucky somebody pulled me orf her.
What! I'd have killed her fer sure!'

'Oh, yes? And got yourself hanged for it, eh?' Emma
was angry and it showed, in her voice, in her countenance, and in the steel-grey of her eyes. 'Do you
honestly think I don't know what Rita Hughes said that
"put your back up"? Do you think I don't know that
there are folks hereabouts who condemn the fact that
Roland Thomas has taken a convict for his wife? *Their*
opinions don't concern either me or Mr Thomas . . . so
they shouldn't concern *you*!' Giving a deep sigh and
shaking her head, Emma came forward to sit beside
Nelly on the narrow iron bed, and gently patting the
back of Nelly's hand, she said with tender feeling, 'Oh,
Nelly, Nelly! Will you always insist on landing yourself

in trouble on *my* account? Don't you know by now that I am capable of fighting my own battles? Do you think you're going to stop folk from gossiping between each other, by attacking them with pitch-forks?' For a minute, there was a deep and profound silence while Emma allowed her words to sink in, and Nelly appeared to be taking them to heart. But then, the silence was broken by Nelly's soft giggling. 'Cor, bugger me, Emma, gal,' she laughed, 'd'yer know, I've only just realised what a narrer escape I've had.' Then, just as Emma thought that her words were having the desired effect, she was told, between spurts of laughter, 'If I'd damaged that pitch-fork . . . I'd have been in *real* trouble with you, wouldn't I, eh?'

Try though she might, Emma couldn't keep a straight face when she turned to see Nelly's lively eyes and homely face all crumpled with laughter. 'Oh, Nelly!' she said, trying hard to suppress the merriment already spreading from her heart. 'What *will* I do with you?'

'Get me outta this bleedin' dark hole for a start!' came the reply. And, because of her new status, together with the fact that she had only just come from the Governor, where her pleas on Nelly's behalf had been accepted – with a warning that 'should it happen again, I'll probably throw away the key!' – Emma was able to secure the hapless Nelly's release.

The two women were a strange yet familiar sight as they made their way from the Convict Depot and along William Street. Emma looked exceptionally smart and respectable, dressed in black boots, bonnet and cape, with the long, flouncy, dark-blue skirt softly swishing with her every step. There was an air of elegance about her, and an absolute confidence that only social standing and the promise of prosperity can bring. Nelly looked the worse for wear, having been deprived of the pretty white blouse and brown skirt that Emma had got her for the wedding, and dressed by the authorities in a plain grey frock, which hung on her narrow frame like a sack from a carcass.

'When we get back to the store, you'd best put yourself in a tub of hot water, and the rags from your back into the rubbish bin!' Emma told her. 'Make no mistake about it, Nelly . . . it's been the devil's own job talking you out of *this* one. If you don't curb that temper of yours, Lord only knows what'll become of you.' Emma was anxious that Nelly fully understand the seriousness of her short temper and complete lack of respect for authority. 'You *do* understand what I'm saying, don't you, Nelly?' she asked.

'O' course I do!' retorted Nelly. 'Stop bleedin' well nagging me. Look here, Emma darlin' . . . if I was ter promise yer that I won't be goaded into fighting again, will that do?'

'It'd be a *start* at least,' conceded Emma, 'as long as it doesn't go the way of all your other promises of a similar nature.'

'Oh, stop worrying, Emma,' Nelly chided, 'it'll be all right, you'll see. When I feel meself heading for trouble, I'll count ter ten . . . how's that, eh?' She didn't wait for an answer, but launched into a tuneful whistling of a bawdy tavern-song. Emma shook her head in exasperation. It was no use! Nelly was her own master, and wouldn't be shaped by any other hand, however loving and well meaning it was. 'Come on,' Emma hurried along, 'let's get you home before the preacher hears what tune you're whistling.'

'The divil himself can hear what tune I'm whistling,' replied Nelly, 'and it won't bother me none at all!' Whereupon she resumed the bawdy tune with even more gusto.

As it happened, 'the divil himself' *was* listening, in the form of Foster Thomas. It was still very early in the morning, the hour when most folks were only just beginning to stir on to the streets. An hour that Emma had chosen well for her errand, because the last thing she wanted was for Nelly to be paraded along the street and to be subjected to people's unkind stares. There had been enough talk as it was: with Nelly choosing to roll about in the dust with Rita Hughes, and to attack her with a pitch-fork, in full view of those guests who were loyal enough to Roland Thomas to attend his wedding. It was planned that it should be a quiet affair, which, in spite of the fracas later caused by the caustic remark made by the blacksmith's daughter combined with Nelly's short temper, had been carried off extremely well. It had delighted Emma to learn that both she and Mr Thomas had a number of genuine supporters.

Little had changed since Emma had been made Mrs Thomas, and subsequently, a 'free' woman. She wore a gold band on her finger; she entered into deep and far-reaching plans for business expansion with her husband; she walked to the church with him on a Sunday, arm-in-arm, and was dutiful as a wife to all intents and purposes. Yet there was no other physical contact between them. Each made no demands on the other. Emma could not bring herself to address him as any other than 'Mr Thomas', as she had done for so long. And the one large bedroom had been divided in two, by means of placing a wardrobe down the middle.

Emma had taken over the duties of housekeeper from Rita Hughes, and a young lad had been taken on to help about the stores and warehouse. Already Emma had been instrumental in securing a more satisfactory warehouse along Cliff Street, and talks were underway to contract a sea-going vessel and reliable crew to run trading goods all along the coast. All in all, the arrangement between Emma and Roland Thomas was proving to be most satisfactory.

In the five weeks following the wedding ceremony, nothing had been seen of Foster Thomas, and no word of his whereabouts was ever heard. Emma hoped he might have crawled into some God-forsaken corner to rot away, but she suspected he had not, for creatures of his sort seemed always to survive, albeit by their predatory nature. She suspected also that, if any one person might know where he was, it would be Rita Hughes who, Emma knew, was besotted with the worthless fellow.

'Back! Get back, you fool . . . outta sight!' Foster Thomas gripped his fingers tight about the arm of his companion before, with an angry snarl, he swiftly drew her into the shadows. 'She mustn't see me,' he hissed through gritted teeth, 'not *yet* anyway . . . not until I'm good and ready!' There was no mistaking the loathing in his eyes, as he ran them over the upturned face of Rita Hughes. Slowly, his eyes narrowed to thin, cruel slits as he raised a finger and drew it along the angry red weal that ran from the corner of his mouth, then down over his neck to the tip of his shoulder blade. 'So!

They think they have cheated me, do they? Well, let them think it! But I'll have what's mine. One way or another, I'll have what's mine.' When he glanced down at her, with the fury alive in his eyes, Rita Hughes was forced to ask herself whether she was doing the right thing in hiding him. When he had turned up some twenty-four hours earlier, there had been no question in her mind that she must help him because wasn't it true that they had cheated him, and that the news of his father's wedding had been a terrible shock. Now, though, she began to wonder just what manner of revenge he intended, and for the first time, she was afraid. Yet, amidst her fears she was filled with a love and longing for him so desperate that she could never refuse him anything! All the same, when he watched Emma out of sight, his eyes following her every move, she wished she could turn from him. But she could not. When he began murmuring in a strange and fearful voice, 'I mean to have *everything* . . . everything that belongs to me!' she knew she would do all she could to help him. Foster Thomas sensed his power over her; sensed it and revelled in it. Yet he was careful not to disclose the fact that, when he vowed to get back *everything* that belonged to him . . . it included Emma. It must include Emma, above all else, because no other woman would do. Emma might have taken his own father for her husband, but she was *his*. When the time was right, he would claim her. But he would need to be devious, and ruthless. That did not bother him. What bothered him was how, when it became necessary, he would discard Rita Hughes, for she was besotted, he knew. No matter, he would use her, like he would use others; when they were of no more use, he would employ whatever means he could to dispose of them. In the depths of his dark and treacherous mind, Foster Thomas had begun a particular train of thought with Rita Hughes foremost in his thinking. It ended with another image looming large. The image was that of Nelly, and with it Foster Thomas saw an easier way to Emma, and to all that had been taken from him. The plan was already forming in his mind. It gave him pleasure and, when he chuckled aloud, Rita Hughes gave a shiver. But when he grabbed her and took her in a passionate kiss, all her doubts melted away. He only had to ask, and she would do anything for him.

'Yer a good friend ter me, darlin' . . . and I don't deserve it.' Nelly was getting ready for bed and Emma had brought her a number of garments chosen from her own wardrobe. These she laid across the back of the cane stand-chair, while Nelly slipped into her nightgown and got into bed. 'How can I repay you, gal?' she asked.

'You just keep your nose clean, and work towards your ticket-of-leave,' Emma told Nelly, 'that's all I ask of you.' She sat down on the edge of the bed, her clear grey eyes roving over that bright, impish face which she loved dearly. 'I'll help you all I can, Nelly . . . you know that, don't you? When I go to England, I want to take you with me. We've been through so much together, Nelly . . . you and I.'

Of a sudden Emma fell into a deep silence and Nelly suspected that she was thinking of a particular night when the two of them had been bundled into a prisoners' waggon, and Emma's newborn daughter had been left behind. Now, when the tears began tumbling down Emma's sad face, Nelly was quickly beside her, her

91

arms about her friend and the tears moist in her own eyes. 'Aw, Emma darlin' . . . let the past go, why don't yer? Please . . . let it go, or it'll tear yer apart.'

Emma was crying softly, and when she turned to look at Nelly, the pain was heavy in her anguished eyes. 'Oh Nelly, she was so beautiful . . . mine and Marlow's daughter.' A faint smile passed over her lovely face as she said, 'How like Marlow she was with that rich, black hair . . . so tiny she was, so very lovely. Oh, Nelly, *why* did she have to die? How could the Lord be so cruel as to punish an innocent babe for *my* sins?'

Emma was sobbing now, and as Nelly held her fast in her arms, she was smitten with guilt. All these years she had let Emma believe, beyond a shadow of doubt, that the child had been lifeless when it had rolled into the gutter. How could she tell Emma otherwise, when even the slightest hope that the child was alive would have made her exile even more of a nightmare!

Nelly was not certain. She could never be certain, because the lamplight had thrown strange shadows on the cobbles that night, and the darkness had been filled with all manner of sounds. But Nelly recalled that, as the waggon sped away to the ship which would take them to the other side of the world, an old tramp seemed to collect Emma's child into her shawl. The child made the crying sound of all newborns. She hadn't told Emma then, and she was afraid to tell her now, for fear Emma would never forgive her. And, anyway, it was far too late now. Far too late! Too much water had gone under the bridge, and there was no turning back. Besides which, it was more than likely that, even if Emma's child had lived on that night, she wouldn't have survived long. It was a sorry thing, but a true one nevertheless.

Part Two

England 1874

Old Hatreds

Repent not you that you shall lose your friend
And he repents not that he pays your debt;
For, if the Jew do cut but deep enough,
I'll pay it instantly with all my heart.
Shakespeare, *Merchant of Venice*

Chapter Four

'Stop thief!' The shrill cry of alarm rang through Blackburn Market Place and, instantly, all eyes were turned in one direction. What they saw was a well-built young woman bedecked in a burgundy outfit of ribbons and velvet, with a fur-trimmed cape and extravagant bonnet, and beside her a boy of some ten years old, both shocked and the one attempting to console the other. From their dress, their manner, and the way in which the woman tenderly sobbed into her silken handkerchief, it was obvious to one and all that they were gentry-folk. 'See!' cried the woman, waving her handkerchief in the direction of a small, dark-haired waif who was making good her escape. '*There* she is! Stop her, somebody . . . she stole my purse!'

'Why! That's Molly!' one stall-holder cried. ''Er as belongs ter the tramp!'

'You *know* the thief?' Martha Trent was sufficiently recovered to confront the burly fellow, her expression one of disbelief and outrage. 'Then you must inform the authorities at once. The ragamuffin must be brought before them . . . put away until she learns her lesson! She had my purse, I tell you!'

'That don't surprise me none,' replied the burly stall-holder, grinning through the gaps in his blackened teeth. 'What *do* surprise me, lady . . . is that you knew about it. What! I've known that little bugger steal the baccy from a gentleman's pipe when it were still in 'is mouth!' He flashed a proud and merry glance into the crowd of gawping onlookers and, knowing the little thief as well as he did and having seen the very event he described, began roaring with laughter. 'Aye!' rejoined another. 'There ain't a pickpocket anywhere as can show *that* scallywag a thing or two . . . why, I do believe she could dodge a'tween a unsuspecting gentleman's legs an' steal the very breeches from 'is arse!'

At this the crowd erupted into tumultuous laughter, which in turn sent Martha Trent into a fit. 'Fetch a policeman, Edward!' she instructed the dark-haired boy at her side. Then, when he hesitated, she nudged him between the shoulder-blades and sent him forward a pace or two. 'Hurry up, child!' she snapped and, lifting her arm above her head, she daintily touched her fingertips over her brow. 'Oh! . . . It's all too much!' she cried, calling the boy back. 'Get me a carriage . . . take me home, quickly!' As the boy turned back and came towards his mother, an older woman in a ragged shawl appeared on the scene. She had a peculiar hopping gait as she made her way to where the boy's mother was feigning a swooning fit. At the sight of the old woman, there were a few soft remarks and a series of little sniggers.

'What's the matter, dearie?' The woman sidled up to where Martha Trent was precariously perched on an upturned orange-box. 'Been robbed, 'ave yer? By! There's some bad rascals about an' that's a fact!' She cooed, becoming agitated when there was a series of giggles from the onlookers. 'Be orf with yer!' she shouted, rounding on them and making a good show of castigating them. 'Yer should be ashamed o' yerselves . . . 'Ere's a fine lady robbed, and there's not *one* o' yer fetched a bobby!' She shook her fist. She also winked her eye. In a moment, the crowd had dispersed, everybody going in separate directions and each one quietly smiling at the old woman's antics. But though she was a scoundrel, they knew that Sal Tanner was harmless enough. Since her brother Marlow had been gone these past nine years and more, the poor soul had had a hard and hungry life. Then there was another mouth to feed! One which didn't rightly belong to Sal, but which she had found in the gutter nigh on nine years back. Right outside the prison gates, or so it was said. Old Sal had called the girl by the name of Molly, and together they haunted the alleyways of Blackburn town, foraging a living where they could and occasionally 'relieving' the gentry of their fripperies and fineries. Oh yes, canny Sal had taught the girl well, until it was hard to tell who was the better thief! Often though, when the work was about, the girl loved to toil along the canal, helping to load and offload the goods ferried about on the barges. She had a deep, natural love of the sea, and often stowed away, or scrounged a ride along the Leeds and Liverpool Canal into the big docks at Liverpool. Old Sal though would go into a frenzy, because she was fearful that Molly would be taken by the sea . . . as she truly believed her brother Marlow had been.

'Now then, dearie . . . let's get yer a carriage, eh?' Sal made to take hold of Martha Trent's arm. 'We'll 'ave yer back 'ome safe an' sound in no time at all.' She stepped closer, and as she stretched out one arm as though to assist the shocked and outraged woman, her other arm came up in a crafty move to pluck the cameo brooch from the lapel of Martha Trent's fur-trimmed cape.

'I'll see my mother home, thank you.' The boy Edward had stepped between old Sal and his mother. He had seen her intention, but made no hue or cry. Instead he smiled into her wrinkled face, met her bloodshot and boozy gaze with firm, dark green eyes, and in a decisive voice that caused her to step back a pace, he said, 'The authorities can't be too far away, for they do patrol the area. Don't worry, my mother will be fine.'

'Of *course* I'll be fine!' rejoined his mother, who, at the sight of old Sal creeping up on her, had made a remarkable recovery. 'Go away, you!' she told the old woman, at the same time holding her silken handkerchief to her nose and wearing an expression of disgust. 'Get away from me!'

'Be on your way, old woman.' Of a sudden, old Sal was confronted by an elderly gentleman dressed in a dark suit and topper, and carrying a walking-stick with a horse's head handle. When he spoke, he waved the stick in the air, 'Unless you want me to summon a policeman?' he asked with a threatening air.

'Not at all, sir!' exclaimed old Sal, being cheeky enough to pat him on the arm. 'I'll be on my way this very instant!' In a minute she was hurrying away. As she went, her ears caught the gentleman's remark to the lady. 'It's Mrs Trent, isn't it . . . daughter of Caleb Crowther? You remember I was introduced to you when I visited Breckleton House last December, for business discussions with your father. Your husband was away at sea, and you were staying with your parents.'

On hearing this, old Sal was stopped in her tracks. 'Caleb Crowther,' she muttered, turning about to look again. 'Caleb Crowther . . . hated Justice o' the Peace, eh?' And this hoity-toity lady, with her fine clothes and plump bodice . . . this was his spoiled brat of a daughter, Martha! Old Sal had no liking for the Caleb Crowthers of this world, not when they took delight at throwing her in prison so reg'lar! Oh, yes, Justice Crowther was a bad one, and no matter how many times old Sal warned little Molly against him, it could never be enough, because it was well known how he had vowed to clear the alleys and streets of 'these undesirable vagrants'.

'Yer bugger! Yer'll 'ave ter *catch* us first!' she chuckled now, quickly hobbling away. After turning a few more corners and making her way down an alley or two, old Sal stopped, leaning against the side of a house and taking time to catch her breath. 'Let's see what we fished from the old gent's pocket,' she murmured as, with a deep-throated chuckle, she pulled a long, thick chain of silver from the depths of her shawl. Attached to the end of the chain was a strikingly handsome silver watch, which she quickly bit against her two remaining teeth. 'Solid!' she remarked to the sky. 'That'll fetch a bob or two, an' no mistake.' Of a sudden, she gave a joyful little skip and began wending her way along the cobbles, hurrying as best she could. Her gait was markedly lopsided on account of the limp, which had been the legacy of a broken leg got from a warehouse fire some years before.

As she went on her way, old Sal Tanner could be

heard muttering in that familiar manner for which she was known, "E were a nice enough feller . . . but if 'e will go about tellin' poor old folks like meself ter "Be orf! Else 'e'll fetch a bobby", well . . . the bugger *deserves* 'is pocket-watch spirited away. She teks 'er chances where she finds 'em, do old Sal, an' she don't give a tinker's cuss whether it's a hoity-toity lady, a fine and dandy gentleman . . . or a dark-'aired little feller wi' a cheeky smile, an' eyes that green as they coulda' been med by the little folks.' Here she stopped and looked upwards to the cold January sky. For a moment she appeared to be turning something over in her mind. Then, having apparently reached a decision, she cocked her head to one side and laughed, 'What d'yer want ter go and give that little feller such emerald-green eyes for, eh?' Laughing louder, she shook her head from side to side and lowered her gaze to the ground. 'Gi' me a bloody shock, it did . . . 'avin' them green eyes smilin' at me . . . I thought it were the little folk come ter claim my Molly, so I did!' The merriment suddenly went from her voice and her expression grew serious as she resumed her journey once more. 'T'ain't right that folks should 'ave such green eyes! Green's the colour o' the little people . . . yer 'ave ter get their sacred permission. Oh, but 'e *ain't* one o' the little people. I'm sure o' that. No, 'e ain't . . . 'cause all manner o' folk 'ave green eyes. I've seen 'em, but I ain't seen none so emerald-green an 'andsome as *that* little feller's.'

In her peculiar and eccentric belief that the colour green was sacred to the 'little people' and must *never* be used or displayed without their permission, old Sal had been taken aback when young Edward Trent had smiled on her, yet, by the same token, dismissed her. She had been surprised also that, having surely seen her intention to make away with his mother's cameo brooch, he had not swiftly raised the alarm. Now there was a strange kettle o' fish, she thought . . . whoever heard of one o' the gentry having a kind heart? Well, one thing was for sure . . . that green-eyed little feller hadn't inherited his grandfather's heart! No indeed, for Caleb Crowther's black heart was unforgiving and wicked. 'To Hell wi' the bugger!' old Sal shouted out at the top of her voice. 'He'll find 'is way there one o' these fine days, an' when 'e does . . . let 'im *rot*, for there's nobody this side o' Hell as would lift a finger ter save 'im!' Not when he watched one of his own transported off to Australia as a convict; not when he didn't lift a finger to help the poor lass; and not when he robbed her of every last penny left to her. 'Oh, yer a bad divil, Caleb Crowther!' old Sal cried out. Afterwards she broke into her hopping gait and moved a bit swifter when she feared her voice might have carried too far.

If young Edward Trent had set old Sal to thinking deeply, so had she left a strong impression on his mind. Yet not as strong as the one left by the dark-haired waif who had robbed his mother of her purse. As the carriage took him and Martha Trent back to Breckleton House, the boy couldn't get the image of her pretty face and strikingly beautiful dark eyes out of his mind. Who was she? Why did she have to *steal*? Was the old tramp her mother . . . where did the girl live? All of these questions he might well have discussed with his mother had she been the kind of mother who was open to discussion. But she was not and though his father would have shown an interest, sadly he was away at sea. A quiet despair filled the boy's eyes as he thought more deeply of his beloved father, Silas Trent. He was away too often these days, and he missed him so. Oh, but the minute he came home, Edward intended to tell him all about the incident at the market. He didn't suppose they would go to the market again, not after today. So he might never see the girl again. Such a possibility made him sad, for he would like to talk to her, this dark-haired girl who cheekily winked at him as she fled away, clutching his mother's purse. He remembered that the big man behind the stall had called her by the name of Molly, ''er that belongs ter the tramp'.

For the remainder of the journey back to his grandfather Crowther's house, young Edward Trent thought of little else but the girl, Molly. A pretty girl with a pretty name who, he felt sure, he would meet again. The thought cheered him a great deal, and when his mother angrily prodded him and instructed, 'Sit up straight, Edward . . .'. I will *not* have you slouching when you think nobody's looking!' he stiffened his back and straightened his shoulders with a smile on his face. His mother was trying to make him feel miserable again, just like she always did when she was in a mood. But she couldn't make him feel miserable *this* time. Not when he had in mind a small, impish face with black laughing eyes and hair as dark as midnight. Molly – he would remember the name well.

'We did well, Molly, me little flower!' Old Sal gave a hearty chuckle and roughly grabbed the girl to her bosom where she rocked her for a moment, before thrusting her away. 'Now then . . . where we gonna hide 'em eh? Like as not, that hoity-toity lady will be spelling out both our descriptions to the bobbies at this very minute! They might come swooping down on us at any time!' Of a sudden she was frantic, rushing from one side of the miserable room to the other and flinging objects aside, then lifting up boxes and peering beneath. 'Oh gawd!' she moaned, swinging round and fixing her bloodshot eyes in a stare on to the girl's face. 'We've had it *this* time . . . I feel it in me bones, Molly darlin' . . . they'll catch us fer sure this time!'

'No, they won't,' replied the girl, taking the old one by the hand and leading her to a battered old stool, where she eased her down on to it. 'They'll not catch us, old Sal . . . 'cause we'll move house, like we've done afore!' She smiled up at the old woman with bright, wide-awake eyes and a look of mischief on her heart-shaped face and, for a fleeting moment which caught Sal Tanner unawares, Molly's dark eyes and black, unruly hair touched a memory in her old heart. A precious memory of another child who used to look up at her with the same bright smile and the very same love shining from big, black eyes. Strange, she thought now, how much this lovely child reminded her of the little lad she had had to raise when their parents had suffered a tragic death. Where was he now, her brother Marlow? Had he gone to foreign parts and made his fortune as he said he would? And had he forgotten the sister he'd left behind? Sal would never believe such a terrible thing, not of Marlow, who had always been as straight and loving as a day was long. No! He hadn't forgotten her at all. 'Twas the *sea*. The sea had claimed him, that was the truth of it! Why couldn't he have listened to her? How many times had she warned him not to lose his foolish heart to one o' the gentry? Time and time again she had told him that his fancy for Emma Grady would be the ruin of him! Then when Emma wed Gregory Denton and it seemed like the best thing to Sal, Marlow had nigh wasted away, pining for what could never be his. Oh, the fool . . . the bloody fool. Aye, 'twas his love for Emma Grady that had driven Marlow Tanner to travel the seas and, though the poor lass met a worse fortune at the hands of her own guardian, Caleb Crowther . . . old Sal couldn't help but hold Emma Grady partly to blame for the loss of her fine brother.

'Allus wanderin' . . . wanderin' about like lost souls we are, Molly darlin', but we'll outwit the buggers, an' that's all as matters, eh?' She was laughing now, having shaken the past away from her thoughts and brought her concentration to matters at hand. 'Get yer stuff together, gal,' she said. 'Let's be off . . . afore the sods come creepin' up on us like a plague o' rats, eh?'

In no time at all, Molly had collected the few things that she and Sal could call their own . . . two chipped enamel mugs, a small oil lamp – which also served to boil a pan on – a box of candles, two best china plates purloined from a fancy store in Manchester, together with two sets of cutlery, a wooden-handled bone comb, two grey blankets and the clothes they both stood up in. After wrapping the articles in one of the baskets, Molly slung it over her narrow shoulders and presented herself before old Sal. 'That's it,' she said, 'there ain't nothing else worth carrying away.'

'Travel light, that's the best thing ter do, me darlin',' chuckled Sal, 'then yer can tek ter yer heels if needs be, eh?' She tousled the girl's short, unkempt hair. 'Mek towards the canal, up by Angela Street,' she said, shuffling towards the door. 'Happen the landlord at the Navigation might slip us a glass o' some'at strong . . . some'at ter warm the old bones.' Then, with a crafty wink, she added, 'Like as not, we'll find us a buyer there, fer the purse and watch. I'm surprised that gentry woman only had two guineas in her purse though . . . still, it'll keep us fro' starvin' fer a while, I suppose.'

Molly nodded, thinking what a good job it was that old Sal hadn't seen her slip a *third* guinea from the purse into her pocket. She didn't like deceiving Sal in that way, but past experience had taught her that Sal's fondness for 'a jar o' the best' often left them penniless and hungry. Slipping a few coins away now and then, when they had hit lucky, was Molly's way of taking care of old Sal. The one thing that frightened the girl more than hunger or not having a roof over their heads, was that the authorities might put her away. And if Justice Crowther had *his* way, she'd be rooted out for sure! Who would look after Sal then? Not the drinking cronies who cadged every last farthing from her to whet their own boozy appetites, that was for sure. And not the folks who laughed at her antics, nor them along the canal who might willingly offer a lift to Liverpool on their barges, but who would not be so willing to offer a bed and board to the likes of Sal, when they knew she could be a real handful while under the influence.

The girl, Molly, had known no other family than the woman they called old Sal, and she loved her with a fierce protectiveness. But, though the old woman would always hold that special place in her affections, many had been the time when Molly had craved to know who her *real* family was. During these times she had asked countless questions, to which Sal would always reply, 'Yer ain't got no family but me, child. I've telled yer afore how the little people sent yer to me . . . found yer in the gutter I did . . . wi' that very watch as yer wear round yer neck. Oh, an' yer must *never* sell that pretty trinket, Molly gal . . . not even if yer close ter starvation! It belongs ter the little folk, d'yer see? Just like *you* do!'

Molly didn't share old Sal's eccentric belief in 'the little people', mainly because she had seen no evidence of them, and perhaps because she knew instinctively that old Sal was different from most folks, in that she often lived in a strange little world of her own. The watch though, which Sal had entrusted to her, was solid and real to Molly, a link with her past and a pointer to her future, she knew. But whenever she looked at it in secret, she felt afraid. It had always remained a mystery to her. *Who* had treasured it before her? Could it possibly be her own mother, or father; or did it in fact not belong to her at all? Was it instead something that had been dropped by a stranger and come across by Sal, at the same time as Sal had come across the tiny bundle of rags that was Molly?

There were things written on that watch, things that would tell Molly of its background, if only she could understand them. But they might as well be written in Latin for all the sense they made to her, because she had never learned to read. Sal couldn't teach her, for *she* couldn't read either. Molly was desperately afraid to show the tiny, delicate watch to anyone else, lest they steal it away forever. No, she must keep it safely hidden inside her vest, touching her skin. At least until she could find a way to master the art of learning words.

'Come on, young 'un!' Old Sal had hobbled down the steps that led from the dilapidated house, and now she was standing in the backyard, making frantic efforts to put a lighted match to the baccy in her clay pipe, and loudly cursing when the cutting January breeze snuffed it out. After a while she gave up trying and rammed both matches and pipe into the pocket of her long, grubby skirt. 'Come on, come on!' she called as the girl came to the steps. 'If we don't find somewhere ter lay us heads fer the night, we'll freeze for sure!'

'You go on . . . I'll catch up in a minute, Sal,' Molly told her, turning on the top step to secure the door. 'When it's quietened down in a few days,' she called after Sal, who was already shuffling her way out into the cobbled alley, 'we might be able to come back and get the stool and a few other things.'

'Aw, bugger 'em!' yelled Sal. 'There's none o' that rubbish worth coming back fer.'

Molly didn't agree. There was the stool, a little cupboard she'd made herself out of an orange-box, and that picture of a sailing ship that she'd found aside somebody's midden. Then there was that old brass clock which had been in this derelict house when they first came here some two months ago. Two months! That was the longest they'd managed to stay in one place and, even though Sal had always told her *never* to look on any place as permanent, Molly had a special feeling for this house; although it wouldn't be long now before they pulled the street down. The folks had all been moved out long since, and there was talk of a mill being built here.

109

As Molly closed the door and turned away to follow Sal, she made herself a promise that when it was safe she *would* come back for those things she couldn't carry now. Oh, but first they had to find somewhere to live and that wouldn't be easy.

'Where's your little people *now*, Sal?' Molly called out as she ran after the bent and ragged figure. 'If you're so pally with 'em . . . ask 'em to find us a place to live!' She lapsed into a fit of giggles when back came the answer, 'Don't be so cheeky, yer young bugger! Ye've got more tongue than what the cat licks its arse with!'

When the girl caught up with old Sal, she hitched up the cumbersome bundle to a more comfortable position across her shoulders and slipped her small hand into that of the woman. 'I wish we could have stayed here for a while longer,' she said wistfully, 'I liked it here.'

'Aw, bless yer 'eart, luv,' replied old Sal fondly, squeezing tight the small fingers clutched to hers. 'We'll find us a place, you'll see.' When she glanced down, it was to see a more contented look on the girl's face. What would she do without the lass, Sal thought as they trudged along towards Angela Street and the canal. The young 'un had been such a companion to her, such a comfort, and she loved the bonny lass, even if at times she were a right little sod! All the same, never a night passed that Sal didn't thank the little people for bringing her such a treasure. In the same prayer when she gave thanks, old Sal whispered a more fervent one, asking that young Molly should never be parted from her because the very thought of such a thing sent her straight for the gin bottle!

Chapter Five

At half-past four on a sultry July afternoon, Molly straightened up from her labours, wiped the sweat from her eyes with coal-smudged fingers, and leaned the shovel against the black, shiny mound of newly delivered coal. 'I think my back's broken,' she laughed.

'I'm not surprised, young 'un,' chuckled the thin, wiry fellow who had been working alongside. 'By! You've done the work o' *ten* your size, an' that's the truth on it. Call it a day . . . here.' He propped his shovel against the gas-lamp nearby, then he dipped his fingers into the pocket of a grubby cord coat which was lying beside it. 'Tek your wages and get off home,' he said, counting out a number of coins from the pocket, and placing them in Molly's outstretched hand. 'Wash that coal dust off your face an' all . . . I'm blowed if yer don't look like one o' them dark wandering minstrels.' His face creased into a grin as he regarded her more closely. She's a grand little worker, he thought, a feeling of hopelessness surging through him. He might have offered the poor little bugger a home on his barge. But she'd only grow up to be a woman. And he couldn't abide women, not at any cost! Give him a dog every time . . . they were less trouble.

Molly was more than glad to call it a day because there wasn't an inch of her body that didn't hurt. The sight of those four shilling pieces resting in the palm of her hand made her feel good inside. They were worth all the coal shovelling, and wouldn't Sal be pleased, she thought. 'Thank you kindly, Mr Entwistle,' she said, her mucky features breaking into a happy smile, and her small even teeth appearing brilliant white against the dark background.

'Bugger me, if you ain't flashing like one o' them there beacons!' chuckled the little fellow. 'You'd give anybody a real fright if they wuz to meet you down a dark alley, an' that's a fact!' He was still chuckling as Molly put away her shovel on the barge and went on her way, whistling a merry tune.

''Ow much did 'e pay yer, gal?' Sal wanted to know. 'An' don't expect any tea, 'cause I ain't got no money!' she grumbled, before Molly could answer her question.

'We shall both have us tea,' Molly retorted good-humouredly, 'because Mr Entwistle paid me *four whole shillings*.'

'*Four* . . . Well, the mean old sod!' Sal had been sitting on the bank with her cumbersome skirt drawn up to her knees and her legs dangling towards the canal water some three feet further down. In a minute she was scrambling up to confront Molly with a look of disgust on her face. 'Ye mean ter tell me as the bugger had yer working all day . . . an' only paid yer *four* shillings?' She shook her fist in the air and took Molly by the shoulder. 'You come wi' me, lass,' she exclaimed, beginning to propel the girl at a smart pace towards the ramshackle wooden hut which they had commandeered as a home. 'Get thi' face washed an mek yerself look respectable, 'cause we're gonna have

112

a few words with your Mr Entwistle!' She gave a loud hiccup and excused herself most profoundly. 'I ain't been drinking, neither!' she bluntly informed the amused Molly. 'So don't think I *have!*' Whereupon she promptly lost her footing and grabbed at Molly for support.

'Oh, Sal . . . as if I would,' said Molly with mock seriousness. 'O' course you haven't been drinking. You told me yourself that we can't have anything to eat, because there's no money. And, if there's no money for food, then there's no money for booze . . . ain't that right?' With Sal's fingers clutching her shoulder tightly, and having to pick her way carefully over the rubble and boulders strewn hereabouts, Molly couldn't afford to glance up at Sal's face, but she felt Sal's round violet eyes turned on her. 'I think Mr Entwistle paid me a good day's wage,' she said. 'He's a nice fella . . . and he always has a good word to say about *you.*' At once, she was brought to a halt.

'About *me*?' Sal demanded, a little smile teasing the corners of her mouth. 'What does he know about me, eh? I don't know the bloke . . . do I?' Her deep, ruddy forehead was creased into a multitude of wrinkles as she struggled to place the name in her mind. 'How come this Mr Entwistle knows me, eh?' She was puzzled. 'An' where might I have made the fella's acquaintance, I wonder?'

'I don't know, but he mentioned summat about a public house,' lied Molly, manufacturing a suitable expression of bewilderment. 'I *think* it was the Sun.'

'Naw, I don't fancy that place too often these days . . . not since the landlord said I were blind drunk and fit fer nowt but causing trouble.' Sal gave a little

113

chuckle, before resuming a serious face. 'Well . . . I might a' been just a *bit* tipsy . . . but there were no call fer the bugger ter set his dog on me!' She fixed her round, marble eyes on Molly's upturned face and, even though they were shot through with tiny pink blood vessels and appeared vague from drinking, Molly thought what a pretty violet colour they were. 'The Swan!' Sal exclaimed, seeming pleased with herself. 'I bet it were the *Swan* 'e were talking about. What do he look like, this fella?' When Molly gave a deliberately inaccurate description, for fear that Sal might still track him down and cause a rumpus, she jubilantly slapped Molly on her back, and grinned broadly, saying, 'There! I've a feeling I know the bloke . . . played cards with him, I expect. And, who knows, it's likely we've supped many a pint together!' She put her hands on her hips and surveyed Molly in the closest manner. 'Yer an ungrateful child!' she scolded in her most serious voice, broken by a series of loud hiccups. 'Four shillings is a very *generous* wage! An' I'll thank you not to call a drinking pal o' mine a "mean old sod". I'm surprised at you, Molly gal. C'mon . . . get orf home an' clean yerself up. Then we'll away ter the Navigation fer a pie and a pint. We'll mek a little hole in Mr Entwistle's four shillings, eh?' She laughed, swaying until Molly was sure she'd fall over.

As they wended their way along the canal bank towards the hut, Molly kept tight hold of old Sal's hand, because the way the old one was swaying and stumbling, it was likely that she'd lose her balance at any minute. When she did, and the two of them ended up fighting to stay upright, Sal erupted in a fit of cackling and shouting. 'Did yer see that, young 'un?'

she laughed, setting her booted foot forward again. 'Yer nearly went arse over tip an' dragged ol' Sal with yer! I reckon you've been at the gin bottle, yer little sod!'

Molly felt herself coming out in a cold sweat when she thought how Sal had been sitting over the canal bank, with her legs dangling down. It was painfully obvious that she'd been drinking, after she'd promised *not* to! What will I do with her, agonised Molly as she took a tighter hold of Sal's meandering figure. Get her back to the hut, and get her to sleep it off, that's what! Oh, and what a good job she'd had wit enough to mislead her about poor Mr Entwistle, for Molly was well pleased with her wage and she knew it to be fair. Besides which, if Sal had gone back and caused trouble, he might not have given her any more work, and that would have been a bad thing because honest work was getting harder and harder to come by.

The hut which was now home to Sal and Molly was situated at the widest area of grassy bank, and was half hidden in the undergrowth. There was a tall stone wall immediately behind, and directly behind that, the vicarage. This fact had given old Sal a great deal of pleasure as she told one and all: 'What more could a body want, eh? . . . I've got the ale house down one end, and the vicar at the other. If I'm tekken bad after a jolly night out, I have only ter whistle and the vicar'll come a'runnin' with his Bible. He'll get me ter the gates o' Heaven right enough. Drunk or sober, the good Lord won't turn me away, I'm thinking!'

When they had first come across the dilapidated workmen's hut, there were chinks between the weathered boarding 'wide enough ter drive a horse and cart through', as Sal had complained. Now, however, the chinks were stuffed with moss which Molly had painstakingly gathered, and the wind couldn't force its way in so easily. On a hot day like today, though, the air inside the cramped hut was stifling. 'Bloody hell, lass . . . prop that door open with some'at!' instructed Sal as she fell on to the narrow bed, this being a scrounged mattress set on four orange-boxes, the whole length of which swayed and creaked beneath Sal's sudden weight.

In no time at all, Molly had filled the pan from the wooden rain-bucket by the door, and brought it slowly to the boil on the oil-lamp. She might have brought some wood and lit the rusty old stove, but it was such a lengthy palaver and, anyway, it was too hot a day. When the water had boiled, Molly tipped a spoonful of tea-leaves into each of the two cups, put three spoons of sugar into both and topped them up with the boiling water. She threw out the milk, which had gone sour. 'Come on, Sal,' she said, fetching one of the cups to where Sal was lying flat on her back, 'you'll feel better when you've had a sup of hot tea.'

'Is there milk in it?' came a muffled voice from beneath a tangled shawl.

'No. It was sour, so I threw it out.'

'Then I ain't having none!' came the surly reply.

Molly knew there was no point in trying to persuade her.

'I'll go to Angela Street and get a gill from the shop,' she promised, returning the cup of hot tea to the floor beside the oil-lamp.

'Go on then, and be sharp about it,' Sal muttered, 'me tongue's hanging out.'

116

Quickly, Molly took up the pan and went running along the canal. It took only a few minutes to arrive at the shop in Angela Street. It was a quaint little place, filled with shelves of all manner and description, and these in turn were filled with jars, tins and other miscellaneous items. Above the wooden counter hung small hams and strings of onions; on the counter were placed huge cheeses and fresh baked loaves of bread; behind the counter stood a short sturdy woman with a broad, welcoming smile and a white floppy mob-cap on her rolled-up grey hair. She wore a severe black dress with starched white collar and cuffs, and the bodice pulled in so tight at the waist that the poor woman had a permanent red face.

'Well!' she exclaimed, on seeing Molly's black face and generally unkempt appearance. 'You look like you've been up the chimney and no mistake!' She kept smiling all the same and took the pan which Molly offered. 'Milk, is it?' she asked. Molly politely requested her to pour in a gill, 'if you wouldn't mind, please . . . and a loaf of bread, with a pat of best butter.' It was done in a minute; the pennies were paid and Molly hurried back to the hut. Sal was fast asleep and snoring loudly, and Molly left her to it. 'The best thing you can do is sleep it off, Sal,' she told her fondly, at the same time perching on the stool which she'd rescued from their previous home, gratefully sipping her tea.

Some time later, Molly went down to the canal and refilled her pan. The month of July had been a dry one and she didn't want to waste good rain-water on washing. When the water had boiled, she mixed it with a pan of cold water in a tin bowl; she stripped off her dress and undergarments, washed herself first and after dipped the clothes. Next, she laid them over the stool and put the stool outside in the sun. Then, very carefully, so as not to wake her, she climbed in beside old Sal. When a long scrawny arm reached out to enfold her, Molly snuggled into it. She was aching all over, and she was suddenly tired. That coal shovelling was hard work, but it wouldn't stop her from turning up tomorrow. Mr Entwistle would probably be laid up till Monday, but there might be other work to be found. If not, tomorrow was Sunday, and that was the day when most of the gentry took to strolling about in Corporation Park up on the hill. If there was no work to be had along the wharf, it was likely there might be a fat wallet or two just waiting to be separated from its owner. At one time, Molly had told Sal how she thought it was wrong to steal on a Sunday because when, out of curiosity she had taken a peep inside the church, there were 'all these grim-faced folk sitting there, and a preacher in a long black frock with beads round his waist, talking to the folk in a terrible frightening voice!'

Molly had never forgotten how he had warned that Sunday was the Lord's Day and a day when all sinners should repent or go to Hell. It had been a glorious summer's day one minute and the next, in the very moment when he bellowed out in that fearful voice, the sky went black and there was a terrible clap of thunder. 'The devil's coming for me, Sal,' Molly had run home to tell her with big shocked eyes, 'the preacher's sent him!'

'Is that right, Molly lass?' Sal had asked with a laugh and a twinkle in her eye. 'Well, the bugger'll have ter get past *me* afore he gets ter you! An' he won't be the *first* divil I've sent packin' . . . nor will he be the last!'

118

But, seeing that young Molly was not convinced, she went on in great detail about how 'the preacher were warning the folk in the church . . . them with their fancy frocks an' pretty bonnets . . . 'cause its folks wi' money as do the most sinning. An' don't you worry none about the divil chasin' yer, Molly lass . . . 'cause the Lord looks after them as looks after themselves. 'That's what *we* do, lass, you an' me . . . we look after us selves. Ain't that right?' Molly couldn't deny it, so she told the Lord that very night, 'I hope them rich folk stop their sinnin' Lord. Me and Sal, we'll go on looking after ourselves, and thank you kindly.' Sal thoroughly approved. 'That's the way, darlin',' she cackled, 'y'see . . . we're doin' these rich folks a favour when all's said an' done. The more money we can relieve 'em of . . . the less likely they are to be sinnin' with it!' And Molly's admiration of old Sal was increased tenfold.

Saturday night saw most hard-working folk hereabouts heading in the direction of the nearest ale house, the Navigation. It was across from the canal bank at the top of Angela Street and it was from there that the jolliest and loudest accordion music emanated, telling its tale up and down the canal and bringing the bargees from their cabins.

'D'yer hear *that*, me darlin'?' chuckled Sal, a deep grin lighting up her wrinkled face, and her feet giving a little joyful skip as she swung from the mattress. 'You stay an' get yer sleep,' she told Molly with a crafty look. 'That coal shovellin' fair wore you out, I know.'

In a minute, Molly had got from the bed and collected her dry clothes from outside. 'I'm coming with you,' she informed Sal, and Sal knew from that determined look on Molly's small face that it was no use arguing.

'All right then, young 'un.' She fetched her flat neb-cap from its nail behind the door and rammed it over her grey wispy hair. 'But I want none of yer naggin', like last time! We've a few bob in us purse, an' I mean ter have a pleasant pint . . . an' happen a game o' cards.' She hurried out of the hut, leaving Molly to close the door and secure it. 'Follow me if yer must. But yer ain't telling *me* what I should an' shouldn't do!'

Molly stayed a small distance behind as Sal's bent and untidy figure scurried away in her odd, dipping gait. Every now and then she would pull the long shawl about her and make sure her flat cap was secure on her head; all of her sharp jerky actions betrayed her frustration that Molly was on her heels and, before the evening was out, would no doubt remind her that playing cards was a fool's game. Had Sal forgotten how she lost her lovely barge through playing cards? Forgotten! Sal hated being reminded of it. How could she forget? *How* would she ever forget losing the barge that had been a treasured home to her and Marlow all those years? She *couldn't* forget, and she had no intention of doing so. But, she did intend winning it back, an' *that* was a fact! It was only a matter of time, that was all. A matter of time.

Molly had grown wise to Sal's moods and tantrums, so she intended to tackle the subject from a new angle, although she hoped it would still get the message across. The opportunity presented itself when a big chestnut cob went by on the towpath, pulling behind it a brightly painted barge, with a swarthy-looking fellow at the tiller, whistling a jolly tune. 'Evenin' to yer,' he called when he saw the two figures hurrying in the direction of the Navigation. 'Lookin' ter cool yerself down and wet yer whistle at the same time, eh?' he laughed.

'T'ain't no business o' yourn if we are!' Sal retorted, jerking her shawl over her shoulders and beginning to mutter to herself. The man took no offence, for he knew of old Sal and her misfortunes. 'Take care o' yerself, Sal,' he called out, 'an' mind out for the young 'un.'

At the last minute before he disappeared away round the curve in the canal, Sal thought better of her surly mood and came to the water's edge to shout after him: 'Thank you very much, bless yer. An' *you* mind how yer go, me darlin'!' Whereupon, seeing him wave an acknowledgement, Sal caught Molly into her shawl, saying with a little laugh, 'See that, Molly? . . . We've still got a few friends, you an' me, eh?'

Molly saw her chance. 'What's it like, living on a barge, Sal?' she asked, looking up with round innocent eyes. She was secretly pleased when Sal took the bait.

'What's it like? Oh, it's *grand*, Molly lass . . . right grand! There's no better life in this 'ere world, than rovin' the waterways in yer own barge . . . wi' yer own pots an' pans an' the treasures about yer.' Of a sudden, her eyes grew sad and a look of nostalgia came into her weathered old face. 'The good Lord shoulda struck me dead fer losin' that grand old barge,' she murmured. Molly was hopeful that Sal would not be tempted to go gambling tonight.

Having arrived at the Navigation on Mill Hill, Molly took her place on the flagstones beneath the window of the snug. 'Shall I look after some of yer money?' she

121

asked of Sal. 'There might be pickpockets and ruffians about tonight.'

'Don't you worry yer little head about *my* purse, Molly lass,' protested Sal, with an impatient wag of her finger. 'Yer talkin' to the best pickpocket an' ruffian in the whole o' Lancashire!' With that, she disappeared inside. A few moments later, the window of the snug was slid up and out came two hands, with a small jug of sarsaparilla and a pork pie. 'Get that down yer, lass,' Sal's ruddy face appeared, 'an' if yer little arse goes ter sleep on them cold flagstones, get yersel' off home. I can find my own way later.'

'Oh aye!' came a man's cheery voice from inside. 'An' 'appen thi' can . . . straight into the bloody cut!' There erupted a roar of appreciative laughter, as Sal promptly told Molly, 'P'raps ye'd best wait fer me after all. When I go ter Paradise, it'll be downing a bucket o' best ale, not a belly full o' canal water!'

''Course I'll wait.' Molly had no intention of going back to the hut without Sal.

'Yer a good 'un,' Sal told her, as she handed over the stone jug and the pork pie. There came another wave of laughter as she added with a chuckle, 'Enjoy yer meal, Molly lass. An' don't forget to thank the gentry fer it!'

Molly settled down as the window was slid shut above her. She wondered what kind of meal the same 'gentry' might be settling down to this very evening. 'Best roast, all steaming and crackly,' she said softly to herself. 'And the finest port in fancy glasses.' All manner of images conjured themselves up in her imaginative mind: one was of a long, polished table and little servants in smart, black frocks with white collars and cuffs, starched so stiff they dare hardly move for fear of cutting themselves. She'd heard folks talking about the gentry, and Molly didn't care much for what she heard. As she bit into the hot, succulent pork pie with its fine flaky pastry, she wondered whether, if one of them should turn up now and offer to change places, she might be tempted. The answer was no! She and Sal hadn't got much, it was true. But they'd got each other, and they didn't go in for lying and cheating, the way folks claimed the gentry did. It was said that the gentry would even rob their own kind if there was a profit to be made. Well, that wasn't the way with proper folk! If one of the gentry was to show his face here and now, Molly would tell it to be off, and no mistake!

There was one, though, that she might exchange a few kindly words with, and that was the boy in the market yesterday. The boy with dark hair and friendly green eyes, whose mammy she had robbed. Molly felt no remorse about taking the woman's purse, because she had seen how that woman had harshly treated the boy when he had accidentally stepped on her expensive boots. Molly's attention had been drawn by the awful fuss Martha Trent made and, feeling upset for the poor boy, had given his mammy the chance to make a fuss for a different reason by stealing her purse. Molly was not sorry about that at all. But she was worried that she wasn't able to get to know the boy. He looked so nice, so friendly, and when he saw her cheeky wink, Molly was sure that he had tried not to laugh. She liked him, but she didn't suppose she would ever see him again. Even if she *did*, it would be safer for her and Sal to keep well out of sight – especially since Sal had told her that the boy's grandfather was Justice Caleb Crowther.

That fellow wanted her put away, and though Molly wasn't afraid of much else, other than her darling Sal falling into the canal on a dark night, she *was* afraid of this Justice Crowther, for it was well known that he was a bad and cruel man, with a particular hatred for bargees, poor folk, and for what he scornfully called 'alley urchins'.

Molly took pleasure from her memory of the boy, yet she felt awfully sorry that he had been cursed with such a man for his grandfather, while she had been blessed with someone like Sal to look after her. But then Molly giggled as she dwelled on that a bit longer, because she wasn't rightly sure whether Sal looked after *her* . . . or whether she looked after *Sal*. 'It's a bit o' both,' she decided at length, taking a healthy bite out of the pie and afterwards enjoying a great nose-tickling gulp of sarsaparilla. 'We look after each other, so we do!'

'Hello, Sal, I ain't seen you in a long time. How's the world treating you, eh?' Sal had turned from the bar with her gill of frothed-up ale, and had almost collided with a thick-set fellow with big, bushy brows and a 'tache which drooped from either side of his top lip to the bottom of his chin, where the ends met to form a closed circle. Sal recognised him as a pal of Marlow's who had deserted these parts for a merry widow, some ten years before. 'Where's Marlow, then?' continued the fellow, stretching his neck and looking about, then, seeing no sign of Sal's brother, he brought his soft, brown eyes to look down quizzically at her. 'The widder got fed up, and threw me out of the door,' he said casually, 'it seems my charm wore off. I got back last night . . . staying in lodgings till I get work and a place of my own. Where is he then, eh? . . . Where's that brother of yourn? If I remember rightly, I owe the bugger a drink.' Here, he threw back his head and laughed aloud. 'He warned me the widder would chuck me out afore she'd wed me. And he were right. I shoulda' listened to him. He always were a sensible bloke.'

Sal appeared upset by the fellow's remarks; his reference to Marlow being 'a sensible bloke' had cut deep. It was true. Of the two of them, *she* had always been the one to get them in trouble, and Marlow the one to get them out of it. Whatever would he have thought about her gambling their barge away? God forbid that he should ever find out; although it wouldn't matter so much if she was to win it back. Oh, but he was gone for good! Marlow wasn't coming back, or she would have had a sign of it before now. The sea had taken him, she felt it in her bones. Emma Grady had driven him to sail the seven seas, and he was lost. Gone forever, and Sal's heart broken because of it.

To hear this fellow talk so fondly of the darling brother she'd lost put Sal in a bitter frame of mind. When she answered him now, it was with a sharp and dismissive tongue. 'Get outta my way,' she told him, clutching her gill of ale and nudging her way past him by the use of her elbows. 'Marlow's gone. 'E's *gone*, d'yer hear? An' he ain't *never* comin' back!' She then sat in the corner sulking, but by the time she'd supped the last dregs of ale from the jug, she was softly crying and muttering aloud, 'Damn and rot every gentry there ever was! Where the bloody hell are yer, Marlow Tanner? An' where's that gormless dog o' yourn, that yer left be'ind ter look after me?' Sal had searched far and wide for Marlow's bull mastiff. But she had never found it after it ran off some three years back. 'I expect it's gone the same way as Marlow,' she cried into her glass, 'an' I shall never see *either* of 'em agin!'

'Cheer up, old un, things are never as bad as they seem.' There was a fine-looking fellow with a spotted scarf about his neck, seated at a table nearby, and he had watched Sal for some time, feeling downright sorry for anybody who could be so miserable about supping a jug of best ale. He had mentioned to another fellow the surprising fact of a woman being admitted into the bar. Straightaway he had been told that Sal Tanner was always the exception, 'being one o' the lads, so to speak'. He was also enlightened as to Sal's misfortunes, in first having her brother leave to make his fortune in foreign parts, and so it now seemed, to have lost his life in the process. 'Marlow Tanner would never have deserted his sister on purpose, you can rely on it!' Then, as if that wasn't enough, Sal had taken very strongly to gambling, and just as folks predicted, she had come up against a better player than herself and lost all her possessions. 'That barge had been in the Tanner family for *generations*. Oh, I can tell you, if Marlow's ghost ever did come back to these parts, it would haunt old Sal to her grave . . . and rightly so, if you ask me!' The fellow was most unsympathetic to Sal Tanner's plight, 'seeing as she brought it on herself. Then, to top it all, she comes back from a hanging with a newborn child that somebody left by the wayside . . . Some whore dropped it there to be rid on it, I expect.' Here he chuckled quietly, after looking to make sure that Sal wasn't listening because he knew well enough that she had a vicious temper when put out. 'Sal reckons the infant was put there by "the little peo-ple" . . . for her to raise . . . as a punishment and a burden for her sins.'

The fellow with the spotted scarf took a more sympathetic view of Sal Tanner's troubles, having always had his own fair share. 'Let me get you another gill,' he offered, leaning over to pat her fondly on the arm and to smile at her with bright blue eyes.

'Yer what?' It was a long time since any stranger had shown a kindness to Sal, and though it made her suspicious, it also cheered her no end. 'Offerin' me a drink, is it, eh?' she asked, her head cocked to one side and her violet eyes twinkling. Of a sudden she was roaring with laughter, then she became quiet and intimate in her manner. "Ere . . . d'yer have a fancy for me?' she said in a low, excited voice. 'Got an urge ter tek me ter bed, have yer?' It was ages since any man had laid her down, and the thought of a tumble had her all excited. 'It'll cost yer a bit *more* than one gill though, me darlin',' she finished with a chuckle and a suggestive wink.

'Don't be so bloody daft, woman!' The poor fellow was shocked. 'I'm offering you a drink out of the goodness of my heart! Whatever gave you the idea that I'd want to take an old soak like you to bed?'

Sal was on her feet in a minute, sleeves rolled up and looking for a fight. '*Old?*' she demanded. '*Old!* . . . You listen ter me, matey! I'm never old . . . Ask anybody in this bar. They'll tell yer as I'm not much above forty . . . an' I'll warrant you yourself is already long past *that*, yer cheeky sod!

'Oh well, pardon me,' replied the fellow with a crafty wink at one and all, 'but you look nearer *eighty*!' At this, everybody there roared their approval . . . with the exception of Sal; however, she did see the funny side to it. What an old fool she was, to think any man could take a fancy to her. Them days were long gone, she was sad to say. 'Ere then!' She banged her empty jug on the table in front of him. 'Fill it up. If yer don't want ter *tickle* me whistle . . . yer can *wet* the bugger instead!' There then followed a great wave of laughter, and various shouts of 'Good ol' Sal!'

''Ave a gill on *me*, an' all, luv.'

Sal took up the offers, and soon she was in high spirits, doing a jig on the bar and showing one and all that she had 'a good pair o' legs on me yet'!

Outside in the growing dusk, young Molly was excited by the feverish hand-clapping and the merry music, and she wished she was old enough to go in and join them. 'It sounds like Sal won't be able to put one foot afore the other when they chuck her out,' she murmured, tapping her feet to the jollity and watching with interest as an old man shuffled by. He had a partly bald head with isolated tufts of grey hair, a long, unkempt beard, and a gaudy, green waistcoat some two sizes too small for his podgy chest. His jacket and trousers were an odd match; the trouser legs stopped short of his ankles and the hem of the jacket came down to his knees. In the light emanating from the pub windows, Molly recognised him as old Gabe Drury, a long-time and loyal friend of Sal's. 'Hello, Mr Drury,' she called out as he was about to disappear into the pub doorway, his legs being the worse for drink and his eyesight somewhat blurred. He reached out both arms to steady himself against the door pillars while he focused on the source of the greeting.

'Well, if it ain't young Molly . . . Sal Tanner's little 'un. Inside, is she?' he asked. When Molly replied that yes, she was inside, he laughed aloud, saying, 'I shoulda' known. The music's allus loudest when Sal Tanner's around.' After a concentrated effort, he manoeuvred himself inside and was gone from Molly's sight. In a moment though, her interest was taken up by the arrival of a two-horse carriage, which drew up some small distance away. In the growing darkness, Molly could see very little of its occupants, although there looked to be two of them, and one appeared to be wearing a top hat. It was a grand sort of carriage, thought Molly, her interest aroused. The kind only used by toffs and the like. She was about to get to her feet and maybe sneak a closer look, when the carriage door was flung open, and out climbed . . . not a toff, but an ordinary-looking fellow with a flat cap on his head and a look of slyness about him. When he came so close to her that she could have reached out and touched him, Molly was taken aback because, in spite of his common clothes and the way he pretended to swagger as if he'd had a drink or two, Molly was convinced that he was neither drunk nor ordinary.

Puzzled by such strange antics, Molly watched him go into the pub, then craned her neck to see whether the carriage might now pull away. But it didn't. Instead, the gent with the top hat seemed to slink deeper into his seat and all was deathly quiet from that quarter.

Molly was so intrigued now that, first of all, she got to her tiptoes and took a peep through the window of the bar. There in the farthest corner was the strange man, his eyes staring at a group of men some three

129

tables away, one being Gabe Drury, who appeared to be holding a few boozy regulars entranced by the story he was telling. Then, even as Molly was taking stock of the man, he got up from his seat and moved to within an arm's reach of Gabe Drury, afterwards conversing with him and showing great interest in every word the old man said.

Turning her attention back to the carriage, Molly had the feeling that even while *she* was watching the fellow in the pub, the other fellow in the carriage . . . the toff, was watching *her*. It was all a strange to-do, and Molly became even more curious. Pretending to look away, she made as though to saunter along in the opposite direction; when she was hidden in shadows, she quickly doubled back and crept along by the canal wall, coming up on the carriage without being seen. But if Molly thought she might get a better look at the gentry inside, she was mistaken, because his face was deep within the dark recesses of the carriage, and he turned his head neither one way or another, so intent was he on keeping his gaze fixed on the pub doorway.

Molly had no intention of giving up though, and, in a minute, she was boldly tapping on the carriage window. 'Hello, mister,' she called out, even beginning to move the handle which would open the door, 'got a shilling, have you?'

At once the driver had swung down from his seat. 'Clear off,' he warned Molly, 'else I'll take my horse-whip to your backside!' However he wasn't quick enough to stop Molly from flinging wide the carriage-door. At the same instant, an arm reached out from inside with the intention of quickly closing the door again, just as the driver was bearing down on Molly. At once, before the flesh might be flayed from her legs, she sprinted away. And with her she took a vivid and disturbing picture of the toff inside the carriage: a big man, whose face and neck were smothered in iron-grey hair, and who had the most vicious, piercing eyes she had ever seen, which stared down on her with a look of pure hatred!

From a safe distance, Molly kept watch on the carriage; she wished that Sal would hurry up and come out, so they could go home to the relative safety of their hut. It wasn't too long before the odd one or two revellers began emerging from the ale house, so Molly kept her eyes peeled for Sal's familiar figure.

But it wasn't *Sal*'s familiar figure that came out. It was Gabe Drury's, together with the fellow who had arrived in the carriage. There they were, arm in arm, the older man swaying and staggering, occasionally bursting into song, and now and then laughing out loud at some genial comment made by the other fellow.

With Molly still watching from the shadows, Gabe Drury was led towards the carriage, and unceremoniously bundled inside it, with the other fellow standing watch outside and talking quietly to the driver. Molly crept nearer, until she was crouched below the door, with her ear pressed close against it. She could hear old Gabe Drury protesting most strongly at being 'brought away from me drinkin' pals!' Whereupon the toff showed great interest in 'the story you've been telling . . . regarding a certain man by the name of Thadius Grady . . . and the murder of a bargee by the name of Bill Royston?'

'What's it to *you*, then, eh?' Molly thought Gabe Drury's voice seemed more sober and suspicious, especially when the toff offered him 'two guineas to repeat the story to me. But, leaving nothing out, mind . . . nothing at all!'

'Two guineas!' Molly couldn't help but gasp softly at the price this gent was willing to pay, just to hear a story! Why! *She'd* tell him a better tale than old Gabe Drury, at half the price. Then she recalled the gent's words – 'the *murder* of a bargee by the name of Bill Royston' – and something inside her froze. The name was familiar to her, because hadn't Sal once revealed that her *own* name had been Royston, but was changed to Tanner when she was a child. Beyond that, Sal would say no more. But Molly had been left with the feeling that there had been a terrible tragedy of sorts, because of the sadness in Sal's face when, on that one occasion only, she had talked of her background, and of her parents, Eve and Bill Royston. Was it the same 'Bill Royston', Molly wondered now. Had Sal's father been murdered? And, if he had, then why was this gent so interested, and what did Gabe Drury know of anything?

Molly was tempted to steal away, lest she should hear something which was best not heard. But she was more tempted to *stay*.

'Let me out. I don't want ter talk to no bloody toffs!' Gabe Drury's voice was trembling with fear, not booze. 'Let me out, I tell yer. I don't know nothing about any "murder" . . . an' I've never even heard of a fellow called Thadius Grady!'

'You're a liar! You've been spreading gossip about the town . . . malicious and dangerous gossip that could have you put away . . . or likely hanged! In fact, I think I'll tell the driver to take us straight to the constabulary this very minute.'

'No, I don't want no truck with the bobbies,' came Gabe Drury's fearful cry, 'I've done nothing wrong, I'm tellin' yer.' When the gent appeared to brush aside the old fellow's fears and to lean out of the window ready to instruct the driver to move off, the old man began blubbering and pleading, 'All right . . . I'll tell you all I know.'

'And I shall see you get your two guineas,' promised the gent in velvet tones.

Molly listened most intently, while Gabe Drury hurriedly spilled out his story, his nervousness evident in the way he halted and stumbled on every other word. He described how, on the day Bill Royston was shot to death, he saw a man fleeing from the place . . . a gent . . . 'much like yourself, sir', but not he, no, not he! 'Blood all over him, and a look on his face as guilty as any I'd ever seen!' The memory of it all was too much, as Gabe Drury pleaded, 'That's all I know. Now, let me be . . . let me out of here!'

'In a minute. Tell me first, and think hard, man, because your life might depend on it. You say you saw Thadius Grady running from the place where Bill Royston lay dead? . . . Did you see anything else, man? Any other person, anyone *else* you could recognise? Speak up, man, speak up or I'll have you hanged, I tell you! There should be enough to bring a charge against you!'

'No . . . I weren't there, sir!' protested Gabe Drury. 'I were in the grass some fair distance from the canal . . . sleeping off a night o' revelry. Oh no, sir . . . I weren't *there*. Not at all. What's more, I never saw nobody else . . . only that gent, Thadius Grady . . .

133

just like I said. An' he's dead an' gone himself now . . . so it don't matter.'

'You're sure? *He* was the only one you saw?' When Gabe Drury reassured him, there was yet another question to answer before he was allowed to go. 'Just now . . . before you entered the public house, you addressed a scruffy urchin?'

'Scruffy urchin?' Gabe Drury's mind was still shot with fear at his experience here this night, and what with the booze, he was having trouble thinking straight. 'Oh aye! Yer must mean young Molly . . . Sal Tanner's lass.' He was relieved to have remembered, but puzzled as to why a posh gent might be interested in the likes of Sal Tanner's little 'un.

'Sal Tanner, eh?' The gent raised his hand and thoughtfully scratched at the mass of hair about his face. Then, leaning forward and looking the old fellow hard in the eyes, he repeated, 'Sal *Tanner*, you say?' He waited for an affirmative, if nervous, nod. 'Hmm . . . the same one who ran her barge from Liverpool and carried coal and cotton to the Wharf Mill?' Again, he waited for the nod. Then, when it was cautiously given he went on, 'The same one who had a brother . . . I believe his name was Marlow?'

'That's right, sir . . . Marlow, a fine young fellow. Went off to seek his fortune and ain't never come back since.' By this time, Gabe Drury was glad that the subject had come away from the night of Bill Royston's murder. Funny though, how two things in particular stood out in the old fellow's mind, in the wake of the gent's questions. First, it was speculated at the time that a *woman's* body had been found alongside Bill Royston's. And, if rumour had it right, it was said that the woman was not one of the usual run, but a well-bred lady of the gentry, no less. But it had been carefully hushed up. Then as if that wasn't enough, here was a fellow of the same class . . . asking about none other than Sal Tanner. Sal Tanner! Whose father was the same Bill Royston that got himself murdered!

'This scruffy urchin . . . you say she's Sal Tanner's daughter?'

'Well . . . not *exactly* her daughter. Sal never had any children of her own. Folks don't rightly know where Sal got the young 'un from.' Of a sudden, the gent was leaning forward again and, when Gabe Drury saw the cunning look in those piercing eyes, some deep instinct warned him to keep his mouth shut. So when he was asked, 'What *more* do you know of Sal Tanner . . . the brother, or the urchin?' he shook his head. 'I don't know nothing else, sir, an' that's the truth. I ain't been round these parts fer a long time, an' I ain't got that many friends ter speak of.' He winced beneath the other fellow's close scrutiny of him. But he was determined that, two guineas or no two guineas, wild horses wouldn't get him to admit that he'd known Sal and Marlow since they were no bigger than a blade o' grass . . . an' he knew their parents, Eve and Bill Royston, a good many years afore that. It wasn't widely known that when their daddy was shot to death and their mammy hanged for it, the two Royston children were whisked away to safety by the barge-folk, and their name changed to that of Tanner. Somehow, Gabe Drury suspected that even this gent 'ere wasn't aware of the connection. But if that was the case, why was he asking after Bill Royston and Sal Tanner in the *same* breath? There was something strange going on here, thought Gabe Drury, although he was convinced that the gent was not aware of the blood ties between Sal and the murdered man. But he felt he might have said far too much, and stopped short of revealing how Sal Tanner had come across young Molly after a hanging . . . found the little wretch right outside the prison gates, or so it was said . . . when it was still wet and warm from its mother's womb.

'You've told me all you know?' The voice had a sinister ring to it, as it came out of the dark shadows in the carriage. 'You're certain that the man you saw was Thadius Grady? You saw no *other*?'

'None at all. Like I said, I don't know nothing else, as God's my judge,' and he hoped God might forgive him for lying.

'Then here's your two guineas.' There was a chink of coins and a grateful 'Thank you, sir' before the carriage door was opened and Gabe Drury set his foot on the pavement. As he hobbled off into the darkness, a song on his lips and thankful that he was at last on his way, the gent himself stepped down out of the carriage and muttered into the ear of the other man, who had kept watch outside. This one now nodded his understanding of the instructions just issued. In a minute he went stealthily after the homely figure of Gabe Drury, the both of them being swiftly engulfed in the darkness.

Having quickly scurried back to her hiding place when she knew the conversation was over, Molly watched everything. She felt afraid, yet didn't know why. But having been taught well by Sal, and not being one to miss an opportunity, she sidled up to the carriage; before the gent could climb back inside, she had slipped her fingers into his coat pocket and stolen away what felt to be an unusually thick wallet. Molly smiled craftily as she crept back into the shadows. Sal will be pleased, she thought, as the carriage moved away. It wasn't too often that the gentry presented themselves so easily for the picking! But how would she explain it to Sal? How could she tell her about the carriage an' all . . . yet *not* tell her about that fearful conversation? Molly thought better of telling Sal about that, because there was something awful about it. From what Molly could understand, old Gabe had seen the fellow who had murdered Sal's daddy . . . and his name was Thadius Grady. There would be no sense in raking all of that up when it would upset Sal, especially since this Grady fellow was 'dead and gone'. And especially since Gabe had seen fit to keep quiet about it up till tonight. Molly supposed Gabe hadn't wanted to upset Sal over it then, any more than she did now. She expected Gabe had been afraid to go to the constabulary before, and Molly could understand that. You didn't go looking for trouble, and the constabulary was trouble, for the likes of folk such as Gabe.

Molly's stomach had turned somersaults when that gent began asking after her and Sal. That in itself was enough to make her keep the whole thing from Sal, because she did like to get to the bottom of things, did Sal. Molly sensed that it could only bring trouble down on their heads. No. The best thing was to forget all about it, and tell Sal that she'd found the fat wallet lying there on the pavement. The thought made her chuckle. Wouldn't Sal be surprised, she thought, taking up her place at the door of the public house, just as the revellers began pouring and stumbling out of it. She kept her eyes peeled for Sal's shawled figure, and she returned a cheery 'G'night' to one and all as they went away down Angela Street, singing and laughing at the tops of their voices – one or two starting a fight, afterwards rolling about in the gutter with a crowd of cheering drunks egging them on. Bedroom windows were flung open, and out came angry instructions to 'Piss orf, yer drunken sods!' and 'Bugger orf out of it . . . else I'll set the dog on yer!' Molly grinned from ear to ear. She'd seen it all before. And many was the time when it was Sal who might be fighting and rolling about in the gutter, especially when she'd had a few too many and lost at cards into the bargain.

As the carriage sped away into the night, leaving behind the alleys and cobbled streets of the old quarter, the gent inside smiled to himself. He had done well, he thought, and covered up his tracks most cleverly. It always paid to keep an informer amongst the riff-raff, because who could sniff out a rat better than another rat? When the news was brought to him that a certain old fellow was spreading a story that could so easily have pointed the finger in *his* direction, there was no other course but to track the fellow down. He had to find out just how much the fool did know of the canal murders which took place all those years ago.

The smile which had crept over the gent's face deepened into a cruel and smug grin. He had satisfied himself that the fellow had no knowledge of any person fleeing the scene, other than the hapless Thadius Grady, who was always a weak and unfortunate fool. Now, had the old man Drury stayed a moment longer on that particular day, and looked in the opposite direction, he might well have seen the very gent who was seated in this carriage now. In fact, if he hadn't been so intent on fleeing from Thadius Grady, he might well have seen a real murderer. And, if he had, thought the man, if he had, then he might not have lived until this night!

Though he was pleased with his night's work, there was something else that played on his mind and set him wondering. It was to do with Marlow Tanner and Emma Grady who, thankfully, everyone believed was no more than a ward to him, left in his care by his wife's brother, Thadius. The image of the small, dark-eyed urchin insisted on troubling him also, and it made him furious inside, firing his avowed determination to rid the streets of these vagrants and thieves!

As his thoughts continued to mull over Marlow Tanner, Emma Grady and the dark-eyed urchin, a distasteful thought began to grow in his mind and to haunt him. Until he murmured out loud, 'No matter! She'll go the way of all her kind . . . to meet a sorry end.' Yet he had not forgotten that Emma Grady was with child when she was convicted and that, according to the report he had received, soon after its untimely birth, the dead infant was abandoned to the gutter and afterwards disappeared. He had believed, as had the authorities, that some marauding dog or hungry rats had carried it off and made a meal of it. He had hoped that such was the case. He was *still* of the same mind. Nevertheless, he suddenly felt uncomfortable.

How much more 'uncomfortable' might Caleb Crowther feel if he were ever to learn that the 'scruffy urchin' was indeed Emma's child and his *own* grand-daughter.

★ ★ ★

'Oh, I can't believe it, child!' Sal had staggered home, moaning and wailing, and giving thanks to the girl on whose small shoulder she leaned her considerable weight.

'Don't upset yourself, Sal darlin',' coaxed Molly, easing the drunken burden from her shoulders and taking it gently to the bed, where she laid it down. 'I'll make us a brew, shall I?' she asked.

'No, no, lass.' Sal had dragged herself into a sitting position, although she appeared a twisted and bedraggled sight. 'Stay aside o' me . . . I don't want ter to be left on me own,' she pleaded, at the same time taking Molly's hand and tugging the girl to sit beside her. 'Oh, I'm that upset, lass,' she cried, rubbing at her eyes until they were puffy and sore-looking, 'an' I were in *such* a good mood when we come outta the ale 'ouse.'

Molly could vouch for that. It was ages before Sal had come out, and she was in such high spirits that Molly couldn't help but forgive her. It seemed that she'd won half-a-guinea, made a new friend, and had a wonderful night into the bargain.

It was when they were some short way along the canal bank and heading for the hut that the hue and cry went up. The outcome of it all was that Gabe Drury's body had been found floating at the water's edge. He had drowned, they said, and had a deep cut on his temple, 'no doubt where he hit the kerbing as he lost his footing and accidentally tumbled in', it was agreed. And Sal Tanner was the very first to curse the old fool for 'wanderin' so close ter the water when he's drunk as a bloody lord!' Afterwards, she shed genuine, heartfelt tears.

Molly however was not so satisfied that Gabe Drury

had 'accidentally tumbled in', though she was wise
enough not to say so. All the same, she couldn't help
but wonder about the gent in the carriage – whose face
she had not seen – and the conversation between him
and the old fellow. Nor had she forgotten how the gent
gave instructions to the other one, who then followed
Gabe Drury into the darkness. She didn't care for the
way things had shaped up, and that was a fact. But she
wouldn't dwell on it too much if she could help it,
because Molly had that same fearful sensation inside:
one that told her to stay well away from that sort of
trouble, and to look after herself and old Sal. *That* was
all that mattered to her, and nothing else. Still and all,
Molly felt sorry about the old fellow, even though she
didn't know him as well as Sal did. But having heard a
few unsavoury truths tonight, she wondered how much
of it old Gabe had brought on himself?

Of a sudden, Molly remembered something, and it
brought a smile to her face. 'Look here, Sal,' she cried,
fishing the fat wallet from inside her tatty dress, 'see
what *I* found!' She was sure it would do Sal a world of
good.

At once Sal was attentive, stretching her scrawny
neck and struggling to see what it was that Molly
clutched so triumphantly. 'What yer been up to, yer
little sod?' she demanded to know, as Molly laughingly
thrust the article into Sal's grubby fist. ''Ere, fetch that
candle a bit nearer,' she instructed Molly, 'I ain't a
bloody bat, y'know . . . I can't see in the dark!' Gabe
Drury's fate was quickly forgotten. 'Feels fat, does
this!' she chuckled, turning the wallet over and over,
and excitedly hoisting herself up to a sitting position.
'Let's see what we got, eh?'

141

When Molly brought the candle and held it close, Sal tore open the wallet, and out spilled a fistful of notes, together with a carefully folded letter and a number of calling cards. 'Bugger me, lass . . . if we ain't hit the jackpot!' cried Sal jubilantly. 'Where'd yer get it, eh?'

'Found it.'

'*Found* it? . . . Well, I'm blowed!' Of a sudden, Sal was rolling her small eyes heavenward, saying in a reverent voice, 'There y'are . . . I *knew* it! It's the little people, tellin' me I'm fetchin' yer up right!' Molly didn't think so, but she wouldn't dream of spoiling Sal's astonishing recovery from the sad news concerning Gabe Drury.

'What's *that* say?' Sal pushed one of the small cards under Molly's nose. 'I can't mek head nor bloody tail o' these words.' She squinted her eyes and looked down the length of her nose at the card.

'Oh, Sal . . . you know I can't read the words either,' protested Molly, making no effort to take the card from Sal.

'Hang on a minute, lass!' Sal pointed a dirty finger-nail at the bold, black capitals printed there. 'I've seen them words afore.' Of a sudden, she had thrown the card down on the chequered quilt and was scrambling from the bed, her eyes wide with fear and her finger still pointing to the card. 'I *know* where I've seen them there words! It were when me an' a few drinkin' pals were fetched afront o' the Justice. It was Justice Caleb Crowther as had the lot on us flung in the cells.' She had backed away from the bed and was standing by the door, her stocky figure held stiff and upright as she told the astonished Molly, '*Caleb Crowther!* That were it. It were them words as were fixed on a board for all to see.

Cissie Bent learned to read when she were in service at the big house down Lytham Way . . . it were Cissie as told me what them words on the boards were sayin'. *Caleb Crowther* . . . same as them words on that card!' The next minute, she shot forward and caught hold of Molly by the shoulders. 'Where'd yer get it, lass? *Found* it, yer say? Tell me the truth now . . . I'll not have yer tellin' me lies!' She proceeded to shake the girl but instead was violently shaken herself when Molly instinctively braced herself. 'Has Justice Crowther been round these 'ere parts? Is he looking fer us? Oh dear God . . . dear God! When will the evil fella leave us in peace!' She was beside herself, and her face had turned bright crimson from the futile efforts she was making to loosen the girl enough to shake her hard. Of a sudden, she gave up the effort and ran round the room gathering up her bits and pieces. 'We shall have ter gerrout o' this place, an' that's a fact.'

'Calm down, Sal,' Molly told her, collecting the few sorry articles from Sal's hands, and replacing them, 'we're safe enough here. Justice Crowther ain't been nowhere near this place.'

'Then where did yer get that there wallet from, eh?' Sal demanded.

'I told you . . . I *found* it!' lied Molly, feeling satisfied in the face of poor Sal's fit of panic that she had done the right thing in keeping secret that meeting between Gabe Drury and the gent. Sal was afraid. *Really* afraid, like Molly had never seen her before. 'So you needn't worry,' she assured her.

Sal needed more convincing and, looking deep into the girl's big, black eyes, she asked, 'Are yer *sure*, lass? Yer not lying? Yer really *did* find that there wallet?'

When Molly nodded, saying, 'It was like I told you,' Sal visibly relaxed. Then in the next minute, she became anxious again, 'Where? . . . *Where* did yer find it?'

Molly had to think quickly, because she daren't frighten Sal by telling her that the Justice was in a carriage right outside the ale house, or Sal would *never* be convinced that he hadn't come to cart every last one of them off to jail: ' . . . so I wandered about a bit, and found myself nearer town. That's where I found it . . . down Ainsworth Street.'

'Oh aye? Well, *that's* where yer gonna return it!' declared Sal, going to the bed and folding everything back into the wallet.

'Return it!' Molly could hardly believe her ears. 'What? Now?'

'That's what I said, lass! You're gonna *return* it . . . right away. My God! The minute that fella finds his wallet gone, he'll not rest till he's found it. What! . . . The bugger'll turn Lancashire upside down if needs be!'

'But if we throw the papers and the wallet away . . . and just keep the money, he'll never know it was *us* that had it,' argued Molly, who was loath to let go of her prize.

But Sal would have none of it. 'Oh, he'll know right enough, my gal!' she retorted, shaking her grey head from side to side. 'He'll *know* well enough . . . 'cause he's got spies *everywhere*! He's a bad 'un, child,' she said, thrusting the wallet into Molly's hand, then frantically wiping her hands down on the fringe of her shawl, as though the very touch of Caleb Crowther's wallet might have left its mark. 'You don't know that fella like *I* do! Long afore the little people sent you ter me, that Justice Crowther had a grudge agin the Tanners.

Why! . . . He even took a horsewhip to my Marlow, when the lad were doing nothing more offensive than talking ter Justice Crowther's ward, a nice enough lass, by the name of Emma Grady. Stripped the skin clear off his shoulders. An' he hounded Marlow ever after . . . sacked him from running goods to his mills . . . not carin' whether we *starved* because of it! Oh aye, he's a wicked, spiteful bugger, is that one.' She opened the door of the hut and pushed Molly towards it. 'That ward of his . . . lass by the name of Emma Grady . . . she were accused o' murderin' the bloke as Crowther wed her off to. An' d'yer know, child . . . that lass were innocent, an' there's plenty o' folk who'd vouch fer it, I'm sure. She were heavy wi' child an' all, when they took her. An' it were said that she begged an' pleaded fer him ter come an' help her. But the bugger never lifted a finger . . . an' he could have done! Oh, aye, he could a saved the lass, I've no doubt at all.' Here, she bent forward to whisper in Molly's ear. 'So y'see, Molly darlin' . . . y'see how dangerous such a fella can be? If yer don't shiver in yer shoes at the very sound of his name . . . then yer bloody well should.'

Molly felt herself being firmly propelled through the door and out into the blackness of the night. With Sal's instructions to 'tek it right back where yer found it, mind!' she took off at running speed in the direction of Angela Street. She had learned a very important lesson, and one which she wasn't likely to forget in a hurry. This fella, this Justice Crowther, was someone to be avoided if at all possible because, if he frightened Sal in that way, then he must be fearsome. 'Blimey!' Molly muttered aloud as she ran along the bank. 'What a good job I didn't tell Sal that he were asking after her. Or she would have gone mad.' She was struck by a sudden thought, every bit as unpleasant. He was asking after *her* as well. Of a sudden, Molly's reluctance to return the wallet didn't seem as strong. In fact, the more she thought of it, the faster her thin little legs ran, because now she couldn't get it back to the spot fast enough.

By the time Molly turned out of the canal banking and made towards the spot where the carriage had stopped, everything was quiet. She supposed that the sorry Gabe Drury had been taken away in a waggon by now, and folks had gone home to their beds. She wondered again about that strange meeting between the Justice and the old fella, but her young mind couldn't make head nor tail of it except to be even more certain that she'd done right in keeping her mouth shut. 'After all,' she whispered aloud, quickly laying the wallet on the flagstones, and looking round furtively before making her way back, 'look what happened to old Gabe Drury!'

No sooner had Molly disappeared into the darkness than a carriage drew up in Stephen Street, some short way from the Navigation. Out of it stepped Caleb Crowther, who moved softly, first to instruct the driver to 'stay quiet', then hurriedly to where he suspected his wallet might have fallen when he had climbed out of the carriage earlier. Coming to the top of Angela Street, he stayed close to the wall of the Navigation. Then, peeping round to satisfy himself that all was quiet, he quickly crossed the cobbled road and began searching the flagstones on the opposite side. It took a moment or two, as there was only one gas lamp lighting the corner, but after a determined and frantic search, he gave a small, jubilant cry and snatched up the wallet.

In a few moments he had made his way back to where the carriage waited in an unlit part of Stephen Street. 'Quickly man . . . get away from here!' he told the bowler-hatted driver in an urgent whisper.

As he settled back into the seat, before going through the wallet to satisfy himself of its contents, Caleb Crowther gave a sigh of relief. On discovering earlier that his wallet was missing, he had half-persuaded himself that the urchin might somehow have picked his pocket, though he could not see how she would have had the opportunity. But one thing was certain, if the little wretch had been guilty of stealing his wallet, it would have been the worst act of thieving she had ever committed. It would have been her *last!* He had been fearful that the wallet might have been ransacked before he could recover it, and with his name on those cards for anybody's eyes to see, he had spent more than a few frantic moments being anxious of the consequences, for they did not bear thinking about.

Agnes Crowther watched from her bedroom window, a tall and solitary figure with a regal head and unbending neck, her two hands joined together in that posture of prayer which was her particular trait. With staring, unfriendly eyes, she followed the carriage as it turned into the drive. Instinctively, she knew that it would not come right up to the house, but would halt some distance away, in order for her husband to disembark and make a quiet return from his nightly exploits. The pattern was always the same: on the days when he was not travelling the circuit as Justice, he would go to the Wharf Mill, for the purpose of satisfying himself that the recently appointed manager was carrying out his instructions to the very letter. Afterwards, he would make his way into Manchester for a long and detailed discussion with his accountant.

Then, usually between the hours of five and six in the evening, he would return to Breckleton House and sit throughout dinner with a surly face and make no conversation. The moment he had swallowed his last gulp of wine he would fold his napkin in a most meticulous fashion (which had become infuriating to the watching Agnes), and with a curt nod of his balding head and a moment to run his fingers through the profusion of hair on his face, he would stand up and take a last lingering look at his empty plate, before going quickly from the room, leaving his long-suffering wife feeling desperately frustrated at the lack of civilised exchange of a few words. In the time it took to spruce himself up and don his outdoor garments, he was gone from the house, and it was always the early hours before he returned.

As the carriage was taken round the back and she heard her husband's footsteps coming up the path, Agnes Crowther stepped back from the window, fearful that he might see her. Always when she enacted this particular scene, it gave her a strange sensation of excitement. This was a cat-and-mouse game, when she had both the patience and the cunning to wait for the right moment to pounce. 'I'll have you in my clutches yet, Caleb Crowther,' she muttered, climbing into her bed. It was a long, lonely time before she could get to sleep, because the thoughts racing through her mind would not let her rest. Agnes Crowther had only recently suspected her husband of bedding other women and the suspicion had festered inside her, until she could think of nothing else. Four weeks ago he had moved his things out of her bedroom on the pretext that, 'I don't want to disturb you on the occasions when I must be late home.' Agnes Crowther was acutely aware of the unkind speculation that was rife amongst the servants, and it was a hateful experience. She had become a more spiteful and bitter person because of it. Yet she found every excuse not to believe what she suspected because, in spite of his hostile nature of late and his lack of affection towards her, she still loved him. It was that sorry fact, and her stiff pride, which prevented her from taking the steps which her instincts urged. The very idea of a private investigator was most distasteful.

If Agnes Crowther had spent a restless night, it did not show when she breezed into the dining-room the following morning.

'Good morning, Caleb,' she said in as amiable a voice as she could muster, smiling sweetly as she poured out her tea and met her husband's eyes across the table.

'Good morning, my dear,' he replied, at once looking away to fix his eyes on the folded newspaper before him. He obviously had no intention of addressing her further. But then he raised his eyes and looked at his wife with a quizzical expression, which both surprised her and caused her to ask, 'Yes? What is it?'

Without laying down his knife and fork which he held like a threat over the liver and bacon on his plate, and without even straightening his neck which was bent forward ready to devour the contents of his plate, he said in a quiet and thoughtful voice, 'We know Emma Grady was pregnant, and that the child was born . . . presumably dead, or so we were informed?'

Agnes Crowther was astonished. It was her husband himself who had forbidden the mention of Emma Grady's name in this house. There had been times when her own conscience had made her think deeply about the girl. Times when she thought her brother Thadius might haunt them for their callous treatment of Emma. Yet now she was intrigued. 'Yes,' she agreed, 'Emma *was* pregnant . . . and the child still-born, as you say.' At this she quickly looked away with guilt written in her downcast eyes. 'It was a great pity that the child did not receive a Christian burial . . . being abandoned in such a way.' She would have gone on at great length about how the officer responsible should have been severely reprimanded, but she knew from past experience that her words would fall on deaf ears.

'The child.' Caleb Crowther was speaking again, but still he had not moved another muscle. 'Is it likely, do you think, that her husband, Gregory Denton, was not the father?'

Agnes Crowther was shocked. '*Not* the father?' She picked up her napkin from the table, dabbed it furtively at her mouth, then put it down again. She could not face another mouthful. 'Heaven forbid that a niece of mine should go outside her marriage in that way.' She was quite overcome. 'And if her husband were not the father, then who was?' Of a sudden, she could almost read his mind as he kept his eyes fixed on her. '*Marlow*

Tanner!' The name sprang to her lips, and as though it had burned her, she put her hand across her mouth, and stared at her husband with unbelieving eyes. 'You think *he* was the father of Emma's child?' she asked through her fingers.

For a moment, Caleb Crowther gave no answer, and seemed to grow more cautious in what he might be suggesting. Lowering his knife and fork, he sliced into the liver, pierced it with his fork and poked it deep into the mass of iron-grey hair around his mouth. When he spoke again, minute segments of the chewed liver shot out in a fine spray across the table. 'It was just a thought,' he grunted, 'We never did find out what caused the terrible row that led to her husband's death, and if you remember, Marlow Tanner had left the area shortly before. It was just a thought, that's all.' He was anxious to assure her, 'Just a thought. Don't worry your head about it.'

But Agnes Crowther did worry her head. Of course it was possible that Marlow Tanner pursued Emma even after her marriage, because it was no secret that he loved her. And Emma would never have married Gregory Denton if it hadn't been for Caleb threatening to have Marlow Tanner transported. Emma loved him so much that she sacrificed herself to save him from her guardian's animosity. That was what it all amounted to. Now, as she was reminded of such distasteful events, Agnes Crowther faced her husband with steely eyes, saying, 'As Emma is a world away and her child no more, I can't see that any of it matters now. Even if Emma were to come back to England, you have been clever enough to secure the mill in your own name . . . so she represents no threat.' She watched him nod his bowed head. But he did not raise it, being so intent on wolfing down his breakfast. Again she spoke, in a quieter, more intimate voice. This time, he raised his head and met her gaze with stiff, angry eyes when she told him, 'I saw you arriving home in the early hours. What manner of . . . business . . . kept you out so late?'

'Whatever manner of "business" . . . it is certainly none of yours.' His knife and fork clattered to the plate while he stretched his neck towards her and spat out the words in a furious voice, 'If you're wise, my dear . . . you'll refrain from questioning my activities. I shall depart this house . . . *my* house . . . whenever I please. And I intend to return at whatever hour I choose. What I do not intend to do is be accountable to you, or to anybody else. Is that perfectly understood?'

'Perfectly.' Agnes Crowther forced herself to smile sweetly, being more convinced than ever that it was not only the likes of Emma Grady who had gone outside of marriage. It was her own husband also. The guilt was plainly stamped on his face, and she loathed him for it.

Caleb Crowther thrust his chair back from the table and rounded on the little maid Amy, who, at that moment, had entered the room and was checking the big silver tureens on the sideboard. 'You!' As she turned round, he shook a fist at her. 'Inform the cook that if she serves such pig-swill up again, she'll find herself finished in this house . . . without references!' When she hurriedly made a slight, nervous curtsy and scurried from the room, Caleb Crowther looked down scathingly on his wife, who deliberately kept her eyes averted. 'Be careful not to question me or my movements again,' he warned, 'or it won't just be the cook who finds herself out of the door.' Then he left the room, slamming the door shut behind him.

'Hmh,' snorted Agnes Crowther, 'you think so, do you?' She laughed softly. 'Well . . . be careful yourself, because I may not be quite the fool you take me for.'

'He said *what*?' Cook's big round face went a painful crimson colour, and Amy feared it might explode. Why should she always be the one made to deliver such messages, she thought with alarm. She would have explained to Cook how the master was already in a terrible bad mood and perhaps didn't really mean it, but Cook didn't give her a chance. 'Pig*swill!* . . . I've never heard the like in all my born days.' The shock was so much that Amy had to fetch her a drop of port wine from the pantry.

'I'm sure it wasn't your breakfast that upset him,' Amy assured Cook. 'I'm sure it was the mistress. They'd been having an awful row . . . some'at about the mistress shouldn't ever question him again.' Oh dear, Amy never did like upsets. There were enough of them when poor Miss Emma was here, and there were always upsets when Miss Martha came to stay. That Justice Crowther seemed to be at the root of any upset. He was a misery. A real misery.

Before Cook had sipped the last of her port, she received another shock, which caught her unawares yet left her in a better mood. It was the sight of Agnes Crowther sweeping down into the kitchen, coming to tell the tearful woman, 'Mr Crowther spoke too hastily, and you are not to take it to heart. As usual, your cooking was exemplary.' After the mistress had gone, Amy declared how good it was of her 'to come downstairs like that'. She also made mention of how the mistress had changed over the years 'since poor Miss Emma were sent to Australia, for murderin' her husband'.

Cook wasn't having that. 'Emma Grady did no such thing!' she retorted, her own dilemma paling by comparison. 'That lass didn't have it in her, to "murder" anybody.'

'No . . . *she* didn't actually murder him, did she? It were that Mrs Manfred.' Amy's brown eyes swelled as she suddenly remembered. 'Ooh! Just think, Cook . . . she were livin' right under this roof as housekeeper. Ooh! . . . We might'a been murdered in our beds.' The thought was so frightful that she clapped both her outstretched hands up to either side of her face, her wide-open mouth and eyes giving her the look of a fish out of water.

'They were neither of them murderers!' exclaimed Cook, losing her patience. 'Get away and clear the dining-room, you little fool,' she told her. Amy knew Cook's unpredictable moods well enough to make a hurried exit.

That night, in the safety and privacy of her own quarters, Cook took an envelope from its hiding place, this being the silk lining in the lid of her portmanteau. 'Murderers indeed!' she muttered, carefully opening the envelope and unfolding the letter from inside. She had read its contents many times before and she knew them word for word. Yet even now it struck her heart cold to read the letter again. It had been delivered by hand only minutes after Mrs Manfred was hanged. It was in her handwriting, though unusually sprawling and hurried. Cook had tried to appreciate how terrified the poor woman must have been with the gallows waiting. But it was beyond her comprehension, and she prayed it always would be. The letter read:

Dear Friend,

There isn't much time left before I meet my maker. I don't know if I am guilty of pushing Emma's husband down the stairs, but I do know I am guilty of having the intention in my heart. My poor darling Emma is innocent of all, except for loving a man other than her husband, and being foolish enough to bear his child.

If there is a victim in all of this nightmare, it is Emma alone, and my heart goes out to her.

You may wonder why I am writing to you, instead of to my only relative. The reasons are these. Firstly, my sister has chosen to believe that I am guilty and has disowned me. Secondly, and for Emma's sake, I feel I must confide in you on very delicate matters regarding Caleb Crowther. Please understand that nothing of what I am about to tell you can be substantiated, or would hold up in a court of law. But I must rid myself of the awful burden which I carry, and I trust that sometime in the future when, God willing, Emma is a free woman, what I am about to reveal might put into her hands an opportunity to question Caleb Crowther, and somehow, to expose the truth which would incriminate him.

I have reason to believe that Caleb Crowther is a murderer!

As I say, I cannot prove anything, and for that reason I have kept silent. Also, God forgive me, I have been cowardly enough to consider my own fate, were I to openly accuse him. I would do it *now*. But I believe my accusations would not only be received with ridicule by those in authority, but would warn Caleb Crowther enough to cover up his tracks.

When I first came to look after Emma, which was very soon after her mama's killing, I was greatly alarmed by snippets of gossip in the area which suggested that Emma's mama had been indiscreet with her affections, and had been unfaithful to Thadius Grady on more than one occasion. Mr Grady himself confided this to me, in a moment of deep despair. Also, I came across the burned remains of clothing in a secluded corner of the garden. It was only later that it occurred to me that the dark iron-like stains on the garments, which I disposed of, might have been *blood* stains. Of course, I instantly dismissed what, I convinced myself, were foolish and dangerous notions. But the discovery of such a fire, and in such a secluded part of the garden so soon after the brutal murder of Mary Grady, left me with many disturbing suspicions. These same suspicions were stirred up by the furtive comings and goings of Caleb Crowther to the house. Also, these visits, when he and Mr Grady would retire to the drawing-room in deep and whispered conversation, always left Emma's papa in a most distressed state of mind.

I have no doubt that, if the two of them were involved in some dreadful secret, then it was brought about more by Caleb Crowther's hand, than by the gentle Mr Grady's. My only concern at the time was for little Emma.

There is something else also. On the day when Thadius Grady died, I was in the linen cupboard. I heard the bedroom door being locked and, on looking out, I saw the ashen, still face of Emma's papa with all life gone from it. And I saw Caleb Crowther, with as guilty a countenance as I have ever witnessed, hurriedly replacing the pillow beneath poor Mr Grady's head. I was surprised and filled with doubt when the doctor saw nothing untoward.

I pray to the Lord that I am wrong in the terrible notions that have haunted me since. And, if I am *not* wrong, then I pray to the Lord for his forgiveness, in being too cowardly to speak up. Yet always in my heart is Emma, and the fear of what such knowledge might do to her. As you know, she idolised her papa, and still deeply grieves for him. So I ask you to be very careful with this information; none of which can be proved, I think.

Yet, if you ever find an opportunity to use it in order to protect Emma from her appointed guardian, do not hesitate. I have a feeling that Caleb Crowther will try to rob Emma of everything her papa left to her. I pray you do all you can to prevent that.

A kindly warden has promised to deliver this letter to you. I trust you will get it. Goodbye and God bless,

Your friend,
Mrs Manfred.

★ ★ ★

The moment her eyes had read the last word and it was etched into her mind, Cook meticulously folded the letter, put it back into the envelope and carefully replaced the awful but precious thing into the silk lining of her portmanteau. On her round, shocked face there crept a look of cunning, as she raised her small pink eyes to look in the direction of her master's quarters. 'Them's terrible words in that there letter!' she murmured, as though addressing someone in person. 'Words as say that *you* . . . a fine upstanding Justice . . . are a thief and a murderer.' Her mouth closed tight and the flabby jowls began working until they actually trembled. Then, lowering her head but keeping her accusing gaze fixed to the ceiling, she said in a grim voice, 'Aye! *Terrible* words. But told by a poor woman who faces the gallows. An' terrible they may be, Caleb Crowther . . . but I believe every last one to be the truth.'

Returning to her work, Cook began muttering to herself. 'I shall guard that letter with me life. It's me insurance against a sorry old age. But you'd best watch your step, else I might be tempted to use the letter afore I intended, Mr fine an' mighty bloody Crowther!' As she whisked the eggs around in the mixing bowl, she chuckled to herself, knowing that she had in her possession the means by which the wind might be taken out of the devil's sails.

Chapter Six

The long harsh winter of 1873 had come and gone. The summer which followed was glorious and, on a day in September 1874, Caleb Crowther received his son-in-law, Silas Trent, into the library. His mood was brighter than usual, believing that this pre-arranged meeting would prove beneficial to himself and improve his finances considerably. The thought appealed to him, and when both he and his son-in-law were seated, he bestowed a rare smile upon his visitor. 'Your business, then?' he asked in a genial voice, and settled back in his chair while his son-in-law, somewhat encouraged by Caleb Crowther's friendly disposition, eagerly outlined the reason for his visit.

Before he had even finished however, Caleb Crowther had sprung to his feet and gone to the fireplace, where he stood with his legs wide apart and his fists clenched by his side. The smile had gone from his face and in its place was a look like thunder. 'You want me to throw good money after bad!' he roared, afterwards storming towards the library door and flinging it wide open. 'I'm surprised that you even had the gall to put such a proposition to me! Good-day to you, sir!' He tapped his foot impatiently as he waited for Silas Trent to rise from the leather armchair, then, when the tall, well-built man with brown hair and military moustache approached him, he added sneeringly, 'Your father left you a thriving shipping line, Mr Trent . . . and in only a few years you have seen fine ships slip through your incompetent fingers, until there is just one vessel left. One, Mr Trent . . . and the *bank* half-owner of it! I trust you have more sense than to let your marriage go the same way, because, to be quite frank . . . I am wearying of supporting your family while you travel the seven seas. If you're not man enough to keep a shipping line successful, then your father should have had more sense than to leave it to you in the first place.'

Silas Trent stood only the smallest distance away from his father-in-law, so close in fact that he could see the delicate criss-cross pattern of purple veins which marbled the whites of the other man's eyes. For a long moment he met Caleb Crowther's vicious stare with steady, unswerving brown eyes, and it ran through his mind what a fool he had been to let Martha persuade him into approaching her father. He felt humiliated and, in the wake of Caleb Crowther's cruel, unjust accusations, he felt a tide of dark anger rising in him. Yes, it was true that he had been left a fleet of proud ships, and that, sadly, that same fleet was now reduced to the *Stirling*, which he himself captained. But what the arrogant Caleb Crowther refused to acknowledge was the colossal cost of running and maintaining a large fleet of ships. While the contracts were plentiful, and there was money enough to take on the crews, there were no problems. But in recent years it was proving more and more difficult to secure good lucrative contracts. There were too many shipping lines chasing too few cargoes which, since the closure of many cotton mills and the stopping of convict transportation, had become more scarce. Indeed, if anything, Silas Trent was proud of the fact that he still ran the *Stirling* at a profit when so many other shipping merchants had lost everything. Then there was the growing threat from faster, iron-built steamers. Recently though, he had heard that a firm in Australia had invited tenders for the shipping of sandalwood to Singapore. There were also opportunities to get in on the expanding wool trade out there. In fact, Australia had become increasingly important for merchant trade, and Silas Trent regretted the fact that he had concentrated on other markets and routes these many years, since losing the government contracts to carry convicts. He had made his one big mistake there, and he was the first to admit it. However, the opportunity to make amends had presented itself. He *knew* he could make the most favourable tender for the sandalwood route from Australia to Singapore, and with careful planning secure the shipments of wool and other cargoes which would bring him back to England and his family. But he needed capital to get him started. He had been to the banks and other lenders without success. Caleb Crowther had been his last hope. Silas had stressed that he would win the contracts to carry goods to and from Australia, if only he could get the financial backing.

He had voiced these convictions to his father-in-law, who had rejected them out of hand. Now, he replied in a firm but cutting voice, 'As for my marriage, don't let it concern you, Mr Crowther, sir. Your daughter and I may have our difficulties like any other couple, but they are not insurmountable. 'Then, being fully aware of the frostiness between Caleb Crowther and his own wife, Agnes, he quietly added, 'When we have a problem, sir, we discuss it. I fully recommend that course of action: you will find that it works wonders.' Before Caleb Crowther could recover from such insolence, Silas Trent gave a courteous nod, bade him good-day, and in a moment had departed from the room, left the house and climbed into the waiting carriage, which went sedately down the drive and out on to the street.

Seated in the ornately furnished drawing-room busy with her tapestry, Agnes Crowther had heard the conversation which had taken place between her son-in-law and her husband. The outcome had been exactly as she had warned her daughter Martha. Yet that foolish woman had insisted on harbouring false hopes and sending Silas on a fool's errand. Silas Trent was a good man and had been a good husband to Martha. He was a wonderful father to the boy, Edward, and if there was a way by which he might recover from his present financial predicament, Agnes Crowther felt confident that he would do it. He must do it, for the sake of Martha and the boy, because it was a certainty that, should the worst happen and Silas Trent lose everything, neither he nor his family would be made welcome in this house. Martha's father had made that very clear on several occasions, when he had stated, 'I believe a man should be responsible for his own family. Martha has passed from my care into that of her husband's, and she must stand or fall with him!' The boy, Edward, however was a different matter: Caleb Crowther saw him as the son he had never had.

Sighing wearily, Agnes Crowther sank her needle into the tapestry and gave it her full attention. But not before murmuring, 'You will find a way, Silas . . . I know you will.' Just as *she* would, she thought. In the past she had done much to be ashamed of, and she had come to dislike her own husband because of it. Yet even now, if the opportunity came when she might make amends, she wondered whether she would be capable of doing so.

'Sell the *Stirling*! There are other ways to earn a living!' Martha Trent was in a fury when she realized that her husband had borrowed money on their home in order to finance his journey to Australia, where he intended to secure his future prospects. 'You'll see us without a roof over our heads,' she accused him now. 'Is that what you want? . . . To see us wandering the streets like beggars?'

'Don't be foolish, Martha. It will never come to that, and you know it . . . even if I have to buy a barge and fight for a cargo up and down the Leeds and Liverpool Canal!' Silas shook his head and came to where his wife was petulantly beating the top of the piano with one hand, and dabbing a delicate handkerchief to her eyes with the other. Taking her by the shoulders, he would have held her close, but she tore away from him, crying, 'Go on then! . . . Go to your precious ship, and sail to the ends of the earth for all *I* care! You don't want me and you don't want the boy . . . or you would not be so heartless as to put up our home for security! You'll never be the successful man of business that my *father* is, and you could do no better than to listen to his advice. Isn't it enough to know that he will not invest in you?'

'You know why he won't invest in me, Martha,'

protested Silas, growing impatient at Martha's hostile attitude. Like father like daughter, he thought. 'Caleb Crowther won't back me, because he has already backed one of my competitors. If I'd known at the time that he was hand in glove with Lassater Shipping I would never have been persuaded to approach him in the first place. I've also recently learned that not only do Lassater Shipping hold long-term contracts to carry cotton from your father's mill and that he is a large shareholder in that shipping-line, but he has passed on confidential information which I confided to him during our conversation. The result being that Lassater Shipping is now a major contender for the sandalwood cargoes from Australia to Singapore. He betrayed us. Do you hear what I'm saying, Martha? . . . Your father who, in your eyes, can do no wrong . . . *betrayed* us!'

'Liar!' In a swift and unexpected movement, Martha Trent swung round, taking the silver candlestick from the piano top and, with a scream of 'Get out!' sent the object flying. Silas Trent was caught unawares, saw the heavy candlestick at the last minute and ducked quickly sideways, but not in time to avoid a glancing blow to the side of his head. When he put his hand up to touch his temple, the blood ran through his fingers and a small pool of crimson dripped on to his jacket.

Martha showed no sign of regret. Instead, she stood stiff and unyielding with bright angry eyes which continued to stare at her husband unflinchingly. He also showed no remorse for the heated argument which had raged between them, nor did he make any move towards her.

In the hallway outside the room the boy, Edward, sat

on the stairs, quietly crying as his parents ranted and raged at each other. Now he got to his feet as his father came from the drawing-room, a look of utter desolation on his face when he saw the boy there. 'Oh, Edward! Edward!' he moaned, quickly covering the boy's head with his two hands and pulling him tight into his body. 'What must you think of us?' he asked in a voice which betrayed his shame. When he received no answer, he went down on his knees and looked into his son's face, seeing the terrible anguish in those dark green eyes, knowing that he had caused it. 'I'm sorry, son,' he said with a sad apologetic smile. 'I'd rather you had not heard all that. But she's wrong, you know . . . your mother. I won't let you down, I promise.' Still there came no acknowledgement from the boy, who had lowered his gaze and seemed unwilling or unable to raise it to Silas Trent's concerned face. After a while Silas released the boy and got to his feet. For a moment longer he looked down at his son's bowed head, then, ruffling the dark hair with the tips of his fingers, he said with a small laugh, 'I'm off to turn our fortunes round.' When there was still no response, he said in a quieter voice, 'Take care of your mother.' In another moment he was gone. Still the boy did not move, his dark head bent to the rich, floral-patterned carpet with the tears falling down his face.

When he sensed a movement close by, Edward lifted his eyes to see his mother standing in the door of the drawing-room. Her face was smudged with tears and there was a look of bitterness in her brown speckly eyes, as she told him through gritted teeth, 'Get upstairs to your room, and don't come down until I send for you!' With a heavy heart he did as he was told.

Behind him Martha Trent angrily issued instructions to their one and only servant, a young woman of stocky build whose blue eyes showed no surprise. 'Master Trent and I will be leaving for Breckleton House straightaway. I dare say we shall be away for several weeks,' adding in a tone too low for the servant to hear, 'and probably for good!'

The maid gave a hurried little curtsy. 'Yes, ma'am,' she acknowledged, thinking as she went about the business of packing how she wouldn't mind being left alone in the house for weeks on end; indeed, if anything, taking into account her mistress's dreadful disposition, she much preferred it. But her heart went out to that poor little lad, dragged from pillar to post and never a friend to call his own. And that tutor who came in of an afternoon to teach him his lessons, well, he were a miserable old bugger an' all. On top of which, the lad were expected to work twice as hard when he got back from these frequent trips to Breckleton House. It were no wonder the poor little blighter looked like he'd got the weight of the world on his shoulders. Still, the lad seemed to have a right fondness for his grandad, Caleb Crowther, and by all accounts that surly-faced fellow had an unusually soft spot for his only grandson, so that was one blessing, thank the Lord.

All was still and pitch black outside Breckleton House when the small figure clothed in night attire rose from his bed. Cautiously opening his bedroom door, Edward Trent listened intently and was pleased to hear no sound other than the slumbering tick of the wall clock on the landing. He knew that his grandfather had gone away on his legal duties, and his grandmother had long ago retired to her bed. Softly now, he crept to his mother's room, peeped inside and satisfied himself that she was sound asleep. Afterwards, he went back to his own room, put on his breeches, with a clean white shirt and green corduroy waistcoat, pulled on his knee-length socks and lace-up ankle boots, which he loosely fastened. Then, grabbing his cap and fixing it securely on his head, he took the handful of coins from his cash-box, and went softly down the stairs and out of the back door.

As he stumbled across the fields, then through the narrow cobbled alleys of Mill Hill, fearful of the strange shadows and of where the dark alleys might lead him, yet even more fearful of his father never coming back, the boy began to sob. He had never seen them fight as fiercely as that before, and it made him unhappy. He didn't want to stay in the house without his father, and even though he liked his grandfather, he also frightened him a little.

He was going to find his way back to Liverpool, to the docks where all the big ships came in. He would find his father's ship, and steal on board. The thought cheered him and he hoped he was going in the right direction, because he did not intend to be left behind again. He hoped that the *Stirling* had not already sailed for Australia. That awful possibility spurred him into a little run when, time and time again, he stumbled on the sharp, jutting cobbles. In the pitch black of the early hours, when he was imagining some kind of monster in every dark, terrible corner, his courage began to desert him. Faster and faster he ran, convinced that he could hear the soft thudding footsteps of his pursuers. When a large shadowy cat crossed his path suddenly, he actually screamed out loud in terror.

The boy's scream echoed against the high, smoke-coated buildings which rose up about him like the walls of a prison. The disturbance created more disturbance as alarmed cats, rats and other creatures of the night fled to safety.

Yet if it alerted some night marauders to run away, it alerted others to stay and watch, in the happy event that it might be turned to their own advantage. Such a pair were engaged in the unlawful entry of a darkened warehouse in this isolated area, but, on hearing the scream close by, promptly abandoned their efforts in the hope of better pickings. Careful not to utter a single word to each other, and using a well-developed system of sign language, they crept from the back-yard and out into the alley. At once they heard the frightened figure of Edward Trent running towards them, his boots playing out a tune on the cobbles, and the coins in his pocket chinking frantically against his leg.

Quickly, the two shadowy figures slithered back into the recess of the wall, waiting for the very second when the approaching figure would be so close that they could leap on it from behind.

Edward Trent never even knew what stopped him in his headlong flight. One minute he had been determined to reach the end of the dark, terrifying alley, so that he might come into a more open and less threatening area. In the next minute, the ruffians had pounced on his back and wrenched him sideways; his head smacked hard against the brick wall, and he crumpled to the ground, a pool of blood trickling from the back of his head to the cobbles, where it congealed to form a dark, sticky stain.

'Bloody 'ell, yer fool!' cried the smaller and younger one of the two in a forced whisper, as he touched his fingers to the stain, promptly snatching them away when the liquid clung to his fingertips. 'Ye've *killed* 'im, dah.'

Quickly now, the older fellow struck a match and held it over Edward Trent's face, which, in the eerie glow of matchlight, looked a sickly shade of parchment. 'It's a brat,' he remarked with surprise. 'Can't be above a couple o' years younger than you, what . . . ten or eleven.' Here he gave a gasp of astonishment as his eyes roved over the prostrate figure, which had not moved even an inch nor shown any flicker of life. 'T'ain't no *ordinary* brat neither! Look at the cut of 'is togs . . . this ain't no street urchin. This is a bloody gentry, I'm telling yer.' He was all for making good his getaway the minute he had emptied the victim's pockets. But his companion had other ideas.

''Elp me strip 'is togs off!' The younger one began tearing at the blood-stained waistcoat. 'These buggers'll fit me. Me an' this feller are about the same size . . . just shows yer, don't it, eh? I bet I'm a good three years older, but no bloody bigger . . . 'cause 'e lives on the best, an' folks such as us . . . *we* live on the soddin' dregs.' There was a deal of hatred in his voice as with the help of the older fellow he viciously stripped off every last garment from the boy, and afterwards, without compassion – but with every intention of fooling whoever came across the lifeless body, and also of diverting suspicion – dressed it up in his own filthy flea-infested clothes. When he prepared to exchange boots though, he realized Edward Trent's were far smaller than his own, so he thought better of it.

'Now, let's get the 'ell outta 'ere,' instructed the older one. In a minute they had fled without a second thought as to whether the boy might be dead, or still alive. It mattered not anyway, because folks hardly ever came this way, and if he wasn't a gonner now, he would be by the time he was found. The younger ruffian was all for rolling the body in the canal because 'it's nobbut a stride away'. But he was dissuaded. 'We ain't got time. An' somebody might come along. The feller's 'ad it anyway.'

So they fled, with only each other and the night as witness to their awful deed.

Chapter Seven

'Well I'm buggered, Molly lass,' cackled Sal Tanner as she watched the girl strip-wash over the bucket of canal water, 'yer nobbut comin' up twelve year old . . . an' already ye've got pointed little tets!' When Molly looked at her in disgust, with a deep uncomfortable blush spreading over her lovely face, Sal rocked with laughter. 'Don't be embarrassed, gal,' she told her, 'at lest, not 'till yer get ter *my* age, an yer tets 'ang down ter yer knees like withered balloons!' She roared again, when Molly hurriedly finished her wash, quickly replacing her panties and misshapen grey dress, which came down to the top of her boots in a ragged, uneven hem. The boots she pulled on had also seen better days, the laces being too short to do up the top eyelets, and the toe of one boot having come slightly apart.

Taking her wooden bone-toothed comb, Molly raked it through her short black hair until it shone blue as a raven's wing. 'I ain't taking no notice of you, Sal Tanner,' she said with a toss of her head, 'you're just trying to rile me, and it won't work!'

Sal had been making a determined effort to chew the small slice of apple which she had just pared with her penknife. Fast losing patience at her inability to enjoy the juicy apple, because it was difficult to chew with your gums when all your teeth had fallen out, she spat

171

it out through the hut window and threw the remainder
of the apple after it. 'Sod an' bugger it!' she yelled. 'As
fer you, Molly lass . . . yer gerring too bloody big fer
yer boots. Aye! Too cheeky, an' too 'igh an' mighty by
'arf.'

Molly paid no heed. She knew that Sal had to take
her frustrations out on somebody, and as she was the
only other one here, then it might as well be her. 'I
shan't wash in the hut anymore,' she told Sal Tanner, at
the same time picking up the handle of the bucket and
lifting its considerable weight off the floor. 'If you're
gonna make fun of me, I'll wash by the canal.'

'Oh aye? That'll be a grand idea, won't it, eh? Gi' the
passin' barges a right old treat . . . show *them* yer little
pointed tets, why don't yer?' Her humour having
returned in the face of Molly's innocent remarks, Sal
Tanner threw her two arms up in the air and began
rocking back and forth in a fit of helpless laughter, her
toothless mouth wide open and her legs the same.
Molly patiently shook her head, gave out a little laugh
at the merry sight, then went down to the canal and
emptied the bucket into it.

When she returned to the hut, she found Sal in a
worse state, filled with panic and trying desperately to
cough up a chunk of apple which appeared to have
lodged itself in her gullet. It took a few frantic minutes
of pushing, pulling, thumping and shaking, but eventually the offending piece of apple was dislodged and
thrown out of the window to follow the rest. 'Have a
little sleep, Sal,' encouraged Molly, who had suffered
quite a fright at the sight of Sal choking.

'Only if yer promise ter wake me up at midday, when
I'm off ter the Navigation fer a tipple,' replied Sal,

carefully sipping the water which Molly held up to her. After a couple of sips she thrust it from her, 'Bloody 'orrible stuff!' she moaned, pulling a wry face. 'Did yer save it from yer washin'-up water?'

When Molly assured her that she had done no such thing, Sal gave a little chuckle and winked a cheeky violet eye at the girl. 'Course yer didn't!' she told her. 'But yer *will* wake me up at midday, won't yer, eh? 'Cause I've a feller ter see!' She winked again, 'A proper gentleman friend, an' I'm fotchin' the bugger back 'ere . . . fer a little . . . quiet session, just the two on us. So mind yer gives us an hour or two on us own, won't yer lass?' She insisted, 'Ye'll do that fer yer ol' Sal, won't yer?'

Molly didn't mind, because she'd promised herself to go fishing down the quiet end of the canal. She had even collected a few juicy worms and got her willow stick all ready, with a good strong twine and a bent nail. All the times she'd been trying, and never once had she caught a fish. Today was going to be different, Molly felt sure. Today, she *would* catch a fish. It must be a lucky day, because at long last Sal had a boyfriend.

Sal's face crinkled into a multitude of crevices as she smiled into those big, wonderful black eyes. 'Yer reckon yer gonna catch us a fish, d'yer?' she said. 'Wi that bent nail an' balin' twine? Well now . . . won't that be a celebration, eh? Fresh caught fish fer us tea!' She didn't laugh at the idea, but kept on smiling.

'You'll see!' returned Molly. 'You'll see!' Then off she went to get everything ready for the big event, quietly closing the door behind her while Sal swung her legs up on to the mattress and settled into the bolster for what she considered to be a well-earned nap. 'Got

173

ter be bright an' fresh fer me new feller,' she chuckled, pulling the shawl about her and folding her arms over her breast. Soon the little hut was filled with the echo of her contented snores. In the heat of a lovely September day, the tiny enclosed hut was also filled with the rancid aroma which rose up from Sal's unwashed body and dirt-laden clothes. But deep in her amorous dreams, Sal was blissfully unaware of such trivialities, because at last she had a fellow to call her very own. Her last thought was of him as she murmured, 'Thank the Lord he ain't one of them particular kind.'

At four minutes past midday, Molly duly shook Sal awake, made her a brew of tea and persuaded her to polish off just one jam butty. But try as she might, Molly could not persuade Sal to dip her hands and face into a bowl of hot, soapy water. 'Gerraway wi' yer!' Sal was horrified: 'Time enough fer soap an' water, when I'm laid out an' ready fer the knacker's yard. I expect the buggers'll throw a bucket o' the wet stuff o'er me then . . . when I ain't in no position ter argue, eh? Till then, I'll thank yer kindly ter keep the disgustin' tack away fro' me!' However, she did allow Molly to comb her wispy grey tufts of hair, saying with a mischievous wink, 'Yer never know, Molly lass . . . me feller might just want ter run 'is fingers through me lovely locks.' Then she rolled about laughing, and couldn't resist adding, 'There's about as much chance o' that . . . as you catchin' fish!'

'Have a good time, Sal,' Molly called after her as she hobbled off towards the Navigation.

'Aye, I will!' returned Sal with a naughty and suggestive wiggle of her bum. 'I've caught my bloody fish. So now, you gerrof an' catch *yourn*!' She was singing merrily when she rounded the corner and went out of sight, and Molly's heart swelled with love. 'Sal Tanner, you're as bad as they come,' she said, shaking her head, her dark eyes smiling contentedly, 'but I wouldn't swap you for all the world.' Then with her willow fishing-stick and a can filled up with fat, wriggling worms, she set off towards the far end of the canal. She had no intention of coming away until she had caught a big, swashy gudgeon to show to Sal!

Molly settled herself in the shade of an old silver birch tree, whose spreading branches gave welcome shade from the hot sun. '*This* is where the gudgeon are hiding,' she murmured with a rush of pleasure. 'They'll be looking for a cool spot, just the same as me.' In no time at all she had wedged her fishing-stick into the bank and kept a close watch as the baling twine sank deeper and deeper into the water, with the fat worm wriggling on the end of it. Many was the time Molly had tackled Sal and other fishermen about how afraid she was the worms might be terrified when lowered into the water as bait. Her fears had been allayed when she had received the very same answer from one and all: 'Don't be so bloody daft, lass . . . 'tis a well-known fact that worms ain't got no nerves, so they can't *feel* owt.' Molly had been obliged to accept this, but it still made her cringe when the worm went out of sight, because she couldn't help wondering how she would feel if she were in its place. Molly had decided that she wouldn't like it at all, no, not at all.

After a while, when she seemed to have been scanning the water for hours, until her eyeballs ached, and

the warm, sultry afternoon made her feel tired, Molly
wrapped her legs round the fishing-stick and wound the
baling twice about her toe, so that if a fish were caught
up on the other end she would know about it. She lay
back in the grass, feeling wonderfully contented with
life, thinking how quiet and peaceful it was here. On
top of which, Sal had a feller and he just might be the
one to look after them both; although somehow Molly
doubted it. There had been other fellers, some long
time back, but they never came to anything worthwhile
either. She wondered how the two of them were getting
along, and she felt sure they must be gone from the hut
by now, in search of a card game perhaps? Unless of
course they had brought a supply of booze with them,
but Molly doubted that as well, because Sal never had
any money, and neither did the fellers she picked up.
Molly gave a small laugh. 'It's a good job I've still got a
few bob tucked away, Sal darling,' she giggled, 'so we'll
not go short of a loaf yet.'

Of a sudden, Molly sat bolt upright as the twine
tightened about her toe. 'Ssh now, gal,' she told
herself, moving with the utmost care as she slid her toe
from the loop and put her two hands around the
willow-stick, which began bending towards the canal,
as the twine was pulled tighter and tighter. In a minute
it was all-out war! If Molly hadn't whipped the stick
from the ground and taken charge, the entire lot would
have gone flying into the water. Unable now to contain
her excitement, Molly began whooping and hollering,
giving the line its head, then drawing it back again.
Inch by inch she shortened the line and wound it round
the stick, bringing her struggling quarry nearer and
nearer until she could see the fish-tail thrashing furi-

ously in the water. 'It's no good you arguing, you old bugger!' she yelled. 'I've got you, and I ain't letting you get away!' At the right moment, she flicked the stick in the air, bringing both line and fish out of the water. With a soft thud the exhausted fish fell to the grass. 'You little beauty!' cried Molly, reverently collecting it up in her hands and gently easing the small bent nail out of its mouth. 'Oh, you're a *real* beauty!' She gazed in wonder at its small sleek body, its silver colour speckled with gold, and the sheen in its tail and fins almost translucent in the light of the sun. 'Oh . . . you really *are* lovely!' gasped Molly, and she knew in her heart that she could never take its life. She was held fascinated for a moment longer, then, when its mouth gasped frantically and its eyes began popping, she knelt down by the water's edge and lowered it back in. When it moved away, slowly at first, then in a rush of excitement, Molly was not sorry. She had caught a fish, and her only thought was to tell the world.

'I *caught* him!' She stood up and yelled at the top of her voice, 'Sal . . . *I caught a fish!*' Without stopping to collect her precious fishing tackle, she sped along the bank like the wind. 'Sal . . . Sal, I *did* it!' There was a fever in her, and the greatest need to tell the only person who mattered in her young life.

When Molly saw the hut in sight, she was spurred on, her whole being alive with excitement. 'Sal! . . . Sal!' she was calling as she flung open the door. Then she was cruelly silenced by the scene which greeted her. Sal was there, and so was her fellow. But they were both stark naked, the small wiry man bending over the bed where Sal was lying, and Sal lying so still that Molly's heart shrank inside her. At once the man swung round,

177

his eyes large and terrified as they stared at Molly. "T'ain't my fault,' he said in a trembling voice, 'we were having a good time . . . a good time, I tell you! Then she couldn't breathe. *Look* at her, oh God in Heaven . . . 'tweren't *my* fault!' He began shivering limb from limb as Molly came further into the room, a look of confusion and horror on her face. All the while he was scrambling into his clothes the man kept repeating in a tearful voice. 'Tain't my fault! We were having a good time, I swear.' When he was fully dressed, he came to where Molly was stooping over her beloved Sal, and touching her gently on the shoulder he promised, 'I'll fetch help, I swear . . . I'll fetch proper help.' Then he was gone in a great hurry.

'Let 'im go, Molly lass.' Sal made no move other than to raise her eyes to Molly's face. There was the twinkling of a smile in them, but only a twinkling, and to Molly it seemed as though somewhere deep inside those bright merry eyes a light had been switched off. 'Oh, Sal . . . what shall I do?' Molly felt torn two ways, because part of her wanted to rush out and find help, but a deeper instinct kept her there.

'Don't do nowt, lass,' murmured Sal, as Molly reverently drew up the blanket to cover Sal's nakedness. 'Yon feller'll get 'elp. But it won't do no good, darlin' . . . 'cause old Sal's gone past being 'elped. 'She made an effort to laugh, but it seemed to cause her pain, as she brought both her arms up and clutched them across her chest; then she smiled a toothless smile, softly chuckling as she went on with difficulty, 'The bugger were right, y'know. We *were* 'aving a "good time". Best good time I've 'ad in bloody years! Only . . . me old ticker let me down, sod an' bugger it.'

Every word was an effort. 'Oh, but it were *grand* ter feel a feller's weight atop o' me after all these years, lass. Pity it's fer the last time, eh?'

Molly didn't think it was such a 'grand' thing. And she wanted Sal to stop talking that way, because it frightened her.

'You're going to be fine and dandy,' Molly said in a choking voice, 'you *are* Sal . . . you are!' The thought of losing Sal was more than she could bear. As hard as she tried to hold back the tears, they would not be held, and as they flowed down her sorry young face, Sal reached up a grubby hand to wipe them away. 'No, Molly lass . . . don't do that on my account.' Her fingers touched the tiny delicate watch that Molly always wore about her neck. 'An' don't yer *dare* to sell that there trinket! It don't belong ter you, y'see . . . it belongs ter the little people. You promise me now, lass . . . *promise* ye'll never sell it!' Molly promised, but with Sal's next words, she wished she hadn't. 'Let the buggers put me in a pauper's grave,' she told Molly, 'it meks no difference ter me, 'cause I'll be past carin'.' Again she would have chuckled, but was gripped with such a fierce pain that it took her breath away.

'Lie still, Sal . . . please.' Molly was also racked with pain, but it was a different kind of pain . . . a sort of terror. 'I'm going to get help for you, Sal,' she said now, beginning to move away.

'No! *Don't leave me*. I want yer next ter me when I go . . . I'm a coward, yer see,' she finished with a tight little smile. 'You stay aside o' me, Molly lass.' Her smile faded into a look of sorrow as she softly added, 'You an' Marlow . . . yer all I've got. An' *that* bugger's gone afore me, I'm thinking . . . 'cause if 'e ain't, then

179

'e's deserted me . . . an' I'll *never* believe that of 'im.
Never!' She had Molly's small hand secure in her own,
and she had no intention of letting go.

'Sal, *please* . . . let me get help,' pleaded Molly. But
then something happened which riveted her to the
spot, because Sal uttered three words to her that she
had never said before, 'I love you,' she whispered.
Then she closed her eyes, and her hand fell back on the
bedclothes. She never heard Molly's terrible cry of
anguish as the distraught girl threw herself into Sal's
lifeless arms.

When the man came back, just as he had promised,
together with an old gypsy-fellow who was renowned
for his knowledge of medicine, they saw the child still
cradling the woman who had been the only mammy she
had ever known. They heard her crying softly as she
murmured a prayer, and they knew there was nothing
left to do but notify the authorities to fetch old Sal away
to her last resting-place. As for the young 'un, well,
she'd have to fend for herself, because times were hard
and folks had enough mouths to feed.

Word spread quickly that very day about how poor Sal
Tanner had gone. 'In the arms of a feller,' said one,
'enjoying herself right up to the very end,' and everybody agreed whole-heartedly that, if Sal had to go, 'the
old bugger wouldn't have wanted it any other way'. All
the same, it was a pity about the young lass, they said,
and an even bigger pity that old Sal led the girl to
believe she'd never had no parents and was 'left by the
little people' because where were 'the little people'
now, eh? Well, nowhere else but in Sal's twisted, merry
mind, that's where! But then where were the lass's

proper parents? For all anybody knew, they might just as well be the little characters dreamt up by old Sal. The top and bottom of it all was that young Molly had nobody. She was on her own, and it was hard enough to survive in this world even when you were a grown-up fellow and had a companion to watch out for you. When you were a lass though, not yet twelve years old, *and* all alone in the world, surviving could turn out to be a nightmare. But everyone had more than their fair share of troubles, and had to work through them the best they could.

'You *cheated* me! And you cheated Sal!' Molly's tear-stained face was raised to the sky and her small fist was clenched and held up as though to threaten some unseen thing. 'I hate you! D'you hear me . . . I *hate* you!' She continued to look upwards, as if waiting for a reply, and when the sky remained unchanged, she crumpled to the ground, sobbing as though her heart would break. 'Give her back to me. Oh, please . . . give me back my old Sal.'

For a long while Molly stayed still on the grass, her heart so filled with grief that she didn't care whether she herself went the same way as her darling Sal. In fact, she would have preferred it to being left all on her own.

'Aw, it ain't so terrible, Molly,' said a kindly voice immediately above her, and when she looked up, blinking her dark unhappy eyes against the bright sunlight, Molly saw that it was one of Sal's drinking cronies, a small, shrew-like creature with pointed features and a narrow body almost completely shrouded in a long, dark cotton shawl. In a minute she was seated on the grass beside Molly, her tiny pea-like eyes swallowed up in the great rolls of puffy flesh which surrounded them. 'None of us can live for ever, y'know . . . 'specially not the likes o' me and Sal, who don't gi' a cuss for nothing and nobody.' She went on, 'Anybody as enjoys their tipple, like me an' Sal, well . . . they're on their way out a sight quicker than most folks, ain't they, eh?' She inclined her head to one side and took a while regarding Molly's slim, taut, little figure, with the promise of great beauty emerging; she looked into the dark oval eyes and saw something unusual and lovely there, and a look of cunning came over her face. 'No, you forget Sal Tanner,' she said, edging a little closer, 'she's laid out in that cold place now, waiting her turn to be put in the ground. Poor old sod . . . *she* won't be knocking back any more jugs of ale . . . no, nor bedding any more fellers neither, unless o'course it's a free-for-all up *there*.' She kept her prying eyes on Molly's unhappy face, while she jerked a thumb heavenwards.

'I'd be obliged if you'd please leave me be,' Molly told her. She didn't care much for the woman, she never had done, and she didn't like the things that were being said now. On top of which there was an awful ache in her heart, and she wanted to be left on her own.

'Oho . . . want rid of me, do you? Well, I expect you're not too keen on company just now . . . and it's only to be understood, in the circumstances, what with poor Sal not proper cold and all.'

The woman watched while Molly went to sit by the water's edge, where she absent-mindedly began to skim small clods of soil into the canal. 'They wouldn't let me go in where they took Sal,' murmured Molly in a forlorn voice, the tears still tumbling softly down her face. 'I wanted to stay with her.' She brought her two small fists up and scraped the tears away. 'But they wouldn't let me.'

'Well, o' *course* they wouldn't let you!' The woman was astonished that anybody should want to stay in a parish mortuary, unless of course they were stretched out and had no option. 'You don't want to go upsetting yourself any more than you need,' she told Molly, who made no response other than to lean forward, fold her arms across her bent knees and drop her dark head into the cradle there. She felt utterly lost, and she knew in her aching heart that nothing would ever be the same again.

The woman sidled closer, all the while regarding the trim attractive figure: all manner of unsavoury thoughts ran through her mind. She was well aware that there was a ready market for young virgin girls, because hadn't she already fattened her purse from it time and time again?

'It comes to us *all*,' she went on, attempting now to move the subject away from Sal, when there might be an opportunity to lead on to other, more profitable matters. But first she had to deal with the girl's hostile attitude towards her. 'Don't take it too much to heart,' she said, 'Sal had a fair old innings. Why! . . . Look at the poor little bugger who got crushed unrecognisably under a coach and four in the early hours of this very morning . . . and not a spit too far from this very spot neither! Came dashing out of an alley they did, two o' 'em . . . the bigger one scarpered when a bobby blew his whistle, but the young 'un, well . . . after the wheels and hooves had gone over him, there wasn't much left, so they say. Funny thing, though . . . y'see,

the undertaker is a cousin of the Navigation landlord . . . an' the word is that the little feller as was
mangled, well . . . he were a *gentry*! What d'you think
of that then? And if that don't top it all, it seems that he
was Justice Crowther's own grandson! Well! . . . It
don't bear thinking about, does it, eh? What would a
young gentry like that be doing out at all hours . . . tell
me that, eh? If you ask me, they're no better than *any*
of us.'

She dug deep into her shawl, drew out a clay pipe
and proceeded to light it, puffing away until her face
grew an uncomfortable shade of pink. When it was
firing nicely, she peeped at Molly, who up to now was
too steeped in her own thoughts to pay any heed to the
old woman's mutterings. 'Well, as I was saying . . .
Justice Crowther's grandson no less! They do say as
how he went wild when he was told . . . and the
mother, she just passed right out in a faint. The boy's
father's away on the high seas, and can't be contacted. I
expect it'll break his heart, because the lad were an
only child . . . happen he ran away or some'at, it's hard
to say, ain't it? Got some fine and dandy togs on, by all
accounts, except for his boots . . . which looked like
they'd trudged for miles, according to the undertaker.
And it was said how the lad had big coarse feet for a
young gentry. Still . . . they don't wear boots in
Heaven, I don't suppose, eh?' She gave a little laugh,
before nudging Molly and saying slyly, 'What have you
done with Sal's boots? I'll give you a pretty penny for
'em . . . her shawl too, if you've a mind?'

'They're not for sale. They're Sal's . . . and she's
keeping them!' Molly had paid little heed to most of the
woman's rantings, but the mention of Sal and her

clothes had caught her attention.

'All right,' the woman was keen to pacify the agitated girl, 'let her be buried in 'em . . . though it seems a terrible shame to let good boots go to rot in a pauper's grave. And what about you, eh? You come and stay with me . . . you'll have plenty of friends, I promise . . . and a chance to turn a pretty penny.' Her pea-like eyes glistened, 'What d'you say?'

Molly was past listening, ever since the woman had said 'pauper's grave'. Now she was on her feet, her black eyes blazing. 'Sal ain't going in no *pauper's* grave!' she yelled, beginning to run in the direction of the hut and calling behind her. 'If that's what you think, you're *wrong*. I won't *let* her go in no pauper's grave!'

'Huh!' Takes hard brass to pay for a proper funeral, you little fool,' returned the woman. 'If you come with me, I'll see you earn it. Then you can pay for a proper funeral . . . I'll even be so good as to *lend* you the money, and take it back out of your earnings. What d'you say?'

Molly said nothing as she sped away into Blackburn town to make sure the parish officials didn't put Sal in a pauper's plot.

The fat bearded man was not altogether unsympathetic. The small dingy office fronted the parish yard where in one small corner stood a red-brick building with long narrow windows and a big black painted door. It was in there that they kept all the 'vagrants' and 'vagabonds' who had departed this world.

'No, I've told you before, you're not allowed in there. Tomorrow though, it won't matter anyway . . . because she'll be in the communal plot behind the

185

churchyard. You'll be able to go and see her there.' He
felt sorry for the pretty dark-haired girl, but rules were
rules, and it was more than his job was worth to let her
in. 'Go on, off you go,' he told her.

Molly stood her ground, her dark eyes beseeching as
they looked up over the desk, her fingers clutched tight
to its edge. 'Sal *ain't* going in no pauper's grave!' she
declared, with such firmness that the fat bearded man
put down his pen, and reached forward to look at Molly
more closely. 'I want Sal to have a proper burial,' she
told him, her gaze unflinching beneath his intense and
curious stare.

'Oh I see, young lady,' he said with a patronising
smile, 'and how do you propose to pay for this "proper
burial"? Got plenty of money, have you? . . . Come
into a tidy sum?'

Only then did Molly realise the enormity of the task
she had set herself. Fleetingly her small fingers toyed
with the tiny watch secreted beneath her dress. But the
thought of Sal, and the recollection of a promise she
had only recently made caused her to feel ashamed.
Yet somehow she would see that Sal was not thrown
into the ground like some dead dog. She and Sal had
come across such a pauper's burial once, and Molly had
never forgotten it. She was determined it would not
happen to her beloved Sal.

Molly told all of this to the man with the friendly
eyes, and though he argued that she was looking to do
the impossible, he did agree to delay Sal's departure
from the yard until Monday next. 'Today being
Wednesday, that gives you a good four days. After
that, she'll have to be put down with the rest of
them . . . or stink to high heaven, and nobody will

want to touch her. And we can't have that, can we?'

Molly thought it unnecessary to say such a cruel thing, but she went away with a lighter heart. All the same, she was desperate as to how she might find the money. 'Two guineas, he said,' she muttered as she made her way back towards the canal, 'and Sal would get a proper church burial.' She hoped that the shrew-like woman was still there on the canal bank because, much as she didn't like the idea of going to live with that one and doing whatever work she was offering, Molly felt she had no choice. Not if she was to get two whole guineas in such a short time. It was true that Molly could pick a few pockets at Blackburn market on Saturday, but there weren't always gentry about, and it would be a miracle if she made *two guineas*. No, she daren't risk it. The woman's offer was her best bet. Once she'd repaid the two guineas, she would be free to go her own way again. But without her Sal. What a frightening thought. Yet her grief was eased by the intention of doing the very best she could for her darling Sal.

There was no sign of the shrew-like creature. So, armed with a vague notion that the woman lived somewhere down George Street, Molly set off again, thinking to look in the window of the Navigation on the way in case she had gone there. She was desperate to find her and she was prepared to do anything to see that Sal wasn't given a pauper's farewell.

Molly was just on the point of stepping from the canal bank and over the short wall – beyond which was the road and the Navigation – when the merest flicker of movement caught her eye and made her turn her head. In that split second she saw a boy on the bank, moving slowly at first, then staggering clumsily until, even as Molly looked, he lost his footing altogether. With a pitiful, weak cry he fell sideways and down, slithering into the water and disappeared out of sight, his small white hand grasping at the air in an effort to save himself. By the time Molly had sprinted the few yards to where he had vanished into the water, there was no sign of him at all, save for an odd bubble here and there, and the scuff mark along the bank where he had fallen in.

In a minute Molly had slipped out of her frock and was launching herself into the air, towards the spot where she had seen the boy go down. Surprisingly the water struck cold as she sliced into it, but the deeper she went, the warmer it seemed. Molly was a strong swimmer, having learned the skill as naturally as she had learned to walk, and often she had scoured the canal bottom in search of the odd coin which might have rolled from a drunk's pocket. Yet in the murky depths a coin might sparkle and catch the daylight from above, whereas there was nothing Molly thought as she swam this way and that, that might sparkle on a drowning boy. Except perhaps the terror in his eyes.

Molly would not give up though. She would go on searching until her lungs came near to bursting. Straining her eyes, she noticed a patch of unusually thick reeds where the fish had been disturbed. Quickly, she kicked her strong legs and swam the short distance, and in a minute she had caught sight of the boy. Thank God, she thought, his lungs were not yet swamped, seeing a thin spasmodic trail of bubbles escaping from within the tangle of reeds. Quickly she had him freed and in her grasp, a rush of relief flooding her heart. At the same time, Molly was aware of the desperate urgency to get him to the surface.

On the bank, Molly pummelled and squeezed him, until he began coughing and spluttering. 'Good!' she told the wet and bedraggled boy, yanking him to a sitting position, before pulling on her frock, and hoisting him to his feet. 'Now, lean on me, because we've a fair way to go afore we come to the hut.'

Later, when his clothes were dried and he was full of Molly's hot tea and jam butties, the boy sat by the rusty stove which Molly had lit to thaw his bones. 'You're a silly bugger!' she chided him. 'What were you doing . . . wandering along the bank like that? Don't you know better?' She had little patience with such foolishness.

The boy gave no answer. He just kept his eyes fixed on the stove and began shivering again. He wasn't sure how to react. In fact, he had no idea *how* he came to be 'wandering along the bank'. He didn't even know his own name. All he knew was that he had found himself in an alley, then he had walked and walked until he came to the canal. It was all a nightmare to him, and he knew above all else that if it had not been for this scruffy girl with the big black eyes and sharp temper he would surely have drowned. But he did not want to speak to her, because he hurt all over, and he was afraid.

'Oh, I see . . . cat got your tongue, has it?' teased Molly. Then, as he bent his head away from her, she saw the deep gash and the hair still matted round it. 'When did *that* happen?' she asked, reaching forward on her stool to take a closer look. 'That's bad!' In a minute, she had gone to fill the pan and, while it boiled, she searched about for a clean piece of cloth with which to bathe the wound. Tearing a strip from the pillow-slip, she tested the water in the pan. Finding it warm enough, she drew the pan away and stood it on the stool. 'Keep still now. I don't want you struggling,' she instructed the boy. He did not move though, and nor did he protest because he felt lost and confused, but he had no intention of betraying his fears to a girl.

'Me and Sal . . . we never light this old stove, because it smokes like the billows and burns up more wood than we can find.' Molly kept up a banter of talk as she swabbed the gash on his head. She wished he would talk back, but she respected the way he must feel. He had suffered a nasty shock, she knew. But what puzzled her most was that the boy couldn't swim. Most children in these parts could swim before their legs were properly grown. That was another thing: Molly didn't think the boy came from here, or she would have remembered him. Yet she hadn't seen his face, not properly, because he kept avoiding her, turning his head away so she wouldn't get a good look at him. She supposed he must feel embarrassed at being rescued by a girl. Boys were like that, she knew. Strange though, how he couldn't swim. And he wasn't the usual sort of scruff because, although his clothes were tatty and probably smelt to high heaven before they got a ducking in the canal, his *hair* was properly cut, and his nails were *clean*. Strangest of all though, were his hands: so small and lily-white, it was plain he had never done any coal shovelling or hard work of any kind!

'Where do you come from?' she asked him now.

'And why were you stumbling along the bank, with such a terrible gash on your head?' A thought suddenly came to her. 'Did somebody *knock* you on the head?' That would account for why he was staggering like he was drunk. 'Is *that* it? Were you set on by somebody?' She was sure of it now. 'You ain't from these parts, are you?' Molly leaned forward as she spoke, hoping she might get a look at his face again, because she was growing more curious by the minute. But he deliberately turned his face from her. The things she was saying made him think, and the things that began creeping into his mind were too unpleasant to dwell on.

'All right then. You lie on the bed and rest awhile. When you're feeling stronger, just let yourself out and shut the door behind you. I've got to go and see about Sal's funeral.' She opened the door and threw out the remainder of the water from the pan. 'You don't have to tell me nothing,' she called to him. When she came back into the hut, the boy was lying on his side, with his back to her. 'You're a strange one,' she murmured, her gaze resting on his tousled dark hair, 'and no mistake!' For a long poignant moment, Molly kept her gaze fixed on him, thinking how she had found Sal in that very bed, not so long ago. Sal, who had always been there, drunk or sober, Molly's best friend. Now she was gone, and the more Molly thought about it, the more desolate she felt. Without her being conscious of it, the tears began filling her eyes, then spilling over to run down her face.

It was then that the boy turned to look at Molly. When he saw her crying, she quickly looked away and pretended to busy herself clearing away the pan and other things. Of a sudden, she was aware that he was

191

taking an interest in the tiny watch that hung forward from her neck as she stooped. 'I'll be on my way in a minute,' she said in a matter-of-fact voice. 'When I come back, I'll expect you to be gone.' When she straightened up to glance at him, he was still looking at her, his dark green eyes resting on her face, and Molly was riveted with shock. She *knew* him! How could she forget those emerald-green eyes and that particular way he had looked at her in the market place that day? Sal too had remarked on the boy's eyes. ''E put me in mind o' the little people . . . gave me a real nasty turn,' she had told Molly afterwards. She had told Molly something else as well: the boy was none other than Justice Crowther's *grandson!*

Molly was mesmerised as her own dark puzzled gaze bore into the boy's face. How could it be Justice Crowther's grandson? Molly began vaguely to recall snippets of what the shrew-like woman had told her only this very day. 'Justice Crowther's own grandson . . . after the wheels and hooves had gone over him, there wasn't much left, so they say.' How could it be then? How was it possible that the boy she had saved from drowning could also be the same boy? The answer was that he could *not*. Molly looked at his quiet face; she saw how clean and decent it was; she saw those eyes and that rich dark hair, cut in the way of a gentry; she remembered how clean his nails were, then how soft and white his hands. And she knew! Knew without a doubt that somehow there had been a trick played on Justice Crowther. She couldn't quite fathom it out, but she was certain of it. *This* boy was Justice Crowther's grandson, not the boy in the fancy togs who was run over by a coach and four. Something else was triggered off in Molly's mind. Something the shrew-like woman had said, to do with the undertaker remarking how the boy who was mangled 'had big coarse feet for a young gentry'. Of course he did, thought Molly now. Of course he did, because he *wasn't* a gentry, that was why!

'How did you come to be wandering along the canal bank?' she asked him now, coming closer to the bed. 'Did you run away? Who knocked you on the head? Somebody did, I'm thinking . . . because there ain't nothing in the water that could have done it.'

'I don't know . . . anything,' Edward Trent replied, meeting Molly's gaze and feeling certain he had seen her before. Of a sudden, he recalled disjointed images of himself sneaking out from a big house, and of running from the devil in a dark alley. But the more he tried to think, the more he became confused. 'I know *you* though . . . I'm sure of it. I've seen you somewhere . . . somewhere.' The pain in his eyes deepened as he struggled to remember.

'It's all right,' Molly assured him, becoming convinced of his identity by the refined tone of his voice and the fact that he had seen her somewhere before . . . in the market place, no doubt. 'You'll be fine . . . after you've rested. You've had a nasty knock on the head . . . and you nearly drowned. It's not surprising that you can't properly recall what happened. Don't you worry. Get some sleep, and you'll be fine, I promise.' A plan was forming in her mind. A daring plan that might be the way to pay for Sal's burial. But she'd have to be quick, or it might be too late.

'What's your name?' the boy asked, settling himself

into the bed as weariness came over him.

'Molly. I'm Sal Tanner's lass.' Molly felt a deal of pride as she told him that. But it was mingled with a deep and painful sense of loss, which betrayed itself in her dark eyes. The boy was quick to notice, and to recall that Molly had earlier remarked that she had to go and 'see about Sal's funeral'. His instincts told him not to talk of 'Sal', or outstay his welcome. 'I want to thank you for what you've done for me,' he said, 'if I can just rest awhile, I'll be gone and I won't be a burden, I promise.'

'That's right,' encouraged Molly, 'you rest, while I go about my business. But you don't need to hurry away.' If her plan was to work, the boy must be kept here. 'Old Sal used to give me a herbal drink when I was feeling under the weather and couldn't sleep. I'll get you a drop,' she told him. After a frantic search, she discovered Sal's gin bottle hidden inside the orange-box. Quickly mixing a measure of it with a drop of water and a sprinkle of sugar, she held it to the boy's lips. 'Here we are. Drink this and you'll sleep like a hedgehog in winter.'

When Molly was satisfied that he was in a deep contented slumber, she covered him over, took one of the shoes which had shrunk to his feet after the canal soaking, then went swiftly from the hut, shutting the door tight behind her. Glancing up to ensure that the window was left open for ventilation, she tucked the expensive shoe into the pocket of her frock and went at top speed along the bank.

Molly was not too proud of what she intended to do now, because she liked the boy. She thought him to be a cut above the other gentry she had come across, but she made herself recall an old saying of Sal's – one which she often used to excuse her more unsavoury activities: when needs must, the devil pays, was what Sal would claim in her own defence. It was what Molly told herself now, as she sped through Mill Hill and on towards the outlying fields. She had a rough idea that she was heading in the right direction. Anyway, Breck-leton House shouldn't be too difficult to find.

'Get away from here, yer little ruffian!' Cook had been summoned to the kitchen door by Molly's insistent knocking, and she was not too pleased at the sight of a filthy little urchin standing there. 'There's misery enough in this house today . . . wi'out us being both-ered by beggars!' She would have slammed the door in Molly's face, but when she was told, 'Justice Crowther's grandson *ain't* dead. *I've* got him!' Cook hesitated, just long enough for Molly to blurt out, 'He's got dark eyes the colour of emeralds . . . and he can't swim.'

'How do yer know *that*?' Cook demanded, inching the door open, yet not coming back out. 'An' when did a filthy little baggage the likes o' *you* see the colour of 'is eyes, eh?' There was no doubt she was intrigued, because it was true that the young master had never learned to swim. There had been arguments about it between his mother, who saw it as being unnecessary, and his father, who claimed that every boy should be given the opportunity to learn to swim, especially when he might follow in his father's footsteps and be a sailor. Martha Trent's reply had been a caustic one, 'I shall *never* let him be a sailor!' From there, the argument had raged on.

195

'How d'yer know all this?' insisted Cook, keeping her sizeable frame secure behind the door.

'I know . . . because he fell in the canal and I saved him from drowning,' replied Molly, beginning to take the shoe from her pocket. '*He* wasn't the one who was run over and killed. I reckon as it was another fellow altogether. I don't know if it were a rogue or a gentry, but it weren't Edward Trent, I'm telling you, missus. Because *I've* got Justice Crowther's grandson, hidden away and safe enough.' She brought the shoe with the shiny buckle from her pocket, and when Cook saw it, she nearly fainted. 'Oh, upon my word . . . it's the young master's boot!' she cried, flinging the door open and making a grab for it.

'Oh, no you don't!' warned Molly, immediately dodging backwards and remaining at a safe distance. 'I ain't giving this shoe to *nobody* . . . anyway, not till you fetch the lady of the house. Don't fetch the Justice, because I'll not tell *him* nothing! I'll only do business with the lady of the house.' Molly had never forgotten Sal's warning concerning Justice Crowther, and the very idea of being confronted by the fellow himself made her shiver in her boots.

'As it happens, yer little dirty baggage . . . there's only the mistress and the boy's mother here. The Justice is at the undertakers, making final arrangements.' She rolled her eyes upwards and made the sign of the cross on herself.

'In that case, he's making final arrangements for somebody else,' Molly reminded her, 'because I've got his grandson safe, I'm telling you. Now . . . if you'd be so kind as to fetch her ladyship?'

'You cheeky little madam!' snorted Cook. For two

pins she would have brought Thomas to see the little wretch off down the road, but there was too much in what the girl said. Cook felt it was more than her life was worth to ignore the evidence of the shoe and all. 'Wait here. I'll see if the mistress is interested in what you have to say . . . but let me warn you: if you're here to cause mischief, you'll be given every opportunity to explain it to the authorities!'

When the door swung to, leaving Molly staring at the grotesque brass gargoyle which served as a knocker, she put out her tongue at it. She went to the window, where she pulled herself up by the wall and sat on the deep stone window-ledge, swinging her skinny legs back and forth, and waited somewhat nervously for the lady of the house to emerge.

Molly did not have to wait long: no sooner had she settled herself than there came a flurry of activity at the kitchen door. 'Where is she?' came a woman's agitated voice. Then, as Agnes Crowther swept out on to the flag stones, one hand plucking the folds of her long taffeta skirt and the other waving loosely in the air, she caught sight of Molly, who quickly jumped down from the window-ledge. Molly's stomach turned nervous somersaults at the sight of this fancy lady, whose husband had the power to have her flayed alive. As Agnes Crowther approached, Molly backed away. 'Don't you come no nearer, missus,' she warned, 'if you try to grab me, I'll make a run for it and you won't see your lad again.'

'No!' Agnes Crowther stopped some short distance away, lifting her hand from her skirt and putting both palms up to Molly. 'It's all right . . . I won't come any nearer.' She gestured for Cook and the maid, Amy, to go back, saying, 'Make sure that my daughter is not disturbed. Let her sleep.' When the two women were out of sight Agnes Crowther turned her attention to Molly. 'Tell me all you know of my grandson . . . please.' Then, in a harsher tone, 'But be careful you tell me no lies, or you will live to regret it, I promise!' She then recovered her composure, stiffened her back and raised her two hands together in a posture of prayer, holding them close to her breast as she asked, 'What *do* you know? Cook tells me you don't believe it was Master Edward who was killed. What makes you say such a thing? The truth, girl. Out with it!'

Her courage returning, and with Sal's predicament paramount in her mind, Molly described how she had seen the boy stumble and fall into the canal. 'He would have drowned, missus . . . he *would*, if *I* hadn't saved him,' she assured Agnes Crowther, who merely nodded impatiently and bade her go on. Molly then explained how, in spite of the boy's clothes, she suspected that he was not an urchin off the streets. 'His nails were too clean, and his hands were too soft and white,' she said. After which she went into great detail regarding his appearance, how dark was his hair, and how deep-green his eyes. She told of the way he had spoken to her. 'Too *posh* by half! . . . And look here' – she snatched the shoe from the depths of her ragged frock – 'this is the boy's shoe!'

All the while Molly had been talking, Agnes Crowther had paid the closest attention, and the more she heard, the paler she became. When the shoe was brandished before her, she cried out and swayed as though she might faint, her posture of prayer broken as she put out an arm to grasp the wall for support. 'It *is*

Edward's shoe!' she gasped, her eyes fixed on the black ankle boot which had a small decorative buckle to the side. 'Oh . . . I had my suspicions all along that it was *not* my grandson lying there in the mortuary . . . but no one would listen. They were all quick to grieve. Too blinded by what they saw before them, and too easily led by what they were told.' Of a sudden she was moving forward, her face a study in compassion, and her arm outstretched as though to take the shoe from Molly's grasp. 'Where is he . . . this boy? You must take me to him at once!' she urged.

But Molly was no fool. She had not forgotten the purpose which had brought her here, nor had she forgotten what a fearfully powerful family she was dealing with. 'Not so fast, your ladyship,' she told her, teasing the shoe away and taking a step backward. 'I *will* take you to where your grandson is, but it will cost you a pretty penny.'

'You scoundrel!' retorted Agnes Crowther. 'I shouldn't be at all surprised if you and your kind hadn't arranged this whole dreadful affair!' The fire had returned to Agnes Crowther's eyes, and for a brief moment Molly's courage began to waver. But it took only a thought of where Sal was and where she might end up to restore her flagging spirit. 'No, I didn't!' she retorted indignantly. 'I might be a thief when things get desperate . . . but I ain't no crook!'

'What is it you want then?' demanded Agnes Crowther. 'If this boy really *is* my grandson . . . and there is no real proof of that . . . you may depend that Justice Crowther will reward you handsomely.'

'I won't do no dealings with *him*!' Molly told her. 'I need two guineas . . . it ain't for me, neither.'

'So! . . . There *is* somebody else. Somebody who has put you up to coming here and telling lies.'

'There's nobody else, missus. The two guineas is to pay for a proper burial for . . . well, that don't matter none. You just pay me now, and I'll fetch the boy from where he's hidden.'

'No. I must come with you, or how can I trust you?'

When Molly saw that Agnes Crowther was adamant, she reluctantly agreed to a compromise. 'You take a carriage to the warehouse at the end of Stephen Street in Mill Hill . . . and I'll fetch the boy to you, within the hour. Mind you . . . if I so much as catch sight of anybody but just yourself, I swear you'll not get him back! And I want paying *now*.'

'Half now, and the remainder when I see that the boy really *is* my grandson.'

So it was agreed. With one guinea safe in the palm of her hand, in exchange for the shoe, Molly set off at a run to rouse the boy from his slumber. Still not fully convinced but filled with hope and excitement, Agnes Crowther hurried indoors to don her cloak and bonnet, emerging some ten minutes later to climb into the carriage, with Cook's words ringing in her ears: 'Yer don't want to get yer hopes too high on the word of a street urchin, m'lady. Set the authorities on the little baggage . . . they'll soon find out what she's up to!'

Agnes Crowther's reply was to remind her of her place. 'Make sure you leave my daughter resting. And, if the master returns in my absence, you are to say nothing of my errand. If it turns out to be a trick I myself will inform Justice Crowther to root the girl out; but . . . if by some miracle my grandson really *is* safe . . . bringing the boy home will speak for itself.'

★ ★ ★

Some time later, after Molly had successfully roused Edward Trent enough to walk him along the towpath and down Angela Street towards Stephen Street, Agnes Crowther was alerted by her driver Thomas. 'This looks like them now, m'lady,' he said, leaning down from his lofty seat and pointing a finger towards the two children approaching. Being a woman not easily given to Christian values, Agnes Crowther had never set great store by prayer and rarely indulged in it with much heart. But when she reached her head out of the carriage window, the sight of those two small and bedraggled figures coming towards her brought tears to her eyes. When she stepped down from the carriage and waited, as Molly had insisted, she actually uttered a heartfelt prayer. Then, as they came ever closer, and she kept her anxious eyes on the boy, the familiar shape began to grow, the manner of his walk, his hair, she began to recognise him as her own grandson. Forgetting that she had promised to stay by the carriage, Agnes Crowther began walking towards them, completely oblivious of the one or two people who hurried by to go about their business.

When Molly saw that Agnes Crowther had gone back on her word, she was unsure as to what to do. The boy was leaning so heavily on her shoulder that, were she to let him go, he would slump to the floor. Besides which, she *must* collect the other guinea. So she stood still and waited. When Agnes Crowther saw this, she hurried her steps until she was almost running. When in a moment she was on them and the boy looked up at her through hazy eyes, she threw out her arms and wrapped them about him. 'Edward . . . oh, thank

God!' For Molly, who had never witnessed such humanity in the gentry, it was a humbling scene. 'I *told* you he was safe, didn't I?' she said. 'He would have drowned if it weren't for me.' She mustn't let them forget that, she thought, *nor* that she was still owed a guinea!

When Thomas had gently lifted the boy into the carriage, Agnes Crowther kept her promise to Molly. 'I don't know whether you've played a guilty or an innocent part in this business,' she said sternly, at the same time handing over the guinea, 'but you kept your word to me . . . and I shall keep mine to you.' Then, before Molly turned and took to her heels, she was given a warning: 'Stay out of Justice Crowther's way. I have no doubt that he would insist on knowing more than you have told me.'

'Goodbye, my Sal.' Molly was on her knees in the churchyard, her small grubby hands lovingly arranging the flowers over the mound of earth. 'I'll miss you . . . and I'll never forget you, not as long as I live.' Her face ran wet with tears, and her sad dark eyes betrayed the pain which racked her heart.

When, reluctantly, she left the churchyard, Molly was glad at least that she had been able to keep her promise to Sal, because how could she rest, knowing that Sal, her one and only friend in this world, was not lying in properly consecrated ground? Now the priest had said the right words over Sal, there had even been a hymn sung in church for her, and Molly's heart was once more at peace as she wended her way home on that wind-blown Tuesday evening.

As she rounded the canal bank and made towards

the hut, Molly thought briefly about the boy, Edward Trent. There was talk on the wharf of how some ruffians had kidnapped him, then held him to ransom, only setting him free when a great sum of money was paid. It was also rumoured that Justice Crowther had vowed to hunt down the 'villains responsible', to bring them to justice and to punish them with the severest penalty that the law would allow. According to the gossips there was a bad rift between the Justice and his wife, Agnes, because of the whole sordid business; the boy himself, though greatly improved, was still under medical supervision and therefore protected from being more closely questioned on the matter. As for his mother, Martha Trent, she was as determined that the 'kidnappers' be apprehended and made to pay, as was her father. Silas Trent, Martha's husband, was away on the high seas, and knew nothing yet of the narrow escape his son had had. As for the lad in the fancy togs, nobody ever found out who he was or where he belonged, because never a soul came forward to claim him, and it wasn't surprising, they said, in view of all the fuss he'd caused, as well as the puzzling fact that he had been found wearing togs that were the property of none other than Justice Crowther's grandson.

Molly had heard all of these rumours, but had paid them little heed. It was a known fact that folks did love to exaggerate.

By the time Molly had brewed herself a pot of tea and finished off the last crust of bread, together with a wedge of cheese, it was already twilight. Later, when she had strip-washed at the bowl and pulled on the well-worn cream-coloured shift which Sal had brought home one day as a surprise, Molly slipped the bolt on the door and knelt by the makeshift bed, her hands together, eyes closed tight and her young heart flooded with memories of Sal. 'Take care of her, please, Lord,' she murmured. 'I know she did bad things sometimes, but she weren't really bad, and she always took good care of me. Sal always said I shouldn't ask for too much in my prayers, Lord . . . but I'd be very grateful if you could please help me to find my own mam and dad. I don't know where to start, because all I've got is this little timepiece.' Here she withdrew the tiny watch from round her neck and gazed at it fondly. 'I don't know what the words say, and I don't know where it came from, but I *must* have a mammy somewhere, Lord,' she went on, 'and I would dearly love to find her.'

It suddenly struck Molly that even if she did have a mammy somewhere and the Lord only knew how it would gladden Molly's heart to see her, there was always the chance that her mammy didn't want her, because hadn't Sal described how she had found the bundle in the street. 'An' it were you . . . left by the little people.' If she *had* been left in the street, Molly knew it wasn't by no 'little people', but by somebody else. And if that somebody else was her own mammy, then it followed that she didn't want her own child, and, if she didn't want it *then*, when it was a tiny helpless newborn, then it was certain that she wouldn't want it now.

The more Molly thought about it, the more desolate she became until, feeling suddenly exhausted and more lonely than ever, she climbed into bed. Life was a funny old thing, she told herself, deliberately shutting out the world and drifting thankfully into sleep. Until this very minute, Molly had not realised just how tired she was. 'Tomorrow,' she promised herself, 'I'll go down to the wharf and see if I can get a regular job.' The thought cheered her no end.

When Molly awoke, it was amidst a barrage of noise and confusion. She knew at once that it wasn't yet morning, because the inside of the hut was dark, except for an arrow of moonlight coming in through the tiny window. 'Who's that?' she shouted, her heart pounding as she swung her legs out of bed and began frantically searching for her boots. There was somebody out there. She could hear all manner of noises, like rats scrabbling to get in, or maybe it was ruffians who knew she was here on her own! In a minute, she had found her boots, and was hurriedly pulling the first one on. 'I've got a shot gun!' she yelled, hoping that might send them scurrying away. 'If you come near me, I'll blow your bloody head off!' Oh, how she wished Sal were here.

Suddenly, two things happened, and Molly was lost. The hut was filled with light directed in through the window and, before Molly could think what to do, the door burst open and in rushed several large figures, at least two of them carrying huge lamps whose halo of light swung eerily from wall to wall. 'Get out of here!' yelled Molly, her hand raised threateningly, and the boot she held aimed at the figure who stealthily approached her, while the others remained both still and silent. She could not see his face, but the tall and grotesque silhouette he made struck fear into her heart. He lifted his arm and made a sign with his hand, a beckoning gesture to call the others on. In a minute,

Molly was surrounded, the lights all seeking out her face, and the silhouette taking on the shape of a man, a man who was unusually large, with a profusion of iron-grey hair covering the lower half of his features, and blue eyes that were both piercing and hateful. When Molly looked up, she instantly recognised the man, and she was in mortal terror. It was the same man who had talked with Gabe Drury before that poor soul was found floating in the canal; the same man whose wallet she had stolen, and was made to return when Sal discovered its awful identity. Molly would never forget how fearful Sal had been on that night: 'Justice Crowther would search far and wide to find you,' Sal had warned her and, instinctively, Molly also had been fearful of him.

Boots or no boots, Molly decided the only thing to do now was to make a run for it. With a cry of 'You ain't taking *me*!' she flung her boot at one of the lamps, and made a frantic dash towards the door. Her swift reflex appeared to have caught the intruders off guard. 'Stop her, you fools!' yelled Caleb Crowther, himself swinging out an arm to catch her as she ducked and dived out of his reach.

Being thin and wiry, Molly was also quick on her feet and she might have made it to freedom, were it not for the constable outside. As she rushed out of the door, he blocked her path and caught her by the shoulders, afterwards holding her aloft by the scruff of her neck with her feet kicking furiously in the air. 'Let me be!' she screeched, lashing out at him with her two fists; 'I ain't done nothing wrong! . . . I *ain't*, I tell you!' She was cruelly silenced by a spiteful blow to the side of her head, as her pursuer stepped from the hut.

'Know when to keep your mouth shut, urchin.' Caleb Crowther took a lamp from the constable nearby, and holding it up high, he looked deep and long into Molly's tearful face. 'Robbery, violence . . . abducting my grandson? . . . You call this "nothing"?' His voice was soft and smooth as velvet, but at the same time intense and terrifying. 'Rogues have *hanged* for less,' he told her, 'but we've got you and, no doubt, we'll soon have your accomplices.'

'I didn't do *any* of those things,' Molly protested, angry that she should be accused. 'He would have drowned if it weren't for me. I found him in time . . . and he already had a gash on his head. Whoever it was that attacked him . . . it weren't *me*!' She was lashing out with her legs and arms. 'I only fetched him back 'cause I needed Sal's burial money. If I hadn't fetched him back, he would have run away . . . he told me! But I can't blame him . . . wanting to run away from *you*. I should have let the poor little bugger go!' Of a sudden, Molly realised she had gone too far and let her tongue run away with her. Sal was right when she always used to warn that 'yer too quick-tempered by 'arf! That tongue o' yourn'll get yer in trouble one o' these fine days, my gal!' She gave up her efforts at struggling, and hung in the constable's fists like a rag-doll. 'I did save him from drowning,' she finished lamely.

'Bind her well,' instructed Caleb Crowther, his face a study in rage. 'Let her escape, man . . . and you won't see daylight for years.'

While the constables set about securing Molly's flailing figure, Caleb Crowther went back inside the hut, his mind working feverishly and his determination to be rid of that dark-eyed urchin made stronger by what he had just seen. His earlier suspicions had been undeniably confirmed, and he was deeply bothered by it. Just now, when he had lifted the lamp, its light had picked out a glistening object on the urchin's neck; he was convinced that the object was the very same watch that had belonged to Emma Grady's mother, Mary. Mary, whom he had loved beyond the grave, whom he still craved for in his sleeping hours, and who had suffered the ultimate penalty for deceiving him with another man.

He recalled having seen that same urchin before, on the very night he had talked to Gabe Drury and, even more disturbing, he now suspected that she might have seen his face; although of course he had kept well hidden, and there was no proof whatsoever of his having seen Gabe Drury. *Who* would listen to a street urchin, already implicated in all manner of the worst possible crimes? No, he was safe enough, he was sure. But that wasn't all, because he strongly suspected that this girl, who bore the same dark features as the bargee, Marlow Tanner, was the child of that man . . . and borne by the woman whom everyone believed to be his niece, Emma Grady! The sight of that watch, which had been Emma's mother's and was still in Emma's possession at the time of her arrest, left him with only one conclusion. The brat was Emma's offspring, and as such represented a threat in the long-term. A threat which was every bit as irritating as Emma Grady herself, and one which he did not intend to tolerate under any circumstances. Here he smiled to himself, as he drew out a small tin of matches from his waistcoat pocket. Fortune was sometimes a wonderful ally, especially when it offered the perfect opportunities to be rid of one's enemies, he mused.

Striking the match alive, Caleb Crowther waited awhile, until the bright yellow flame was rearing and spitting. Then, with the smile deepening his features, he dropped the lighted match on to the mattress, afterwards going to the door and watching while the mattress gave up a fierce and rosy glow.

Before they dragged her round the corner and away from her beloved canal bank, Molly glanced back, towards the hut which had been her and Sal's home. When she saw the flames and smoke reaching to the night sky, she was filled with shock and horror. In that moment, she saw the look of satisfaction on Caleb Crowther's face, and for the first time in her young life, she felt real hatred in her heart. When, in a moment, they were bundling her into the waiting waggon and her sobbing was pitiful to hear, Molly knew that she would never forget this night. Nor would she ever forget, or forgive, the man they called the Justice.

Caleb Crowther kept a close eye as Molly was ushered into the jail-cart along with other miscreants who had been dragged from their beds this night. He had not forgotten the delicate watch around her neck, or his intention to take it discreetly from her at the first opportunity. But he must not be seen in the act of securing it from her, or that might well arouse too much interest.

'What did the buggers get *you* for, eh?' Molly felt herself being nudged by the person thrust in next to her, and when she turned to see who it was that was so interested in her, she was pleasantly surprised to be faced with a pair of smiling eyes and as handsome a fellow as she'd ever seen. Besides which, he appeared to be not much older than Molly himself, about four-teen she reckoned.

'They've accused me of robbery, and of abducting Justice Crowther's grandson,' she replied, always being one to tell the truth when it mattered. Though, if Molly thought the fellow might be shocked at the charges against her, she was not wrong.

'*What?* Robbery and abduction . . . and the grand-son of the Justice, no less!' Of a sudden, he was rocking with laughter, and so were the other two captives in the waggon. 'Yer having me on, ain't yer?' he chuckled. 'Why! There ain't two-pennorth of yer, and that's a fact!'

Molly would have been amused too, if it weren't for the fact that it was she who was in this terrible predicament, and not him. 'It's all right you laughing,' she said, 'but *I* don't think it's so funny!'

'Aw . . . it ain't so bad, you'll see.' He had lowered his voice, so the two accompanying constables might not hear. 'In a few minutes we'll be crossing Mill Hill bridge at the top of Parkinson Street. The horses don't like it, on account of it being narrow and having a sharpish turn. They'll slow right down, you mark my words . . . *that's* when we'll make a run fer it.'

'Stop that whispering!' thundered the constable seated at the front, and for a moment everything was quiet.

'Are yer game?' insisted the fellow, nudging Molly again and whispering close to her ear.

It only took Molly a second to give her reply, because, truth be told, this handsome likeable fellow might be her only chance to get away. What was more, she had taken a real liking to him. 'What d'you want

210

me to do?' she asked, then sat rigid and silent when the constable leaned forward to see who was being so insolent as to go on whispering in the face of his instruction.

When, in order to distract the constable's attention, Molly developed a seizure of coughing, the fellow beside her murmured quietly, 'Just be ready, that's all!'

Molly knew the Mill Hill bridge well, and she kept her eyes glued to the open slats in the wooden cage, constantly looking ahead for when they would pass the bottom of Stephen Street, on the approach to the hump-backed bridge. The journey seemed painstakingly slow as the cart wheels picked their way over the small uneven cobbles. Molly's heart was thumping fearfully, because she knew that if the escape bid were unsuccessful, both she *and* the handsome fellow would be made to regret the effort. Yet, in spite of the instincts which warned her always to be on her guard, Molly trusted the lad sitting next to her, and she had unusual confidence in him. Wasn't it strange, she thought, how sometimes a body warmed to a stranger without ever knowing why.

As the waggon approached the bridge, the horses instinctively slowed down.

'What's the delay?' called Caleb Crowther, leaning out of the carriage window behind. He sounded highly impatient.

'It's the bridge, sir,' replied the constable in the rear of the waggon as he climbed out to monitor the situation more closely. 'The horses . . . they don't like it, being so narrow and sharp, like.'

In a minute, Caleb Crowther was out of the carriage and striding towards the waggon, which at this point

211

was stationary, the horses having come to a standstill. 'Drive them on, man!' he roared. 'Don't let them have their head!' At the front of the waggon, the driver could be heard cracking his whip and threatening the terrified animals with all kinds of terrible fates.

'Quick gal . . . get ready!' The young fellow took hold of Molly's bound hands, gripping them tightly as he urged in a frantic whisper, 'Wait till the Justice has his back to us . . . then *jump!* Run for all you're worth and don't let go of me.' No sooner had he spoken the last word than Caleb Crowther engaged the constable in a row, turning his back to the waggon and demanding the fellow's explanation as to why he had come this way at all, instead of going straight down Parkinson Street and out by way of Havelock. Not being as familiar with the Mill Hill area as was the constable, he was unaware that the dark narrow viaduct at the bottom of Parkinson Street would have sent the horses into even more of a blind panic.

'Now!' the fellow cried, and Molly felt herself yanked from her seat and propelled forward at a furious pace. Before she knew quite what was happening, the two of them were launched from the waggon and sailing through the air. 'Run, me darling!' the fellow yelled, as their feet crunched to the ground. Suddenly, all hell was let loose. The constable shouted, 'The prisoners are escaping!' The horses bolted in fright, and the constable still in the waggon, together with the remaining hapless prisoners, was flung from side to side as the waggon went careering over the bridge, with the first constable taking up chase.

Molly scrambled to her feet, with her hands still securely held by her companion. She laughed out loud at all the commotion and thought the whole escapade to be a real treat, until, with a cry of rage, Caleb Crowther darted forward to grab her, viciously, by the neck, at which point she felt herself being tugged in separate directions as the fellow and the Justice pulled with equal determination. It only took a few seconds, but to Molly it seemed like a lifetime before the fellow gave an extra tug and she was yanked free. Unfortunately, she felt the precious timepiece ripped from about her neck as she sprang forward close on the fellow's heels. But there was no going back. The uppermost thought in her mind at that moment was that she must run like the wind, until safe out of harm's way. Behind them they could hear the constables' whistles piercing the night air.

When at last the fellow brought himself and Molly to a standstill at the bottom of Myrtle Street, they were both coughing and wheezing, gasping for air and dangerously unsteady on their legs. Molly truly believed that she would never walk again.

It was a long and painful few minutes before either of them could get enough breath to speak. It was Molly who recovered first. 'He took it . . . that awful Justice broke the chain and took my timepiece.' She felt desolate.

'Timepiece? What . . . yer mean a pocket watch?' The fellow seemed surprised that a scruffy girl should keep something as useless as a 'timepiece'. 'Aw, it don't matter none, gal. Who cares about it, eh? I'll get yer another.' He discarded the binding which had secured Molly's wrist and watched with curiosity while Molly gathered together the bits of broken chain which had tangled about her neck. 'Steal it, did yer? Why didn't yer sell it, then? It ain't no use round yer neck, is it?'

'I *didn't* steal it!' Molly retorted. 'It belonged to *me* . . . ever since I was born.' Now she would never find her real mam and dad. 'There were *words* on it,' she told him in a tearful voice.

'Words? . . . What did they say?'

'I don't know,' replied Molly, 'but I would have found out one day.'

'Yer mean yer can't *read*?' He was suddenly proud of himself. 'I learned ter read when they put me and me mam in the workhouse . . . after the old fella ran away. The beadle made all us children say our prayers and learn ter read. Then he threw me out on the street when my mam died.' He seemed momentarily lost in thought. 'Was it worth a bob or two . . . that watch o' yours?'

But Molly didn't want to discuss it. It was too painful. 'What's your name?' she asked instead.

'Jack . . . Jack-the-lad they calls me; what's yours?'

'Molly . . . Tanner,' came the hesitant reply, because Molly had never used the name 'Tanner' before. She had only ever been known as 'Molly . . . Sal's lass'.

At once the fellow's face broke into a wide and attractive grin, and, in the light from the street gas-lamp, Molly saw that his eyes were a warm shade of brown, and his teeth were surprisingly white and even. 'I like your name . . . Molly,' he said, chucking her under the chin and making a cheeky suggestive wink, and I like *you* . . . I reckon yer a real good-looker, with that coal-black hair and them big midnight eyes. You'll do for me,' he said boldly.

'Hmph! You've got a bloody nerve,' Molly told him sternly, thinking he was one of them certain 'charmers' that Sal was always warning her against.

'I have! You're right, Molly gal. I have got a bloody nerve, and I'll tell yer some'at else . . . I'm gonna *marry* yer just as soon as ever I can!' Then, before Molly could get her breath, he took her by the hand, pulled her towards him and planted a loud hearty kiss on her mouth. 'Yep,' he said, shaking his head and drawing his lips together, 'you'll do fer me, Molly gal! First though . . . we've to steal yer some togs, 'cause I ain't having my future missus wandering the streets in her nightshift.'

Molly bit back the caustic retort which rose to her lips. With his warm, strong hand clasped over hers, and the feel of his kiss still burning on her mouth, it did seem peevish to be so ungrateful. Besides which, she had a warm, contented feeling inside that even the thought of losing Sal, or being hunted down by the Justice . . . or even losing her precious timepiece . . . couldn't spoil. Molly liked him. She *really* liked him, this 'Jack-the-lad'. 'Where we going?' she asked as they trudged along.

'Never you mind, darling,' came the reply, with a comforting squeeze of his hand. 'We'll make a good few miles before daybreak . . . leave Blackburn town behind and go where the buggers'll never find us.' He stopped and turned to look at her. 'That's a fault o' mine,' he said, with surprising shyness; 'me mam allus said I were a bossy bugger. What I want ter know, Molly gal, is . . . them plans o' mine, how do they sound ter you? Do they suit you?'

Molly returned his warm, quiet smile, and when she

215

spoke it was with a song in her heart. 'Whatever you say, Jack,' she told him. For a while, he simply looked at her, his smiling brown eyes reaching into her trembling young heart. 'Oh yes, Molly gal,' he said at length, 'you'll do fer me!'

As she followed him, not knowing where and not really caring, Molly felt comfortable in his presence. Oh, but her precious timepiece. She opened the palm of her hand and glanced down at the dainty mangled chain with its pretty petal fastener. 'Don't you fret, Molly lass,' came Jack's voice in her ear, ''cause I'll mend that for yer. And I shall keep me eyes open for a new watch along the way.' Molly thanked him. But her heart was sore at the tragic loss of that watch. How will I ever find my mam now, she wondered with a stab of regret. If you're listening up there, Sal . . . have a word with your 'little people'. Happen they'll know what to do. She laughed in warm memory of Sal's antics. Then, with softly spoken words, she murmured, 'You shouldn't have left me, Sal . . . you shouldn't have left me.'

Part Three

Australia 1876

Always Searching

The times I have dreamed,
The dreams I have known,
Will stay within my heart.
I will cherish them
And cherish you,
Loathing the miles
That keep us apart.

J.C.

Chapter Eight

'Where are you bound for, mate?' The handsome dark-haired sailor swung his knapsack to the ground, glad to be relieved of its cumbersome weight, even though the August day was one of the coolest he had known. The breeze blowing inland held the threat of rain. 'Captain Trent, isn't it?' he asked of the sturdy looking figure with quiet brown eyes and military moustache who was making his way down the gang-plank towards him.

'That's right . . . Silas Trent's the name.' He fixed the sailor in his sight, noting at once how able-bodied and pleasant the fellow seemed. He also sensed something very sad, or lonely, in his countenance. When he dropped to a level footing with him, he took the hand which was outstretched and, closing it in his own strong fingers, he shook it warmly. 'This is my ship, the *Stirling*,' he said, inclining his head sideways. Then, with a laugh he added, 'My wife, Martha . . . she accuses me of being in love with the old hulk.'

'She's no hulk,' remarked the sailor, envyingly roving his dark eyes over the ship's lines and noting that she was as good a barque as he'd seen in a long time. 'She's a fine vessel. You're a lucky fellow, Captain . . . and owner, I take it?'

'That right. And yes . . . she *is* a "fine vessel". The

219

last of a grand sailing fleet built up with sweat and blood by my own father, and left to me when he passed on. Unfortunately I've come on harder times than he ever witnessed . . . fiercer competition, and capital finance being that much harder to acquire. It's the larger lines who call the tune now . . . They're the ones who get first crack at the best cargoes. On top of which, all the experienced crews are lured away by better wages.' He shook his head and thoughtfully stroked his 'tache, before saying in a quieter tone, 'It's been two years since I've seen my wife and son . . . Edward's going on sixteen years old now, away at school he is. I'm glad to say he's a better bookworm than I'll ever be. It would have been grand though, if he had the sea in his blood, like me, and his grandfather before him. But he's not interested . . . wants to be a doctor, he says. Well, each to his own, I expect. My lad had a nasty experience a while back . . . set on by some ruffians and very nearly drowned in the process. It left its mark on his mind, I dare say. All the same, I intend to build my father's fleet up again . . . it's a promise I've made myself.'

The dark-eyed sailor smiled, a dashing, gypsy-like smile, when all the sadness went from his face and only the eyes betrayed an inner conflict. 'We all make ourselves promises, Cap'n,' he said; 'only some of us don't have wives and children to go home to. I do have a sister, though . . . and I've promised myself that I won't go back to her empty-handed. I'll make my fortune, I'm sure of it.' He laughed out loud. 'The only thing is . . . it's taking a bit longer than I thought! Yet, if I went home now . . . I wouldn't be going altogether empty-handed.'

'Looking to sign on, are you?'

'I am. I've just come in on the *Augustus* . . . see there?' He pointed to the three-masted barque berthed alongside. 'I've finished a three-year stint with her . . . Calcutta out of Melbourne mostly . . . wool and sandalwood. The skipper landed a good contract from one of the big traders.'

Silas Trent knew of the ship. It belonged to the Firth Line and was one of four. 'I know that well enough,' he said, wincing. 'That was the very contract I was chasing when I came out here. Why aren't you staying with her?' He was curious to know.

'She's making ready for England. I'm not about to go back yet.'

'Then you won't want to come aboard here either, because Liverpool is where I'm bound. Liverpool and good old England . . . first tide in the morning; we're already battened down and the last of the crew are due back any minute.' When he saw the disappointment on the sailor's face, he pointed to a clipper which was lying off shore. 'You might try the *Linesman* out there. I believe she's headed for Swedish waters.'

The sailor shook his head and swung up the knapsack to his shoulder, saying, 'No luck there, I'm afraid. She already has a full crew . . . I made enquiries about that one soon as ever I came off the *Augustus*.'

'What are your plans then?'

'A jug of ale and a good night's sleep at the tavern. Like as not I'll get me a ship on the morrow. Good day to you, Cap'n.'

Silas Trent nodded his head and touched the neb of his cap as he watched the sailor walk along the jetty and round the corner towards the inn, thinking that the fellow was not the usual coarse type of sailor he'd come across. When, out of the corner of his eye, he caught sight of his first officer returning with the authorised papers, he gave him his full attention. 'Everything in order?' he asked.

The officer nodded before making a gesture after the sailor whom he had seen leaving. 'Taking him on, are we?'

'Unfortunately no . . . we're one man short and could have done with that fellow. But he won't be bound for England.'

'Aye, and you couldn't have done better than him if you'd searched from one end of Australia to the other. He's a good man.'

'You know the fellow, then?'

'Did a year's stint on the *Eleanor* with him about four years back. He goes by the name of Tanner . . . Marlow Tanner. Pity he won't sail for England with us, but he's intent on making his fortune.' He laughed softly, but not with malice. 'Fine bloody chance o' that, I'm thinking. If he ain't made his fortune these past fifteen years, there's not much chance of him making it at all!'

'Marlow Tanner, you say?' Silas Trent was racking his brain. He knew the name, but where? . . . When?

It was some time later when Silas Trent recalled the name of Marlow Tanner, and where he had come across it before. Wasn't *that* the fellow who, according to Martha, had been 'Emma Grady's downfall'. Of course! By all accounts, Emma was in love with Marlow Tanner, even after she was married off to Gregory Denton, and he was crazy in love with her, so much

that he had left England on the news of her marriage. A terrible and riveting thought crossed his mind
as he continued on his way. How unpredictable the
hand of Fate was, to bring Marlow Tanner to the very
place where Emma lived, and neither of them aware of
it.

He felt himself to be in a great predicament for, even
on this very evening, he was heading for the house on
Phillimore Street where Emma lived with her husband,
Roland Thomas. Since her marriage to him some eight
years back, Emma had expanded the firm of Thomas
Trading Company beyond the boundaries of Australia,
with shipments of wool, sandalwood and other cargoes
being commissioned to the likes of him. She had
worked hard, he knew. Who didn't know of her
admirable progress in the trading world? The results of
her determination and the incessant ambition which
drove her to succeed were most evident in the house on
Phillimore Street, a grand, white-painted place, with
impressive well-kept gardens and massive pillars fronting the main verandah. But for all that, Emma was
neither happy nor contented. She had made a comfortable home for her husband, who, following a bad fall
from the loft in his old shop, was unfortunately confined to a bath chair. He was a good man, but, like
Emma, he kept quiet in his sorrow. He had never really
come to terms with the loss of his beloved first wife, or
his guilt arising from it. Added to that was the fact of
his crippled legs which cruelly robbed him of his
freedom and dignity. Then there was the tragedy of his
son, Foster Thomas. His only son, who, because of his
rakish and deceitful nature, had forced his father to
throw him out of the house on the very eve of his

mother's funeral. To this day, Roland Thomas had never forgiven him.

Emma's discontent stemmed from three things: the fact that her husband's state of health prevented her from returning to England, where she had long planned to confront her old enemies and seek out those who had loved her; the pain of always remembering how she had lost her one and only child; and lastly the futile love she carried in her heart for the child's father, Marlow Tanner.

Here, Silas Trent paused in his thoughts. Should he tell Emma that the man she craved was no further away from her than the inn at the docks? Or would it be a cruel and spiteful thing for her to know? Silas Trent decided against telling her. He would not be the one to cause her unnecessary heartbreak, because even though his heart still belonged to his wife Martha he was more than a little in love with Emma himself.

As usual, Emma was delighted to see him, but as she swept across the marquetry floor of the spacious entrance hall, looking slim and attractive in a bustled dress of burgundy, her rich auburn hair swept back with two mother-of-pearl combs, it struck him how pale she looked and how subdued her strong grey eyes.

'Oh, Silas, I'm glad you came. I thought you might stay on the ship this evening. I know you intend sailing on the first tide.' Emma's lonely heart was always gladdened at the sight of him. In this last year she had found a friend in Silas Trent, and whenever they were together, she would ask him of England and the way it was when he had left. And always, he would avoid talking of his wife, and of his father-in-law, Caleb Crowther, because he knew of their callous treatment of Emma, and he felt ashamed. Emma, too, avoided the subject, in order to spare him embarrassment. But she revelled in news of his son, Edward, and had been horrified to hear of the unfortunate incident which had befallen him, the news of which was relayed to Silas in some distant port. Silas had not been home since, and Emma knew how very much he was looking forward to it. 'Just think,' she told him now, leading him towards the library, where she regularly spent many long hours at work, 'if you're not laid over too long at Singapore, you'll be home well in time for Christmas.' She added softly, 'Oh, how I envy you!'

Silas had not missed her gentle utterance, nor the longing behind it, and his heart went out to her. 'How is Roland, Emma?'

'He's fine,' she said, gesturing for him to help himself to a tot of rum from a tray on the sturdy oak dresser. When he had poured himself a drink he extended the sherry decanter towards her. Emma nodded and then gratefully took the half-filled glass which he handed to her.

When they were both seated in brown leather armchairs situated either side of a large, rather ornate dark-oak desk, Emma told him, 'Roland is no worse . . . and he's no better. But there are times when he has these unpredictable moods of deep depression and, to be honest, I don't know how to handle him.' Emma deplored her husband's awful predicament and was determined to do all she could to make life comfortable for him. But it was not easy. It was never easy.

'You'll cope, Emma,' she was told now. 'But you're driving yourself too hard . . . you know that, don't you?'

Emma knew it. She knew also that, without her work, she would grow slowly crazy. 'My work keeps me sane,' she said, sipping the sherry but hating the taste of it. 'Talking of which, I have a proposition to put to you. I've thought on it long and hard. Roland and I have discussed it, and as usual he's left the decision to me.'

'A proposition, Emma?' Silas Trent was intrigued. 'What kind of proposition?'

'One that will benefit us all.' Emma put her sherry glass on the desk before getting to her feet, where she walked slowly and deep in thought around to the back of her chair. Here, she put her two hands on the chair and leaned forward to look at Silas with a direct and friendly gaze. 'As you know, the Thomas Trading Company handles increasingly vast quantities of goods . . . all manner of goods pass through our hands every working day. In these past two years alone, we've doubled the business. Eighteen months ago we invested heavily in the running of pearl, wool and sandalwood . . . prize cargoes for which we commissioned ships such as yours, to carry far and wide . . . we're expanding all the time, you know that.'

'Everybody who's involved in shipping or merchandise knows it.' Silas Trent was already following Emma's thinking, but he dared not let himself believe it. 'What exactly are you getting at, Emma . . . how does all of this involve *me*? Apart from being fortunate enough to secure a cargo from you wherever possible, and being well paid for it too,' he gently laughed, 'though I do believe I'm honest and reliable enough to deserve it!'

'You have certainly proved that, Silas . . . in fact, if that *wasn't* the case, I wouldn't be talking to you now, and I would not be about to offer you a stake in a new venture. Perhaps even a partnership later on, if all goes well.' Her steel-grey eyes never left his face.

'*Partnership!*' Of a sudden he was on his feet.

There came the sound of a voice from the doorway. 'That's right, Trent, a partnership . . . of sorts and all in good time.'

Seeing that it was her husband being pushed in his bath chair by the nurse hired to care for him, Emma went quickly to his side. 'Mr Thomas!' she gently reproached him. As always Silas Trent was amused to hear Emma address her husband as 'Mr Thomas'. Not once, since discovering that Emma Grady as was, was now Mrs Thomas, had he heard her call him by the name of Roland. It was an odd thing, but apparently accepted by them both. 'I thought you were sleeping.' Emma had given strict instructions that he was not to be disturbed.

'Couldn't sleep,' returned Roland Thomas, affectionately patting Emma's hand which rested on his shoulder. It always seemed to Emma to be a very cruel thing when she saw how helpless he had become. Her husband was still a striking figure, tall with large bones and a strong-featured face which was shaped harder by a coarse beard around his mouth and chin. Yet, if a person looked closely enough, it was not difficult to perceive the futility in his deep-set eyes, nor to see the weary stoop of his once broad and powerful shoulders. To Emma, and to those who knew him well enough,

Roland Thomas was not a happy man. Yet Emma kept alive his interest in the business by actively involving him in day to day routine affairs, while ensuring he was involved with the greater issues – of which the proposition to Silas Trent was one example. In such a way, and by promising that she would stay by his side for as long as he needed her, Emma had successfully rekindled his passion to see the Thomas name 'up there above the rest'. She was well on the way to fulfilling his long-held ambition, an ambition which had been interrupted by the fateful accident he had suffered. The same accident that had cost Roland Thomas the use of his legs. By the same token, it had also cost Emma very dearly.

Because of it, all of Emma's carefully laid plans were now postponed, for how could she leave him and return to England? It was his greatest fear, and only when Emma had fervently given her word that she would not desert him had he acquired peace of mind. But if he had gained peace of mind, Emma had not. Often, in the solitude of her room, she would think about the man who was her husband, the man in the specially-adapted room downstairs, and she was torn a multitude of ways. Without him, she would likely never have had the opportunity to see a company grow and prosper, and to be an integral force in the excitement of it all. She would not be on the way to becoming wealthy, nor would she be in such a respectable and envied position. Emma knew all of this, and was thankful for the unique opportunity which the kindly Roland Thomas had put her way. On the other hand though, Emma sometimes wondered whether the price she was asked to pay was too high. There was no love in her life, only the ever-painful memory of Marlow. She had been blessed in her life with only one child, and that child had been snatched away for ever. She had no real friends, with the exception of Nelly, who, in spite of the frustrating habit she had of landing herself in trouble, was always a delight and great comfort to Emma. In all truth, she longed for freedom of spirit, and she longed for home.

Yet, there were times when Emma was forced to ask herself just where her home was. Here, she had risen above the pit into which her enemies had thrown her, and she had forged a life of some consequence. She had Nelly, and Roland, and she had her work. Why then did she crave for England? Was it only because there were things to settle there and questions to be answered? Was it for revenge, which in all truth, had long been her driving force? Was it in hope of a long desired reunion with a lover she could never forget? Or was it simply because England was her home, her roots, the land of her birth, from which her body had been torn, but in which her mind, heart and spirit would ever dwell? All of these considerations caused Emma a great deal of agonising . . . until she had decided that her deep longing to return to the homeland was a combination of all these things.

The one truth that grew ever stronger in her heart was that on a day in the future, she knew not when, she *would* return. When she did, all the questions which had tormented her would be answered. Until that day, she must remain patient and stay true to her ideals, for if she did not, then she would be as much a prisoner now as on the day she was brought here in exile.

Dismissing the nurse by asking that she arrange for refreshments to be sent in, Emma wheeled Roland to the desk. She and Silas Trent also took up their places there. 'Perhaps you would explain to Mr Trent what we have in mind?' Emma asked of her husband. She knew how such a suggestion would please him.

'I'll do that . . . of course I will, Emma,' he replied, afterwards turning his serious gaze on the man seated before him. 'Let me make it plain, Mr Trent . . . when Emma first made the suggestion I was dead set against it, but as always, she made me see the advantages of her plan.' He smiled warmly at Emma, before returning his attention to Silas Trent. 'I won't beat about the bush, Trent,' he said. 'Since you've been running cargo for us, you've proved yourself to be a reliable, honest fellow with an appetite for hard work. Now then . . . Emma has it in mind that we're missing out, by commissioning the odd ship at a time. She sees the big shipping companies regularly snatching valuable cargoes right from under our noses . . . because they don't have to commission the odd barque or clipper. They have the advantage of sailing their *own fleet*, so they're not subject to the same limitations and frustrations as we are. The consequence being that, whilst the Thomas Trading Company is rapidly expanding overland, we haven't made as much headway on the shipping of goods. It's not an area that we've ever had that much experience in, you see.' Here, he winked at Emma, saying, 'But Emma intends to change all that. Y'see, she's a woman who don't like to be beat, and I reckon she's just itching for a fight with the big boys . . . ain't that right, Emma?' He appeared to grow excited at the prospect.

'You know it is,' she laughed. Then, as there came a light tap on the door, heralding the entrance of a short, sturdily built maid carrying a tray of food and drink, she got to her feet and cleared a place at the desk. 'Thank you, Judy,' she said, watching while the young woman gingerly put down the tray before quietly leaving the room. It was when Emma had poured the tea and prepared to hand a cup to her husband that she noticed how pale he had suddenly become and how his face seemed pinched as though in pain. 'Are you all right, Mr Thomas?' she asked, putting down the cup and saucer and hurrying to his side. She had seen these attacks before and recalled the doctor's warning: 'The paralysis isn't the only problem, Mrs Thomas,' he had told her soon after the accident. 'There will always be pain, I'm afraid, and the risk of spinal deterioration. That in turn will bring its own more dangerous complications. There's very little we can do and, in the circumstances, your husband is not likely to survive beyond five years.' That was almost three years ago, when Emma had decided to devote herself to making her husband's life as easy as was humanly possible. He himself had insisted on being told the truth and, knowing it, he had come to lean on Emma all the more.

'Don't fuss!' he told her now, putting his fingers to the stiff collar of his shirt and frantically loosening it. He was acutely aware that Silas Trent was also on his feet, looking concerned. He cursed the paralysis which seemed at times to creep into every corner of his being, squeezing and torturing him until he felt like screaming out in the rage which it wrought within him. He fought it with every ounce of the strength he had left, but it was not enough; it was never enough.

Over the years, Emma had come to recognise the signs, and now, seeing him writhing in the chair with a look almost of hatred on his face, she sensed the onset of a deep depression, and her heart went out to him. 'Mr Trent,' she said, in a deliberately calm voice, 'would you be so kind as to summon the nurse? . . . You'll find her in the room adjacent to that of Mr Thomas.'

'Right away,' Silas agreed, going at once from the room and hurrying down the corridor which led from the hallway to the east side of the house. He knew the direction, because he had visited Mr Thomas in his room on previous occasions, when that unfortunate fellow had been confined to his bed.

By the time the nurse was alerted and both she and Silas Trent hurried back to the study, Emma was already on her way, pushing the heavy weight of her husband and the cumbersome bath chair before her. In a matter of minutes the protesting Mr Thomas had been whisked off to his room and one of the servants sent to fetch the doctor.

Some short time later Emma was seeing the doctor from the house, thanking him, and quietly nodding her head as he explained, 'He'll be fine now, Mrs Thomas. It's just as I told you . . . he will become more subject to these attacks as the illness takes its hold. At present they only last for a very short time, but they will worsen, I'm afraid.' He smiled reassuringly. 'No man could be cared for better than you care for your husband. Good day, Mrs Thomas.'

Silas Trent patiently waited in the study. He had watched the incident, been a part of it even, and he was filled with admiration for Emma. How unlike his own wife she was, he thought, for as much as he loved the petulant Martha, he could never imagine her making the sacrifices for *him* that Emma had made for her husband. It was made more remarkable by the fact that she did not love him, nor, he suspected, did her husband feel for Emma what a man should feel for his wife. Silas recognised the marriage for what it so obviously was . . . Purely a business arrangement, because there was no doubt that it was Emma who was the brains and force behind the business which Thomas Trading Company had become; Emma had initiated the big deals that had propelled the company ever upwards. But it was also plain to see that, without the finance and opportunity supplied by her husband, Emma would have been very hard put to have achieved her astonishing business coups, and to have become so well regarded in what was essentially a man's world.

Knowing how heavy Emma's burden was, Silas Trent's heart urged him to tell Emma of Marlow Tanner's presence here. But his head warned him against it.

'He's sleeping peacefully now.' Emma returned, full of apologies and eager to continue the discussion. Silas Trent noted for a moment how the light had gone from her lovely grey eyes. Then, when she began to outline her plans, the excitement was there again, in her voice and in the whole of her manner. 'I don't pretend to know the first thing about shipping, ships . . . or the moods of the ocean with which you have to contend. But I *do* know about merchandise and the market value of it. I know how to acquire your cargoes, even if I don't know one end of a hold from the other. If Thomas Trading Company had its *own* fleet . . . by God! I'd give the big boys a real run for their money.'

'A fleet of your own!' Silas Trent was astonished at

the ambitiousness of Emma's plans. But he was also enthused by it, sitting forward on the edge of his seat, his brown eyes alive as they looked at Emma with awe. 'Do you have any *idea* how much you're talking about?' he asked her. 'Why, it would cost a fortune! Every penny you have.'

'Every penny we have, maybe. A fortune . . . perhaps not.'

'How then? . . . At any rate, Emma, it sounds too much like a gamble to me.'

'It *will* be a gamble,' Emma conceded, 'but that's how fortunes are made, Silas . . . nobody ever grew rich by hiding their capital under the floorboards. I know we'll have to start off with the very basics . . . ships that are seaworthy without being too fancy or expensive. Ships tailormade to our immediate needs . . . then, as we prosper in that direction, we can begin to plan for better ships, and more of them. Do you see what I'm getting at?' Emma's enthusiasm was so contagious that Silas Trent, being greatly moved by it, jumped to his feet and immediately began pacing up and down, all the while ramming one fist into the other, appearing deep in thought.

'You're right, Emma . . . of course you're right!' He came to a halt and swung round to face her. 'The big companies do sell off their vessels occasionally . . . but no, they ask too much money for them. But the single owners like me . . . who captain their own ships, *there* lies our chance, Emma!' He was no more than three feet away from her now, and when Emma saw the corresponding excitement in his face she knew that she had chosen the right man. 'I know of at least two who have run into trouble and are hanging on by the skin of their teeth. A good offer for their vessels would make the decision for them: Oh, they're not ships of great beauty, because they've seen better days. But they *are* seaworthy, and still have a few sailing years left in them.'

'I'm all set to move into coastal shipping in a big way, Silas . . . already I've paid for vessels to carry many thousands of pounds of cargo. But the cost of commissioning vessels to carry it is crippling my profits. Oh, I'm well aware that running and maintaining my own fleet will draw heavy on the purse-strings . . . but I calculate that such expense will be offset by the fact that, not only will I be in a position to take a greater slice of the trade, but that the decisions as to when and how often the cargoes go, and how big a cargo it will be, will not be dictated by the vessel's captain but by me . . . and you, Silas. Roland and I want you in on this venture . . . the three of us . . . each with an equal share.'

'But I have no money.'

'I know that. But you do have a ship, and if I'm right, you do have it mortgaged?'

'Unfortunately, yes.'

'How heavily?'

'The bank owns a fifty per cent share. I own the remainder.'

Here Emma gestured for him to be seated opposite her. 'What I propose then is this . . . presuming of course that you're interested?'

'I certainly am!' He was no fool. This could turn out to be the chance of a lifetime, the break in his fortunes that he had prayed for!

★ ★ ★

It was an hour later when Emma walked Silas Trent to the door, and already it was coming twilight outside. 'You're satisfied with our arrangements then?' Emma asked. 'I can go ahead and have it drawn up, ready for you to sign on your return?'

'The sooner the better,' he agreed,' wondering how he could ever thank her, for words alone seemed so inadequate. 'Meanwhile, I'll try and make contact with the two owners concerned . . . and I'll explain the entire deal to the bank. I'm sure they'll be delighted . . . as I am.'

'You don't mind relinquishing full ownership of the *Stirling*?' Emma asked.

'To become a full and active part of the Thomas Shipping Line? It's more than a fair exchange, Emma . . . and I really don't know how to thank you for your trust and confidence in me.'

'You have *earned* it, Silas. And the decision was based on the fact that, while Thomas Trading has a wealth of experience in merchandise . . . *you* have the experience in seafaring. To be honest, we couldn't really do it without you. It's only the beginning though, I do promise you. Today, your barque and one other, together with the large clipper ship you mean to acquire for us. Tomorrow, who knows . . . we could grow to be bigger even than Lassater Shipping.' She laughed, but Silas Trent had every confidence in Emma's prediction. She had created for him also a unique opportunity. Instead of being half-owner of one vessel, he could go home with the wonderful news that he was about to become a part-owner of a newly formed shipping line. His great joy was momentarily clouded by the fact that, at some later date, it might be necessary for him to be based here in Western Australia, and, whilst he himself was enthused by the possibility, he knew how strongly attached his wife Martha was to England and to her parents. However, he would cross that bridge when he came to it.

'God speed,' said Emma, smiling up at him with encouraging eyes. For a moment, Silas Trent was sorely tempted to lean down and kiss that warm, perfectly shaped mouth. But his respect and admiration for her would not let him take such a liberty. Instead, he gently lifted her hand in his, and gazing deep into those sad grey eyes that so touched his heart, there was an even greater temptation growing inside him. A temptation which, God help him, he could not resist, for he believed that Emma had earned the right, by the sacrifices she had made, to grasp every opportunity for happiness.

'Is there something troubling you, Silas?' Emma had sensed the struggle within him.

'Yes, Emma . . . it's you . . . *You* are troubling me.'

'Oh.' Emma felt the need for caution, but she was not sure why. Stepping away from him, she opened the front door, saying with a smile as she returned her attention to him, 'Now, why should you be troubling yourself about me?'

For a moment he gave no reply, but came to where she waited with the door open and her hand resting lightly on the glass knob. 'Emma, please forgive me if it seems I've taken too much on myself in thinking that you are not happy.' She put up her hand with the intention of interrupting him, but he shook his head, saying more firmly, 'I have more respect for you, Emma, than I have *ever* had for any other woman.

You're not only spirited and ambitious, but you are loyal, kind and, when the occasion demands it, always prepared to put others before yourself.' She softly smiled and lowered her head, as he continued in a gentler voice, 'I know how you grieve for your lost child and . . . I know about Marlow Tanner.'

Emma jerked her head up, her eyes wide and surprised as she stared at him. 'Marlow Tanner!' She was afraid that somehow he had discovered that her late husband was not the father of her child. The shame she felt in that moment was all-engulfing. '*What* do you know of Marlow Tanner?' she demanded, instinctively casting her eyes towards the room that was her husband's. 'Mr Trent . . . the agreement between us does *not* give you the right to discuss my private life!' Emma opened the door wider. 'I think you had better go, and we'll just forget this conversation.' She was astonished, though, when he made no move.

'You *do* love him, don't you, Emma?' he said softly. 'You love him still . . . after all these years.' He watched her small, stiffened shoulders relax. He waited whilst she slowly closed the front door, and he remained perfectly still and patient as she kept her back to him. He had triggered something very deep and precious in her, he knew. He wished he had not done so. When she turned to look at him, with imploring eyes that were softened by the touch of tears, he fervently trusted that he was doing the right thing. 'I will *always* love Marlow,' she told him simply, 'and I have never kept that truth from my husband.'

'Forgive me, Emma, but I don't talk of these things merely to pry, but because . . .' He was unsure as to how he might reveal that the fellow was here, without shocking her too much. ' . . . I wasn't going to tell you, Emma, but I must! I couldn't leave with an easy conscience unless I had told you that I met Marlow Tanner very recently.'

'You . . . *met* him?' Emma's heart soared as the image of the man she loved rose in her mind. Oh, how very clearly she could see him, with his tall powerful figure and those black laughing eyes. It had been so long, so very long, and her heart ached for the sight of them. '*Where* did you meet him? How long ago? Was he well?' The torrent of questions poured from her. There was so much that she needed to know. And, seeing the joy light up her eyes, Silas Trent was convinced that he had done the right thing. 'Oh, Silas . . . where did you see him, and when?' Emma asked breathlessly.

'He is well, Emma, I promise you. At least he seemed well enough some hours ago, when I saw him on the jetty.'

Emma was visibly shocked by his words. 'Some *hours* ago? . . . You saw him then? Here, in Fremantle?' She could hardly breathe for the pounding which stifled her throat.

'He had just arrived . . . wanted a return ship. When I told him I was bound for England, he said he might well spend the night at the inn and seek a ship on the morrow.'

In a moment, Emma was hurrying away in the direction of the nurse's room, after saying to Silas, 'Please wait. I'd be obliged if you would walk me as far as the jetty.' Silas began warning her that she should not walk the streets at night. But Emma had already gone. In another moment, she returned with her

239

bonnet and cape on. 'You're sure it was Marlow? How could you tell? I wasn't aware that you and he were acquainted,' Still she could not believe it.

All the way to the jetty, Silas was made to answer the detailed and persistent questions which Emma directed at him. Now, as they stood at the foot of the Stirling's gangplank, her courage began to desert her, and once again she insisted on going over the incident when he had met Marlow, while Silas Trent unsuccessfully made every effort to dissuade her from going to the inn alone.

Marlow felt the need for sleep coming on him. He had intended enjoying a tankard of ale before retiring, but suddenly he had no appetite for it. Then, at the very moment when he was about to get to his feet and make for the attic room which was his for the night, an old Darwin fellow sat alongside him and engaged him in conversation. 'Looking for a ship, I hear,' he said. 'Anywhere but England, is it?'

'News travels fast round here,' returned Marlow in a friendly voice. 'But yes . . . I *am* looking to sign on, for Singapore if I can find a ship that's bound that way.'

'Well now, mate . . . I reckon you've struck lucky, because there's a clipper due on the morrer . . . the *Statesman* . . . belongs to the Lassater Line. I'm looking to sign on myself.'

'Oh aye?' came the caustic comment from a nearby table. 'Well, you'd best be quick about it, the pair of you! There's a rumour going about that Mrs Thomas has set her sights on putting Lassater's outta business.' He laughed out loud, and straightaway there were others, making similar observations and enjoying the whole thing, seemingly at the expense of Lassater Shipping. 'Well, for my money,' said one, 'I'll back Mrs Thomas. If past experience is anything to go by . . . the poor buggers don't stand a chance.'

'I reckon there's a lot of truth in what they say, mate,' the Darwin fellow told Marlow. 'There have been rumours right enough, and if it's right that Mrs Thomas intends moving into the shipping business . . . the big boys had best keep their wits about 'em. She's a sharp one, that.'

Marlow had heard of Thomas Trading, because they were rapidly making an enviable name for themselves wherever goods were bought and sold. But now he was intrigued to know more about this 'Mrs Thomas' who, according to the talk here, was a formidable force.

'She's well respected round these parts,' obliged the Darwin fellow. 'Never been known to cheat nobody . . . gives a fair price and always deals above board. Oh, there was a Thomas Trading Company long before *she* came on the scene. Roland Thomas had built a nice little business up for himself, but that's how it would have stayed . . . a "nice little business", if he hadn't married again.' Pausing, he took a swig from his jug of grog and made a noisy celebration of licking it from his lips, before wiping the back of his hand across his mouth and continuing. He described to Marlow how poor Mr Thomas had suffered one thing after another. First having his wife killed by robbers, then being forced to throw his only son out on to the streets. 'Rotten to the core, that one,' he said, with disgust. Then he outlined the events which followed, of how Roland Thomas's son, Foster, had gone from these parts to roam the outback. 'There was even talk that he'd taken to robbing and the like . . . though of course nobody ever really knew.' All they did know was that some six months ago, he came sauntering into Fremantle, boasting about having made a wad of money and that he wouldn't rest till he'd put his father outta business and claimed what was rightfully his. 'Some folks reckon he doesn't *only* mean the Thomas Trading Company, which is signed over completely to Mrs Thomas should anything happen to her husband, but that he's got his eye on another prize! He's a bad bugger . . . a real bad bugger. Furious he was, when old Roland up and wed the girlie who worked in his stores . . . but, if you ask me, that was the best thing Roland Thomas ever did! He's a good man, and it was a crying shame when he took a bad fall which crippled him. Still . . . that wife of his, she treats him like a lord . . . always the best for her husband, and that's a fact.'

'Mrs Thomas . . . she runs the company, does she?' Marlow had never heard of any woman actually running such a company, and he was intrigued by the fascinating story he was being told.

'*Runs* it?' The Darwin fellow gave a small chuckle. 'Why, she made it what it is today! And I'll tell you summat else, bucko. I reckon she'll not stop there, oh no. Not if she's a mind to go into shipping!' He took another swig of his ale. 'And that ain't bad, is it mate? . . . Not for an ex-convict who was shipped out here at the tender age of seventeen.'

'An ex-convict?' Marlow was astonished. 'She's English?'

'Through and through. Emma she's called . . . Emma Grady as was . . . convicted of having a part in killing her husband, Gregory Denton. Oh, it's well known . . . but it's hard to believe that girlie killing anybody.' The Darwin fellow turned to see if Marlow was still listening and to exaggerate the point he was making that Emma was incapable of 'killing anybody'. But his companion was long gone, having been struck with shock by what he had heard, and consequently being desperate to escape outside, where he might breathe the fresh air and compose himself enough to reflect more sensibly on the news of Emma, news that had devastated him.

Once outside, Marlow just walked, with no particular destination in mind. He was like a man in a trance, possessed of a nightmare which seemed to be choking the very life from him. Emma! His darling Emma! Transported as a convict! The things he had been told by the Darwin fellow raced through his mind and churned his stomach, until he felt physically sick. 'Oh, Emma!' he murmured with a voice that was both savage and tortured. 'How could I know? Oh God . . . I should never have gone away . . . never have left you, my darling.' His thoughts careered back over the years, to the night when he and Emma had found such perfect and wonderful love, when he had taken her to himself and she had given both heart and soul to him. He thought of how desperately he had pleaded with her to leave her husband and come away with him. What he had suggested was morally wrong, he knew that at the time, and he knew it now. He remembered the anguish he had put Emma through, by asking such a thing of her, and oh, he had loved her all the more because of her loyalty. But now he was forced to ask himself whether his selfish act might have triggered off a life for Emma that eventually proved to be unbearable.

Marlow tormented himself with all of these things, but in his deepest heart, he could never believe that Emma had taken a hand in killing her husband, Gregory Denton. She had a temper. Yes, he knew that well enough, and she was frustratingly stubborn. But she was also kind and loving, with the greatest loyalty and compassion, these were the very virtues in her that he so adored. In his travels he had known other women, fought with them, and slept with them. But he had never loved them. How could he, when his heart would always belong to Emma? Emma, who was *here*. And *married*! It was all too much at once, far too much for him to come to terms with.

As he walked, Marlow felt as though he were in a frenzy. What should he do? Should he go and see her? Back came the answer. No! He must not do that, because she had been through enough. And she had been through it alone, because he had not been there when she needed him most. How could he ever forgive himself! Also, Emma was married, and heading a thriving business. He was not surprised that she could build up such a concern, for she was always known for her tenacity and ability in that way. But *married!* Did that mean that she had forgotten him, that the glorious love they had shared, and which was still so alive in him, had meant less to her? He had no way of knowing, but the longer and deeper he dwelt on it, the more despondent he became.

Instinctively, as always when he was deeply disturbed, Marlow headed for the sea. There was something in watching the waves roll over, and listening to the peculiar sound they made, that had the greatest soothing effect on him. He had no intention of going back to the tavern just yet. He had a need to be alone, and there was no sleep in him now. He wondered whether he might ever again feel the need for sleep.

The daylight was being slowly covered by the darkness as, his thoughts in a turmoil, Marlow headed towards the far end of South Bay, where he hoped to find a quiet, isolated spot where he could sit awhile and think over the events which, even now, he could hardly believe. But it was *true*. It must be true.

As Marlow walked with a determined stride, yet not in a hurry, towards South Bay, Emma – who *was* in a great hurry – rounded the corner from the direction of Arthur Head. She saw the figure some way along South Bay. In that split second her heart leaped, and her every instinct urged her to turn back before it was too late. Yet she could not. She could turn back now no more than she could deliberately stop breathing.

All the same, the sight of that figure brought Emma to a standstill, and a tremendous surge of panic went through her. It was *him*. It was Marlow. But he was changed. Older. Yet he was *not* changed. The long years rolled away. Into her mind's eye came the image of how he had been. The way his strong, lithe figure had moved, that rich black hair, and the way he had had of holding his head erect and looking straight ahead as he walked: all of these characteristics were long etched on her heart and as familiar to her as the act of putting one foot before the other. It was also true that she had come to love her husband over the years. But in a very different way, a tender, compassionate way. Not at all in the all-consuming, passionate way in which she loved Marlow.

She watched him now, and her heart was paralysed. Time had frayed his youth, and there were lighter shades in his hair, and a slower purpose to his step. But the essence that was Marlow remained strong. She wondered at the manner in which he had arrived here. But then, she knew he had gone away to seek his fortune all those years before. Australia was an exciting place to be now. It was only natural he would find his way here. In her heart she gave thanks for it.

After agonising over what to do, how to approach him, and what she might say when he looked at her with those intense dark eyes that had always seemed to reach into her very soul, Emma was plagued with doubts. Would he even want to see her? Did he still love her in the way that she loved him? Or had he forgotten her? After all, it was some sixteen years since that wonderful, unforgettable night when she had conceived his child, and, when she refused to leave with him, he had gone away wretched. It was even possible that he might still be bitter and would never want to see her again.

For another moment, Emma's courage began to desert her. But never being one to accept defeat or to turn away from life's cruelties, she began walking, this time with more urgency, towards the curve of the beach round which Marlow had by now disappeared.

It was the most beautiful evening. The air was warm, yet cooled by the incoming breeze, and the sea lay still and glistening like a stretch of sky littered with sparkling stars. Here and there the soaring seagulls were beginning to seek a haven for the night, and their cries were strangely subdued, making a weird haunting sound which softly echoed in the twilight. The sky was the deepest blue, streaked with ribbons of white and black, and on the horizon where the sun was already going down, the myriad of colours shot the sky purple and red.

It was a most awe-inspiring and magnificent sight, which lifted Emma's spirits as she drew nearer to the figure hunched on the small rise of cliffs beside the beach. He looked a lost and forlorn soul, and Emma's heart went out to him as, softly, she came ever nearer. She wondered how much of a shock it would be for him to discover that she was here, in this place, and it crossed her mind how uncanny was the hand of fate, which had torn them apart so long ago, only to bring them together on the other side of the world. Life was a strange and unpredictable thing, she thought. It also occurred to Emma that Marlow may well have returned to England at some time or another during his travels, and maybe he did know something of her fate. It was *possible*, because she remembered how sensational her trial had been and the great interest it had aroused, because of her relationship to Justice Caleb Crowther.

When Emma came close enough to see the strong profile of the man she loved, and even sense the utter despair which was so evident in his manner, all the determination and courage she had mustered drained away. She must not go any further, for she loved him too much. She was married, committed to a life which had been shaped for her here, so how could she bring herself to cause this man any more pain, which, if he *still* loved her, she would certainly do. In all of her life, Emma had been called upon to make many painful sacrifices, but none of them . . . *none* of them was ever so painful as the one she must make now, as slowly and reluctantly she turned away. She had seen him, almost touched him. It was another poignant memory to carry her through the years. And yet . . . and yet.

Lost in thoughts of Emma, and agonising over their cruel destinies, Marlow felt the deepest despair. But then, of a sudden and for no reason that he could ever recall later, every instinct within urged him to turn his head to look over his shoulder in the direction of the small narrow beach path which over the years many footsteps had trod. What he saw there was the very image which had flooded his mind this past hour, which had brought him both joy and torment, and which was now hurrying away. After all this time, he couldn't really be sure, but something in his heart told him that it was Emma! Not a girl any more. Not young. But his lovely Emma all the same.

In the same moment when Emma heard the soft, rushing footsteps coming up behind her, she heard also the sound of her name, soft and caressing like the breeze, and filled with such longing that it made her heart turn over. 'Emma.' It was Marlow's voice, and it struck at her like the blade of a knife, bringing shock, surprise and a sense of something awful. Yet at the same time, it was something else entirely, rippling through her being with delicious urgency and making her want to cry.

When she stopped and the hand touched her shoulder, she shivered, afraid to turn round, yet compelled to do so. Lowering her head and keeping her gaze to the ground, she moved her body until it was facing his. She saw the long, black-clad legs, and the boots on his feet all spattered with sand; she felt the warmth and presence of his body, and her heart reeled beneath the gentle touch of his hand on her shoulder. Yet she kept her gaze to the ground, because, however much she longed to look up and see again that strong, handsome face that she knew so well, she dared not, for though she was exhilarated, she was also afraid, and that fear betrayed itself in the trembling of her hands which now Marlow took tenderly in his own. 'Look at me, Emma,' he softly urged, and the voice that she had remembered was just the same. It touched her heart so deeply that, without her even being aware of it, the tears ran from her eyes and spilled down her face. Still she dared not lift her gaze to his.

Now he moved her hand until the long, lean fingers of his own were wrapped about both of her small fists; then, lifting his free hand to her face, he tenderly wiped away the tears, afterwards cupping his fingers beneath her chin and slowly raising her head.

When, in a moment, her heart pounding fearfully inside her, Emma's gaze was brought to mingle with Marlow's, she thought that never again in the whole of her life would she experience anything so beautiful, so astonishing. It was as though, in that precious moment when they gazed on each other, the whole world stood still. It was she and Marlow, just as they had been fifteen years ago. They were both older, perhaps wiser, and the flush of youth was long past. But now, in this moment of time, none of that mattered. What really mattered was the youth and joy in their hearts. Their love had not changed with the passing of time. It had only grown stronger. Emma thought that if ever it were possible to choose the moment when she might depart this earth, it would be in this split second when she and Marlow were united, not only in the flesh, but in their very souls, each being the essence of the other.

When, with a broken cry, Marlow caught her to him, and buried his head in the curve of her neck, Emma felt the warm, sticky wetness of his tears against her skin, and she knew beyond all doubt that he loved her with all his heart, as she did him. Lost in each other's arms, they found such contentment as neither had known in many a long, long year. The moment was too deep, too precious for words, so, keeping one arm about each other, they walked together to the small cliff where Marlow had been sitting. There, in a deep recess which gave them privacy, they rekindled a love that had been forbidden when they were very young, that had driven them both to despair and forced them apart. A love that had conceived a child, now lost to them, and that had spanned longer than fifteen years, not suppressed by those years, nor by the great distance between them . . . only growing stronger, and more dangerous.

Emma was not afraid, nor would she sacrifice this precious time with Marlow. When eagerly, yet with the softest touch, Marlow unclothed her, and took her into his own magnificent nakedness, Emma was ready. When she felt the warmth of his skin mingling with her own and saw how his dark eyes burned as they roved over her body, she was proud. When she heard him murmur in the most tender of voices, 'I love you, Emma . . . *adore* you,' she knew the feelings that were stirring within him, because those same feelings stirred within herself. When his warm eager mouth covered hers and he slid on top of her, oh, she wanted him so desperately that everything which had governed her life until then was as nothing. She clung to him and coveted him. She caressed him, kissed him with a passion that frightened her and when, with a fierceness to match her own, he entered her, Emma experienced a tide of exquisite pleasure that forced her to cry out. It was like a dam had burst open inside her, a huge rolling wave surged through her emotions, taking with it all the loneliness, the heartache and the pain she had ever known. She arched herself into Marlow's demanding nakedness and she gave of herself without reservation, but she took also, drawing both strength and passion from her man. There was a rhythm between them, like pulsating music which enveloped them both and pushed their pleasure senses to the limit.

As the waves of sensation washed over Emma time and time again, she thought she couldn't bear it, because in the pleasure and the fulfilment, there was also pain. Yet, it wasn't a physical pain, but a suffering that came from deep within herself. It was the pain of the heart, and which was both destroyed and created by love itself. Because of it, she clung all the more tightly to her lover, being fiercely loath to let him go.

Later, when the urgent passion had subsided, and all that remained was the different passion of a deep, abiding love, Emma was content to lie in Marlow's reassuring arms, and together they talked of all the things that were in their hearts. Emma explained the tragic events which had brought her to Australia. She told him everything, how Gregory had died and not by her hand. She outlined the reasons for her marriage to Roland Thomas, and told him of the unfortunate Nelly, who had been a staunch friend, and whom she considered to be just as much her responsibility as was her

251

crippled husband. She assured him of the great love she would always feel for him. All the things which had befallen her she told him; all but one, and that being the one which still haunted her dreams. She did not reveal that he had been a father, or that the child was lost, because she knew that he would suffer the same guilt and anguish which she had suffered ever since. At least she could spare him that. And so she did. Neither did she tell him of her suspicions regarding Caleb Crowther, for that would serve no purpose. Besides which, she herself must deal with that, when the time came.

'You've been through so much, Emma. If only I'd known . . . if only I had stayed.' Marlow saw the guilt and failing in himself, and was angered by it.

'You couldn't have changed anything,' she told him. 'Please believe that.'

'All the same, I should never have deserted you.'

'I sent you away,' she reminded him, and he could not deny it.

Of a sudden, he sat up straight, and taking Emma by the shoulders, he swept her to her feet, standing before her and looking with sudden determination into those strikingly beautiful grey eyes. 'I must go back,' he said with a surge of enthusiasm, 'back to England. To my sister, Sal . . . because, even though I left to seek my fortune and make a better life for her, it seems to me that I deserted her also!'

'No.' Emma could see that he was unjustly punishing himself. 'You never deserted *anybody*, my darling. You're not capable of that. Everything you did was with others in mind.'

'All the same, Emma . . . I must go home, and seek

another kind of "fortune" there. It's strange, I think, how you come to realise what good fortune really is. It isn't gold or material things . . . it's having a family who needs you . . . it's enjoying good health and contentment. And it's having the hands and strength to toil for a living.' Here he paused and his gaze lingered on her face awhile, seeming to search for something there, yet knowing he could not find it. 'Most of all, my darling,' he went on, 'good fortune is loving someone until your heart sings . . . and having your love returned. I know you love me, Emma . . . I've always known that, and if I never hold you in my arms again, you've given me the greatest joy a man could ever know.'

'Don't, Marlow . . . please.' Emma was close to tears.

Now, he gazed at her long and hard, stroking the palm of his hand down her tumbled auburn hair; then, as he looked on that fine and lovely face and those grey eyes that smiled at him so, he thought how fresh and youthful she was, how still like the girl of fifteen he had first met by the canal. The years in between had taken nothing from her beauty, only enhanced it.

'I can't bear to let you go again, Emma,' he told her, gripping her shoulders more tightly, 'yet I can't stay here knowing you're married, loving you as I do.'

'I know,' she said, the sadness rising in her eyes. She was aware of the impossibility of it all and, as she looked at this man who had matured and grown even more handsome with the years, she was sorely tempted. But it could not be. There were too many entanglements, too many people to be hurt, and how could she live with her conscience if she chose the way he would have her go? She began to explain, but he put his hand to her mouth and afterwards pulled her to him, leaning forward and tenderly kissing the top of her head. 'Forgive me, Emma . . . but I want to take you here and now, from this place. I'm afraid that if I don't, I'll never see you again, and I couldn't bear that. I couldn't!' He held her more tightly, for only a moment, before easing her away from him. 'I asked you once before to come away with me. I'll never regret that. But I won't ask you this time, Emma, because you know in your heart what I think and feel. Whatever you decide to do, I must wait for that decision and I promise you, my love . . . I will abide by it. I don't want to cause you pain, or to put you in an impossible situation.' He put his two hands one either side of her face and tilted it up towards him. 'You do know that, don't you, Emma?' When she gave no reply, instead turning her sorry eyes away, he told her, 'The *Stirling* leaves for England on the morrow. If the cap'n will sign me on, I'll be aboard and headed home. Unless, Emma . . . unless you ask me to do otherwise. I'll look for you, my love . . . before she sets sail and, if you're not there, I'll understand.'

When Emma brought her gaze back to look on his face, and he saw the tears in her eyes, Marlow's heart turned somersaults inside him. Dear God above, how he loved this woman! How he needed her!

As Marlow reached down to kiss her, Emma was filled with sadness at their predicament, and she knew there could be only one ending to their glorious reunion this night. She raised her lips to his, she put her arms about his neck and clung to him as though she would never let him go. When, after a long and exquisitely painful moment, he released her, she put her hand up to stroke his face tenderly, that strong and familiar face that, even if she were to die a very old woman, she would never forget.

No more words were spoken between them then, before Emma tore her gaze from the dark pained eyes that never left her face for even a second. Then, with scalding tears running down her face, she turned away and left him standing there. The interlude was over, the dream was short-lived, and the future just as uncertain as it was before.

Marlow watched her go and his heart went with her, but he made no move to stop her. Instead, he waited until she was out of sight, before turning to trudge along the beach to the other side, where he knew the *Stirling* to be berthed. He felt certain that Captain Trent would sign him on, and yet he prayed that he would not sail for England with her on the morrow. He *would* return home, yes, but he hoped above all else that when he did, it would be because Emma had made him a happier man. Yet even as he dwelt on the possibility, he realised how impossible it was. All the same, he would keep watch before the tide carried him out to sea. He could never give up even the slimmest hope.

As the *Stirling* got underway, Marlow kept his eyes peeled towards the shore for signs of Emma. But she never came, and he was a man lost. He could not have known how, in the hour when she knew that he would be gone from these shores and from her life, perhaps for ever, Emma sat in her study with the door locked against the outside world, quietly sobbing.

After a while, she got to her feet, wiped her eyes and composed herself. Then, with her small, straight shoulders set in a stiff, upright stance, and wearing the expression of a woman with a purpose, she threw open the curtains, telling herself in a firm voice, 'Come on, my girl! There's a business to be run!' She had learned the art of making the head rule the heart. She had learned it well.

Chapter Nine

Emma suspected that she was pregnant! These past two months and more, since she and Marlow had made love, had proved to be one of the most difficult times in her life. Not only was she plagued by the physical consequences, such as nausea and a general feeling of being unwell, but she was haunted also. Here she was, a woman past the age of thirty, and carrying a child that was not her husband's. She would not be able to hide that fact for very much longer, because once the outward signs of her pregnancy became evident, it would also betray the truth, that she had been unfaithful to Roland Thomas, because how could a man who was paralysed from the waist down father a child? There would be questions, Emma knew, and gossip of a spiteful nature; yet for all that, Emma was filled with a great happiness and every day had taken on a new meaning. It struck her how curious and condemning it was, that she should have been married to two different men, yet the children she had conceived were not fathered by either of them. It did seem as though, in spite of the many obstacles put in their way, her and Marlow's paths were meant to cross. Emma nurtured and cherished the tiny life that was forming inside her, and she wanted to believe with all her heart, that it was the Lord's way of compensating for the child she had so cruelly lost. But then, she reminded herself, what she and Marlow had done was wrong. No amount of soul searching could change that. Emma knew that she should be tormented with guilt and a sense of shame, but she was not. What had happened was the culmination of a wonderful love, which she could never deny, whatever the consequences.

At seven o'clock on a balmy October evening, Emma stood by the jetty, with the keen warm breeze blowing about her skirts and lifting the hem of her dress into a gentle arc which whipped the air and revealed the layers of her cream-coloured petticoats. She had slipped off her bonnet, leaving it fastened about her neck and resting on her shoulders, and, as the breeze teased both the long strands of her rich auburn hair and the flowing blue ribbons of her bonnet, she made a strikingly lovely figure, with the evening sky silhouetting her still slim and shapely form.

The torment that countered Emma's joy showed in her eyes, those strong grey eyes that so vividly reflected her every mood. Now there was a sadness in them, as she gazed out across the sea towards the horizon, her thoughts dwelling on Marlow, and the way in which their love had been beset by insurmountable problems all these years. How wonderful it would be, she thought, if things were different and Marlow could share the miracle of this little life already beating within her. Why is it, she asked herself, that bearing his children must be painful and forbidden Emma did not know the answer, only that it was so.

For a long time Emma kept her eyes fixed to the horizon, wondering where Marlow might be at this very minute. There was a strange calmness in her heart as she thought more deeply about this man whom fate seemed determined to keep from her, and Emma marvelled at the peace she felt. It was as though some quiet instinct told her that, when Marlow had instilled in her that most precious seed of life, there had also been created a hope for their future. Even though Emma could see no possible way in which she and Marlow might be together always, the murmurings of optimism would not be denied.

Chiding herself for being foolish enough ever to believe that her future lay with Marlow, Emma turned from the ocean which had taken him from her, and sighing deeply, began her way towards Cliff Street and the warehouse. Marsh Williams was back with the waggon train which did the regular run into the outback and she must have his report firsthand. Besides which, there was news of a pearl-lugger having been lost, taking with it a deal of shell which was destined for the Thomas Trading Company, and some twenty-five men were reported to have lost their lives. The cargo was extremely valuable, but it was to the unfortunate men and their loved ones that Emma's heart went out.

As always, Emma's arrival at the warehouse was greeted with mixed feelings. Most of the men respected her for being the fair-minded and clever business-woman she was. But there were those who bitterly resented having to take orders from *any* woman, yet were shrewd enough to make an effort at disguising their feelings; after all, the Thomas Trading Company now had the edge on most of the competition, and the wages were the best around. There wasn't a man among them who could honestly deny that it was Emma herself who had achieved this.

When Emma first acquired a large warehouse on Cliff Street it was a single unit. Now the company owned almost a third of all the property down the left-hand side of Cliff Street, and every inch of space was used to its full. By the time Emma arrived, the whole place was a hive of activity. Already the two largest waggons were hitched to and loaded with all manner of tools, such as shovels, galvanised buckets, oil, candles and other basic necessities. The last items – twelve sacks of flour – were being carried out one by one aloft a burly labourer's shoulders who, on sighting Mrs Thomas, gave a wide grin and an awkward nod of the head. 'G'day,' he called, and Emma returned the greeting. Afterwards, hurrying through the noise and organised chaos within the busy stores, where there was a deal of counting, checking, stacking and carrying going on, Emma found Marsh Williams out in the rear yard where the big geldings were stabled. He was a large and fearsome-looking man, with unusually wild red hair, yet he had the gentlest manner and a considerate nature, which belied his formidable appearance. He was so deep in conversation with the warehouse manager – a tall, thin and authoritative man with a surly face called Oliver Barker – that neither of them saw Emma approaching. It was only when Emma said, 'Good morning, gentlemen, that they turned in surprise.

'Mrs Thomas . . . I might have known you'd be out bright an' early to catch me before I'm off again,' remarked Marsh Williams. Mr Barker suggested they should 'seek a quieter place to talk', whereupon the three of them made their way to the office at the far end of the warehouse. Here Emma was informed that all had gone well on the previous trip. 'But I'm telling you, Mrs Thomas,' said Marsh Williams with some excitement, 'I reckon if we'd taken twice the merchandise we could'a sold it.' He thrust the signed dockets into her hand, then, as she thoughtfully perused them, he went on, 'There's more and more prospectors setting up an' looking fer a fortune . . . an' *settlers* too.' He thrust another paper on to the pile of dockets in her hand. 'See that? . . . That's a list of goods we hadn't got room for. Orders . . . mostly from the women folk . . . cloth, an' fancy things like pictures and china stuff. There's even a request for a *tablecloth*, would you believe? . . . And a tapestry frame.'

Emma's sharp business instincts told her that here was something of real interest. Her trading post already dealt in stock of the items mentioned. But up till now there had been no call for such things actually to be carried to the customer. This was a market created not by the frantic search for gold, or by farmers who looked to scratch a more down-to-earth living from the land, but a demand from the women who had bravely uprooted themselves in search of a better life. What was more natural than that they should want to retain a degree of civilisation, even though they might be in a raw and primitive land where, often, the code of culture and behaviour was lost in the struggle to survive?

'We must supply this demand,' Emma told her manager now. 'Get these women their cloth, and their china plates! If we can't cater to them, there are others who will.'

'And what should we leave behind in order to make the space?' asked Mr Barker, with a touch of sarcasm in his voice. 'The flour and sugar? . . . Or perhaps the tools which they so desperately need? You're wrong, Mrs Thomas, there isn't a trading outfit in the whole of Western Australia who would supply these women's fripperies. There's little profit in it, and there are other, more important priorities.'

Emma saw it differently. She knew how a woman might influence her husband to her way of thinking. She felt also that any woman who had courage enough to brave the adverse elements of this demanding land had a mind of her own and would not rest until she had those things about her which, however much they might be seen by some as 'fripperies', made life tolerable to her. Emma was quick to realise also that, because other traders might not agree with her, there was a unique opportunity here to get in first, and to build this particular market up, before the others became aware of its potential. Oh, it was true that, once they saw it opening out, they would make every effort to secure a large slice for themselves. But Emma knew from experience that if a trader got in first and gave full satisfaction, the customer tended not to change to another supplier. It was an opportunity not to be missed. Yet, there was a difference of opinion here, between the warehouse manager and herself. Such a situation, though it at times caused little difficulty, was of paramount importance in this instance, because if she were to make strides into this promising market, she must have his full backing. Most of all, it was important that he viewed the project with enthusiasm.

Giving nothing of her own opinion away, Emma asked him now: 'So you think it's of little consequence?' Mr Barker had only been with Thomas Trading for a very short time and he came with good references. But he had a surly disposition and he had yet to prove himself fully to Emma. 'I reckon it's just women's fancies . . . won't come to nothing. Anyway, we're short of waggons as it is . . . *and* the men to drive them. Good men are always hard to find.' With the heat of the morning already beginning to tell, and the small office being somewhat stifling, the door had been left open. Outside, two of the workers heard Mr Barker's comments and one observed to the other, 'It ain't surprising the bugger can't keep a good man, when he treats 'em like dingo shit!' The other nodded in agreement, spat out his chewing tobacco through his teeth, and the pair of them went about their work.

'You leave me in no doubt about *your* feelings in this,' Emma told Mr Barker, purposely keeping her own opinion to herself. Then, turning to Marsh Williams, she asked, 'And you, Mr Williams . . . are you of the same mind as my manager, bearing in mind that he has had some long experience in the trading business,' she warned him deliberately.

'Well . . . I reckon it don't matter too much what I think.' Marsh Williams knew he might be treading on delicate ground here, but he was an honest man, and must give an honest answer. 'In my opinion, most women know what they want, and more often than not they get their own way. I think that if we were to ignore that fact . . . we could end up by losing out. The women in the outback ain't got fancy money, and they ain't got easy ways of getting to town. But it won't always be like that.'

'So, you're saying that we should go all out to satisfy

their modest demands?' When he nodded without hesitation, she went on, 'And if we *did*, how do you imagine we could provide enough waggons and good men to drive them . . . a problem which Mr Barker so rightly pointed out. It's one thing catering for the town's women who come to the store . . . but we'll need extra waggons, horses and these "good men" to take the goods to the customer.'

'I don't see it as a problem, begging your pardon, Mrs Thomas. Waggons are easily secured and the horses we can find well enough. I don't deny that the men might not be so easy to locate, but I think it's worth a hell of a try!'

'And so do I, Mr Williams!' Emma took the two men unawares by her bold admission. 'In my experience, small, seemingly unimportant markets have a canny knack of growing into a lucrative business . . .' Here she turned her sharp grey eyes on Mr Barker, telling him in a firm angry voice,' . . . but only for those who have the guts to get in there first!'

When Emma left Cliff Street two hours later, she had gone through the books thoroughly, and given Mr Barker the opportunity of taking on Marsh William's job as lead driver; when, infuriated he had refused, Emma put him under notice and appointed Marsh Williams as the new manager. His first task was to secure the services of top drivers, who were not afraid of giving a hard day's work for a good pay-packet. On her way out through the warehouse, Emma was stopped by several men, who had overheard her instructions. From what they told her, it was plain to Emma that not only had she made the right decision – which some ventured to say was long overdue – but that there should be no difficulty in recruiting the kind of men required, once they knew that Barker had been shown the door. Her next stop was the trading post, to see how Rita Hughes and Nelly were coping. Emma always looked forward to spending a few hours in their company, in the comforting knowledge that the Thomas Trading post was in better hands than hers.

'Pregnant!' Nelly's brown eyes popped out of her head as she stared at Emma. ''Cor, bloody hell, gal. I *knew* it! The minute yer told me about that meeting with Marlow Tanner . . . I just *knew* it!' She was so agitated that she swept herself up and out of the cane chair in the little room that she once shared with Emma and which was her own abode now. 'What yer gonna do, Emma? . . . How in God's name d'yer think yer can keep a thing like *that* to yerself? What! . . . You'll be as big as a ship in a few months, and how are yer going to hide yer belly then, eh? Oh, yer silly bugger . . . yer silly little bugger!' She turned to look at Emma, who was astonished to see that Nelly's friendly gaze was wet with the threat of tears. 'Oh, Emma . . . you've got yerself in a right pickle, and no mistake,' she wailed.

Emma had not been prepared for the fact that Nelly might feel fearful for her, only that Nelly would give her a proper telling-off. Now, however, she found herself in the position where it was she having to comfort Nelly. 'Come and sit down, Nelly,' she said, going to put her arm round Nelly's shoulders and drawing her back towards the chair, where she persuaded her to sit down. After they were both seated, facing each other, Emma told her how she intended to 'talk to Roland about the whole business, when he's in a better state of health. I realise he will have to be told the truth,' she said quietly. 'But he knows about Marlow . . . and I'm sure he will understand.' She prayed that he would.

'He bleeding well *won't*, y'know!' exclaimed Nelly. 'Not if my experience of men serves me right. And, even if he does . . . there are others in this town of Fremantle who'll be only too glad to point the finger at you. Oh, I'm telling you, me darling . . . yer don't know what you've let yerself in for!' Nelly was full of woe, but Emma would not be depressed. She clung to the belief that all would come right in the end, because she had no intention of ever being separated from the child she was carrying. Not by hell or high water.

Feeling that her problem was one that only she and she alone could contend with, Emma deliberately directed her attention to other matters, of how pleased she was that Nelly and Rita Hughes got on so well, and how well the store was doing. 'But are you sure that you wouldn't prefer to come and stay at the house with me, Nelly? There's plenty for you to do there, and it would be nice to have you close by.'

'Naw . . . it ain't that I'm not grateful, Emma gal,' Nelly replied, pulling a face, 'but I'd be lost in that grand place, and what's more, I like working the store and meeting people. Besides . . . you ain't so far away, and I do see you every day, don't I, eh?' Nelly could not be persuaded so, as on previous occasions when Emma had raised the matter, she pressed it no further. All the same, Nelly's reluctance to come and live in the house was surprising. But then, when they had both returned to the store, Nelly to her tasks and Emma to her business discussion with Rita Hughes, something happened which gave Emma grave reason to fear for Nelly. It explained also Nelly's reasons for not wanting to leave the store, in favour of lighter work at the house.

'Morning, Mrs Thomas . . . beats me how you always manage to look cool in this blistering heat,' called a portly little fellow who was at the counter, busily heaping a wad of 'baccy from the jar and into his pipe. He had a ruddy face with a blue neb cap perched on his bald head in a jaunty manner, and Emma recognised him as a nearby settler who insisted on buying his 'baccy only by the pipeful, having developed a raking cough and rationed his 'smoke' because of it. When Emma warmly returned his greeting, he paid for the 'baccy and left, whistling a merry tune.

The store was busy, with customers constantly milling in and out, when Emma murmured her intention of perusing the ledgers to Rita Hughes, and afterwards went into the office. She made copious notes about various things which she would need to discuss with Rita, but on the whole, she was delighted to see that everything was in good order and the business running smoothly. Emma congratulated herself on seeing the potential in Rita Hughes, and following her own judgement in offering her a responsible position here. Rita had not let her down.

It was about an hour later, just coming up to midday, when custom had slacked off enough for Emma and Rita Hughes to retire to the small office together in order to discuss the points which Emma had noted. 'You'll be all right on your own, Nelly?' asked Emma. 'We shouldn't be above an hour. Then you can get straight off for your break.'

'You two bugger off from under me feet,' instructed the incorrigible Nelly, ''course I'll be all right!'

Rita Hughes and Emma looked at each other with amusement, but they were not surprised by Nelly's familiar light-hearted abuse. They had grown used to it, and saw no offence in her attitude, for there was none intended.

'I gave up on her years ago!' laughed Emma, shaking her head.

'She's a good worker and harmless enough,' rejoined Rita Hughes, as she followed Emma to the back office, 'though I do have to keep my eye on her with the likes of Marjorie Hunter and her snooty cronies. Given the opportunity, they would report Nelly to the authorities and have her reassigned to cleaning out the prison pigsties.'

Emma knew this Marjorie Hunter well. She was a social climber who had nosed her way on to every committee that was formed, and Emma made a mental note to have a word with Nelly before she left. That woman, and others like her, could prove to be Nelly's downfall if she weren't very careful, and it would be tragic if that were to happen, because lately Nelly had made every effort to mend her ways. In fact, Nelly had earned her ticket-of-leave, gone out of her way to appear more disciplined and it had been *months* since she'd been in any kind of trouble. Emma was full of praise for her friend, but there was something which bothered her. This was Nelly's unusually quiet manner on the occasions when Emma began talking of her future, and of how one day she would take Nelly home to England and 'find you a handsome husband there'. At one time, Nelly's jubilant reaction would have been to prance about her little room, with a mischievous look about her, and the comment, 'What 'andsome feller could resist a little beauty like meself, eh? Oh . . . I'll show the bugger a thing or two and no mistake!' Lately however, Nelly seemed to have other things on her mind, so that when Emma talked of England and their future, Nelly's quiet indifference was both astonishing and disturbing to Emma.

The reason for Nelly's curious behaviour was made painfully evident to Emma, when both she and Rita Hughes emerged from the office in less time than Emma had anticipated, having concluded the business discussions with satisfaction and efficiency. It was Emma who saw them first, and she couldn't believe her eyes! The store entrance was closed up and the shutter pulled down. There, with her back against the door was Nelly, her arms stretched round the bent form of a man, and the two of them locked in a kiss which was so obviously passionate that Emma felt her own cheeks flaming.

Rita Hughes had been walking alongside Emma, paying careful attention to Emma's suggestions for display, her own eyes looking downwards to a sketch in her hands which Emma had made to emphasise her point. When, of a sudden, Emma came to a halt, Rita Hughes looked up at her briefly, before following Emma's startled gaze to where the two figures were so rapt in their enjoyment of each other that neither had heard the two women approach.

'Nelly! What in God's name do you think you're doing?' Emma demanded, lifting the cumbersome folds of her skirt with both hands as she swept forward in anger. As she did so, the man, whose back had been to

269

her, now swung round and Emma was so shocked to see who it was that she came to an abrupt halt, exclaiming in a voice that was filled with horror. 'You! . . . Foster Thomas!' At that point, Rita Hughes made a loud gasp, afterwards coming forward on hesitant steps to face him. 'No! . . . I won't believe it. You and . . .' Here she inclined her head towards Nelly, who had stepped up to half-hide herself beside Foster Thomas. ' . . . and *Nelly*!' So terrible was her voice that Emma quickly glanced at her. She was riveted by the awful look on Rita Hughes's face, which was drained white, her odd-coloured eyes stark with panic. Emma knew then, without any doubt, that Rita Hughes adored this man, this fiend who had it in him to force himself on a woman who was ill and helpless, and who was as low as any man could get.

'Look here, girlie,' Foster Thomas appeared unperturbed by the intrusion as he half-turned his murky blue eyes to Nelly, with a sly smile moving over his lean handsome face, which was marred only by the thin low scar made by the lick of his father's whip, 'I reckon we've been caught in the act.' He laughed, a quiet sinister sound which chilled Emma's heart. She had not forgotten how Roland had disowned this man, and how it was common knowledge that he sought to avenge himself on Emma who had been made full heir to all that was 'Thomas Trading'.

'Get out!' she told him now, going in a rage towards the door and flinging it open. 'Get out . . . and *stay* out!' she told him, her grey eyes ablaze.

'It ain't all his fault, Emma!' Nelly protested, running forward in his defence and touching Emma on the arm. She was amazed when Emma shrugged her off, never once taking her stony glare from the man she had every reason to loathe. 'I'll only tell you *once!*' she warned him in a dangerously quiet voice.

'All right, Emma my beauty. There's no reason for me to stay now, is there?' He smiled down on her, his blue eyes boring into her face, 'Not when you've spoiled my fun.' He turned to look at Rita Hughes, who was softly crying and for whom he had always felt a certain repugnance. 'Sorry, girlie,' he said without feeling, 'but y'see . . . Nelly's a better bet.' He now glanced at Nelly who was beside him. 'Ain't that right? Through you . . . I'll definitely achieve so much more.' Nelly giggled foolishly, taking his words to mean that he loved her as she loved him, heart and soul.

But Emma was under no such illusion. She recognised his words for what they really were, a threat against herself and against his father, her husband. She knew in her heart that he would stop at nothing to get to her in any way he possibly could. Nelly was such a way, a poor gullible creature with a heart of gold, and it was filled with love for him. He knew well enough that Emma adored her friend Nelly. That she had watched out for her all these years, and that it would bring her the greatest joy to see Nelly free and settled with a good man who could give her the love and care she so much deserved. To see her entangled with a monster like Foster Thomas was devastating. He was cruel to the point of being sadistic, and Emma knew that he would use Nelly, break her spirit in the process, then fling her aside as though she were nothing.

Emma was tempted to accuse him loudly of these things in front of Nelly, to show him up for what he was and to goad him into revealing his real character. But she gritted her teeth and said nothing, because she suspected that to belittle him in front of Nelly would only fire that foolish young woman to leap to his defence. Instead, she opened the door wider and stepped back for him to pass. As he did so, he leaned down to murmur in her ear, 'It's too late, Emma. *I have her!* I'd rather have you . . . but one thing's for sure, I'll make you suffer. All of you!' Then, as he blatantly bent to kiss Nelly full on the mouth and she, with adoring eyes, followed his long lean figure as it went down the steps, Emma was frantic. When he turned round to tell Nelly with an intimate wink, 'I'll be back for you, girlie,' Emma's worst fears were realised.

'I won't listen to you!' Nelly pressed her hands over her ears, before running to the far end of the room to which Emma had brought her. Emma deplored the havoc Foster Thomas had already wreaked here: Nelly growing more agitated by the minute, and Rita Hughes quietly serving the customers, with a look of abject sorrow on her face, the light gone from her eyes. Foster Thomas had a great deal to answer for, and if Emma had her way, both these foolish women would see him for what he was. Yet Nelly was besotted beyond the point of reason, and Rita Hughes would not even discuss the matter. Whatever Rita's thoughts, she obviously intended to keep them to herself.

'The man's no good for you, Nelly!' Emma argued now. 'Can't you see that he's *using* you? Using you to hurt me. Oh, Nelly . . . be sensible. He'll only break your heart.'

'He *won't!*' yelled Nelly, taking her hands down and flinging herself into the cane chair. 'Foster Thomas loves me. And I love him!' Then, in her anger, she said

272

something that cut Emma's heart to the quick. 'You're jealous, that's all! Don't think *you're* the only one who can have a husband, Miss High and Mighty . . . with your fancy house and all your money!' At once, a look of horror spread over her face, and when she saw how deeply wounded Emma had been by her cruel words, it seemed for a moment as though she might go to her and make amends. But when Emma murmured in a tearful voice, 'Oh, Nelly . . . Nelly,' her back stiffened, and the resolve returned to her face. 'You've got it all, Emma Thomas,' she said in accusing voice, 'and you're carrying your lover's child to prove it!' She turned her eyes from Emma's face because she could not bear to see the pain she had caused. Yet Nelly was convinced that Foster Thomas *did* love her. She was certain also that Emma would stop her from seeing him if she could. Well! In these past months she had earned her ticket-of-leave, and she had the right to choose her own employer. For the first time in her life, Nelly was head over heels in love, and being convinced that her man truly returned her love, she was adamant that *nothing* would come between them, not Emma, not anybody. Oh, she loved Emma like she was her own sister, but what she felt for Foster Thomas had seeped into her every nerve-ending, every bone of her body, and it had given her life new meaning, and a fresh purpose. How could she let it be spoiled? Emma hated him, she knew. And, truth be told, there was every reason, for wasn't she herself a witness to how he had taken Emma when she was desperately ill and lying unconscious? But he was drunk at the time! She had questioned him on this very issue, and he had told her how he was filled with remorse that he should have done such a dreadful thing. Oh, he was no angel, Nelly knew that. But then, neither was *she*.

'I'm leaving. I'll report to the authorities and find new work in Fremantle.' Nelly's voice was cold and unfriendly, but still she could not lift her eyes to Emma. 'I'd be obliged if you'd piss off . . . go on! Leave me be, and let me live me own bloody life!'

Emma stared down at Nelly's familiar brown unruly hair, and she could hardly see for the tears which swam in her sorry eyes. In a moment, she had taken a step forward, her hand outstretched as though she might stroke Nelly's bent head. When Nelly sensed Emma's intention, she looked up to meet Emma's unhappy gaze. For a while, she said nothing, a great and terrible struggle going on inside her. Then, when Emma asked, 'You don't mean that, do you, Nelly?' she got to her feet, quickly rummaged about in the room to collect a few belongings, then brushed past Emma, turning at the door to tell her in an angry voice, 'You ain't gonna piss off . . . so *I* will. Don't come after me, and don't contact me . . . 'cause I've washed me hands of yer. Yer turned yer back on my feller . . . so, you've turned yer back on what I want most in life. That tells me that yer ain't the friend I took yer for. Don't you ever interfere in my life again!' She flounced out of the room, and slammed the door, leaving the only person in the world who genuinely loved her totally devastated by her parting words, 'Don't contact me and, don't ever interfere in my life again.'

That night, when Emma lay in her bed looking back on that most dreadful scene, she felt a deluge of sorrow within her that she had not experienced in a long, long time. She knew that she had no right to go against Nelly's furious insistence that Emma should not contact her, and if truth be told, Emma was convinced that she could never change Nelly's obsessive love for Foster Thomas . . . in the same way that Nelly would not change Emma's own loathing for him. She had hurt Nelly badly, she had threatened what her friend saw as her only chance of happiness, and Emma wished that it could have been different. She feared for Nelly. But there was nothing to be done, except to pray that no real harm would come to her, before the truth of Foster Thomas's character was revealed. Love was a cruel master. Who should know that better than Emma herself!

Even while Emma cried herself to sleep, Nelly was settling down in the attic of a nearby inn where she had found work. She too was desperately unhappy because of the terrible things she had said to Emma. Yet she would stand by her decision now. She wouldn't contact Emma and she wouldn't retract any of those things which had been said, because she loved Foster Thomas too much to risk losing him. In fact, when she had found him to tell him how she had been so cruel in saying those things to Emma, he had been quick to defend her and to reassure her of his love. What was more, Emma had been wrong in saying that he was only 'using' her. Because this very day, he had asked her to marry him! The authorities were duly informed and soon Nelly would be Mrs Foster Thomas . . . a *free* woman. So much for Emma's warning, she thought bitterly.

Nelly was convinced that she would never come to regret the path she had chosen. But if it had been

within her power to see where that path might lead, she
would never even have taken the first step!

Chapter Ten

'It's no use you keep worrying over Nelly . . . you're only making yourself ill!' Roland Thomas reached his arms up to the wooden bar which Emma had arranged to be fitted to his bedhead, and with a determined effort he pulled himself up to a more comfortable sitting position. 'She's married . . . made her own choice, and I reckon she'll have to live with it.' He pursed his lips as he looked from Emma to gaze thoughtfully at the chequered eiderdown, and all the while he was cursing whatever ill-fortune it was that had brought him a son like Foster Thomas.

'If only she would answer my notes, Mr Thomas . . . if only she would show willing to make amends between us, that's all I ask.' Emma was standing by the window, looking out on to the verandah and occasion-ally lifting her eyes to scour the distance beyond the road which led down to the sea. Always, when she let her thoughts wander over the horizon, the image of Marlow would flood her heart and, like now, she turned away. It was no use craving for what could never be. She had come to realise that much, and to be thankful for whatever blessings the Lord saw fit to bring her.

With her naturally slim figure, and being sensible enough to choose dresses that were not nipped in too tight at the waist, Emma's condition was not easily evident. But she knew that in another few weeks, when she came into the fourth month of her pregnancy, there would be no hiding it. Already Mr Thomas had remarked how pinched and pale her face was. He had put it down to one thing only. The very same issue which he was raising now. 'Come and sit beside me, Emma,' he suggested in a kindly voice.

Emma turned from the window, momentarily surveying the bedroom, which was Roland Thomas's own little world. Following the accident that had crippled him and which dictated the need for a downstairs room, Emma had chosen this one, because of its spaciousness and because it was always flooded with light. It was a lovely east-facing room, having large windows with a triple aspect, and from his bed Mr Thomas had a wonderful view of Queen Square. Emma had employed a man to work on creating a garden which was riotous in colour and, on a summer evening, when the windows were flung wide open, the scent from the shrubs and flowers would permeate the room. It was the most delightful room in the whole house, made even more pleasant by the chintz fabric and articles of light-coloured wood furniture which Emma had imported from England. Indeed, the decor of this room, and the drawing-room where Emma received her visitors, had made such an impression on certain people of social standing that Emma had built up a strong line of sales in various furnishings which she brought in from the homeland.

'Listen to me, Emma.' Roland Thomas reached out his hand to where Emma was now seated in the wicker armchair by his bed and, gently touching her shoulder, he went on, 'Nelly went into that marriage with her eyes wide open. Oh, I know she's prone to do silly things, and she often jumps in with both feet without looking where she's going . . . but, she's a grown woman! You can't watch out for her forever, girlie.'

'I know,' Emma conceded, 'but there have been rumours ever since she and Foster took on that small store in Perth. Word has filtered back that things are not well between them . . . and *that* doesn't surprise me!' Emma added bitterly, 'But *why* won't Nelly answer my letters? Every time the mail coach comes back, I feel positive that this time there'll be a reply . . . but there never is.' Of a sudden, Emma sat bolt upright in the chair, then she was leaning forward, her grey eyes alight with enthusiasm. 'I'm of a mind to go there, Mr Thomas,' she declared. 'I'm certain she'll talk to me . . . if we're face to face.'

'No, girlie.' Roland Thomas closed his homely brown eyes as though in pain, and shaking his head, he told her, 'You're only hurting yourself in thinking that. You've known Nelly a good deal longer than I have . . . and, by God, you've been through some terrible times together. But I'll tell you this. In the years that I have known her, Nelly has shown herself to be foolhardy and stubborn. *I'm* fond of her too, you know that, Emma . . . but you can't deny that if she sets her mind against some'at, well . . . she's hard put to change it. And I know it's painful for you, Emma . . . but the truth is that Nelly's set her mind against you! You'll drive yourself into the asylum if you don't accept it. And you know as well as I do, *that's exactly* what that no-good son of mine planned right from the start.'

279

'But he's using her, Mr Thomas.' Emma felt so utterly helpless and wretched. 'He has no feelings for Nelly! He'll make her life a misery. And I must do something . . . I can't just watch it happen and do nothing!'

'There isn't a thing in this world you can do, Emma. You've written to Nelly and you've offered both friendship and support. If she chooses to throw it all back in your face, then I'm afraid . . . you must respect her wishes.' He saw how distraught Emma was, and he despised his son all the more for it. 'Y'do see that, don't you, Emma?'

Emma reluctantly nodded, for she knew that he was right in what he said. She got up from the chair and, assuring him that she would try to put it all from her mind, she went to the door and was on the point of closing it behind her when Roland Thomas said in a strong convincing voice, 'Mark my words, Emma, Nelly will seek you out, I'm sure of it. One of these days, she'll come to realise what a good friend she has in you, and she'll turn up on the doorstep. She will. You see if I'm not telling the truth.'

Emma smiled, nodded to him, and softly closed the door. If only that were true, she thought sadly, realising how Foster Thomas was so cruelly right when he promised to make her suffer because, since that day when she and Nelly had parted on such awful terms, there had been no real peace in her life. Oh, if only Nelly *would* seek her out, Emma thought, as she composed herself to brace the long business meeting which even now awaited her in the study, in the form of her accountant and a representative from the Jackson Chandlers Company, a modest but promising little concern situated in Fremantle. Emma had challenged the Lassater Shipping Line in making a bid for Jackson Chandlers, which she saw as a natural addition to the newly formed Thomas Shipping Company. However she must be very cautious, because only yesterday she had received the news that Silas Trent had met up with the two shipowners whom he and Emma had discussed and it seemed that, for the right price, they were willing to sell. That would greatly deplete her financial resources and, though a Chandler's business would be a great asset, she had to gauge the price right, without losing the chance of acquiring it altogether.

As Emma bade the two smiling gentlemen good morning, her thoughts inevitably lingered on what her husband had told her. If only it could be true, she thought, if only Nelly would 'turn up on the doorstep'. What a joyous day that would be.

Three days later, on Saturday, the twenty-fourth of October in the year of our Lord, 1876, the promise which Roland Thomas had made to Emma came true, but instead of being the joyous occasion which Emma had hoped, the unexpected arrival of Nelly heralded a series of tragic consequences.

The day had been particularly harrowing for Emma, because as yet she had been unable to replace Nelly satisfactorily in the store. Since Nelly's departure, there had been one new employee after the other, a young girl from Bunbury, a lad who had served some time on a whaling ship, and a middle-aged woman from the prison. Each and every one of them had proved to be a disaster in one way or another. The girl had shown herself to be bone idle, the lad to be accident-prone, and the woman to have a weakness for thievery and argument. The last straw for Emma was when, that very morning, Rita Hughes was made to fend off a vicious attack from the prisoner, who had every intention of splitting Rita's head open with a pickaxe. Apparently, Rita had quite rightly made the comment that the floorboards needed a fresh sprinkling of sawdust. The employee saw this as the very excuse she had waited for in order to pick an argument. She replied that she had other jobs to do, and if Rita Hughes wanted more sawdust down, then she'd better 'do it yer bloody self'. A raging row erupted and Rita Hughes was seen to flee into the street, to escape serious injury. Emma was given no choice. The woman had to go, and she herself was obliged to take her place. That didn't worry Emma though, because she was never one to be afraid of work.

What *did* worry Emma was the way Rita Hughes appeared to be letting herself go in these past weeks. As a rule, she was meticulously dressed, her collar and cuffs always starched and sparkling, and her entire appearance of such trim smartness that was beyond reproach. Her hair, which was now more marbled with grey, would be neatly secured into a roll and fastened tightly in the nape of her neck. Her small dark boots were highly polished and she was most particular never to be seen with a hair out of place at any time during her long working day. The same pride and joy which she took in her tidy appearance was always extended to include the execution of every task she did, however demanding or menial. People used to admire her for it, and make regular comment on it. Now, however, their admiration had turned to curiosity and their comments had turned to whispering in little gossiping groups, about how sloppy Rita Hughes was becoming and how little she seemed to care for her appearance of late. 'Why, you'll never believe it,' declared the butcher's round-eyed wife, 'but a pin actually fell from her hair and into the salt-bin only the other day. And did she take the trouble to retrieve it and to secure her hair from her face? No, my dears . . . she did not!' There was much speculation and on two occasions at least, the customers had seen fit to complain quietly to Emma. 'Whatever's the matter with the poor woman?' asked the kindly seamstress. 'Is she ill?' Emma promised that she would certainly have a discreet word with Rita, and so she did; after which Rita Hughes appeared to make a great effort to improve, or to be seen to improve. But Emma was not fooled. She knew well enough that Rita had been devastated by Foster Thomas's preference for Nelly, though if she had her own suspicions as to his motive, she kept her thoughts to herself.

'Are you all right, Rita? You do look very tired.' Emma was seated on the tall stool which was pulled up to the bureau in the back office; she was about to close the ledger after making the stock entries, when she glanced through the glass partition to see Rita Hughes gazing out of the window. 'Rita . . . it's been a very long day, I know –' Emma was by her side now '– you go on home. I'll lock up.' Normally they would have closed the store some hours before, but this was the last Saturday in the month and the stock-taking must be done.

'It's getting dark,' came the reply. Of a sudden, Rita Hughes had swung round to face Emma and it was plain to see that she had been crying. Now though, she displayed a half-smile and told Emma in a brisk voice, 'I wouldn't dream of leaving you to finish up on your own. There's still the stock to be brought through from the back, and the displays to be set up ready for Monday morning.' She donned a serious expression on her face as she swept past Emma, saying, 'Better get on with it then . . . the two of us will make light work of it and be done in no time at all.' She fetched two lamps from beneath the counter, lighting them both, then placing one on top of the counter and hanging one from the hook in the beam situated over the bureau. It was only then that Emma realised how rapidly the daylight was fading. No wonder she had a throbbing headache, when she had been poring over the ledgers in half-light.

An hour and a half later, at a quarter to ten, everything was done, and the two women prepared to leave. 'I don't think I've ever felt so tired in my whole life!' Emma declared with a warm smile to Rita Hughes, who was fussing about the way her cape just would not sit right on her shoulders. 'My head aches . . . my feet are on fire, and I could fall asleep on the spot!' She put out the lamp in the office, before coming through to the store. 'I expect you feel exactly the same, Rita.' She looked at the other woman, who seemed painfully preoccupied, and Emma felt a rush of compassion for her. 'Thank you for the hard work you've put in,' she told her warmly, 'I'll see you're suitably rewarded, you know that.'

'Of course. Thank *you*, Mrs Thomas. An extra guinea or two is always very welcome. It's a shame that we've found no one to take Nelly's place . . . I know you have more than enough to do, without having to take up responsibility here.'

'Well, I can't deny that there are never enough hours in a day, Rita. Still . . . I am seeing that young man from Perth next week. He seems to be very keen on coming here to work, and he has sent exceptionally good references. Let's just hope he's a distinct improvement on the other three, eh?' She smiled, and was surprised when Rita Hughes actually laughed out loud, saying, 'Make sure he doesn't have a weakness for chasing women with a pickaxe!'

The two women were still softly chuckling as they made their way towards the door, with Rita Hughes carrying the lamp and Emma beginning to sort out the right key from the bunch in her hand.

When the door suddenly burst open, both women were taken completely by surprise. In the few seconds of confusion which followed, Rita Hughes screamed out and dropped the lamp to the floor and Emma's first thoughts were that the intruders were robbers, who obviously knew that she had the day's takings on her person. When the dark shadowy figure lunged at her, and Rita Hughes continued screaming, Emma began fighting it off, aware all the while of the flames which had erupted from the broken lamp; fortunately the oil had not been spilt. But then Emma heard a familiar voice calling her name, 'Emma . . . oh Emma!' At once she knew the voice. It was Nelly, Nelly, who had burst in through the door and who had fallen against her, Nelly, now slumped in her arms and sobbing her name as if it were her salvation.

Quickly, and without panic, Emma took stock of the situation. The flames must be put out before anything else, or the whole place would go up. Easing the figure from her, she yelled to Rita Hughes to 'put the flames out! Use your cape . . . anything!' She had already whipped off her own cape and was frantically smothering the fire, which thankfully had not got a proper hold, but was a fearsome thing all the same. When she saw Rita being quick to follow her example, Emma ran to the back wall where the water buckets hung, and in quick succession she used all six of them, dousing the flames and afterwards satisfying herself that enough water had been poured through the cracks between the floorboards. She had seen other disasters from fires that were thought to be put out, but which smouldered under the building until finally flaring up again when least expected.

'Rita, do you think you could find your way to the office, and fetch the lamp from there? There are matches in the top drawer of the bureau.' While she spoke, Emma could see the outline of Nelly in the faint light from the street lamp outside, and when the figure didn't move from the floor where it had fallen, Emma's fearful heart turned somersaults. Stooping down to look more closely, Emma slid her two arms beneath her dear friend's arms and, with all the strength she had left, she raised Nelly to a sitting position. By that time Rita Hughes had come back with the halo of light from the lamp going before her. 'It's *Nelly*, isn't it?' she asked in a trembling voice. 'What's wrong with her, Mrs Thomas?' She raised the lamp and as she did so, the light fell on Nelly's face. 'Oh, my God!' she cried out, the lamp trembling in her hand. '*Look at her face!*'

Emma had seen, and was both shocked and sickened by the sight of Nelly's bruised and battered body. One of her eyes was so swollen as to be virtually unrecognisable; there was a deep, vicious indentation on her forehead that might have been imprinted there by the shape of a ring, so sharp were the edges; and the gash along her cheekbone was all the more misshapen by the blood which had dried on it. From her right temple to a cut on her lip there was a long, meandering red trail, which was not so much a deep cut as a mark made by a blunt instrument being drawn along it.

Emma saw that Nelly was not unconscious, but sapped of all strength, in pain, and obviously filled with terror. Emma now tried to help her to her feet, saying in a gentle, soothing voice, 'It's all right, Nelly . . . it's all right. Don't be afraid, I'll take care of you.' Nelly began shaking violently and the tears rolled down her sorry face as, lifting her brown eyes that were normally so merry and were now terribly scarred by her ordeal, she kept saying over and over again in a small trembling voice, 'It ain't the first time, Emma darling . . . it ain't the first time he's got drunk and thrashed me.'

'Ssh!' Emma clung to her friend, yet she could hardly see for the scalding tears which blurred her eyes. 'Ssh now, Nelly. He won't "thrash" you again. You have my word on that!' In that moment, if she could have placed her bare hands on the worthless creature who had done this, she wouldn't have been responsible for her own actions.

'Oh, Mrs Thomas,' Rita Hughes had gone a deathly shade of white, and for one awful moment, Emma thought the poor thing was about to faint. 'She won't *die*, will she? Oh, she can't mean that *Foster* did this to her . . . she can't!' She peered closely at Nelly, who was leaning all her body weight on Emma's slim form. With her tiny eyes stretched open in horror and her

287

voice filled with awe, she said again more softly, 'She won't die, will she?'

'She might,' Emma told her in a firm voice designed to jolt her senses, 'if you don't give me a hand to get her up to the house!' At once, Rita Hughes came forward to take some of Nelly's weight from Emma; then, with Nelly's bedraggled and sorry figure supported between them, they went at a careful if hurried pace towards the High Street and the Thomases' residence. Emma hoped they would not disturb her husband, who had suffered a great deal of pain and discomfort these past few days, and was at the end of his patience.

'If you have any idea who did this, then it's your duty to inform the authorities!' The doctor's expression was severe as he spoke to both Emma and Rita Hughes; the latter found it difficult to tear her eyes from Nelly's scarred face even though she had helped to wash and clean the wounds which so offended her.

'I ain't sure who did it, doctor!' Nelly called out from her bed. 'And it ain't no use you asking them two neither . . . 'cause they don't know who it was no more than *I* do!' Nelly sensed from the look on Emma's face that she had every intention of telling the doctor that it was Foster Thomas who had battered her friend, and so great was Nelly's fear of that man, so deeply had he instilled in her a riveting terror of him, that she would have crawled from the bed on her bended knees to prevent sending the authorities after him. Nelly believed that if she allowed that to happen, she would be signing her own death warrant. 'That's right, ain't it, Emma . . . ain't it Rita? . . . You ain't got no idea *who* attacked me, have you, eh? No idea at all. You make sure the good doctor knows that!' She didn't recognise her own voice as it sailed through the room from her bruised and swollen lips. In her anxiety to keep secret the name of Foster Thomas, she pulled herself up from the bolster, crying in pain as she did so.

'You lie still!' instructed the doctor. 'I'm afraid you have a broken rib or two. Lie still, or suffer the consequences.' He watched while Nelly fell back on to the pillow, her face contorted with pain and misshapen by the beating it had taken. Yet she kept her frightened brown eyes on Emma, willing her not to betray her.

'Now then, Mrs Thomas . . . do you have any idea who did this? She knows, I'm sure,' he cast a concerned glance at Nelly, 'but, for some reason, she won't confide in me.'

Emma was suffering a bitter conflict. She *should* tell. With every bone in her body she wanted to see that fiend pay for what he had done to Nelly. But now, as she looked towards her friend and saw the desperate pleading in her tearful eyes, she was torn a thousand ways. 'She has told me very little,' she replied, convincing herself that Foster Thomas would be made to pay, if not tonight, then tomorrow, when she would persuade Nelly that the authorities must be told. Nelly was back, and she was safe, thank God. Tomorrow, she might be ready to see things in a different light. She saw the great rush of relief and gratitude in Nelly's face as she buried it in the pillow and began quietly sobbing. 'Thank you so much, doctor,' Emma said now, showing him to the door, 'I'll talk to Nelly when she's rested.'

Emma waited while the doctor attended to her husband. He had unfortunately been woken by all the comings and goings, and demanded to know what had happened. Emma told him the truth, that Nelly had taken a terrible beating, but she deliberately kept his son's name out of it. 'You can't hide the facts from *me*, girlie!' he had told her scathingly. 'It's him that's beaten her, that's right isn't it? That no-good son of mine who's never done anything worthwhile in his life. But he can take up his bloody fists to a helpless woman! By God! There'll come a day when he'll drive me too far!' At this point he had thumped his clenched-up fists time and time again into his lifeless legs. 'Curse these useless things! If it weren't for these, I'd show him a beating all right. Man to man . . . not man over his helpless wife.' He had worked himself up into such a pitch that Emma had to ask that the doctor see *him* as well as Nelly.

'He's sleeping now, Mrs Thomas.' The doctor's face was grave however. 'I'm afraid his pain will soon be beyond medication.' He watched the light go from Emma's wise eyes, and he was filled with admiration for her courageous spirit. She was a fine woman, a woman who never stinted in her friendship or loyalty, and she was rightfully well respected hereabouts. 'I've done all I can. Your friend won't scar . . . although she'll be some long time mending, I'm afraid. But as for your husband, Emma' – he had never addressed her by her Christian name before and the point was not lost on Emma – 'he won't mend at all.'

When the doctor's carriage had gone from sight, Emma glanced down at herself and was strangely surprised by the fact that her dress was blackened by the smoke from when she had beaten out the flames from the lamp. Strands of her hair hung loosely about her neck, and the hem of her skirt was still damp from the water which she had flung on to the flames. Strange, she thought, how none of it seemed to matter now. And oh, she felt so very, very tired, her whole body was stretched with a weariness she had never experienced before. She supposed it was because of the child she carried inside her. Of a sudden, she remembered Rita Hughes, and it struck her how late in the evening it was.

Going to her husband's room, Emma made certain that he was sleeping. She was satisfied also to see that the nurse had made herself comfortable in the wicker chair and was keeping watch. 'Call me if you need anything,' Emma whispered to her; when the chubby-faced nurse gratefully nodded, Emma went softly up the stairs to where Nelly was in a deep, healing sleep.

'I'll get Taylor to walk you home,' Emma informed Rita Hughes. 'Your family will be frantic, wondering why you're so late.' She collected a long fringed shawl from the chair back and wrapped it loosely about her shoulders.

'Thank you, yes, I would like to go home and clean up. My parents won't be worrying though because they're away visiting an aged uncle in Perth. They're not due home until tomorrow.'

'Oh, I see. Well . . . if you'll just watch Nelly a while, I'll go and rouse Taylor to accompany you along the streets. There's no safe place in the dark for a woman on her own.' She left the room and began her way down the wide dogleg staircase, her path lit by the four oil-lamps, strategically placed atop of each of the four thick oak posts which supported the stairs. In the flickering light, Emma wondered what a dishevelled sight she must look. There hadn't been even a moment since Nelly had arrived to wash and spruce herself up. No matter, she told herself, lifting one hand in an effort to tuck her straying auburn hair into a more disciplined appearance, there'll be time enough when Rita is safely on her way. The thought of a hot tub followed by a good night's sleep sent her feet hurrying down the thickly carpeted stairway, as she began to wonder whether Taylor, the handyman, might still be awake and pottering about his room above the outbuildings. She would collect a lamp from the kitchen on the way out, because the area directly behind the house was exceptionally dark.

Two steps from the bottom of the stairway, Emma halted, inclining her head to one side and listening hard. What was that slight sound that had disturbed her? Emma stood still a moment longer, not daring to move, her fearful heart pounding. She turned her anxious eyes towards the gloomy hallway below, as she held her breath and waited to hear the sound again. But the air was silent and brooding. I must have imagined it, Emma told herself, yet she was not fully convinced and, if it hadn't been for the fact that she was anxious to see Rita Hughes safely on her way, so that she herself might be bathed and asleep that much quicker, Emma might have been tempted to go back up the stairs and ask that good woman to accompany her on her errand. But no, Rita had done quite enough for one day, and did not deserve to be put on any further, Emma decided. Besides which, there would be no one to keep an eye on Nelly in the next few moments. Emma had already made up her mind that she would spend the night in the chair in Nelly's room, in case she needed her.

Emma resumed her descent into the hallway, chiding herself for letting her imagination run riot. Now she convinced herself that there had been no noise, except perhaps for the rustling of her own silk skirt as it swept against the stair-treads. She even smiled to herself, saying in a small whisper, 'You should be ashamed, Emma. Fancy! A woman of your thirty-two years being afraid of the dark.' Emma would not have been so 'ashamed' had she known that someone was hiding below, listening to her words, and smiling.

What happened next was done so swiftly that Emma was not even able to cry out. As she stepped into the hallway, the figure sprang from the shadows, clamping one hand over her mouth and gripping her two arms behind her back with the other. As the intruder forced her along by the wall which skirted the drawing-room, Emma kicked and struggled, but she was held so fast that her attempts were futile. She was being dragged round the corner and into the narrow passage, where the door to the left led to the room that was Roland Thomas's and the door to the right went into the drawing-room. Whoever it was who had her in a grip of iron was both immensely strong and obsessively determined that she be given no opportunity to raise the alarm. The hand which smelled of stale tobacco and which had her silenced was stretched from her nostrils to her chin, holding her lips tightly together and preventing her from getting even a pinch of skin between her teeth to bite through and shock her attacker into releasing her.

Emma realised that, if she were to summon any help

at all, she must use her feet, even though her legs were swept from the floor. There was no other way. When her assailant pushed her beyond Roland Thomas's door, Emma's frightened eyes saw that the door was half-open. She knew also that, situated on a small table outside the drawing-room, was a large pot plant. If only she could kick out and upset the table so that the plant fell to the floor, surely to God *someone* would come running.

When Emma's chance came, she was ready. But it was unfortunate that the drawing-room door was also partly open, because if the intruder had been made to relax his hold on Emma's arms in order to open the door, nothing on this earth could have held her. As it was, she was pinned fast. But in that split second when he used Emma's body to push open the drawing-room door Emma took her bearings. Praying that she would not miss, she lashed out with her foot in the direction of the pot plant. Her heart soared when she felt that she had made contact and she waited for the crash which must surely follow. But, except for a scraping noise where the pot plant moved along the table only a few inches, there was no loud crashing sound that could summon help to her side. She knew at once that her captor was enraged by her attempt, when he cruelly pushed his hand tighter into her face and gave her arms a spiteful twist. She felt herself being dragged into the room, and her terrified heart sank within her when she realised that the door was softly closed behind them, and that she was alone with her assailant in a room that was pitch black. All Emma could do was to offer up a silent prayer and believe that somehow her ordeal would be over quickly. Her heart bled for the tiny life which beat inside her, and she had to trust in the Lord that he would not be so cruel as to let her lose *this* child.

Emma struggled as her hands were bound so tightly together that her wrists felt as though they were being sliced in two. When a rag was thrust into her mouth and secured there by the broad hessian binding, Emma was totally helpless. Her terror was heightened when she felt herself being pushed to the floor, and her arms tied to the table leg. In a minute, she was left alone while the creature who had brought her here busied himself opening wide the long tapestry curtains which had shut out the moonlight. When, after an instant, he returned and knelt before Emma, he smiled to see her startled grey eyes as they stared at his face in the revealing light of the moon.

'Surely you ain't *surprised*, are you, my beauty? You should have known I'd come back for you!'

Emma found herself looking into the worst evil she could imagine. It was Foster Thomas, handsome as ever, but in that wicked, smiling face with its deep blue eyes, there was a depth of ugliness of the kind that came from within, a hideousness which clung to him like a mantle. His eyes bore deep into Emma's, and she shivered as they touched her soul. Quickly Emma looked away, wondering what dreadful tortures this madman had put Nelly through, and what awful intentions he had towards her this God-forsaken night.

Of a sudden, he began giggling, and it was plain to Emma that he was either drunk out of his senses, or he had completely lost his mind. Either way, she was riveted with the most awful and compelling belief that neither she nor her unborn child would ever see the morrow.

The thought made her frantic, and she desperately searched her mind for ways in which she might escape, or alert others in the house. It wouldn't be too long before Rita Hughes went looking for her, she told herself; have faith, Emma, trust in the Lord! But if Foster Thomas intended killing her, Emma knew that he could do it easily, in a moment, before the door could be opened. She knew it and was terrified.

'Don't turn away from me, Emma.' She felt his rough fingers beneath her chin as her head was yanked back. She felt his booze-laden breath fanning her face, but still she kept her gaze lowered from him. She would have thumped her boot heels against the carpet, but he was crouched on her legs, his weight keeping them secured. He was devious. But then, madmen usually were. 'So Nelly came running to you, did she?' he asked in a whisper, still smiling. 'I knew she would. I planned it that way, y'see.' The smile went from his face and, to Emma's horror, he began slowly undoing the buttons of her dress. When she struggled and squirmed, he fetched his hand up and slapped it hard across her temple. 'No, Emma . . . you're not to struggle against me. You're mine, y'see . . . you've *always* been mine, I've told you that so many times and still you fight against it!' His eyes were wild as they stared at her, yet they were vacant also. In that moment Emma knew that he was completely and utterly mad.

'That Nelly . . . she knows too much for her own good.' He was talking in a whisper as he leaned close towards her, all the while undoing her buttons. 'She saw me, y'know . . . the night my mother was shot. I set the whole thing up, but it went wrong.' He laughed very softly as he slid his hand into Emma's dress and began caressing the warm firmness of her breast. Emma felt physically sick, but she knew that if she were to save herself and her child, she must not goad him, for he was quite capable of sliding his hand to her throat and squeezing the life from it. 'If things had gone well that night . . . then *I* would have Thomas Trading . . . and all this.' He waved a hand to encompass the whole room. 'But there's still hope. Oh, Emma . . . you and me, we can do anything we set our minds to!' He looked into her face as though searching for some sign of encouragement. When he saw only hatred and fear in Emma's accusing eyes, he made a curious expression, like an animal in pain, Emma thought; then without warning he placed his two fists one either side of Emma's dress and, with a low growl sounding deep in his throat, he ripped the bodice apart, exposing her bare breasts, now scarred red by his fingernails.

In that same instant, the door crashed open. Foster Thomas scrambled to his feet, his wild eyes picking out the figure of his own father, who was lying twisted on the floor. He was exhausted by the immense and determined effort it had taken for him to get from his bed – without waking the nurse – take his hand gun from the drawer, then to crawl along the passageway, hampered by the dead weight of his legs, and finally to reach up and open the door. The terrible ordeal he had gone through showed on his face, which was contorted with pain. But when he stared up at this man, this terrible coward who was his own son, Roland Thomas's heart was filled with a strange guilt. Somehow, he imagined, the blame must lie with him. He had spawned this worthless creature, and only he could make amends. He raised the gun and pointed it at his son's heart.

'No!' Emma's terrified scream stayed trapped in her head. But there came another sound, a loud ear-splitting sound, when the room was pierced with fire. Foster Thomas stood perfectly still for a split second, then, with his startled eyes staring into his father's distraught face, he crumpled silently to the ground, his eyes fixed in a round, surprised expression.

The silence which followed was eerie, but then there came the sound of anxious voices and running feet in the distance. Emma saw the nurse first, as holding a lamp before her, she came to a halt by the twisted, sprawling figure of Roland Thomas. Her unbelieving eyes went from her patient to the body lying nearby – its vacant stare seeming to fix itself upon her – then, her mouth falling open as though in slow motion, she rested her shocked gaze on Emma's bound and gagged figure, with the dress almost torn from it. She saw the devastation in Emma's terrified eyes and was paralysed by it. Emma's paramount thoughts were of her husband, who had been made to commit a terrible crime, murdering his own son!

It was as though Emma's heart had stopped beating when, her eyes drawn once more to the face of Roland Thomas, she saw that he was softly crying. It was with a rush of horror that she realised the dark intent in his expression, yet she was powerless to stop him. The frantic protest which was cruelly stifled in her throat found an outlet in her eyes, as they pleaded with the nurse to lower her gaze and see what dreadful thing her patient was about to do. But the nurse was already giving urgent instructions to the servants and to Rita

Hughes, who had also heard the shot and had come to investigate.

In those few vital moments when the frantic expression in Emma's grey eyes conveyed itself to her husband, it was already too late. He looked at her, smiled gently and moved his lips in a silent whisper. Emma read those two words as easily as if they had been shouted from the rooftops: 'Forgive me,' her husband asked. Then he turned away.

When remembering it over the years to follow, Emma thought it strange how very quickly the whole thing had happened – in the space of mere minutes – but how tortuous and endless it had seemed.

She relived that awful night many times before she could finally rid herself of the look in her husband's tragic eyes when he had mouthed his pitiful words; of the sound which his bath chair made as Taylor hurriedly trundled it down the passageway towards the nurse; and of how, even as Taylor and the nurse prepared to arrange it in order to lift Roland Thomas more easily into it, a second shot rang out. Emma was haunted by the vision of the nurse's starched white dress all spattered with crimson, and that poor woman's scream rang in Emma's dreams for some long time afterwards.

Later, when the authorities had completed their investigations, and she sought solace in Nelly's room, Emma fell like a child into her arms, clinging to the one person who knew her almost as well as she knew herself. 'Oh, Nelly . . . *why?*' she sobbed. 'Roland was such a good man.'

Nelly held her tight, nuzzling her own bruised and battered face against Emma's hair. Like Emma, she had witnessed things that would long torment her. 'Who knows why, Emma darling,' she murmured. 'When the good in us is faced by terrible evil . . . who knows what we might do?'

Chapter Eleven

'It's a boy, Emma!' Nelly had watched the final moments from when the small dark head had first appeared. Now, as the tiny shoulders came into sight and then the baby's whole perfect little form slithered into the world, she was unable to contain her joy and excitement. 'Aw, Emma . . . you should see the little bugger! He's gorgeous!' she shouted gleefully, her brown eyes watching Widow Miller's every movement, as she collected the tiny babe into her arms. Holding the squirming bundle upside down, the plump woman gave it a number of short, sharp spanks on the buttocks, smiling broadly when its loud cries filled the room. Then, taking it to the dresser, she quickly washed it, wrapped it in a shawl and came back to the bed, where she placed it in Emma's arms. 'Nelly's right,' she said with a kindly smile, 'you have a beautiful son.' She then set about washing Emma and making her comfortable.

When the tiny bundle was put into Emma's outstretched arms, she was so full of emotion that she could only nod her gratitude. When she took the child to her breast and lowered her gaze to see its tiny face, her vision was blurred by the tears of joy which sprang from her heart. There were no words which could convey how Emma felt in that most precious moment.

301

Here, in her arms, warm and real, was her son, Marlow's son, as perfect a boy as she could ever have wished for. In her heart she gave thanks to God for her baby's safe deliverance, because, in the weeks following the tragedy which had unfolded right before her eyes, there were anxious times when the doctor feared that Emma might lose her child. Yet never once did Emma lose her faith. She made herself believe that this child was meant to be, that she and Marlow were meant to be, and that if there was a merciful God, he would bring her through the ordeals which he had set her, for she had weathered them in as courageous and determined a manner as was humanly possible. Surely now he would help her to find a kind of happiness and peace of soul. In her son, he had answered her prayers.

'He don't look like you, Emma gal.' Nelly had waited for the Widow Miller's departure before sitting on the bed alongside Emma. 'He ain't got your auburn hair . . . and he ain't got your grey eyes neither!' She was fascinated.

Emma smiled up at Nelly's homely face, which was as jubilant as though the infant might be her very own, and her heart was touched by memories of Nelly's dreadful ordeal at the hands of Foster Thomas. For just a moment her joy was marred. She knew that, even were she to live to a ripe old age, there could never be anyone who would be as close to her in friendship as Nelly. Impulsively, Emma held the child towards this woman whom she had loved like her own flesh and blood, for more years than she cared to remember. Together they had been through so much, yet all their ups and downs had only served to bring them even closer. 'Hold him, Nelly,' she offered now, 'feel how warm and soft he is.'

'Oh, Emma! . . . Can I? Aren't you afraid I'll drop him?' Nelly's face was a picture, as her brown eyes grew big and round and she put her hands behind her back to prevent them from grasping the child until she was good and ready. 'Ooh, look at him,' she laughed, 'I do believe the little bugger's smiling at me. No! I won't take him, Emma . . . I just know I'll drop him.' When Emma insisted, she gave a sheepish grin and brought her two hands from behind her back. Taking a few moments to prepare herself, she vigorously wiped the palms of her hands on the deep folds of the blue silk dress which Emma had bought her. Then, after a deal of nervous coughing and throat noises, she held out her arms, a look on her face that amused Emma: a mingling of bliss and sheer terror. 'Tell him not to wiggle, Emma gal,' she muttered, taking the bundle and holding it close, 'it's been a good many years since I held a young 'un, and I might have forgotten the right way to do it.'

'Isn't he beautiful, Nelly?' Emma gazed at her son, her adoring eyes following his every feature. Nelly was right. He did not have auburn hair or grey eyes, because in that tiny face there was a wonderful likeness to his father. He had hair as black and rich as Marlow's, and the eyes, though touched with sapphire blue, were dark also. Even the strong lines of his face, the shape of his nose and that straight set chin were reminiscent of Marlow, and Emma's happiness was overwhelming. Yet in her great joy, there was a tinge of sad regret when she thought of that other babe which she had borne, a little girl with the same dark colouring, and

303

who would have been a sister to this son of hers and Marlow's. But that was over sixteen years ago now, and if the child had lived, she would be almost a woman. Emma let her thoughts dwell on that for a while, looking to find some measure of consolation in the knowledge that it was all too far in the past now, too late. But it only made her pine all the more, as she made herself think about a girl of seventeen, a dark-haired girl with the striking vivacious looks of Marlow, and perhaps having also some measure of Emma in her character. The years had not diminished Emma's loss nor her pain, but only intensified it. She would have to learn how to live with the memories and not let them cause her pain. In time, maybe, she would be able to, Emma thought. But she could never forget.

'Here, Emma . . . you'd best take the little darling back.' Nelly placed a gossamer kiss on the infant's forehead. 'I do love him, Emma. He's precious,' she said.

Emma collected him in her arms. 'Thank you, Nelly,' she said, gratefully squeezing her friend's hand, 'he *is* . . . very precious.' She thought that nobody in this world could ever know just how much. Now there were plans to be made, exciting plans which she had kept to herself these past months, but which were now pushing themselves to the front of her mind. 'Nelly,' she said quietly, afterwards seeming lost in thought, as she looked for the best way to broach the subject, in view of Nelly's excitable nature.

'Yes? . . . What's on yer mind, gal?' Nelly had got to her feet, but now she looked down at Emma with a puzzled frown. 'Oh look! Yer ain't worrying about the business and such, are yer?' she demanded. 'Rita

Hughes is doing a *grand* job at the store . . . she's a changed woman since that . . . awful business.' Nelly's face became crestfallen as she was forced to remember. But then, in that way she had of pushing away anything which disturbed her too deeply, she went on, 'And that Silas Trent . . . well! If yer don't mind me saying, Emma . . . the bugger's work-mad! I mean it, darlin' . . . yer couldn't fault him. He's running that business like it were his own! What! . . . I'm telling yer . . . yer couldn't do better yourself!'

'I know that, Nelly.' Emma wondered how she could ever repay Silas Trent for giving up the sea in order to watch over her interests while she herself had been unable to.

'You'll be up and about in no time now,' Nelly reminded her, 'but o' course . . . you'll have this little 'un here to look after. What name are yer giving the lad?' she asked.

Emma had not decided on that issue yet, because she was torn between her own father's name, Thadius, and Marlow's father's name, which if she remembered right, he had told her was Bill. It would have been lovely if she could talk it over with Marlow. But as yet, Silas's enquiries as to his whereabouts had been unsuccessful. The news from Blackburn, Lancashire, was that he had left the area on learning of his sister Sal's demise. It was said that he had been heartbroken. Emma did not intend to give up though, and had told Silas that Marlow must be found. He was not alone in the world any more, because here was a woman who loved him. And he had a son! What better purpose was there for a man to live?

'You ain't to worry about the business, Emma,'

Nelly reminded her now, 'it's being well taken care of.'

'No, I *wasn't* worrying about that,' Emma assured her. 'Silas has it all in hand. I know that, from his weekly reports to me. Also, Mr Lucas from the bank has expressed his admiration for Silas Trent's business acumen. Thomas Shipping has proved to be a very profitable venture all round . . . and we're picking up inland trade all the time. No, I'm not worrying on that score, Nelly. In fact, there are only two things that concern me now. One is that Marlow hasn't yet been found.'

'And the other?'

'The other is *you*.'

'Me? Oh, Emma . . . what have I done wrong now? Look here, if that parlour maid's been telling tales about me breaking that white statue on the mantel-piece . . . she's a little liar. I know nothing at all about it!'

Emma was amused to see that Nelly's face had gone a bright shade of pink. She knew all about the statue, which Nelly *had* broken, and which the maid had reported, but Emma had dismissed the matter. 'I don't know what you're talking about,' she lied, to save Nelly's pride. 'What I have in mind has nothing at all to do with a statue.'

'What then? If she's accused me of something else, I'll *do* for her . . . I bloody will! Just you tell me what she's been saying. What's on yer mind, Emma . . . come on, me shoulders is broad enough, and I'm ready fer anything?'

Emma was really enjoying herself, putting on her most serious face, she beckoned for Nelly to sit down on the bed once more. Then, when her friend was seated and looking at Emma with a bold, defiant expression, Emma asked, 'Ready for *anything*, you say?'

'That's right, me girl! You just tell me what's on yer mind! But I'm telling you right now . . . I didn't do it!'

'Would you be ready to set sail for *England*, I wonder?' Emma blurted out, watching with amusement as Nelly's whole face appeared to fall open with surprise.

'England!' Nelly was on her feet in an instant, looking down on Emma with disbelieving eyes, as she asked in a voice filled with awe, '*We're setting sail for England?*' Her voice tailed off and caught in a strange little choking sound. When she spoke again it was in a whisper, and the tears were spilling down her face. 'D'yer mean it, Emma gal? . . . We're really going home?' The sight of Nelly's tears and her obvious happiness touched Emma's heart. She swallowed the lump which had straddled her throat and when she nodded, Nelly threw herself down on her knees, her two arms stretched out to embrace both Emma and the child. 'I can't believe it!' she cried through her laughter. 'We're going home. Oh, Emma, Emma! At long last . . . we're going home!'

The torrent of emotion created by Nelly's simple delight engulfed Emma, moving her also to tears of joy. 'It's been a long time, Nelly,' she murmured, holding her son fast on one arm and stroking Nelly's bent head with her free hand, 'but yes . . . at long last, we're going home.' These two devoted friends clung to each other. They cried a little and laughed a little, and the hardships they had endured fell away.

Outside, it was growing ever dark and on this June

evening there was a wintry nip in the air. But in the room where Emma's son had been born, there was warmth of a human kind, there was sunshine and hope. Soon there would be a new dawn, when long cherished dreams might be realised.

'You can count on me. All will be well taken care of in your absence, Emma.' Silas Trent looked around the ship's cabin, then, satisfied that Emma and her son would be comfortable on their long sea voyage, he swung the two large tapestry bags up on to the bunk. 'Nelly's beside herself with excitement,' he laughed, 'I've just left her examining every nook and cranny in her cabin . . . there isn't a dial that she hasn't twisted, or a cupboard or drawer that she hasn't investigated.'

'Leave her be . . . she'll soon tire of it and come looking to see what I've got that *she* hasn't!' Emma's laughter was light-hearted and, with her son in her arms, there shone from her lovely eyes a peace which Silas Trent had not seen there before. 'If the weather is kind to you, Emma, you should arrive in Liverpool on or about the 16th of September. If our information was correct and Marlow receives the message I sent to the Navigation pub, he should be waiting when you disembark. God speed, Emma. And don't concern yourself about matters at this end.' He smiled broadly, saying, 'Now that you've made me a full partner . . . I wouldn't dare let you down.'

'You won't let me down, I know that,' she told him warmly, adding, 'or you would never have been made a full partner!' Emma had no qualms where Silas Trent was concerned, because she knew him to be a man of integrity and honour.

'All the same . . . that fellow at the bank has his beady eyes on my every move!' he laughed, wagging a finger at Emma.

'And so he should!' Emma chided with a smile. 'After all, where would we be without the darling man?' Of a sudden, Emma grew serious, as she asked, 'Has your wife promised to come out?'

'Not yet. Martha's ties with home are too strong for her to let go, I'm afraid.' There was disappointment in his voice, and a sorry look in his dark eyes, 'I haven't given up though. Edward has expressed the wish to come and see me before he pursues his own career . . . I'm counting on him to persuade his mother that her place is here with me.'

'And are you so sure you don't want to return to England . . . to be with her?'

'I've already made it clear to Martha that I'll *never* go back.' Here he leaned forward to kiss first the child, then Emma. 'She knows that I love her, and would welcome her here with open arms. She also knows that my mind is made up . . . Australia is the place I want to be. It's my home now, and my future is here. If Martha loves me, she'll want to share my life, and that means breaking away from her parents long enough at least to give this country, and me, a chance to prove ourselves.'

'You're a good man, Silas Trent.' Emma knew no better. 'Martha is a lucky woman.'

'Martha is not made of the same stuff that you are, Emma . . . unfortunately!' There was anger in his voice as he turned and walked to the door, 'But I love her. I always have.' When he had stepped out of the doorway, he looked back at Emma. The smile had returned to his craggy, moustached features and his brown eyes

309

were twinkling, 'Take care of young Bill. I've no doubt he's got the makings of a sailor in him.' He gave a chuckle and a wink, then was gone and Emma was left staring at the oak-panelled door.

Of a sudden, the door burst open to reveal Nelly's bright excited face. 'Cor, bugger me, gal!' she cried, rushing into the cabin and tugging at Emma's arm. 'Ain't we posh, eh? Quick, gal . . . let's get topside and wave at the folks on the jetty!' Before Emma could resist, she found herself being propelled out of the cabin, along the dark narrow gangway outside, then up the short flight of steps which took them to the upper deck. Here there were crowds of people all milling in one direction, towards the railings, from where they could see the jetty below.

In this month of August, the sun was at its winter's height and folks were well wrapped up against the cool breeze. Most of the women wore short flouncy capes over their wide skirts and boaters or peaked bonnets fastened with ribbons. Others were swathed in long fringed shawls which were pulled up right over their heads and caught fast beneath the chin. The men wore tall straight top-hats or trilbies with wide curved brims; their long jackets were dark and severe, as were their trousers. Most of them sported great sprouting moustaches, or beards, or both, and all eyes were turned to the shore as, frantically, they scanned the multitude of upturned faces below, searching for the one which was most beloved and familiar. From one end of the deck to the other handkerchiefs fluttered like flags. There were murmuring voices, people tearful and laughing, and occasionally a loud cry when a loved one was spotted.

Such was Nelly's cry now, as she excitedly tapped

Emma on the shoulder. 'There he is!' she called out,
taking off her bonnet and waving it in the air, until the
breeze caught it and whipped it away. But Nelly's
enthusiasm was not dampened. 'Silas! Up here . . .
look up here!' Whereupon, dozens of eyes did as she
bid them, afterwards looking away when they saw a
stranger, but smiling at the woman's obvious excitement and being all the more enthused by it. 'Here,
Silas . . . to your left!' Nelly shouted, and when at last
he caught sight of the little group, he snatched off his
hat to make a wide circle in the air, his face wreathed in
a smile and his eyes playing now on Emma and the
child in her arms. Emma saw his mouth move, but such
was the din all round that it was impossible to hear
what he was saying. Securing her small son in one arm,
she waved enthusiastically with the other. She kept on
waving, even after the vessel began moving away, until
Silas was at first a tiny speck in the distance, then he
merged with the others until no one face was distin-
guishable.

Long after the other passengers had left the railings
and gone in their different directions, and Nelly had
taken Emma's son to the cabin, Emma stood alone, her
knuckles stretched tight as she gripped the rail, and her
thoughtful grey eyes scanning the horizon as the shore-
line rapidly disappeared from her view. The sea is a
solitary place, she thought, as a great feeling of loneliness suddenly took a hold of her and her gaze roved
across the distance. It was a humbling and terrifying
experience to be completely surrounded by deep, dark
waters, stretching out from all sides like a glittering
carpet that looked solid, yet was not. Emma shivered.
She was not a good sailor, though she did love to see

311

the fine ships and the colourful vessels that hustled for space in the docks. There was something uniquely fascinating about it all and now, as the seagulls soared above, calling, and following the ship for as far as they dare, Emma thought how peaceful it was. Her thoughts were back on the shore, as they wandered over the years she had been exiled in this beautiful land of Australia; it was with a shock that she realised how the years amounted to almost half her lifetime! In this land to which she had been forcibly brought, she had suffered indignities and fear; she had known terror and hopelessness, poverty and deprivation. Yet through her hard work, determination and strength of character, she had also achieved a great deal to be proud of, and she was thankful for it. Her long struggle had been an uphill one, but she had never given in.

Now, as Emma relived those years in her mind, she came to understand how, perhaps even without knowing it, she had sunk her roots deep in this great new land. She had achieved almost everything her heart had desired. Yet if she were to set those achievements against being with Marlow for the rest of her life, the choice was simple: everything she had would be less of a prize than their life together, with the many children who, God willing, would surely follow.

All the same, as the ship sailed further and further away from the shores of Australia, Emma felt a pang of sadness, for she knew in her heart that she would never return. At least, not before she was a very old woman, who might wish to show her grandchildren that part of her life which came about long before even their parents were born! For now though, she was going home – sailing towards her ultimate dream and praying that when the ship came into dock in the port of Liverpool, she would see Marlow waiting there.

When the tears crept into her eyes, Emma blamed the stinging sea-air, but she knew that it was a memory which had stirred her to tears; the memory of a young boy swimming in the canal, a young handsome lad who teased her and laughed with her, and because of that, was later cruelly beaten until his back lay open. Even then, Emma's heart had been lost to him, just as hopelessly as it was now. Now that same boy had become a man, and she was a grown woman. But the deep abiding love between them was still as young and strong, indeed, had bound them together over the turbulent years which had cruelly parted them.

Emma looked up at the great expanse of sky above her. She watched the small puffy clouds scurrying in and out of the blue pockets, she saw how beautiful and serene it was. Something deep within told her that beyond the sky that she could see, some almighty force was at work. She murmured a small prayer of gratitude for having come so far, and she asked that the thought of revenge against her old enemies might not drive her too hard. Above all, she asked for Marlow to be waiting for her, and that they might be blessed with a new life ahead. Her deepest regret was that they had been robbed of seeing their first-born grow up to be a woman.

'Are you gonna stand there all day, Emma, gal?' Nelly's abrupt interruption surprised Emma from her thoughts. 'The lad's flat out exhausted for now,' she said, adding with a shake of her tousled head, 'but there'll be blue murder when he wakes up, screaming fer his tit . . . and his mam's out here star-gazing!'

313

'Go on with you!' Emma laughed out loud, coming towards the steps which would take them down to the cabin. 'Perhaps we'll have a minute to unpack before young Bill Tanner demands his supper!'

As Emma followed the chattering Nelly along the gangway, there was a song in her heart and a spring to her step. When the ship gave a gentle roll and Nelly, laughing, said, 'This is the life, gal! Rolling about like a drunken sailor, and not a tot o' bloody rum ter show fer it!' her heart was flooded with laughter, and she felt fortunate to have such a friend by her side.

Nelly, too, had suffered bad times, thought Emma, but, thank God, she had emerged without lasting damage. Certainly, her liking for the opposite sex was beginning to return, if her behaviour on the jetty earlier this morning was anything to go by. She had taken a real fancy to what Silas had called 'a rough-looking bloke with a koala bear on his shoulder'. It was only when the fellow got carried away by Nelly's amorous attentions that he proudly drew a snake from his jacket pocket. Nelly had turned all shades of green, before making a hasty retreat behind Silas and Emma, saying in a wounded voice, 'Did y'see that bloke pestering me? . . . I've a bloody good mind ter report him to the authorities!'

Part Four

England 1877

New Hope

Joy and grief were mingled in the cup;
but there were no bitter tears:
Charles Dickens, *Oliver Twist*

Chapter Twelve

'Your father is a fool. You are *not* going to Australia . . . I forbid it!' Caleb Crowther slammed his clenched fist on to the desk, rose from his seat and, with a look of thunder, he fixed his piercing blue eyes on his grandson's face, saying in a threatening voice, 'While you and your mother choose to live under my roof, you will do as I say. Your father deserted you both, as far as I'm concerned, and this . . .' he snatched a letter from the desk and crumpled it in his fist, ' . . . *this* is what I think of him and his letter!'

'Excuse me, sir. My father did *not* desert us.' Edward Trent met his grandfather's stare with a forthright expression. 'He's worked hard over the years to build a future for me and my mother. He wants us there, with him . . . and, if anything, it is we who have deserted *him*! I've disappointed my father by choosing a career other than the sea . . . but he hides that disappointment and gives me great encouragement in my chosen profession, even though it means we remain far apart. As for my mother, he begged her on his last voyage home to return to Australia with him. She refused, and since then, my father has written many letters, pleading with her to join him, but still she refuses. No, sir . . . it is not my father who has deserted us, but the other way round in my opinion. You have seen the letter which I

317

received only this morning, arranging for me to visit him in Australia before I embark on my studies. I owe him that much . . . and if I may say so, sir . . . I intend to go, with or without your blessing.' The whole time that he was speaking, Edward Trent kept his dark green eyes intent on his grandfather's face, and even though the older man continued to test him with a challenging stare, the young man never once flinched or hesitated in his defence of the father he loved.

'The devil you say!' Caleb Crowther stormed round the desk and came to a halt only inches away from his grandson, who believed for a moment that he was about to be physically struck. Instead, he was surprised to see a devious smile uplift the other man's face as he said in a goading manner, 'So . . . you intend to go with, or without, my blessing, do you?'

'I'm sorry, sir, but yes . . . I do. My first duty is to my father.'

'Hmh!' Caleb Crowther's unpleasant expression grew even more devious. 'And do you intend to go with, or without . . . my money?'

'I have money of my own. A regular allowance sent from my father,' Edward Trent reminded him.

'Indeed you do . . . you do!' agreed his grandfather, still smiling as he stepped towards the desk, where he eased himself back on to its edge, his eyes drilling into the young man's face. 'And . . . as I understand it, your mother is trustee of this money?'

'She is, yes, sir.'

'Then you *won't* go, I'm afraid!' Caleb Crowther's smile broadened as he watched the puzzled look come on to his grandson's handsome features. 'You see,

Edward . . . you might be prepared to go off to the other side of the world . . . with or without my permission, but my daughter, Martha, is another matter. Like the dutiful woman I have raised her to be, she will do *nothing* without my permission.'

Edward Trent's heart sank within him. What his grandfather was saying was sadly the truth. He had his daughter exactly where he wanted her and if he instructed that Edward's money was not to be released, then nothing would persuade her to go against her father's word.

'May I go now?' Edward asked, trying not to let the disappointment show in his voice. 'It seems our conversation is at an end.'

'Oh, look here, Edward,' Caleb Crowther knew well enough that, as always, he had won the day. The boy would stay here, in Breckleton House, until the day he would leave for London and his studies. That was as it should be! But it did not please him to be at odds with his only grandson, whom he admired as a likeable and worthy young man. 'Please understand that I'm doing this for your own good. Who knows what dreadful accident could befall you on such a long and arduous journey? It really is foolhardy and selfish of your father even to suggest it!' Rogues and ruffians abound everywhere . . . waiting to pounce on such innocent fellows as yourself! Have you both so easily forgotten how you were set upon and almost killed by such people?' He waited a moment before continuing, 'Well, let me tell you, Edward, my boy, that *I* will not forget so quickly! That urchin girl who had you secreted away will not elude me forever, believe me.'

'The girl did me no harm, sir. I told you that, the

very moment it all started coming back to me. She was the one who found me . . . she saved me from drowning, and afterwards, she returned me safely to my grandmother.'

'Of course she returned you! Half-dead . . . and for a *price*!' Caleb Crowther could not contain his rage at the girl who had escaped him that night, when he thought he had her safely in his clutches. Like always, when he was made to think of it, his reason became impaired by his fury at being so easily outwitted by an alley urchin, and, if he suspected right, by the offspring of Marlow Tanner and his own sinfully begotten daughter, Emma Grady!

'You have it wrong, sir,' insisted Edward Trent, 'the girl is innocent of everything. Her only crime, if indeed there was one, was in asking the price of a friend's funeral . . . someone she dearly loved, and who otherwise would have been buried in a pauper's grave. I ask you, sir, how can that be a crime?'

'Don't be so gullible, boy! She's no better than the worst rogue who might roam the streets. But I have her face imprinted here.' He tapped his temple, before going on with conviction, 'She won't escape me for ever, make no mistake of that!'

'Why do you hate her so? I'm no liar, sir, yet you will not believe me when I tell you that this girl committed no crime against me. She only did all she could to help me. Have you another reason for wanting her put behind bars?'

When Caleb Crowther realised the way in which his grandson was looking at him, and even questioning his true motives for wanting the girl put out of the way, he grew more cautious. 'Leave such matters to me,' he said abruptly. 'Now you may go. Ask your mother to come and see me . . . about better investing your allowance. I was wrong to let her handle it in the first place. Put all nonsense about going to Australia out of your head. In less than a year, you'll be immersed in your studies. Until then, you can better prepare yourself, and perhaps find time to become more involved in the day-to-day running of a textile business . . . which, I might remind you, will no doubt be your own one day.'

It was Saturday, the second day of September, and Cook was in a bad mood. 'Don't talk nonsense,' she snapped at the scullery-maid, 'wherever did you hear such utter rubbish . . . electric lighting indeed! I'll not see the day when they put it in *my* kitchen . . . I shall be kicking up the daisies first, I tell yer!'

'Well, I know what I heard!' retorted Amy. 'When I went past the dining-room last night, the door was partly open and I heard the master's guests talking about it . . . honest I did.'

'Get away with you!' snorted Cook, brandishing her rolling-pin and causing the maid to scurry from the room into the pantry, where she made an act of cleaning the shelves. 'If your hands worked half as hard as your ears, my girl, we'd get things done a lot quicker round this place!'

'It looks like I've arrived at a bad time.' Edward Trent poked his face round the door, saying with a half-smile. 'Shall I come back later?'

'No, lad.' Cook was always pleased to see this young man, who had a likeable character and a winning way with him. 'Get yourself in here.' She inclined her head towards the noise which was coming from the pantry. 'Amy!' she called.

'Yes?'

'Away upstairs and see to the fire-grates. There's a nip in the air and the master will want the fires lit tonight, I've no doubt. Find the housekeeper . . . tell her you've done your tasks in the kitchen, and I'll not have idle hands about me.' When the little figure had gone, as quickly as her legs would allow, across the room and up the stairs, Cook turned to the young man with a hearty laugh, 'Poor Amy doesn't move so fast as she did some twenty years ago!' She shook her grey head and cleaned the flour from her hands, in order to fetch the big enamel teapot from the tressle by the fire. 'Still . . . we're none of us getting any younger, my lad . . . I'm sure it won't be long now, afore the master sends me packing through them doors.' She filled up two rose-patterned teacups and pushed one towards him. 'If there's one thing I'm really afeared of, young Edward . . . it's growing too old to be of use, and being left to rot in some dingy back room down some dark forgotten alley.' She was in a very sorry and melancholy mood, on account of the fact that her old bones were beginning to stiffen, and her eyesight wasn't what it had been.

'That won't ever happen to you.' Edward Trent thought his own troubles seemed like nothing when compared to the dreadful fate which Cook anticipated. 'I've heard my grandmother say often how marvellous you are, and how she could never find another like you in a month of Sundays.'

'Oho! . . . It ain't the mistress who I'm afeared might chuck me out, lad. Oh no! It's your grandfather as worries me. Me and him have never really hit it off, y'see, we're allus . . . suspicious . . . of each other. I'm no fool, and I knew fer sure that, given the proper excuse, he'd take real pleasure in seeing me pack me bags!' She took a moment to squeeze her sizeable frame into the wooden armchair situated at the top of the table, then, taking a noisy slurp of the hot tea, she made a small grunting noise and shook her head. 'My! He's a sour-tempered man is your grandfather . . . if you'll pardon me saying so?' Yes, and a rogue of the worst kind into the bargain, she thought to herself . . . a murderer too, if that precious letter was anything to go by!

'I'll even say it *myself*,' rejoined Edward Trent. 'I know he's fond of me . . . and I have a certain respect and liking for him. But he will ride roughshod over anything he takes a dislike to . . . however much he might be upsetting others.'

'My very point exactly!' remonstrated Cook, putting her cup on the table and leaning her great chubby arms on the table ledge. 'Been at loggerheads, have you . . . you and your grandfather?'

'He insists I won't be going to Australia to stay with my father a while. He's talking to my mother at this very minute . . . forbidding her to finance the venture.'

'Oh dear!' Cook pursed her thin lips into a perfect circle of wrinkles.

'But it's *my* money . . . sent to me by my own father!'

'Makes no difference, lad. Still . . . I can't say I'm surprised he won't let you go. Not if it's true what they say . . . that your father's set up in business with Emma Grady.' Of a sudden, Cook realised how she was letting

323

her mouth run away with her. Emma was forbidden talk in this house . . . had been these many years.

But Edward Trent's interest had been aroused by the mention of Emma Grady's name, and not for the first time. His father had spoken highly of the woman who had gone into business with him. Edward himself recalled when he had shown curiosity about Emma, in a communication he had intended sending to his father. But it had been snatched from him and flung into the fire. His mother had been very agitated and had straightaway sat herself at the bureau, where a letter had been angrily written, instructing his father never to mention that woman's name again. In all the letters Edward had received since, there had never been one single reference to 'Emma'. 'Who is Emma Grady?' Edward asked now, his eyes intent on Cook's anxious face.

'Why, I'm sure it's none of my business, young Master Trent,' Cook replied in a jolly fashion. 'Now then . . . off with you, and let a poor soul get on with her baking!' When she saw how unhappy he looked, Cook's old heart was sorry at his plight. 'Aw, look here . . . talk ter yer grandmother, why don't yer? Why! Yer the very apple of her eye, and I'm sure if it were only a matter o' money that prevents yer from visiting yer father, well . . . she'll help, I'm certain of it. Y'know, the mistress don't *always* agree with what yer grandfather says, and she's allus had a special liking fer Silas Trent, 'cause he's a good man, and she knows it.' A slight noise on the stairway caused her to gasp out loud and clutch at her chest. Seeing that it was only Amy returning, she visibly sagged with relief. 'Oh my poor heart!' she cried, sinking back against the wall.

Then, fixing her small worried eyes on Edward Trent, she told him, 'Go on! Do as I say, lad. But, don't you mention to anybody that you and me were discussing yer grandfather's business . . . else me life won't be worth living!'

'Why, I swear the thought never even crossed my mind.' Edward Trent laughed, and put a finger to his closed lips. Halfway up the stairs, he called back in a quiet voice, 'Thank you for your suggestion, all the same. It's the very thing, I'm sure.'

Amy had watched Edward Trent go, then, leaning her whole body across the table, she whispered something to Cook which made that woman's kindly eyes grow big and round with astonishment. '*What* was that you said?' she demanded, not being at all certain that she had heard right the first time.

'It's true!' Amy nodded, her face alive with excitement. 'I heard the mistress and Martha Trent. They were talking just now . . . in the drawing-room. Ooh! In a real fit that Martha was . . . and Mrs Crowther well, she was pacing up and down, not knowing what to do. After all, her and the master were partly to blame for what happened, weren't they? If they'd helped poor Emma when she begged 'em to . . . the authorities might not have transported her!' She gave a delicious little giggle, as she reminded Cook, 'Emma won't have forgotten how they turned their backs on her! No wonder the buggers are shivering in their shoes at the news, eh? Oh, and what news it is. After all these years, *Emma Grady's coming home!*'

Chapter Thirteen

Emma was coming home! Marlow must have read the letter a dozen times and more; each time his excitement grew. He could hardly believe it when the landlord of the Navigation had given him the envelope. Apparently, the good man had received it the week before, with a letter addressed to himself and requesting that the enclosed be given to Marlow Tanner at the earliest opportunity, as it was of the utmost importance. 'What you been up to, you bugger?' the landlord had laughed, and when he saw Marlow's face drain of colour on reading it, he gave him a jug of ale on the house. 'Oh, I'm sorry, mate,' he said, 'bad news, it is?' Then, when Marlow had told him how it was the best news, the very best he'd ever heard, he poured *himself* a jug of ale and drank to Marlow's good fortune.

That was two weeks ago. Now, it was the fourteenth of September and the ship bound from Australia was due to dock at Liverpool on the morrow. Tonight Marlow was seated in the corner of the Navigation, listening to revelry all around him and thoughtfully sipping his ale.

'Funny that . . . you're sitting on the very bench where your Sal used to sit, God rest her soul.' The man was of medium build, with tufts of grey hair above each ear and a large expanse of baldness between. He had warm blue eyes, a large loose mouth and long square teeth, from which protruded a clumsy, curved clay pipe. 'Shame about old Sal . . . she were a good sort,' he went on, settling himself beside Marlow, who inched along the bench in order to make more room.

'The *best*!' Marlow rejoined. 'There'll never be another like her.' His handsome dark eyes clouded over.

'From what I hear, she would have been proud o' you, Marlow Tanner. I hear you've done right well for yourself since coming back from seeking your fortune. I heard tell that you had to come right back to your own front doorstep afore you made good. Started off by getting your own barge back . . . at twice what the bugger were worth! Then you worked like a dog, 'till you've now got three cargo barges . . . everyone kept busy from contracts fetching and carrying goods from the docks. Atop o' which, or so rumour has it, you've brought one o' them big houses up Park Street. Is that the truth, mate? Have I heard right?'

'You have, but don't think it came easy. Anything that's worthwhile never comes easy!'

'Don't I know it. You're a bit of a legend in these parts, Marlow Tanner, and, if I've heard a dozen things told about you, the one that's told most often is about the way you've sweated blood to make your way up. And good luck to you, that's what I say! It can't have been easy to come back home and find your only family buried in the ground . . . oh, and the fellow who knew you both since you were toddlers . . . what were his name, Gabe Drury? Aye! . . . Drowned not twenty feet from this 'ere pub!'

Marlow didn't want to hear any more. He was so

filled with excitement and dizzy with thoughts of Emma that talking of the bad things which happened would only spoil it all. He didn't want to be depressed. Not tonight. Not on the very eve of Emma's return. 'I'll say goodnight, then,' he told the man, at the same time getting to his feet.

'Aye, well . . . mind how you go.' He nodded and slid further along the bench, saying as Marlow negotiated his way round the table, 'That were a funny business, though . . . about the urchin, I mean. Strange, how nobody knew where she came from . . . Sal would insist as how she'd been left by the little people, but then, *you* know how fanciful Sal's imagination could be.'

'I expect it was some poor little foundling Sal came across,' Marlow told him, 'she always did have a heart of gold.' He too had heard all about the girl, and for a while his own curiosity had been fired. Weeks upon weeks, he'd searched for the girl and enquired after her, until all trace of her had vanished and he was forced to give up. The last he had heard was that, when the girl had somehow found the money to pay for Sal to have a proper burial, she just disappeared. There was talk of her having fired the hut where she and Sal had been living, then gone from the area. Nobody knew anything more. Marlow would have liked to have found the girl, if only to thank her and to repay her for taking care of Sal's funeral. It would have broken his heart to come home and find his sister in a pauper's grave. Marlow made mention of these things now, in view of the fellow's kindly interest. And he was alarmed to hear something he had not known before.

'By all accounts, she thought the world o' your sister,

and the lass did find the money to bury her proper. But, if you ask me, she went about it the wrong way because, for some reason, she set herself up badly with no other than Justice Crowther.'

'How was that?' Marlow resumed his seat. 'Where does that loathsome fellow come into it?'

'Don't rightly know, and folks tend to keep their mouths shut tight when *his* name's mentioned. But, not long back, I spent a term behind bars. There was an old lag there who got dragged from his bed one night, and thrown in the waggon. He saw things, he said . . . to do with that girl and Justice Crowther. The lass ran off, with another fellow who was in the same waggon. The old lag reckons as how Justice Crowther swore and vowed to track the urchin down.'

'This "old lag" . . . where can I find him?'

The man gave a strange little laugh as he told Marlow, 'Huh! In the very pauper's plot the urchin saved your sister from, I shouldn't wonder!'

'You're telling me that he's dead?'

''Fraid so . . . had his guts rotted by the drinking . . . or so I heard tell.'

Of a sudden, the accordian music started up, and someone called for Marlow and the fellow to join in the singing. While the fellow did so, with merry enthusiasm, Marlow chose that moment to leave, and to walk home at a steady pace while he pondered what the fellow had told him. It was a few years since his Sal had passed on and the girl had gone from the area. He supposed she must be many miles away by now, and doing well. Yet Marlow could not forget what that girl had done for Sal and he realised how much she must have loved his wayward sister. God knows, thought

Marlow, Sal was no angel, and if truth be told, there's no doubt he would have given her the sharp end of his tongue for having gambled away the barge that had been their parents' and their grandparents' before them. But, as always, he would have forgiven her, because he loved her. No doubt just as the girl had done.

As he let himself into the grand front door of his Park Street house, Marlow thought how proud he would be to tell Emma of his achievements. Lady Luck had smiled on him and he was grateful. Now, he must force himself to be patient until the morrow when he would be waiting on the docks for his Emma. He wondered what Silas Trent had meant when he spoke in the letter of a 'wonderful surprise' which Emma was bringing with her. He was filled with excitement at the prospect of seeing her, of holding her, in this land where they both belonged.

Marlow tried hard to push away the thought of that girl whom Sal had raised, and to whom he owed a debt. With Emma paramount in his thoughts, it was not difficult after a while. But he could not entirely quell the curiosity within him, as he recalled what the fellow in the pub had said. 'For some reason, she set herself up badly with no other than Justice Crowther . . . the old lag saw things that night.' Marlow couldn't help but wonder what it was that the old lag had seen. If in fact he had seen anything at all, or if he had seen it all in the bottom of an ale-jug. Folks did like to talk and gossip; even more so if there was the price of a drink in the offing.

All the same, Marlow thought there were questions left unanswered – like who were the girl's real parents?

And *had* Justice Crowther a vendetta against the girl. If so, why? He hoped it was all just idle speculation, because who should know better than himself, and Emma, what it was like to be hounded by that man!

Marlow came into the hallway and lit the lamp on the small circular table. 'Wherever you are, young 'un,' he murmured in a serious voice, 'if you really *have* made an enemy of Justice Crowther, don't ever come back to this area. And may God keep you safe!'

332

Chapter Fourteen

'Cor, bugger me, gal! It's like a bleeding sale at the fishmarket, ain't it?' Nelly cried out when her toe was trodden on and a great surge of bodies sent her along at a faster pace towards the gangway. 'I'm blowed if these impatient folk won't send us arse-uppards into the water any minute!' She flashed an angry look at one burly woman who was so intent on pushing her way to the front, that she actually took Nelly a few paces along with her. 'Did y'see that?' Nelly demanded of Emma, who was some way behind. 'I've a bloody good mind to fetch 'er one!'

Emma was caught in a crush of her own, when her only thought was to keep safe the child in her arms, and to emerge intact from the excited throng of passengers who were, understandably, excited at the prospect of meeting their loved ones waiting on the Liverpool quayside. 'Just watch where you're going!' Emma called back to Nelly. 'If we get separated, wait for me at the bottom of the gangway.'

Within the hour, Emma and Nelly were reunited, having come to no harm and gone safely through the process which awaited all disembarking passengers. Now they had their luggage on the ground beside them, a small trunk, five portmanteaus and three large tapestry bags. They were both utterly exhausted, and the child, who up to now had been content in Emma's arms, was beginning to fret. 'The young 'un wants his tit, I expect,' Nelly told Emma in her usual forthright manner, being quite oblivious to the disapproving stares of several elderly women who happened by. 'Look!' She pointed to a sign over the far wall. 'There's a waiting-room across the way. You'll not be disturbed there. Go on with yer. I'll stay here and keep watch.' She lowered her voice and smiled at Emma in a knowing way. 'Don't worry, gal,' she said, 'you've told me enough about yer fellow fer me to pick him out in any crowd. I'll keep me eyes skinned . . . and I'll fetch yer the minute I suspect he's come a-looking fer yer.'

But Emma would not be budged. Looking down at her son, she saw that he was not upset in any way. It was true that he'd become more fidgety and was beginning to make protesting noises, but Emma believed that was more a consequence of being pushed and shoved in every direction, and being made hot and uncomfortable because of it. 'He's fine,' she told Nelly. 'As soon as Marlow finds us, we'll be on our way.' She raised her anxious grey eyes to scan the crowds, who were still milling around them. Nelly's eyes were anxious too, as they gazed on Emma and saw how determined she was to make no move until Marlow Tanner came, as Emma fervently believed he would.

'Aw, look Emma . . . don't get yerself all worked up, darling. Fellers is the same the world over. He may not come, y'know. Yer have ter be prepared fer that. I mean . . . it's been a year and more since he left Fremantle. Yer told him then that there was no chance fer the two of yer. Yer sent him off without so much as a goodbye . . . oh, and quite right it was, at the time.

But that poor feller may not have got the message sent by Silas Trent. For all yer know, he might a' got wed. I'm sorry, gal, but yer have ter think o' these things when all's said and done.'

'Please, Nelly.' Emma had turned to look at her friend, and there was reproach in her eyes. Did Nelly think that all the things she was saying had not already run through Emma's mind? Of course they had, every day and every night, even before she had embarked on the homeward journey. There had been no word from Marlow, there had been no time. Yet Emma had hoped and prayed that he *had* received the message, and that he was here now, searching for her just as desperately as she was searching for him. Beyond that, Emma dared not think. 'Marlow *is* here, somewhere,' she said in a strong, quiet voice, 'I know it!' In a minute, she had placed the child in Nelly's arms, saying, 'I'm going to find him, Nelly.' Then, with a squeeze of Nelly's hand, she smiled. 'Don't move from this spot,' she said. 'I'll be back as quick as I can.' She wrapped the shawl more securely around the infant, and fussed awhile.

Nelly saw the tall handsome fellow with black shoulder-length hair and intense dark eyes, even before Emma had turned her head away. He had come upon them from the rush of people and was now standing directly behind Emma, his eyes willing her to turn round, and a look of such profound love on his handsome features that Nelly's own heart was moved by it. She said nothing, yet she could not take her eyes off him, any more than he could take his eyes off Emma.

When Emma saw how transfixed Nelly's gaze was, and how she was smiling in that infuriatingly secret way

335

she had, Emma knew. Some sixth sense from deep inside her told her that it was *Marlow* who had captured Nelly's attention. She swung round, and fell straight into his open arms. 'I *knew* you'd be here,' she cried through her laughter. 'I prayed you wouldn't let me down!'

'Oh, Emma, how could I let you down?' Marlow swept her tighter into his arms, taking off her bonnet and showering her with kisses. 'I've only lived for this day, ever since I knew you were on your way home. Wild horses couldn't keep me from claiming you.' He gripped his hands about her small shoulders to ease her away. When she was looking up at him, her lovely face wet with tears and the joy in her heart shining through, he spoke in the softest voice, telling her, 'I love you, Emma Grady . . . adored you for so long that nothing existed before you. And now, at long last, my darling, we're really together. Oh, Emma . . . I've waited for this day *all of my life!*' He held her gaze a moment longer, before bending his head to her upturned face. 'I love you so,' he murmured against her mouth, and when he drew her towards him, kissing her and holding her fast against him, Emma knew what happiness really was.

Seeing the warmth and joy of such a reunion, Nelly also was softly crying. And when she sniffled noisily, juggling the child in her arms in order to wipe her face with the cuff of her jacket, Emma drew away from Marlow, saying to him, 'I've brought you something, Marlow . . . something very precious.' She smiled at the puzzlement on his face, as she reached over to collect the child from Nelly's arms. Then, uncovering the tiny face, she held the small squirming bundle out to him, saying softly, 'This is Bill. Take him, Marlow, for *he's your son*.' Marlow's dark eyes grew wide, going from Emma to the child and gazing at the infant for a long painful moment, then the tears started to rain down his face and a small cry escaped him as he cradled the boy to his chest.

'He's beautiful, isn't he?' Emma murmured. 'And so like you.' She reached out to touch Marlow's face, which was still bent in fascination towards that tiny being, his own son! Now as he looked up to meet Emma's loving gaze, his dark tearful eyes held wonder. 'God bless you, Emma,' he said in a voice filled with awe, 'I have all that a man could ask for.' He placed an arm around Emma and drew her close, and for a moment there was no need for words.

From a short distance away, a girl of some sixteen years watched the tender scene unfold; black-eyed she was, with long loose hair dark about her narrow shoulders and a pinched hungry look in her features. She was painfully thin, and clad in a calf-length threadbare dress, covered by a brown shawl. There was a sadness in her eyes as she watched, and loneliness in her voice when she clutched the fair-haired toddler in her arms. 'See that, sweetheart,' she told the child, 'happy, ain't they, eh?' She kissed the child and pointed its attention towards Emma and the little group. 'That's a *proper* family . . . not like you and me. Oh, but at least you've got a proper mammy, eh? And I love you more than life . . . so, you're better off than *I* am! Y'see, Sal, darlin' . . . I never had no mammy, nor daddy neither. Oh, you got a daddy sure enough, but that Jack-the-lad lived up to his name right enough, didn't he, eh?

337

Cleared off and left the pair of us! Still, I expect he'll turn up again . . . like he's done afore.'

Molly chuckled as she swept the child on to the bony part of her hip. 'Hold on tight, lovely,' she told its pretty trusting face, ''cause we've a crust to earn . . . aye, and happen a bit o' fast footwork to do and all!' She was still chuckling when she passed within an arm's reach of Emma and her family. Molly had pondered on relieving the pockets of the dark-haired gent, but she decided against it, telling the little girl, who was presently twisting its mammy's thick black hair round its fingers, 'It'd be a shame ter spoil such a lovely reunion, wouldn't it? Besides which . . . the gent looks fit and able enough ter catch me, and we can't be having that, can we, eh?' Her dark eyes swept the milling people, passengers, workers, visitors and seamen alike, until eventually they came to rest on a bent old gentleman in top hat and long-coat. He carried a walking stick and wore that particularly arrogant and surly expression which characterised most wealthy toffs. 'I reckon we can outrun *that* old geezer.' Molly chucked little Sal under the chin, tucking her in tight and pulling the shawl taut about her. After which, and with her eyes kept fixed on the old gent, she went into the throng of people and disappeared from sight.

'Well now, ain't we the posh ones?' Nelly climbed into the carriage and turned about to collect the child from Emma's arms. 'When yer think, Emma gal . . . how, so long ago, the two on us were packed off from England as branded criminals . . . outcasts in society . . . and look at us now, eh? . . . I'm buggered if we ain't come back like a pair o' queens!' She winked at Marlow, who handed the luggage up to the carriage driver and was greatly amused by Nelly's forthright manner. He turned his dark smiling eyes to Emma, who smiled back and blushed a little, as she prepared to follow Nelly into the carriage.

Of a sudden, there was a hue and cry, with some kind of skirmish going on a little way along the quayside. 'What the bleedin' 'ell's that?' asked Nelly, leaning out of the carriage door and gawping towards the source of the noise in the distance. 'Well . . . will yer look at that! It ain't but a ragamuffin got herself in trouble!'

By this time, Emma had come to stand beside Marlow and the carriage driver, as everyone's attention was drawn by the sight of a strapping bobby with a red angry face, and a great deal to say to the girl beside him, a dark-eyed girl with an infant clinging to her. 'You've been warned before,' he was saying in a breathless voice, 'but this time you've been caught red-handed, my girl. You'll soon find out that the law doesn't take kindly to pickpockets!'

Emma turned, curious, as the carriage driver gave a low chuckle. 'I fail to see anything amusing in a young girl having to resort to thievery!' she said, in a disapproving voice. 'Why the poor thing can't be above fifteen or sixteen . . . and she has a child to look after.' She turned to Marlow. 'Can't we do something to help her?' she asked, looking up at him with concern.

Before Marlow could reply, the carriage driver had something else to say. 'Don't you worry your pretty head about yon lass. She's a quick-witted one is that, and I'll tell you some'at else, lady . . . that there bobby, as big and forceful as he is, *he* won't hold her!' He shook his head and chuckled aloud. 'A whole army wouldn't hold that one! Oh, I've seen the lass before, many a time . . . here at the docks and wherever a busy crowd might gather. She ain't no fool . . . and she slides a gent's wallet from his person like nothing I've ever seen before. It's a pleasure to watch the lass at work . . . though I keeps my own wallet well and truly safe when she's around, I can tell you.'

No sooner had he finished speaking than there came a shout and the sound of running feet. Emma was astonished to see that the girl had broken free of the bobby and was heading straight towards them, the child tucked tight into her hip and, judging by the broad grin on its face, thinking the whole thing to be a wonderful adventure.

The bobby was in close pursuit, blowing his whistle and growing more red-faced with every step, while the girl ran like the wind, with various do-gooders and would-be heroes grabbing at her as she skilfully dodged them. For a minute, Emma could see the girl's face clearly, and she was greatly moved by it. Why, she's lovely, Emma thought, seeing how strong and proud the girl's features were. Of a sudden, Molly's dark eyes were attracted by Emma. She smiled and winked, then was quickly lost to sight, leaving Emma with a warm feeling, and a sense of admiration.

'Who is she?' Emma asked of the carriage driver, for her curiosity was greatly aroused.

'Dunno, lady,' came the matter-of-fact reply, 'just an urchin . . . and Lord knows, the alleys is full o' the blighters. Cut your throat for sixpence, some of 'em would, but *that one* . . . I dunno. Just an urchin, like I said. We'll not see her round these parts again though . . . not now she's had her collar felt . . . you can depend on that! Don't you give it another thought, 'cause her kind can take care o' themselves, believe me.'

In the carriage, with Nelly seated opposite, her son in her arms and her beloved Marlow by her side, Emma thought how very fortunate she was. There had been times during her life when it seemed all hope of true happiness had gone. Times when she had despaired and been wretched. Times when only the thought of revenge had kept her going. She had not forgotten how those she trusted had deserted her when she was most in need of their help. Nor had she forgotten that her dear father had entrusted his daughter and his entire life's work to Caleb Crowther, who had betrayed that trust. What kind of man was he, Emma asked herself, who would see his own niece transported, and not lift a finger to help? And her father's hard-earned business – what of that? In all these years, there had been no word from her uncle regarding her father's assets. But Emma had learned the art of patience. She could be patient a while longer, because there were other matters more close to her heart that took precedence. She had every intention of confronting Caleb Crowther, because there were many questions she must ask of him. Questions which demanded answers, without which Emma knew she would never truly have peace of mind. But, for now, Emma dismissed these disturbing thoughts from her mind. *Nothing* must be allowed to mar the joy of her homecoming. At last she really was home, with her man by her side, and her family about her. At this point in her thoughts, Emma recalled what Nelly had said earlier, that they 'were packed off from England as branded criminals . . . outcasts in society'. And oh, how true that was, Emma thought now as she relived the awful experience in her mind. Above all else, the greatest horror had been the tragic loss of her first-born. She had her family about her now, yes that was true, thank God, but how truly complete it would have been if only her daughter was here beside them.

Sensing that Emma was lost in some deep private place, Marlow leaned his dark head down towards her. 'Are you happy, my love?' he murmured.

'Oh, yes . . . yes.' Emma gazed up at this man whom she would always adore, and her heart was brimming over. 'If only you knew,' she told him with tearful eyes. 'Oh, Marlow, if only you knew how very happy I am.' When he clasped her hand in his and tenderly brushed his lips against her forehead, Emma gazed down at the quiet face of their son. Even in the joy he brought her, there was a sadness in Emma's heart which would not be denied, for in his dark eyes and in that rich dark hair that was so like Marlow's, she saw another face, that of a new-born daughter. Emma tried to imagine how that tiny girl might have grown into a woman. Would she have the ways and manner of herself, she wondered, or would she be more like Marlow?

Realising the futility of remembering and tormenting herself about what was gone, Emma shook all thoughts of her first-born from her mind. She was glad that Marlow had learned nothing of what had happened, because, at least, he would be saved the heartache which knowing would surely bring.

Somehow, Nelly sensed that Emma was reproaching herself for the past, and, bending forward, she put her hand over Emma's, saying in a soft whisper, 'It's all over now, me darlin' . . . it's all over.'

Emma smiled at her, leaning into the curve of Marlow's loving arm. 'I know,' she said gratefully, 'bless your heart, Nelly, I know.' If only Emma had known also that she had been within touching distance of her 'lost' daughter, and even her first grandchild, how wonderfully complete her happiness would have been.

But is it not written that if we believe and if our faith is strong enough, then all things will come to pass.

Vagabonds

To three lovely women,
good friends whom I love very much:
Jane,
our delightful new daughter-in-law;
Madge,
a real trooper who is the salt of the earth;
Barbara Arnold,
who would happily scour the world for my books!
God bless them.

Part One

England 1885

Don't be afraid
When dark clouds gather.
Somewhere, the sunshine
Is breaking through.

J.C.

Chapter One

'Be off with you . . . we don't want no beggers at *this* door!' Cook's round, homely face was full of disgust as she glared at the young woman who was loitering on the outer step. 'Go on, I say . . . be off with you, afore I call the master. You'll show a clean pair of heels then, I'll be bound.' She had been up to her armpits in flour when the knock had come on the door. Now she began frantically wiping her chubby hands on her pinnie and flapping the corner of it towards the ragged, offending creature who seemed unwilling to make a move.

The young woman stood her ground and eyed the agitated cook with bold black eyes. 'I'm no "beggar"!' she retorted, drawing the tiny infant closer into her arms and reaching down to take the frail hand of the small child by her side. 'I don't want charity, missus. I'm willing to do good honest labour for a reasonable wage . . . and I'm a lot stronger than I look, so don't go thinking I'm afraid of hard, heavy work. I can do whatever's needed of me.' Molly was desperate, and it showed in her voice.

'Oh, it's work you're after, is it?' Cook's temper began to recede as she quietly regarded the young woman before her. 'These your two brats, are they?' She let her small, round eyes rove over the two children; the girl she ascertained to be somewhere in the region of three or

3

four years old, and the infant in arms probably not yet a year old. As for the young woman, she looked the most starved of all three. She was painfully thin, but had the kind of face that held a particular strength, with dark, striking eyes that somehow held a body mesmerized. Cook didn't hold with folks knocking on her kitchen door, especially when they might want something for nothing. 'Where's the father of these two?' she asked sharply.

'He's run off.'

'Run off . . . ? The devil he has.' Cook wasn't surprised. All men were the same in her eyes: either wasters or womanizers. The same thing applied whether they were beggars or kings. 'Well, I'm sorry, young lady . . . there's no place here for extra hands. Oh, we could do with somebody, I'm not denying that . . . but the master don't see it the same way as them that have to do the work.'

'Couldn't you at least *ask*?' Molly believed that beneath her sharp and unkind manner, the old lady might have a soft spot.

Cook shook her grey head. 'No. It wouldn't do no good.' Her small piggy eyes fell to the fair-haired child, who promptly smiled at her, melting her heart. 'Poor little tyke,' she said, thinking how all three made a sorry and pitiful sight. 'Look . . . wait here a minute,' she told the young woman. 'I know there's no work to be got, but there's a larder just bursting with certain goodies that would never be missed by them upstairs.' She jerked a podgy thumb heavenwards. 'I'll not be a minute,' she chuckled, tousling the child's unkempt curls before she turned to go quickly back into the kitchen.

As good as her word, the old dear returned within a

short time, bearing a strawberry basket tucked under her arm and filled with food from the larder: a crusty loaf, a tub of butter, two rosy apples, a chunk of pork pie and three slabs of her best cherry cake. 'Here, take this and make yourself scarce. If we're found out, there'll be *four* of us going down the road to beggary . . . you mark my words!' She thrust the basket over the young woman's outstretched arm and, without another word, stepped back into the relative safety of her own kitchen. 'Lord love and preserve us!' she was heard to mutter, before hastily making the sign of the cross on herself and shutting the door against the sight of that poor young woman with her two fatherless brats.

'Thanks very much, missus.' The young woman smiled and began walking away down the long narrow path that would lead her to the outer lane.

Satisfied that they were far enough away from the big house, she stopped and sat on the high bank beside the ditch. The children sat beside her, waiting for something to eat. Breaking two chunks of bread from the loaf, she gave a piece to each of the children. 'There you are, my beauties,' she said in a soft, loving voice. Then, at the sight of them both happily tucking in to the old cook's generous gift, she laughed aloud, throwing her arms round them and declaring with delight, 'Just follow your mammy's example . . . and you'll never go hungry. What . . . if that old woman had offered me a job in that big posh house, I'd have fainted on the very spot!' When the two children took pleasure in Molly's infectious laughter, she hugged them all the more tightly, her heart bursting with love and a prayer of thanks to the Lord that, somehow, he always managed to see them through the hard times.

From the window of the kitchen Cook had watched the pathetic ensemble as it went away down the path. 'There's always somebody worse off than yourself,' she murmured, feeling guilty that she had spoken so sharply to the young woman at first, because there was something about the creature that seemed to put her above the usual beggar or vagabond. She shook her head thoughtfully and turned her attention to the baking of the day's bread. But the image persisted awhile, until she deliberately pushed it from her mind. They'd be all right, she told herself, them sort had a way of surviving. She was astonished though, to think that a young woman of such attractive looks should be made to wander the streets like that. Oh, and what sort of a fellow would 'run off' and leave his woman and children to fend for themselves?

How much more astonished Cook would have been to learn that the 'vagabond' she had just dismissed from the house of Justice Caleb Crowther was no other than Molly . . . lost daughter of Emma Grady. Emma, the niece of Caleb Crowther, and now his bitter enemy.

'Oh, I say . . . such terrible tempers. And them being gentry and all.' The words were uttered in a soft and fearful whisper as, afraid yet strangely excited by the fearsome row that was raging inside Justice Crowther's study, the maid dithered by the door. A petite and plain woman with a thin, worn face and bright round eyes, she was burning with curiosity; yet she was also amazed by her own boldness in lingering here, her mind in turmoil and her ears singing in anticipation of the boxing they would get from Cook if she loitered in her duties.

Oh, but how dare she barge in on such a terrible

uproar with the master in as black a mood as ever she'd known, and the mistress giving him as good as she got? Why! The idea of disturbing them was *unthinkable*, and if a lowly scullery-maid such as she were suddenly to show her face with the intention of cleaning out the firegrate, like as not the two wolves at each other's throats on the other side of that door might just as easily turn on *her*! The thought was so real and terrifying that Amy clutched at her own throat and turned tail to scurry away. She would have liked to stay a while longer, but no matter; she had discovered enough.

As she went along the corridor and towards the stairs which led down to the kitchen, a wicked and devious smile came to her face. Even now, she could still hear the angry, raised voices behind her. The nearer she came to the narrow stairway, the faster went her thin little legs and the brighter shone her eyes. Oh, but she had such a tale to tell Cook! Such a juicy, satisfying tale!

'At last we know the worst. Emma Grady wants her pound of flesh right down to the blood and bones!' Caleb Crowther sank his ageing but still formidable figure into the leather-bound chair behind the desk, his piercing blue eyes marbled with fear as he glared at his wife's anxious face. 'Damn the woman!' he snarled, clenching his teeth and feverishly stroking his long thick fingers over the mass of iron-grey hair which covered the lower half of his ungainly features. 'When she was transported some twenty-two years ago to the other side of the world, I prayed we'd seen the last of her. But I was a fool. I should have known better. I should have made sure that she was *hanged*!' He fell forward on his desk, burying his balding head in the depths of his hands and making low, intermittent sounds that betrayed the hatred simmering inside him. Hatred, and something else . . . *fear*. The crippling fear that Emma Grady's return had wrought in him. 'Over three years since she set foot on these shores again. Uncertain years . . . littered with solicitors' correspondence and mounting fees to be paid at the end of it all.' He raised his head and began drumming his fingers impatiently on the desk-top. 'She has deliberately kept me guessing as to her real intentions . . . toyed with me . . . no doubt found it amusing to think of me squirming.' Suddenly he was sitting bolt upright in the chair, his narrowed eyes searching his wife's face as he judged her reaction to his next words. 'Now, she's moving in for the kill!' Snatching up the offending letter, he flung it across the desk. 'Read it, woman,' he snapped at his wife, 'this affects us all.'

'You seem very sure that she can hurt us . . . you surprise me. I thought you had prepared for every eventuality . . . including Emma Grady's possible return?' Agnes Crowther smiled knowingly, and with contempt.

It was a gesture that infuriated him. 'There'll be nothing for *any* of us to smile about if she succeeds in her little game,' he reminded her angrily, 'and make no mistake about it . . . she means to beggar us. We underestimated her once. We'd be downright idiots not to see her for the dangerous enemy she's become. Emma Grady went away a young, naïve creature who could be easily manipulated . . . she's returned an influential and powerful woman with a curiosity for certain answers and a thirst for revenge. Mark my words, she won't rest until she has us at her mercy!'

'Strange, don't you think . . . how the tables turn?'

There was cynicism in her voice, and a trace of fear. With calm deliberation, Agnes Crowther came forward from the casement window where she had been gazing across the beautifully tended lawns, quietly indulging in memories of long ago. Her troubled thoughts had carried her back some twenty-five years to when Emma Grady had played and walked on these same lawns; a young girl tormented by the fact that her beloved father, Thadius Grady, was wasting away. With his eventual passing, Emma's torment had not ceased. So many bad experiences had assailed her; so much tragedy and heartache that might have destroyed a lesser soul. 'What makes this letter frighten you so?' Agnes Crowther kept her unflinching gaze on his face. 'There have been others . . . and always you've satisfactorily dealt with them. Why should this one be any different?'

'Because it touches on deeper issues . . . deeds and titles regarding the mills that Thadius left to her. Up to now, her solicitor has been cleverly laying the groundwork . . . probing . . . making sure of his case regarding his client's claims. Now he's digging to the real issues, making demands . . . requesting certain documents. Uprooting things that go back too many years.'

'These . . . "documents" . . . surely you can supply them?' She let her gaze remain on his face a moment longer. Only now did she fear the worst. 'Or is there something there to incriminate you . . . to incriminate *all* of us?' She had always trusted his judgement in these matters; after all, he was a man of the law and well versed in such legalities. With a jolt, she was reminded of how he had cunningly secreted Emma's inheritance and almost lost it in the recession. It was true however that he had then salvaged enough to sell off the derelict cotton mills and to buy a considerable share in the Lassater Shipping Line. If that enviable income were now denied them, it would be nothing short of disaster. Certainly, her husband's comparative pittance, as Justice of the Peace, would not sustain their pampered lifestyle. Suddenly incensed by the prospect of losing everything she valued, she rounded on him. 'This is *your* problem,' she told him in a cold voice. 'It was not me who chose to marry Emma off to an employee of my brother's, a man who was socially inferior to Emma Grady. Is it any wonder that it ended in tragedy? Though I must admit I never really believed that she had a hand in murdering the unfortunate fellow.' In her deepest heart, Agnes Crowther could never see her brother's daughter committing such a foul and cold-blooded crime; the girl was too loving, too warm and sensitive to ever deliberately hurt another soul. Yet it had been these very qualities which had alienated her from Emma. She had seen in her brother's child all of those admirable traits that were sadly lacking in her own daughter, Martha, who was almost the same age as Emma. She could not suppress her bitter resentment of the fact that while Emma was strong and forthright, Martha was weak and deceitful.

When Emma's mother had died in tragic circumstances, and later, when her father Thadius was gravely ill and brought Emma to live with him in this house, both Agnes and Martha had set about making Emma's life miserable.

After her brother's death, Agnes Crowther vented all her bitterness on Emma, not protesting at Martha's spiteful treatment of the girl, nor intervening when Emma was so unsuitably married off. All along, Agnes had suspected that her husband had deliberately planned to cheat Emma, yet she had not once argued on Emma's behalf. Not even when she realized that Caleb had played a hand in the verdict that demanded Emma's transportation as a convict.

For a long, uncomfortable moment it seemed as though Agnes Crowther might read the letter. But then she lifted her hand and joined it with the other at her breast, the fine bony fingers pointed upwards in that posture of prayer which had long been a familiar and peculiar trait of her unbending character. 'I will not demean myself by reading that mischievous letter, and thereby giving credence to Emma Grady's vindictive proposals.'

'You *will* read it!'

'I will not!'

'What are you saying, woman . . . that you refuse to support me in this bitter fight with Emma Grady? You seem to conveniently forget, my dear, that she is after all *your* kith and kin. And, more importantly, that the inheritance she now lays claim to should by rights have been left to *you* in the first place. Why your father struck you out of his will in favour of your younger brother, Thadius, is quite beyond me!'

'No doubt he had his reasons,' came the curt reply. She could have reminded him that the main reason she had been so cruelly disinherited was because she had stubbornly rebelled against her father's strong disapproval of Caleb Crowther. 'The man is little more than a fortune hunter,' he had warned his daughter, 'but mark my words . . . I will see to it that he never gets his hands on a penny of my money!' Agnes Crowther had loved her father. But, much to her later regret, she had loved Caleb more. She smiled now at the bitter irony of it all,

11

because even though Thadius had been the main beneficiary in their father's will, he had foolishly appointed Caleb as trustee and executor of his estate. As Caleb had so often remarked in the months following Thadius's passing, 'I could not have planned it better myself . . . see how conveniently the inheritance has fallen into my lap.' When the mills were later foreclosed by the banks and the money almost gone, Caleb had felt no regrets for Emma, who by now was 'safely' out of the way. His only concerns were these: that he should salvage enough money from the failing textile business to forge a new company in his own name, which would serve to finally sever the links between himself and Emma Grady, and that he should cover all traces of his illegal acquisition of Emma's fortune. He had believed himself to be cunning and thorough. But now, with Emma returned, vengeful and determined to expose his treachery, he had been made wary and afraid. Yet he was equally determined that she would not beggar him. He would see her ruined first. *Or dead!* There was no remorse in Caleb Crowther's heart for the callous way in which he had treated Emma Grady. Only hatred, and now a deep haunting fear that would not go away; he despised himself for harbouring such fear. After all, she was only a woman, however rich and influential she had become.

'So, you mean to defy me?'

'In this matter, I am afraid so.'

'Then you are a fool!' Infuriated, he got to his feet. 'Must I remind you that we're in this together. If I am to be hounded by this upstart, I can assure you, my dear . . . you will keep me company in the workhouse.'

'You think so?'

'I do indeed.'

With a wry little smile, Agnes Crowther turned away, her next words dripping softly in her wake as she moved gracefully across the room, a slim and regal figure in a bustled dress of dark blue silk. 'Oh, my dear . . . you know very well that the workhouse would not suit me. However, I must leave the matter of Emma Grady to you,' she told him icily. 'You know how hopeless I am at such things . . . and how I have no head for what is essentially "a man's business" . . . as you yourself have so painstakingly pointed out on the rare occasions when I have offered an opinion.'

'This is different,' he argued, with all the dignity he could muster in the face of her defiance. 'This concerns you as well as me.' He was puzzled by her bold attitude, but not altogether surprised. The further they had drifted apart over the years, the more independent and rebellious she had become. It was quite infuriating.

'And what would you have me do?' She turned at the door to sweep her cold, green gaze over his angry features. 'Should I go and see her? Put myself at her mercy and beg forgiveness for robbing her of her birthright, afterwards turning our backs on her when she was thrown into a prison cell, charged with murder? Do you think I should chastize her for seeking to hurt us? Or would you rather I tried to explain how sorry we are that we ignored her desperate pleas for help when she was labelled a criminal of the worst kind . . . faced with exile from the shores of her homeland when she was heavy with child . . . a child that was soon lost to her in unfortunate circumstances. And when she asks where her fortune has gone, what should I say? That it was squandered . . . but that enough was saved for investment in the Lassater Shipping Line . . . now a thriving and prosperous company, and one of Emma Grady's most bitter and dangerous rivals?' She smiled sweetly and quietly opened the door. 'Somehow I don't think I would be well received in my niece's house . . . do you, my dear?'

In a moment she was gone and the door was firmly closed behind her. Caleb Crowther went to the window, where he lit his pipe and furiously puffed on it. It seemed to him that, whilst his enemies began to close in on all sides, he stood alone, deserted and friendless. No matter, he thought defiantly, there were still those rats who had no choice but to stand by him . . . or go down with the sinking ship. He had not 'gone down' yet. Nor had he any intention of doing so. Certainly not because of Emma Grady! Or Emma Tanner as she was now called, since her marriage to that fellow Marlow.

In the privacy of the drawing-room, Agnes Crowther was also quietly meditating. Not too long ago it would have been unthinkable that she should defy her husband in such a way. But that was before she had discovered how deeply he had shamed her. She could not bring herself to forgive him for the way he had cheated on her, taking other women to his bed on those long journeys away as circuit judge and not even having the decency to deny it when she had confronted him. She could hear him now, lamely trying to justify his sordid affairs. 'You yourself are not altogether blameless, my dear,' he had told her. 'When a wife turns her husband away . . . fails to do her duty by him . . . then that same wife must not be surprised when he seeks his comfort elsewhere.' It was true that she did not enjoy his advances and his infidelity was only to be expected. But the idea that she should indulge in such undignified behaviour between the sheets was particularly obnoxious to her, considering that she was already in the autumn of her life. As for Caleb, he would never see sixty again and therefore should know better than to shamelessly cavort with members of the opposite sex. To make matters worse, it had come to her knowledge that he had even been seen in the company of street women. *Whores, no less.* She positively bristled at the thought, murmuring aloud, 'And you think I care what ruin Emma Grady brings down on you? You don't care what terrible shame you bring down on *me*, you old fornicator! And as for threatening me, let me tell you I will *not* be "keeping you company in the workhouse". These past years I have carefully put away a small nest-egg. You may rot in the workhouse, Justice Caleb Crowther . . . but I shall keep my dignity.' The thought pleased her and she chuckled deliciously.

It pleased her also to see her husband's astonishment at the manner in which she had stood up to him. At one time she would have been too afraid to be so bold, but, since Emma's return the tables had turned; however much he might deny it, Justice Crowther was quivering in his boots, and his wife, the long-suffering but equally devious creature, was emerging the stronger of the two.

'Why, you little fool . . . giggling and glorying in such a thing, when you should be trembling at what it could all mean!' Cook's reaction was not what the maid had expected, and she was completely taken aback when, after gleefully imparting the news of how she had heard the mistress saying that 'Caleb Crowther was a forni-cator and would rot in the workhouse without her, if Emma Grady was to ruin him', she had been angrily attacked by the normally amiable cook, whose chubby face had grown bright purple, the ladle in her fist sent whistling towards Amy's ear with intent to knock her sideways.

'*But it's true* . . . I swear it!' protested the astonished Amy. 'I ain't being fanciful . . . not this time. The mistress really *did* say all those things.' She kept her distance from Cook's anger, her bottom lip quivering and the curiosity gone from her eyes; in its place was the same expression Cook had seen on a big stray dog that she'd found sitting on the kitchen step some days ago. Lost it was, and starved of both food and affection. The constable had later returned it to its rightful owner, but Cook still recalled how it touched her old heart with its round, soulful eyes. 'Oh, you gormless thing,' she told the cowering maid, 'sit yourself down. I'll make us a brew of tea, and you can tell me what the mistress did say, word for word.' Amy waited until Cook had dropped the ladle on to the surface of the big pine table, then, quietly snivelling, she slid into one of the stand-chairs and pulled it up to the table. 'It were just as I told you,' she mumbled, carefully watching Cook's every move. She could do with a cup of tea now, she thought miserably, because the old bugger had frightened her so much that her mouth had gone all dry!

'You're a silly, innocent little fool,' Cook placed the tray on to the table and edged her ample frame into a chair set directly opposite the maid, 'but I shouldn't have jumped at you like that . . . and I'm sorry.' She cut a wedge of apple pie and scooped it on to a small china plate, which she then pushed in front of the little woman. 'Get that down you,' she ordered in a kindly voice, and, shaking her grey head, she added more severely, 'You'll never change, will you, eh? What were you when you

16

first came to Breckleton House . . . fifteen . . . sixteen? That were over twenty years since, and you're still as daft as a brush!'

'I ain't daft.'

'Aye well . . . happen not "daft" . . . but you've still not learned the way of things.'

'What do you mean, Cook . . . the way of things?' Amy didn't feel quite so threatened now, so she took a hearty bite of the apple pie and leaned forward, the better to hear Cook's next words. For the life of her, she couldn't see what she'd done wrong.

'First of all . . . I don't doubt for a minute that the mistress said those things.' Cook smiled to reassure her. It was sad but true that Amy had never been what might be considered 'intelligent'. And the older she got, the less she seemed to stop and think things out. 'But there's some'at you need to realize, Amy, and it's this.' She chuckled good-humouredly when the maid began frantically nodding her head and urging Cook, between mouthfuls of pie, to 'go on . . . I'm listening.' Poor, misguided soul, thought Cook, as she went on in a discreet voice, 'What you heard upstairs . . . well, it could likely affect all our livelihoods, and that's a fact!'

''Ow d'yer mean?' The poor thing stopped chewing the pie. Somehow she wasn't enjoying it quite so much.

'Well, if you think about it . . . it's as plain as the nose on your face, Amy,' Cook said in slow, deliberate tones, the frown deepening in her forehead and causing Amy to grow anxious again. 'If Miss Emma does succeed in beggaring the master and he's left to live on what he gets from being a circuit judge, you and I both know it won't be enough for him to keep this big house . . . nor his servants.' She saw the light dawning in Amy's widened eyes, as she added cautiously, 'That means the house-keeper, the parlour maid . . . then me and you . . . we shall *all* of us end up in the workhouse together if the worst comes to the worst.'

'The *mistress* won't,' Amy thoughtfully corrected, ''cause I heard her say as how she had "a small nest-egg put away" . . . Oh, Cook! What shall we do? *I* ain't got no "nest-egg" put away, and I don't expect you have neither.'

For a short while there came no answer from Cook, who had lapsed into deep thought on the scullery maid's last words. Well, Amy was wrong, thought Cook, because a 'nest-egg' was just what she *had* got put away . . . safe and secure these many long years. But her 'nest-egg' wasn't bonds nor money, nor anything that might at first glance buy a roof over her head. Dear me, no! It was nothing more than a letter written to her by Mrs Manfred, the former housekeeper at Breckleton House. Poor Mrs Manfred who had been hanged over twenty years since for her part in the 'murder' of Miss Emma's husband, Gregory Denton. All the same, that letter was the roof over Cook's head in her old age, and the food in her belly, and a few guineas to make life comfortable too. It was a sad and sorry letter written by a gentle soul about to face the gallows and, as a body might want to do in such a terrible situation, Mrs Manfred had poured out all her innermost fears in that same letter. Not only her fears, but her dark suspicions regarding the master himself, whom she believed to know a great deal of the circumstances surrounding the death of *both* Miss Emma's parents. The letter indirectly accused Caleb Crowther of being a murderer, no less!

'I said . . . I don't expect *you've* got a nest-egg put by

any more than the rest of us . . . and as you told me yourself, you're well past sixty-five,' remarked Amy, who always regarded the elderly cook to be a fountain of all wisdom. 'So what will we do if the worst comes to the worst?' There were tears in her voice, and her eyes were suspiciously bright as they implored the round, aged face across the table. 'What shall we do, Cook? Where can we go?'

'Now don't you fret yourself,' warned Cook. 'The worst hasn't happened yet . . . and if it does, then we shall have to think again, won't we, eh?'

'Oh, Cook, d'you think Miss Emma really will take all the master's fortune away?'

'Well, if she does it'll be no more or less than he deserves. But you have to remember that Miss Emma's been back a while now, and she hasn't managed it yet.' She chuckled aloud and fell back in the chair, her great arms wrapped one around the other as she gleefully hugged herself. 'Oh, but hasn't it been a pretty thing to watch, eh . . . the master's face draining chalk-white every time one o' them letters from Miss Emma's solicitors comes a-tumbling through the door.' Her face was a study in delight as she revelled in Caleb Crowther's discomfort. 'But he's a crafty old fox . . . and he's had longer at the art of being devious than Miss Emma has. I'll wager the feud between 'em is coming to a head at long last.'

Suddenly, the elderly woman realized that it might be foolish to delay much longer in fetching out that particular nest-egg and collecting payment on it. But – just as it had done since Emma Grady's return – some deep instinct warned her to bide her time for as long as she could. The reasons were many. Firstly, the master was a dangerous man . . . a Justice . . . and if he were to learn of such a damning letter he might somehow steal it from her and see to it that she was locked away until she rotted; that was a fearsome prospect that gave her nightmares. It were a delicate situation, and one that she hadn't quite fathomed out. Of course, Emma herself might likely pay money to have the letter in her possession, but Cook had firmly resisted that particular course because it didn't seem right to ask *her* for money, besides which the letter referred to the suspicious deaths of both her parents and was bound to cause her a great deal of distress. Then there was the mistress, Agnes Crowther. Now, she would *certainly* be interested in the contents of that letter, but she was a stiff and easily shocked woman of rigid principles, and if she were to be asked for money against the letter, it might end up with its owner being flung in prison on a charge of blackmail.

No. The whole thing had to be done proper, decided Cook. For the minute, she had to watch how this wrangle was developing between Miss Emma and the master, and be sure to keep her distance from both of them. One thing was certain. She must be careful not to move in too quick, nor to leave it too late. It were a delicate thing indeed, that it was. Meanwhile, she was thoroughly enjoying the sight of the master squirming beneath the pressure of Miss Emma's boot.

Chapter Two

'D'you really mean to see him in the workhouse, Emma?' Nelly came into the garden where Emma was seated by the rose-arch, her quiet grey eyes gazing towards the distant green landscape and her thoughts reaching back over the years. There was sadness and regret in her downcast features. But when she saw the familiar and homely figure of Nelly, her face lit up in a lovely smile. 'I don't know, Nelly,' she replied, waiting for the other woman to be seated on the bench opposite. 'I do despise him for the things he's done . . . turning his back on me when I needed him most, betraying my father's trust in him, and using my inheritance as though it were his own. I can't forget these things and, God help me . . . I can't forgive him.'

'Oh, Emma gal, I do wish you would let the past go!' Nelly's brown eyes were beseeching, and Emma's heart was warmed by the sincere and loving soul that now implored her. 'Let it go, darling . . . before it becomes a blight on the happiness you've found with Marlow and the little lad.' Nelly blinked her eyes in the warm April sunshine as she prayed that, this time, Emma might be persuaded to leave her uncle, Caleb Crowther, to his own devices, and in time no doubt his wickedness would catch him up and be the end of him. To see the gentle Emma so bent on revenge was a terrible thing.

'It isn't so easy, Nelly,' murmured Emma. 'Oh, in time I might be able to forget . . . and perhaps even forgive all the things I've mentioned. But how can I forgive him for the worst thing of all?' Her voice fell to a whisper and the grey eyes softened with the threat of tears as she gazed longingly on the face of her beloved friend; a friend made in the fearful prison cell to which Caleb Crowther had committed Emma all those years before; a good and loyal friend who had helped her through her long, traumatic exile in Australia; a dear and cherished friend who, Emma hoped, would always be close by. In fact, Nelly was like the sister Emma had always longed for.

'Aw, Emma.' Nelly's gaze bathed Emma's troubled face. 'You're still brooding on that newborn girl-child, ain't you, eh?'

'I can't help it, Nelly. I try so hard to put it out of my mind, but it won't leave me. Not the sight and feel of that tiny, dark-haired bundle in my arms . . . nor the awful pain in my heart when the child was wrenched away and left in the gutter.' Emma's grey eyes shone like hardened steel and her voice stiffened with anger. '*He* did that, Nelly! . . . I begged him for help, but he left me in prison to rot. He could have arranged for me to at least have my baby in a safer place, where she might have had a chance to survive. Oh, Nelly, Nelly, how can I ever forgive him?' Now she could not hold back the tears that trickled down her face.

'All right, Emma, darling.' It hurt Nelly to see Emma's tears. 'Do what you must . . . but don't do anything you might live to regret, eh?'

Emma gave a small laugh as she wiped away the tears. 'Bless you, Nelly,' she said, 'you sound just like Marlow.

22

He thinks I'm only punishing myself by pursuing this business with Caleb Crowther.'

'Well! There you are then. And there ain't two people who love you more in all the world than me and your fella.' She shook her head and the wispy brown hair fluttered about her face. 'Tain't no good trying to reason with you though, is it . . . you're just as stubborn as you've allus been!' She chortled softly and the curve of her features was lost in a multitude of fine wrinkles. Nelly was not yet in her fortieth year, but the ravages of a hard life and earlier years of terrible neglect ·had written the passage of time cruelly on her. Even though she was considered shapeless and her face was more plain than pretty, there was something warm and de-lightful about her, a particular essence that endeared her to everyone she met. There was a world of joy and love in her merry brown eyes, and a childlike wisdom.

'I know that you and Marlow mean well and have only my interests at heart . . . but in this particular instance, I must follow my instincts. Caleb Crowther is a bad one, Nelly. It wouldn't seem right to let him go unpunished.' Emma rose to her feet. Slightly older than Nelly, she made a very pleasing figure, slight and softly curved in an expensive dress of blue taffeta with pretty white ruffles at the throat and cuffs. Her long chestnut-coloured hair was exquisitely coiled into the nape of her neck, where it was secured by two dainty mother-of-pearl combs. When she moved, it was with a natural grace and elegance. Now, as she began walking away, Nelly also got to her feet and quickly took up her place beside Emma.

Content and comfortable in each other's company, Emma and Nelly meandered through the garden, a lovely place of stately old trees and spreading shrubs already heavy with buds. At the farthest end, away from the house, there was a small orchard bursting with fruit trees of all descriptions. The entire garden was surrounded by a wall six feet high and supporting every kind of climbing flower imaginable: the beautiful cascading wisteria, the heavily scented jasmine, clematis, rambling roses and many more. One or two had already begun to open their buds in the April sunshine, but the whole magnificent panorama of colour and perfume would not be evident until mid-summer, when Emma would spend many contented hours in her favourite spot, the small paved area which was bound on three sides by tall, elegant spruce trees. In its middle was a small pond teeming with life, two fancy wrought-iron benches and a circular table. It was in this place that Nelly had found her just now.

From here, Emma could look across the garden and through the tall, wide gate with its open network of railings and scrolls. Beyond the gate was Corporation Park, an undulating expanse of green lawns and wide open spaces, the sight of which filled Emma's heart with nostalgia. It was here, in this lovely old house, that Emma had spent a good deal of her childhood with her beloved father, Thadius Grady. On returning to England, she had been delighted to see that the house on Park Street was up for sale. It seemed like the hand of Fate to her. She and Marlow had bought it, restored it to its former glory, and Emma spent many precious hours wandering from room to room and picturing herself as a child running free within its walls; a child without a mother, but cherished by the father who adored her, and cossetted by the unforgettable Mrs Manfred, who had come to be her nanny. It was in this house that Emma had known great happiness, then heartache when her father had told her of his plan to live at Breckleton House with the Crowther family.

Now, as Emma dwelt on these unpleasant memories, the pain was too much. Thank God for my own family, she thought, and for such a loyal friend as Nelly.

'I'm surprised Silas Trent don't take offence at the way you're badgering old Caleb Crowther,' remarked Nelly in her usual forthright manner. 'The old bugger is Silas's father-in-law after all.' Nelly intended to use every means at her disposal to dissuade Emma from feuding with her uncle because, although she herself loathed what that wicked man had done to Emma, Nelly could see nothing good coming of it all. She felt instinctively that it would be Emma herself who was likely to end up with a bloody nose, however much she was in the right.

Emma was not persuaded by Nelly's latest arguments regarding the man who was both a friend and business colleague and to whom she had recently sold the Australian-based trading company. 'Silas understands,' she replied, 'he knows it is something I have to do.'

Nelly shivered and made an unpleasant face. 'Y'know, Emma gal,' she said in a softer voice, 'I've allus regretted not having a father to talk to . . . somebody I could tek me troubles to when I were growing up . . . if y'know what I mean. But I'll tell you this, gal . . . I'd rather be orphaned and homeless than have a fella such as Caleb Crowther for me father!' Her mood was more indignant as she added, 'I might have understood Martha being swayed by her father's authority when she were younger . . . 'cause when all's said and done he's enough to frighten anybody. But it ain't as though she's still a snotty-nosed kid now, is it, eh? The woman's the wrong side o' forty, be buggered . . . and she still hangs on his every word!'

She hurried her pace to keep up with Emma, who had caught sight of her son's small dark head through the drawing-room window, where he was just about to be released from his afternoon's studies. Soon, he would be ready for full-time tutoring; thank goodness she and Marlow were in agreement that young Bill should not be forcibly sent away to boarding-school. 'When the time comes, we'll let the lad decide for himself,' Marlow had said, the 'time' being when Bill would be nine years old, Emma sighed. It did seem a long way off in the future, but she knew from experience how time had a nasty habit of running away all too quickly. Lately though, life had been good to her: she and Marlow were now man and wife, and they had a wonderful son in young Bill. Also, they were financially secure, what with the sale of her own business and the continuing success of Marlow's transporting concern along the Leeds and Liverpool Canal. In this last year alone he had increased his fleet of barges to twelve in all. Although Emma was always mindful of how fortunate she was, all the wealth and security in the world could never compensate for what she had lost.

Walking beside her, Nelly was aware of Emma's quiet thoughts; she heard the deep troubled sigh and knew at once that her dear friend was thinking of the newborn girl-child that was lost to her on a grim and terrible morning almost a lifetime ago. She knew also that Emma would always hold Caleb Crowther responsible, and rightly so. But, not for the first time, Nelly's conscience troubled her, because all these years she had allowed Emma to believe that her child was born dead, when in fact she herself suspected that the little girl had lived. The image rose in her mind now of how she had embraced the unconscious Emma in the prison wagon that sped them away after the birth, and of how, in the vanishing distance, there had appeared an old woman who had stooped to collect a bundle from the gutter, *a bundle that cried out*. Nelly had never been certain, and was loath to reveal her suspicions to Emma in case it made her term of exile that much more unbearable. Later, when Emma was a free woman, so many years had passed it seemed futile to delve too deeply into what was long gone and, to Nelly's mind, should be forgotten.

In a thoughtful attempt to dispel Emma's brooding countenance, Nelly raised another issue that was close to Emma's heart, that of a young woman, a thief they had encountered at the Liverpool docks on their return to England some three years ago. The unfortunate girl in question had cunningly outwitted the police officer who apprehended her then, much to Nelly and Emma's relief, had made good her escape, giving Emma a cheeky wink as she fled past them with a grubby child held fast to her thin, ragged figure. Emma had since agonized over the young woman's plight and when, a little over a month ago, Nelly had caught sight of that pathetic soul scouring the market-place here in Blackburn, Emma had implored her to enquire after her, 'Nelly . . . we must find her and make life more bearable for her and the child'. She had not been surprised when Nelly pointed out, 'Oh, but she has *two* nippers now . . . the first one big enough to run as fast as ever her mammy can, and a little scrawny thing clinging to her like a monkey.'

'What I *really* came to tell you' – Nelly's chirpy voice shattered Emma's painful thoughts – 'was that I didn't have no luck at all in finding that young woman. Nobody seems to know who she is . . . or, if they do, they're not about to tell no stranger.' She snorted with disgust. 'Hmh! . . . it ain't as though I look like a villain or a troublemaker, is it, eh . . . ? On top of which I even offered the buggers a handful of silver for any information regarding her whereabouts. Huh! . . . the way they stared at me anybody'd think I'd been sent by the law or some'at!' The idea was shocking to Nelly who, many years ago, had herself perfected the art of 'defying the law' at every opportunity.

'Did you find no one who might help?' asked Emma anxiously. 'Did you explain that you were on a kindly errand . . . that you meant her no harm?'

'Course I did . . . till I were blue in the face,' Nelly replied with an injured look, which soon gave way to a deep, thoughtful expression as she went on, 'Funny thing, though . . . how them bargees along the wharf clammed up the minute I described her, and I'll tell you what, Emma me old darling . . . I ain't finished with the buggers yet!'

'Oh, you *must* keep trying, Nelly . . . keep on trying till you find her,' urged Emma, her own troubles fading beneath the visions which now flitted through her mind: a young girl burdened with a child, both ragged and hungry-looking. It pained her to think that the poor unfortunate now had another mouth to feed and, according to Nelly, was 'every bit as thin and scruffy as the first time we saw her'. She recalled how the girl had winked at her even as she had led the police officer a merry dance. What a striking face she had, with those big black eyes and strong features. Something about her had touched Emma's heart. 'We mustn't give up,' she told Nelly now, 'I won't rest until we've found her.'

At that point, Emma's son came running from the house to greet her and she was saddened by the fact that she had not been blessed with more children. As she swept the laughing, sturdy little fellow into her arms, Emma felt a pang of guilt. He was so strong and healthy, so cherished and provided for. How very different must be the lives of those two children that Nelly had described. How hard must be the existence of a young mother who was made to steal in order to feed her babies. In her prayers, Emma never failed to give thanks to God for having made her life easier. Now she prayed he might help her to find this young woman so that life might also be made a little kinder for her.

Chapter Three

'Well, if it isn't Molly! A sight to brighten a fella's day. But I'm surprised you dare show your face in broad daylight, you tinker. What shameful antics have you been up to *now*, eh?' The friendly, taunting voice sailed along the wharf, causing the dark-haired young woman to stop and turn around. When her black, mischievous eyes alighted on the familiar brightly coloured barge moored nearby, she began sauntering towards it, her unhurried pace dictated by the tiny infant in her arms and her steps hindered by the slight, fair-haired girl trotting closely beside her. 'You're never meaning *me*, are you?' she laughed. 'Why! . . . I'm an angel if ever there was one.'

Straightening from his labours aboard the barge, the burly young man regarded her closely as she drew near. 'There were a fancy lady asking after you, Molly, my darling,' he said, with a lop-sided grin, 'done up like royalty she were . . . and real keen to make your acquaintance, I reckon.' Mick Darcy was mesmerized by Molly's dark beauty, and by that particular graceful way she had of moving. The nearer she came to him, the more his heart turned over. She may be painfully thin, he thought, and dressed in threadbare rags, but there was something magnificent about her; classy was how he would describe the lovely Molly.

Classy, and, as far as he was concerned, sadly unattainable.

Mick lost count of how many times that waster, Jack-the-Lad, had run off and left her, only to return and put his feet under Molly's table again. The truth was, she loved the blighter. And love had a nasty way of blinding a body until they saw only what they wanted to see. It irked him though to see how Molly had been used by that rascal time and again. By! If the fellow was here right now, at this minute, likely as not he'd get the full weight of a fist in his lying mouth! The bugger didn't deserve such a loyal, bonny lass as Molly. Oh, if only she'd give *him* the chance to look after her, he would make her life that much more comfortable, treat her special, he would. But her heart belonged to Jack-the-Lad, and there seemed no way of winning it over. All the same, he wouldn't give up. He wanted Molly, *loved* her. He had patience enough to wait for the right moment in which to make his move.

As she drew nearer, Molly could not help but be impressed at the fine figure aboard the barge. Mick Darcy was a tall, well-built man, and standing on the deck at this moment, with the sunshine lightening his earth-coloured curls and those long, strong legs wide apart for balance against the rolling vessel, he made a handsome sight.

With a wide, cheeky grin, Mick pushed the flat cap back on his head and lowered his voice as she looked up from the quayside. 'You little devil, Molly,' he laughed, 'what have you been up to, eh . . . that some fine lady should be asking after you?'

'I ain 't been up to *nothing*,' she retorted good-humouredly, hitching the dark-eyed child more securely on to her bony hip and keeping a tight hold on the small girl by her side.

'Well, if you ain't been up to nothing . . . how come the gentry are stalking the market-place and offering good money to know your whereabouts, eh? You tell me *that*, sunshine . . . ! You must have been up to something.'

'*I tell you I ain't.*' She smiled and her dark beauty startled him. Then, laughing, she added, 'At least . . . no more than usual . . . a fat wallet or a fancy purse here and there, gently confiscated from them as can afford it. Only enough to keep body and soul together, mind.' Of a sudden, the small girl at her hand broke free. 'Now then, little Sal,' Molly warned in a sharp voice, 'don't you go wandering off . . . else like as not you'll end up in that there canal!' When the child broke into a run, Molly started after her. 'Stop her, Mick!' she yelled.

'Whoa, my little beauty!' Mick Darcy chuckled as he swept the frail, scruffy bundle into his arms and flung it high in the air. When it began laughing and squealing, he pressed it to the floor of his barge, playfully prodding its flat little belly until it curled in a heap and hid itself in a tight hug, at the same time letting out bursts of uncontrollable giggling. That is, until Mick came towards her, his fingers pointed from his forehead in the shape of two long horns and his voice wailing like that of a ghost. At that point, the twitching bundle clambered to its legs and ran screeching and laughing towards the galley hatch, where it disappeared into the quarters below.

'You terror, Mick Darcy,' chuckled Molly, who had delighted in the whole episode. 'The poor little thing'll have nightmares for weeks!' Taking care not to become entangled in the paraphernalia of ropes that cluttered

33

the deck, she climbed aboard. 'Got the kettle on, have you?' she asked, going in the same direction as little Sal. 'My throat's parched.' She cast an accusing glance up to the blue, cloudless sky. 'There still ain't no sign of cooler weather,' she moaned. 'Have you ever known such a muggy, dry May in all your born days?'

'Can't say as I have . . . and I can't say as I haven't, Molly darling,' he replied, at the same time putting a strong lean hand on her shoulder and gently drawing her to a halt. 'There . . .' he stretched out his arms, 'give the babby to me. I don't want to see the pair of you tumbling headlong down that narrow flight of stairs.' His teeth showed white and straight against his tanned skin as he smiled down on her. 'Besides . . . knowing you, you'd like as not fall on my old mammy's best china, and she'd haunt me from the grave.'

'Huh! You ain't got no faith in me at all, have you, Mick Darcy?' She returned his smile and there was a wonderful warmth between them, which made Molly nervous and put her on her guard. She drew the child away. 'The little devil's wet her pants,' she warned, looking quickly aside when she saw the tenderness in those searching, amber eyes. 'Thanks all the same, Mick,' she said, starting her way towards the first step, 'but she's a bit touchy . . . teething she is . . . and she'll happen kick up a fuss.'

'Away with your excuses!' he told her, encouraged by the sight of the little one holding out her arms to him. 'Look there . . . the bairn's no fool, she knows she'll be safer with me,' he laughed. Whereupon Molly graciously handed the child over and they all descended to the lower cabin.

A few moments later, Molly was seated on the bench

by the table, with little Sal kneeling beside her. The smaller bairn was contentedly sleeping between two plump red cushions which Mick had carefully arranged in the narrow bunk that was just visible from the living quarters. Little Sal was growing excited by the increasing number of barges now navigating their way into the narrow waters fronting the many warehouses and cotton mills along Eanam Wharf; at the sight of each new arrival chugging in, little Sal would press her nose to the porthole and squeal with delight. From the galley, Mick could be heard whistling jauntily. Occasionally he would put his head round the wood panelling to reassure Molly and the girl. 'Won't be long now, my beauties . . . bacon and eggs, sunny side up.' The delicious aroma of sizzling bacon soon permeated every corner of the barge.

'You really don't have to feed us,' protested Molly, even though she hadn't eaten a proper meal in days and her stomach was rumbling with hunger.

'It's my pleasure,' he said, placing the hearty breakfast in front of her and little Sal, who suddenly lost all interest in the barges outside as she tucked into the meal with unashamed enthusiasm. 'If you'd only let me, Molly . . . I would take on the responsibility of you and the two bairns tomorrow.' His voice was quiet and serious as he studied her with imploring eyes.

'Well, we ain't your responsibility,' Molly was quick to remind him. 'We never could be . . . and you know it, Mick Darcy. These two little lasses and me . . . we belong to Jack.' She lowered her gaze and patted herself below the waist, 'Not forgetting the little one who's not yet shown its face.'

'*Oh, Molly!*' He put his breakfast plate on the table

and fell heavily on to the bench opposite. 'He's never left you with another?'

Molly nodded her head, and he could have sworn there was a merry twinkle in her black eyes. 'It happened when he found his way home just before Easter . . . "recovering from a run of bad fortune", he said . . . two weeks later he won a packet on the horses and went off to celebrate. I haven't seen him since.' She laughed out loud at the expression of horror on Mick's face. 'Oh, don't fret yourself,' she told him, beginning to enjoy her meal, 'if my calculations serve me right, the bairn should arrive some time round Christmas Eve . . . What d'you think to that, eh? It's not everybody as can look forward to such a special Christmas present, is it? Oh, and like as not, its daddy will have turned up long afore that.'

'The bugger deserves a thrashing!'

'Hey, watch your language afront of the little ones,' warned Molly with good humour. 'Come on, eat your breakfast and don't look so shocked . . . I'm not about to drop it here and now!' she laughingly reassured him.

'It wouldn't matter if you *did*, Molly darling . . . you know it would be made welcome.' There was a world of love in his voice.

'I know.' Long, slim fingers reached out to cover his hand in a warm gesture. 'You're a good friend to me and my bairns, Mick Darcy,' Molly murmured, 'and there's nobody else I'd ever share my troubles with. I can't deny what you say . . . Jack will never be any good . . . he'll always gamble his money away; he'll drift from place to place like the vagabond he is, and I know in my heart that there's no future for us together . . . he's not the kind to put down roots. But I love him. And I can't help the way I feel. Oh, it's not so bad . . . I can put up with his coming and going, and his gambling, because I know he'll aways come back, to hold me in his arms and tell me there's no other woman for him. It's only crumbs, I know . . . but it's all he can give, and it's enough. So long as he's faithful, and there's no other woman in his arms, I'll put up with all his failings.'

'And if there ever *was* another woman?' Mick had no reason to believe that Jack had deceived the trusting Molly, but the fellow was a worthless bounder who was capable of anything.

For a while, Molly remained silent, pushing the curled bacon round her plate with the prongs of the fork and deeply considering Mick's question. Of a sudden, she stabbed the fork into the bacon and raised her black, tempestuous eyes to his. 'I'd *kill* the pair of them,' she said with alarming calmness; after which she went on to finish her breakfast as though the subject had never arisen. All the same, her hands were trembling and her heart was beating furiously inside her at the thought of some other woman in her Jack's arms.

'I can't think how you ever got tangled up with the likes of him . . . you never have told me the full story.' Mick had seen the pain in Molly's eyes, and he called himself all kinds of a fool for having planted the seed of doubt in her mind with regard to her fellow. All the same though, he knew that Molly was no fool. The idea that Jack had ample opportunity to be unfaithful to her must have presented itself. 'You do realize that one of these days, Molly . . . he just may not come back?' Somewhere, in his deepest heart, he prayed for that day, but then he was filled with remorse, knowing how devastated Molly would be if ever Jack finally deserted her. He couldn't understand how she went on forgiving this man who used her badly at every turn. But then, love was a funny, unpredictable thing. Look at *him*, for example. Look how he adored Molly beyond all else, knowing that she would never look at any man other than Jack; Jack, who had lumbered her with three kids, and left her to fend for them as best she could, knowing full well that every time he went away there was always the danger that Molly and the young 'uns could be thrown on to the streets. However, if the truth were told, eviction might turn out to be the lesser of two evils, because that grim, God-forsaken place on Dock Street could never be called 'home'. If Molly were to lose that place she only had to ask and he would gladly take her in. But she *wouldn't* ask. He knew that, and it saddened him. Yet in spite of everything, he still loved and wanted her. So when it came right down to it, he did understand how one soul could adore another, even if it were a lost cause.

'You're wrong, Mick.' Molly's gaze was defiant, albeit a little desperate, he thought. 'Jack will *always* come back . . . he'd never leave us for good.' There came into her eyes a faraway look, and, as always, she was out of his reach. 'He loves us, you see.' Turning from Mick's earnest gaze, Molly looked out of the porthole, her dark eyes scanning the wharf as though searching for someone. When the infant stirred behind her, she quickly glanced round to assure herself that the child was safe enough. Then, facing Mick, she went on in a quiet voice, 'You don't have to tell me how worthless Jack is . . . I've known for a long time. You ask how I ever got "tangled up with the likes of him", and I can only tell you that he came to my help when I desperately needed someone. I were all alone in the world, Mick . . . very young and very frightened.' Here she paused. Images of an old woman came into her mind – a limping, bedraggled woman with thin, tousled hair and a kindly face that was ravaged by a rough life and a particular love for 'a drop o' the ol' stuff'. Old Sal Tanner had been Molly's anchor in life, her mammy, her friend, and the kindest, dearest, most cantankerous lady on God's earth. Leaning back in her seat, Molly fought down the tears. 'You know of old Sal Tanner . . . her as brought me up from a babe in arms?'

'I don't come from these parts but I know of old Sal right enough.' He smiled that broad smile which some-how disturbed Molly in spite of herself. 'Who *didn't* know of her? The old tramp's become a kind of legend in these 'ere parts. It's a strange story, Molly . . . how she always told that you belonged to the little people . . . how she found you in the gutter and all.' His voice grew more serious as he asked, 'Did she ever reveal your true parents?'

'She didn't know, bless her. She had strange ideas, did old Sal, but she was very special to me.' The memories came flooding back. 'There was this timepiece she used to keep hidden . . . a pretty, delicate little thing it were . . . with writing on the case. Old Sal would show it to me from time to time . . . almost afraid of it, she was . . . said it were right next to me when she found me in the gutter . . . "A sign from the little people", she claimed. At first, I believed everything she told me. But then, as I got older and realized that Sal's ideas were a bit stranger than other folks', I got to thinking about that there timepiece. I wondered about the writing on it, and promised myself that, one day, I'd learn to read. Then I might find out where I *really* came from, and where I belonged.'

'Where is it now . . . ? This timepiece? Will you show it to me?'

'It's gone . . . gone, long before Jack taught me to read.'

'Gone? You mean you sold it?'

Molly shook her head. 'No. I would never do that . . . not when old Sal made me promise never to part with it.'

'Then where is it?'

'Snatched from round my neck by Justice Crowther.'

'*Crowther!*' Mick recoiled in disgust. That was a name to foul anyone's lips. 'How in God's name did you tangle with *him*? Most folks know how to steer well clear of that particular devil.'

Molly told him everything: how, when she was very young, she'd found Justice Crowther's grandson dazed and wandering, and how he fell into the canal and would have drowned if she hadn't dived in and saved him. 'I didn't know who he were, till I took him to the cabin to recover . . . he didn't look like no gentry to me . . . dressed in filthy rags he were, and looking like the worst tramp.' Then she explained how it turned out that he'd been set upon by ruffians who had stripped him of his own posh clothes and swapped them for the rags he wore when she found him. 'Only a few days before, old Sal had left this wicked world and was lying in the mortuary . . . waiting for a pauper's grave unless I could come up with the money to bury her properly. Well, it were like Lady Luck smiled on me when she led that gentry lad to my door.' Molly told how she had contacted Justice Crowther's wife, and been reluctantly paid for the return of her grandson, Edward Trent – 'a really nice lad he was'. While Mick listened, enthralled and astonished, she went on to describe how Justice Crowther then blamed her for kidnapping his grandson, and hunted her down without mercy. 'It was the very night when he seized me and burned old Sal's cabin that he snatched the timepiece . . . when I was escaping from the prison-cart with Jack-the-Lad. He saved me, my Jack . . . kept me with him all the time we were on the run, even though I slowed him down and might have been the cause of both of us being captured and clapped in irons for the rest of our miserable lives.'

Mick shook his head. 'The story of how Justice Crowther's grandson was "brutally kidnapped" went far and wide . . . I remember something of it when I was working the Manchester waterways. But, my God, Molly . . . I didn't know . . . why haven't you ever told me all this before?'

'Because it's a dangerous thing to let loose. I've a feeling in my bones that if Justice Crowther were ever to find me . . . he'd *still* get pleasure from clapping me in irons. I only told you so you'd understand how much I owe Jack, and how he'll always come back.'

Mick nodded, though he was not convinced about Jack's loyalty. 'You say the timepiece was snatched from your neck, Molly?' When she nodded, he went on. 'Are you *sure* of that . . . ? I mean, could it not just have been accidentally broken in the struggle, and fallen to the ground?'

'No. Some time after, when we thought it might be safe, Jack and me went back and searched . . . Jack knew how much it meant to me. There was no sign of it. I'm convinced that Justice Crowther still has it . . . perhaps he thinks it might lead him to me in time.' She dipped her two fingers into the neck of her dress and drew out the black string that hung from her throat.

Knotted at the end of the loop was a tiny gold clasp in the shape of a petal cluster. 'When the chain was torn from my neck . . . this fastener got caught in my hair.'

'It's very little to go by, Molly.' Mick was surprised that she had not sold the pretty gold cluster. After all, it must be worth a guinea or so. Then he realised the depth of her love for old Sal Tanner, and the promise she had made the old woman. No, it was *not* surprising that Molly still cherished the tiny piece, for it obviously meant more than money to her. A sudden thought chilled him. 'Are you telling me that this fancy lady . . . the one who's been asking after you . . . is *sent by Justice Crowther* to root you out?'

Molly gave no answer for a moment, seemingly lost in deep, tormenting thoughts. She gently stroked the child's fair head and was suddenly fearful for the future. After a while, she looked up to meet Mick's anxious gaze with a rush of defiance. 'Who else could it be?' she asked. 'Of course she were sent by the Justice. But I tell you this, Mick Darcy . . . they can search high and low, but they'll not find me . . . I've learned when to keep my head down. And I've grown as crafty as a fox when it comes to dipping and diving.'

'You'd be safer moving away from these parts.' Mick was afraid for her. 'Come away with me, Molly . . . you and me . . . we could make a good life together.'

Molly got to her feet. 'You know my answer to that,' she said cuttingly, 'and if you want us to stay the good friends we are, don't ever ask me again.' She turned to draw the child into her arms. 'Come on, Sal my darling . . . it's high time we went.'

'Forget what I said, Molly . . . it's just that I'm afraid for you. You can understand that, can't you?'

Molly thought hard before answering. 'It's forgot then.' Her smile was warm, though not intimate. 'What I told you . . . about the Justice and all that . . . it won't go no further? There are times when a body can't tell friend from foe.'

'You can count on me.' He reached the infant before Molly did, and as he tenderly raised its sleeping form into his capable arms, his eyes were drawn to Molly, who was looking at him in a strangely unsettling way, her black eyes following his every move. When she realized that Mick had been made curious by her close observation of him, she was suddenly self-conscious and, irritated by the soft pink glow that suffused her neck and face, she quickly lowered her gaze to the floor.

Mick brought the child to her, yet made no attempt to give it into her arms. Instead, the two of them stood for a moment, he gazing down on her, and she with her eyes averted. When in a while she raised her eyes to his he was astonished to see them bright with tears. 'What is it, Molly, me darling?' he asked softly. 'Why were you watching me like that?'

Something in the tone of his voice cautioned her. She must never unwittingly give him hope. But, oh, what a grand, heartwarming sight he had made just now, when he had so lovingly raised her sleeping child into those strong arms; arms that were more used to raising the cripplingly heavy loads that lined the wharves. He was a good man, she thought. A better man than Jack could ever be, but she dared not tell him that, for fear he misunderstood. 'It's not important,' she said in a deliberately matter-of-fact voice. 'I were just thinking, that's all . . . just thinking.'

Before he could persist in his questions, Molly turned

away and climbed the steep, narrow steps that led up to the deck. Little Sal, full and comfortable from the hearty breakfast, trotted behind her mammy, and Mick brought up the rear, cradling the infant close to his chest. This was how it should be, he thought, me and Molly, with the bairns round us and Jack-the-Lad out of the picture altogether. Yet even while his fancies took hold of him, he knew that that was all they were. Fancies. All the same, it made him tremble to think how close he had come to frightening Molly away. He would watch his tongue in future. Somehow, he had to keep his emotions in check or he'd lose her friendship altogether. He couldn't bear the idea of not having her pay the occasional visit, when they could sit and share their troubles like two old friends. Such times were precious to him, and if he had to settle for that or nothing at all, then he would content himself with the strong friendship that existed between them.

As he watched Molly leaving the wharf, Mick's love for her was never stronger, a frustrating love, and one which he knew would continue to cause him pain. A spiral of anger rose in him, but it was tempered by a sneaking admiration. Molly was too independent by far! Too proud, and too bloody loyal to a man who wasn't worth salt. So what if Jack *had* saved Molly from the bobbies? Any man would have done the same, given the opportunity. God almighty . . . ! It didn't mean she had to devote her whole life to him because of it, and it didn't mean she had to close her eyes to his many failings.

At the corner of the warehouse, Molly glanced back. When she saw that Mick was still watching, she waved and smiled. Then she was gone. For a long, aching moment, Mick stared at the place where she had paused, before issuing a deep, weary sigh. 'Aw, Molly . . . my lovely Molly,' he murmured, but there was a smile in his voice, and in his heart a warm anticipation of their next meeting.

'Good morning . . . looks like we're in for another glorious day.' The fellow addressed Mick in a firm, friendly voice as he strode towards the front office of one of the bigger cotton mills.

'Top o' the morning to you, sir,' replied Mick, while observing how, even though the man was dressed in casual togs, they were not the togs of a labourer, but the easy attire of a gentry. This one was a puzzle, though, because he had a winning smile and a manner that was not hostile to the likes of himself. Growing curious, he clambered from the barge and sought out the advice of a bargee who was securing his vessel nearby. 'Who's that fellow?' he asked, adding with a chuckle, 'If he were fitted out in cords and rolled-up sleeves, I'd swear he was a bargee the same as you and me . . . there's something about his manner . . . and the cut of his swagger. Though I dare say he's never done a day's work in his life, eh?'

'Well now, that's where you'd be wrong, fella-me-lad!' The old sailor came forward to lean against the rail where he took off his cap, slung it over a nearby strut and leisurely proceeded to light up the tobacco in his pipe. Mick was amused to see how the old one was in no particular hurry to satisfy the curiosity of a stranger. In fact, he seemed to be positively relishing in withholding the information just that bit longer. When his pipe was lit and he himself engulfed in billowing grey smoke, he went on, 'That there fellow knows more about barges and working these waterways than you and me put together.' Here, he leaned over and pointed to the sign heading his barge. 'See that?'

'The sign, you mean?'

'Aye . . . see the name written there?'

Mick studied the sign, before reading it aloud – *'Tanner's Transporters'*. He glanced back to where he had seen the man disappear. 'You're never telling me that *he* owns this barge?'

'I am that. This barge . . . and nigh on a dozen more like it. And I'll tell you some'at else, matey, Marlow Tanner may not *look* as smooth and smarmy as the next gent . . . but he's a better gent than ever you're likely to find. A proper credit to the blokes who work for him. There ain't one of us who wouldn't stretch ourselves to the limit if he were to ask. Teks care of us he do . . . through thick and thin. You'll never find a better gaffer than Marlow Tanner.' He pursed his lips into a multitude of wrinkles and nodded his head as though agreeing with himself. 'And that's the very truth!' he concluded, making ready to resume his labours.

'A dozen such barges, you say?' Mick had been working this particular stretch of the Leeds and Liverpool Canal for almost a year now, and was curious to know how it was that he had not come across a 'Tanner Transporter' until today.

'Aye, that's right. Up until a year back, we were regular between here and the big docks . . . but the gaffer secured a juicy contract, which meant us coming up outta the Yorkshire side.' He chuckled, displaying a jagged row of tobacco-stained teeth, 'Earned us all a bob or two extra, that did.'

'I see.' That would explain why he hadn't shared a berth with one of these barges before. 'But didn't he lose the contract *this* side, if he shifted operations like that?'

'Naw . . . he's too bloody canny a businessman for that,' remonstrated the old one. Of a sudden, he was eyeing Mick's barge alongside. 'That yourn, is it?'

'It is.'

'And you've been working this particular stretch . . . ferrying cotton to the Liverpool Docks?'

'I have.'

The old one laughed out loud. 'Then *you've* been paid by Tanner . . . just like the rest of us . . . and all these single barge-owners hereabouts.'

Mick shook his head. 'No, old man. You've got it wrong . . . my pay packet comes from the owner of that there mill.' He pointed to the very building into which he had seen Marlow Tanner disappear. Suddenly, the light began to dawn. 'Well, I never . . . ! Are you saying *he* owns the mill?'

Thoroughly enjoying himself, the old fellow gleefully pointed out how Marlow Tanner not only secured every available barge-owner for the period of one year, but when the owner of the largest cotton mill loudly protested at what he claimed was a 'threat to free enterprise', he promptly bought the mill as well! 'Made the fellow an offer he'd a' been a fool to turn down.'

As Mick went thoughtfully back to his own barge, two things crossed his mind. One was paramount in his reckoning. If his own services had been secured for a year – which they had – and if the Tanner barges were now back in force – which they seemed to be – how long would it be before he was summoned to Marlow Tanner's office and told he was no longer needed? It was a daunting prospect, especially since the fellow was also busy buying up the mills that had hitherto supplied a living to the likes of himself.

Deeply concerned, Mick decided not to wait for Tanner to lay him off. He still had a living to make, and he wanted to make it *here* in these parts, where he could keep an eye on Molly. No, he couldn't afford to wait. The matter had to be settled. The sooner the better, to his mind. Straight away, Mick changed his direction and went hastily towards the mill office.

The other matter that had crossed his mind was the name *Tanner*. Surely it couldn't have a link to the old woman who had raised Molly from a child? No, he told himself. Old Sal Tanner was a drunk, a tramp who had no one but Molly . . . or so he had heard. He'd better watch his tongue, if he were to obtain more work from this fellow. Besides, Tanner was a common name hereabouts. He laughed softly to himself. The very idea that a mill owner, a wealthy fellow such as Marlow Tanner, was in any way connected with an old soak who imagined that 'the little people' had brought Molly to her, well, if he didn't want to be laughed at and run off the wharf, he'd best keep his foolish mouth shut!

Mick was still chuckling to himself as he entered the building. Some moments later, he was face to face with Marlow Tanner, a fine able-bodied fellow of some forty years and more, with sincere dark eyes and hair as black as coal. For a fleeting moment, Mick was put in mind of Molly's own similar dark features, and his heart ached a little.

'Sit down, Mr Darcy.' Marlow Tanner recalled greeting the young man earlier, and he had already guessed the nature of his urgent visit. 'No doubt you're wondering where you stand now that the year's secured work is almost finished?' When Mick answered that yes, this was so, Marlow Tanner immediately put him out of his misery by reassuring him, 'There'll always be work for them as wants it.'

As the discussion got underway, Mick's admiration and respect for this man was increased by the minute. He was pleasantly surprised at how quickly the older man put him at his ease. His surprise, however, would have turned to astonishment if he had known that Marlow Tanner was Molly's father.

There were things of the past that neither of them was aware of. Not Mick, nor Marlow. Nor certainly Molly, who had long given up the idea of ever finding her true parents.

Chapter Four

It was Christmas Eve. Blackburn Market had been a hive of activity all day long, but now the snow, which had been gently falling since late morning, was beginning to settle more thickly on the cobbles. Overhead the sky was grey with the promise of more severe weather.

As the snow grew thicker, the crowd of shoppers grew steadily thinner, with people cringing from the cold, scurrying away to the warmth of their own cheery fire-sides. Seeing their customers hastily depart, a number of stall-holders began to pack up their wares and load the waiting carts which would carry them home. The more seasoned and determined merchants, however, stood their ground, their lusty cries desperately tempting the remaining shoppers to 'Get yer hot chestnuts 'ere, missus' or 'rabbits for the Christmas pot . . . skinned and ready'. For those whose purses were fatter there was the offer of 'fresh, plump turkeys to grace any lady's table'.

At the sight of a well-heeled and expensively attired gentlewoman standing not six feet away, the man with the turkeys saw a likely customer and at once began besieging her with umpteen reasons as to why 'yer daren't go home without one, missus!' He was instantly struck dumb when back came a sharp retort in a broad Cockney voice, 'And I daren't bleedin' well go home *with* one, neither . . . else I'd be flung out the kitchen and no mistake!' Nelly might have gone on to explain that Emma would not thank her for interfering in what was Cook Parker's domain. But the outburst had provoked much laughter from the shoppers within hearing distance, so she merrily winked at the astonished stall-holder and wandered away to continue her browsing, finally coming to rest at the bric-à-brac stall where she purchased a small quantity of pretty coloured lace.

Not being naturally born to the genteel manners of a lady, Nelly loved to meander through the market, revelling in the shouts of the barrow-boys and other traders, and losing herself amongst the ordinary folk. She had another purpose also: to keep an eye out for the young woman who had crossed Emma's path and left such a deep, lasting impression on her; on Nelly too and that was a fact. Today, though, she had scoured the many faces which had thronged the market place, but none of them had matched the face of that young woman, with her strong, lean features and big black eyes that held a world of tragedy.

Over by the market clock stood the very person who was proving so elusive to Nelly: a poorly-dressed creature with a thin, anxious face and a belly swollen with new life. Beside her stood little Sal, a child of fair face and angelic blue eyes.

'There y'are, darling,' Molly told the child eagerly, 'the barrow-boy's making off soon . . . there'll be a few juicy titbits left lying on the ground when he's gone. You see if I'm not right.'

'Can we have a Christmas tree, Mammy?' Pinched by the cold, little Sal huddled into Molly's shawl.

'We'll see, sweetheart, but you're not to count on it,

mind.' Molly knew that even if they did 'find' a tree, it was more than she dared to drag it all the way back to Dock Street. Not with the birthing so close, and not with her feeling as weak as a kitten, the way she did. It was strange, she thought, how all the while she had been carrying little Sal and young Peggy, there hadn't been a day's discomfort. But *this* time it was different. Right from the start, she'd been violently ill of a morning, and the bairn seemed to lie so heavy inside her that it was like a dead weight pulling her down. There was something else too; a feeling that something wasn't quite right. She had scolded herself for even entertaining such depressing thoughts. 'The others were lasses . . . this little rascal must be a lad,' she had laughingly convinced herself. 'It's a known fact that fellas cause all the trouble in the world!'

'If we get a tree . . . I can put my rag dolly on it . . . then she can pretend to be a princess, like the ones we saw in the shop window.'

'Ssh, I've told you, we'll have to see.' Christmas was the worst time for Molly. It always hurt her when she couldn't provide the things that made a child's Christmas that much more special. But then, as far as she was concerned, Christmas was *not* special, it was no different from all the other days that ran into each other. Apart from the children's birthdays. She always made a little fuss then, because if anything at all was worthwhile in her life, it was her babies. Glancing down at the child, she softly called her name. 'Sal, you'd really love a proper tree, wouldn't you, darling?' When the fair, curly head nodded eagerly, Molly squeezed the tiny hand clutched in her own. 'Then your mammy will get you one, sweetheart,' she promised, thinking how it should be possible to pick up a few fallen branches and bundle them together to make a little tree.

Of a sudden Molly thought of Mick and was instantly beset by feelings of guilt. If she had taken up his kind invitation, their Christmas would have been that much brighter; there would have been proper food on the table, maybe even a fat, proud turkey. Little Sal would have had a tree. Molly quickly dismissed the pang of guilt. In her heart she believed that she had done right to turn down Mick's offer that she and the children spend Christmas aboard his barge; she had done right to tell him a lie, that Tilly Watson from next door had got there with an invitation before him, and that she had already accepted; so how could she be so ungrateful as to turn the woman down *now*, she had argued, after all the work she had put herself to? Like the gentleman he was, Mick had reluctantly agreed. 'I *did* do right!' Molly muttered under her breath. After all, what if she was enjoying a hearty Christmas in another fellow's home and Jack were to come back, only to find the house cold and empty. It wouldn't be right. Molly didn't fool herself that Jack was likely to come home laden with presents, but that didn't bother her none; Jack himself would be the best Christmas present, and the children would have their daddy for Christmas. Mick had been disappointed, but he'd get over it soon enough, she decided. Besides which, there were two other reasons why she could never have accepted. Firstly, the birthing was too near. Then there was this thing about Mick and her: him trying so desperately to hide his feelings for her when she only had to look in his eyes and his love was shining there like a beacon for all to see. It made her feel bad and uncomfortable. As though his pain was all her fault. Well, it wasn't, she told herself now, and much as she valued Mick's friendship, it might be better all round if she were to steer clear of him from now on.

A short time later, after filling their hessian bag with bruised but still edible titbits collected from the cobbles, Molly and little Sal were busy foraging for the longest branches from beneath the Christmas tree stall. Of a sudden, something happened to take Molly unawares and to put the fear of God in her. Something that triggered off a series of tragic events which no one, not even Molly, could have foreseen.

Having completed her small shopping expedition, Nelly was preparing to make her way home. The square was fast becoming deserted, and already the scavenging animals were slinking in to devour any juicy morsels that might be left lying beneath the food stalls. Feeling the effects of the cutting breeze that nipped at her face and froze her fingers, Nelly hurried towards the other side of the square, to where a line of horse-drawn carriages waited along Victoria Street for any would-be passengers. It was when Nelly stopped to glance about and make sure there were no traders' carts hurtling in her direction that she caught sight of the two bent figures busily collecting the strewn Christmas tree branches. 'It's her!' she muttered aloud. 'The *very* gal I've been searching for!' So excited was she that, in a moment, she might have called out. But caution and instinct warned her not to, for fear the young woman and her child were frightened off. Good Lord, Nelly told herself as she went on wary steps towards where Molly and little Sal were preparing to leave with their precious hoard, Emma would never forgive me if she knew I'd caught sight of the creature and then *lost* her.

It was little Sal who first saw the stealthily approaching figure; Nelly's fox-fur neckpiece and fancy feathered hat held her mesmerized. When Molly looked to see what was so intriguing as to hold the child's attention in such a way, her heart almost stopped beating at the sight of the figure making its way towards her, and, to her mind, looking devious into the bargain. 'Jesus, Mary and Joseph . . . it's the gentry!' she cried, her black eyes wide and fearful. 'Quick, Sal, *run*! Run as fast as your legs'll take you!' Flinging the branches to the ground, Molly grabbed the child's hand, chiding her when she began crying for the precious Christmas tree which now lay in ruins on the cobbles. '*Leave it!*' yelled Molly, frantically tugging the sobbing girl away. 'The gentry's after us . . . and if I'm caught it won't be a blessed *tree* you'll be crying over . . . it'll be your poor mammy, 'cause they'll likely lock me up till I'm old and grey!' There was real fear in Molly's heart as she took to her heels, fear that lent wings to her feet as she and the young one sped away over the cobbles with never a look back.

'Stop! Stop!' Nelly took up pursuit, cursing at the long heavy hem of her expensive dress and thinking how, if she were twenty years younger and unencumbered by the fancy attire of a 'gentlewoman', she would never have been left so far behind.

Seeing that others, alerted by her cries, began to follow the chase, she yelled for them to 'mind yer own business . . . she *ain't no thief!* It's a private matter, so bugger off!'

'Blow me down . . . she might look like a lady, but the old trout sounds more like a sodding *fishwife*!' shouted one, being frustrated at having the only excitement of the day ended so abruptly. Just as quickly as they had joined in the fray and now looking somewhat affronted by the vehemence of Nelly's verbal attack, the pursuers loped off. All but a snotty-nosed lad who took great delight in pelting Nelly with anything he could lay his hands on – unfortunately for Nelly the articles included two split and not very fresh eggs which left their sticky mark all down the front of her skirt.

Nelly might have stopped to 'cuff your grubby ear'ole' but she still had sight of the two runaways and was bent on catching them if she could. In fact, if the truth were told, Nelly was thoroughly enjoying the entire episode. She couldn't remember when she'd felt so alive. Her mind rolled back to when she herself was no older than the unfortunate quarry she was now chasing and she couldn't help but chuckle at the memory of her own narrow escapes from the law and gentry alike. Oh, they were the days! Ducking and diving, grasping her opportunities as they came and never giving a tinker's cuss for the fact that she had neither home nor family. It was a hard life, but it had its moments, she recalled: the worst one being when the authorities clapped her in irons to be shipped off to Australia as a no-good vagrant and petty thief. The best moment was the fateful day when she met another poor soul who was branded with the same iron, but, unlike her, was as innocent as the day was long: Emma Grady. Her darling precious Emma, who had been her one and only family ever since.

'*Stop*, yer little fool!' she yelled now, her breath feeling cut off at its root and her steps already beginning to slow to a painful trot. 'It's a *lady* as wants ter talk ter you . . . Emma Grady as was, who's Emma Tanner now. She only wants to *help* you!' When she realized that the two ragamuffins were long gone, she repeated bad-temperedly, 'Wants to help you, she does . . . though Lord knows *why*. After the merry dance you've led me, you ungrateful urchin . . . I'd not cross the bloody road to help you, I wouldn't!' Yet she knew that her words were no more than hot air and frustration because now, after seeing how terrified the young woman was, and how she was foraging for the discarded bits of Christmas trees, and also that she was heavy with child, Nelly was as anxious as Emma to find her and do what she could to make her sorry lot that much easier. But she wouldn't find her again today. Not today. Maybe not ever again, now that the poor creature had the measure of her. She would be more on her guard than ever now, and that was a fact.

Despondent, Nelly gave up the chase and turned away, feeling both irritated and decidedly uncomfortable from the effects of her short burst at running. She promised herself that, now she was in her forties and a bit longer in the tooth than during her wilder days, chasing vagabonds would definitely *not* be one of her future activities. All the same, she would dearly have loved to talk with that young woman, if only to assure her that she had no reason to fear either herself or Emma, who, in Nelly's opinion, was one of God's chosen angels. 'Though she can be a real terror if she puts her mind to it,' she promptly reminded herself with a chuckle. 'And Lord only knows what she'll say when she sees me looking like something out of a shipwreck, with me hair bedraggled and me skirt stinking to high heaven of rotten eggs!' Anticipating a healthy exchange of words between herself and Emma, she promptly climbed into the nearest carriage and instructed the bemused driver, 'Park Street, my good fellow . . . and be quick about it!' When he appeared to hold his nose at the rich and unpleasant smell that wafted up his nostrils, she fell back into the seat, quietly chuckling. By God, when that young vagabond was finally brought to account for what happened today – and she *would*, of that Nelly was determined – she'd get the sharp end of Nelly's tongue and that was a fact! Still and all, even though Nelly had thoroughly enjoyed herself, there were serious issues here. She hoped the unfortunate young woman had not been too frightened by all the attention, nor pushed too far to her limit. After all, she had another little soul tripping along beside her, and the added burden of being heavy with child. On top of which, the pair of ragamuffins looked as starved as scarecrows, and couldn't have two penn'orth of strength between them. 'Ah, but they gave *you* a good run for your money, Nelly my gal, that they did,' she laughed, throwing a cutting look to the driver when he turned to regard this strange and smelly passenger. 'You look where you're bleeding well going!' she told him. 'Ain't you never seen a lady afore?'

'Quick, darling, run and fetch Tilly Watson . . . tell her to be as quick as ever she can!' Molly fought against the gripping pains that raged through her with a vengeance before spasmodically ebbing away, leaving her breathless and bathed in a film of sweat. The bairn was fighting to be born and there wasn't a moment to lose. It was the frantic chase through the market that had brought on the spasms, and at first Molly had hoped they might subside once she reached the relative safety of Dock Street, but, if anything, they had intensified. Molly's churning thoughts came to dwell on the woman who had chased her and Sal through the market. A gentry, but with a voice and manner that contradicted her fancy clothes. Molly recalled the words she had shouted after them, 'Stop, yer little fool . . . it's a *lady* as wants ter talk ter you. Emma Grady as was, who's Emma Tanner now!'

Molly knew she and little Sal had made a lucky escape, though she had wondered since whether the frantic run in her advanced condition had complicated matters for the poor mite inside her. Molly wasn't certain, because she had long felt that things were going wrong. All the same it was unfortunate, and whether the circumstances had brought her labour about that much more quickly, she really did not know. What she did know was that she and little Sal had done right to take to their heels. '*Emma Tanner*,' the woman had shouted, '*Emma Grady as was.*'

Molly's fears were threefold. Firstly, she knew the name Tanner well enough. Marlow Tanner was a big name hereabouts. She also knew that he was the brother of old Sal Tanner, whom Molly had adored, and who had suffered a great deal of heartache when her younger brother, Marlow, had 'gone orf to 'Merica ter seek 'is fortune'. Years she waited for him to return. Years of trouble and worry, when she never lost her faith in him. But when there came no word from him and she began to believe he had been 'snatched from the face of the earth', old Sal finally gave up hope of ever seeing him again. But she never blamed him, saying, 'My lad wouldn't desert me on purpose, Molly gal . . . if 'e ain't able ter come back an' see 'is old sister as fotched 'im up like both mam and dad to 'im, well . . . it's 'cause the poor bugger's lying dead on some foreign soil, or 'e's been swallered up by the ocean!'

Now though, Molly knew better. Marlow Tanner *had* deserted old Sal, because some time back he'd returned to his roots and built up a big fleet of trading barges along the Leeds and Liverpool Canal. Molly had seen him many a time, and many a time she had been tempted to accuse him on old Sal's behalf, and to tell him how his sister would have been buried in a pauper's grave, but for her. *She* had stood by old Sal, while *he* had deserted the darling woman. But Molly couldn't bring herself even to talk to him. She knew in her heart that old Sal would have forgiven him in a minute, but she never would! She loathed him; even the thought of conversing with him turned her stomach over.

Besides, in Molly's opinion, Marlow Tanner had made matters worse by marrying the one they called Emma Grady. In spite of the fact that the hated Justice Crowther had done nothing to stop her being transported as an accessory to murder, and there was now a feud said to be raging between them, Molly saw that particular woman as an enemy to be feared. After all, rumours ran rife and happen Emma and Caleb Crowther were not 'at each other's throats'. After all, he *was* her uncle when all was said and done, and there was no denying that Justice Caleb Crowther would like nothing better than to clap Molly in irons and leave her to rot. 'But oh, not if Molly keeps her wits about her!' Molly declared aloud now. 'They'll not catch me and mine while there's a breath in my body.'

Molly and the Justice had crossed paths on that particular night when he had snatched the precious timepiece from round her neck and burned old Sal's cabin to the ground. It was Molly's avowed intent that her enemies would never get the better of her, nor would the one who had joined them . . . old Sal's treacherous brother, Marlow.

Drenched in sweat and anxious for her baby, Molly waited for Tilly to come to her. The time for thinking was over. The child was on its way and there was much hard work ahead. If Tilly didn't hurry up, Molly knew she'd have to do it all on her own. There was no doubt that the birth was imminent. That in itself wasn't a bad thing, reasoned Molly, because this particular child had been the worst of all to bear. She would not be sorry to see it parted from her aching body and lying warm beside her. But it was hard! Dear God in heaven, it was hard to take such persistent and crippling pain; worst of all to make herself suppress the cries that might help to make the ordeal a little more bearable. But she must *not* cry out, not in front of little Sal, who would likely be horrified to hear her mammy in such pain.

As it was, the girl knew well enough that 'my babby' was on its way, for Molly had been careful to satisfy little Sal's curiosity regarding 'the bump' in her tummy; although she had kept her explanations short and simple, assuring the child that the babby she would insist was hers was a precious gift to her mammy and daddy from the Lord above and that the 'bump' was the cradle where the tiny being would stay warm and safe, until it was big and strong enough to come into the world and say hello. Little Sal was content with the explanation and never tired of hearing it. 'I hope she says hello to *me* first,' she had told Molly with an old-fashioned look in her soft blue eyes, ''cause I was here before Peggy, so my arms are bigger to hug the babby . . . and I won't let the babby fall, will I, Mammy?'

On Molly's frantic instruction, little Sal had raced out of the house to fetch Tilly Watson from next door. In a surprisingly short time she was back, with the small wiry figure in tow. 'Jesus, Mary and Joseph, Molly gal!' gasped Tilly, one look confirming her suspicions. 'You don't give a body much warning, do you, eh?' At once she ushered little Sal from the room, saying kindly, 'It's all right, sunshine . . . your mam'll be all right. Take yourself off to my place, child, and tell Joey to give you the eggs I've left on my plate. Seeing as you've dragged me away from 'em and they'll be cold and dried up when I get back.' Enthused by the prospect of an egg butty, little Sal promptly forgot about the 'babby' she had already claimed for her own, and went skipping out of the door, only to pop her head back round it a moment later to remind Tilly, 'You have to fetch me when the babby comes . . . you won't forget, will you?'

'*No, no, Sal!* Tilly won't forget.' Molly struggled on to the bed, gasping hard when the squeezing pain in her back became unbearable. 'Go on . . . go on, child!'

Sensing something beyond her understanding, and reassured by her mammy's promise – although puzzled why it should be given with such impatience – Sal quickly set off again. But not before she had discreetly glanced back at the sight of Tilly Watson's bedraggled brown head bent over the bed, and her thin bony hands busying themselves in helping Molly out of her garments. Sal didn't like that. Not at all, and, shutting out the image of her mammy's face all twisted and uncomfortable, she went on her way, her blue eyes thoughtful and a look of concern on her small, heartshaped face. She would have a word or two to tell that naughty babby when it came, hurting her mammy like that!

At the open door of Tilly Watson's house Sal paused, listening to the crescendo of noise emanating from inside, where the three younger Watson brood were indulging in a free-for-all, or, as Tilly called it when the three of them began wrestling in earnest, 'having a bloody bundle!' For a moment Sal was tempted to leave. However the thought of that fried egg just sitting on Tilly's plate and waiting for her was too much. Anyway, above the squeals and shouts could be heard the excited cries of little Peggy and the firm voice of Joey Watson, who had taken over the role of father since the demise of Tilly's husband. So, knowing that Joey would soon have things under control, little Sal entered the house, praying that none of the other children had pinched Tilly's precious egg, because if they *had*, she might just be ready to punch somebody on the nose and start them fighting all over again!

From across the road, and being careful to stay well out of sight, Jack-the-Lad watched the frail-looking girl go into Tilly Watson's house and close the door behind her. Chuckling softly, he circled the woman's waist with his arm and pulling her into him, he said quietly but with some amusement, 'That little lady ain't half as delicate as yer might think . . . and when it comes to her mam and young Peggy, just let anybody try and hurt 'em. *Then* you'd see what a little tiger that Sal can be.'

'Sal? . . . That your kid, is it?' The woman was past her prime, thickening in figure and brassy in countenance. She snuggled into his embrace.

'That's right, darling,' he confirmed, with an intimate

chuckle. 'Sal's the eldest, then there's Peggy. *Sodding gals!* Still . . . there's another on the way, so happen *that* one'll be a lad, eh?' He nuzzled her ear, and began pushing himself against her in a gently suggestive, rhythmic movement. 'Don't care much for gals,' he murmured. 'Well . . . not until they start bursting out in all the right places,' he laughed. 'Naw! Kids is a bloody nuisance . . . too much like responsibility, I say.' There he chuckled again and his voice fell to a sensuous whisper. 'I don't care much for 'em once the little buggers is here, but I can't deny I enjoy *making* 'em.'

'You randy bugger, Jack!' laughed the woman, playfully shaking him off. 'But I'm not complaining.'

'I should think not, sweetheart. Not after I've shown you a good time, eh?' He dug his hand into his trouser pocket and drew out a silver coin which he gave into her out-stretched hand. 'Get off down the boozer, gal,' he told her, gesturing towards the end of the street. 'Turn left at the bottom of Dock Street and you'll see the boozer on the corner . . . you can't miss it. Wait there till I fetch yer. Think on – you stay there till I fetch yer. Have yer got that?'

She nodded, but asked, 'How long d'you think you'll be?'

'No longer than necessary. It's Christmas, ain't it? I have to show me face . . . leave her a few bob . . . let the poor sod know I ain't dead or nothing.' He kissed her hard before thrusting her from him. 'Don't you fret, darling. I'll be down the boozer to fetch yer afore yer can say Jack Robinson. Then we'll find us a quiet dark place where we can have a bit o' rough and tumble, eh?'

Feigning embarrassment, she thumped him on the shoulder. 'Go on with you, Jack Tatt,' she said, 'no wonder they call you Jack-the-Lad!' She pushed the silver coin into her purse, then, without a backward glance, she bounced away to waddle at a furious pace down Dock Street, leaving her charming but devious colleague to saunter across the cobbles towards the house. Inside, in her terrible labour, Molly had cried out his name several times, only to be told by Tilly Watson, '*He* ain't coming to help you, my gal. The likes of that one don't even deserve thinking about!' Being a practical woman who could never understand what Molly saw in that useless man of hers, Tilly was loath to admit that, on this particular occasion, the good Molly might benefit from the sight of Jack's no-good face. Because on this particular occasion Molly needed her mind taken off the awful pain she was suffering and the unnaturally long time it was taking for the young 'un to show its face. She'd birthed many a newborn in her day, had Tilly Watson, and she had come across all kinds of complications. But none like this. There was something badly wrong here. Badly wrong, and very frightening. If the bairn didn't soon make an appearance, she might have to leave Molly and get help, but the thought of leaving Molly for even a moment was very frightening, because those few precious moments could mean the difference between life and death. For Molly, or the child. Or both.

Outside, Jack leaned against the wall and wondered what his reception might be. After all, he'd been gone a long time on his latest spree, and for all Molly knew he might be dead and buried. Of a sudden he was pierced by a stab of conscience, but like always, it was only momentary. 'Molly knew what she were tekking on . . . I never lied to her about the gypsy in me, never once,' he murmured to himself. Ah, but he *had* lied about other things, he reminded himself. Things that were just as precious to him as having his freedom when the wild blue yonder called; things like his insatiable appetite for a bawdy woman, and the need of a man to sow his wild oats before Old Father Time caught up with him. There was something else too, which he had never told Molly. One of the rare things in life that he was ashamed of. He hadn't the courage to tell her. Not yet anyway. All these things he had deliberately kept from Molly, because, trusting, genuine article that she was, Molly would neither understand nor forgive him. By! He trembled in his boots at the thought of her ever finding out how he had bedded one floozy after another; sometimes *two* at a time when he'd been too drunk to know any different. What! Molly might be an adoring and gentle soul, but she had one hell of a temper and would rip his eyes out if she knew how he was doing her down behind her back. He had only ever seen Molly's temper once, and that was enough. He remembered the occasion well and the remembering sent shivers down his spine. It was in that very boozer where he'd just sent the floozy. Him and Molly were not long wed, and he'd taken her into the bar to show her off to his drinking cronies, when in came a brazen hussy he'd been foolish enough to have a bit of a fling with, not two weeks before. The silly cow made a beeline for him. Thank Gawd for the fact that the floozy was legless drunk and couldn't remember his name, or the fur would really have flown, and no mistake! As it was, he managed to convince Molly that he was innocent as the day were long, and he had 'never clapped eyes on the silly bitch afore'.

Molly had never since broached the subject and he often wondered whether she believed his story, or whether she might just harbour a deal of suspicion towards him. However, she never showed it, and he made it his business to reassure her constantly of his undying love for her. Funny thing was, he *did* love Molly. He loved and respected her a great deal. She was a good woman, a good mother, and had always been exceptionally loyal to him. If the truth be told, Molly was the most beautiful creature he'd ever come across. If she had any faults at all, they were the strength of her love for him, and the way she trusted his word. Yes, Molly was good, while he was a waster, a womanizer, and too much of a bloody coward to face a man's responsibility towards his family. He was a useless wretch, no good at all, a Jack-the-Lad if ever there was one.

Jack's rugged, handsome face broke into a self-satisfied smile and suddenly all trace of self-recrimination was swamped by the good feeling that washed through him. It were no use fighting it. A Jack-the-Lad was what he was born to be, and a Jack-the-Lad was what he'd be till his dying day. He straightened up, spat into the palm of his hand and smoothed it over his unruly fair hair. Then, with a merry tune on his lips and a bright twinkle in his warm brown eyes, he went jauntily into the house.

Inside the bedroom, the scene that greeted Jack was a grim and serious one. Even before his shocked eyes had taken in what lay before him, he was made fearful by the atmosphere in the room. Slowly and silently he came forward, the merry tune stilled on his lips and a look of puzzled astonishment in his brown eyes.

The room, like the rest of the house, was sparsely furnished. There was a big old dresser and a broad, sturdy brown wardrobe; over by the window stood a marble wash-stand containing a bowl, a matching jug, and other bric-à-brac. At the far end of the room was a huge, high bed with four iron posts topped by spherical shiny brass knobs. Over the bed was a small, dark crucifix that Molly had found on the tip and which she would not let him throw away, and placed next to the bedhead was a little wooden cupboard with an unlit candle on top.

Jack's eyes were drawn first to Molly, who lay so still in the bed it frightened him, and whose dark, tousled head was turned sideways from him. At the foot of the bed lay a tiny bundle, tightly wrapped from head to toe, and horribly still also. Seated on the bed, her head bent to her hands and emitting a soft, crying sound was the woman he knew as Tilly Watson. It was she who looked up and saw him first. '*You!*' The word was a mere whisper, but it might have been a shouted accusation for the awful guilt it wrought in him. 'You're too late,' she said, 'always too late!' When she got to her feet and looked deep into his shocked eyes, it was with unconcealed malice. Without speaking another word, she collected the small, still bundle from the bed and, coming to where he had stopped in horror, she gently placed it into his arms. 'This is your son,' she told him in hostile voice, 'cursed he is . . . and barely breathing. The poor little soul nearly took his mam with him and all.' The next words were spat out in disgust. '*She needed you* . . . called out time and time again. I told her . . . you ain't worth the ground you walk on.'

When the door banged shut behind the furious woman, Jack made no move. In his arms he could feel the feather-light weight of the child and a faint warmth exuding through the shawl. Afraid and hesitant, he lowered his gaze to the tiny being now writhing in his arms. Instinctively, he drew back the shawl to reveal its tiny limbs. What he saw there shocked him to the core. The nausea had started like a clenched fist in the pit of his stomach. Now it spiralled up through him, touching every part of his being. The infant's legs were grotesquely odd, one shorter than the other, with a twisted foot, the sight of which was deeply repugnant to the man's senses.

Suddenly aware of the painful sobbing that filled the room and touched his sorry heart, Jack lifted his gaze towards the bed. Molly was looking at him: her big, black eyes were the most tragic he had ever seen and her tears were like purgatory to him. When she began to speak, he ventured forward. 'Look at him, Jack,' she pleaded brokenly, 'look at your son . . . *our* son.' The sorrow in her voice hung in the air like an enveloping vapour. 'Don't be afraid, Jack. Don't turn away from him . . . *please don't turn from him.*' For an endless moment she was silent, then in a painful whisper she told him, 'I needed you . . . *why* weren't you here?'

'Oh, Molly, can you ever forgive me?' He sat beside her, holding their son between them and reaching out a comforting hand. 'I'm no good for you, Molly . . . but I do love you. You *know* that, don't you?' Molly knew. He was here and that was enough. For now. Together they held the innocent babe. Together they cried. Together they took comfort from each other; but not even her beloved Jack's presence could dull the awful bitterness in Molly's heart when she had seen how dreadfully crippled their son was. It was too savage, too unfair. Yet hadn't she known all along that something was wrong? Known it, and been afraid. She told Jack as much now. '*Why* weren't you with me?' she murmured again, but deep in her heart she knew it would have made no difference to the outcome.

'There are two kinds of men in this world, Molly my love,' Jack said. 'There's the kind a woman can rely on to watch out for her and his kids . . . he'll provide for them and see them through the bad times. Then there's the likes of me.' He sighed and drew her closer. 'Like I said, Molly, I'm no good and I never will be. Oh, I love you and the kids right enough . . . but I'm too much of a coward to face up to my responsibilities. If I was anything of a man, I'd leave this house and never show my face again. Because if I was to stay and try as hard as ever I could, to be the man you deserve, I know it wouldn't work, Molly. I'd only end up making your life that much more miserable.' When she made no reply, he buried his head in her shoulder and for a while they remained silent, each lost in their own particular thoughts; she with her face pressed close to that of her child, and he with his arm embracing the two of them.

Molly offered the child her breast milk, but it had small appetite and soon, exhausted and emotionally spent, she drifted into a fretful sleep. For a while, Jack watched her and the infant. But he could not bring himself to touch it again. When it began softly whimpering, he fetched Tilly Watson. 'Don't wake Molly,' he told her, 'let the lass sleep.' After that, he went to the boozer on the corner. The tall, boldly-painted floozy had gone, so he emptied every coin from his pocket on to the counter. 'Let the booze run till the money's all gone,' he instructed the barman. Word had spread fast about Molly's crippled bairn, and the landlord understood Jack's forlorn mood.

At five minutes before midnight, they brought Jack

home and, with Tilly Watson's reluctant help, made him comfortable on the parlour couch. Soon after, Tilly returned to her own brood, who were temporarily subdued by the arrival of Peggy and little Sal.

In the dark early hours, Molly attended to her son. Then, carrying the lit candle, she went carefully down the stairs to the parlour. For a long, unhappy moment she stayed by the door, gazing down at the unconscious, spreadeagled form of her wretched husband. As she continued to gaze on his handsome face, he moaned and wrapped his arm over his shoulders like a child might do. A well of love bubbled up in Molly's tired heart. 'Oh, Jack! . . . Jack!' she chided softly. Molly suspected his pain was every bit as great as hers. But not his loneliness, she thought with a stab of bitterness, never his loneliness.

After a while, she turned away, her sorry heart that much heavier. There were so many things she had wanted to talk over with him. So much that was still unsaid. Dear God, didn't Jack know how much she needed him? Or that they could have helped each other so very much?

Lying in the dark, desperately tired yet too disturbed to sleep, Molly thought long on her son. She thought on the heartfelt words that Jack had spoken to her earlier. She recalled all manner of things from that fateful day, and, remembering with a small shock that it was Christmas, she cried for little Sal who would not have her tree after all.

Molly had known a good teacher in old Sal. 'Never let the buggers get yer down, Molly, gal', was her favourite instruction. 'Don't shed tears fer them as ain't worth it!' Molly smiled at the memory of that eccentric and cantankerous old darling. Her smile became a chuckle, but it wasn't long before the sound of Molly's soft laughter melted into sobs. Life was a trial. Her young bones ached like they were ninety years old and her heart felt like a lead weight inside her.

Suddenly, Molly had the strongest yearning to hold her newborn close to her heart. When he was tucked up in the bed beside her, she told him, 'Don't you worry, little fella . . . there's nothing for you to worry about. Not while you've got your mammy who loves you.' For the first time in as long as she could remember, Molly cried herself to sleep. Strangely for the first time also, she shed heartfelt tears for the parents she had never known.

It was Christmas. After a long, unsettled night of discomfort, Molly woke to a strange silence in the house. For a moment she was confused, but then she remembered that the girls were next door with Tilly Watson. One glance at the infant assured her that he was contentedly sleeping.

'Mammy . . . Mammy!' The sound of little Sal's voice gladdened Molly's heart. Suddenly the girls burst into the room and were running towards her; little Sal quickly hurling herself on to the bed, and Peggy, struggling to clamber up, only to have her chubby legs left dangling in mid-air as she clung tenaciously to the eiderdown, before slithering to the floorboards again. She was a sturdy child, more solid than little Sal, and having a bold, round face with large oval eyes, the same mud-brown colour as her thick, straight hair. She squealed with delight when Molly grabbed her two stocky arms and hoisted her on to the bed.

'Couldn't keep them away, Molly.' Tilly Watson stood at the foot of the bed, her thin, bony arms folded across her pinnie, and a smile on her mouth which Molly thought did not light up her eyes. 'By! You look better for a night's sleep, and that's a fact,' she told Molly. But there was something she was not telling, and Molly sensed it. 'I'll bet yer starving, aren't you eh . . . ? I'll tell you what, there's a bit of smoked bacon left in the larder. I'll fry it up with a piece of bread, and we'll top it off with a brew o' tea. Oh, I know it's not much, Molly . . . but it's the best we can do for now, eh?' She turned to leave.

'Wait a minute, Tilly.' Molly was afraid, but she had to ask. 'Something's worrying you . . . is it Jack?' It was there again. That feeling of nervousness and insecurity whenever Jack made his way home. Almost as though the happiness he brought was too good to last.

For a moment, Tilly Watson stood still, nervously twirling a knot of her skirt through her fingers. She brought her gaze to bear on the children, who were laughingly tumbling against each other and seemingly unaware of the tense atmosphere. Suddenly, the newborn was awake and thrashing his tiny arms in the air. Tilly swallowed hard and looked at Molly again; at the pitiful sight she made, with her reed-thin figure dressed in an old nightgown of Tilly's, and her surprisingly rich, black hair tousled about her ears. In her dark eyes there was more living than a woman twice her age should experience. Poor little bugger, thought Tilly, and how she wished it wasn't her who had to impart the sorry news. It *was* left to her, and there was only one way to tell it, and that was straight out. 'He's gone,' she said quietly, flinching inside when she saw the surprise, then sad resignation wash over Molly's face. 'I'm sorry, dearie, but the bugger's done a bunk. I can't say I didn't see it coming, and I dare say it'll be a long time, if ever, before he shows his cowardly face round these parts again.'

'Thank you, Tilly.' Molly glanced at the girls, her voice betraying nothing of her shocked thoughts. Thank goodness the children seemed not to have heard. 'I really am hungry . . . a bacon butty and a pot of tea will be fine.' Enough had been said in front of the children, and she didn't want Tilly to see just how hard the news of Jack's going had hit her. She had intended making the effort to get out of bed, but now the spirit had left her.

'Right then.' Tilly knew when she had been dismissed. She didn't mind, not in the circumstances. 'Poor little sod,' she murmured, closing the door behind her. 'What a bastard that man of hers is . . . to run off and leave 'em again, and after what she's been through . . . *Men!* I'd spit on 'em soon as look at 'em, and that's a bloody fact!'

At midday, Molly got up from her bed and checked that the newborn baby was sleeping soundly in his cot. After which, she put on the blue serge dress that had already seen her through four winters, and made her way downstairs.

'Now that's very foolish, Molly lass, if you don't mind my saying so,' Tilly Watson remarked with a wag of her finger. 'It'll serve you right if you start bleeding . . . and there's every danger of it, you mark my words. I do know what I'm talking about . . . I've seen more bairns born into this world than I can count. Most of the little blighters come easy, but . . .' she hesitated, afraid to harp on the awful circumstances of Molly's birthing,

'. . . well, you *have* been through a bad time, Molly, and Lord knows there ain't two-penn'orth of you.' Coming to where Molly had eased herself into the upright horse-hair armchair, she threw her hands up in despair, saying, 'You listen to what Tilly's saying, there's a good girl. Don't worry about the two lasses, because they'll be all right lost amongst my brood.' When she realized that Molly had no intention of going back up the stairs for a while, she shook her head and went to the door. Here she reached up to the nail where Molly's shawl hung, and taking it down she hurried across the room to fling it round Molly's small shoulders, saying with a degree of irritation, 'Very well, you must do as you think fit. Don't take no notice of me!' Her tone was unusually sarcastic.

'Aw, Tilly, don't take offence,' Molly pleaded, reaching out her hand and clutching the older woman's thin, muscular arm. 'I know you mean well, but I really am feeling stronger.'

'Huh! Stuff and nonsense!' Tilly snorted, taking Molly's frail-looking hand and putting it firmly back in her lap. 'Just *look* at yourself! What! I've seen *corpses* with more flesh on their bones and colour in their faces . . . you can't deny it. Not when you're sitting there, looking at me with them big black eyes that have lost the light God gave 'em. If you will insist on staying down here, my girl . . . then you must abide by two conditions.'

'Anything you say, Tilly.' Molly knew that if Tilly were to take her by the arm and escort her back upstairs, she would never find the strength to resist. Besides which, she was right to be concerned, because the mere effort of getting dressed and finding her way down to the parlour had all but drained Molly of her strength.

'First of all, you're not to move one step away from

this 'ere fireside.' She indicated to where her newly laid fire was already emitting a cheery glow. 'It'll warm your poor bones once it gets a proper hold,' she promised.

'You have my word, Tilly . . . I won't budge from this chair.' Molly couldn't, even if she wanted to, because she realized now that Tilly was right. She *had* got up from her bed too early.

'Right then. And think on, when I fetch you a bite to eat . . . happen a bowl of hot, nourishing soup . . . I want no argument about that neither. You'll eat every last morsel?' When Molly nodded, she appeared satisfied. 'Want to see the lasses too, I expect?' Without waiting for a reply, Tilly went to the fireplace where she took up the poker and began agitating the coals in the grate. When she swung round again, it was to see Molly staring up at the mantelpiece where, propped up against the brass candlestick-holder was a folded piece of paper, upon which was written the word MOLLY in big, black letters.

Molly's heart had turned somersaults when she saw her name glaring back at her. The name, *Molly*, had been the very first word that Jack had taught her to read. After that, she learned his name, and then the letters of the alphabet. Although it was a trying and laborious process, Jack had taught Molly the rudiments of reading and writing. She had loved him all the more for it.

'I forgot that were there,' Tilly said in a sullen manner. '*He* left it, afore he ran off!'

'You should have told me, Tilly. You should have told me straightaway.'

'Happen,' Tilly grudgingly conceded, 'but if I was to tell the truth and shame the devil . . . I hadn't made up my mind whether or not to burn the blessed thing!'

'Then shame on *you*,' Molly chided, but it was a gentle and kindly reprimand. 'Will you pass it to me now . . . or must I get it myself?'

'You stay where you are!' warned Tilly, reluctantly fetching the letter and giving it into Molly's outstretched hand. 'I'll leave you to read it then. But only ten minutes or so . . . then I'll be back with a bite to eat for you.' At the door she chuckled. 'And no doubt with the children in tow.' With a flourish of her skirt and a lingering look of disgust, she was gone.

Molly raised her quiet eyes from the closed note clutched in her hand. She wanted to open it and yet she was sorely tempted to fling it into the flames, where it would be quickly devoured. Instead she sat very still, gazing into the fire's glow and wondering how Jack might justify his leaving them all yet again, and at a time when they badly needed him. 'Oh, Jack . . . when will we ever be a proper family,' she murmured, now unable to stem the tears that rolled down her face. After a few moments she steeled herself to open the letter, and read:

Can't face you, Molly. Last night, I tried to drown it all in booze, but it was no good. *I'm* no good, as I've tried to tell you many times. I'm a waster, and like they say, I'm a Jack-the-Lad who'll never settle down.

It's not that I don't love you, Molly darling, because God knows *I do*. And that's the trouble, you see. *That's* what keeps fetching me back to hurt you and turn your poor world upside down. You know yourself, you'd be better off without a bastard like me.

If it were in my power, I'd have you done up

like the lady you are . . . with dandy clothes and a
fine house, with no worries to mar them lovely
black eyes. But it ain't in my power, and it never
will be. All I can bring you is trouble and
heartache. But because you've shown me how
things can be if only I might change me ways, and
because I love you more than I could ever love
any other woman, I'm asking you to be patient
with me, darling. Don't give up on me altogether.
But, if you find yourself a decent bloke while I'm
gone, then it'll be my loss. Don't miss out on any
chances because of me.

    If I get lucky, I'll send some money, I promise.
Till then, God bless, and look after yourself.

Jack

You know, I always wanted a son to be proud of.
Life's a bastard, ain't it, Molly darling.

'Oh, and so are you, Jack. SO ARE YOU!' Molly
sobbed. There had risen in her a terrible rage as she read
the letter. Now the rage became a cold, hostile sensation, and pulling herself up by the arms of the chair,
she went on slow, painful steps to the fireplace. There
she screwed the letter into a hard, round ball and threw it
into the flames. 'You're so right,' she said in a contemptuous whisper, and with bitterness in her heart such as
she had never known before. 'You *are* a bastard, Jack
. . . and a coward! And I don't care if I never see you
again!' She watched the letter blacken and curl. 'I hate
you. Don't come back. Don't *ever* come back!' She
thought of the good times they had known in the early

days, and that special way he had of making her laugh. In her mind she pictured his wayward fair hair and those dark brown eyes that twinkled. She recalled how passionate he was in lovemaking, yet so tender and thoughtful. He loved her. Molly knew that without any doubt, because it was not something that could be faked or hidden. And, God help her, she loved him. Enough to wait? She wondered. Enough to give him the one last chance he was asking? She tried to imagine what it would be like if she were never to see him again. Never to look into those laughing brown eyes, and never to have his arms embrace her. She weighed that pain against the pain he had caused her today, and which he caused her every time he left them. There was a greater pain now, because of their son, because of the children who might have had a proper Christmas, because he was too much of a coward to face life head on. Oh yes, there was pain and heartache, and bitterness. Yet beneath it all remained Molly's steadfast loyalty and love for Jack. Steadfast and deep-rooted. She couldn't deny it. Not yet. Maybe not ever.

Of a sudden, there was so much noise and confusion outside the room that Molly's turbulent thoughts were shattered. Above the din sailed little Sal's excited voice. '*Mammy . . . ! Mammy . . . !* See what we've got!'

Molly turned her head as the child ran into the parlour, and following behind was Tilly Watson with Peggy in her arms. '*Here's* something to buck you up,' she laughed, putting the child to the floor and pulling her to one side as all eyes turned on the door.

Molly was astonished when the figure of a man began pushing its way in. For a moment she couldn't see his face, because he was weighed down with a Christmas tree in one arm and a plump hen in the other. Her first thought was that *Jack* had come back to mend his ways and her heart warmed with gladness. She laughed out loud, the tumult at the door turning into a blur through her tears of joy.

'Happy Christmas!' he shouted, coming forward to the table where he laughingly off-loaded his wares, before swinging Molly into his arms. Her heart sank. It wasn't Jack. It was the bargee, Mick. Mick, with a broad smile on his handsome face, and two very excited children clinging to his trousers. *Mick, not Jack*. The realization cut through her like a knife.

'Come on, Molly sweetheart . . . let's have you resting!' he told Molly while leading her gently back to the chair. There was a special tenderness in his voice and a knowing look in his amber eyes, which told Molly that he knew what had happened: the night's trauma, the boy-child, even that her husband had deserted them. No doubt Tilly had sent her son, Joey, to let Mick know what had taken place here. Though Molly would be eternally grateful that the children would have a proper Christmas after all, she wished that it could have been Jack who had provided it. As it wasn't, she wondered how she could ever forgive him.

Chapter Five

'You pay me to advise you, Mr Crowther, and I am advising you now . . . stay as far away from Emma Tanner as you possibly can. Now that the date for the court hearing is set, you can only make matters worse should you even consider approaching her.' Mr Dunworthy leaned forward across his vast desk-top and, peering intently through his tiny spectacles at the grim-faced man before him, he repeated in a softer yet more penetrating voice, 'Stay away from Mrs Tanner, or be prepared to face the consequences.' His voice was authoritative and free of emotion, but in the privacy of his own thoughts, the man was only just beginning to realize how very much he disliked Caleb Crowther: once a justice who was feared and hated by all who were brought before him, but now retired and soon to be at the wrong end of a courtroom himself.

'To hell with it, man!' Springing from his chair with such anger that it was sent spinning on its axis, Caleb Crowther stormed back and forth across the office, his fists clenched tight behind his back and his head bowed to his chin. In spite of his fierce response to Mr Dunworthy's instruction to 'stay away from Mrs Tanner', there was an air of despondency about his bent countenance, and more than a suggestion of fear. Suddenly he swung round to face the small, fish-like face behind the desk. 'I *should* go and see the bitch . . . confront her and warn her off for her own good. This business is all wrong and you know it. The damned woman's vindictive . . . got her facts all wrong. If you ask me, her brains have been addled by the Australian sun. She spent too many years amongst the convicts . . . there's not a manjack who was ever transported that did not claim they were innocent. Emma Grady was no different!'

'So you're still convinced she had a hand in the murder of her husband?' Mr Dunworthy was not of the same mind. He never had been.

'*Of course* I'm convinced!' Caleb Crowther knew that Emma was not capable of such a heinous deed, but it had served him well to uphold her guilt. It served him well now. 'There is not the slightest doubt in my mind that she killed the unfortunate fellow . . . a most upright and respected citizen if ever there was one. Damn it, man, that was why I gave no objection when he approached me for Emma's hand in marriage.' He was very careful not to disclose that it was he himself who had put forward the proposal. His reasons had been twofold – firstly, he wanted Emma off his back because she was a thorn in his side, and secondly, she had been a constant painful reminder to him of her mother, Mary. God, how he had loved that woman, exquisite and desirable as she was. Also a temptress who drove him crazy with her insatiable appetite for other men. Not satisfied with her devoted husband, Thadius, Mary Grady had bewitched the young, virile Caleb Crowther, a man on his way up in the world. A man who, at the time, was able to lay the world at her feet. But he was married, and afraid to risk a scandal which would most certainly have wrecked his judicial career. When he refused to leave his wife, Agnes, it was then that Mary deliberately drove him to distraction by taking a lover: a bargee by the name of Bill Royston. Caleb Crowther visibly trembled as he remembered the terror and awful carnage that resulted.

'Sit down, Mr Crowther.' Mr Dunworthy was astonished to see the beads of perspiration break out on the other man's face. 'I'm afraid you're working yourself into a shocking state. Look . . . you must leave this matter with me. There is very little that you can do. Please rest assured . . . I will do all I can to safeguard your interests, Mr Crowther.'

'Yes, yes!' Caleb Crowther was appalled at having let his guard down in front of this eagle-eyed fellow. From now on, he would have to be very, very careful. For, if the terrible truth were ever to come out, of what happened all those years ago, well . . . it just did not bear thinking about. 'But believe me when I say there's an evil and vicious streak in Emma Grady . . . Emma Tanner now, since her marriage . . . a particularly nasty streak that stems from . . . from . . .' He could not bring himself to finish the sentence, or he would have said 'from her mother, Mary'.

He could not say it, because his deep, all-consuming passion for Emma's mother was still too alive in him. To betray her memory now would be tantamount to betraying himself. His courage was too small, his mind too filled with her image. What would she have said, he wondered now, if she knew how he had used her innocent daughter, Emma, for his own greedy, despicable ends? Married her off to an insignificant clerk so that he could be rid of her, and, if that wasn't punishment enough for the young, helpless girl, he had given over only a small part of her dowry, by duping the pitifully gullible young man who was to be her husband.

After the marriage Caleb Crowther had plundered Emma's entire inheritance. Then, when Emma's husband had met his untimely end and the law was baying for blood, he had made it his business to point the strongest accusing finger at Emma. Terrible things he had done against her. None of which he regretted. Only the thought of Mary had made him quake to his stomach, only the idea she might be watching from her grave; only the memory of what had taken place on a particular night some forty years and more before. Even now, the awful knowledge of it, and the part he himself had played, still brought nightmares. He felt the horror of it now. In a swift and trembling movement, he grabbed his hat from the desk and rammed it on his head. 'I must be away,' he told the surprised Dunworthy. 'Good day to you.'

As he strode from the room, leaving the door wide open behind him, Caleb Crowther could hear Mr Dunworthy's voice anxiously entreating him, 'Heed what I say, sir . . . make no attempts to approach your niece, or I might be obliged to wash my hands of this case altogether.'

The departing man made no outward response, other than to mutter angrily beneath his voice, 'The devil take you both, you pitiful fool . . . you and the bitch who would sink me to her level!' Once out on the street, he took a moment to quieten himself. He felt greatly agitated and spoiling for a fight. 'Stay *away* from her?' he sneered in a twisted smile. 'Not *me*, sir . . . ! Not the Justice Crowther!' Stepping out to the kerb he hailed a hire carriage, and, to the approaching driver who urged his ensemble towards what might be the likeliest fare of the day, Caleb Crowther made a formidable sight with his tall, bulky figure and large-boned face. This was made all the more awesome by the prolific and bushy growth of iron-grey hair that spread across his unpleasant features like a creeping mantle.

As the carriage clattered over the cobbles towards him, Caleb Crowther raised his arm across his forehead to shield his eyes from the late afternoon sun. He hated the summer and the tiresome August heat. It sought to rob a man of his dignity. On top of which, he was still smarting from Mr Dunworthy's instructions. So, when a small lad came careering into his path and foolishly rolled his wooden hoop into the gentleman's leg, the next thing he knew was the gentleman had whipped him sharply across the shoulders with his cane. There then followed a terrible uproar when the fearful lad began screaming for his father, who was some way behind. Seeing his son unjustly attacked, the incensed fellow launched himself at Caleb Crowther with vicious intent. The upshot was that he also got a cane sliced across his head, and was promptly taken into custody by a passing officer of the law, who had recognized the Justice Crowther. Therefore he lost no time in collaring the 'offender' who had dared set himself on such a solid and respected upholder of the law. By which time Caleb Crowther had climbed into the carriage and, with much irritation at having been so affronted, gave the astonished driver a curt instruction to 'make haste to Park Street – the Tanner residence'.

The Justice was so agitated that even when the horse and carriage went forward he could not relax, clinging as he did to the very edge of the seat and straining his narrowed eyes to the road ahead, as though he might will it to shrink so that in only a minute he could step down to the path that would lead him to Emma Tanner's front door. Yet he knew well enough that the journey through the busy centre of Blackburn and out on to the Preston New Road which would carry him to Corporation Park and the street beside it was all of three miles, with a deal of narrow roads and congested alleys to slow him down even before the carriage left the heart of Blackburn itself. He knew that. Yet still he could not settle.

It was when the carriage was making its way up Town Hall Street and on to King William Street that Caleb Crowther's searching eyes were drawn to the kerbside. There was something disturbingly familiar about the thin, dark-haired ragamuffin who was absorbed in arranging the colourful blooms which, now and then, she offered to strolling passers-by. 'Only a shilling . . . fresh as the morning,' she called out, and the two children happily playing beside her added their chirpy persuasion, 'Only a shilling . . . only a shilling,' whilst giggling uncontrollably in between. Molly smiled patiently at their antics.

Hearing the approach of a carriage, Molly hurriedly got to her feet and propelled the two small girls to a safer distance from the road, instructing them to 'stay there'. Then snatching up a particularly large bunch of flowers from the bucket, she approached the carriage, which had been forced to a slower pace by the many traders' barrows that lined the narrow, cobbled street. 'Fresh blooms, sir,' she called out, running alongside the carriage and holding up the flowers to the gent inside. 'Fresh blooms for the little lady,' she coaxed, peering inside to where Caleb Crowther was eyeing her intently, and desperately trying to recollect where he had seen the ragged creature before; he *had* seen her before, he was sure of it.

Deeply curious and strangely disturbed, Caleb Crowther leaned his ungainly form nearer to the open carriage doorway. Already there had been stirred in him a host of unsettling memories: of a dark and deadly night when he and his officers had scoured the canal banks for the criminal who had snatched his own grandson for a ransom. That same night he had found the culprit: a young street-urchin with big bold eyes as black as coal, and known to have been brought up by another no-good creature, who went by the name of Sal Tanner. Oh, but he had enjoyed snatching the young wretch from the makeshift home, which was a derelict workman's cabin on the canal banks. What a sight it made as it burned to the ground! However, his joy had been short-lived, for the urchin made good her getaway even before the prison cart had delivered her to the jail. He had never forgotten. *Never forgiven*, and he was not a man to leave old scores unsettled.

Instinctively, Caleb Crowther's hand went to his breast, his trembling fingers searching out the tiny and delicate timepiece that had once belonged to Mary Grady, the dead woman whom he was bound to love until the end of his days. All these years since the night he had torn it from the grubby neck of that street-urchin, he had agonized over how she had come by the timepiece, when he himself had seen Thadius Grady give it to his daughter Emma on his deathbed.

Caleb Crowther had argued with himself that the urchin could have stolen it, like the thief she surely was. But then, he reminded himself, how could she have stolen it when Emma Grady had been transported from

Her Majesty's prison to the other side of the world, some years before: at least as long ago as the urchin was aged in years.

Likely as not the old tramp, Sal Tanner, had stolen it. But no, he had decided against that theory, because all the time Emma Grady was incarcerated in jail in England, she had the timepiece with her. His discreet inquiries revealed the truth of that. *What then?* He had asked himself time and time again: how did Mary Grady's timepiece get from her daughter, Emma, into the hands of a street-urchin? For Caleb Crowther, only two real possibilities remained: one, Emma had either given it to someone inside the prison or it had been stolen there, when it afterwards changed hands again, and finally fell to Sal Tanner's thieving paws; or – and for Caleb Crowther this was the explanation that he had come to believe – the street-urchin was Emma Grady's *own daughter*!

Caleb Crowther had privileged information regarding Emma Grady's last moments before she was bundled into the prison wagon, and afterwards on to the convict ship in Liverpool Docks. It was discreetly reported to him that Emma had been delivered of a girl-child, on the cobbles, right outside the prison gates. The officer in charge, believing the child to be stillborn, had ordered Emma into the waggon, leaving the child behind at the mercy of scavenging dogs. It then happened – or so the officer thought (only *thought*) – that as the wagon sped him and his charges away, he might have heard the thin, painful wail of a newborn. However, he could not be sure, he said. As the years grew longer, his memory had become dimmer, until now he put it all down to a feeling of guilt and an over-active imagination.

Caleb Crowther, on the other hand, had been plagued by the whole episode ever since. After all, in the years when Emma Grady was safely out of the way, and he lived a high, handsome lifestyle at her expense, it disturbed him to think that there was at large a grubby alley urchin who was the legal heiress to everything he had robbed from Emma.

There was something else that crossed Caleb Crowther's deep and conniving mind, as he struggled to get a good look at the dark-haired girl who was now cajoling him to 'buy the pretty flowers'. The urchin who had long been a thorn in his side had encountered him on one other occasion, *previous* to his snatching her on that dark, unfortunate night when he had so foolishly lost her again.

The occasion in question was when he had believed himself to be securely hidden in a carriage which was discreetly stationed beside a certain public house called the Navigation. On that night he had with him a dubious and murderous villain who was on a particular errand for him: he was to commit one Gabe Drury to the murky depths of the canal, where his silence would be assured. Gabe had been unfortunate enough to see many years ago a particular 'gentry' leaving the site where heinous murders had been committed. Murders involving Mary Grady and her illicit lover, the bargee. Murders involving others, who as yet were undetected. It was Caleb Crowther's intention that they would remain so.

It had been imperative to Caleb Crowther that he silence the old drunk, Gabe Drury, once and for all. The deed was suitably executed. But on the night of its doing, *that same street urchin* had peeped inside his carriage. From that day to this, Caleb Crowther could never be sure whether he had been recognized. To his thinking, the surest way of safeguarding himself would have been to eliminate the luckless urchin; to dispatch her to the deep along with the luckless Gabe. But up until now, he had never again set eyes on her whom he suspected was Emma Grady's lost daughter. The irony of it all gave him a deal of satisfaction because he had been told by his own wife how desperate Emma had been to have another child. Now it was too late. For that very reason, he had not revealed his suspicions regarding the street urchin. The pleasure he got from thinking how a daughter of Emma Grady's was sleeping rough and scraping a living alongside thieves and vagabonds was too enjoyable. Besides, if he had his way, that particular urchin would never live to be old bones!

'Come on, sir . . . you'll not find fresher blooms in the whole of Blackburn. A shilling . . . only a shilling!' Molly took a breath as the carriage slowed to a creeping pace. The smile on her face was dazzling as she raised it to bestow on the gentry. A stab of astonishment made her gasp as she saw how intensely he was staring at her. For an awful second, their eyes met; his tiny eyes slitted to study her all the more closely, and her black eyes stretched wide with curiosity. The cry sprang to Molly's lips almost without her realizing. *'God Almighty . . . ! It's the Justice!'* For a second she was riveted with fear. Then all hell seemed let loose, as Caleb Crowther realized that here was the very urchin he had sought after all these years. *'Stop, thief!'* he yelled, in an effort to recruit the help of passers-by. But Molly was never an easy quarry and there was no one willing to take up the hunt. Not on such a hot and sultry day, when they had better things to do than wear themselves out helping a fancy gent in a carriage.

Before she took to her heels Molly flung the bunch of flowers in Caleb Crowther's face, causing him to stagger backwards on to the seat with a great thump that rocked the carriage violently. This in turn startled the horses, which reared into the harness, whinnying and thrashing. They started forward at breakneck speed as terrified screams rent the air and fleeing bodies scattered in all directions.

When at last the unhappy ensemble came to rest some considerable distance on, Caleb Crowther struggled to the doorway where he peered up and down the street, cursing all the while and lashing out with his cane at anyone who ventured a helping hand. All he craved was to have the black-eyed vagabond in his grasp. But it was not to be on this occasion: Molly and her young ones were long gone. And safe. For the moment.

Heaping hell and damnation down on everybody's heads, the trembling and furious Caleb Crowther fell back on to the carriage seat, threatening the hapless driver with all manner of charges should he be reckless enough to persist in demanding a fare. 'Get me to Breckleton House, you fool!' he ordered churlishly. 'At a steady trot, or you'll face the consequences!'

As they went sedately along, Caleb Crowther's temper was not improved. He would not give Emma Tanner the satisfaction of seeing him so shaken, he mused. But she would keep. Until he could confront her with a cool and level head.

The court hearing had been set for early in January 1887, so for the remainder of this year he must carefully examine all the possibilities which would enable him to bring that particular vixen to heel. There was time enough. Besides, if he had learned anything at all during his dealings with the 'lower' orders, he had learned one thing above all else, and it was this: *there were more ways than one to skin a cat!*

Meanwhile, whatever Emma Tanner was up to at this moment, he hoped against hope that life would treat her badly and hound her with all manner of misfortune.

Molly was shocked. The news was awful and, even though she considered Emma Tanner to be her sworn enemy, Molly's heart went out to her as Tilly Watson's tale unfurled.

'So there you are, Molly,' concluded Tilly with a grave shake of her head, 'it doesn't matter whether you're a lady or a washerwoman, rich or poor . . . when your child's taken from you in such tragic circumstances, the pain is just the same for one as it is for the other.' She leaned back in the horse-hair armchair and stared at Molly seated opposite, whose dark eyes were moist with tears. 'You know, Molly . . . it's a strange thing how life has a way of turning full circle.'

'What do you mean?' asked Molly quietly, afterwards glancing at the door to make certain the children had not crept down from their bedroom. When Tilly had come in from next door to relate how Emma's son had been killed in a shocking accident, Molly had quickly taken the girls away to their beds. There was enough heartache in their little world without them listening to others' tragedies.

'What I mean is this . . . there's an old saying which warns, "Be sure, your sins will find you out". There's another . . . "Vengeance is mine, saith the Lord".'

'You're talking in riddles, Tilly,' chided Molly, 'what are you getting at?'

'Well, I'll tell you. I'll tell you something now that I've never told anybody . . . not for a long time anyway.' She had lowered her voice to a whisper, glancing behind her towards the door, as though fearful of being overheard.

'Go on.' Molly was intrigued. She knew that Tilly Watson liked a 'drop of the old gin'. She knew that Ada Loughton had been the one to come round to Tilly's house with the dreadful news concerning Emma Tanner's son. She also knew that whenever Ada Loughton paid a visit to her old friend, like as not there was a bottle of gin tucked discreetly under her shawl. The result being that, some hours later, Ada Loughton would waddle away down Dock Street, swaying from side to side and singing out like an old sailor. As for Tilly, the gin always loosened her tongue, like it had now.

'What's on your mind?' insisted Molly.

'You promise it won't go no further, if I tell you?' demanded Tilly, casting an anxious look about.

'Promise,' Molly reassured her, 'and who would I tell anyway, Tilly?'

'You might tell the bargee, Mick. After all, he has been calling on you a lot of late . . . and the two of you seem to be getting real chummy-like.' She fell forward, throwing her arms about and loudly cackling. When Molly glanced towards the door, Tilly noticed. At once, she fell silent, pressing a bony finger to her lips and afterwards whispering, 'Sorry, young 'un . . . I forgot the lasses were asleep.' When Molly nodded her head and said nothing, she went on in hushed and secretive tones, 'You know how Emma Tanner . . . Emma Grady as she was then . . . was convicted of having a hand in her husband's murder?'

'Yes. I've heard it said,' agreed Molly. It only confirmed what she already believed – that Emma Tanner had the bad blood of Justice Crowther running through her veins.

'You know *that* much, Molly girl,' chuckled Tilly softly, 'but there's something you don't know. *I was there . . . I SAW IT ALL!*' She revelled in the way Molly's big eyes opened wide with astonishment. 'And my old man with me . . . Lord rest his soul!' She quickly made the sign of the cross on herself. 'We saw the buggers struggling atop the stairs . . . Emma, her husband, Gregory Denton . . . and that old nanny of Emma's, Mrs Manfred, the one they hanged.'

'*You saw them murder him?*' A thin, cold shiver ran down Molly's spine. For some inexplicable reason, she felt so afraid that it was almost as though she herself might have been there. Now she also made a hasty sign of the cross on herself.

'Did we see them murder him?' repeated Tilly thoughtfully. 'You might well ask. What we saw that night was enough to put the fear of God into any decent soul.' Something in Tilly's voice reflected the turmoil that was going on inside her. There had been times over the long, hard years since that dreadful night when she had feared for her own soul. She feared for it now: if the truth ever came out, it would reveal that what she and her husband *actually* saw on that night was no more than a struggle between three people, when one of them was unfortunate enough to lose his balance and go hurtling down the stairs to his death. Oh, it was true that Mrs Manfred was fighting like a tiger to protect Emma, there was no doubt of *that*. But Emma herself had nothing to do with him tumbling down the stairs, Tilly was certain of it. Yet, because she was desperate and times were hard, she had told the authorities otherwise, therefore pointing the finger at Emma in as final a way as her own worst enemy might have done. She had lived to be ashamed of it, but never to admit the truth to a living soul. Dear me no! That would be a very foolish thing to do!

The reason for Tilly's betrayal of somebody who had been a good and loyal friend to her was a tin box. A tin box that she had secretly taken from the deathbed of Gregory Denton's mother, soon after the latter had witnessed her son lying in a heap at the foot of the stairs. Tilly found the box to contain a few old documents that she had no use for at all, and a deal of money that she had a dire need of. So, she kept her mouth shut about thieving the box, and opened the same mouth as wide as she could, in order to see Emma arrested. That way her own secret would be safe: there was no danger that Emma might find out about the box and lay claim to it.

When Emma was transported, Tilly spent many a sleepless night. Later though, she took a strange comfort in making herself believe that Emma *was* guilty. Indeed, she told Molly the very same now. 'She murdered the poor unfortunate fellow. You have my word on it. Me and Emma lived next door to each other. Soon after she and Mr Denton were wed, and he brought her to live on Montague Street, I was called in to look after the old woman . . . bloody cantankerous old sod *she* were and all. But now, do you see what I'm telling you, Molly?' Molly shook her head and Tilly went on to explain, 'What I said earlier was that it's strange how life turns full circle.'

'I see what you're getting at now.'

In her mind, Molly quickly ran through all that Tilly had revealed. And it did seem like a horrible justice. Somehow, she did not take the same pleasure in it as did

Tilly. 'You're saying that Emma Tanner's son was killed in a manner that was uncannily like the way in which she helped murder her husband?'

'Vengeance is mine, saith the Lord!' Tilly threw her arms in the air and, clapping her hands together, she cried jubilantly, 'Emma pushed her husband down the stairs to his death . . . and now, over twenty years on, her own son meets a sorry end, by falling down a cliff face in Corporation Park.' Puffing out her narrow, bony chest, she shook her head and, just for a second, seemed about to express some small sympathy. But then she remembered her own part in Emma's conviction all those years ago, and caution took over. She must always be careful to remind folk of what a callous woman Emma Tanner was. 'Like I said, Molly . . . it's the hand of justice, don't you think?'

'It's a cruel hand all the same . . . that takes an innocent child from its mammy,' Molly murmured. The news of young Bill Tanner's tragic accident had subdued her. Being a mother herself, she could understand how devastating it must be to have the child you adored snatched away. She thought of her own lasses, little Sal and Peggy; she thought of her newborn who, crippled though he was, had not lost his life. For a moment, that part of her that was a mother went out in sympathy to Emma and Marlow Tanner. But then she remembered how Emma had been convicted of helping to murder her own husband. She thought of how Marlow Tanner had betrayed his own darling sister, old Sal, who had brought him up after they had lost their parents in strange and mysterious circumstances. Molly was made to remember all of this. And more besides: how Emma Tanner was blood kin to Caleb Crowther, and how that fiend had set out to make Molly's life a misery from when she was a child – even now he was hell-bent on destroying her, should she give him the chance.

Molly's hackles were up. Caleb Crowther would *not* be given the chance to destroy her, because this very day she had vowed to tread more carefully in future. Since the other day, when she had come upon him in that carriage, Molly had been in a state of panic, even considering whether or not to move out of Dock Street. She had decided against that. Her reasons were twofold. Firstly, she was certain that she had not been followed, and secondly, should Jack ever come home again, it would be to this little house on Dock Street. So, for the time being at least, she had no plans to up sticks and take to the road.

She didn't tell Mick about her upset with Caleb Crowther. He might renew his pleas to get her and the lasses living aboard his barge. Her mind was as stubborn as ever on that particular issue. Mick Darcy was to keep his place where Jack's family were concerned. He knew that now, and that was the way Molly preferred it.

All the same, Molly was forced to admit to herself what a good and loyal friend Mick was to her and the young 'uns. In fact, of late she found herself comparing him more and more to Jack. *Jack!* A spiral of anger and disillusionment rose up in her. In all this time there had been no word. Soon, she promised herself, he'll come home. In spite of everything, she knew that she would be waiting.

Long after Tilly returned to her own brood next door, Molly's quiet thoughts strayed to Emma Tanner, who, according to Tilly, had lost a son. Though Molly's sympathy was tempered by her fear and loathing of that particular family, she hoped, with a mother's heart, that the Lord might ease the awful grief which Emma Tanner must now be suffering.

On the second of September, in the year of our Lord 1886, the son of Marlow and Emma Tanner was laid to rest. Afterwards the many mourners filed through the big wrought-iron gates, each one with heavy heart and bowed head. Each one to pause at the gate, where they took Emma's black-gloved hand into their own and murmured their genuine condolences at such a tragic waste. Throughout the whole, sad ordeal Emma stood upright and dignified, loyally supported by her dear friend Nelly on one side, and her beloved husband Marlow on the other. He also was grief-stricken at the loss of his adored son. But he had vowed to remain strong for Emma's sake. Emma was crippled beyond redemption at having lost her son, Bill. Her precious son. Her pride and joy. The one child with which the good Lord had blessed her, only to snatch him cruelly away. Just as he had robbed her of the girl-child all those years ago.

Of a sudden, Emma felt incredibly old. On that day only last week, which seemed a lifetime ago, a shining light had gone from her life. Oh, she loved Marlow as much as any woman could love a man. He was her rock, the strong anchor that had sustained her faith for all the years when she was alienated from her homeland. He was everything a man could be to a woman, and life without him was unthinkable. But there had been another part of him that she had cherished with all of her heart – his son and hers. Bill was the living creation made out of their deep, abiding love for each other. In his stalwart and gentle character, he was all that Emma could ever pray for in a son. Now that he was gone, how could she face another day without his eager, shining face to smile at her and his boyish ways to vex and try her?

'God! Oh, dear God,' she prayed inwardly now, 'if you really are there in your heaven, tell me why you've taken his young and innocent life? *Why?* WHY?' Only the muffled sound of shuffling feet answered her, as one by one the mourners gave their love and sympathy. 'There is no answer from God,' she thought bitterly, 'because there *is* no God. And for me, there never was!' All the trauma and tragedy of her life came rushing back to haunt her. So many mountains to climb. So much heartache. Would it never end? A tide of weariness surged through her and for the briefest moment her strength wavered. Leaning into Marlow's loving embrace she whispered, 'Take me home. Please, take me home.' But then she realized with a stab of pain that there would be no small welcoming face there to greet her. Never again. *Never again!* No laughing bundle of joy to come eagerly running at the sight of her. In her house there were no children. The cruel words seared into her mind. No children. *In her house there were no children*. Now, there could be no *grandchildren* either!

Softly, Emma allowed herself to be taken on Marlow's arm along the path towards where the long line of carriages waited. They made a splendid and sombre sight against a cloud-dappled sky, with their dark-curtained windows and magnificent black horses bedecked with grand funereal plumage, and seated atop, the serious-faced drivers in top hat and tails. Lost in her most inner thoughts, Emma could see nothing before her but a small boy's face. She would *always* see it. Always cherish it. Like the one before. The one before.

'Mr Tanner . . . Mrs Tanner.' The soft, lilting voice caused Marlow to pause and turn around. Emma did not look up. Instead she kept her gaze to the ground. The voice was an intrusion.

Marlow reached out to take the priest's proffered hand. 'I must get my wife home,' he said quietly, 'she needs to rest.'

'Of course, of course . . . I understand.'

Suddenly Emma raised her grey eyes to him, and he was astonished to see how they fastened on his face with naked accusation. He was visibly shaken when, in a stiff and remarkably calm voice, she told him, 'No. You do not "understand". How could you?' Emma's white, stricken face betrayed little of the heartbreak she was suffering. Nor did it reveal the extent to which her faith in God had been shattered. Her next words, however, were delivered with such contempt that even Marlow gasped. 'Although I respect your intention, Father Mason, I'm afraid you bring me no comfort. Nothing you can do or say will change what has happened. In your prayers you may ask your God why he should rob a young innocent of his life. You may pray . . . just as I have done. And, just as I have done, you will be greeted with silence. Go back to your church, Father Mason, and seek your own comfort. There is none for me . . . no sanctuary in your master's house. *No place for me here.*' Her words rained down on him relentlessly. 'You will never see me cross your threshold again in my lifetime!'

'No, no . . . Mrs Tanner . . . Emma, *please*,' he entreated, 'think long and hard about what you are saying!' The colour had drained from Father Mason's face. As he stepped forward, Emma recoiled from him.

'Good day,' she uttered quietly, with no hint of regret in either her voice or her countenance as she moved away. Devastated by Emma's cold outburst, an astonishing outburst in view of her extraordinary faith in the Almighty, Marlow gave his apologies to the priest and hurriedly took up his place beside his wife. Later, when she had recovered enough from her grief and was made to reflect on her bitter words, Emma would relent. He was certain of it.

Some short way behind, Nelly quietly followed her darling Emma. The anguish in Nelly's heart was unbearable, and as the tears flowed down her face, she asked, *Help her, Lord*. She hasn't stopped loving yer . . . she never could. But oh, yer bugger, Lord . . . yer have put Emma through the mill, ain't yer, eh? So don't cross her off yer books yet, will yer? . . . 'Cause she'll be sorry for what she said to Father Mason, soon as ever she teks the time ter think on it.' Her heartfelt prayer broke into a fit of sobbing and, for a moment, Nelly found shelter behind a broad oak tree. Here, she plucked up the corner of her cape and dried her eyes on it. Then, before emerging in a more composed manner, she asked one other thing of the Lord. 'Should I tell Emma what happened all them years ago at the prison gates, when she gave birth to that bonny lass? If yer remember, Lord, there were an old tramp who collected the child from the gutter and made off with it . . . and I swear I heard the cry of a newborn. Oh, dear Lord, what shall I do, eh? *Shall I tell her?* Will yer help me ter decide fer the best? You think on it, Lord, and let me know.'

When the flurry of clouds quickly shifted to reveal a bright, smiling sun, Nelly took it as a sign that the good

Lord had heard her, and was thinking on it. With a lighter heart, she followed the path to where Emma was being helped into the carriage. In that moment, it struck Nelly how slow and pained were Emma's movements; not only bowed with grief, but something else. 'Yer ain't no youngster no more, Emma, me old darling,' she murmured with affection, 'we none of us are.' Old age has a nasty way o' creeping up on a body, she mused, because here they were, her and Emma, well into their forties. It was right what they said . . . 'time and tide wait for no man'. 'Nor no *woman* neither,' she murmured with a sigh. It seemed like only yesterday when she and Emma first met, in a dingy prison cell. Ridiculously young, they were, and terrified of what life might have in store for them. Well, they had come through those terrible times and found some sort of peace here in Blackburn: she with Emma's stalwart friendship over the long hard years and Emma with Marlow and their son. 'Oh, Emma, *Emma!*' Nelly could only guess at Emma's heartache and, beside it, her own sorrow paled in comparison.

On the slow, respectful journey back to Park Street, Nelly glanced often at the stiff little figure of Emma, with its straight, narrow shoulders set against the world, and her pale, drawn features that were like cold marble. She dared not imagine the fire that raged beneath.

Nelly thought about the accident that had taken the life of Emma's son, and she still could not shake off the feeling of guilt that had haunted her since that awful day only a week ago. It was a day bursting with all the warmth and colour of a splendid summer. A day when Emma and young Bill had jumped at Nelly's suggestion that they should picnic in Corporation Park . . . 'go right to the top where the Crimean guns were sited', and afterwards meander the long winding path down. It was on the way down that the accident happened.

Against Emma's light-hearted warnings to 'stay on the footpath', the excited boy had clambered on to the brink of a dangerously steep cliff-face, whose surface made a deep and sheer drop to the rockeries below.

Nelly thought she would hear Emma's unearthly scream for as long as she lived. When they rounded the corner to see him balancing on the jagged protrusions above the slate face, it was something she would never forget. The mischievous smile on his face as she and Emma dashed forward. Then, in an instant, the boyish smile turning to horror as he lost his balance and went crashing to his death. It was instantaneous, or so they said. But not to Emma, and not to Nelly, for those few fleeting seconds seemed like a lifetime. A nightmare that would go on.

Nelly had to make a decision. One of the most difficult she had ever encountered. Would it help Emma, in her grief, to believe that *somewhere* she might have a daughter? Oh, it was true that, if the newborn *had* lived on that fateful night, she was no longer an infant but a full-grown young woman in her twenties. And what kind of young woman was she, Nelly wondered. Why! She might turn out to be the worst kind of gold-digger, who cared nothing for who her real mammy might be, only how much she was worth. The idea frightened Nelly. Besides which, she reminded herself, after all these years it would be nigh on impossible to trace Emma's daughter. It might be as well then to leave it be. Let the past and its secrets lie buried where they couldn't do no harm. 'Who are *you* to decide on it?'

Nelly asked herself indignantly. 'It's fer Emma ter decide.'

But before Emma could decide, she had to be told, Nelly mused. If she were to be told now, after all this time, she might just want to know why she had not been told years before, why all that time ago Nelly had lied to her. Would she understand that Nelly had only kept the truth from her in order to make her exile that much easier? Or would she condemn Nelly for betraying her? Nelly was in a terrible dilemma, because Emma's friendship meant more to her than anything else in the world. Yet she knew in her heart that Emma had a right to know the truth, especially now, when she believed herself to be childless. But then Nelly asked herself another question: suppose Emma's grief were eased by the news only to discover that the young woman had disappeared off the face of the earth and couldn't be traced – wouldn't that only add to Emma's pain?

'Oh, dearie me, Lord,' Nelly murmured, peering out of the carriage window to the shifting clouds, 'you'd best tell me what to do soon . . . 'cause I ain't got no idea at all which way to turn!' She knew that, either way, it would not be easy for Emma. On top of which, in a few months' time there was this blessed court case involving Emma's uncle, Caleb Crowther. Nelly bristled with anger at the thought of that man. She believed beyond a shadow of doubt that all of Emma's troubles were securely rooted in his black heart. 'May the devil take you,' she muttered through clenched teeth, 'for it's with *him* that you belong.

Chapter Six

'You little sod!' Tilly Watson wrenched the boy from the
cupboard, where he was on tiptoe in the process of se-
creting a freshly-baked jam tart into his trouser pocket.
'*One each* . . . you know well enough what Joey said, my
lad! And it's his hard-earned money that keeps us all
from starving . . . so you'll do as he says, you greedy
little bugger, you!' When he twisted his fat little body
from her and attempted to stuff the whole tart in his
mouth at one go, she snatched it from him and lashed
out with a swipe of her left hand – as a consequence
the tart was well and truly mangled in the tussle. When
Tilly's random swipe caught him a good cuff round the
ear, the boy was sent reeling sideways to fall in a heap on
top of the two small onlookers, who were filled with glee
at seeing their greedy brother well and truly chastised.
When he landed on them and all three crumpled to the
floor in a jumble of arms and legs, they collapsed into
fits of hysterical laughter that had both Tilly and Molly
laughing also. Peggy and little Sal hugged each other and
quietly giggled; though they carefully hid behind Molly's
skirts and seemed unsure as to whether Tilly's temper
was safely spent.

'Get out and play, the lot of you!' Tilly yelled now,
running at the heap of fighting, squirming bodies, until
they began squealing in make-believe horror and

emerged upright to scamper out on quick little legs. 'Play in the yard till Joey gets home from work . . . then I'll call you for your teas,' she told them. After which, she fetched the big iron kettle from the hearth, part-filled it with water and returned it to the cheery coals, where it soon began to sing.

'Are you sure it's all right to leave Tom and Peggy with you?' Molly asked. 'You do seem to have your hands full.'

'*Of course* I'm sure, dearie.' Tilly Watson gestured for Molly to sit down at the big, square table in the centre of the room. 'I'd soon tell you if I didn't want the young 'uns,' she said, 'but, like I've said many a time, I might as well have *thirty* as three like my brood . . . little sods they are, every one!' She laughed to see Molly's two hiding behind their mammy's skirts. Her laughter subsided at the sight of the small bundle in the curve of Molly's arms. The boy was some eight months old, yet he was so small and thin-looking that he could have been mistaken for an infant much younger. He was a happy child though, in spite of that crippled leg. Handsome too, with the same black eyes as his mammy, and crisp dark curls that tumbled freely about his heart-shaped face. 'By! . . . That child is the outright image of you, Molly . . . uncanny it is . . . the very same hair and eyes, the same jaw-line, and even a temperament to match his mammy's!' Tilly shook her head sadly. 'Such a lovely, cheery little chap,' she said quietly. But then she noticed how deeply her words were affecting Molly, and she changed tack. 'He's a strong child . . . you mark my words, Molly . . . he won't be held back by no crippled leg, you'll see!'

'*No, he won't*,' declared Molly, turning the boy on her

knee and kissing the outstretched fingers that came up playfully to touch her face, 'because I intend to get his leg seen to, soon as ever I can!'

Tilly was in the process of pouring the boiled water on to the tea leaves in the two mugs when Molly's statement pulled her up short. 'Aw now, don't go living no pipe-dreams, dearie,' she warned in a firm, shocked voice. 'Such things as . . . well, fixing the boy's leg . . . it takes more money than you and me will see in a lifetime, I dare say.' She shook her head vigorously, before marching to the window, where she stared down into the yard. Knocking hard on the window she yelled to the maraud-ing group below, 'Stop that screaming! . . . And *you*, Walter . . . leave your sister's ears alone!' The noise subsiding, she came back to the table and finished the task of brewing tea. When the kettle was put back in the hearth and both she and Molly were in possession of a mug of steaming liquid, she broached the delicate sub-ject again. 'Like I say, don't lose yourself in impossible day-dreams, dearie . . . there's *nothing* to be done for the boy, and it's best that you accept it.'

Molly resented the older woman's complacency, al-though she realized that Tilly Watson could not be expected to understand her feelings in this matter, which was so close to Molly's heart. After all, she told herself, how *could* Tilly understand, when all of her own children were so vigorously healthy. All the same, Molly did not want to discuss the issue so openly in front of the girls. 'You two . . . would you like to go and play in the yard with the others?' she asked. When they both eagerly agreed and ran off towards the scullery, where the steps led down to the yard below, Molly was quiet for a while, holding the boy up in her arms and watching with pride when he pressed his feet to her knees and tried unsuccessfully to draw himself up. It disturbed her to see how unbalanced and difficult his stance was. She did not fool herself that he would ever be able to walk in a natural manner, because it was painfully obvious that whilst his right leg was developing normally, the left one remained both stunted in growth and twisted away from his body. The foot was perfect in shape, but bent at a peculiar angle, so that when he pushed it against her lap it was not with the sole but with the inner ankle. To see this delightful and happy child so deformed was a great source of distress to Molly. She refused to believe, as Tilly did, that 'there's nothing to be done'. She said as much now.

'Stop fooling yourself!' Tilly Watson regretted not having snuffed the child's miserable life out when she had the opportunity. '*Look at yourself* . . . you're a young woman with no fellow, and three children looking to you for all their needs! You've told me yourself that you're a two-week behind with paying the rent.' She wagged a finger at Molly and, scowling, said, 'You listen to me, dearie. That landlord of ours is a mean and moody old sod . . . what! 'E'd have you out on your ear soon as look at you! Come to your senses, Molly . . . don't be a bloody fool. There's more important things to think about than that there twisted limb.' She pointed an accusing finger at the boy, who was playfully turning somersaults in Molly's arms; she thought the sight of his deformed leg hideous. 'To my mind, it's more important to have food in your larder and coal on your fire of a winter's night.'

Molly gave no reply. There would be no use, because no one could understand how she felt. Not Tilly, not any one. She changed the subject. 'So you will keep an eye on Peggy and the boy? Just for a few hours, while I see if there's money to be made in town.'

As usual, Tilly Watson did not hesitate. '*Of course* . . . I don't even notice them amongst my own brats. I expect you're after a few flowers, or an odd job or two, eh?' She evidently approved. 'Every shilling keeps the roof over your head and fills the belly,' she said. 'That's what's important, dearie . . . not trying to change the body the good Lord sees fit to give us.' She collected the child from Molly's arms. She would not have been squeamish in pinching the breath from its body soon after it was born, but unfortunately, the opportunity had been short-lived. So, now the child was here, and claiming a place in the world, there was no point in harbouring regrets. 'They'll be fine with me, as well you know,' she told Molly, 'and you're very welcome to leave little Sal alongside them . . . that eldest of yours is a godsend. You'll not be surprised when I tell you that she organizes *my* lot, with the force of a sergeant-major!'

Molly was not surprised, and laughing at Tilly's observations, she explained, 'My Sal's a puzzle, right enough. She can be shy and wary of strangers, but put her in amongst them that she knows, and she'll take complete charge in a minute. There's no denying that she's a born madam.' Just like her mammy before her, thought Molly with nostalgia, and just like her darling, eccentric namesake, old Sal Tanner.

'Will you leave the lass, then?'

'Oh, I don't know about that.' Molly had grown accustomed to Sal tagging along with her everywhere she went. Of a sudden though, she was reminded of her true errand today. It was not in search of a few half-dead flowers from a market-barrow which the seller had flung to the cobbles, nor was it to land herself a few hours' labour for a shilling or two. *No!* She had more ambitious things on her mind today than selling a few flowers or toiling in the market, lifting and stacking crates until her back ached. The money earned from these ventures would never bring enough to pay the rent, fill the larder, and put aside a tidy bit towards getting Tom's leg seen to. Molly had despaired at Tilly's warnings in that quarter, because hadn't she already told herself that it would take years, perhaps for ever, to accumulate enough money to pay for an operation. On top of which, Molly didn't even know whether there was such an operation that would put Tom's leg to rights, nor that there was a surgeon in the whole of Lancashire who was capable of such a delicate thing. But she had to believe, for Tom's sake, because how could he be a man amongst men and labour alongside them if he were a cripple? Molly had therefore set herself an enormous task. Until Jack took up responsibility for the boy, Tom had no one but her to rely on. And, God forgive her, she would employ every means at her disposal in order to see Tom become a whole being.

Realizing the dangers in what she intended doing that day, and being herself somewhat nervous of the consequences, Molly thought long about Tilly Watson's suggestion. She came to the conclusion that it might be wisest, after all, to leave little Sal with Tilly on this particular occasion. After all, Tilly could be relied on to keep the children occupied and to see that they came to no harm. Her mind was made up.

* * *

'All right, Mammy . . .I'll stay here with the others and see they're not naughty.' Little Sal's blue eyes smiled up at Molly. 'I don't want you to leave me behind *all* the time,' she declared, 'but I'm a big girl now, aren't I? . . . So I'll stay, if I can be in charge.' She peeked at Tilly Watson, who was standing at the top of the stone steps that led up to the scullery. It was obvious to the two women that Sal was seeking reassurance, and, perhaps, in her own small way, issuing an ultimatum.

'Well, *of course* you must be in charge!' agreed Tilly, casting a wary glance at the other children, who had stopped their yelling and fighting to view the proceedings. 'Isn't that so, you lot?' Tilly asked them. 'Sal must be in charge.'

'Only if I can be a soldier!' replied the chubby, fair-haired boy.

'And me, too,' chirped the smaller boy, who had a definite crossover in his speckled green eyes. The baby of the group, who was not much younger than Peggy, said nothing. Instead, she stood slumped against the back wall, sucking her thumb and using her free hand to hitch up the pee-stained knickers that had slipped to her knees.

'There you are then, Sal. It's agreed,' confirmed Molly, bending down and taking the two girls into her arms. 'Give your mammy a kiss.' She almost lost her balance when they flung themselves tight into her and rained her with kisses and hugs.

As she climbed the stone steps, Molly was made to pause when Sal's voice called out, 'Promise you'll be quick as you can?'

'I promise, sweetheart.'

'And will you bring us something?' Peggy chipped in.

Molly smiled at the difference in the character of her two daughters. All Sal wanted was for her mammy to come back quickly. That was enough. Peggy wanted her mammy back also, but she preferred her to return with a present in her pocket. 'I'll see what I can do,' she told the eager, uplifted faces. When she saw that little Sal was not altogether satisfied, she added a message just for her, 'I promise I'll be back as quickly as possible.' She warmed at the child's smile, and watched as she happily returned to the others, quickly beginning to stand them up against the wall and issue orders to 'get into a straight line, and no fighting'.

Thinking how much she adored her children and how empty life would be without them, Molly left the house and went away down Dock Street with a determined heart. She hoped the good Lord would understand why she was about to go back on a promise she made to him soon after Peggy was born. At that time, Molly had thought long and hard about the responsibility of having two children, one of whom was old enough and quick enough to follow her mammy's example, whether it be good or bad. Pickpocketing and stealing at every given opportunity was a bad example for little Sal, Molly had decided. She knew well enough that her older daughter was already beginning to acquire certain traits that would lead her into a life of street crime; just as she herself had done while under the influence of old Sal Tanner, albeit a loving and protective influence.

So Molly had stopped her thieving and turned to more honest ways of earning a living. Such as selling flowers that were past their prime, and moving crates in the marketplace, or singing outside a public house on a Saturday night – that was the most lucrative of all. But none of these enterprises ever allowed Molly and her offspring more than just a meagre existence. In fact, as Tilly had rightly pointed out, Molly had fallen behind with the rent and was having to dodge the landlord for fear he would give her notice to quit.

The last time Molly had been two weeks in arrears with the rent, he had made a lewd and improper suggestion. Nauseated by his proposition, Molly had worn herself to a frazzle that week, humping and shifting crates from early morning to when the market shut down. By the time she had paid the arrears and given Tilly a small sum for minding the children, there had been precious little left for food and fuel. Sometimes Molly despaired. Now she had the added burden of Tom's awful handicap. It was a combination of all these things that had made up her mind. She wasn't proud of her plans, not at all, because she intended to rob the fattest wallets and steal the most handsome fob watches, in order to accumulate enough money so she could take Tom to see a doctor who could put his leg to rights. She was even prepared to sell her precious gold clasp if it proved to be necessary. That particular prospect was the most daunting of all.

As Molly passed the Church of All Saints, she quickened her step and averted her eyes, while murmuring softly, 'I know it's wrong, Lord, and I'm sorry . . . but it was *you* that gave my boy a crippled body! You've left it to me to put right. And, if you don't mind me saying so . . . it's better if I *steal* than to earn money the way my landlord would have me do!' To Molly's thinking, she was employing the lesser of two evils, and considered that there must be some small merit in that.

Hurrying along the cobbled alleys, by way of Hart Street and Cicely, Molly's thoughts were drawn to two men in her life: Jack, the husband she still foolishly adored, and the bargee, Mick, who foolishly adored *her*. How different they were, she mused. And isn't it cruel the way Fate stirs things up into such an unhappy muddle. Molly was unpleasantly aware how Mick kept creeping up in her mind of late. In fact there were times when he, *and not Jack*, figured prominently in her thoughts. It frightened and worried her. She might be presently deserted by her husband, but she had grown accustomed to that and as a rule he always came home after a while. And she might be a thief, but to tell the truth, Molly could see little alternative in the circumstances. She was poor, and often desperate. That could not be denied. But she was not the kind of woman to go cap in hand to anyone. Neither was she the kind of woman to go from man to man, in exchange for a degree of security. She was a very simple and straightforward being, with an equally uncomplicated view on life: although he lacked a certain strength of character, Jack was her *husband*, and she loved him. But that was not to say he wouldn't get the length of her tongue when he did come creeping back! Until then, it was up to her to do the best for the children that it was in her power to do. Thanks be to the Lord, she was young and healthy, with a strong enough back to carry the particular load he had placed on it. As for Mick, well he was just a friend. A very *special* friend, there was no arguing. But Molly had every intention that he must remain only that.

'Gorra penny ter spare, 'ave yer, darlin'?' The thin and pitiful plea caused Molly to glance down. What she saw almost stopped her heart. It was a young man of about fourteen years, although he might have been older. It was difficult to tell, because he was horribly hunched at the shoulders and beneath the flat peaked cap, his narrow face was gaunt, with huge pleading eyes that stared up at Molly and touched her deep inside. He was seated on a makeshift trolley, just large enough to carry the small pathetic figure with only stumps for legs. *In her horrified mind, Molly saw her own son, Tom.* 'Ain't yer gorra penny ter spare fer a poor soul?' he insisted.

At once, Molly reached beneath her shawl and drew out the purse there. 'It's all I have,' she said quietly, giving it into his outstretched hand, 'take it . . . and God bless.' As she hurried away, the tight painful lump in her throat suddenly broke, and the tears welled in her eyes. She could feel the young man's bulbous eyes staring after her, but she dared not look back. 'That could be Tom,' she whispered over and over. Her determination was resolved: it would *not* be Tom. *NEVER!* She wouldn 't allow it.

Molly quickened her steps towards the railway station. There were always easy pickings to be had wherever folks congregated. It was a known fact.

'I wish you were coming with us, Nelly.' Emma took her old friend into a loving embrace, holding her close for a while and gently patting the trembling shoulders, while she herself fought against the emotion of their parting. 'But the time will fly . . . you'll see. We'll be back before you know it.'

Nelly drew away and began frantically fishing about inside her cape until, in a moment, she produced a bold, white handkerchief, with which she promptly dried her eyes and afterwards blew her nose. 'Oh, don't take no notice o' me Emma gal,' she said with deliberate flourish. 'I'm just an old mardie arse!'

Emma laughed, but it was a mirthless and sorry sound. 'Just look at yourself!' she gently chastised, smiling into Nelly's round, brown eyes that were pink at the edges from crying since early morning, and at the strong, straight nose that was bright red and sore from the constant friction of the handkerchief. 'You'll only make yourself ill if you go on like that!' There was genuine concern in her voice. It came to her, with a stab of astonishment, that since their first meeting in that prison cell more than twenty years ago, her impending trip to Australia would be the first and longest time that she and Nelly had been truly parted. 'I know how you feel, Nelly,' she murmured now, 'don't think I *wanted* to leave you behind . . . Oh, Nelly! Why did you insist on remaining behind, if you knew it was going to upset you so?'

'You know why!' Nelly exclaimed, hating the idea of Emma going all the way to Australia, but fearing even more the thought of going *herself*.

'Because she's a loyal friend.' Marlow stepped forward from his discreet vantage point some way beyond where the two ladies were saying their farewells. He had seen how Nelly's unfortunate outburst had affected Emma, and at once he was greatly concerned that even now, at this late moment in time, Emma might refuse to make the long journey to the other side of the world. As it was, he'd had the devil of a job convincing her to undertake this trip in the first place. It was both the doctor's sound warning with regard to her health and his own desperate pleas to Emma that had finally persuaded her of the need to get right away from all that reminded her of their son, and of what might have been. Since Bill's tragic accident, Emma had withdrawn deeper and deeper into a dangerous, twilight world, until Marlow lived in fear of losing her also. His own heart was empty and heavy with grief at the loss of the son he'd idolized. But, unlike Emma, he had made himself come to terms with that dreadful loss, if only to help Emma out of her own, crippling grief.

In these last few weeks since the boy's funeral, he had privately shed many a tear and, strangely enough, the shedding of those tears had somehow eased his heart-ache. But Emma's grief had turned inward. She had not spoken one word about their son: she would not be drawn into any conversation regarding him, nor had she cried a single tear on his behalf. It was as though she had locked his memory and his precious image into that secret part of her where he would be kept safe, intact and still alive. But in doing so, Emma had created for herself another place, another time, where she and the boy remained aloof from the world, where he lived out his life in her mind, and that mind was beginning to lose the boundaries between what was real, and what was not.

'*Must* we go, Marlow?' Emma pleaded now. 'You know I would much rather stay at home.'

Nelly was horrified! Filled with mortification at having betrayed her emotions in front of Emma, she resolved to make amends. 'Don't you talk such stuff and nonsense, Emma, my girl!' she chided in her most authoritative voice. '*What!* . . . And spoil my chance at being the "lady of the house"? You wouldn't do that to yer old friend, would you? No, you get off to Australia . . . say hello to that Silas Trent for me . . . and make sure the buggers take proper care o' the business you built up with your own sweat and blood!' She laughed and winked, casting a cheeky glance to where Marlow was silently thanking Nelly for her splendid efforts, when he knew it was tearing her apart to see Emma leave. 'You and Marlow . . . well, you know what I mean, Emma, gal . . . it's so romantic, ain't it, eh? Gazing over the ship's rail into the horizon, and watching the moon play on the water. Oh, and when you *get* there . . . to Australia, there'll be long, sultry nights . . . all that sun and gently strolling along the beach.' Of a sudden she laughed out loud, and clutching her cap tightly about her, she began shivering and chattering her teeth, 'While us poor mortals are left to suffer an English October!'

Emma saw through Nelly's ploy. And she loved her all the more for it. Reaching out her arms, she gripped Nelly's shoulders and, keeping her at arm's length, she gazed into her friend's twinkling brown eyes with a veil of nostalgia in her own strong, anxious gaze. Those merry eyes had carried her back to when she and Nelly were young. All the joy of that time, all the pain, all the defiance, it was still there, as if it were only yesterday.

Fleeting images paraded through Emma's turbulent mind, and paramount in these were the images of two children: one a newborn girl-child, and the other a boy already maturing towards manhood. Both children were hers and Marlow's. Both had been conceived out of wedlock, and worse, they had been conceived when she was married to other men! Both were now lost to her and Marlow for ever.

Now Emma asked herself the same question she had asked time and time again since the death of her son: *was she being punished for her sins?* In her terrible grief, she had denounced God. Now she wondered whether there really were an Almighty that was unforgiving, more cruel than any mere mortal could conceive, totally without mercy. If that were so, then she had been *right* to denounce a God in his heaven, for such an awful and powerful force could never be described as anything other than malicious. Therefore she regretted none of the harsh words which she had spoken in the churchyard on the day of her son's funeral. The only truth that now stayed with her was that she had sinned, and she was being punished. Beyond that, her reasoning refused to go.

'All right, Nelly . . . but take good care of yourself, won't you?'

'Don't I allus?' Nelly wrapped her two fists round Emma's gloved hands and tenderly lifting them from her shoulders, she squeezed them in a frantic gesture, saying in a dangerously trembling voice, 'Ooh, Emma, gal . . . let the good Lord smile on yer and bring yer both home safely.' She was not surprised when Emma quickly withdrew her hands. But her mention of the 'good Lord' had been *deliberate*, because she had prayed with all her might for Emma to return to the faith. And she would go on praying.

'Goodbye, Nelly.' Emma leaned forward to kiss the weatherworn and ageing face that she knew as well as her own. 'Just remember what I said . . . take good care of yourself.' Nelly clung to her for a moment, and then they were parted.

Having suppressed her tears for Emma's sake, Nelly's resolve melted as the train pulled away in a rising cloud of steam, and soon she could no longer see Emma's fluttering handkerchief for the blinding tears that tumbled down her face. 'God keep you both safe,' she murmured, in between rubbing at her eyes with the now soggy linen square.

After a few moments the train had gone from her sight. With a bowed head and heavy heart she turned away towards the ladies' cloakroom. Here, she regained her composure, straightened her bonnet and smoothed out her cape. Then, fearful of the long, empty days ahead without her Emma, she emerged on to the platform once again.

Only now had Nelly come to realize just how very long Emma would be gone. *Four months.* Four endless months that, to Nelly, would seem like a lifetime. Oh, she knew that Marlow had been right in applying for a postponement of the court hearing between Emma and the infamous Caleb Crowther. In her weakened and distressed condition, Emma could never have defended herself properly against her uncle. The authority had conceded to this and, in view of Marlow's request, together with the recent bereavement of their only son, the hearing was duly posponed to the thirty-first of March, in the year of Our Lord 1887. Marlow intended to keep Emma away until the month before, especially as the groundwork for the case was already prepared.

'Come on, Nelly gal . . . get yer pecker up and stop maudlin'!' Nelly told herself, in a loud whisper that drew a number of curious glances from passengers awaiting their respective trains. 'Oh, yer may well gawp and wonder,' she told them, unaffronted, 'but none o' *you* buggers have just seen yer darling off ter the other side o' the world, I'll be bound!' When all she received in return were haughty looks and a few disgruntled murmurs, she snorted aloud and stormed away, saying in a loud, firm voice, 'Miserable buggers!'

Lingering awhile by the flower-stand and debating to herself whether to purchase a posy, Nelly was interested to hear a conversation taking place nearby. The tall lady – with a head full of feathers and flowers that were tied beneath her chin with a wide extravagant bow – was relating to her smaller, plainer colleague a most detailed explanation of the 'disgusting affair . . . when a decent, respectable gentleman or lady could not attend their normal business without being robbed. And in broad daylight!' She was most indignant.

Amused by the manner of the two ladies who, in Nelly's opinion, were 'hoity toity and too blessed with their own importance', Nelly would have left the station there and then. But the woman, still speaking in loud and injured tones, drew her colleague's attention to the culprit. 'Oh, my dear!' she declared, sounding as though any minute she would fall down in a dead faint, 'What a *dirty*, despicable ruffian that young woman was . . . thin and undernourished of course. But I am quite certain to have nightmares about her, quite certain, my dear. Such large, piercing eyes she had . . . *black as the devil's*, and a look about her that quite unnerved me. Why, my dear! When the officer escorted her into the station-manager's quarters, I believe she was quite capable of putting a curse on him . . . fighting and spitting like a demon, she was!'

At once, Nelly was convinced that here was the very girl she had been seeking these many months: 'thin and undernourished . . . large black eyes', and by all accounts, possessed of a bit of fire in her character. Yes! It was the same thief, of that Nelly had no doubt. Putting on her sweetest smile, and sidling up to the two ladies, she imitated the tall one, saying 'Oh my dear . . . do excuse me, but I could not help overhearing. How *frightful* for you!' It was all she could do not to burst out laughing.

Both ladies seemed momentarily taken aback by the interruption, carefully regarding Nelly's expensive cape and bonnet, and seeing how altogether refined she did appear. Accepting that she was a woman of quality, they were soon spilling out the entire story of how a well-to-do gentleman had raised the alarm when 'this ragamuffin' dipped her hand into his pocket. The outcome was that he caught hold of her and was determined not to let her go until someone in authority was summoned. Upon the officer's arrival, the gentleman, together with the thief and a member of the public who was thought to have witnessed the unfortunate event, were quickly ushered into the station-manager's office. 'And, as far as I know . . . they are still in there,' remarked the tall lady. By this time, drawn by this particular lady's shrill, uplifted voice, a small crowd had gathered to add its voice to the proceedings.

'Really!' Nelly was marvellous in her condemnation. 'Whatever is the world coming to, my dear?' Suitably shaking her head in disillusionment, she swung away and swept through the crowd of bodies, loudly tut-tutting as she went. A little smile crept into her heart as she made her way to the station-manager's office. At long last, here might be the opportunity to help this unfortunate creature. And wouldn't Emma be pleased?

Anxious to approach the 'injured' gentleman before he preferred charges, Nelly was mortified to discover that 'both the gentleman and the thief have been taken to the constabulary.' But being Nelly, a woman who was not easily thwarted, she promptly gathered up her skirts, ordered a cab, and instructed it to take her quickly to the police station. Once there, she had no intention of leaving without the young woman in question!

Chapter Seven

'Who *is* this woman, Molly? And why would she persuade the gent to drop charges against you?' Mick had been shocked when Molly told him what had happened, and he had made her promise never to go thieving again. He was also very hurt when he realized that she was prepared to resort to such methods rather than turn to him for help. He knew, however, that the limited help he could offer her would never be enough to get Tom's leg put right, and he could understand how desperation had driven her to go picking pockets. He knew what an awful thing it was, to be so desperate. Because didn't *he* feel the same way? And hadn't he lost many a night's sleep on account of his all-consuming love for Molly? And now, because of that same desperation, he had come to a decision. The hardest thing of all was how he might bring himself to tell Molly. Her visit to the barge on this chilly November Saturday had been a pleasant surprise, which he intended to enjoy to the very full, before breaking his news to her. He would have told her today anyway, because, if she hadn't turned up here, he would have gone along to Dock Street some time later that evening.

'She's an odd sort,' Molly replied in answer to his question. 'Her name's Nelly . . . and she's a sort of "companion" to Emma Tanner.'

127

'Tanner?' Mick was surprised. 'The same Emma Tanner who's wed to my boss?'

'The very same.'

'Well, I'm blowed . . . it's a small world when all's said and done!' A thought suddenly occurred to him. 'I remember you telling me that you had no time for the likes of Marlow Tanner . . . though you never said why? And here you are, working for his wife . . . or his wife's companion.'

'You're right, Mick . . . I *don't* have any time for the likes of Marlow Tanner.' Molly had never explained why she felt this way towards Mick's employer, and it was something she did not feel able to discuss with anyone. If the time ever came when she had to speak her mind about the way Marlow Tanner had deserted his own sister – the old dear who had raised her from a child – then it would be to the *man himself*. Oh yes, it would be interesting to see how Marlow Tanner reacted to her accusation. But she had no desire to exchange words with him, not on that shameful matter, nor on any other.

'He's always been a good employer to me,' Mick argued. 'Honestly, Molly, you're a strange little thing and no mistake. What in God's name has Marlow Tanner ever done to *you*, eh?'

'He's never done anything to me,' Molly said truthfully. It was old Sal Tanner whose heart had been broken by his callous disregard for her. 'And the reason I'm working for his wife's companion is because I've got no choice.' Molly's gaze reached beyond Mick's bulky frame in order to check that the children were not up to any mischief in the forward cabin. When she saw that they were happily playing with the small saucepans that Mick had given them, she relaxed into the seat and supped on the hot broth which Mick had dished up for all of them. The children had quickly finished theirs, before scampering off to lose themselves in the paraphernalia that cluttered the bulkhead quarters. Molly resumed her conversation. 'If I don't turn up every day at the big house on Park Street, this "Nelly" has threatened to persuade the gent to charge me after all . . . on top of which, the constable told her to let *him* know if I didn't behave, because he released me into her custody and he's taken her word that she'll keep me out of trouble.' There was anger and resentment in Molly's black eyes as she looked up into Mick's kind, handsome face. 'Bloody cheek!' she said. 'I'm a grown woman. I don't need no guard dog.'

Mick laughed. 'Well, *that's* a matter of opinion, me beauty,' he said. 'But how long does this Nelly expect to keep you working there?' He also did not like the thought of Molly being made to report there against her will.

'Three months, she said. We came to an understanding about it. I'm to work there as a general help for three months . . . after which time I'm free to leave, and nothing said.' Here, Molly chuckled. 'She thinks I'll stay on, of my own free will, when the three months is up.'

Mick was intrigued. 'And *will* you?'

'No!' Molly was adamant. But then she lapsed into deep thought: how she had actually come to *like* Nelly, and how, in spite of herself, she had begun to look forward to her mornings up at the big house. And there was something else as well. Something that was very precious to her, and for which she had grown exceedingly grateful. She explained to Mick. 'Though little Sal wasn't too pleased,' she said in a low voice. 'It weren't fair to ask Tilly to mind all *three* children while I did my duties at the house . . . so I told Nelly that I'd have to fetch little Sal to work each day, because I'd nowhere to leave her.' She chuckled. 'I was sure she'd refuse, and so *I* couldn't come either . . . then she'd have no hold on me. But she weren't a bit worried. Now she thinks the world of Sal . . . and she's even *teaching* her things . . . reading words, and writing. She tells her stories and she plays in the garden with her.'

'Aren't you jealous?' Mick laughed.

'Oh, you might tease, Mick Darcy,' Molly chided, 'but *yes* . . . I *was* jealous. But Nelly's not the sort to try and steal a child's affection . . . she's really taken to Sal and me. To tell you the truth, she's not a bad sort . . . rough and ready she is . . . just like us.'

'No, Molly . . . not "like us",' Mick reminded her quietly, 'she's rough and ready maybe, because she was a convict with Emma. But now she lives the life of a lady, in a fine house with fine things round her. And, like as not, mixes with high, influential people.' Mick was concerned that Molly was in danger of losing sight of the real issues here. 'Don't forget *that*, me beauty, and don't forget that she *forced* you to go and work there. Keep your wits about you, Molly. These gentry have to be watched . . . and they harbour some very strange ideas. I don't know that you should let her take up so much of little Sal's time. Remember, there's been a child lost in that household . . . the Tanner's son. They're too old to have any more children.' He glanced round to reassure himself that Sal had not overheard, before looking into Molly's uplifted face. 'You do know what I'm saying, don't you, Molly?'

Molly knew right enough. The very same idea had

crossed her own mind and she had been made to recall her other fear, regarding Justice Crowther and the fact that he *was* kith and kin to the Tanner household, whatever the rumours said. She had broached the matter with Nelly, who had vehemently assured Molly 'that devil will not set foot in this household you have my word on it!' But then, she had gone on to ask awkward questions, such as why was Molly so intimidated by the Justice? . . . Had they ever locked horns? . . . Why should he be interested in a ragamuffin such as herself?

Afraid that she might reveal too much of her lawless past, including the fact that the Justice had hounded her badly, Molly cautioned herself, and from that point on, she remained vigilant and wary of letting her tongue run away with her. In spite of Nelly's assurances, Molly's suspicions were not altogether allayed. Yet, for all that, she still had a sneaking liking for Nelly, who had a straightforward and winning way about her. As for Emma Tanner though, and her husband Marlow, Molly was thankful that they were on the other side of the world. By the time they returned, she intended to be long gone. Three months, Nelly had said, and Molly was obliged to agree in the circumstances. Three months. And not a minute longer!

'Penny for them.' Mick clicked his fingers, and Molly instantly gathered her thoughts. 'All I'm saying is . . . be careful, Molly. Money and authority bring their own brand of law, and folks like you and me . . . well . . . be very careful, Molly lass. You never can tell what you're up against.'

'I'm nobody's fool,' Molly retorted, but not without a measure of gratitude in her voice; though Mick need not be so concerned. She was a survivor, and her instincts had always served her well. They would now. She would not relax her vigilance, not for a moment.

'Are you paid well?' Mick wanted to know, and was satisfied when Molly told him that yes, Nelly did pay her well. Fourteen shillings and sixpence a week; enough to keep the family fed and the rent up to date, besides giving Tilly a small payment for minding the two young ones.

'And did you buy *that* with your wages?' There was a softer, more intimate tone to Mick's voice as he pointed to the blouse that Molly had on. It was a high-necked garment in the warmest shade of burgundy, with full sleeves and pleated shoulders, and a row of tiny mother-of-pearl buttons from collar to waist. The deep, striking colour brought out the fire in Molly's dark eyes. Now, as she softly blushed beneath Mick's admiring gaze, he reached out and would have wrapped his strong hand over Molly's small fist.

Sensing his intention, she put her two hands into her lap and plucked at the grey serge skirt with its black hem. 'See this?' she said, cleverly drawing his loving eyes from her face. 'Nelly gave me this . . . and the blouse. She's got this chest in the attic . . . *stuffed* with clothes and things that don't fit her no more.' Molly smiled as she recalled how Nelly had explained: 'There was a time when I were thin as a pikestaff and fancied mesel' with the fellers . . . but now I'm lumpy as a cart-horse and the fellers would sooner strap a bag of oats ter me nose than put their arms round me!' Suddenly, in the wake of Mick's timely warning, Molly felt all the old suspicions rushing back. 'I'll give the blouse and skirt back . . . I should never have accepted them in the first place.'

'No, no . . . don't be foolish,' Mick said. 'Keep the

clothes. There's no reason why you shouldn't. If they don't fit her any more, then they're no use at all to her, are they?' His gaze mingled with hers, and Molly's heart turned over. 'Besides, me beauty, you look a picture of loveliness in 'em.' In that instant, the light of day caught his eye, and Molly was astonished to see her own image reflected in his strong, loving gaze. It frightened yet excited her at the same time.

When, somewhat shaken, she lowered her eyes, he stood up and touched her on the shoulder. 'Will you come up top with me, Molly? There's something that needs to be said . . . away from the children.' He collected her shawl from the nearby bunk and, taking it by two corners, he held it out. When Molly stepped forward, he wrapped it round her with great tenderness and, for a heart-stopping moment, she thought he intended to kiss the top of her head. Instead, he straightened his broad shoulders and gestured for her to go ahead.

On deck, Molly drew the shawl tightly about her. The mid-morning breeze had gained momentum, slicing the air with spite, and chilling her face. She shivered noisily. However, when Mick put his arm round her she instinctively drew away, although in truth Molly would have liked to snuggle into him. There was a feeling of great strength and protectiveness about this big, kind man.

'What is it you want to tell me, Mick?' Molly asked, looking up at him and thinking how ruggedly handsome he was. But he wasn't *Jack*, and he *wasn't* her husband. The three children inside the barge were not his either. He was a friend, a dear friend and that was all. Molly was disturbed to find that she was having to reassure herself of these facts more and more of late.

'Just listen, Molly . . . don't say *anything* until you've heard me out.' He paused, as though waiting for her to protest. When she did not, he went on in a quiet voice, all the while looking down at her lovely face, and fighting a terrible compulsion to grab her by the shoulders and force his lips on to hers. Dear God, how she haunted his every waking thought! His first words told Molly what she had long known, and been afraid of. '*I love you, Molly* . . . more than I've ever loved any woman. All I want in this life is to care for you and the children . . . to take you on as a family . . . *to belong.*' He raised his head and cried out softly as though in pain, '*Oh, Molly, Molly!*' Kicking his foot against the rail post he swung away from her, his two fists wrapped over the post and his tall, strong figure bent forward, the shoulders slumped wearily and his voice filled with despair as he told her, 'That husband of yours is a damned fool! I can't understand a man who could turn his back on a woman like you . . . leave his children . . . not giving a cuss whether they're cold or hungry.' Suddenly, he groaned aloud and came back to grip her by the shoulders. 'I know it hurts you to hear these things, Molly . . . but it's the truth, and I wouldn't be much of a man if I didn't say what was on my mind.' He sensed Molly's irritation and felt her shoulders stiffen beneath his hands. 'All right . . . all right.' He stepped away, keeping his eyes on her face, frantic that he was doing and saying all the wrong things, when he had spent these past few days planning how he could best win Molly over. He knew it would not be easy. She was fiercely loyal, worse, she loved her husband in spite of his roving ways.

'I'd best be going.' Molly took a step forward. She did not like the way things were developing.

'Don't do that, Molly,' he pleaded. 'Look, I've gone about this like a bull-headed fool. A minute . . . one minute more, and I promise I'll not mention him again.' His whole being relaxed when Molly stopped right beside him.

'It's simple enough,' he murmured in her ear, 'I love you and I'm asking you to come away with me. Let me take care of you, sweetheart . . . you and the young 'uns?'

In spite of herself, Molly was touched by the desperation in his voice. She knew he had not meant to slander Jack; in her heart she had to admit that he had spoken only the truth. It was strange that things had come to a head in this way, because she had intended telling him that, after today, she would not be coming to the barge anymore. Jack may be a coward, with the wandering heart of a gypsy, but he also had a vicious streak in him. It was wrong of her to see so much of Mick. It could lead to trouble. Besides which, she was not being fair to Mick by continuing these meetings, because, just as she had suspected, and in spite of his assurances to the contrary, they were encouraging Mick to believe that something more permanent might develop between them. Now she half-turned, her heart skipping a beat when she realized how close Mick's face was to hers. 'Please, Mick,' she said, her dark eyes melting beneath that intense, adoring gaze, 'you know you're asking the impossible.' He made no reply, but held her attention a moment longer until she became mesmerized by the softness of his gaze; there was something compelling about his whole countenance, keeping her there, trapped and helpless in the deep emotion that drew them together.

Molly could never remember exactly how it happened, but, suddenly, she was in his arms and he was pressing his mouth to hers. And she was willing him on, reaching up to wrap her arms round his neck, gently moaning as he rained frantic kisses on her face, her ears, her neck; all her resolve was was washed away in a tender and exquisite tide of ecstasy. 'Say you'll be mine,' he coaxed, 'just say the word, Molly.'

Suddenly Molly saw a movement out of the corner of her eye. It was little Sal! With a shock, Molly sprang from Mick's embrace, a wave of remorse sweeping through her when Sal said pointedly, 'I want to go home.'

It took Molly only a few moments to prepare the children, and soon they were clambering down the gang-plank on to the wharf. As Molly passed by him, her gaze fixed ahead and a tinge of embarrassment warming her face, Mick reached out, to draw her tenderly to a halt. 'I can't go on this way,' he told her softly. 'I must *leave* this area. With or without you.'

Molly did not look back. There would be too much between them, too much pain in his eyes. So she told him as gently as she knew how, and not without regret, 'Then it must be without me.' She felt his fingers grip into her shoulder, and, for a moment, she was afraid that he meant to swing her round to face him. But then his hand slid away and she was free to go.

Without another word, Molly walked on, away from the barge where she had spent many happy hours, away from a man who was both good and sincere, and along the wharf until, at the far end, she turned. She had thought to see his strikingly handsome figure standing astride the deck, with his passionate brown eyes seeking her out. When there was no sign of him, it was as if a lead weight had filled her heart. 'God bless and keep you, Mick Darcy,' she murmured, 'wherever you go.'

As she turned away, realizing that she might never see him again, Molly wondered at the feelings she had experienced in his arms. Warm and wonderful feelings that left her still trembling. But she could not accept that it could be love. 'I'm lonely,' she told herself, 'that's all.' Then, with a surge of anger, she said through gritted teeth, *'Jack, you bugger!* . . . It's high time you came home.' In fact he had been gone so long that, if he were not home by the time she had served her three months up at the big house, she would make it her business to track him down.

Molly loved the clinging, flowery smell of beeswax; as she polished the lovely walnut dining table, its particular perfume filled the air and made her think of spring sunshine. Of a sudden she was softly humming a tune, every now and then peeping out of the window to stare across the lawns towards the summer-house. Little Sal was sitting there, browsing through a picture book that Nelly had lent her.

Seeing the deep and contented look on her daughter's face, Molly paused in her labours to gaze a while longer. Outside the sun was shining and there was no breeze at all. There on the sundial was perched a tiny robin redbreast, dipping his head this way and that, and occasionally letting out a thin, piercing chirp. There was a freshness about everything, and a wholesomeness that lent a deal of content to Molly, who was lost so deeply in the wonder of it all that, when the door was flung open, she gave a small cry and swung round with her black eyes big and fearful. 'Oh, Miss Nelly!' she cried, visibly sagging with relief.

'Heavens above, gal!' retorted Nelly. 'Yer nothing but

a bag of nerves.' She sauntered to the window where Molly had been standing until, upon Nelly's arrival, she had quickly resumed her polishing. 'It ain't like a *December* day, is it, eh?' she said, gazing at Sal who had caught sight of her and was frantically waving. 'More like spring, I reckon,' she said, cheerily waving back.

'That's just what I was thinking,' agreed Molly. She did not stop work, but began softly humming the pretty song again. However, when Nelly came to sit beside the table saying, 'Your Sal is a bright and quick little gal,' Molly was at once attentive. Putting her cloth on the table and straightening her back with a little groan, she looked directly at Nelly, a lovely smile on her face and a mother's pride in her voice. 'Oh, she is! She is! . . . Right from when she were so high.' Molly stretched out her hand to indicate a figure not much taller than Tom was now. 'She wanted to know *everything*. Whenever she found something to puzzle about, she'd ask "Why, mammy" . . . "Why" . . . all the time "*Why?*"' Molly laughed softly at her own private memories. 'Drove me nearly crazy with her questions.' Suddenly, she was regarding the older woman with a more serious expression. 'You've done wonders for little Sal,' she murmured, 'we'll never be able to thank you properly. If it weren't for you . . . little Sal would not have had any learning. Certainly not from *me*, because I'm a very poor scholar myself . . . though, thanks to my Jack, I can read a little.'

'Molly, please come and sit aside o' me for a minute . . . let the polishing wait. There ain't nothing important about putting a shine on a table. Come and set yersel' here.' Nelly pulled out the chair next to her. 'I want us to talk a while.'

Whenever anyone told Molly they wanted to 'talk', she always assumed the worst. 'There's lots more to be done yet,' she argued, remaining where she was, 'and it's almost midday . . . I've to be back home within the hour. Can't it wait, whatever it is?' Her heart sank when Nelly slowly shook her head. Reluctantly she walked round the table to the other side and seated herself on the standchair, her slim back as stiff as a rod and her dark eyes anxious as she asked, 'What is it you want to talk about, Miss Nelly?'

'Aw, fer goodness' sake, gal!' Nelly threw her hands into the air in an expression of frustration. 'Ain't I asked yer afore . . . time and again . . . *don't* call me Miss Nelly! Yer mek me sound like a bleedin' *gentry*!' She poked Molly's arm with a stiff, angry finger. 'How would *you* like it if I kept calling *you* Miss Molly, eh?' When she saw Molly's face break into a smile, she slapped her chubby hand to her knee and roared with laughter. 'There y'are then . . . it sounds bloody daft, don't it, eh? *Miss* Nelly this, and *Miss* Nelly that!' Here she gave a cheeky wink, saying in a furtive whisper, 'Mind you, gal . . . I don't complain when the *servants* call me by that title, 'cause my good friend Emma . . . well, she's telled the buggers, "You must address my companion as Miss Nelly!" Oho, what a to-do there was, when Emma heard the housekeeper telling the scullery maid how "that Nelly woman is no better than we are" . . . well! My Emma were up in arms. Told 'em she did . . . not to refer to me in such an undignified way again.' Nelly chuckled. 'I would 'a loved ter see the face on that cook when Emma telled her off . . . miserable, po-faced bleeder she is – I never have liked her.'

Molly really did have a soft spot in her heart for this

outspoken and unpredictable woman. Now, as Nelly ranted on about Miss Warburton, the cook, Molly quietly observed her. She wasn't certain how old Nelly was, although she thought it must be somewhere not far off fifty years; yet there was such life and enthusiasm about her that a body could be forgiven for thinking she was much younger. Only the deepening wrinkles etched into her face, and the streaks of grey that coloured her wispy brown hair belied the possibility. She had told Molly how 'I used ter be thin as a pikestaff in me younger days', but there was little evidence of that now, because the 'pikestaff' was thickly padded with round, bulging parts and a somewhat 'bouncy' bustle. Even in her pretty silk and taffeta dresses with their ribbons and frills, Nelly could never be taken for a 'lady'. But it took more than fancy clothes to make a 'lady', thought Molly now; if she were ever asked, she would say that this genuine, warm-hearted creature sitting here now was more of a 'lady' than any one of those living in their posh houses and riding in their coach-and-four.

'I said . . . why is it that yer never want ter talk about yersel'?'

Nelly's question surprised Molly, who straightaway was on her guard. She must never forget that Nelly was Emma Tanner's very best friend, and that this was the Tanners' house, where every wall had ears. And where there were ears there were mouths, and where there were mouths there was gossip. Gossip had hanged many an innocent creature before now!

'What do you mean?' Molly asked, feigning ignorance of the older woman's intention to draw her out.

'Don't you come *that* business with me!' Nelly chided good-naturedly. 'I've done it too often mesel' not to know what yer up to. What I said was . . . yer never talk about yersel', do yer? Keep yer secrets close ter yer chest, don't yer, eh?' She stared at Molly in a forthright manner, and when Molly stared back with a defiant look in her shining black eyes, Nelly laughed aloud and rocked in her chair. 'Yer little bugger!' she declared, wagging a finger. 'Yer don't intend giving much away, I can see that. But yer ain't gonna get the better of me.'

'I'm sure I wouldn't want to do any such thing,' Molly replied quietly. 'I don't talk about myself because . . . there's nothing to talk about. There aren't any "secrets" to "keep close to my chest",' she lied.

'All right then, me darlin' . . . don't get agitated.' Nelly was irritated with herself, because she had succeeded in frightening the lass . . . the very thing she'd wanted to avoid. Her old heart was touched by the way Molly was unthinkingly twisting her apron round and round her finger. And those eyes! Dark, handsome eyes that seemed to see right inside you. Of a sudden, Nelly was astonished to be thinking of *Marlow Tanner! He* had eyes like that, black eyes that spoke volumes. A funny little shiver ran down her spine as she slyly regarded Molly, with her thick, dark tousled hair and so exceptionally beautiful; even with black lead up her arms from doing the firegrate, and with that stiff, unattractive apron over her secondhand clothes. Nelly felt instinctively that there was something here, some strange, inexplicable quality – or secret – about this young woman that she hadn't yet fathomed. But she *would* get to the bottom of it, because she wouldn't rest until she did.

'Look, Molly, luv . . . yer'll have ter forgive a nosey old bugger like mesel', but . . . well, I've tekken a real liking ter you and the little 'un. At first, I just wanted ter do right by them as is less fortunate than mesel' . . . just as my Emma taught me. But since I fetched yer here agin yer will some six weeks back, like I say . . . I've come ter like yer a lot.' Nelly had Molly's attention now, so she went on, 'Yer don't need ter tell me anything that yer don't want to, but there's one thing I can see with my own eyes, gal . . . and it's this. Yer've had a hard life . . . it's written in yer face, and in that quick, defiant manner yer have . . . just the same as *me* when I were living rough an' ready after me parents died.' Here she was intrigued by something which had not until now occurred to her. In a gentler voice, she asked Molly, 'Ain't yer got no parents, child?' When Molly lowered her gaze and gave no answer, she thoughtfully nodded her head. 'I see,' she murmured although in truth she wasn't quite sure what she *did* see. 'Tell me one thing,' she asked now, 'do yer trust me? Answer me truthful, mind!'

Molly raised her head and looked directly into the older woman's eyes. What she saw there was real compassion, and more honesty than she had ever expected. Yet still she was not certain. So much had happened in her young life, so much to destroy her natural trust. So many things that warned her always to be wary, to suspect *everyone*, or suffer the consequences. She liked Nelly. Liked her a great deal. But she didn't *know* her. Not really.

Molly had been asked to answer truthfully, and she did. 'I don't know whether I trust you . . . or whether I don't. I *want* to. But I can't . . . not altogether.' Molly hated the sound of her own words. And yet they were straight from the heart, as 'truthful' an answer as she was able to give.

'Fair enough, Molly gal, I can't say I'm surprised yer won't confide in me. Not when I fetched yer here agin yer will . . . threatening all kinds of retribution and punishment.' Nelly paused, looking into the troubled face of the young woman beside her, and a great surge of sympathy flooded her heart. She reached out and touched Molly's slender fingers. 'Aw, look here, darling,' she said softly, 'I would never have reported yer to the authorities like I threatened, should yer not turn up here . . . *Never!* That were just a ploy ter frighten yer . . . all I really wanted to do were to *help* yer, honest ter God.'

Impressed by Nelly's obvious sincerity, Molly looked at her searchingly, before asking, '*Why?* Why would you want to "help" me? . . . You don't know me.' She couldn't deny the suspicions that still persisted.

Nelly made a small noise, which sounded like a muffled laugh, or a groan of frustration. She took her hand away from Molly's fingers, and getting to her feet, she said, 'It's a long story, gal. It goes back ter when me and Emma were younger even than you are now . . . to a bad time, and a bad place.' Here she smiled and slowly shook her head. 'There are things in life that are best forgotten. But because life is by nature unpredictable, certain things that happen in the past have a direct and cruel influence on both the present and the future. Try as yer might, it's hard ter ever put the past completely behind yer.'

'I understand that,' Molly said now, being aware of certain parts of Nelly and Emma Tanner's past, such as them being sent as convicts to Australia. Molly couldn't help thinking that if the authorities still transported unfortunate wretches today, she would no doubt have been clapped in irons along with the rest of them. As it

143

was, she could expect a sorry end if ever Justice Crowther had his way! Oh yes, she could understand how frightening and shocking were the circumstances in which Nelly and her Emma had been taken all those years ago. But what she could not understand was this: 'What has all that to do with me?'

'Well, it ain't got nothing ter do with you,' Nelly replied, 'but what I'm trying ter say is that when a body's been as low and sorry as it can be, then it gets ter thinking. Me and Emma came through all our trials and bad years.' She stopped, remembering how broken-hearted Emma was at the loss of her son, and how that same loss had shaken them all to their very roots; besides shaking Emma's faith in the good Lord who had given her the strength and determination to soar above her earlier hardships. 'Emma's done well for herself . . . all done by hard work and pure grit! And all through it, she's never lost sight of her own unhappy start, nor has she forgotten how cruel and unjust life can be for the poor wretches at the bottom of the layer, much like yourself if yer don't mind me saying. She's a good woman.' Nelly's love for Emma was obvious in her voice, and in the proud look on her face. 'We saw you once before, my gal . . . did yer know that . . . *winked* at Emma, yer did.'

Molly was intrigued. She could not remember doing anything so inexcusable. 'Winking' at the niece of her most dangerous enemy? *Never!* 'I'm sure I did no such thing!' she retorted. But then Nelly chortled and went on to describe how on the very day she and Emma had arrived back in England, they had seen with their own eyes how Molly had been 'collared' by a constable, for picking pockets at Liverpool Docks. *Molly remembered it all.* She had had the fear of God put in her on that particular day, some years back now. Nelly's tale unfolded; she explained how Molly went running past her and Emma, with the child tucked to her hip. 'And when yer came alongside us, why! . . . Yer cocked the cheekiest wink ter Emma, just like it were all a bloody game!'

Suddenly it was all coming back to Molly. She recalled how this smart and beautiful woman stared at her with astonished and admiring eyes and yes, she did recall winking! A ripple of fear went through her as she asked incredulously, '*That* was Emma Tanner?'

'It was! You made a big impression on her that day . . . she never stopped talking about the incident all the way to Blackburn.' Nelly explained, 'She kept saying as how she would have liked to help you . . . you and the young 'un. But nobody knew where you'd come from, or how yer might be found . . . or at least, they weren't telling if they did know. Honour among thieves, I suppose. Anyway, what with her boy and her new husband, Emma's thoughts were busily occupied elsewhere fer a while. But then, one day not too long back, I clapped eyes on yer agin. There were two bairns with yer on that particular day . . . well, I told Emma what a bag of bones you looked and, after that, she wouldn't take no for an answer. My orders was ter find yer. Emma was gonna help yer . . . whether yer liked it or not. So *that's* why I got yer released into my custody, y'see. It were an opportunity for me ter do what Emma would have done if she were here . . . see that yer had a shilling or two in yer pocket . . . and proper work ter keep yer out of mischief.'

'Does Emma Tanner know I'm here?' Molly believed Nelly. But for old reasons, she dared not trust Emma

Tanner; it was possible that, unbeknown to Nelly, Justice Crowther was *using* Emma to capture the urchin who, he was wrongly convinced, had snatched his grandson.

'No. I have written to Emma of course, but I've said nothing about our arrangement. Emma hasn't been well since her son's tragic death.' She smiled sadly and for a moment was lost in thoughts of a reunion that couldn't come too soon for her. 'It'll be a lovely surprise fer her when she gets back. But for the minute, she's got too much on her mind to worry about what's going on here.'

'You said she won't be back till March . . . I'll be *long* gone by then,' protested Molly.

Seeming somewhat surprised at Molly's outburst, Nelly eyed her curiously. 'So yer won't stay on, eh?' She seemed genuinely upset. 'Aw, that's a real shame, gal . . . I thought we were getting on right well and all. And what about little Sal? . . . She's coming on champion with her learning . . . yer ain't being fair ter the poor little soul, are yer, eh?' Her look was imploring. 'Yer *will* change yer mind, won't yer? . . . Aw, Molly gal . . . *say* ye'll change yer mind.'

To Molly's reckoning, what Nelly was doing now was nothing short of blackmail. Fancy trying to persuade her to stay by using little Sal. 'No, I won't be staying on.' Her basic, intuitive fears urged her to get to her feet and argue. 'Soon as ever I've served my time . . . I'll be going.' She was adamant.

'What d'yer mean . . . "served yer time" . . . yer make it sound like a prison sentence!' Nelly had taken umbrage at the younger woman's rigid attitude. When back came the reply that Molly saw her time here as being exactly that . . . a 'prison sentence', Nelly was made to realize how, if *she* were in Molly's shoes, she too might feel the same way. 'All right, gal,' she said in a softer, more understanding voice, 'I don't want it said that I'd ever hold a body against its will. So, yer can go whenever yer like. *Today*, if you've a mind.' She gazed for a moment longer at Molly's surprised expression, then swinging round, with her full, stiff, taffeta skirt making an angry swishing sound, she went to the door, pausing there to tell Molly in injured and clipped tones, 'I could have sworn you were content in yer work . . . and what with the young 'un making such great strides in her learning, I was sure you'd be with us fer a long time.' She was puzzled by Molly's attitude, and suddenly a thought crossed her mind. 'It ain't the wages I pay yer, is it? . . . Yer don't think the wages is mean, and yer can't manage on them, is *that* it?'

'No, no, it isn't that,' Molly told her. 'The wages are very generous and I manage well enough. No, it's nothing to do with wages. And as for the learning you've given little Sal, well, I really *am* grateful.' Molly hesitated. For one stupid, careless minute there, she had felt so guilty and hated herself for the way Nelly seemed so upset, that she had almost confided her fears. Thank God she had bitten her tongue in time, because how could she tell this woman who had been so kind to her that she suspected Emma of deceiving them both. How could she say that Emma's uncle, the hated Justice Crowther, was baying for her blood, and that he might have recruited Emma to find her?

With her justifiably narrow and prejudiced view of the gentry, Molly found it hard to believe that any one of them – even someone like Emma Tanner who had been reduced in fortune for a while – would actively seek out a pickpocket, in order to 'help' her. Oh, Molly had heard the rumours of a terrible rift between Emma Tanner and the Justice. But two things warned her not to be too easily fooled; firstly, the Justice was Emma Tanner's kith and kin, and it was a known fact that every family had its rows, and quickly made up again. Secondly, when it all came down to it, blood kin tended to stick together against outsiders; especially when that outsider was thought to have snatched one of their children, in order to demand money.

Molly had survived by following her instincts. She had to follow them now. So, with regret she told Nelly that yes, under the circumstances, it would be best if she and little Sal left straightaway. It suddenly occurred to her, however, that Emma Tanner and Justice Crowther might not give up so easily. She must be very careful to put them off the scent; there might be just one way. Quickly, she added in a convincing voice – even putting a little smile on her face – 'Anyway, I would have been leaving soon,' she lied, 'because my husband doesn't want me working no more.'

'Oh!' Nelly could not hide her astonishment. 'I was under the impression that yer fella had left home a long while since? . . . . Are yer saying he's back?'

Molly rebuked herself for having revealed that she was a woman on her own, although she had never told Nelly the circumstances of Jack's leaving. In fact, she had closely guarded all information concerning her life outside of these four walls, and had instructed little Sal that under no circumstances was she to talk to Nelly about where they lived, or tell her *anything* at all about the family. The girl appeared to have done as she was told, except on one occasion when she had mentioned how her sister Peggy had hid in Tilly Watson's cellar and 'frightened everybody to death, because they all thought she'd got lost'.

'He's been back some time,' Molly went on, desperate that Nelly should believe she was telling the truth, and sad that it was sometimes necessary to deceive people with a lie. 'He's brought good news too! My man's been offered a job down south . . . with a little house besides. So we'll be moving away in no time at all.' She painted a happy smile on her face, but her dark eyes remained troubled.

A great silence fell over the room and for what seemed an age Nelly showed little response to Molly's words, other than to look out of the window to where little Sal's fair head was bent over her picture book. As though sensing that someone was looking at her, she raised her head and, seeing that it was Nelly, she waved her hand again, before returning to the book which Nelly had given to her. 'I'll be so sorry to see the young 'un go,' Nelly murmured, looking at Molly with regret, 'and you too, Molly.' Suddenly, there was a smile on her face, and coming back into the room, she astonished Molly by grabbing hold of her in a rough embrace. 'But I'm glad at yer news, child,' she said in a curiously gruff voice. Suddenly, as though embarrassed, she thrust Molly from her, saying a little too loudly, 'O' course yer must go with yer fella . . . and find happiness where yer can. There ain't enough of it in this world, and *that's* a fact.'

Within the hour, Molly and little Sal were turning out of the long path from the big house; the girl unusually subdued by the unexpected and unhappy event, and her mammy wondering whether she had made the right

149

decision; after all, Emma Tanner was not due back for some many weeks. On top of which, Molly dreaded losing the regular wage she had brought into the wretched little house on Dock Street. All the way down Park Street Molly agonized over her decision. Nelly had been such a help to her. She seemed such an honest and straightforward person, and wasn't it unlikely that such a person would love another woman like her sister if that woman were deceitful? Could it be possible that Emma Tanner was *not* doing Justice Crowther's dirty work after all, and therefore Molly's suspicions were totally unfounded?

For a moment, Molly's resolve began to falter. There was little Sal to be considered and the child's bewilderment was written clearly on her face. Had she done the right thing? Molly asked herself now. Had she acted too hastily? Couldn't she safely have stayed on, at least until just before the Tanners returned? Nelly's unhappy face came into her mind and now Molly stopped, her thoughts churning round in her mind. Surely a few more weeks wouldn't matter, she argued with herself, and she did need the money, there was no denying that.

Molly's mind was made up. Gripping the child's hand tightly in her own, she began walking back towards the big house, slowly at first, then more hurriedly. 'Where are we going, Mammy?' Sal asked, her little legs running to keep up with Molly's long strides. 'Are we going back to Nelly's house, are we, eh?' She was obviously delighted by the prospect.

'You'll have to wait and see, won't you?' Molly teased, a warm smile lighting up her lovely features as she looked down at the girl's eager face.

When Molly raised her eyes towards the grand iron

gates of the Tanner residence, the smile slid from her face, and in its place there came a look of fear and horror. There, climbing from a carriage which had stopped at the roadside right outside the big house was the unmistakable figure of Justice Caleb Crowther. Molly's heart missed a beat and she stopped in her tracks. All manner of emotions tore through her: shock, disbelief, fear and repugnance. So! She *had* been right about Emma Tanner all along! And what of Nelly? For it seemed as though she also had been deceitful, and was no better than the rest.

As he strode towards the gates, Caleb Crowther seemed to cast a glance in Molly's direction. Terrified, she pulled little Sal behind an overhanging laurel bush, warning her to 'stay very still and don't make a sound!' Sensing the fear in her mammy's voice, the girl did as she was told.

Not daring to show themselves, for fear that Justice Crowther might suddenly spring on them, the two stayed hidden, pressed deep into the shrubbery and hardly daring to breathe. From high up on his seat, the carriage driver could be easily seen. Molly's fear of discovery was heightened when suddenly he stretched his neck as though searching the very spot where they were secreted. Terribly afraid, Molly clutched the girl to her and pulled her down into an uncomfortable crouching position. Through an open patch in the laurel bush, she saw the driver relax in his seat, draw out his pipe, which he proceeded to fill with strings of tobacco from his pouch, and afterwards lean lazily into the seat, head back, eyes heavenwards as he took great sensuous pleasure in the puffing of his pipe.

The carriage driver's pleasure was short-lived, however, when suddenly there came the sound of slamming doors and angry voices, followed by the unsightly appearance of Justice Crowther as he rushed out of the gates and instructed the flustered driver, 'Breckleton House . . . and be quick about it!' As he climbed into the carriage he was clearly heard to say, 'So, she's gone, has she?' Then he laughed out loud. 'Well, she can take refuge where she likes, but she'll never get the better of Caleb Crowther! *Never!*' Yelling out another instruction to 'make haste, you fool . . . there's no time to lose', he flung himself into the seat and slammed shut the door.

In a moment the carriage was thundering past the very spot where Molly and the girl remained, not daring to move a limb. When little Sal glanced up at Caleb Crowther's stern, granite-like features, she instinctively cowered, clinging to her mammy's skirts and holding her breath until the carriage was out of sight.

After what Molly considered to be a safe passage of time, she and the girl emerged from their hiding place and went at hasty speed down Park Street and on into Blackburn town. Molly's dark thoughts were relentless in their condemnation of Nelly, who had very nearly tricked her into believing that she was a genuine friend. How cleverly Emma Tanner's companion had wormed her way into Molly's confidence. How despicable that the woman had used little Sal in such a way; plying her with books and 'learning' when all the time it was probably a way of trying to gain the child's confidence, loosening her tongue, hoping to pry valuable information out of her, with regard to where they lived and other useful snippets that would lead the Justice right to their front door. Oh, dear God above! What now? Molly's mind was in turmoil. *What now? What now?* The question had no sooner come into her mind than it was

on her lips. 'Sal . . . did you ever speak of Dock Street to
Nelly?' She drew the girl to a halt. 'Did she ask you
questions? Did you tell her anything?'

Little Sal shook her head, her vivid blue eyes looking
up at Molly, a deep frown etched into her forehead. 'I
never told her about Tom,' she said, 'and I never said
anything about Dock Street.' A look of guilt wrote itself
across her face and she lowered her gaze.

'But you did say *something*, didn't you, Sal?' Molly
had sensed her daughter's fear and was careful to speak
more softly. 'What did you tell her? I need to know. Did
she ask you questions, Sal? . . . What did you tell her?'
Her voice was marbled with such anxiety that the girl
lifted her gaze.

'I only said about that time when Peggy hid in the
cellar and we all thought she was lost.'

'*What else?*'

'I told her it was *Tilly Watson's* cellar.' The girl
hesitated, before adding quietly, 'and I said we sometimes go down Eanam Wharf and play on Mick's barge.'
She smiled brightly, as though a weight had been taken
off her small shoulders. 'I never said no more, honest,
Mammy. I haven't got us in trouble, have I?'

'It's all right. It's not your fault, darling,' Molly assured
her, although there was a crippling knot of fear in her
stomach at hearing Sal's 'confession'. Oh, that Nelly had
been cunning! She had not managed to worm the name
of their street out of little Sal, but she might as well have
done, because she knew the name Tilly Watson, and she
had learned about Mick, living in a barge by Eanam
Wharf. Molly suspected there was more than enough
information there for her to be tracked down. By now,
Mick was long gone, probably to southern parts where

work was plentiful. He would not be so easily found, she supposed. Thinking of Mick brought a strange fleeting sadness to Molly.

But there was no time for dwelling on regrets. Molly realized that she was in great danger. Her *family* was in great danger. Her one thought now was to get them all to safety. But *where?* Where could they go, with only the week's wages given to her by the devious Nelly – Judas money! Molly called herself all kinds of a fool for having been so gullible! Still, she did have fourteen shillings all told, and it was better than nothing. Ah, but there was something else, she reminded herself. There was the gold petal-clasp that old Sal had entrusted to her. As she and the girl hurried towards Dock Street, Molly dipped her fingers into the neck of her blouse, feeling for the gold droplet. She would be loath to part with it, because it had been on her person ever since the day old Sal was buried. Besides which, she had promised the old darling that it would stay with her always. Up till now, Molly had managed to keep that promise. But here was a very bad and frightening thing that was happening now. She hoped old Sal would agree that pawning the clasp was preferable to being pounced on by the Justice, when she and the children would be horribly punished, she was certain. With the money got on the clasp, Molly might go further afield in order to escape his clutches. Suddenly, Molly drew the girl to a halt.

'What's the matter, Mammy?' Sal saw how Molly's face had drained of colour and she was frantically searching in the neck of her blouse. It was gone. *The clasp was gone!* For the first time in a long while Molly wanted to cry. She felt desolate. Unbeknown to Molly, the clasp had been plucked from the carpet by Nelly, who, not realizing it was Molly's, had assumed that it belonged to Emma, and had put it safely away. 'Mammy . . . what's the matter?' little Sal insisted, her bottom lip quivering. For a moment, Molly continued to forage for the clasp, but stopped at once when she saw little Sal's fearful face.

Realizing what a frightening experience the child had just endured, Molly got to one knee, and taking little Sal into her arms, she said, 'It's all right, sweetheart . . . it's all right. Nothing for you to worry about.' In a brighter voice, she added, 'Let's hurry home, eh? We've all kinds of exciting plans to make . . . and as you're the eldest, I'll be looking for some good advice from you. I know you won't let me down, will you?'

'I have to be growed up, don't I, Mammy . . . 'cause I'm older than Tom and Peggy, aren't I, eh?'

Getting to her feet, Molly nodded, and actually laughed aloud. What a little madam you are, my Sal, she thought proudly. But then, as they rounded the corner of Dock Street, Molly's 'pride' turned to shame. What would her daughter say when she discovered that her mammy meant to take her away from the only home she had ever known – miserable though it was – and that they had no other place to go? Molly had been heart-stricken at the loss of her precious clasp; now she was more frantic at the daunting future that lay ahead. Here she was, with only a few shillings to her name, three children – one of them a cripple – and being hounded by a Justice and his spies, who all wanted her blood. Hounded on to the streets; forced to find a safer place.

Molly's thoughts came back to Nelly, and for a moment she was saddened. But then her sadness quickly turned to anger. That woman had almost duped her.

Almost! But Molly thought she had her measure now all right! No wonder she was able to persuade the authorities to release a pickpocket into her custody. Why! She probably told them that she was acting on Justice Crowther's instructions. Right from the start it must have been a devious plan. Nelly had been playing with her all along; probably getting little Sal's confidence too, so that she could lay claim to her for the Tanners. Molly could not fathom out why the Justice was not summoned to move in on her before today. Perhaps he, like his niece, had been out of the country, or possibly he had been trying to discover where she lived, so they could take the whole family into custody. But here Molly had taken precautions because, being made by nature and circumstance a suspicious person, she had cleverly varied her path home, dodging this way and that, in case she was being followed.

When the front door of her small, dilapidated house was in sight, Molly breathed a sigh of relief and gave thanks to whoever had watched over them that day. She and her family were still free, in spite of the woman called Nelly. With a sense of disgust, Molly imagined the scene that had taken place in the Tanner household when the Justice had come to collect his quarry, only to find it had flown. The thought of his fury gave her a small rush of satisfaction.

As Molly went into Tilly Watson's home to collect the children, her feeling of satisfaction at having outwitted both Nelly and the Justice might have turned to regret if only she had been aware of what had *actually* taken place between Nelly and Caleb Crowther that morning.

Caleb Crowther was beside himself! Having heard nothing all these weeks, except notification that the court case was postponed he saw the delay as being another trick by Emma Tanner to unnerve him. When he could stand it no longer, and against the advice of his solicitor, he had gone to the house on Park Street with the intention of thrashing the whole thing out once and for all. How infuriated he had been to be told not only that Emma Tanner had gone blithely off for an indefinite period. On top of which the common and repulsive creature she had left behind had actually ordered him from the premises. *Him!* A distinguished Justice of the Peace, albeit retired. He would not have budged one inch were it not for the awful uproar she was making, and the threat he knew she would not hesitate to carry out – 'to shout and yell blue murder and fetch the bleeding authorities down on your head!'

All day long the thought of how Emma Tanner meant to ruin him ate into his thinking and filled him with fear, an emotion with which he had never been too familiar. Yet here he was, a man much older and worn with the passage of time, whose comfortable lifestyle was threatened because of what had taken place so many years before; a man who was always used to being the victor, yet in this instance could well be defeated and, consequently, reduced to poverty.

Everything he owned, every penny he had, could be forfeited if the courts found in favour of Emma Tanner. It was a possibility that he must face. Caleb Crowther had never fooled himself on that score. But he would fight that damned woman with every means at his disposal, legal or otherwise. Even though, in his deepest, darkest heart he was made to acknowledge his own guilt. He *had* betrayed a dying man's wish and married Emma off to a totally unsuitable young man, in order to cheat her out of the marriage settlement her father had bequeathed her. He *had* plotted to have her convicted of murder and afterwards transported to the far-off shores of Australia. When she was safely despatched there, he had lost no time in looting her entire inheritance, selling the assets and converting them into hard cash which was duly deposited in his own name. All of these things he had done, it was true. But no one would ever know the *full* extent of his corruption concerning Emma. Because it went much, much deeper. So awful, so terrible and damning were the deeds he had committed that, even now after long haunting years, he would relive those heinous crimes in his uneasy slumbers, waking in a cold sweat of fear and shame, and horrified for the sanctity of his very soul.

Suddenly that same horror and shame was on him now. Leaning forward in his chair, he dropped his grey, balding head to the desk-top, his small pink-rimmed eyes staring upwards at the ceiling and, for a moment, he seemed almost demented, his eyes beginning to roll and the chilling sound of soft laughter emanating from his loose, open mouth. In that moment, he saw how foul and murderous was his character. In that moment, he was made to relive every terrible act over again. Now, when he screamed aloud and tore his fingernails into the flesh on his face, there was madness in him.

When there came an urgent knock on the door, he snatched himself to an upright position in the chair, desperate to compose himself, for he was trembling uncontrollably, and still in the grip of his terrible thoughts.

'Grandfather . . . are you in there?' Edward Trent's anxious voice penetrated Caleb Crowther's troubled mind, and at once the change in him was astonishing.

Springing from his seat with a surge of energy, he hurried to the door, quickly unlocking it and, with a smile on his ungainly features and a brighter light in his eyes, he flung open the door to greet his beloved grandson. These two did not always see eye to eye, but underlying their many differences was a degree of love which was forged many years ago and which had somehow survived the numerous upheavals between them.

'Edward! . . . Oh, my boy, it's good to see you.' Caleb Crowther slapped one large hand on the young man's shoulder, and with the other he took Edward's hand into his own, gripping it hard and shaking it enthusiastically as, at the same time, he propelled his grandson into the study, kicking shut the door behind them. 'What's brought you here today? . . . Why aren't you at the infirmary? . . . Are you with your mother? . . . Is Martha here?' His questions tumbled out one after the other, until, realizing he had hardly given the young man time to draw breath, he laughed aloud. 'Forgive me,' he said, 'but I really am so very pleased to see you.' He gestured to the deep leather armchair on the near side of the desk opposite his own seat. 'Sit down . . . do sit down, Edward,' he urged. Then, when the young man had done so, he went quickly to the walnut cabinet by the fireplace, and here he part-filled two tumblers with whisky. 'Drink up, my boy,' he told the young man, who reluctantly took the glass. 'We'll drink a toast to *me* . . . your grandfather . . . who will soon show the Emma Tanners of this world that they take on too much when they take on Caleb Crowther!' He swung the glass up high in a gesture of salute, before putting it to his mouth and emptying the fiery liquid down his throat. A look of consternation crossed his features when he saw that, instead of following his grandfather's example, Edward had put his own glass to the desk. '*What?* . . . You won't drink to your grandfather's victory over a wretched creature who would see him paupered?' He stared penetratingly at his grandson, before drawing a hard, long breath that swelled his chest to enormous proportions. Noisily releasing the air through flared nostrils, he slammed his glass on to the desk. 'What ails you?' he demanded, suddenly realizing from the serious look on Edward's face that his grandson was here for a particular reason; one that was not too pleasant if his quiet and disapproving manner was anything to judge by. 'And what brings you to Breckleton House . . . if it isn't to console your old grandfather?'

He spoke with an injured tone as he sat heavily into his chair and continued to stare at the young man, grudgingly thinking how he would forgive him almost everything. Edward was his only grandson and, thankfully, had inherited none of his mother's petulant and selfish ways. Martha was a weak-willed, grasping and repulsive creature, who had alienated her father from a very early age.

From the day of Martha's birth – and for very secret reasons to do with Emma Tanner's lovely mother, Mary Crady, whom he had adored beyond reason – Caleb Crowther had taken a deep dislike to his daughter. Martha did not earn his love when she was a new-born in his wife's arms; she did not earn it when she was a child; and she had not earned his love when she became a woman. If anything, she had earned only his intense loathing. There were times when Caleb Crowther was forced to examine the unpleasant and shamefully weak traits in his daughter's character and to question himself about their origin. Certainly they were not inherited from her mother, for Agnes Crowther could never be described as weak, or petulant. Grasping perhaps. And devious on occasion. But by and large she was a strong-willed and determined woman, who was not afraid to show her claws, a characteristic that had greatly irritated him of late.

With deepening concern, Caleb Crowther regarded the young man who was his grandson; he let his anxious eyes rove over the familiar straight and strong features, the dark, well-groomed hair and those intense green eyes that gave Caleb Crowther the odd impression that his grandson was able to see right through him. 'There's something on your mind, isn't there?' he said now, keeping his gaze on the young man's face. 'Out with it, then . . . let's hear what you have to say!' He sensed an imminent battle. All the familiar signs were there. They had battled before on many issues, and no doubt they would battle again on many more. But there was one particular issue on which they could never agree, yet which would not go away. Caleb Crowther's instincts told him that the very same issue was about to raise its ugly head now.

'I had a letter from my father this morning,' Edward began.

'Oh, yes! . . . And no doubt he had some very damning things to say about me, *did* he?' Caleb Crowther had not expected his grandson to bring Silas Trent into the conversation, nor did he like it. The man was an upstart! Arrogant and obstinate in the matter of his wife, Martha who – encouraged by Caleb Crowther – adamantly refused to leave England in order to join her husband in

Australia. Since buying out the trading business which Emma had built up over many years and in which he had been generously offered a partnership, Caleb Crowther's son-in-law had taken it from strength to strength until now he had secured shipping contracts right around the globe. His only remaining ambition was that Martha, whom he adored in spite of her childish, obstinate ways, should join him in Australia, where they could enjoy the fruits of his labours together. Now that their son Edward had fulfilled his own lifelong desire to qualify as a doctor and had moved out of the family home to be nearer his work, Martha *might* have been persuaded to go to her husband and remain by his side, if it weren't for the strong influence exerted over her by her own father.

Caleb Crowther cared not whether Martha should disappear from the face of the earth, so obnoxious was she to him, but he saw her as a means by which he might make Silas Trent pay for having joined forces with his old enemy, Emma Tanner . . . or Emma Thomas as she had then been. Silas Trent's unbelievable success, and Emma's part in it, was a thorn in Caleb Crowther's side. He could not forgive his son-in-law for going against his advice to 'stay clear of that woman . . . there is no love between us, and I want no kin of mine kowtowing to a creature of that sort.'

It was true that Silas had asked Caleb Crowther for a loan in order to save his own dwindling fleet of merchant ships, long before Emma had put her own propositions to him, and it was also true that Caleb Crowther had callously refused his son-in-law's desperate plea out of hand. Yet he saw Silas's acceptance of Emma's offer as being both traitorous and rebellious. He had never forgiven him. He never would!

'My father made no mention of you . . . only of my mother, who refuses to answer his letters.'

Caleb Crowther impatiently waved his arm in a gesture of dismissal. '*Enough!* . . . I am not interested in your father's domestic squabbles. If Martha has turned her back on him, then it's no more than he deserves!' Secretly he was delighted, and if his constant interfering was worsening matters between his daughter and her husband, then so much the better.

'Did you know that Emma was in Australia? . . . And that she and Marlow Tanner have met up with my father?' Edward Trent eyed his grandfather closely, gauging his reaction and hoping against hope that the animosity between this man and his own beloved father might diminish with the passage of time. However, Caleb Crowther's next words dashed his hopes to the ground.

'Always the traitor, eh?' The news had been an unpleasant shock. That blasted woman at the Tanner house had not told him that Emma had sailed to Australia, only that she was 'out of town'. Damn and bugger it! What was Emma Tanner up to? . . . What devious little game was she playing at? He had been furious when the courts agreed to Marlow Tanner's request of a postponement of the hearing on the grounds that Emma had suffered a tragic bereavement. *He* stood to suffer more than that! And *would* if she had her way. He wanted this business over and done with, and to that end he had gone to a great deal of trouble and expense in falsifying certain 'evidence', some of which would show how Emma had systematically robbed her own father while he lay dying. *That* was the most difficult of all the manufactured documents, but a guinea or two extra had been enough to procure them. Now, when he had all these little surprises in store for her, she had upped and departed, leaving him floundering and frustrated. Oh, she was a wily one! Now here she was, hobnobbing with his traitor of a son-in-law. What were they up to? What in God's name were they up to? Not knowing her next move was more than he could bear. 'What else did your father have to say with regard to that creature?' he demanded to know. 'How long does she intend to rob me of my moment in court . . . when I mean to turn the tables on her!' He chuckled, but was quickly silenced by the condemning look on Edward's face. '*What* . . . you don't see the funny side of it? Oh, you will . . . believe me, *everyone* will! She may have been the one to instigate proceedings, but *I'll* be the one to finish them.' His smile was darkly unpleasant. 'I intend to see Emma Tanner regretting the day she ever locked horns with such a fellow as me.'

There followed an uncomfortable silence, during which time the two men regarded each other with a degree of hostility. 'I want you to end this dispute with both my father . . . and Emma,' Edward declared in a quiet and serious voice. 'She is a good woman . . . and have you forgotten that she has recently lost her only child?'

'What is that to me?' Caleb Crowther rose to his feet and, curving his fists round the desk edge, he leaned forward in an ominous posture. 'And don't you dare tell me that she is a "good" woman,' he thundered. 'To my mind, she is no better than a common criminal . . . an opportunist . . . of no more consequence than the wretched women who roam the streets in the dark hours!'

Now Edward also was on his feet, glaring at the older

man with stony, condemning eyes. 'It does not become you . . . a distinguished Justice . . . to be so prejudiced, so vindictive . . . *and to one of your own blood kin!*'

Edward Trent could not have known what terrible effect his last words would have on Caleb Crowther, for he was not aware of certain dark secrets that had lain heavy in his grandfather's guilty heart these many years. When Caleb Crowther reeled at Edward's accusation, his face growing distorted as though in crippling pain and his clumsy bulk falling backwards into the chair as though pushed by some unseen hand, Edward's medical training convinced him that his grandfather was suffering a heart attack. Rushing forward, he would have grabbed at the older man's stiffened collar and frantically tried to loosen it, but his efforts were angrily shrugged off. 'LEAVE ME BE!' Lashing out at the young man, Caleb Crowther sprang from his chair and breathing unnaturally hard, he snarled, '*You!* I thought at least you would stand by me in this. But it's plain to see that you're no better a man than is your father. Get out . . . *GO ON! Get out!* I don't care if I never see you again.'

Edward knew the futility of trying to reason with Caleb Crowther when he was in one of these terrible moods. He had hoped to convince his grandfather to make good the relationship between himself and Emma, who was after all his own niece. But as he might have expected, his words had fallen on deaf ears. Some time ago, before the death of her son, Edward had tried desperately to persuade Emma to think again about the case she was relentlessly pursuing against her uncle, Caleb Crowther. But she had been no more receptive to his pleas than had his grandfather..

Dejected, Edward left Caleb Crowther angrily storming to and fro across the room. He consoled himself with the thought that at least he had tried. Tried, and failed. It was painfully obvious that this vicious feud between Emma and his grandfather, in which his own father was caught up, had gone on too long and was too ingrained in both their lives to be so easily resolved. He prayed it would not end too harshly, although somewhere deep inside him Edward Trent had the uneasy feeling that it would all end in tragedy.

Martha Trent and her mother Agnes had been deep in conversation in the drawing-room when the furore between the two men disturbed them enough to send them rushing into the hall. Seeing her son striding towards them from the study, Martha hurried forward, her round face pink and flustered, and her chubby hand to her heart. 'Whatever is the matter, Edward?' she asked, as he came to a halt before the two women. Suddenly she gripped his arm as though to lead him into the drawing-room, her small brown speckled eyes boring into him with disapproval. 'I hope you haven't been upsetting your grandfather!' She added angrily, 'I trust you had the good sense to keep the contents of your father's letter to yourself. There is no one in this house who wishes to know that Emma Tanner and your father appear to be as thick as thieves.' She tugged at his arm, but was incensed when he remained rigid and unmoving. 'You *did* tell him, didn't you?'

'Yes, mother . . . I did.' Edward did not regret his actions. 'It's high time that Grandfather was made to see sense.' He took Martha's hand gently from his person. 'I hope I am never forced to take sides between them, because I honestly could not say where my sympathies would lie!'

'*Really, Edward!*' Martha's face had grown so red it seemed she might explode. 'You can't know what you are saying!'

'What I am "saying", mother, is that my father . . . *your husband* . . .' he felt the need to remind her '. . . is one of the few people who enjoys Emma's confidence. What I am *also* saying is that she has suffered a very tragic life . . . we *all* know that. It would be useless to deny it.' He had seen his mother open her mouth to intervene and at once he flashed her a warning glance. 'You *least of all* cannot deny the truth of it! . . . Only very recently she lost her son in a tragic accident. Yet still grandfather heaps loathing and retribution on her head. *One* of them must be made to see sense.' Seeing his mother's expression harden, he looked beyond her to the tall, dignified woman who had made no remark throughout, but who had listened with great interest. 'Grandmother . . . surely you agree? A family must not fight within itself.'

At this point Agnes Crowther stepped forward, a regal figure with greying hair bound tight to her head with expensive mother-of-pearl combs and, as always, her long slim hands held together in a posture of prayer. She made no answer to Edward's question. Instead she turned towards the dumpy, plain figure beside her and in a patronizing voice, instructed, 'Leave Edward to me, dear . . . you go and pacify your father.'

'Of course,' Martha replied, nodding her head in a serious manner and going quickly towards the study, her voluminous skirts swishing angrily against her ankle boots as she quickened her step.

Agnes Crowther watched her daughter disappear into the study and waited until the door was closed before addressing her grandson. 'Your grandfather is unlikely to heed your advice, I'm afraid,' she told him with a half-smile, which belied her delight in the fact that her husband did not always persuade this young man to his own thinking. 'He does not listen to anything *I* say . . . and as you should know, he will insist on doing things his own way . . . however unpleasant the outcome.'

'So you're of the same opinion?' Edward asked, glad to have at least one ally in this spiteful business. 'You believe the outcome *will* be unpleasant?'

Agnes Crowther gave a small, cynical laugh. 'Oh, my dear Edward . . . there is no doubt in my mind at all!' she told him. 'But *whom* will it be more "unpleasant" for, I wonder? After all, between you and me, Emma Tanner has a very good case. On the other hand, your grandfather has a number of excellent contacts . . . both in the legal world . . . *and* in the criminal world.' Here she smiled at the disbelief on his face. 'Don't feel too sorry for him, Edward, because he is not a man to be crossed lightly. Rather, he is a man who will employ *any* means in order to rout his enemies.'

'Are you saying he would resort to *criminal* means to answer Emma's charges?'

Agnes Crowther realized that she had said enough. She would have liked to have said more. She would have liked to have shattered Edward's image of his grandfather once and for all. Such a thing would not prove too difficult. All she had to do was reveal the *truth* of how Caleb had set about destroying Emma's life. But then she would have to confess *her own* part in it: how she was the one who kept Emma locked in her room while her dying father called out for her to come to him. She would have to explain why it was that she had stood idly by while Caleb submitted Emma to a catalogue of injustices. Agnes Crowther had since grown ashamed of her own complicity in these events. But she had also grown older, and her courage was not so strong that it would allow her to go to Emma and ask forgiveness. Such a humble act had never been in her nature. It was not in her nature now. Far better to let things lie, for they could not be undone. 'Come and keep me company, Edward.' Agnes Crowther's instincts warned her to change the subject, as the two of them made their way into the drawing-room. 'Tell me about your father's letter . . . how is he? . . . Does his business still flourish? . . . You do know how I feel about Martha refusing to join him out there, don't you? Silas is a good family man and has always been an excellent husband to my daughter . . . to my mind, she should at least make the journey to Australia . . . if only to spend a short time with him. I have said as much to Martha, but well . . . you know how disagreeably stubborn she can be.'

Edward knew only too well. He knew also that his grandmother had cleverly diverted the conversation from the more important issue that had brought him here, that of his grandfather's continued loathing towards both Emma and his father. A crippling and unreasonable loathing that touched on the whole family and lingered in the air like the poison it was. Though he did love his grandfather, Edward could not deny that there were times when he positively disliked him. His unbending and vindictive attitude was something Edward saw as being both frightful and dangerous.

Now, as he followed his grandmother into the

drawing-room, Edward was made to recall a time when he was but a boy and had foolishly run away from home, after his father had gone to sea. He had been set upon by ruffians and later safely returned by a small, ragged girl. He still carried the memory of the girl's face in his mind: small and heart-shaped with big black eyes, and unkempt hair as dark as midnight. He remembered how she took money from his grandmother, money which would be used to save some old 'friend' from a pauper's grave. He often thought of her, but for some inexplicable reason he could not bring himself to discuss her with anyone. Except of course when he felt obliged to defend her to his grandfather, who would have hunted the girl down and had her severely punished. That was the first time Edward had witnessed Caleb Crowther's terrible, almost insane obsession with his own sense of power. It was not something to be admired. Edward thought of the scene which had taken place between them just now. He thought of Emma, and of his father, who could do nothing right in Caleb Crowther's eyes. He thought of his mother, whose own behaviour towards her husband was somewhat callous. Edward thought of all these unfortunate people whose lives were, either directly or indirectly, influenced by his grandfather to some degree or another. He secretly acknowledged that all around him there seemed to be an air of conspiracy, and his loyalties were painfully divided.

Martha's loyalties, however, were not divided. She adored her father and though the affection had never been mutual, she had spent the whole of her life trying to please him. Caleb Crowther had preyed on this weakness in his daughter. He preyed on it now. 'Silas Trent deliberately went against my express wishes when he accepted Emma's offer of a partnership in the Australian trading company,' he told her in injured tones.

'I know that father . . . and I did my utmost to prevent it.' Martha was mortified for fear that he might hold *her* responsible. 'That is the sole reason I refuse to acknowledge his letters . . . nor will I ever be persuaded to leave these shores at his request!' She was desperate to pacify this man who, in her eyes, could do no wrong.

'Ah!' Caleb Crowther swung round from the window, where he had been looking out on a crisp, dry morning and churning over all manner of possibilities in his mind. One in particular, stimulated by Martha's declaration, brought a devious smile to his face. 'So . . . you will not leave these shores to please your husband, eh?' he asked coyly, coming towards her and pausing before her chair, where he stooped in order to look directly into her brown-speckled eyes. 'But will you leave these shores in order to please your old father, eh?' He smiled a wicked and intimate smile that seemed to unnerve her momentarily.

'What do you mean?' She was obviously perplexed by his remark. She began stuttering, a characteristic that betrayed Martha's insecurity where her father was concerned. 'I . . . I don't un . . . der . . . stand.'

'Oh, it's very clear, my dear. Apparently, *your husband* and *my niece* have once again joined forces . . . or so it would seem. It therefore follows that they must be up to something, don't you think?' When she appeared lost for words, but eagerly nodded, he went on, 'I strongly suspect that those two would not hesitate to conspire against me. Do you agree?'

'Yes, yes . . . they both would like to see you ruined, I'm certain of it.'

171

'Then don't you also agree that *someone* should be out there to keep an eye on them? . . . Someone who might *naturally* be amongst them without arousing suspicions, and therefore in a position to report everything back to me?'

'How clever. *Yes . . . yes.* With the court case raising its head in the not-too-distant future, you need to be aware of what that vixen, Emma, is plotting against you.' *Still* she did not suspect her father's intention.

Caleb Crowther was pleased with himself. Stretching noisily, he smiled down at her and, keeping his eyes on her keen upturned face, he seated himself on the edge of the desk. What a fool you are, Martha my dear, he thought with repugnance. What a naive, addle-brained little fool! But useful to him at times. Like now, when he would plant a spy on his two unsuspecting enemies. A pair of eyes and ears, and an observer who would duly report back to him without question. 'Have a sherry, my dear,' he offered sweetly, 'and then we must talk. I have a proposition to put to you, for I am sure that the last thing you would want to see is me and your poor mother in the debtors' prison.'

It was late evening when Caleb Crowther emerged from Breckleton House and climbed into the waiting carriage. He had succumbed to a driving need in him to visit old haunts where there were women who would be only too eager to satisfy the basic urges that had come on him. 'All the way to London my good man!' he called in a jocular voice as he climbed into the carriage. He felt good. Anger was an invigorating emotion that suited him well. Besides which, the gullible Martha had been like dough in his hands. Within the week she should be setting sail for foreign parts. He chuckled aloud at the thought of having manufactured yet another little plot that just might prove to be most rewarding to him. What was even *more* amusing was that the effort required on his part had been nothing at all. Let other fools use up their finances and their strength, he mused; the cost to him was only a little scheming. *That* was always a very gratifying pleasure.

As the carriage swiftly conveyed him out of Lancashire and along the highways to London town, Caleb Crowther was bloated with his own cleverness. It might have sadly deflated him to know that even at that moment he was not heading for pleasure or gratification, but was hurtling headlong towards catastrophe.

'It's too late, sir . . . we closed the doors at two o'clock this morning.' The young man's spotted face pushed itself closer to the small grille in the door. What he had first seen on looking out was a man too intoxicated for his own good, so intoxicated in fact, that it would be inadvisable to allow him into even this club, which was notorious for its inebriated membership. What he saw on closer inspection was a drunk who was well dressed and 'possessed of an air of authority'. He thought it wise to address the toff with more caution – after all, a body could never tell *who* were knocking on these doors! It could be royalty, millionaires from America, or even the law in disguise. 'I'm afraid I'm not allowed to let you in, sir . . . it could cost our licence if we opened these here doors after two in the morning.'

'Damn and bugger your licence, man!' Caleb Crowther rapped his cane into the grille, causing the poor fellow to snatch away his face for fear of losing an eye. '*Open* these doors, I tell you!' There then followed a loud and abusive exchange, which in turn alerted the proprietor of the establishment, who came rushing to the door and at once pushed his well-fed face to the door, instructing the offender to 'clear off . . . or I'll call the law.'

'Oh, you will, will you?' demanded Caleb Crowther, whilst swaying in his boots. 'You'll call the law . . . *to see off the law!*' He began laughing uproariously and clattering his cane up and down the door panels, until the sounds echoed in the dark early hours like an approaching army.

'Good lord! . . . It's *Justice Crowther*.' The proprietor now recognized the great bulky figure who, in his time, had spent many a long night and many a handsome fortune in these very same premises. 'Open the door, you fool,' he ordered the flustered fellow who was cringing behind him. 'Get this bloody door open this instant! Have you any idea who our guest is? . . . Well, I'll tell you . . . it's none other than the eminent Justice Crowther!' The door was quietly swung open and the dead weight of Caleb Crowther fell into the proprietor's arms. 'I might tell you also that this distinguished figure of the law was a regular client beneath this roof some years ago.' He also recalled that this same uncouth and spiteful character had caused them a deal of trouble on occasions, even scarring one of the girls when she had displeased him. That same girl was still employed here, though she was an embittered woman of more mature years, who had never been the same since her looks were so cruelly spoiled. She was not much in demand afterwards, and had been glad to accept an additional position in the kitchens. It crossed the proprietor's mind to keep these two well and truly apart. Yes indeed, the

Justice was a man who brought trouble with him. But he also brought enough guineas in his waistcoat pocket to compensate for such a curse. And as the proprietor's only concern was that these guineas should be suitably and properly transferred from the pocket of the Justice to his own, then a body must allow for a small upset now and then.

'I fancy one of your harlots! . . . No rubbish, mind!' Caleb Crowther steadied himself between the two men, addressing the fat, balding proprietor who was short enough to be looked down on. 'I prefer a whore with a bit of quality . . . I'm not after catching the pox, neither!' he warned.

'Now, now, Justice . . . sir . . . we don't keep that sort here, you should know that . . . you being familiar with this establishment.' The proprietor's hardened senses were surprisingly offended, both by Caleb Crowther's manner, and by the stench of stale booze that emanated from him. It was obvious that the Justice had been on a prolonged drinking spree, and had only happened here as a last resort, probably drawn by the smell of cheap perfume and the promise of willing, wide-open legs.

'A *redheaded* whore,' chuckled Caleb Crowther with an unseemly and lecherous expression, 'the redheaded ones give a bit more than their money's worth.' Somewhere in the back of his memory he recalled another redhead on another night, in this very same club. But it was long ago and the memory was no more than an irritating blur; besides which he was presently under the influence of too much whisky. 'Never mind what colour hair she has,' he ordered now, his temper darkening at his own inability to remember, 'just get on with it, man . . . like I said, make sure it's quality . . . don't want *any* old tramp!' He began giggling as the proprietor gave instructions to the clerk, 'Take the Justice up to the best room. If there's anybody in there . . . shift 'em down the corridor. Any trouble, and you fetch *me*, straight away. We want nothing but the best for the Justice.'

'Nothing but the best for the Justice,' repeated Caleb Crowther as he ambled drunkenly towards the staircase, 'nothing but the best.' He swore aloud when the clerk tripped beneath the heavy, lumbering weight that leaned against him. 'Get off, you damned fool!' he roared, staggering against a nearby table and drawing angry looks from the clients seated there. Infuriated by the manner in which the lady and gent were eyeing him up and down, he skimmed his arm across the table-top and sent every object crashing to the floor. At once there was uproar. The lady began screaming and the gent was all for launching himself at the drunken intruder; he *would* have done, were it not for the intervention of the frustrated proprietor, who calmly transferred the agitated couple to another table, where they were to be given 'anything they wanted on the house'.

As Caleb Crowther was discreetly ushered upstairs, the proprietor was made to ask himself whether the 'distinguished' client was worth all the trouble he had brought with him, yet again! Still, he consoled himself with the belief that, before the Justice finally left these premises, he would likely have paid handsomely by way of compensation. If his memory served him right, Justice Caleb Crowther was not only a big man, but a big sinner, and a big spender. After all, when it came right down to it, nothing else mattered but the size of a client's wallet. And they didn't come much bigger than this client's! Let him have his display of bad temper. The proprietor had seen many such displays but, as a rule, they were short-lived and made no lasting damage, at least not so far as the proprietor himself was concerned.

In the few hectic moments when Caleb Crowther had made his presence known, he had provoked both anger and amusement amongst the gathered clientele, who saw this great arrogant drunkard as something to be either spat at, or laughed at, but in any event soon forgotten.

There were two observers in particular, however, who had been deeply shaken by the sight of Caleb Crowther: one being filled with alarm, and the other shot through with a terrible loathing of him. From a safe distance, the two watched as Caleb Crowther was led away, swearing one minute and laughing the next.

The woman was tall and slim, wearing a crimson gown and black feather boa. In her late thirties she was still an attractive figure, her striking countenance marred only by the angry, jagged scar that ran down one side of her face. The scar was a legacy from over twenty years ago, inflicted on her in this very establishment, by the then much younger, but equally obnoxious, Caleb Crowther. Then, as now, the redhead had been employed in the capacity as 'hostess' to the many pursuers of pleasure who frequented this seedy London club. She had been young and tender when Caleb Crowther had disfigured her in one of his uncontrollable rages. At the time she had been highly desirable and extremely popular with the clients. Ever since that night her popularity had plummeted. Now she was called on only as a last resort, to serve those who were either half-blind, short of money or too drunk to know or care what they were paying for.

The proprietor had kept the redhead on, but not altogether out of the goodness of his heart. It was his business to cater for every kind of client, providing that client had enough money. There were a number of these more undesirables whom his other girls refused to 'serve'. The redhead, however, had no such choice; *Caleb Crowther had seen to that.* No other club would employ her, and she knew no other way of earning a living. Girls such as her often ended up on the streets and from there there was no place else to go but down.

The redhead survived, being used by the worst dregs in society, and filling her time in between by working in the club's kitchen. Life was hard, and degrading. Over the years she had grown more bitter, eaten up by her hatred of the man who had so drastically altered her life. She had always promised herself that one day her chance to settle the score would show itself. When that happened, she vowed to be ready. *She was ready now.* At the sight of Caleb Crowther, drunk, floundering and ravaged by the years, her mind was in a fever, planning the revenge for which she had waited so very long! For the moment, the redhead was not quite certain what form that revenge would take. But of one thing she was sure: that man, that monster who had scarred her, would not see the dawn without her having repaid him in full.

'Do you know him?' The young man kept his arm round the redhead. He would have preferred a much younger and prettier whore, but on this night she was all he could afford and besides, when they were abed with the lights out, it wasn't her face that interested him.

'I *did* know him . . . a long time ago,' she replied thoughtfully, forcing a smile and taking him slowly across the room. 'Let's not talk about him, eh? . . .

You're here for a good time, aren't you?' She tousled his hair and winked at his merry brown eyes which were suddenly troubled.

The redhead could not have known how the unexpected appearance of Caleb Crowther had also brought back fearful memories to her young colleague. Memories of being captured by the law one dark night when he was not yet a man. Memories that made him tremble when he recalled the Justice in charge that night; the same Justice whom he had just clapped eyes on and who, though more aged and sodden with booze, was every bit as formidable as he had been those many years before.

'Come on, let's see you get your "good time", darling,' the redhead urged. She wanted this one over quickly; after which she would be free to retire to her own bed. She needed to be alone; there were things to be sorted, things to be done. She grew excited at the prospect of revenge.

The young man followed. But the urge to gratify his ardour had diminished the moment Caleb Crowther had appeared, bringing back those unpleasant and unwelcome memories. Because with the memories had come the image of a small, ragged figure: a girl with eyes as black as coal, and a heart of gold. A girl he had saved from Justice Caleb Crowther's clutches, and whom he had grown to love, in a way he could love no other.

Suddenly Jack was swamped with guilt. A guilt that tore at him like so many claws. What kind of man was he, he asked himself, to treat Molly in the shabby way he had done, ever since the day he had taken her virginity? In all that time he had not been a proper provider; nor had he shown himself to be a good father. He recalled the last occasion when he had deserted Molly, and his shame was like a weight inside him. How could he have done such a thing, when only hours before she had given birth to his son? But then he reminded himself that the boy was a cripple. *A cripple!* He could not come to terms with anything so grotesque. He was too shocked by it. Too repulsed. Suddenly, his guilt and shame were smothered by the spiral of horror that rose up in him. He wanted *nothing* to do with that incomplete being. He could never belong to it; never truly acknowledge it. So, he had done right to leave, and it was likely that he would never go back. But what of Molly? Molly, whose strong black eyes had the power to melt him, what of her? How in God's name would she cope? His sorry heart was squeezed inside him at the thought of how Molly seemed born to suffer. Softly, the guilt began creeping back. *No!* He mustn't let it. It was no good, because he would never change, however much he adored her. He was a loner; a man born to wander.

As the redhead urged him onwards, turning to the small, cheaper rooms on the ground floor, Jack wrapped his arm round her, laughingly squeezing her narrow waist. 'Mind you cheer me up, sweetheart,' he told her, ''cause I'm feelin' a bit miserable, d'you see?' He quickened his step, propelling her along with him. He had not forgotten that the Justice was upstairs and, drunk or sober, he was a powerful enemy. Jack believed it was in his own interest to leave that place as soon as he could. Oh, but not before he'd tasted the delights of this here redhead. Not before then!

In the darkest hours before the dawn, the redhead saw Jack from the premises. 'Take care o' yourself, darling,' he told her merrily. 'Keep yourself warm for the next time I'm feeling lonely.'

'Any time,' she replied with a suggestive wink, 'any time at all.' When the door was closed and bolted, she leaned against it for a moment, all manner of schemes running through her mind. The night was almost gone, and soon the various clients would begin to creep away under cover of darkness, to scurry home before the daylight fell on them. The Justice would be among them.

Stealthily the redhead made her way towards the kitchen. Once there, she paused for a while, gathering her thoughts. Uppermost in her mind was her intention to make the Justice pay for what he had done to her.

As she stood there in the vast, eerily silent room, its darkness penetrated only by the soft glow from the oil lamp she carried, it came to the redhead that she must demand payment *in full* from the Justice. SHE MUST KILL HIM! It was the only way. Having mulled over the alternatives – including blinding or crippling him – she always returned to the obvious. But she had no intention of swinging for the deed. Not her. Because no man was worth that. Not even scum like the Justice. So she must be very careful.

Quickly, the redhead crossed the kitchen, going silently towards the big, dark-wood dresser, where the longest, sharpest knives were kept. Here she positioned the lamp on top of the dresser, so that its light shone directly into the drawer. Taking malicious pleasure in the choosing of the instrument, she spent a moment or two picking up the knives one by one and turning each one over in her hand, before deciding on a long, slender, meat-boning tool. The feel of it seemed right to her, and she was satisfied that, when it entered his heart, the Justice would have no time to struggle.

A wicked smile lifted her scarred features as she began her way upstairs. It had occurred to her that, if he had spent himself well in his night of debauchery, the Justice should, by now, be in a deep slumber, as would the whore who had been unfortunate enough to bear his weight on top of her. She would not disturb either of them, so quick and silent would she be. Better still if the Justice had sent the whore away when he had finished with her, she thought.

The redhead knew well enough which room the proprietor would have allocated to such a 'distinguished' client as the Justice. The best room was situated at the end of the long corridor. Tiptoeing on bare feet she went quickly there, pausing outside the door, her courage fast deserting her. She had never been more afraid! But *what* was that? Someone crying out? A muffled, frightened sound, like someone was choking!

'Get a hold of yourself, girl,' the redhead murmured. 'Do what you've come here to do . . . then show a clean pair of heels before some nosey bugger claps eyes on you!' She would have turned the door handle there and then, but her feet seemed fixed to the spot. *She couldn't do it!* Not kill somebody in cold blood. Disheartened, she turned away. But then she raised her hand to run the tip of her finger along the scar that had drawn itself deep into her cheekbone. *He had done that!* Oh, but murder? Could she really *murder*? With her luck, she would be bloody sure to be hanged for it, she argued with herself. Yet she wanted him to suffer, like she had suffered. Slicing his face would have given her great satisfaction, but even that could never be enough to compensate. Suddenly some slight noise drew her attention. What was that? There . . . there it was again. A muffled sound, and a whole flurry of noises, as though in a struggle, 'or passion-starved bodies going at each other like there were no bleedin' tomorrow!' she whispered, making a small snigger.

The noises were coming from that room! The room where, the redhead was convinced, lay the Justice and his whore. Intrigued, she bent her ear to the door and, on hearing the sound she had first recognized as a 'muffled, choking sound', she suddenly stiffened with alarm. It *was* coming from inside. But it weren't no sound made by pleasure . . . more like the sound of a body having the life choked out of it! No, no. She was letting her imagination run away with her. It were all that fever in her mind, and the obsession with getting her own revenge on the beast in that room. A terrible sensation of fear took hold of her. The sounds had stopped. All was silent from within. But it was a strange, uneasy silence that put the fear of God into her. Yet there was something else it put into her. Curiosity. She had to see for herself what was going on in there.

Slowly, and with trembling fingers, the redhead tried the door handle. It could well be locked from the inside, she thought, but that was not always the case. Locking a door bespoke shame, and many of the clients who frequented a place such as this were without shame.

The door handle moved easily beneath her touch. Trembling softly and with bated breath, she inched the door open, until, in a moment that seemed like a lifetime, she could see right into the room. And what she saw there stopped her fast in her tracks, her mouth wide open and her eyes narrowed into thin dark slits that seemed to want to shut out the scene before them.

It was the Justice right enough, even more repulsive in his nakedness. The whore was with him, a slim, dark-haired thing with white thighs and crimson lipstick besmirching her face. But her face was stark white and her naked body was awkwardly spread-eagled over the edge of the four-poster bed, her legs stretched wide apart and there, lying between them, was the Justice. The two of them might have been ecstatic in the throes of lovemaking – were it not for three things which were immediately obvious. The room was in a shocking shambles, as though someone in a terrible fury had vented all their rage on it; there was not a single item that hadn't been broken, torn, or split asunder. The whore was too still, too limp. The Justice was raised above her, staring down in horror, his two hands still wrapped about her throat. Now, as he turned to see who had entered the room, he began whimpering like a baby.

'Christ Almighty! . . . *What have you done?*' The redhead's voice was hushed with shock. Coming quickly into the room, she instinctively let the knife fall to the carpet and dropping the lamp on to the dresser, she rushed to the bed, viciously pushing aside the mound of blubber that was shaking with terror. '*You bastard!* . . . You've done it this time!' Even as she spoke, she saw that it really *was* a night for revenge after all!

'She's not dead, is she? . . . She *can't* be dead!' Caleb Crowther still had the dulling effects of booze on him as he began frantically to pull on his clothes, all the while stumbling and crying. 'We had an argument . . . nothing really. She teased me . . . poked fun at me. Oh, but she can't be dead. Not *dead!*'

'Shut up, you fool!' The redhead put her finger and thumb to the whore's neck, feeling for any sign of life.

She had seen nakedness many times, and she had witnessed most things that were both shameful and corrupt. But she had never encountered murder before. It was not pleasant, nor was there any dignity in it. Part of her wanted to scream at the top of her voice and alert the whole house. Yet a deeper instinct made her hesitate. Suddenly it was there. A pulse beneath her fingers . . . hardly noticeable, but there all the same. 'My God!' she exclaimed, the cry of gratitude already rising in her throat. But in the same breath, she stopped herself from declaring that the whore was still alive. Instead, she twisted her face into an expression of disgust and loathing. 'You've killed her! *Murdered* her.' She deliberately began to raise her voice, but not so high that it would go beyond that room.

'I'll pay you! *Anything!*' Caleb Crowther was beside himself with fear as he sidled up to her. 'Keep quiet about this . . . we'll get rid of her. Name your price . . . *anything, I tell you!*'

Coolly, the redhead eyed him, making him wait. Making him suffer, and secretly revelling in the sight of it. Yet she dared not linger too long, for fear the whore on the bed might start recovering. That mustn't happen. Not yet, or the sweetness of her revenge would all too soon turn sour. 'I could see you *hanged* for this,' she said in a hoarse and terrible whisper. 'There'd be no wriggling out of it . . . "Justice" or no "Justice" . . . caught red-handed at it . . . you can't deny it. Oh, I know they wouldn't take *my* word . . . a *whore's* word . . . against yours,' she sneered at the fleeting and conniving look that spread over his ungainly features. 'But you'd do well to remember that I only have to raise me voice to bring all and sundry running to see what terrible mischief you've done . . . they'd see it written in your face like the guilty fellow you are.' She chuckled to see the light of fear heighten in his eyes. 'And I dare say there'd be a judge or two come a-running . . . and happen even a constable from the streets. Oh, and what would the world say, to see an upright and legal fellow like yourself in a place like this . . . with a *dead* whore in your bed?' Her confidence had grown. 'Anything, you say? . . . You'll pay me *anything?*'

'Just name your price. Only keep your mouth shut about what you've seen here tonight!' There was a touch of arrogance in his voice, and even the suggestion of a threat.

The redhead cocked her eye at him, taunting, 'Or *what?*' she demanded. 'Or you'll shut it for me? . . . Strangle me, like you strangled this poor sod, eh?' She cast a sideways glance to where the whore's body lay. And she was alarmed to see the eyelids momentarily flutter. 'I'm no fool!' she told him now, coming forward in order to block his view of the whore. 'The minute you've gone, matey, I intend to write out a detailed story of what took place here, in this room. Oh, I *can* write, sweetie! I ain't the complete fool you take me for. Then I shall put that story in a place where neither you nor anybody else could find it, unless I was to suddenly disappear, o'course! Try double-crossing me, matey,' she warned, her loathing of him evident in her every word, 'and you'll live to regret the day!'

Caleb Crowther knew that she had him at her mercy. He had been all kinds of a damned fool. He was under no illusions but that he would have to pay the price. For now at least! Later though, when he was in less of a torment and had recovered enough from the ordeal to contemplate it, there might be something he had overlooked. Some liltle thing that could alter the situation to his advantage.

For now, though, he had no option but to play along. The club was too full of prying eyes and, as this bitch had pointed out, there was a danger of betraying his compromising situation to those who were enemies of old. Enemies who would take great pleasure in seeing him charged with murder, even though their own reputation might be damaged by their presence in such an establishment. Such a one was Bartholomew Bent, a legal man of considerable influence who had once been brought under severe pressure by Caleb Crowther, and who had a particular dislike of the fellow. He was here! Caleb Crowther had seen him with his own eyes some hours ago, though he had managed to keep discreet his own presence here. 'You have my word,' he reluctantly conceded. 'What are we to do about . . . about . . .' He pointed to the bed, but was too cowardly to look at it.

'You just leave that to me,' she retorted, at the same time throwing the corner of a blanket over the 'body', yet being careful not to cover the face. 'Take your shoes up!' she told him. 'I'll see you off the premises. *Hurry! Hurry, you fool!*' She waited impatiently until he had flung his cape over his arm and gathered up his cravat, white silk scarf, and the black polished shoes that were stuffed with socks and suspenders.

Quietly opening the door, the redhead gestured for him to go before her, out into the corridor. As he did so, she caught sight of a fat wallet protruding from his back trouser pocket. The wallet itself was of secondary importance to her, as were the notes within, although she could certainly make good use of them. But what prompted her to snatch it away were the gold initials etched into it: his initials. A vital piece of evidence as far as she was concerned. And, if that in itself wasn't enough, she plucked out the contents of one of his shoes; it had struck her as being amusing that many a gent took pride in displaying his initials on the fastener of his sock suspenders. A quick glance told her that this 'gent' was no different .

'Damn your eyes. Give them back!' Her swift and unexpected move had taken him by surprise.

'Ssh! . . . We don't want to wake the others now, do we, eh?' she goaded maliciously. The two objects would serve her better than they would serve him, she thought. Where he might claim that his wallet had been stolen in some public place, he could hardly give the same explanation for how one of his *sock suspenders* came to be missing: 'Now you go on, m'lud,' she sniggered, 'softly to the front door, and away to your fancy home . . . before your "nanny" comes a-looking for you.' When he glowered at her, she suddenly changed mood, her expression becoming dark and nasty. '*Get out of my sight, Justice* . . . or I might change my mind and rouse the whole household after all!'

'All right, all right . . . you give me little choice,' he whispered gruffly, his piercing, hate-filled glare devouring her every feature.

There was such naked animosity in his eyes that for an uncomfortable moment the redhead secretly questioned the wisdom of what she was doing, for here was a powerful, mean man, who could also be a powerful and destructive enemy. Yet even that fear of future retribution was not enough to dissuade her from her ambitious scheme. Not only had she stumbled upon the opportunity for revenge, but by some quirk of fortune – or *mis*fortune – she had also been afforded the opportunity to make her miserable life more comfortable. The thought was unbearably pleasant, even thrilling, as she followed the nervous, sweating figure down the stairs and onward, through the foyer, where the desk clerk was fast asleep.

Before closing the front door on him, the redhead held the lamp high on Caleb Crowther's face. 'Don't forget . . . *you've done murder here this night!*' She smiled as he seemed to cringe beneath her words. 'Oh, but don't you worry . . . I'll take care of everything. And I'll be in touch. Oh, yes . . . I'll certainly be in touch. *You can depend on it!*'

As Caleb Crowther slunk into the night, the woman's words kept coming back to haunt him. '*You've done murder here this night!*' What on earth had driven him to such dreadful extremes? The night was cold, but the sweat ran down his face as he questioned whether that redhead could 'take care of everything'. *But she must!* She must or he was lost.

Hailing a carriage, he climbed in and hid in the darkest corner. There must be no newspapers allowed into Breckleton House. He couldn't bear to think of reports describing the discovery of a body. At this minute, with his every limb shaking uncontrollably, he could only think of his own precious skin.

Part Two

1887

Life is a thread;
So easily broken.
                    J.C.

Chapter Eight

'What d'you mean . . . "she's gone"?' Mick Darcy's face fell with disappointment. '*Where's* she gone? When will she be back?'

His heart sank inside him as the young man slowly and solemnly shook his curly head. 'I'm sorry, Darcy, but Molly *won't* be coming back . . . "not to these parts ever agin" was what she told me mam.' Joey Watson's tone softened when he saw what a devastating effect his words were having on the bargee. 'Didn't she let you know? I were given to understand that you an' Molly had a, well . . . a particular understanding?'

'No.' Mick smiled, but it was a sad and sorry expression. 'Not that *I* wouldn't have welcomed a closer understanding between us. But if you knew Molly at all, you must know how devoted she is to that husband of hers.' He suddenly realized that he was openly discussing Molly's private affairs and he was shamed. 'Me and Molly had *no* such understanding, young man. It was my privilege to be a good friend to her, that's all . . . as I know your mother, Tilly, was.' He paused, allowing his statement to sink in. 'So, you've no idea *where* Molly might have gone?'

'None at all, and if me mam were in, she'd tell you the very same . . . Molly was cagey about where she was headed.' He rubbed his thumb along the dark fuzzy stubble on his chin, at the same time scrutinizing the bargee. He knew well enough how this broad, handsome fellow idolized Molly from next door because hadn't his mam said time and again, 'that Mick Darcy thinks the world o' Molly . . . tek her and the three kids at the drop of a hat he would, and he's a fine catch by any woman's standards. By! If that Molly had any sense at all, she'd bar the bloody door agin that useless husband of hers . . . and snatch Mick Darcy's hand off with his offer! Oh, but she won't! Not while she's besotted with that waste o' timer, Jack-the-Lad. But mark my words, our Joey . . . she'll come to regret waiting for that bugger. Oh, yes, there's no doubt she'll come to regret it. Tuh! If *I* were in that gal's place, you wouldn't find me turning down a fella the likes o' Mick Darcy!'

'Taken all her belongings, has she?' Mick glanced towards the unkempt little house that had been Molly's pitiful abode.

'Well, she didn't have *much* to take, but yes, she went away pushing a cart piled up with bits o' this and that. The littlest o' the lasses were sat atop the jumble, with the cripple. The one called Sal trotted alongside her mammy, helping to push the cart.' He shook his head and pursed his lips, making a sucking sound. 'They made a sorry sight and no mistake.' He deliberately kept back one significant piece of information. It wasn't often that folks hung on his every word, and even though he felt a measure of sympathy for the bargee – who was obviously head over heels in love with Molly – he was enjoying being the centre of attention.

'Thank you for your trouble,' Mick told him now, beginning to turn away. 'If by any chance Molly *should* ...e back . . . you will tell her I was here?' When the young man nodded, he went on, 'Happen I'll wander about a bit . . . keep a look out for her. I'd hate to think she was in need, or trouble, or anything of that sort . . . what with three young 'uns looking to her.'

'Oh, I shouldn't bother yerself about any o' *that*, matey,' interrupted Tilly Watson's eldest. He thought it just the right moment to reveal his 'snippet of information'. 'Molly ain't on her own, d'yer see? Because, according to what she told me mam . . . she's given the house up fer the very good reason that her Jack's got himself a job some fifty mile away . . . and there's a *place ter live* goes with it. That's where Molly's taken herself and the brats. She's gone ter set up home with her wandering husband.' He felt pleased with himself, until he saw how the colour had drained from the bargee's face. Thinking himself a heartless bastard, he said, 'Molly seemed in good spirits when she left Dock Street, mate – happiest I've seen her in a long time. Look . . . she'll be all right now her fella's seen sense enough ter put down roots. Her and the young 'uns . . . they'll be well looked after. That's what you want, ain't it? You being a friend?'

'Oh, that's what I want, right enough,' Mick was hasty to reply. 'It's what Molly would want too. Her husband and young 'uns all under the same roof, and him set up with a steady job.' He was lying. It *wasn't* what he wanted at all! If he had his way, Molly and the bairns would be under his own roof, and it would be *him* looking after them, not that vagabond Jack-the-Lad. Still and all, it was Jack who was Molly's choice and not himself. He had lost her. Her undeserving husband had won her back. For Molly's sake, he must accept that and be glad for her. But it was a hard thing. A painful thing that beat him down inside.

All this time, Mick had hoped that Molly was missing him, and that she would come to realize how much better a man he was than the useless article she had married. He had deliberately stayed away, giving her time and distance, so she might be watching when he returned. Instead of which, he had come back to find her gone from these parts 'never again' to return, if this young man's account was anything to go by. Well, he'd left Molly with a question to consider. She had given her answer, and it was clear enough to him. She kept no place in her life for Mick Darcy. He was not one to force himself on a woman. Molly had shown him the door, and he would stay out, even though his heart was broken.

But before he took his leave of this well-informed young man, there was one thing that needed to be said. In a firm and condemning voice, Mick told Tilly Watson's son, 'By the way, fella-me-lad, you'd do well to remember that the "cripple" you mentioned has a name . . . just as you have! *His name is Tom*. Don't forget that in future, will you . . . "matey"?'

'O' course not . . . the name escaped me fer the minute, that's all.' The young man had detected tne warning in Mick's voice. It was a warning he would heed, for who in his right mind would want to get on the wrong side of a bloke who was built like *this* one? Not him, and that were a fact. 'Tom, y'say? Nice, cheery little fella too.'

With a nod and a nervous smile, the young man quickly shut the door, leaving Mick Darcy to gaze longingly at the sorry little house nearby, with its partly boarded-up window and peeling paintwork, and the ᵕudged whitestoned step where Molly had spent many ᵕr bent to her knees. In his mind's eye he could see her there, scraping away with the whitestone and carefully marking the edges. She didn't have much, he thought, but she had worked hard to maintain at least a degree of dignity. Stubborn, independent and proud, she was a woman of rare breed. To his mind, the lovely Molly had only one fault: she loved the wrong man. Still and all, he reminded himself now, Jack *was* her husband, and the father of her children; while *he* was an intruder. Oh, yes, he thought the world of her and would lay down his life for her if she wanted him to. But she didn't. Nor did she love him.

He stood outside Molly's house on Dock Street, watching the door and willing her to appear. When she did not, he walked away, an unhappy figure with bowed shoulders and reluctant step. For him – without any hope of winning Molly – life had suddenly lost its meaning.

However, life must go on. There was always work to compensate a man. Now that he was back in the area, he would go to the mill on Eanam Wharf. When Marlow Tanner had taken his wife Emma on a long sea voyage after the tragic loss of their only son, he had left a good and loyal man in charge during his absence.

Mick Darcy quickened his step. That was where he was headed: to ask this 'good and loyal' man for work. Molly had gone to Jack, and, according to Tilly Watson's eldest, she was 'happiest I've seen her in a long while'. It was poor compensation for his own unhappiness. At least she had gone to Jack of her own accord and, at long last, it did seem as though she'd got her heart's desire. There was little he could do but to wish her well, and pray that the Good Lord would watch over her.

* * *

'Why can't we stay here, Mammy?' Little Sal was close to tears as she helped Molly to pile their pitiful bits and pieces on to the cart.

'Because we're going to find somewhere *better*!' Molly was at her wit's end. Since fleeing Dock Street and not even daring to confide her reasons to Tilly for fear that the Justice was closing in on her, Molly and her bairns had traipsed all over the north west, sleeping in derelict houses, rat-infested warehouses and even setting up home in a shed behind a laundry. Each time something had driven them on: either a curious constable or taunting children, and in the case of the shed at the rear of the laundry, an official who threatened to call higher authorities. The most recent abode was a condemned property in the centre of Liverpool, a good spot because the people there minded their own business.

Recently though, this block of condemned houses had begun to attract all manner of undesirables, layabouts and loud-mouthed drunks who had come to take an unhealthy interest in Molly and the young ones, particularly in little Sal, with her wide blue eyes and yellow hair. Only last night two men, the worse for drink, had come stumbling into the room which Molly had made surprisingly cosy. They made it clear to Molly that it was Sal they wanted. They offered money, promising to 'fetch the little angel back when we've done'.

Terrified, Molly had yelled and screamed at them, flinging every missile she could lay her hands to, until being the cowardly fellows they were, the two intruders took to their heels.

Molly suspected these fornicators would be back. ~h foul creatures were not easily deterred. So, weary ~rt, yet ever strong in spirit and determination where the safety of her bairns was concerned, at the first light Molly began gathering their belongings together.

Before the dawn lit up the sky on another cold January day, Molly could be seen pushing the cart along the alleys of Liverpool. When Peggy echoed little Sal's remark, 'Where we going, Mam?' Molly reassured them both. However, in her heart, she could see no comfort for any of them. She had to make plans, this much she knew; for now, her only aim was to keep her bairns safe.

With that in mind, Molly kept her eyes on the road ahead. She had no idea where it led; only that she must follow it, and hope against hope that, at the end of it, she would find her Jack.

Chapter Nine

On the fourth of March, in the year of our Lord 1887, Emma stood on the highest point in Corporation Park, thoughtfully surveying the scene below. It was a strange sort of day, with a keen breeze cutting the high ground, and the sun shining brilliantly from a spiteful, shifting sky. It was neither warm nor cold, and at half-past two in the afternoon neither light nor dark. The sharp, bitter wind was erratic, dying down in one instant and whipping up to a frenzy in the next. The sun's brilliant bright rays were piercing to the eye, but they held no warmth. There was a peculiar agitated mood about the wind, and a disturbing unpredictability about the weather in general. Emma thought it matched her own mood.

Against the drifting patchwork of grey and white clouds and surrounded by vast unbroken stretches of grassland, Emma made a lonely figure high up on the pinnacle beside the Crimean guns. She was impeccably dressed as ever: in a burgundy coat nipped in at the waist and chased with dark lace at the hem. On her feet were the daintiest black pearl-button shoes, and showing at her throat was the exquisite silken collar of her ivory-cream blouse. On her shining chestnut hair, which was loosely curled into the nape of her neck, she wore a large, soft tammy of the same striking colour as her strong grey eyes, which now were roving the streets and by-ways below, drawing in the years and reliving precious moments of long ago.

Even in her mid-forties, Emma was still an astonishingly attractive woman. She possessed a unique blend of dignity, grace and loveliness that would compliment any woman half her age. Yet she was never proud nor vain, and it was always others who acclaimed her beauty, while Emma saw nothing special or admirable about the way Nature had fashioned her. If she consciously strove to preserve any part of her character, it was that strength of spirit with which she had been blessed, and which had brought her through so many traumas in her eventful life.

So often, when life had sought to bring her to her knees, that special strength within her had helped her through. Always there for her to call on, never once had it failed to sustain her. *Until now*.

Since her return from Australia, Emma had made every effort to accept the loss of her son. But somehow she could not come to terms with it. Angry, bitter and confused, she fought against a natural grieving process. There were no tears to ease the awful pain inside her. Instead, there was only a hard core of resentment in her heart. She had built a wall of destructive emotion around her memories, which no one, not even Marlow, could penetrate.

In these past weeks, Emma had taken to frequenting Corporation Park, where she, Nelly and the boy had spent many happy hours. Always she came alone, staying sometimes the whole afternoon, when she would wander the meandering walkways, avoiding the spot where young Bill had tumbled to his death. Marlow had remarked so often how, if only Emma could bring herself to look again on that place, she might realize how final was the parting between herself and the boy she adored. But nothing would persuade her in that direction. Nor would she be drawn into any conversation regarding either the tragic incident or her own thoughts on it. Even now, after all these months, she refused to visit that corner of the churchyard where he had been laid to rest. The priest's well-intended visits to the house on Park Street had been greeted with such hostility that, at Marlow's request, he had ceased to call, entreating both Marlow and Nelly to 'do what you can to persuade Emma into the House of God where she must surely find a measure of peace'.

Emma had resisted all efforts to restore her faith in the Almighty. In her bitterness she could not forgive him; though outwardly she showed little sign of her turbulent feelings. Instead she appeared cool, reasonable to a fault, and stalwart in her support of Marlow's continued success in the transporting business. But, as Nelly had pointed out to Marlow only the other day, 'The *spark* seems to have gone out of our Emma . . . and it breaks my heart ter see how she's quietly torturing herself.'

Marlow had reassured the anxious Nelly; in truth he also was deeply concerned for Emma's state of health. She adamantly refused to see a doctor. To Marlow's heartfelt plea that Emma must 'reconsider this awful business between you and your uncle, Caleb Crowther . . . raking up so much bitterness and pain from the past with which to further torment yourself', she would only concede with great reluctance to 'delay the setting of a new date for the hearing'. Because, to Emma's mind, the very *root* of her pain was Caleb Crowther himself, and when a root was so rotten that it contaminated all it touched, then that same root must be mercilessly chopped out and destroyed.

All the same, Emma was in no great hurry to bring her despicable uncle to task, for to her way of thinking, the longer the delay, the more he would be made to suffer. Let him believe that she was having second thoughts about the charges she was bringing against him. Let him wallow in a false sense of security. The shock to his conniving heart would be all the greater when he was eventually made to answer her allegations.

After a while, when the clouds began to grow dark and threatening overhead, and a few isolated spots of rain warned of the deluge to come, Emma began her way down the steep incline towards the exit.

For the past twenty minutes and more, Nelly had been nervously pacing back and forth to the side window in the drawing-room. From there, the side gate leading out of Corporation Park was just visible, and now, when she saw the small familiar figure of Emma approaching, Nelly went rushing into the hallway to greet her, pausing only to poke her head in through the kitchen door with the instructions, 'Mrs Tanner's back. Be so good as to fetch a pot o' tea to the drawing-room. And a plate o' sandwiches . . . *proper* sandwiches, mind! We don't want none o' them silly little things as disappear with one bite!'

When Nelly's homely face had gone from the doorway, impatient glances were exchanged between the plump, round-eyed maid and the cook – who appeared a most unlikely candidate for the position of 'cook', being thin as a barge-pole and so tall that she had to bend from a great height when attending to her tasks at the big pine table. She had a gaunt, sour face and an equally sour disposition. But her culinary skills were second to none, and she had never been known to panic. Her name was Miss Warburton. Nelly disliked her intensely, and much to Emma's consternation, there was a great deal of friction between them, each one constantly looking to put the other in a bad light with the master and mistress of the house. Miss Warburton had been reduced to tears on more than one occasion, when Nelly had told her quite categorically to '*piss orf!*'

Just now there were other, more important things on Nelly's mind. 'Where've yer been all this time?' she demanded of Emma, who took off her coat and tammy, and at once had them snatched from her hands by the anxious Nelly. '*Two hours* you've been gone, yer bugger!' she chastized, hanging up Emma's outdoor clothes while still keeping a disapproving eye on her. 'I don't like yer going off on yer own fer hours at a time! . . . Wandering about in the park. Why! There could be *anybody* just waiting ter jump out at yer.' She frightened herself with such a terrible thought, 'Robbers an' murderers . . . them buggars are *everywhere.*'

'Don't exaggerate, Nelly,' Emma smiled at the wide-eyed face that glared at her so disapprovingly. 'I'm perfectly safe. You know as well as I do that there are *no* "robbers and murderers" in Corporation Park.'

'I don't know any such thing, my gal,' Nelly declared firmly, 'and neither do *you.*' She touched Emma lightly on the arm. 'There's tea an' sandwiches on their way,' she said, 'let's you an' me set in the drawing-room, eh?' She swung away, swerving towards the kitchen door where she screeched, 'Ain't that tray ready yet, Miss Warburton? *Be so kind as to get a move on!*' When

Emma cautioned her, she turned round and, squeezing her head down into her neck, she made a wicked and mischievous face. 'It's allus best ter keep the buggers on their toes,' she said in a loud whisper. ''*Er* type especially needs ter be reminded who's boss!'

When, some ten minutes later, Emma and Nelly were seated in the pleasant comfort of the drawing-room, with the tray duly placed on the table between them and the door closed against intrusion, Nelly picked up on the argument of Emma wandering Corporation Park alone. 'Why ever don't yer let me come with yer, darlin'?' she asked in between long, noisy gulps of her tea. 'Yer really *shouldn't* be going about them narrow little walkways all on yer own.'

Emma considered Nelly's argument for a while, before explaining in a firm and serious voice how she needed to be on her own occasionally, and how these frequent walks through the park were as good as a tonic to her. Although she dearly valued Nelly's companionship, there were times when she craved solitude and peace. 'Times when I can quietly contemplate and assess the way of things,' she said to the anxious Nelly.

Nelly put down her cup, at the same time closely regarding Emma. 'Did you go to the cliff face, Emma gal?' It was a delicate and daring question, but one she needed to ask.

At once, Emma was on the defensive, deliberately ignoring Nelly's pointed question. 'I think we're in for a storm,' she said, replacing her own cup on the table and getting to her feet. 'I'm going to my room for a while, Nelly. Marlow should be home within the hour . . . we can talk then, if you like?' She despised herself for walking out on Nelly's company. But she despised even more the prospect of being 'interrogated' by a persistent Nelly, who meant well, but whose questions were painful to Emma.

'Go on then, darlin' . . . you go and put yer head down fer a while.' Nelly realized she had frightened Emma away, and she was angry with herself. 'I might even do the same meself,' she chuckled.

'Bless you, Nelly . . . you're a good friend.' Emma reached out to take Nelly's hand in her own. There were so many things she wanted to say. So much that she needed to confide to this dear woman who had been like a sister to her. Oh, they had often talked for hours, of the past and their many adventures. They reminisced about years ago and the people who had crossed their eventful lives. She and Nelly had laughed and cried together; they had despaired and hoped together. There had *never* been anything between them that was awkward, or secret, or forbidden. Until now.

Nelly clung to Emma's small, slim fingers. She had seen the pain in her beloved Emma's eyes and she hated this terrible thing that was splitting them asunder. Like Marlow, she feared for Emma's peace of heart. Now, as she looked up with bright, tearful eyes she asked softly, 'Will yer not talk ter me, darlin'? . . . Stay and talk ter me, eh?'

'Oh, Nelly, Nelly!' Emma gazed down at the round brown eyes that were now encased in soft, wrinkly folds of flesh. She remembered them when they were young and vivacious, rudely alive with mischief and following everything that wore a pair of trousers; always shining with that very special love that had grown between her and Emma over the years.

Looking at her now, Emma realized with a rush of

compassion that little had changed with regard to the incorrigible Nelly. The eyes still held a measure of mischief, and few handsome men were safe in her company. There was no denying the affection with which she gazed on Emma now. No, Emma thought warmly, Nelly had not changed, she probably never would. Not even the ravages of time would change her except to broaden the already dumpy figure, or to couch those bright, honest eyes in fleshy cushions. Nelly was just Nelly. And you either loved or loathed her. Emma *loved* her.

'Stay with me, Emma gal,' Nelly pleaded now, 'and I promise not to chastize you no more.' In truth, although she didn't come right out and say it, she was pledging not to question Emma about things that were painful. They both knew what she was really promising. For Emma, it was enough. Sighing, but with a smile that warmed Nelly's heart, Emma sat down again. 'Oh, there's a good 'un!' Nelly cried. 'You can tell me again about your trip to Australia . . . about how that cousin of yours turned up unexpected . . . that dreadful Martha! Oh, and d'yer *really* believe as how her husband, Silas, has struck up a close relationship with Rita Hughes? By! I'll bet that mard arse Martha didn't like her nose being put out of joint, did she, eh? Oh, but she's only herself to blame . . . leaving a reg'lar fella like Silas on his own out there. Go on,' she urged, 'tell me *everything*. Don't leave nothing out.'

'I must have told you at least *four* times,' Emma protested. But then, seeing that Nelly was perched on the edge of her seat, all agog with excitement, she sighed and smiled, and outlined the highlights of her long journey yet again: the seemingly never-ending but peaceful sea voyage; the joy of having Marlow all to herself when business was so far away that it could not part them; the strange feelings of both excitement and regret at setting foot on those same shores where she and Nelly had been delivered as prisoners too many years before.

'Y'know, Emma gal . . . I've made me mind up good an' proper . . .' Nelly had grown thoughtful all the while Emma was describing how 'it was strangely unsettling to be walking the streets of Fremantle . . . seeing the prison where we were kept and the house where we later enjoyed our freedom; little has changed, although the convict system will shortly be a thing of history'. Now, Nelly was made to cry out, '*I never ever want to go back there* . . . wild horses wouldn't drag me, I'm telling yer!' Nelly was adamant, shaking her head and looking altogether terrified at the very idea.

'We did have awful experiences there, didn't we, Nelly?' conceded Emma. 'And I can understand why you would not want to go back. But we came out of it all very well, you can't deny that. And Australia is very beautiful.'

'Oh, I ain't denying *that*, gal. But they say Paradise is beautiful too, don't they? And I ain't ready to go there *neither*!' Nelly's face was deadly serious and to Emma, who understood her friend's horror of what she had endured, it was obvious that she would rather die than ever again leave the shores of her motherland. 'But go on, go on, darlin',' Nelly urged now, 'what about this here business between Silas and Rita Hughes . . . her that manages the trading post? . . . Y'say they fancy each other, eh? And that the sour-faced Martha walked right in on it, eh? Oho! . . . I'll bet *that* shook the bugger up, what!' Nelly was positively beside herself with excitement at the thought.

Emma couldn't help but laugh. 'Really, Nelly, you are incorrigible!' she chastized. 'That was *not* how I told the tale . . . well, not exactly,' she had to admit. 'What I said was soon after our arrival in Fremantle, both Marlow and I noticed how dependent Rita Hughes was on Silas . . . and how he seemed always unusually attentive to her. It was very clear to me that the two of them had grown close, enjoying each other's company.'

'Right! That's what I said . . . They were sweet on each other. Then what? Martha caught them at it?'

'Oh, Nelly, you do have a blunt way with words, and you mustn't let your imagination run riot,' Emma told her firmly. 'It was all very unfortunate. Silas planned a lovely farewell evening in Marlow's and my honour . . . a dinner dance for about a dozen people or so. Now, I'm not quite sure what actually took place, but it seems Martha had not informed Silas she was on her way to Australia. No one knew that she had arrived that very evening. It was quite a shock, I can tell you, when she appeared . . . then disappeared in search of Silas. Apparently, she found him out on the back porch . . . with Rita.'

'Kissing and cuddling, eh?'

'Yes, Nelly . . . "kissing and cuddling".'

'Oho! Then all hell was let loose, eh?' Nelly sat, wide-eyed and thrilled, while Emma described how there had been a shrill cry and the sound of an argument coming from the porch. Then, after a few seconds, Martha had flounced into the room and out of the front door, her face a bright red study in rage and embarrassment. Soon after, Silas had followed her, and Rita Hughes made her excuses to leave. Before she and Marlow had boarded their ship the next day, Silas had confided that he had been deeply attracted to Rita, and now he was caught in the dilemma of having divided affections. He was genuinely very fond of Rita – a hard-working and unusually loyal woman who had been lonely most of her adult life – but now that Martha had answered his more fervent plea, to join him in Australia, he was a man torn in two.

'Poor sod,' Nelly exclaimed, but with a cheeky twinkle in her brown eyes.

'He's a good man, Nelly, you know that. I can't help but feel for him.'

'He is a good man,' Nelly readily agreed, 'too bloody good fer a miserable sorry thing the likes o' Martha Crowther. Rita Hughes is worth *ten* o' that one! If Silas Trent had any sense at all he'd give that troublesome woman her marching orders and set up home with Rita. That's what *I* say!' Not being able to remain in serious mood for too long at a time, Nelly began chuckling, 'Oh, but I would a' loved ter see that Martha's face when she caught 'em at it.'

'We don't really know *what* they were "at" on the porch, Nelly, and like I said, it doesn't pay to let your imagination run away with you.' Emma picked at one of the sandwiches, but soon replaced it on to the plate, her appetite not being what it was. 'But what about *you*, Nelly . . . we've had no real opportunity to talk since I've been back. How did you cope, being left here in charge? Did you enjoy the experience?' Emma realized with a pang of guilt that it was *her* fault and not Nelly's that they had found no opportunity to talk. In truth, she had actually avoided discussions of any kind since her first day back. She had been too preoccupied with thoughts of her son, and when the weather permitted, she had spent most of her time wandering about Corporation Park and losing herself in memories.

''Course I enjoyed it; did a good job too, I did . . . kept that bloody cook in order an' all.' Nelly went on in great detail about how things had 'run very smoothly', assuring Emma that she need never fear about leaving her in charge ever again. But the one matter she did not discuss was that of Molly having worked here for a while. Nelly had already confided the whole story to Marlow, who had confirmed Nelly's belief that it was better not to trouble Emma with the details of that particular episode, on account of Emma's present unreceptive mood, together with the fact that there was a child involved. To know that Molly's young daughter had played and laughed in this house and had used the very picture books that belonged to her son might have proved to be too painful a reminder for Emma. It was therefore decided *not* to acquaint Emma with the facts at all. Indeed, Nelly had been surprised at how intrigued and upset *Marlow* had been on learning about the dark-eyed Molly and her daughter, Sal, though he made little actual comment on the two.

'But just 'cause I looked after things so well in yer absence, don't go thinking yer can swan off an' leave me agin, my gal,' Nelly rebuked Emma with a stern wag of her finger, ''cause *next time* I'm coming with yer . . . so long as it ain't to the other side o' the world.'

'You needn't worry, Nelly,' Emma suddenly felt very weary, 'I have no plans for travelling anywhere.'

'That's all right then.' Nelly settled back in her chair to sip leisurely at her tea. She felt pleased with herself at having cajoled the reluctant Emma into a long conversation. All the same though, she would have liked to tell

Emma about Molly and the child. Yet she dared not; her instincts warned her that Marlow was right. Young Bill was too fresh in Emma's heart for her to accept that a strange child had been enjoying his things. Nelly dared not take a chance in telling her. Perhaps later, sometime in the not-too-distant future.

'I think I will go to my room for a while, Nelly . . . until Marlow comes home.'

'Aye, well . . . yer do look worn out. It's all that trudging about in the park. I've telled yer afore, my gal . . . *we none of us* ain't as young as we were!' She watched as Emma began her way across the room. Suddenly she was on her feet, calling her back. 'You'd best tek this bit o' jewellery up with yer,' she told Emma, who paused by the door at Nelly's words and was looking at her in a curious way: Emma was never a lover of jewellery, and she was intrigued by Nelly's remark. 'Yer must 'ave dropped it afore yer left fer Australia, gal,' Nelly said, coming towards Emma with out-stretched palm that displayed a tiny gold clasp which she had retrieved from the drawer. 'Yer lucky it weren't lost, my gal . . . or trod on. I found it on the carpet soon after you'd gone, so I picked it up and kept it safe in the sideboard . . . though I can't see how yer could 'ave worn the necklace that it come from . . . not with its clasp missing.' She placed the clasp into Emma's hand. 'D'yer know, gal, I've scratched me brain ter think which piece o' jewellery it came from. Yer don't have that much, do yer? And I swear *I* can't recall seeing it afore. But it must be yours, Emma, gal . . . 'cause it ain't *mine*. And I'm sure it can't belong ter none o' the staff, 'cause by the look o' the markings on it, that there clasp is worth a tidy sum.'

Nelly's voice ranted on. But Emma had stopped listening. At first, when Nelly had put the tiny clasp into her hand, Emma's instinct had been to give it back, saying that it was definitely not hers. Now, as she turned it over and over in the palm of her hand, *her blood ran cold*. The feel of the gold clasp against her skin was like a series of shocks going through her. She was confused and trembling, afraid and hopeful all at once. THE CLASP WAS HERS.

On close examination of it, Emma soon realized that it belonged to the tiny timepiece that her father had entrusted to her many years ago, just before he passed on. Her feverish thoughts sped back over the years. She recalled the twilight hours when she and Nelly were hurriedly bundled into the wagon which would take them to the convict ship. In her mind's eye, she could see it all. The same sensations that she suffered then rampaged through her now: terror, pain and anger. She could almost *feel* the prison warder dragging her towards the waiting wagon, merciless in his duty, even though she was already in the throes of giving birth. She remembered how Nelly had pleaded on her behalf, and how, in that cold, darkened alley, she had given birth to a most beautiful baby girl, whose dark eyes haunted her still.

It was only later that Emma had realized how she must have lost her precious timepiece in that same alley. For years she had bitterly blamed herself for losing the one thing that had meant more to her father than anything else in the whole world – and consequently was dearer to Emma than the greater fortune her father had left to her. Fortunes could be made and lost and made again, but the timepiece held so many memories and so much love that it was irreplaceable. Emma had cherished it, for it had belonged to her mother, Mary, given to her by Emma's father, Thadius, when they were young and he idolized her so. Now, by some inexplicable quirk of fate, *here in her trembling hand* was part of that same timepiece.

'Good grief, Emma darlin' . . . whatever's the matter?' Nelly had seen how shocked and white Emma's face was.

'This gold clasp . . . tell me again, *where did you find it?*' Emma's voice was soft, but strange and fearful to the listening Nelly. When she shook her head and was about to remind Emma that she had only just this minute explained how she found the gold-piece on the carpet, Emma reached out and actually shook Nelly by the arm. 'Nelly! Where *exactly* did you find it?'

'Well, like I said . . . I found the blessed thing on the carpet.' Nelly was completely taken aback by Emma's attitude. She couldn't ever remember Emma shaking her like that; not in all the years they had known each other. Not even when they were in Australia, and Nelly was constantly getting them both in trouble with the authorities. 'There . . . on the carpet . . . not far from the spot where we're standing at this minute! It were just lying there, I tell yer.' A thought suddenly occurred to Nelly, and it was decidedly unpleasant. 'Hey! You never think I *stole* the bugger, d'yer?' She was deeply hurt at the prospect of Emma believing that she had reverted to her old bad ways.

'No, no . . . I don't think that, Nelly,' Emma reassured her, 'but I can't understand . . . how this clasp came to be in this house.' Her voice trailed off as she lowered her confused gaze to the carpet; after a while she went to the nearest chair, where she sat stiffly, staring at the spot where, a moment before, she had been standing. Her forehead was creased into a deep frown, and even from a distance away, Nelly could clearly see that Emma was trembling.

'It is *yours*, ain't it, gal?' Nelly didn't know what to make of it at all. She sauntered to where Emma sat, her own face twisted into a frown as she looked down on Emma. 'Like I said . . . it ain't mine. So, does it belong ter yer, or don't it?' When Emma gently nodded in response to the direct question, Nelly was still not satisfied, insisting, 'Then if it's yourn . . . whatever's the matter? Ain't yer glad ter gerrit back? By! The way yer paled at the sight o' that gold-piece, anybody'd think you'd seen a *ghost*!'

'A ghost?' Emma repeated in a wondrous shocked voice. 'Yes, Nelly, that is what I've just seen . . . a ghost.' Suddenly, Emma was on her feet and confronting the anxious Nelly. In quiet and intimate mood, she asked Nelly to cast her mind back to the day of their transportation, to the very moment when Emma had been delivered of a girl-child and afterwards been bundled into the wagon, leaving the newborn for dead in the gutter. Nelly remembered it all, and for more reason than did Emma – for it was she who had misled Emma into believing that the infant had been stillborn, when in truth Nelly had long suspected that the child had lived.

'Go on, Emma gal,' she urged now, being caught up in Emma's growing excitement.

'You may or may not recall the delicate timepiece that I kept hidden in my boot?' When Nelly lapsed into deep thought, then vigorously shook her head, Emma went on, 'It was the only thing I had of my father's, Nelly . . .

and it was my secret. I was mortally afraid that it might be discovered and confiscated.' Emma clutched her small fist about the gold clasp and raised her eyes heavenwards. When she looked again into Nelly's puzzled face, her lovely grey eyes were swimming with tears. 'On that unforgettable day when I lost my girl-child . . . I also lost the timepiece.' She opened her hand to disclose the tiny clasp. 'This was part of it, Nelly and *I have not seen it from that day to this*.'

'*That can't be!*' Nelly gasped. 'Yer must be wrong, darling . . . somehow, yer must be wrong!'

Emma slowly shook her head, saying in hushed tones, 'I can't understand it, Nelly. How on earth has it come to be here . . . in this house . . . so many years later?' She was greatly puzzled. 'You found it on the carpet, you say . . . soon after Marlow and I left for Australia?'

'That's right.' Nelly pointed again to the very spot. 'Just there, like I said. So if it is the same as yer lost that night . . . what's it doing back here? . . . And who fetched it, that's what I can't understand. *Who* fetched it into this house?' She shook her head, telling Emma, 'Naw, gal . . . it *can't* be the same trinket. There must be hundreds like it . . . thousands, I dare say.'

'Not like this one, Nelly,' Emma told her, 'my father had the timepiece and the chain especially made for my mother. He told me himself . . . it was his own design.' She raised the clasp between her finger and thumb. 'See the shape and curl of the petals, Nelly? *It is the very same*. I would stake my life on it.' Suddenly she was entreating Nelly. 'Oh, Nelly, Nelly . . . *think hard*; how could it come to be here? Did you entertain any visitors? Did any gypsies call? . . . It is possible that some wandering vagabond found the timepiece and sold it on.

Oh, Nelly . . . I must know. I must recover it if it is humanly possible.' She was frantic. '*Think, Nelly! Who* did you bring into this house?'

'There weren't no gypsies nor vagabonds, I can tell you that . . . what! Some o' them buggers would slit yer throat fer a shilling.' Nelly was filled with confusion. 'Aw, look darling . . . I don't know *how* that there came ter be in this house, I really . . . don't.' Her voice tailed off and her heart-beat quickened. She felt the colour drain from her face. *Molly! Of course.* Molly and the lass, little Sal. But no! If Molly had come across a gold-piece like that, she would have quickly sold it! Nelly's thoughts raced ahead. But Molly was a pickpocket all the same, there was no denying that! Happen she'd raided some gentlewoman's purse and was holding on to the clasp until it might seem safe to sell it on.

'What is it, Nelly?' Emma had seen the look of astonishment creep over Nelly's face and she saw it as a sign that Nelly had remembered something, or *some-body*. Now, as Nelly glanced up, Emma saw the rush of guilt in her homely face. 'Out with it, Nelly. Who was it? WHO DID YOU BRING INTO THIS HOUSE? . . . Was it a ruffian? A thief? *Who*, Nelly? WHO?'

Nelly was beside herself. Marlow had agreed that Emma should not be told about the young woman and her child. But oh dear, dear! What to do? Nelly was made to recall how, years before, she had kept certain things from Emma; how she thought the girl-child had cried out and was plucked from the gutter by a passing vagabond. She had lived to regret keeping that informa-tion from Emma and then as the years passed, it was too late to do anything else. Now here she was, faced with *another* dilemma! Should she tell Emma about the young woman and the child who had used her son's belongings like they were her own, or should she confess to Emma only a part of what took place . . . how she had tried to help Molly – just as she believed Emma herself would have done? *What to do?* Being afraid of hurting Emma in even the smallest way, and realizing that in revealing the truth to Emma, she would be going against Marlow's sound advice, Nelly blurted out the first excuse that came into her head. 'There was a ruffian here! *And a thief too*: Justice Caleb Crowther!'

Emma was shocked. '*He* was here?'

'Came banging at the door, demanding ter see yer . . . ranting and raving he were, but I told him to sod orf out of it!' A tide of relief washed through Nelly on having given Emma enough to occupy her mind, while at the same time not having actually lied to her.

'Caleb Crowther came here?' Emma was quietly digesting this information; yet she could see no real link between her uncle, and how the clasp came to be here. 'Did he come inside the house, Nelly?' she asked.

'Tuh! . . . A likely chance! Oh, he *would* have done if I hadn't kept the bugger where he belonged . . . *on the doorstep*.' Nelly thought the danger regarding Molly and little Sal had passed. But she made the mistake of looking too pleased with herself, too relieved, and too guilty – especially when she now saw Emma observing her with curious eyes. 'I sent him packing, Emma gal,' she finished lamely, visibly squirming beneath Emma's scrutinizing gaze.

There followed an endless and uncomfortable moment, during which Emma looked directly into Nelly's reddening face, and Nelly nervously fidgeted with her podgy fingers – a sure sign that she was feeling guilty.

'You're not telling me everything, are you?' Emma asked softly. Again, the ensuing silence was awkward.

'Don't know what yer mean . . . I've just telled yer what happened.' Nelly was on the defensive, and to Emma, who knew her only too well, Nelly was displaying all the old familiar signs of guilt. Emma had lost count of the times in Australia when Nelly had committed some misdemeanour or other, and had always managed to worm her way out of it. Not *this* time though, vowed Emma, 'I shan't budge until you tell me what it is you're keeping back,' she told Nelly now. 'You *did* have somebody in this house. Look . . . all I have to do is go and ask Miss Warburton . . . or the maid. They're not blind . . . there isn't much that goes on in this house they're not aware of,' she warned, 'but I know you'd prefer me not to give your "friend" Miss Warburton the chance to gloat. Am I right?'

'Yer a bugger o' the worst order, that's what *you* are!' retorted Nelly, but she knew how stubborn Emma could be if the mood took her. Her idea of going to the servants for information though would not bear fruit, because Marlow had given instructions that they were not to admit to the woman and child being in the house.

'*Please*, Nelly.' Emma's voice was pleading. 'You can't have any idea how important it is to me that I find out how this part of my father's timepiece came to be here. If there is the slightest chance that I can recover it all, it would mean so very much to me.'

Nelly couldn't bear to see Emma so desperate. She should tell her everything and suffer the consequences, she thought. Or live to regret deceiving this darling woman for the second time. But what about Marlow's instructions? Oh, she would deal with that when the time came, she told herself. For now, Emma was asking for the truth, and she deserved nothing less.

Nelly told her everything, reminding her about the little thief who had winked at Emma on the day when they had arrived in England some years back, and how Nelly had saved her from being flung in a cell during Emma's absence. She explained how Molly had come to work at the house, and she confessed that little Sal read young Bill's picture books and spent many happy hours playing with those toys which Emma herself had bought for her beloved son. Nelly left nothing out, and at the end of it all, she felt greatly relieved and hopeful that she had done the right thing. 'I don't know how, gal, and I'm blessed if I can believe it, but it is possible that Molly might have owned that there gold-piece. There was nobody else admitted to this here room, except me, the servants . . . and Molly.' There! It was all off her chest, and she felt better for it.

There was relief in Emma's voice too. 'Thank you, Nelly,' she said, adding firmly, 'and though I know that you and Marlow meant well, you had no right to keep this from me.' Her emotions were in a turmoil. The thought of another woman's child in her home created a murmur of resentment in her. Yet there was also a warm glow and a feeling of comfort that gladdened her heart; amidst all of that was so much pain and bitterness, so much love for the boy she had lost.

Now though Emma had a purpose. It was to speak to this 'Molly'. She needed to know how the young woman had come by the clasp. And she needed to know *now*. 'Where does she live?' Emma asked, hurrying from the room.

Nelly ran after her. 'I don't know. Not the name o' the

street . . . nor even the area. She never gave none of her business away. But I do recall the child talking about a neighbour by the name o' Watson. And a fella, by the name o' Mick . . . lives on a barge down Eanam Wharf!' She was astounded to see Emma put on her overcoat and tammy. 'Where yer going, Emma gal?' she asked, at the same time grabbing her own outdoor clothes.

'Eanam Wharf. *That's* where I'm going, Nelly,' Emma replied stoutly, and it occurred to the astonished Nelly that she had not seen Emma in such a determined and purposeful mood for many a long day. 'We're going to talk to Marlow,' declared Emma now. 'He knows all the bargees out of the wharf . . . and so he surely must know the one called Mick.'

Emma spent a moment eyeing herself in the long arched mirror of the ornate hallstand, tipping her tammy this way, then that, until, having secured it with a hatpin at just the right angle, she went smartly out of the front door, with the frustrated Nelly chasing after her, shouting abuse at all and sundry as she struggled to fasten the dark cape about her shoulders. 'Cor, bugger me, gal . . . when yer make yer mind up, there ain't no stopping yer, is there, eh?' she shouted, going down the path with a curious half-running, half-skipping gait. 'Wait on, wait on. I ain't got me bleedin' breath yet!'

From the window of his office, Marlow looked down into the mill yard. He had only just finished going through the ledgers with Joe Turney, the manager. Things were looking good and business was prospering. Cotton shipments were on the up and up, and the Tanner Transporting Concern was positively flourishing. Life had been good to him in so many ways. He had worked his way up from being a bargee who struggled for a living, going cap-in-hand to such men as Caleb Crowther who once owned most of the mills along the wharf – property that, by rights, had belonged to Emma. He had been broken-hearted when he could not have Emma all those years ago, afterwards sailing the world as a deck-hand in order to find his fortune. He had not found that fortune in foreign parts though, but right here in his own backyard, doing what he knew best. In addition, he had the love of Emma. Here he was master of all he sur-veyed, while Caleb Crowther, by all accounts, was on a downward slide. Yes indeed, it was strange how fate and fortune swung its pendulum from one man to another.

There was an uneasy mood on Marlow this day: a disturbing and melancholy mood that would not let him rest. Part of it was the deep and lingering grief at the death of his boy, and part was because of something Nelly had told him.

For days now he had reflected on the news which Nelly had rightly confided in him, and which concerned the young woman and the child who had come to the house on Park Street in his and Emma's absence. When Nelly had first brought the news to him, wondering whether she ought to keep it from Emma, he had quickly instructed that Emma should not yet be told of the incident, especially as there was a child involved and Emma's grief was such that he dare not risk causing her any more pain. Once he and Nelly were agreed on that particular issue, he had seen no reason to pursue the matter any further.

But certain facets of Nelly's story had stayed with him, to tease and torment him, and now he could not put them out of his mind. Nelly had described Molly as being

223

'thin as a sparrer . . . with big black eyes and hair the colour of wet coal. The poor creature's had a hard life, I reckon . . . having ter pick pockets and forage for a living since she were growed enough ter outrun a constable.' Marlow reflected on Nelly's words, and the more he did so, the more he was made to recall other descriptions, of the waif who had been found and raised by his own sister, Sal, when he himself was forced to take to the high seas. One of the greatest and most painful regrets was discovering on his return that old Sal had passed away.

Over the ensuing months, Marlow had learned of the small girl who had seen to it that Sal had been given a proper and Christian burial. A girl who, according to various sources, was 'thin as a reed and dark in features . . . possessed of big black eyes, and a rare talent fer picking the gents' pockets'. All of Marlow's efforts to find the girl had been in vain.

Now, because of Nelly's tale regarding the one called Molly, the yearning to find that particular waif was once more raised in him. There was something else too, though he was not convinced enough to discuss it with anyone else – it had occurred to him that maybe, *just maybe*, this 'Molly' and the waif raised by his sister might be one and the same.

Marlow was not entirely satisfied though, because in this town, as in all other industrial areas, there were any number of vagabonds and pickpockets. It was sad but true. All the same, there was one other reason why Marlow had become more and more persuaded that he should go and talk to this 'Molly'. Her description tallied so closely with that of the waif's, it was true, yet more importantly, it was the name by which that young woman called her own child that intrigued him. Oh, Sal was a common enough name, to be sure. And yet. *And yet.*

Marlow's curiosity and his deep instinct determined that he would talk to the young woman. After all, what was there to lose by it? If his suspicions were wrong, then he would simply apologize and that would be an end to it. If he were right however, and this Molly *was* the child who had ensured that old Sal was not buried in a pauper's grave, then he owed her a great deal. But he must be careful, he reminded himself, because according to Nelly, the young woman had been caught picking pockets on that day when Nelly came to her rescue. She was obviously in poor straits and desperate enough to lie, cheat and steal in order to better her station. While he had every sympathy and was not averse to helping the more deserving amongst the unfortunates of this world, he had no desire to be made a fool of, nor to be misled by the quick tongue of a conniving thief, who saw him as an opportunity to be exploited. He must not rule out the possibility that the unfortunate creature whom Nelly took in was *not* the one who had been raised by old Sal, nor that, given enough information, she would not hesitate to claim otherwise, in order to pick his pocket in much the same fashion as she had picked many another.

The first thing he must do, though, was to talk again to Nelly, and see whether she knew anything at all of the young woman's upbringing. Besides which, he would need to find out where she lived, and whether Nelly would accompany him to that place. Now that he had made up his mind to talk with the young woman, and was determined to be cautious in his approach, Marlow felt easier than he had done for days.

* * *

From the mill yard below, Mick Darcy had seen the solitary and thoughtful figure of Marlow standing behind the office window and surveying all below. He thought for a moment of the troubles that might haunt a man in Marlow Tanner's position – a wealthy and successful businessman, yes, but at the same time just a man, a father who had recently lost his only son, and a husband whose wife was so stricken with grief that it was rumoured she hardly set foot outside the grand house on Park Street.

Bending his back to the stack of bales that needed loading on to his barge, Mick sighed and shook his head, thinking how, even for all the lands and fortunes that Britain was presently adding to its vast empire, he would not want to be in Marlow Tanner's shoes.

Mick Darcy would be the first to admit that he had never worked under a better man than Marlow Tanner. It occurred to him in that moment how, if the opportunity were ever to present itself, he would be quick to help his employer in any way he could, though for the life of him he could not see how such a situation would ever arise.

Thinking how he had better get a move on if he were to finish and have his load secured for the morrow. Mick concentrated his efforts and brought his thoughts back to his own heartache: the woman he adored and whom he was hardly likely ever to see again. Every night since Molly's going, he had dreamed of her. And every morning when he woke, she was the first thought in his mind. All the day long he carried her lovely image in his heart. The longing hadn't lessened with the passage of time; if anything, the pain of losing her was even sharper. Yet, for all that, Mick had to remind himself how Molly had freely made her choice between him and that waster, Jack-the-Lad. She had chosen her wayward husband and there was nothing else to be done. He had to resign himself to that fact, together with the belief that Molly had found happiness in her choice. All that remained now was for Mick to pray that her happiness was of the lasting kind.

Mick Darcy paused in his labours to glance at the carriage that now drew into the yard. He was surprised to see two women alight: one a dumpy, homely person with a quick, busy manner, and the other a more refined yet equally pleasant creature who had the kind of mature beauty that was both gentle and strong. When the grey eyes fleetingly smiled at him, Mick believed the woman to be the one and only Emma Tanner – no other woman could possibly answer the description by which he had come to recognize her. There was something admirable and especially lovely in her countenance.

As the two women made their way into the mill, Mick glanced up to where his employer had been standing a short while ago. Now he had gone from the window, and in a moment could be seen in the darker interior of the mill, his familiar figure rushing down the stairs that led from the office; a figure still tall and handsome in spite of the fact that he was no longer a young man. From where he stood, Mick heard Marlow Tanner call out Emma's name, and in such a way that betrayed both his shock and delight at seeing her here. Together, Marlow and Emma climbed the stairs, with the ever-attentive Nelly only two steps behind, and eager to add her own chatter to the conversation.

Suddenly Mick's attention was drawn by the comment

of a mill labourer, who had been transporting the bales
to the mouth of the warehouse. 'Well, I'll be buggered,
mate. It ain't often yer see *Emma* Tanner down here.
Must be some'at important, I'll be bound. Did you see
the look on 'er face, eh? Like as not, that bloody uncle of
hers has been up to his mischief again. By! He's a bad
'un, if ever there were.' He tipped his flat cap back and
wiped the sweat from his eyes, glancing again to where
Emma had disappeared into the office with Marlow. 'I'll
tell you what, mate . . . I wouldn't mind being a fly on
the wall o' that there office. Oh, aye! . . . It's some'at
urgent that's fetched Mrs Tanner down ter these quarters . . . some'at terrible important, if it couldn't wait till
her husband got home!'

In spite of himself, Mick's curiosity was also aroused.
The fellow was right. It *had* to be something of great
urgency that brought Emma Tanner to the wharf. He
hoped it wasn't bad news.

Mick's curiosity was heightened when, much to his
astonishment, he was quickly summoned to the office.
As he made his way upstairs, how much *more* astonished
Mick would have been to learn that the 'terribly important' matter to be discussed was none other than his own,
precious Molly!

Chapter Ten

Molly scanned the faces at the table, just as she had done night after night, week after week, hoping to catch a glimpse of Jack. But he was not there. He was never there. Now she had begun to despair of ever seeing him again. She felt weary and heavy of heart, not certain what she should do next, or where she should search.

Since coming to Liverpool and taking the waitress job in a dockland café, Molly had worked like a slave; but she didn't mind the work, because she considered herself fortunate to have found an employer who had given her and the children an outhouse which Molly had made into a little makeshift home for the four of them. All the same, life was far from comfortable. The outhouse was crammed with piles of books, tools and crates at one end, and the wind whistled in through the many chinks in the wooden walls. At night, the mice could be heard scampering over the flour sacks, and all in all, there was little privacy to be had.

Her employer's self-righteous and interfering wife constantly harped on about 'your eldest daughter should be learning the Bible and how to sew . . . not gallivanting about like a common vagabond.' She even thrust a book into little Sal's hands, saying, 'Study that, my girl, or you'll end up useless.' The book was a fount of knowledge, entitled *Magnall's Questions*. To Sal it was a fearsome, daunting thing, to be promptly wedged in one of the draught holes, where it would serve a better purpose. But for all that, Molly was saddened by the incident.

She recalled how much little Sal had enjoyed being schooled by Nelly, and she wondered what in God's name would become of them all.

'You're not dreaming of that husband of yours again, are you, Molly?' The large, friendly fellow with the weather-worn face and huge appetite shook his head at Molly before hurriedly tucking into the meal of steak pie and vegetables that Molly had put before him.

'You haven't come across him on your travels, then?' Molly had made the mistake of confiding in the old bargee, who ran a regular route between Liverpool and Manchester. He had not betrayed her confidence, but the mere fact that she had revealed her purpose here made her uneasy. Not a day or night passed when she wasn't reminded how there were certain people who would give *anything* to know her whereabouts.

'I ain't seen hide nor hair of the fellow answering this Jack's description,' the big man told her in hushed, fatherly tones, 'but I reckon a man who could leave a pretty little thing such as yourself ain't worth salt.' He rammed a forkful of red meat into his mouth, before adding kindly, 'Go home and wait for him there, why don't you? It ain't right that you should be working in a place where fellows congregate . . . not a young, good-looking girl like you.' He indicated a nearby table, where a group of young seamen appeared to be taking a little too much interest in Molly's slim, shapely figure. 'This is dockland, Molly. I've got a daughter myself . . . not much younger than you, and I wouldn't want her within ten miles of this place.' He smiled and nodded his greying head. 'Look . . . you take yourself off home and I promise you . . . if I *do* clap eyes on that husband of yours, I'll send him back to you with a swift kick in the breeches. Molly gave no answer, other than to smile at him and turn away. 'You think on what I said, Molly girl,' he urged, 'think on it real good.' His warning duly given, the man returned his noisy attention to the food on his plate.

For the rest of the day, Molly continued to search the faces that frequented Bill Craig's café; there were faces that had grown familiar to her, new faces both hostile and friendly, old faces and young ones. But none of them belonged to Jack. For all Molly knew, he could be miles away and she had been looking in the wrong direction. 'Go home and wait for him there,' the big man had told her. Molly smiled at the irony of his remark. She could have explained that she had no home. She could have told him that in the outhouse behind the café were three children belonging to her and Jack – whom the big man had said was 'not worth salt'. Three adorable bairns who deserved something better: a crippled boy aged one year and a half, a mischievous girl going on three, and little Sal, not yet seven years old, but made to grow up before her time.

Here, Molly paused to think how very much she had come to rely on Sal, a darling little creature who took care of her brother and sister during the hours when Molly worked in the café. At first, Mr Craig, the owner, had insisted that Molly work both mornings and evenings, to cover the busiest times serving breakfasts and suppers. When she protested that she would have to leave, he relented, getting someone else in to do the breakfasts. His motive was purely selfish.

Molly was one of the best workers Bill Craig had ever employed at the café; the pay was not so handsome and most waitresses spent too much time chatting up the customers. Molly, however, preferred to just serve their meals and get on with her duties. He considered Molly to be well worth keeping for as long as possible – in spite of the fact that she came with three brats on her coat-tail and was not as friendly to *himself* as he would have liked. When all was said and done, she was a tasty little article, and in view of the fact that she had no man to satisfy her needs, Bill Craig fancied she might come to enjoy his company between the sheets.

So far, the opportunity had not presented itself. To-morrow, though, his good wife was making her monthly visit to her ageing mother in Yorkshire, and he did not intend to let his chance slip by. The thought of taking Molly's naked body in his arms caused him such great excitement that he had hardly been able to contain himself these past few days.

Whenever Molly had a minute to breathe between the rush of customers, she used that minute to dash back to the outhouse and check that the children were soundly sleeping. Now, when there came a suitable lull, she looked into the kitchen to tell Bill Craig that she was 'just making sure the bairns were all right'.

'Sure, Molly,' he told her altogether too sweetly, 'quick as you can, mind . . . we don't want a riot in here.' He was a long, thin man with a pencil-trim moustache and angular features. His dark eyes were disturbingly penetrating and constantly darted about so as not to miss anything. Molly kept her distance. He was her employer. His wife had not begrudged her and the children using the outhouse. For that Molly was grateful, but, for reasons she found difficult to define, she did not like this odd couple.

Opening the door softly, so as not to disturb the sleeping children, Molly crept forward towards the makeshift beds. Outside the keen April wind teased and rattled at the walls of the outhouse, whistling eerily down the chimney and wailing like a lost soul in torment. At once, the gentle sound of children slumbering comforted Molly. In the soft glow of moonlight which filtered in through the four small panes of the room's only window, Molly could easily recognize the familiar shapes of the three small figures all huddled together in the bed: there was Sal, her fine golden hair making a gossamer cloud on the bolster; to the right of her was Peggy, a sturdy little frame tucked into the protective crook of her sister's arm, her mouth wide open and emitting a strange whimpering sound, which was something between a whistle and a snore.

The only lad was on the other side of Sal. Molly had always believed Tom to be an unusually handsome baby, with his thick black hair and dark laughing eyes. Tilly Watson likened him to Molly herself, and now Molly wondered about their distinguished dark features. It was true that Tom had her looks. But where had they come from? Not from old Sal, because Molly knew that the old dear was *not* blood kin to her. Again, she was made to think on her true parentage. It was obvious that her own dark hair and eyes, and those of Tom, were inherited from one or both of her real parents: Tom's grandparents. Certainly, Tom did not get his own dark features from his daddy, because Jack's hair was fair, and his eyes a pale brown colour. Peggy was the nearest to Jack's colouring. As for little Sal, well, Molly had often been puzzled by her blue eyes and golden hair. It was a funny thing but little Sal so often reminded Molly of that *other* Sal, the old lovable and eccentric tramp who had been everything to Molly in her formative years. There was something about her older daughter that really did put Molly in mind of old Sal Tanner. It was a curious thing, especially when Molly knew that old Sal had been no blood relation to her at all, a very strange and inexplicable thing to be sure.

As always, Tom was restless, tossing this way and that, throwing his little arms in and out of the coarse grey blanket and rolling from one side of his body to the other. Molly's heart went out to him. She wondered at his restlessness, suspecting that it stemmed from the discomfort which his deformed leg caused him. She had discovered that, if he laid for too long on that grotesque little stump, the feeling would go from it. On other occasions, he would be gripped by a cruel and vicious fit of cramp, which only his mammy's loving fingers could massage away. It pained Molly's heart to know that here he was, only a few months away from his second birthday, and she was no closer to getting Tom's crippled leg mended than she had been on the day of his birth; when his own daddy had run away at the sight of his son. When his daddy had run away! *When Jack had run away.*

Of a sudden, Molly was filled with disgust and dread. Spiralling up in the midst of all these painful emotions was a surge of guilt. *Guilt* because she had somehow failed not only Tom, but all of her precious children. It was because of her and the misdemeanours in her past that she was now forced to drag these little innocents from place to place. And what of their daddy? What of Jack? Jack, who had never grown up. Jack, whom she had fallen in love with on the night of their escape from Caleb Crowther's clutches, and whose children she had lovingly conceived and born. *Where was he now?*

Lately, Molly had come to ask herself why she was driven to search for him. Just as often, she had come to wonder whether or not she really wanted to find him. If, one day, he walked into that café, what would she do? What would she say to him? And – more importantly – would he be pleased to see her? All of these questions Molly tormented herself with. But there was one in particular which would not go away, and which caused her the greatest torment of all. Did she still love Jack? It was as though, in her desperate longing to find him, Molly had lost the real reason as to why she scanned every face in every crowd. Somewhere along the way she had begun to lose faith in her children's daddy. Little by little, that feeling she had for him, and which she called 'love', began to dwindle, until there was only shame and anger left.

If Jack's memory was shrinking in Molly's tired heart, there was another whose image was becoming more and more cherished. These days Mick Darcy was closer to Molly than he had ever been. In the late, dark hours when her duties were over and she lay in the narrow bunk some way from her children, Molly would remember the many happy times she and Mick had shared with those infants. All of her instincts told her that were she to search the world over, she would never find a better man; a man who had never wanted anything more than to take care of her and her babies. A good and loyal fellow. Certainly no other man could love her more deeply than Mick had loved her.

Molly derived great comfort from the knowledge that, though one man had shamefully deserted her, there was another who had offered her everything he owned. *Did she love Mick Darcy?* Molly dared not dwell too deeply on it. She could not deny that his memory was precious to her, nor could she deny those long, lonely nights when she imagined how wonderful it would be to feel his strong arms secure about her. Occasionally, she would recall their last meeting, when he had kissed her. The thought of his lips against hers brought a warm glow to her, and made her pleasantly embarrassed at the very real memory of it all. So real in fact did it seem in that moment when she gazed lovingly at her slumbering brood that Molly instinctively put the tips of her fingers to the outline of her lips. Mick's kiss had been so gentle, yet angry and possessive at the same time. Suddenly she was swamped with a terrible sensation of loneliness and regret until, impatient with herself, she turned about, going on tiptoe across the room. She was on the point of opening the door to leave when a small tired voice whispered into the darkness, 'Will you be long, Mammy?'

Checking the persistent feeling of guilt that pulled her down, Molly came back to where little Sal was raised up in the bed, leaning on one skinny elbow and peering at Molly through sleepy eyes. 'Ssh . . . go back to sleep, sweetheart,' Molly said in a whisper, bending forwards to kiss the child and tuck her back beneath the blankets. 'I'll be back in no time . . . no time at all,' she promised.

Molly's promise was enough. In a moment, Sal was snuggled up once more, and contentedly drifting off to her slumbers.

At the door, Molly whispered, 'Goodnight, God bless,' and was surprised to hear Sal reply dreamily, 'Night, Mammy . . . don't be long.'

For the remainder of the long, demanding evening,

Molly was rushed off her feet. Saturday night was always a busy time, but for some reason, on this particular Saturday the café was bursting at the seams, with loud groups of men who found Bill Craig's establishment a good stopping-off place before congregating at the public house. Here they could fill their bellies with food at a reasonable price, whilst exchanging snippets of gossip, and generally putting right the world at large. The more they swilled down the food with the cheap booze illegally supplied by the ever-enterprising Bill Craig, the noisier became their discussions, and the sooner they developed into aggressive arguments.

All manner of subjects were put forward, to be shaken, bandied about, denied or confirmed, but never resolved in any way whatsoever. Molly had witnessed them all – how industry was suffering a terrible depression and 'times can only get worse'. There were those who firmly supported Sir Randolph Churchill's claims that the iron industry was 'dead as mutton'; the silk industry had been 'assassinated' by foreigners; the cotton industry was 'sick'; the shipbuilding had 'come to a standstill' and that in every branch of British industry there could be found 'signs of mortal disease'.

The arguments raged and tempers became hotter. 'Not bloody true,' cried one; 'Churchill wants ter get his facts right afore he goes shouting fro' the rooftops,' said another, this one pledging allegiance to another public figure by the name of Alfred Marshall, a Cambridge economist. This 'educated' fellow claimed that while there had been in the previous ten years 'a gradual depression in prices, a depression of interest and a depression of profits' for those above working-class status, there had been 'no considerable depression in any other respect'. In fact, it was becoming widely accepted that the working-class were beginning to enjoy a 'much better quality of life'.

'Oh, aye?' interrupted a somewhat irate and weary man, dressed in a threadbare jacket that was too small, trousers that shone with wear and a cap whose peak was limp with age. 'It's all very well tekking notice o' those plump, well-to-do fellas with their airs an' graces, an' the smell o' money up their noses . . . but let the buggers do what us dockers 'ave to do day in an' day out! They'd have quite *another* smell ter contend with . . . an' it wouldn't be half so bloody pleasant neither. I wonder how long the sods would last if *they* had ter turn up at these 'ere docks in all weathers, four times a day ter the call-on, eh? . . . An' there may be work, an' there may not! Oh, aye, they'd change their tune then, I'll be bound . . . hanging about at the docks, begging an' hoping fer a bit o' work an' thinking usself bloody lucky if we get six hours' work in a week!' The cry was quickly taken up, and so the heated arguments continued.

Molly was often used to bounce grievances off, but she was always very careful not to get involved. She had enough of her own problems to contend with, and anyway, she thought, it wouldn't matter whether she agreed or disagreed, *her* opinion was unlikely to alter the dockers' grievances; in truth she did believe their arguments were not without foundation.

'That geezer's had his eye on you all night long. You ain't been encouraging him, have you? . . . You know how Bill frowns on that sort o' thing!' The accusing voice belonged to Nell Casey, the fair-haired girl who came in of a Saturday tea-time, waiting-on for three hours, when the crush of customers was at its worst. Molly had taken an instant dislike to the brazen, sour-tempered creature. She in turn made every attempt to belittle Molly in front of the customers, and she particularly resented the way Bill Craig ogled the beautiful Molly when he thought no one was looking.

Nell Casey had almost collided with Molly when the two of them had returned to the counter to collect their respective orders. Molly felt uncomfortable beneath the other girl's hostile stare. 'I don't encourage *no one*!' Molly told her quietly. 'You know that.'

'Well, what the 'ell's he staring at you for then, eh? . . . I'm telling you, he ain't took his eyes off you all night!'

Molly shrugged her shoulders, collected her order and began weaving her way in and out of the tables. From the corner of her eye she saw the man that Nell Casey referred to. He was obviously a seaman, young, bold-looking, and just as the other girl had described, he was deliberately watching Molly, following her every move with sly, calculating eyes.

Molly was suddenly gripped with fear. The way he was staring after her was not the usual flirtatious way in which a man might hanker after a woman. His manner was too furtive, too curious. Beneath those sly, narrowed eyes, Molly felt her heart shrink inside her. Who was he? Why did he seem so interested in her? And what devious game was he up to?

'Hey! Watch what you're doing, me beauty.' The laughing, surprised face peered up at Molly as she disentangled her feet from the chair leg that had protruded across her path and nearly brought her tumbling to the man's lap. As it was, the bowl of soup on her tray slid dangerously to the edge and would have spilled over the protester's ginger curls, if he had not been quick enough to steady Molly by the arm. 'Are ye trying to ruin me love life, or what?' he chortled, much to the delight of every manjack there. 'By God . . . there's no telling *what* dreadful damage a bowl o' hot soup can do to a fella's pride.' When Molly mumbled her apologies and hurried away, he huddled towards the group of men close by and began whispering. Molly heard their lewd laughter echo across the café, and her lovely face burned with shame.

It was some time before Molly had time to glance again towards where the seaman had been sitting. When she did look across, it was to see his seat empty. He was gone, and she should have felt relieved. Somehow, she did not. In fact, his abrupt disappearance unnerved her almost as much as the knowledge that he had been watching her so intensely.

Molly tried to console herself with the knowledge that she had never seen him before and, so far as she could recall, he had never seen her. Besides which, her enemies were not here in Liverpool, but some miles away in Blackburn town. 'You're being foolish,' she told herself, 'letting your fear and imagination run riot.' All the same, she could not shake off that insistent little warning voice – the same voice that told her how one waterway led to another, and how waterways carried vessels, vessels carried men, and men carried all manner of talk. How was she to tell whether the Justice had not put spies out after her? . . . Or offered a substantial reward? It was the kind of thing such men might stoop to. So the whisper might have been put out, and that whisper carried far and wide. Molly's terrible fear was heightened. Dear God, was there no safe hiding hole?

From his place behind the counter, Bill Craig also watched Molly. He saw how suddenly nervous she was, and how her anxious dark eyes kept flitting towards the spot where the young seaman had been. Mistaking Molly's anxiety for interest, his own appetite was teased. He thought she looked especially bewitching tonight, with that blush on her face and those exquisite black eyes so filled with secrecy. Her short coal-black hair was thick and incredibly rich . . . the kind a man was tempted to run his hands over. Unashamedly, he feasted his eyes on Molly's trim little figure, thinking how it should be dressed in silks and furs, instead of a worn-out dress of brown calico that covered her ankles and stole the colour from her face. Even the apron she wore was ill-fitting – having belonged to his own rather too ample wife. But when Molly leaned forward to serve at table, the glimpse of her slim and shapely ankles more than compensated for the ungainly manner of her dress. Even in the calico smock and the small, worn boots, he thought Molly to be the loveliest creature he had ever set eyes on.

Bill Craig was greatly excited. He could hardly wait for the morrow, when his wife took off on her travels. Deep inside him, there was a great longing, a burning that had to be satisfied. The only one to satisfy it was Molly!

The young seaman went along the docks in a jaunty manner, a merry tune on his lips, and a crafty gleam in his eye. He felt good. The money put up by Marlow Tanner would shortly be sitting in the pocket of this here seaman. Rightly so, he prided himself, rightly so! Because wasn't he the most diligent and observant fellow? Hadn't he just seen with his own eyes the very merchandise that Marlow Tanner wanted? Oh, yes! At first light, he would be on his way to carry the good news and to lay his claim to that there money. But for now, he had a crippling thirst on him, and a need to celebrate. A few jugs of ale and a floozy for the night seemed like a just reward for the minute. Tomorrow would be here all too soon, but tonight was Saturday. A night for making merry, and letting tomorrow look after itself!

Molly sat on the edge of her bunk. Through the grimy window panes she watched the dark, lazy clouds against a silver-shot sky. Every bone in her body ached and she longed for sleep. But sleep would not come. Her mind was in turmoil. So many things came to haunt her. Disturbing images had kept her wide awake when she might have enjoyed the rest which she had honestly earned.

All the night long, Molly had softly paced the room, pausing only to gaze at her sleeping children and occasionally to glance out of the window. Dawn would soon be breaking. Outside, there was no breeze nor movement of any kind. It was as though life had run out of time and the earth had died. There was a terrible, sad atmosphere that shocked Molly, and made her wonder at it.

But then she was made to look closer. It was not the night, nor was it the earth that had died; they were merely slumbering. No. The sadness and the awful loneliness were not out there beyond this room. They were in here, in the room itself, and in Molly's own unhappy heart. All that had died was the hope she had fought to keep alive: that faint hope which had kept her going, kept her searching for her man. It had always been a delicate thing, but now, that tiny flame of hope had fluttered its last. *Jack was not here*. He was no place where she had been, and now a cruel and shattering reality came to her like a savage blow. It sent her heart reeling, for after all this time Molly finally admitted to herself that, somehow, somewhere along the way she had lost that which had been very precious to her. The awful realization had crept up on her without her knowing, and now it shone through her thoughts like a blazing beacon. She did not love Jack any more. *She did not love Jack any more!*

'Mammy . . . I'm cold.' In the half-darkness, little Sal had seen the familiar outline of her mammy, bent forward on the edge of the bunk, with her head resting on up-turned palms and a look of dejection about her weary frame. Now, when Molly raised her eyes to glance at the small figure climbing from the bed, the child faintly perceived the tears rolling down her mammy's face. 'Don't cry, Mammy . . . please don't cry,' came the little voice.

'Cry?' At once Molly was on her feet and surreptitiously wiping away the tears. Opening wide her arms, she caught the child lovingly to her breast. 'Whatever makes you think I'm crying, sweetheart?' she asked softly.

'You *are* crying,' little Sal insisted, twisting her body round in Molly's arms and peering into the dark luscious eyes. '*I saw you!*'

'No,' Molly lied. 'Why should I be crying . . . when I've got the three loveliest children in all the world?'

For a long, brooding moment the girl pondered deeply, then in that open innocent way that children do, she said, 'You haven't got Daddy, though, have you, Mammy? . . . and I know you miss him.' Her two skinny arms wound themselves tightly round Molly's neck, as she asked in a small tearful voice, 'When is he coming, Mammy? . . . *When* is Daddy coming to find us?'

Molly was mortified! This was the very first time that

Sal had mentioned Jack in that way. Suddenly it was painfully obvious to Molly that she had been greatly unfair to little Sal – taking her for granted, making her grow up before her time, leaning on her as though she was another woman, instead of a small child who missed her daddy. She wondered now how often little Sal had woken up during the long dark hours when she herself was earning the money that fed and sheltered them. Had her daughter been afraid and lonely without her mammy close by? Was Molly placing too much of a burden on those narrow shoulders, by depending on Sal to mind her brother and sister? Had there been times when either of them had woken in a nightmare, looking for their mammy and, finding her gone, then turned to their elder sister for comfort? Every painful question stabbed at Molly's heart and made her desperate. In that moment, she came to a crucial decision.

'I don't know when Daddy is coming to find us, sunshine,' she told the clinging child, 'but, somehow, I don't think we'll find him here in Liverpool.' She put the girl to the floor and, keeping her voice soft so as not to disturb the sleeping babes, she asked, 'Do *you* miss him, too?' When little Sal slowly nodded, Molly smiled and went on, 'Well then . . . where do you think we should look for him, eh?'

'In *Dock Street*, because if he goes there . . . looking for us, he won't know where we are.'

Molly smiled at the simple logic. 'You're right, sweetheart,' she agreed. But her heart sank to her boots. If she *were* to return to Dock Street, it might not just be Jack that found them! She should have been elated at the thought of Jack being reunited with them. Instead, she felt cold and confused at the prospect. Yet she could not go on as she had done since fleeing the house on Dock Street, especially not now, having seen the true depth of her daughter's feelings. It was possible that Jack might return to Dock Street looking for them – although, somehow, Molly thought it highly unlikely. With the thought came a spiral of disgust.

Thrusting aside her better instincts, Molly promised the girl, 'We *will* go back to Blackburn, Sal. But maybe not to the house on Dock Street.'

'Why not?'

Molly had to think fast. She didn't want to frighten the child by explaining how there were certain people, bad people, who meant to harm them. Instead she told her, 'There'll be new tenants living in the house now . . . the landlord wouldn't let it stay empty, not when there are plenty of people willing to pay for a roof over their heads.'

'Can we lodge with Tilly Watson then? She will let us . . . I *know* she will, Mammy!'

'No, sweetheart. You're quite right, though. Tilly would not refuse to take us in, but it wouldn't be fair . . . she already has a house full of her own brood.'

'Can we ask Nelly then? She's got a big house.'

'No. We can't do that either . . . you *know* we can't!' In spite of deliberately trying to sound matter-of-fact, Molly couldn't disguise the sharp edge to her voice. She saw the girl's blue eyes grow bigger and knew instinctively that the flicker of pain in them was an unpleasant memory: a particular memory, of the day when the two of them were forced to hide in the shrubbery outside the Tanners' house in Park Street.

'Was that man Nelly's friend?' Sal had asked the same question many times during the weeks following the frightful incident. 'I don't like that man,' she uttered now, her voice hushed and cautious, as though she were afraid he might suddenly appear.

'I think he must have been.' Molly wondered whether her own fear of Caleb Crowther had transmitted itself to little Sal, or whether the girl's horror of him was a virgin horror, impressed on her mind by that one, close sighting of him. Certainly he was a fearsome figure, not only grotesque to look at, but sending before him an atmosphere of terror. 'Yes, darling, I think he *must* be a friend of Nelly's . . . or she would never have let such a man cross her doorstep. No, we can't go to the house on Park Street either.'

'Where will we go then?'

'Ssh, darling. Don't you worry your pretty little head about that. You just go back to sleep now, and leave all the worrying to your mammy.' Easy words, thought Molly, but words would not feed them nor put a roof over their heads. Thoughts of Mick came over her. She smiled inwardly at the pleasure his company had brought her; images of the cosy barge insisted their way into the upheaval of her mind, of his tall, manly frame bent over the stove, warming up the stew he had made, or brewing a strong measure of tea. Whatever he did for her and Jack's children was always done graciously and with a loving smile. With the warm, contented memories came a flurry of pain and regret to Molly's young, lonely heart.

How many times had she lain awake in that hard, uncomfortable and lonely bed, reliving that last tender scene aboard Mick's barge, when he had taken her in his arms and murmured, '*I love you, Molly*'? How often had Molly questioned the wisdom of her decision to turn her back on that fine man? So often that she could not count the times.

Now, when little Sal put the question, 'Well, can we go

to Mick, then? I *like* Mick, Mammy,' Molly could find no words to answer. Instead, she gently put her finger to the child's lips. 'Ssh, sweetheart,' she whispered, taking her by the hand and leading her to the bed, where she coaxed the child in and tucked her up. The other two were sleeping so soundly that they were not disturbed; only Tom fidgeted, making a strange little noise as he struggled to roll himself over.

In a while, when she was satisfied that Sal was sleeping, Molly took off her boots and dress, and the cotton under-garments that were more practical than comfortable. In a moment, she also had climbed into the bunk and was heavy with sleep. She wasn't altogether surprised when a stocky little figure climbed in alongside her and nestled close to her heart. It was strange how Peggy seemed to know instinctively when her mammy was ready for sleep. Molly closed her arms about the child, and, in no time at all, the room was quiet, save for the soft, rhythmic breathing of slumbering souls.

Outside, the wind gained momentum, shivering against the walls of the outhouse and pushing in through the many cracks in its aged walls. Soon the rain was spilling down with a vengeance and the night was quickly lifting into daylight. Molly, though, was oblivious to it all. The sleep she had denied herself was upon her at last, refreshing her, and preparing her for the upheavals to come. Upheavals that would try her courage and strength to the full, and of a kind that not even Molly in her worst nightmare could have envisaged.

'But I want to leave *today*, Mr Craig!' Molly protested. 'I was hoping you would pay me my week in hand, and let me go right away.'

'I'm sorry, girlie. I can't do that.' Bill Craig had been up since early light this Sunday morning; first to accompany his wife to her regular service at nearby St Mary's Church, and afterwards to see her safely to the station. It was ten in the morning when he was summoned to the door by Molly's insistent knocking. The sight of her standing there with a freshly scrubbed face and her pretty figure looking especially desirable in that brown, swinging skirt and grey shawl, beneath which was her best ivory-coloured blouse, sent a delicious thrill right through him.

'I've made up my mind to go, Mr Craig,' Molly told him, with a defiant gleam in her dark eyes. 'Please be so kind as to pay what you owe me, and I'll be on my way.'

Unfortunately, the man was equally adamant. He had particular reasons for refusing Molly's demands. And they were very different from the ones he stated now. 'Look, Molly, I don't mean to be harsh. You know I'd pay you up and wish you a safe journey, wherever you mean to go.' He waited, as though for Molly to explain her destination. When it became plain that she had no intention of doing any such thing, he went on, 'But y'see, if you was to up sticks and leave me in a minute's notice like this . . . you'd have to go *without* your pay, I'm afeared. First of all, it's the wife who sees to the wages and such like. And, I'm telling you, girlie, if I was to interfere in her cash-box, you wouldn't be the only one travelling down the road, 'cause she'd throw a blue fit when she got home a Tuesday, and with the black temper she's got, I'd be kicked out that door in no time!' He smiled sweetly and scratched his head, feigning to think of a way out of his dilemma for Molly's sake. 'Naw. Like I say, I'm sorry, but I daren't open that there cash-box . . . it's more than me life's worth, an' that's the very truth.'

Molly was no fool. She knew that he was deliberately lying. Yet if she were to insist on leaving today, it would have to be without her wages for the week she had worked in hand. She could not afford to do anything so irresponsible. And yet, she had promised Sal that they would be leaving just as soon as she had told Mr Craig and collected her wages. 'You *must* have money of your own!' she said now, ignoring his smile and thinking it too greasy by half. 'My wages aren't so great that you need to raid the cash-box.'

'Oh, but they *are*, because, y'see, the wife keeps *every penny* under lock and key.' He shrugged his narrow shoulders. 'I'm no good with money. It's *her* that takes care of all that, and you know yourself how sharp she is.'

Molly couldn't deny the truth of that, because Mrs Craig might be small and wiry, but her tongue was spiteful at times and she did have a very domineering way with her. All the same, Molly could not bring herself to believe that Mr Craig bent entirely to his wife's demands. She had seen him defy her too often in the café for that to be so. But, be that as it may, Molly was *not* leaving without her wages, and she told him so in no uncertain terms.

'And I don't blame you, girlie,' he said in a mock serious voice. 'I'd be the very same meself. But you'll have to wait till the wife gets back.' Suddenly, his mood changed and he eyed Molly in a resentful manner. 'Y'know I'd be within me rights to send you packing without a penny don't you?'

'How's that?'

'Huh! It's easy to see that you don't often take up an honest day's work, ain't it?' he sneered. 'Else you'd know that it's quite in order for me to insist on a week's notice.'

249

'I've only got your word for that,' retorted Molly, thinking how soon he had betrayed his true, obnoxious character.

'Oh, it's right enough! Just ask around . . . you'll see I'm telling the truth. And besides that, don't you realize what a terrible problem you're setting me, by clearing off without giving proper notice, eh? Where am I gonna find somebody to replace you in a matter o' twenty-four hours?'

'That's your problem.' Molly resented the way he had begun to make her feel guilty. 'The plain fact is, I can't stay on. Me and my young 'uns have a particular place to go.' Suddenly she remembered how kind Mr Craig and his wife had been when she and the children turned up here, cold, hungry and homeless. It wasn't in her nature to be thankless. 'I *am* grateful for you giving me a job and a roof over our heads,' she said in a softer voice, 'really I am, Mr Craig. But I have to move on . . . my children aren't all that happy here, and I dread leaving them on their own when I need to work. You do understand how I can't go though – not without my wages. I've no other money, except the twenty shillings you paid me for *this* week's work. And that won't last long, as well you know.'

'Look, Molly.' He stepped aside and beckoned her with a thin, heavily veined arm. 'Come inside where we can talk things over,' he suggested in a fawning voice. 'I'm sure we can come to an agreement of sorts.' He touched her on the shoulder, appearing astonished when she shrank from him.

'*Can I have my money?*'

He stared at her, dropped his arm and inhaled an almighty breath which he noisily exhaled through his nose. 'You're a stubborn little bugger, an' that's a fact!' he said, with a small chuckle. He stared a while longer, drinking in Molly's dark beauty and calculating how he could take it to himself. Presently, his bony face split into a grim smile. 'All right, girlie,' he said, at the same time stepping aside. 'You'd best come in. I can see you'll not budge till you've got what's due to you.' When she looked both surprised and suspicious, he quickly urged, 'Come in, I tell you . . . it'll take me a minute or two to get the box open.'

'All right, Mr Craig, but I can't stay no longer on account of the children being on their own.' Something about him made her feel uncomfortable. 'Happen it might be better if I were to come back when we're all packed and ready to go.'

'You'll do no such thing! I'm not dithering about waiting for you to knock on the door when it suits you! You'll come inside now, and wait while I get your wages, or you can be off and leave me to think on how I'm gonna find a replacement for you at such short notice.' The smile had gone from his face as he proceeded to close the door.

'A minute or two, then,' Molly reluctantly agreed, 'but no longer.'

It was the first time Molly had set foot in her employer's house. It was a big old house, with stained-glass windows, a regal air, and a sense of desolation about it. There was something especially forbidding about the outside – as though it was brooding for the grander age to which it belonged. It was rumoured that, at one time, the house had been the home of an industrialist who came on hard times and was forced to sell. That was the beginning of its descent. Over the years the house and its land were separated; the land was quickly developed, afterwards leaving only a narrow stretch behind where the outhouses stood, and a wider area to the side where the diner was erected, to serve the dockers and other passing trade.

Molly felt like a trespasser. The house was deep inside, with a long narrow passage going down to the sitting-room. She felt on edge, reluctant to stay for even one minute. But she so desperately needed her wages, and after all, she and the young 'uns would soon be on their way. 'A few minutes' – that's how long he said it would take to get her wages together; a few minutes, and she would be gone from this house into the fresh air again. Quietly, she followed his long, thin figure, listening to his meaningless chatter and hoping that Sal would be all right with her brother and sister for the little while she would be gone.

'You sit there . . . I'll not be long.' The man gestured towards a sprawling black horse-hair chair beside the fireplace. 'The cash-box is kept upstairs. I'll fetch it.'

Shivering from the damp atmosphere, Molly made no move to do as he bid. 'I'll wait here,' she said.

His eyes raked her face, then, shrugging his shoulders, he muttered, 'Suit yourself.' Afterwards, he turned away and hurried from the room, leaving Molly with a bad feeling. She was tempted to run from the house before he returned, but the thought of heading for the open road without her wages kept her there. 'They're *my wages*,' she whispered into the room, as though justifying her intrusion. 'I worked myself ragged for them . . . and I'm not leaving here without 'em, no sir!'

As good as his word, Bill Craig was back downstairs wihin a very short time, the cash-box tucked under his arm. 'Can't find the key,' he told Molly; 'Like I said, the wife's a canny bugger . . . keeps it on her person, she does.' He put the cash-box on the table and opened the cutlery drawer beneath. When he had drawn out a small, bone-handled knife, he smiled at Molly, telling her, 'You'll have to grip the box tight, while I prise the lock open.' He clasped his long fingers around the box, pinning it to the table. 'Like this,' he said, 'you keep it still, mind. I don't relish the idea of slicing a finger off !'

Against her better instincts, Molly felt compelled to do as he said. After all, it was true that he could not hold the box and lever the lock open at the same time because the box was secured by a large, free-hanging padlock. He would therefore need one hand to hold the padlock, and the other to prise it apart. All the same, when she came to his side and took hold of the box between her hands, it was with growing trepidation.

'That's right, girlie. You just keep it from dancing about, while I get to grips with this bloody lock.' He chuckled, and to Molly – who was decidedly nervous at being in such close proximity to him – it was a disturbing sound.

As he worked on the lock, grunting and quietly swearing, Molly could feel the warm stench of his breath on her face. Disgusted, she turned her head to one side, all the while telling herself that at no time in all the weeks she had worked for him had Mr Craig made any unseemly suggestions, or been anything other than polite and impersonal. Somehow, she was reassured.

In a moment, though, the reassurance was shattered when Molly inadvertently glanced into the mirror which hung on the wall opposite. *What she saw there made her tremble!* It was his face. A face filled with longing, a face supposedly bent to its task, but instead gazing at Molly, the narrowed eyes intent on her hair, then lowered to her breast where they lingered a while. In that split second when Molly saw the terrible danger, there came a sharp click, and the lid of the cash-box sprang open. Instinctively, Molly pulled away, already backing towards the door, her dark eyes accusing and bright with fury. When he came forward, smiling down at her, his two arms outstretched and a certain look in his eye, her one thought was to get out of there, get away from him! Turning, she made a run for the door.

'Oh no you don't, girlie!' With astonishing speed he was on her and slamming shut the door. When Molly began struggling and biting into the hand that was over her mouth he laughed aloud. 'Struggle an' shout all you like, Molly darling. There ain't a soul to hear you. Unless o' course you want to frighten your brats? But then, what could three young 'uns do, eh? Except cry for their mammy an' wonder what she were screaming at.' He shoved her towards the table, putting her back to it, and thrusting his body against her. 'Naw! . . . I'm willing to gamble that you won't scream an' carry on, girlie. I reckon you ain't the type to frighten three little innocents that way.' He saw the horror in Molly's eyes and, pushing his face close to hers, he laughed in a low, sinister voice. 'I won't hurt you, girlie. But, y'see . . . I won't rest either . . . not till I feel you naked against me.' He began unbuttoning her blouse, pausing only to hold out his unsteady hand in front of Molly's eyes. 'Look there, I'm that excited I can't stop trembling. You're a real beauty, y'know that? The kind a man hankers after in the dark, early hours. Oh, I bet your skin's got the touch o' velvet, ain't it? . . . An' you know how to treat a man, I reckon; know how to pull him into them slim thighs an' allow him a deal o' pleasure he'll not likely forget in a hurry.' His eyes were heavy with longing, his lips partly open, moist and reaching for her. He groaned when Molly struggled against him. 'No, no. Don't spoil it, girlie,' he murmured, pinning her tight in his strong, thin arms. 'Look, see this?' He dragged her to where the open cash-box lay, its contents bulging. 'Bank notes, an' silver coins,' he said. 'You cooperate with me . . . make it worth me while, and I swear I'll give you *three* times your wages. What d'you say to that, eh?'

Molly's reply was swift and painful. With fierce determination that took him by surprise, she twisted herself far enough out of his grip to reach the cash-box. With her fingers locked round it, she brought it upwards in a straight line towards his head. There was a brief instant when his eyes opened wide with surprise at the bank notes fluttering to the carpet. Then, as the sharp edges of the tin box came crashing to the side of his head, the eyes darkened with fury. Molly felt his grip tighten round her throat, and she knew that it was either him or her! She felt herself choking, the room was spinning round and her senses were failing fast. But she found within her a mighty strength born of desperation. Again and again she brought the tin box against his temple, until at last his grip was relaxed. Yet still she could not move, because his whole weight had her trapped beneath him and the table. Slowly, she inched her way from beneath him, and when he slid silently to the floor, the awful horror of what she had done came over her. As she stared down, wide-eyed and disbelieving, her every limb was shaking uncontrollably, and a tide of nausea flooded her senses. Was he dead? Dear God, she hoped not! Her shocked eyes followed the trail of blood, crimson splashes everywhere; on the tablecloth, on the carpet, on the bank notes littered there, on her. *On her!*

Terrified, Molly threw down the bloodstained cash-box and ran into the passage. From there, she found the scullery, where in a frenzy, she dabbed at the blood spots on her blouse with a wet flannel, until the spots became large, shapeless dark patches. After she had splashed clean her face and hands, she would have run from the house with never a glance back. But she could not. In spite of the fact that he had meant to ravage her, how could she leave him, not knowing whether he were alive or dead? Molly knew that if she was to leave now, her conscience would never let her rest.

Shivering with fear, she went out of the scullery, down the passage and back into the sitting-room. On hesitant feet, she came to where the figure of Mr Craig lay sprawled beside the table, the open cash-box only a short way away where she had dropped it, and its contents spilled over a wide area. Even though she was in desperate need of those silver coins that were strewn about, Molly could not bring herself to touch them. 'Mr Craig.' Her voice trembled in the terrible silence. She came closer, peering down at his face to see whether there was any sign of movement. There was none. Panic took hold of her. 'Dear God, what have I done?' she whispered into the eerie silence, and back came her own horror-stricken answer, 'I've killed him. *God above, I've killed him!*'

For a long and seemingly endless moment, Molly stood there loudly sobbing, her hands spread against her throbbing temples and her disbelieving gaze fixed to the man's pale, upturned face, with all manner of terrible thoughts raging through her. She had committed *murder*! There was no doubt in her own mind that she would surely hang for it. Suddenly, above all else came the thought of her children. And it was this thought that quickly sobered her. She must protect them at all cost, for they had no one but her. No one at all.

Quickly, Molly dried her eyes and composed herself. Sal was quick to notice when anything was wrong, and Molly did not want the child to suspect. She took one last look at the man who had so viciously attacked her, and still seeing no signs of life, she went quickly from the house, consoling herself with the facts that no one had seen her go there, and no one had seen her come out. He would not be found until the next day, by which time she would be long gone. But Molly knew that the awful memory of it all would never leave her, neither would the fear. These she would carry with her, wherever she went, always hiding, always the hunted.

The sound of the front door closing echoed through the house. There was no other sound. No movement – only the signs of a bitter and fierce struggle having taken place. But then, after a while, there did come a small sound, a pitiful and weak cry that became a groan. The groan subsided, and in its place emerged the sound of laughter, wicked, spiteful laughter, and amidst it, the softest of murmurs. 'So, you reckon you've done for me, d'you, girlie? . . . Well, you just take that thought with you. *And may it haunt your every waking hour, you little vixen!*'

Bill Craig stood unsteadily before the mirror, ill and dazed, angrily beholding the deep, uneven tear along his temple. 'Little bastard,' he muttered. 'I hope the divil don't give you a minute's peace.' He might have deserved it, but that was no comfort. He might have saved a whole week's wages that belonged to her. Even so, there were only two things on his mind right now.

Firstly, he wished every curse on earth might pursue the bitch. And much more importantly, he had his work cut out to clean this place up before Mrs Craig returned. She was a clever, shrewd woman, who'd already accused him of hankering after Molly. As it was, he had to explain why she'd gone so sudden. Damn her eyes! Women were a curse, and that was a fact!

It was some weeks later when Mick came into Bill Craig's café, asking after the one called Molly. He spoke to the surly proprietor at great length, but was made to depart heavy hearted when he learned that Molly had left some time ago. And no, there was no man with her. Just three young 'uns.

He had thought to find her here, after the seaman had so vividly described her. The unfortunate thing was that the seaman had carried the information too long, having 'met this lovely little floozy and spent a while drinking to me good fortune'.

Mick, though, was undeterred as ever. He would find his lovely Molly: for his love of her, for the Tanners who seemed so very anxious to talk to her and who had launched their own enquiries, and not least, for Molly's own sake.

Chapter Eleven

The children's laughter was a tonic to Molly's heart. She had watched their playful antics and enjoyed their squeals of delight these past twenty minutes and more; minutes that had gone all too quickly, each one ingrained on her memory for all time. If she had nothing else in this world, she had her children and she thanked the Good Lord for them.

Seated at the top of the stone steps that led down from Tilly Watson's scullery to the enclosed yard below, Molly looked a sorry little figure. After those long weeks of hiding and scraping a living any way she could, her already slim figure was now pathetically thin, with the threadbare clothes hanging on her like a shapeless sack. Even the long, respectable shawl given to her by Tilly could not disguise the undernourished form beneath. But for all that, there was a unique strength about Molly's pale, almost gaunt face, and a particular beauty that drew a body's attention; especially the black eyes which were now drawn up towards the radiant sky of a lovely May evening. Certainly, to the young man who was closely regarding her from the parlour doorway, Molly's special beauty outshone even the dazzling sunshine that spilled over her upturned features highlighting the exquisite loveliness of that familiar face and awakening in him a deep aching desire that he could no longer suppress.

For a moment longer, Joe Watson let his eyes rove over Molly's unsuspecting countenance. The more his gaze lingered on her, the sharper became his need for her. At last, he thrust his two hands into his jacket pocket and turned away sharply, consoling himself with the pleasing thought that there would be time enough to show Molly how strong were his feelings towards her. Time enough, *later*, when the Watson brood were all abed and Molly's three were also tucked up for the night.

In the short time that Molly had stayed under his mother's roof, Joe Watson had come to know her routine like the lines on his own hand. After she had made sure her offspring were quietly sleeping, Molly would creep through the silent house to the back steps, to the very spot where she sat even at this minute – there she would stay until the night grew darker and colder, wistfully looking up to the shifting sky and its scurrying shadows, searching for some elusive distant thing that was known only to herself.

During these dark, quiet hours, Joe Watson had stayed hunched against his bedroom window above, watching, needing, and wonderfully intrigued by the lovely secret creature that was Molly. Of late his longing for her had become an obsession that he could no longer control. Any feelings of decency and respect that he might have had towards his mother's unlikely lodger were in danger of being hopelessly smothered by other, more urgent feelings: of greed and lust, of selfish appeasement and the driving desire to take Molly to himself, even against her will if needs be. The ugly strength of his feelings were a disturbing revelation to him.

Now, as he left the house to make his way to the

nearest public bar, Joe Watson smiled to himself. 'Oh, yes, Molly me beauty . . . there'll be time enough for me to tell you how much I want you, when there's only you and me . . . and the dark to hide in, eh?' He chuckled aloud and went on his way with a livelier step at the thought of Molly, naked, leaning into his arms and gazing up at him with big dark eyes ablaze with a desire to match his own.

By the time he strode into the bar, Joe Watson had convinced himself that the lovely Molly wanted him every bit as much as he wanted her. Oh, that wasn't to say that she had ever given him any encouragement, because she had *not*, other than to indulge in a friendly conversation and to express her gratitude at his willingness to 'put up with me and the young 'uns for a while'. No, he could not claim that Molly had ever betrayed her deeper emotions to him. But then, she was one of those rare women who possessed a quiet tongue and kept her innermost secrets to herself. And wasn't it a known fact that often, when a woman said no, she was only being coy and meant yes all along?

Deep down, Joe Watson knew that Molly felt the same way he did. Knowing it made him bolder, filled him with arrogance and caused him to be so impatient that the hours before darkness seemed to stretch before him like never-ending years. But he comforted himself with the belief that the waiting would be worth it when he had Molly close in his arms. Oh yes, the waiting would be well worth it! And who knows? He might even be so foolish as to take her for his wife. Oh, but that might be going a bit *too* fast, he cautioned himself. After all, she had three young 'uns from her estranged husband. And tying yourself up for life to one woman wasn't all that wise. Especially if you could take that woman to your bed whenever the fancy came on you. *No*. First things first. In these past weeks, Joe Watson had cursed the fact that Molly already had a husband and he himself might be made to wait for her hand in marriage. Now, though, he was quietly grateful for it.

'Mammy, tell Tom to behave himself!' little Sal moaned. 'He won't let us play nicely.' With a loud sigh, she put down her side of the makeshift skipping rope and ran to where Tom was mischievously wrenching the other end from Peggy's determined grasp. 'I've showed you how to skip in the middle of the rope, you bad boy!' she scolded him. 'And you have to take your proper turn. If you don't want to play, then go and sit on the steps with our mam!'

'*Bad boy*,' echoed Peggy, stubbornly refusing to let go of the rope, '*not* your turn!' There then followed a bevy of jeers and calls from Tilly Watson's assorted offspring, who were dutifully lined up to wait their turn at running into the gyrating rope, where they might manage a few quick skips before getting their little legs hopelessly entangled, at which point they were promptly banished by Sal to hold the rope while others took their place at the end of the line.

'Do as Sal tells you, Tom,' Molly instructed, beginning to come down the steps, stopping only when she saw him turn from the indignant Peggy and scurry in that dipping, lopsided fashion to the back of the queue, his face spread wide in a happy, mischievous grin. Flattening himself against the wall, he looked up at Molly with such laughing eyes that she didn't have the heart to chastize him further. Instead she smiled back at him, shook her head in exasperation and began her way back up the steps, resuming her cold seat at the top and thinking how it would soon be getting dark.

'Little sods!' Tilly Watson had come to the scullery door to see what all the shouting was about. '*You lot buck yer ideas up!*' she yelled, wagging a finger to the upturned faces. 'Any more arguing an' you'll be put to bed afore yer time . . . d'yer hear me?' When the colourful assortment of heads – including those of Molly's three – all frantically nodded, she mumbled quietly to herself, before yelling again, 'Yer soon coming in anyroad, yer buggers . . . it's not long to yer bedtime as it is!' This observation produced a trail of loud moans and groans, which she stopped short by threatening, 'Yer can give over belly-aching . . . else I'll march the bloody lot of yer up these steps this very minute!' Silence descended. 'Huh! So think on!' she finished, cunningly winking at the amused Molly, who dared not look down at the small, fearful faces in the yard, for fear they might see how much she was enjoying Tilly's 'fierce' banter.

It was little over an hour later when the children were all herded in, moaning and pleading to stay out 'just a bit longer'. They whined all the way up the steps in the fading daylight; they argued round the big old table when Molly and Tilly dished out the last of the bread and preserve; they cajoled and cried when their hands and faces were being washed, and en route from the parlour to their beds they blamed each other for their curtailed enjoyment. 'It's all *your* fault, Tom!' Tilly's eldest complained, glaring at the unconcerned and misleadingly 'innocent' face of Molly's crippled lad. '*You* started all the trouble!'

'*Weren't* Tom's fault!' defended Peggy, furiously scratching at her arm, then beginning to bawl when she saw how red and sore it was.

'*Now* see what you've done!' accused little Sal, taking her small sister into her embrace, her vivid blue eyes drilling into Tilly Watson's eldest.

'She did it *herself*!' came the retort. 'Serves her right, an' all.'

Suddenly it was a free-for-all, with everyone squaring up to each other and heated threats of 'I'll smash yer in the gob', and 'Oh yea? Just try it on, matey!' being flung about.

'Whoa!' Molly quickly intervened, putting herself in the midst of pushing, squirming bodies. In a surprisingly short time, she had them despatched to their respective bedrooms and peace was restored – for another day at least.

'How much longer will we have to stay here, Mammy?' Little Sal leaned up in bed on one elbow, a troubled look in her eyes. 'Why can't we find our *own* house, eh?'

Molly smiled and after putting her fingers to her lips, she murmured, 'Ssh, sweetheart . . . don't wake the young 'uns.'

'But I want us to have our own house,' Sal insisted in a harsh whisper.

'We will,' promised Molly.

'When?'

Molly was always surprised by her daughter's directness. She seemed never to be prepared for it. 'When your father comes back,' she told the attentive child.

'*He's not coming back!*' In the flickering candlelight Molly saw the tears in Sal's eyes and her heart turned over. For a long, painful moment, she searched for a suitable answer, but she could find none. Her own unhappy gaze mingled with that of the girl's, who, throwing her small thin arms round Molly's neck, told her gently, 'I do love you, Mammy.'

Hardly able to talk for the painful lump that leapt into her throat, Molly held her daughter very close, very tight, gathering strength from that slim, seemingly fragile frame and knowing in her own heart that between the two of them in that precious minute, *Sal* was the stronger. 'I love you, too,' she whispered now, gently releasing the clinging child and easing her back into the bolster. 'Go to sleep, sweetheart,' she urged, stroking the girl's forehead until the tired blue eyes closed and it seemed that, at long last, Sal was ready for slumber.

'Good night, God bless, Mam,' came the weary, unhappy little voice.

'Good night, God bless, sunshine,' Molly replied, bending to place a kiss on the smooth, tear-stained face. After satisfying herself that Peggy and Tom were sound asleep, she went to the window and looked out at the gathering darkness. The gas-lamps in the street below threw out eerie yellow haloes, whose lights flickered in the shadows and brought the darkening corners to life.

For a while, Molly was held entranced, her face pressed hard against the cold, stiff window and the glow from the candle in her hand creating a strange image of herself in the window-pane. She gazed at the reflection for a long, curious moment, being both shocked and comforted by what she saw there. *Shocked* because of the gauntness of her features and the weariness in those dark eyes that stared back at her; *comforted* because, in spite of the gaunt features and the weariness, the image was *her*! It was her face, her eyes, *herself*. None of that had changed, only the outside. Inside she was still Molly. She had her wits and her strength. She had her children. With God's help she could go on.

Up to this point, Molly had been deluding herself that perhaps Jack might come along looking for them. Maybe, wherever he was, he might wake up one morning and remember that he had a wife and children who needed him. Now though, Molly had stopped deluding herself. Jack was not coming in search of them. *He never would.* Stranger still to Molly was the realization that she was glad; she never again wanted to set eyes on him! But her love had not turned to hate. Worse still, it had become a cold indifference.

Just now Molly had told little Sal they would have their own place when Jack came home. It was a lie. Molly hoped the good Lord would forgive her. She had known for some long time now that, if she and the young 'uns were ever again to have a place of their own, it would be by her own efforts. There was no other way. But how? *How?* She had lost count of the long, lonely nights when she had sat on the scullery steps, searching for a way, agonizing over what to do, which way to go, or how she might earn enough money to secure and keep a roof over their heads. As it was, life was difficult enough. Tilly had been good enough to take them in when they had arrived here, tired and afraid. But it was a situation that could not last for much longer – 'Only temporary, mind . . . just till yer get fixed up. Two weeks at the most,' Tilly had said.

Tilly had already extended that 'two weeks' to four. Though she never made an issue of it, it was clear that her patience was wearing thin. After all, she had her own troubles, and this little house was bursting at the seams.

Molly suspected also that Joe was impatient to see the back of them. He hadn't said as much, but now and then she would catch him staring at her with a strange look on his face. It made her feel uncomfortable. Oh, she didn't blame him! He was a hard-working man who had tended to the family when his father died. He had every right to come home to a house free of lodgers. Molly understood that. If the house next door – which had been hers and Jack's – had not already been let to an elderly couple, she might have been very tempted to climb in through the back window and lay claim to it. Silly thoughts though, she now reminded herself, because if she wasn't able to pay a proper rent, the landlord would soon fetch in the strong-arms to put her on the streets. No, she had a lot to thank Tilly for, and she was very grateful. Molly hadn't forgotten how desperately ill she was that night when she and the young 'uns arrived at Tilly Watson's door. No sooner had little Sal rattled on the door than her mammy slumped to the ground, wasted and ill, swamped with relief at having safely delivered her babies to a familiar place, and not caring anymore whether she lived or died.

After two weeks of Tilly's care and attention – and the good-natured observation that Molly had better get well for 'I ain't being lumbered with *another* brood o' brats!' – Molly was well enough to get from the bed she shared with Tilly. A few days after that, she was pottering about and gaining strength by the day.

'You still look like a bag o' bones, gal,' Molly told her reflection in the window. The black eyes had begun to twinkle though, and the strong lines of her lovely features were not quite so sharp. Her hair, however, was a pitiful sight – still thick and black as midnight, but hacked short by Tilly who believed 'hair harbours lice, my gal . . . an' I ain't got no time for picking 'em out.' So she had brought the meat knife from the scullery and while Joe held out the rich thick hanks of Molly's hair, Tilly had chopped away at it. At the time, Molly hadn't minded. Now though she winced to look at it. It had cheered her when Joe told her, only the other day, how he thought it suited her short like that and 'fetches the beauty of yer eyes out'. Tilly had laughed out loud, saying how comical it was that Molly had been at death's door, and 'here yer are, worried about yer crowning glory!' Molly had laughed too, feeling vain and foolish. Since Jack wouldn't be coming back, and she had thoughtlessly sent Mick away, what did it matter whether she had shining black hair to be proud of, or a tangled shocking mess? It didn't matter. Not one little bit.

All that really mattered to Molly now was how soon she could be on her way with the children, so as not to be a burden on Tilly any longer? This was her dilemma. There was no one she could turn to for help. Two things she did know though: she had to find a way of making money and she had to leave this house. And it must be soon! For Molly was indeed convinced that she and the young 'uns had out-stayed their welcome. All the same, she wished she felt a great deal stronger and able to easily shoulder the load that was about to fall on her.

On tiptoe, Molly went across the bare floorboards to the big brass bed where her three children were fast asleep. The bed was really Joe Watson's but he had given it up to Molly's three and was content to sleep downstairs on the couch in the front parlour. Molly thought him a fine young man. Somehow, though, she always thought of him as being much younger than herself, when in fact he was a little older. She supposed it must be because of his laughing, wayward manner, which put her in mind of young Tom.

Before leaving the room, Molly took a moment to glance round, holding the candle high, and wrapping her shawl tighter about her when the air struck damp and chilly. This house was the same as the one next door – small rooms with high ceilings and crooked floors; upstairs were three bedrooms, each with a long walk-in cupboard and tiny fire-grate. Downstairs were the front parlour, always a cold, empty space, and the back parlour with its huge, black oven range and steps leading down to the coal-hole. Following on from that was the scullery, with its stone-flagged floor, big pot-sink and outside door to steps leading into the yard below.

Molly closed the bedroom door behind her, thinking how Joe Watson's room was nicely furnished in comparison with the same room next door; at least when she and Jack lived there with the children. All *they* had in that same room was a bed and a chest of drawers, while this room had a wardrobe besides, and a comfortable armchair with a square matting covering the floorboards beside the bed. Tilly's bedroom was the same, but with a row of nails along the picture rail on which to hang her clothes. To Molly, it was all sheer luxury, and her respect for Joe had grown when Tilly claimed, 'My lad's looked after us well since his father died'. Molly thought how grand it would be if she were to have somebody to look after her in the same way. Yet she knew there was no one but herself. And wasn't likely to be.

* * *

'Where've yer been, Molly gal? I thought ye'd fallen asleep on the bed, trying to get the young 'uns off.' Tilly Watson had been rocking herself back and forth in the wooden rocking-chair by the fire-grate. When she saw Molly coming through the door from the passage, she slowed the rocker to a halt and reached down for the pint-pot which had been standing on the fender. Holding it out to Molly, she said, 'Make us a fresh brew, there's a good 'un . . . we've time for a sup or two before our Joe gets back.' Here she chuckled, 'I expect he's got caught up in a game o' cards. Oh, he's a bugger for the gambling, but he'll never go beyond the coppers in his pocket,' she added quickly, with a firm shake of her head. 'Sticks well within his limits, does our Joe. Oh aye! I know that, because old Bill the knocker-up goes there reg'lar . . . *he* likes a game o' cards too. And he has nowt but good ter say about our Joe. First and foremost, Joe looks out for his family. *Then* he enjoys what few coppers he has left!' A self-satisfied smile spread over her features, as she reminded Molly, 'It's a pity your Jack weren't as responsible, the bugger! He wants his arse kicking, and no mistake!'

'Do you want milk in your tea, Tilly?' Molly had been deeply wounded by the other woman's thoughtless observation and was deliberately making no response to it. She knew Tilly meant no real harm. She was not by nature a spiteful person. Besides, Molly reminded herself, Tilly's comments were only the truth, and she herself had come to recognize that more and more. Jack had been her whole world and she would have lain down her life for him. Now he had deserted her, and the children were all she had left. *They* were now her world, and these little innocents had no one else to look to but her. She would not let them down.

When Molly returned from the scullery with Tilly's tea, she was told in a kindly voice to 'sit down. There's things we need to talk over'. Molly's heart sank to her boots. It's time, she thought, time for me to be sent on my way, for Tilly's patience is at an end.

'I know what you're going to say, Tilly,' Molly ventured, doing as she was bidden and seating herself in the upright standchair by the table, 'and I can't blame you. Me and the children have put on you long enough, but I've got plans in hand and we'll be on our way soon.' She hoped that Tilly would be kind enough to give her at least a couple more days, because she still felt incredibly weary and bone tired. Besides which, she had been exaggerating when she told the other woman that she had 'plans in hand'. She had plans to leave, yes. But she had not the slightest idea of where she and the children would go. Somehow the thought of roughing it yet again in a derelict house or a disused factory was terrifying to her. But happen she would have no choice in the matter, for the truth was that she and the young 'uns were beggars. Beggars could not be choosers. Oh, if only she were strong again! If only she could shake off this feeling of tiredness, when every bone in her body hurt and there were times when it was a terrible effort just to put one foot before the other. 'You've been good to us,' Molly said now, 'and I'm grateful for that.'

'That's as may be.' Tilly Watson peered at Molly through quizzical eyes. 'But if I was to tell you the truth . . . I'd say as how I've really enjoyed having another woman in the house.' Here she chuckled and fell back in the chair. 'Even if I'm a good twenty year older than you,' she reluctantly admitted. Her gaze remained intent on Molly's face, and when Molly smiled, it came to her not for the first time how astonishingly lovely this young woman was. Wasn't it strange, she asked herself, how the most gentle and beautiful of souls were always the most vulnerable and how they were ill-used by others. But then, she reminded herself, wasn't it always the very same? The fiercest and most cunning would survive on the blood of those meeker, gentler creatures. Yet wasn't it also true that the Lord himself promised, 'The meek will inherit the earth'.

For a moment longer the older woman took quiet stock of Molly: the roughly shorn hair, the thin figure that was still very seemly even wrapped in a threadbare shawl which Tilly had intended throwing out, and that hauntingly lovely face with its strong lines and big, expressive eyes. There was something very special about Molly. In spite of everything – the many weeks on the road, the suffering she had been through and the illness that had taken its toll – there was still something at the core of Molly's being that was strong, determined and most admirable.

While musing to herself and thinking on Molly's particular character, it came to Tilly how she was reminded of another such creature; one who had been 'used' by others and thrown to the wolves, as it were. One who had suffered more than any other woman she had ever known, and yet had risen above it all to emerge even stronger and wiser. That woman was *Emma Grady* – now Emma Tanner. That one, and this one, known as Molly. They were two of a kind. Like peas out of the same pod!

Tilly Watson's conscience had long since bothered her where Emma Grady was concerned, for she knew beyond a doubt that it was *her* own testimony that had helped to convict Emma Grady and consequently get her transported to the far side of the world. And all for shameful greed. For the taking of a cash-box belonging to Emma's ma-in-law on the night her son was killed – 'murdered' by Emma and the woman who was Emma's only friend. O' course, it were more of an accident than murder. But at the time, it suited Tilly Watson to claim how she had 'seen it all! . . . He were pushed, your Honour. *Murdered* right before me eyes!'

The bank notes which Tilly had taken secretly from the tin-box were long ago spent; most of them on furnishing this very house and affording a set of nice clothes for her and her entire brood. Because of them bank notes, the pantry had never been bare. Oh, the money was long gone now, but it had set the Watson family up well enough, and buried the old man in a decent fashion. Now, what with Joe fetching home a good wage, they managed well enough and, compared to other unfortunates, they had few worries.

The only worry that plagued Tilly was her conscience. She was beset by nightmares about having helped to convict a young, innocent creature who had no parents and was cursed with more enemies than friends. Yet it was a long, long time ago. Too many years had fled, and too much water had passed under the bridge for her to make amends.

All the same, it had eased Tilly's mind when Emma had returned home, a wealthy and influential woman. She might have gone to her there and then and confessed her wickedness. But what good would it have done? It was too late. Emma had endured her ordeal with courage and had done well. Tilly accepted that she too must endure her own particular ordeal of guilt, for it was self-imposed. Apart from which, she had come to believe that it was wiser to keep her own counsel than to foolishly reveal how she had deliberately lied to the courts. Emma's own uncle was a Justice! You had to be very careful with the likes o' them, because they'd clap you in jail soon as wink at you! On top of which, that Marlow Tanner adored Emma, and though he was well known as a likeable and fair-minded fellow, there was no doubt he'd be up in arms at how Tilly Watson had put the finger on his Emma. No. It were always wisest to keep your own counsel in such cases.

All these years, Tilly had wanted to make amends for her terrible deed, yet was unable to. Helping Molly – who to her mind was another Emma in the making – had done a great deal to banish the nightmares that had haunted Tilly Watson.

Now Tilly revealed as much as she dared when she said, 'It's been grand having you here . . . hand on my heart, Molly, you've done me more good than you know.'

'Bless you for that, Tilly,' Molly leaned forward to squeeze the older woman's shoulder, 'but I know what a strain it's been . . . all these little bodies underfoot and more mouths to feed. I don't fool myself that the few shillings I earn here and there are anywhere near enough to fill their bellies.'

'I won't deny that there have been days when I'd be glad to see the back of you . . . when the buggers have been scrapping and my head's felt like it's been jumped on! But I'm not chucking you out on the streets. I'd rest easier in my bed of a night if I knew you had somewheres to go.' She felt Molly move her hand away and she saw the forlorn look in her face. Eyeing her severely, she asked point-blank, '*Have you?* . . . Have you somewhere to go? Come on, the truth, now!'

'No.'

'So, you intend to leave here and take to the roads, is that it?'

'We'll be fine, Tilly. I'll find a place for us now that I've got my strength back.'

'Be buggered!' Tilly snorted. 'Have you looked at yourself lately, eh? . . . Thin as a poker and weak as a kitten! Oh, I've watched you . . . trying to put on an act. But the truth is you're nowhere near fit . . . certainly not fit enough to be trudging about the streets in all weathers.'

Molly could see the other woman's dilemma. On the one hand, she was obviously concerned that Molly and the children should be all right. On the other, she was secretly relieved at the thought of having her little house returned to the bosom of her own considerable brood. All Tilly wanted was a reassurance from Molly that there was nothing at all for her to reproach herself for. Without hesitation, Molly gave her that assurance. 'You are *not* to worry yourself over us, Tilly!' she told her firmly. 'In spite of the fact that I'm still a little thin, I feel better than I've felt for a long time. You remember I was talking to the chimney sweep when he came to clean the flue last week?'

'Aye . . . I thought the pair of you had a lot to say to each other. It took the bugger long enough to do a simple job and *that's* a fact!' replied Tilly good-naturedly.

'Well, he told me how he'd heard there were these big hotels in London . . . crying out for chambermaids and kitchen hands.'

'*London!*' Tilly was horrified.

'It's a chance, don't you see, Tilly? A chance for me and the young 'uns to make a fresh start.' Molly had been quietly churning the idea over in her mind and now that it was out in the open, she was greatly enthused by the idea. Though she would not easily admit it, somewhere in the back of her mind were the last words spoken to her by Mick, before they parted. He had expressed his intention to leave these parts and, as far as she knew, he also had gone south. Perhaps as far as London. Who knows, she might even come across him there?

In these past weeks, when Molly had at first been too ill to leave the house, then later, when she had hesitantly ventured out, she had been most careful to stay well away from the wharf. Her reasons were twofold – firstly, knowing that Mick had left the area some time back, she felt it would be a sad, lonely place without him there; secondly, she had to be most careful not to show her face in places where she might be seen and recognized. Certainly she had to avoid the wharf, if only because of the fact that Marlow Tanner was a regular figure there; Marlow Tanner meant *Emma* Tanner, and Emma Tanner meant the *Justice Crowther*! Her blood ran cold at the very thought of him. Especially now, since she had been forced to flee Liverpool. She had not forgotten (how could she?) that man in the café left for dead. And she had killed him! She was more of a fugitive now than ever. There could never again be a moment's peace.

Molly was not so much concerned with her own safety as with that of the children. So now, when Tilly made a suggestion, she was instantly tempted to reject it out of hand, but then felt compelled to consider it more carefully. 'Oh, but Tilly . . . how could I leave my children behind? It's unthinkable!' The very idea shrank the heart inside her.

'If you ask me, my girl, it's the most sensible thing you can do!' Once Tilly had made her mind up, there was little shifting her. 'You go to London and find that job you were talking about. Get yourself a place where you can all stay together. *Then* come back and collect the young 'uns. They'll be content enough here, I promise . . . no harm will come to them.'

Molly was mortified at the thought of what little Sal would have to say to such a suggestion. 'Oh, I don't know that I could leave them behind, I really don't.'

'Then *don't* go to London . . . or anywhere else. Look for some'at round these parts . . . and I'll help you.' She was curious as to why Molly would even *think* of going to such a fearful place as London, so far away, and full o' strangers.

'I can't stay round these parts, Tilly . . . I *must* get away.' Molly's desperation and fear betrayed itself in her voice.

'What is it, Molly?' Tilly had suspected for some time that Molly was hiding something, afraid, maybe even running from someone. Certainly, when she arrived here at this door some four weeks since, she had the look of a haunted soul.

If ever Tilly Watson saw real fear and desolation in a body's eyes, she saw it when Molly first recovered after being close to death's door for nigh on a week. She felt *then* that Molly was driven by a dark secret. *She felt it now.* Her curiosity got the better of her. 'I weren't born yesterday,' she said in a chastizing voice, 'and I ain't so stupid not to know when somebody's on the run. What

277

have you been up to? What are you afraid of, eh? Who's after you?' Encouraged by Molly's astonished look, she insisted, 'A trouble shared is a trouble halved, they say. You can trust me . . . I took a liking to you the same day you moved in next door with your family . . . though I never did think much to that bloody fellow o' yourn! Strange though, how I don't know all that much about you. As a rule, I like to know all about them as live next door. But you, you little sod! . . . You're a right secretive bugger an' no mistake!' Suddenly, she was deadly serious, telling Molly, 'But you're in trouble. I can tell. There is something badly wrong. What is it? Somebody on your tail, is it? After money, are they? Or have you done something unlawful . . . is *that* it, eh?' When Molly remained silent, she threw her arms out wide and shook her head. 'All right. It's none o' my business, I suppose. I've got no right prying.' She began to get from the chair, looking surprised and relieved when Molly put out a hand to press her back.

'Please, Tilly, don't take offence,' entreated Molly, feeling ashamed that it might appear she had thrown the older woman's genuine concern back in her face.

'I was only trying to help . . . in my own clumsy fashion,' Tilly told her, at the same time settling back into the horse-hair armchair and looking up at Molly with a slightly wounded expression.

'I know,' conceded Molly gently, 'and you're right . . . I *do* owe you an explanation.' After all, Molly told herself, she *had* turned up here with three young 'uns and taken every advantage of Tilly's kindness. 'No doubt you've been wondering where I *really* went when I left next door?'

'Ah, well now . . . it *did* cross my mind that you hadn't altogether told the truth when you said you were making a new life with your Jack . . . that he'd got himself a job an' a place for you all to stay. The bugger never did strike me as a suitable provider. And what with you clearing off so quickly . . . like you were running away . . . well, it did set me wondering, I must admit. Oh, I were right glad for you, dearie . . . and nobody wanted you properly settled more than me, honest to God! But, well . . . I had my doubts if you must know. Then, when you turned up on the doorstep four weeks ago looking like you were on your last . . . riddled with a fever and half-starved, well!' She pursed her lips and seemed to sink into the memory of that particular day. Suddenly she was accusing, looking at Molly sternly and wagging a finger. 'I expect you let yourself go hungry in order to keep the children fed, didn't you, eh?' Without waiting for an answer she went on, '*Don't deny it!* And, if I were to tell the truth, I'd say as how I would do the very same. Us mothers . . . we're all alike, and that's a fact.' Without warning she fell silent, and folded her arms while keeping her attention on Molly's thoughtful face. She was obviously awaiting an explanation of what had taken place between the day Molly left the street and the day when she came to Tilly's door seeking refuge.

Molly felt obliged to give that explanation. Besides which, it was all a great burden on her sorry heart and maybe what Tilly had said was the truth – 'a trouble shared is a trouble halved'. And so, with no small reluctance and a deal of trepidation, Molly opened up her heart to this kindly woman. She described how she had in fact fled the area because 'someone meant harm to me and the children'. She went on to explain how she lied about going to Jack, for fear that Mick might be tempted to follow her, 'and because there were *others*, more sinister, who might also make it their business to track me down'.

'But surely Mick the bargee would never hurt a hair on your head, child?' Tilly was astounded. 'You're right, though. He *did* come a-looking for you . . . but I could have sworn it were only because the fellow thought the world of you. I've *always* been given to understand that he wanted nothing more than to look after you and the children . . . *adored you* . . . that's what *I* thought!'

'You're right, Tilly. Mick wanted me to go south with him. He told me how much he loved me and the young 'uns.'

'What then? . . . You didn't love *him*, is that it?'

'Oh, no. I *did* love him . . . I *do* love him! Only at the time I was too blinded by my feelings and loyalty for Jack.' A sadness came into Molly's dark eyes. 'I had an idea that I could find Jack and when I did, everything would be all right. But I was wrong.'

'Then it *weren't* the bargee who meant you harm?' When Molly shook her head, the older woman nodded, as though satisfied that she had not misread that man's character. 'Who were it then? Who frightened you enough to make you up sticks and take to the road with three children . . . one a cripple!' she loudly demanded. It was obvious that she was ready to do battle.

Engrossed in their conversation, neither Tilly Watson nor Molly heard the front door latch being lifted and the door opening to admit a certain young man whose head was light from the booze he had tasted, and whose heart was pining for want of a woman. That woman was Molly. The young man was Tilly's eldest son, Joe. Being suddenly intrigued by his mother's emotional outburst, he came on unsteady tip-toes to the parlour door, where he pressed himself against the wall and strained his neck so as not to miss a single word. What he heard held him rigid and astonished.

In the space of a few minutes, Molly had confided everything to this woman whom she instinctively felt she could trust. She told how Justice Crowther had hounded her over the years and of the manner in which Jack had saved her from that man's clutches when Crowther had snatched her from the hut which had been home to her and old Sal, the lovable tramp who had found her as an infant. She revealed her terrible fear of that man and the awful consequences were he ever to ensnare her again.

The more Molly confided in Tilly Watson, the more she felt a great burden being lifted from her shoulders. It was true that 'a trouble shared is a trouble halved'. Only Molly had more than *one* trouble. She had a whole batch of them, and each one had bred another, until now – try as she might – she could see no way out of the cage they had made for her!

'Ah, you poor little sod!' exclaimed Tilly, her eyes popping out like bright buttons at the awful tale. 'And you've kept all this to yourself this long time? Why! It's a wonder you've not gone crazy with it all.' She patted Molly's hand affectionately. 'You poor little sod,' she repeated, gawping at Molly in wonderment. 'Mind you . . . I'd rather it were *you* than me who's made an enemy of that Justice Crowther. By! He's a right evil bastard and no mistake!' A look of horror crossed her features, until in a tick, she was staring at Molly again, urging her, 'Go on then, Molly . . . so where did you go from here? What adventures befell you? Oh, and *what* in God's name made you come back . . . when you knew that the Justice might still be looking for you? No wonder the first thing you did when you came out of that fever was to beg me not to tell anybody you were here!' She felt herself break out in a cold sweat and began feverishly dabbing at her forehead and face with a grubby hankie snatched from her pinnie pocket. 'Oh, dear Lord! . . . To think what might have happened if he'd found out! *What!* . . . the bugger might have even come bursting into this very parlour!'

'Now can you understand why I have to leave your house, Tilly? The last thing I want is that you should get involved.'

'I see.' Tilly Watson was never one to be intimidated and, as suddenly as she had broken out in a fearful sweat, she was calm again, and outraged that Molly should have been so persecuted by that fiend of the law that she had been forced to flee her own home. She said as much to Molly, and was reluctantly understanding when it was then explained to her that 'I wouldn't have been able to keep the house anyway, Tilly, because I couldn't afford the rent after Jack went off . . . leaving me with yet another mouth to feed.'

As Molly finished her story, she held nothing back. In complete and utter trust of this sympathetic woman, she told everything; describing the weeks of living rough, her constant fear that the law was waiting round every corner; her hopeless search for Jack and, last of all, with heavy heart and in such a small, fearful whisper that even the silent listener in the passage could not hear this awful confession, she described how Bill Craig, the café proprietor, had attacked her . . . how they had struggled and she had struck out. 'He fell to the floor . . . lifeless.

Oh Tilly, I killed him! When they catch me, *I'll hang for sure.*' The tears flowed down Molly's face as she thought of the three innocents sleeping upstairs. 'What of them?' she asked. 'What of the children?'

Tilly Watson was shocked. In her time she had cheated, lied and stolen in order to keep a roof above their heads. But Molly! *Molly had done murder!* No wonder she had to keep on the move. No wonder there were times when she seemed afraid of her own shadow. She glanced at Molly's dark untidy head bent into the long, slender fingers; she saw how distressed and desperate the unfortunate creature was, and to her mind there was only one solution.

Getting to her feet, she put her two arms around Molly's trembling shoulders, saying stoutly, 'They'll not harm you while you're in Tilly Watson's house, I can tell you that! From what I can see, my girl, you've already decided right . . . get to the big city and make a new life . . . change your name. Do what you have to do. But like I said before, Molly . . . the young 'uns will be best off left with me until you've got work and found a place to stay.' She sensed that Molly was about to resist that particular idea and was quick to intervene. 'All right, I'll tell you what. Let's call it a day and get a good night's sleep on it, eh? Tomorrow, you can tell me what you want to do.'

'You're a good woman,' Molly said now, gently kissing Tilly on the cheek and smiling when it blushed fiercely. 'Like you say . . . I'll sleep on it.' She turned away. 'Good night. God bless. We'll talk in the morning.' Going to one of the brass candleholders on the sideboard, she took up a match from the tray close by, struck it alight on the rough-edged side, and put the flame to the candle-wick.

With Tilly Watson only a few steps behind, carrying the oil-lamp, Molly went up the stairs to where the children were soundly sleeping, calling back softly when Tilly bade her, 'If yer gonna be a while afore you come to bed . . . mind you creep softly in beside me. I don't want you waking me up once I've gone off!'

After a while the house was quiet, the deep silence perforated only by the soft, distant snoring coming from Tilly Watson's room.

As a rule, Molly would sit a while with the children before tiptoeing out of the room and down the stairs to the back steps, where she would enjoy the cool solitude of the evening, indulging in thoughts of the past and all that might have been. It was at times like these when she sorely missed the eccentric old woman who had raised her from a babe-in-arms.

Old Sal had been Molly's heroine, her mammy and her world. Yet for all that, she had never given Molly the one thing she had always longed for – the truth of her origins. *Who was she? To whom did she belong?* How many times had she asked those questions? Old Sal had not been able to tell Molly the truth – simply because she herself never knew, always believing that the girl-child she found in the gutter had been left by the little people. '*Now I'll never know*,' sighed Molly, gazing fondly at her own three babies. 'But, if I don't belong to anybody else, *I belong to you*,' she told them. The tears sprang to her eyes as she leaned forward to kiss each tiny face in turn: little Sal, her first-born, named after the old dear whom Molly had adored, little Sal, with her vivid blue eyes and bold, forthright manner. Then came Peggy: sturdy, stocky little thing, blessed with thick, rich hair the colour of midnight and dark eyes so like her mammy's. And young Tom, possessed of a happy mischievous nature, lovable and infuriating all at the same time, yet cursed with a pitiful deformity that must hamper him for all his life.

Molly's children were uniquely different, each with their own special personalities and physical traits. She loved them all with fierce protectiveness. They were her life. Her reason for living. Because of these three helpless innocents, she had to stay free, and shrug off the weariness that had settled on her.

On this night, when Molly could so easily have climbed into bed and let the welcoming waves of slumber ebb over her, she found herself going back down the stairs. There was too much on her mind, and important things to be decided. Tomorrow she must answer Tilly's suggestion that she leave the children in her care for as long as it took Molly 'to find a place'.

In her heart, Molly had already decided. She could not leave the children behind. But wasn't that a selfish decision, she argued with herself. Wouldn't the children be safer and happier here, with Tilly and her brood, at least until Molly could fetch them? And, if Molly had her way, that would be sooner rather than later. So her heart led her one way, and her reason another.

There were other things to be carefully considered also: in particular, where did she intend going? London, she had said. But why not further *north*, instead of south? Did it matter, so long as she could isolate herself and the young 'uns? Where the Justice Crowthers and Emma Tanners of this world could not pluck her out? Ah, but remember what the chimney sweep had said: 'The big hotels in London are crying out for chambermaids and kitchen hands'. He'd also said that they had attic rooms and such like, where a body could make its own little nest. And a nest for four needn't be much bigger than a nest for one, isn't that right, Molly asked herself, as she placed a candle on the scullery window-ledge.

It was a beautiful night. The sky was a dark, velvet ocean pitted with dancing stars and lit by a crescent-shaped moon. All round were strange and familiar sounds; the scurrying of little feet in the cellar below, the whistling of a cool breeze squeezing through the many chinks in the high stone wall that skirted the yard. And the gentle rush of the nearby canal was like a soft lullaby on the night air. Molly cherished these snatched moments of an evening; it was so peaceful here, so private and sheltered. For a moment, she pushed all the worrying and urgent thought to the back of her mind, and opened her soul to let in all things lovely.

Strange, how the first emotion that filled her with joy was the memory of a tall, handsome fellow standing proud and straight aboard the barge that was his home and could have been hers also – Mick. His name murmured itself on her lips and the memory was sweet. 'Oh, Mick, whatever will become of us?'

While at the back of the house Molly's thoughts were engaged in memories both bad and pleasant, there was another who also indulged in deep thought.

Joe Watson feverishly paced the pavement at the front of his mother's house, now and again leaning on the street lamp and allowing his senses to imagine all manner of secret fancies. Only a short while ago he had returned home delightfully intoxicated and boldly enter-taining the prospect that not only would he make a play for Molly, but that when he did, that young woman would be so flattered she would eagerly fall into his arms, ready and willing to please him in any way he chose.

Now though the excited fellow had been shocked almost into sobriety, and made to see that there was more to Molly than he had at first imagined. The conversation he had secretly 'overheard' between his mother and her young lodger had certainly given him food for thought. From all that had been disclosed, one article in particular stood out bold in his mind – for some reason which he had not quite grasped, *Molly was a fugitive!* And worse still, it was the Justice Crowther whom she'd come up against!

'God Almighty,' Joe uttered, 'of all the enemies she could have been dealt, it seems she's drawn the worst.' Suddenly he was made to weigh his fancy for Molly against his fear of the most hated and reviled fiend ever set on this earth. 'Do I want Molly so much that I'd take on her enemies an' all?' he asked himself. And back came his own answer – '*Do I bloody hell as like!*'

There was no doubting that Joe Watson had a very real and very urgent hankering for the lovely, desirable Molly, who – though presently a bit too thin and scruffy for his usual liking – had a certain presence and grace that only made her loveliness more magnificent. Yes, he wanted her right enough, he decided. But whereas just over an hour ago he would have taken her with all her needs and troubles – three kids an' all – now it was a different tale altogether. There wasn't a woman alive who could be worth getting tangled up with the Justice for? *Not even the lovely Molly!* Oh, but that wasn't to say that he couldn't strike up a little fun and frolics with her, now was it, eh? he asked himself. And again, back came his own answer. 'O' course not! It's obvious the wandering Jack ain't fulfilling his manly duties, so like as not Molly would welcome this fine fellow as a substitute.'

Joe Watson had always prided himself on being a quiet favourite with the women. It was very plain to him that Molly was first and foremost a woman. Therefore, like all women, she had natural desires. That's where *he* came in – to satisfy those desires, and in the process, to fulfil his own deep-down needs. Needs that were getting more urgent by the minute, and which, even with the name of Justice Crowther still buzzing in his mind, gave him the courage to softly push home his key in the front-door lock, quietly let himself in and, on tiptoe, creep along the passage, then through the living quarters out to the scullery steps . . . where he knew instinctively Molly would be sitting alone, counting the stars and thinking about things that were private and precious to her.

The night had grown chilly. Shivering, Molly drew the shawl close about her shoulders. She had sat there on the hard steps, their marble coldness striking into her and penetrating her very bones.

It seemed like an age that she had stayed there, thinking and worrying, searching for so many answers that would not come. Only one thing was certain to her. She had no choice but to make a new life for herself and the children, and in a place so big and which teemed with so many people that she and the children would be as difficult to find as a raven up a chimney.

London Town! The decision was made, and Molly felt better for it. *But when?* Dare she wait until she was stronger and perhaps got together a few shillings? Or was time running out too fast now? Was the law closing in on her at this very minute? The thought made her tremble. And what to do about the bairns? In her deepest heart, Molly knew that Tilly was right. If she were to head for London with three young 'uns on her skirt-tail, it would certainly make things that much more difficult. But then, Molly reminded herself, she had travelled many foot-weary miles, through town and countryside alike, every step of the way followed by three pairs of little feet, all as determined and brave as her very own.

All of these memories brought a gentle smile to Molly's face, and a grateful warmth to her heart. But she could not ignore Tilly Watson's warning. She would be all kinds of a fool not to realize that trudging the roads and finding the occasional stopping-off place was altogether different from searching for both a permanent home and a secure position which would provide for them all. What employer would take her on with three young children beside her? And one a cripple. It was hardly likely.

Try as she might, Molly could not resolve her dilemma. Her task might prove impossible with the children along, but, oh dear God above, how could she leave them behind? Even in the safe hands of the good woman who had taken them in.

Suddenly Molly's terrible anxiety was thrust away by the thought of Jack. Jack-the-Lad! *Jack the Waster!* The boy who had never become a man. Too much of a coward to face up to life. The dreamer who had cruelly deserted them.

Molly had no illusions left where that was concerned.

Jack would *never* be back. She knew that now, and all of her worries were swamped by the anger such realization brought. Molly had loved him so. *Idolized him!* And in her blind love she would never have dreamed of a day when her feelings could be any different.

That day had been in the making when Tom was born and her man had fled at the sight of his tiny, deformed son. It hurt Molly to remember. She wondered whether she might ever forgive Jack for that. One thing she *did* know: her love for Jack had begun to die on that night, until now there remained in her heart only a cold, empty place where that love had been. To set eyes on him now would never revive that love. Instead it would only bury it forever, along with any future they might have had.

Yet if the thought of Jack brought distress to her, the memory of someone else made her weary heart soar. To her mind now came the image of Mick, strong and virile, protective and caring.

In a moment, Molly recalled something that dear old Sal had told her: 'We're all of us entitled to one big mistake in us lives, Molly darlin'.' Only now did Molly realize the profound truth of those words. Because hadn't she already used up her entitlement to 'one big mistake' when she had sent Mick away? To Molly's mind, she could never make a greater mistake than that one.

Where was he now? Molly tortured herself. Was he in some other, wiser woman's arms? Had he forgotten her entirely? What a fool! What a blind, ignorant fool she had been! And now, it was all too late. Suddenly the tears were burning in Molly's eyes, spilling over and trailing down her face. 'Oh, Mick! Mick! If only you knew,' she murmured into the darkness, leaning her

head into the palms of her hands and gently swaying in
the manner a child might do when comforting itself. Her
sobs were so soft that they fell away on the still night air,
unheard – except by Molly herself, and by the other
who, for these past few moments, had stood at the top of
the steps, discreetly out of the candle-light, becoming
angered by the name he had heard on Molly's lips.

Joe Watson knew more of Mick the bargee's whereabouts than did either Tilly Watson or Molly herself. He
knew, for instance, that Mick seemed very well in with
the Tanners these days, or so the ale-house gossip had it.
And that Mick's barge had been laid up at Liverpool for
some time, while the fellow himself was said to be
'tramping the country like a soul with a purpose'. There
had been much speculation. But nobody appeared to be
familiar with the true facts as to what ailed Mick Darcy.
None dared ask, for Mick was a very private fellow, it
was said.

Since the day when Molly had arrived on his mother's
doorstep, Joe Watson could so easily have mentioned
the gossip concerning Mick Darcy. But being the cunning fellow that he was, his instincts had warned him
to stay quiet. After all, he knew how the bargee had
a liking for Molly and he suspected Molly was not
altogether unimpressed by Mick Darcy's attentions.
And since he himself had growing designs on Molly, it
wouldn't do to discuss possible rivals, now would it?
And deep down, Joe Watson had wondered whether it
wasn't Molly herself that Mick Darcy was searching for!
With all this in mind, he had not even confided in his own
mother. What! Old Tilly would turn stark grey in a
minute if she believed her own provider was considering
taking on another woman – a woman with three brats an'

all. Imagining the ensuing confrontation between himself and Tilly, and still somewhat under the influence of the jugs of ale he had sunk that night, Joe Watson was made to quietly chuckle.

'*Who's there?*' Molly thought she heard something and would have clambered to her feet if Joe had not quickly stepped into the moonlight. 'Oh, it's you, Joe.' There was relief in her voice. As he came down the steps towards her, she discreetly dried her eyes on the corner of her shawl. For one awful minute, Molly had imagined it might be little Sal standing there. Her eldest daughter had an uncanny knack of knowing when her mammy was most in need of comfort. Molly had been careful of late not to lean too heavily on that darling girl. For she was only a bairn, however much she tried to be 'growed up'. To her shame, Molly had been in real danger of forgetting that. Then there was the matter of schooling. Tilly mentioned only the other day that the authorities were sending men round to check on the children. It was all becoming a real nightmare.

'You're a strange one, Molly darling.' Joe eased himself on to the same step as Molly, casually smiling into her dark eyes and thinking how beautifully they sparkled in the soft moonlight. The tears were still bright in the blackness of her gaze as she returned his smile. Encouraged, he gently insisted, 'You ain't fooled me . . . I heard you crying, gal.' He was careful not to reveal that he had also heard her call out Mick's name, and that he could easily have strangled her because of it.

'Oh, don't concern yourself,' Molly was quick to tell him. She was embarrassed that he had seen her crying. 'Women do get weepy sometimes.' Her smile deliberately brightened as he continued to gaze at her. She wanted no sympathy. Though she was grateful that Joe had not complained about her and the children being here, she was in no mood to discuss her personal problems.

'So, it's mind me own business, is it?' Joe teased, boldly taking Molly's hand in his, and being pleasantly surprised by the warmth in those long, fine fingers. 'You needn't worry,' he told her with a cheeky wink, 'Joe Watson knows when not to poke his nose where it don't belong.' His hand on hers remained steady, even though inside he was trembling with excitement. 'Y'know, Molly . . . I've never said this to any woman, but *I admire you*. The way you manage to cope without a fellow . . . and you being made responsible for three young 'uns. There's not many women as'd gladly shoulder such a burden. Mind you, them three bairns o' yourn . . . well, they're great little troopers. Just like their mammy,' he grinned, priding himself on knowing the surest way to Molly's heart was through the brats. 'They do you credit, gal. And don't think I ain't seen how you spend many an hour walking young Tom up and down the yard . . . encouraging him to make the best use of his bad leg, so's he might grow up without being altogether crooked.' Here, he shook his head and was obliged to be truthful. 'You mustn't fool yourself on that score though, Molly, because it's as plain as the lovely nose on your face that one o' Tom's legs is a terrible lot shorter than the other.' When he saw the light dim in Molly's eyes, he cursed himself, 'Aw, now . . . I ain't saying as all your efforts is in vain, or that you should give up. No indeed!' Seeing his slender chances slipping away, he tenderly squeezed her hand and filled his voice with compassion. 'Take no notice o' me, Molly. You just carry on doing what you think best. It's amazing what a body can do, if they put their mind to it. There ain't a single thing wrong with a body holding faith in miracles . . . an' who says they can't happen, eh? Who says that? Not *me*, an' that's a fact!'

Molly was made to laugh at his desperation to make amends; although she did think he had held her hand quite long enough. 'We all have to hope for miracles,' she told him, gently drawing her hand from his grasp. 'I won't ever stop believing that one day something *will* be done to help my Tom.'

'O' course, Molly!' He was downhearted that she had felt the need to tuck her two hands beneath her shawl. If he were not careful, Molly would be up and away to bed, taking a golden opportunity with her. Oh, but not if he were cunning. Tread gently, Joe old pal, he told himself, or your chances of bedding this tasty creature will come to a sorry end. He could just imagine it! Milk-white skin, smooth and warm against his nakedness, open, inviting thighs waiting to draw him in, and soft round teats hardening beneath the tip of his tongue. Oh! It was all too much. How could he stop himself trembling? Why didn't he take her here and now, *against* her will if needs be? No! No, he wouldn't dare. Not with his mother in hearing distance. Besides, if he were wily, he might get far enough into Molly's good favour that she'd want him to bed her on a *regular* basis. Now then, wouldn't that be a fine thing, eh?

'Joe . . . I haven't really thanked you for letting me and the young 'uns stay under this roof so long,' Molly said, shifting her position so that she was looking full into Joe's face.

'Aw, you're very welcome, Molly,' he replied, thinking

how she'd be like an innocent child in his hands. 'Besides, don't forget . . . it ain't really *my* roof. It's me mam's.' He sidled closer. Molly's eyes were so unusually lovely, so darkly entrancing.

'I know, but it's *you* who keeps the family and pays the rent. Tilly's told me that often enough.' Molly was well aware that one harsh word from Joe might have obliged Tilly to turn them out on the streets. Although, to be fair to Tilly, she did have a strong mind of her own, and could be infuriatingly stubborn when she wanted. Many was the time Molly had witnessed a real clash of wills between mother and son. But these two had a great deal of love and respect for each other. She had seen that also.

'I'm not denying that I'm a good provider and a hard-working man,' boasted Joe Watson, deciding to play along that particular line. He had an instinct that Molly would be most impressed by that, being as her husband was neither, and because of it, Molly and the young 'uns were the ones to suffer. 'Oh, yes. To my mind, it's a man's duty to take care of his family.' He kept his voice soft and his gaze gentle. 'I'm not a fellow to shirk his duty, I can assure you of that!' Oh, how he ached to grab her into his arms!

'You're a good man, Joe. There's no denying it.' Molly was faintly amused by his glowing self-opinion. All the same, it was nothing less than the truth. He was a hard-working man, and he certainly looked after Tilly and her brood. 'Any woman would be proud to have you as her man. When the right girl comes along, Joe, well . . . she'll be very fortunate, that's for certain.' Molly began gathering the tails of her shawl together. The night air had grown bitterly cold and she found herself shivering.

Greatly encouraged by Molly's words, Joe reached out both hands, placing one on Molly's slim shoulder and the other beneath her chin, cupping it gently so as to raise her face towards him. When Molly looked at him with big, surprised eyes, a thrill raced through him. Quickly he asked, 'Would *you*, Molly? Would *you* be proud to have me for your man?'

Molly had been astonished when he had put his hands on her. She was even more astonished by his question. 'I didn't mean you to take my words that way,' she told him. 'I'm sorry, Joe . . . you misunderstood me.' She wriggled uncomfortably, but he made no move to release her.

'But you do like me, don't you Molly?' he murmured, his face so close to her that Molly could feel his warm breath against her mouth. The taint of booze filled her nostrils. *So, that was it!* Tilly's eldest had been drinking and was full of false courage.

'Well, of course I do. You've been very kind to me and the children.'

'And, you think me a pleasant-looking fellow . . . handsome, wouldn't you say?' His voice was low and caressing.

In her own mind, Molly could not deny that Joe Watson had a certain charm, a special attractiveness that might appeal to women; with that thick, wavy hair, warm blue eyes and his lithe, muscular figure, there was no doubt he had swept many a girl off her feet. All of this raced through Molly's mind, but in this situation she was most reluctant to voice it aloud.

'You *do* think I'm handsome, don't you, Molly darling? . . . Happen you even *fancy* me a bit, eh?' As he leaned forward, and Molly sensed his intention, she made a determined effort to break free. Even then, however, being conscious of the fact that he was under the influence, she must be careful not to make him lose his footing. A tumble down the stone steps and into the flagged yard could easily prove fatal.

As it was, Molly found herself struggling more to keep Joe Watson upright than to ensure her own escape. 'For God's sake, Joe . . . let me pass!' There was a moment when the pair of them nearly went headlong. But instead of giving Molly the leeway she needed, Joe Watson was determined not to let his moment go. With a laugh, he swooped her to him and before Molly could even object, he kissed her full on the mouth – a long, demanding kiss that filled her with alarm.

His need of Molly was most obvious by the manner in which he pressed himself against her, pushing her back against the wall, and beginning to fumble at his trousers with his one free hand. In his growing excitement, his teeth sank into Molly's lips, causing a slight trickle of blood to escape.

With a last, determined effort, Molly twisted herself away from him, gasping with horror when he made a frantic grab at her and lost his balance! She was helpless as he stumbled sideways and fell on to the steps, before sliding ever so slowly over each stone rising, until with a muffled thump, he came to rest at the bottom, his jacket tangled round his neck, and his trousers limp round his boots.

For one awful minute Molly was petrified, staring down at the misshapen lump and fearful that he'd drawn his last breath.

When she hurried down the steps to investigate, however, Molly's fears were stilled. Joe had come to no harm, 'Come the morning, every bone in your body'll ache,' Molly told his prostrate form, 'and it's no more than you deserve, Joe Watson!' She couldn't help but chuckle at the poor fellow. Yet, all in all, the experience had not been a pleasant one. Certainly not one which she would ever hope to be repeated.

As Molly returned to the parlour, where she collected Joe Watson's greatcoat from the nail on the door, she recalled the ardour of that young man. The more she thought about it, the more serious her mood became. There was no doubting that Tilly's eldest had a yearning for her. A yearning that she had not been aware of. Until tonight.

Oh, it was true that Joe Watson had been influenced by the jugs of ale he had downed at the ale house. But wasn't it also true that, while the ale might have plucked up the courage for him to make advances to her, the wanting itself was already in him? That particular thought disturbed Molly a great deal. Suddenly she was made to recall how, on occasions, she had caught Tilly's eldest staring at her in a strange manner which she took to be disapproval of her and the young 'uns being there. Well! It was plain to see that *that* was *not* the case at all. The simple truth was that Joe Watson had a hankering to bed her! There could be trouble in that, thought Molly. Real trouble. Of a kind she could well do without!

On swift, silent feet, Molly returned to the place where Joe Watson still lay, open-mouthed, loudly snoring and out to the world. Where she had been amused before, she was now troubled. 'You've made my mind up, Joe Watson,' she told him, while carefully draping the heavy greatcoat over his figure, and tucking in his limbs out of the cold. 'I can't stay here another day. It's London Town for me. And the sooner the better!'

For some reason she couldn't fathom, Tilly Watson suddenly woke up in the early hours. Climbing out of bed, she went on bare feet to the window, shivering and moaning when the cold floorboards struck chilly to her toes.

At the window she peered out into the sky, still quite dark, but beginning to shimmer at the edges where the sun was coming up. 'Bloody cats, I shouldn't wonder!' muttered Tilly, wondering what had disturbed her at such an unearthly hour. 'Climbing atop o' one another . . . mating and marauding! Waking decent folk from their beds.'

Opening the window she leaned out, ready to throw the first thing to hand at any moving shadow. 'Get away with you!' she said in a loud whisper, shaking her fist and almost toppling over the window-ledge when she saw a movement in the yard below. Curious, she peered harder. 'That ain't no bloody cat!' she muttered. 'I'm buggered if it ain't a *fella*!'

Quickly Tilly closed the window and rushed back to the bed where she wrapped herself in a shawl. Grabbing the oil-lamp, which she had lit on waking, Tilly went from the room, satisfied herself that all the children were fast asleep, and then began her way downstairs. '*And where's that Molly?*' she muttered. 'What the devil's going on?'

On reaching the parlour, Tilly's temper was not improved by the discovery that her eldest son was not yet tucked up asleep on the couch. 'There'd best be some good reason for such goings-on,' she told the empty couch, 'or my name's not Tilly Watson!'

Passing through the back parlour to the scullery, Tilly was shocked: as she swung her lamp by the big table in the centre of the parlour, she caught sight of a folded note with the name 'TILLI' written on it in big, bold letters.

Setting down the lamp on the table, Tilly carefully unfolded the note, screwing up her eyes in typical fashion as she read, with great difficulty, the following large scrawl:

Tilli,
I've gon to London.
Pleez mind my babis til I can fetch them. Tell them
    I luv them.
I've put my trust in you and God.
Luv, Molly.

'Well, I'm buggered!' Tilly was so overcome that she felt the need to fall into a nearby standchair. 'Well . . . I'm buggered!' Suddenly it came to her that something untoward must have happened for Molly to have made such a swift and fearful decision to leave her precious young 'uns behind. Oh Molly knew right enough that they'd be well looked after and kept safe by Tilly – there was no question. 'But she were so *agin* it!' Tilly said aloud in a shocked voice. 'I thought she'd *never* agree to leave them young 'uns . . . though o' course *I* knew that it would be for the best. Oh aye! They'd be much better off with me . . . tucked up in bed of a night, with a proper roof over their heads and some'at substantial in their bellies. *And* they'll be waiting here when their mammy comes to fetch them.' Tilly had no qualms that

Molly had done the right thing. What she could not understand was what in heaven's name had driven Molly to run off in the middle of a cold, dark night? It weren't like the lass. Not at all. Molly were the sort who would have waited till morning, when she could have talked her plans over proper, and explained to the bairns why it were best to leave them with Tilly. 'And has she even a shilling to her name?' Tilly wondered out loud, 'Or a bite to eat with her?' A quick rummage in the pantry revealed that Molly had taken nothing from there. 'Though the Lord only knows, there ain't much in there to *begin* with!' tutted Tilly. Then Tilly received a second shock.

'Molly, you bugger . . . what did you push me away for, eh? I'm the best fellow *you're* likely to get in a hurry! . . . The *only* one, I shouldn't wonder. Come here, you flighty bitch!' Joe Watson stumbled up the steps and into the half-light of the scullery, one hand struggling with his falling trousers, and the other making a clumsy grab for the shawled figure which turned, startled, from the pantry door.

When Joe Watson's bloodshot eyes caught sight of the woman's disbelieving face, he almost fell back out of the door with astonishment. '*Mam!*' His voice was incredulous.

In a second, he was frantically drawing up his trousers, apologizing profusely and entreating Tilly, 'I didn't know what I were saying, Mam, honest! I've sunk too many jars at the ale house . . . went into the yard for a pee and . . . I must'a fell over or some'at.'

Tilly was having none of it! So! *Here* was the reason for Molly fleeing into the night. This bugger had tried it on. Frightened her. Made her feel it wouldn't be safe to stay where she was easy game. '*Why! You filthy swine, our Joe!*' Tilly was incensed that a lad of hers could take advantage of somebody who'd come to this door for shelter. '*Bloody men!* You're all the same . . . look at a woman and all you see is a bare arse!'

Time and again Tilly lashed out at the hapless fellow, who was losing the battle to hold up his trousers with one hand and fend her fierce blows off with the other. 'Well, she's run off to London Town! . . . You've frightened the poor little sod away. So, now you can work a bloody sight harder and feed the three extra mouths she's left behind in my care. And you'd better hope she comes back for them sooner rather than later.' With each word she landed a resounding clap round his ears. ''Cause they're not going short of *nowt*, d'you hear? Molly's three are to be treated the very same as my own, for as long as they're under this roof. *D'you hear? You fornicating bugger!*' She pushed him aside and angrily slammed and bolted the back door. 'Get out of my sight. You're not only drunk . . . You're shameful. *Shameful!* That's what you are!' She grabbed up the oil-lamp and swept past him, pushing him away with a look of disgust when it seemed he might fall against her. 'You want to thank your lucky stars that your dad ain't here to see this day, Joe Watson,' she called on her way through the parlour, 'because the thrashing *I* just gave you wouldn't be nothing to what you'd have had from him! *He* were a good man. Not the sort to take advantage of an unfortunate young woman deserted by her old man and left with three bairns to worry about. Well, now *you* can worry about them, can't you, eh? . . . Till their mammy's able to fetch them away!'

Alone in the darkness of the scullery, Joe Watson

leaned unsteadily against the wall, cold and aching in every inch of his body, both from the time he had spent crumpled at the foot of the steps, and from the angry attack made on him by Tilly.

But now Joe Watson was angry too. And smarting. And deeply humiliated. There was something painfully belittling in being thrashed by a woman, even if it were his own mother and he couldn't hit back, and even if he *had* deserved it! On top of all that he couldn't forget how Molly herself had also belittled him. Joe Watson never dreamed the day would come when he was turned down by *any* woman, let alone one who must be starving for want of a fellow. '*You bitch!*' he hissed into the darkness. A well of fury rose in him. 'You bloody trash, Molly! I'll not forgive you . . . and I'll not forget how you've turned my own mother on me!'

Long after Tilly Watson's gentle snoring sounded through the house, her eldest son lay on his couch downstairs, his anger and humiliation a burning pain inside him. His greatest fear was that the blokes at work or in the ale house might find out what had taken place here this night, and how he'd been so badly used by two women. If it was ever made public knowledge, his life would be made hell. The thought of all that had happened was like a sore inside him, a terrible hatred that simmered and spread until he could think of nothing but revenge.

Suddenly it came to him! And with such clarity that he was forced to sit upright in his bed, a smile of delight on his face, and a feeling of satisfaction in his wounded heart.

'The brats!' he cried in a whisper. '*Molly's three brats.*

So *I'll* be the one to provide for them, will I?' He chuckled. 'Like bloody hell I will!' He had no intention of doing any such thing. But how to rid himself of them, now that was another matter entirely.

Like a bolt from the blue it came to him. While mulling over the conversation he had overheard between his mother and Molly, Joe Watson was made to recall a name. A certain name that made even him shiver in spite of himself. Justice Crowther. Molly's self-confessed sworn enemy. 'Oho, Molly my darling . . . you'll rue the day you ever stirred up trouble in this house!' His laugh was awful to hear, but not so awful as his cruel intent.

'But when's me mammy coming back? . . . I want her to come back!' Little Sal's vivid blue eyes swam with tears as she looked up at Tilly beseechingly.

'Aw look, sweetheart. If I've told you once this morning, I've told you a hundred times . . . your mammy won't leave you here a minute longer than she has to.' Tilly had been under siege from the girl's questions ever since she'd got from her bed. She'd felt bad enough about leathering poor Joe the way she had; got up special early an' all, to make friends with him, she had. Although her intention was to make it plain that she thoroughly disapproved of the way he'd behaved! All the same, she hadn't behaved very well herself either going at him like that. After all, he was a grown man now. No, she'd done wrong, and meant to tell him so. But when she came down, all ready to mend the rift between them, he weren't there. The bugger had gone, and not even his snap-can with him. It worried Tilly, because Joe did a long, hard day at work. And if he had no snap-can with him, what would he have to eat, eh? After a while of fretting, Tilly decided that he must mean to come home at midday for some'at to eat. She'd talk to him then. Everything would be all right between them; she was sure of it. But then, she was *not* sure of it. 'Oh, Sal . . . I'm telling you, your mammy's only gone to get herself some work . . . and a place where you can all live.' She was wearied by little Sal's insistent questions, although she felt a deal of sympathy for the lass.

'Will she be back tomorrow?'

'Not tomorrow, no,' Tilly told her firmly. 'That don't give her much time to get it all sorted out, does it, eh?' She took her hands from the sink, where she was up to her elbows in dirty breakfast crockery, and with a gentle sigh she wiped them on her pinnie before resting them on the girl's small shoulders. 'Has your mammy ever left you before?' she asked.

'No.'

'Would she leave you at all, if she didn't have to?'

'I don't think so . . . *no*.'

'Your mammy loves you bairns more than anything in the world. You know that, don't you?'

For a long, painful moment there came no reply, and it was obvious to the onlooking woman that the child was fighting inside herself. When suddenly little Sal burst into tears and flung herself forward into the woman's arms, Tilly crushed her tight in a loving embrace. 'Go on, young 'un,' she said softly, 'you bawl your little heart out if you want.' Which the child did. After a while she stepped back from the haven of Tilly's arms. Wiping her eyes on the back of her hands, she looked up at Tilly, and the woman was astonished at the resolve in Sal's face. 'All right now, are you?' she asked.

Instead of an answer, she got yet more questions.

'Me mammy's not been *taken* away, has she? She's not in trouble, is she? That awful man from Miss Nelly's hasn't got her, has he?'

'Why! . . . I ain't got the slightest idea what you're talking about, sweetheart.' Tilly thought Sal's 'Miss Nelly' and 'that awful man' must belong to some misadventure or other that Molly and her young 'uns had experienced during the time when they were trudging the streets. She might have gone deeper into the matter but she was presently more preoccupied with her son, Joe. Something was troubling her. Something that wouldn't let her be. 'Your mammy *ain't* in no trouble . . . you've got my word on it.' Quickly, she fished Molly's note out of her pinnie pocket. 'Look here. Your mammy wrote this . . . she left it on the table for me to find. It were there when I got up this morning.' She handed it to the girl, who flattened it out on the slopstone, trying desperately to make head or tail of it. Thanks to Nelly, Sal could read a few words. Molly's spelling, however, posed a difficulty for the child.

'Well?' Tilly was amused to see how Sal turned the note every which way in order to decipher it. 'Can you tell what it says?' She assumed that Mollly must have taught the girl about words.

'I know my mammy's name,' Sal said proudly, pointing to the word 'Molly' at the bottom of the note, 'and I think that's your name there?' She showed Tilly her own misspelt name.

'That's a clever lass,' encouraged Tilly, pointing to the main body of the note. 'Can you tell what all *that* says?'

'Not properly,' Sal admitted.

'Right then!' Tilly ran her finger along each word,

carefully reading it for Sal's benefit. When she had finished, there was a brief silence, during which Sal was thinking hard on what her mammy had said. When at last she returned her attention to Tilly, her eyes were much brighter, and there was a little smile on her face.

'Are we going to live in London then?'

'It would seem so . . . *if* your mammy finds work and a place for you all.'

'She does love us! . . . And she *will* come for us soon, won't she?'

'She said so, didn't she?' Tilly asked kindly. When Sal eagerly nodded, she told her, 'There you are then. Now! . . . Can a poor woman get a bit o' peace round here? You go off and play in the cellar with the others. Keep them all outta sight mind . . . because that schooling fellow might come a-searching these 'ere parts!'

With serious face – that told Tilly how the girl would not be altogether happy until Molly was back – Sal went down the scullery steps towards the cellar, from where there came enough noise to satisfy her that Molly's two younger bairns were not fully aware that their mammy had gone so far away.

Tilly knew that Sal would not stay long in the cellar. After a short while, she was proved right when Sal emerged to seat herself on the front doorstep, where she gazed wistfully up the cobbled street, watching for the familiar and much-loved figure of her mammy to come round the corner at any minute.

If it weren't for her brother and sister depending on her, and the fact that she didn't know the way to London, Sal might have been tempted to follow her mammy there and then.

Though little Sal stayed on the doorstep for the best

part of the day, she was not rewarded for her vigilance. At suppertime she was told by Tilly, 'Come in off that cold step, my girl . . . you've been out there quite long enough!' Feeling both cramped and hungry, little Sal made small protest.

No sooner had little Sal sat herself round the big table in the centre of the parlour than Joe Watson let himself in the front door. On hearing his familiar footsteps, Tilly rushed into the passage. 'Don't you lot touch none of them muffins!' she warned the little hungry souls assembled round the table. 'Joe's here now. We shall *all* enjoy us supper . . . when grace is said.'

There was such a forbidding, sullen look on her son's face that Tilly's joy at having him home was cruelly quashed. 'Are you all right, Joe?' she asked, watching him take off his flat cap, which he flung over the nail in the door. She was concerned to see what a strange, brooding mood he was in. 'What's kept you so late? . . . I've been worried. D'you know what the time is, eh? It's gone eight o'clock.' Still he made no response. Instead, he pushed past her and made straight for the front parlour. His foot was already over the threshold when Tilly urged, 'Don't be surly, Joe. Supper's already laid out in the back parlour. We've none of us started, because I insisted that we wait for you.' Coming closer to him now, she was deeply disappointed to realize that he had been drinking again. 'Aw, Joe, you've never been drowning your sorrows in that ale house, have you?'

'What if I have?' His manner was strange to her, and most disturbing.

'Look . . . I'm sorry we had a fight, Joe. I was wrong to tackle you the way I did. And *you* was wrong to try and take advantage of Molly. You must have really worried her . . . else she wouldn't have gone off like that in the middle of the night. Oh, she *had* to make a move, I know that . . . and I'd already asked her to leave the bairns with me till she were settled. But I don't like the idea that you forced her hand, Joe. I don't like it at all!' All this time, Tilly had deliberately kept her voice low, because of small, curious ears not too far away. 'She's a good sort is Molly. And she's had a bloody hard time of it.'

'Leave me be!'

'Aw, lad . . . don't keep bad blood between us,' pleaded Tilly. His answer was to close the door in her face. 'Have it your way,' she called out, 'but you did wrong, Joe Watson. You think on it, and you'll see your old ma's right. *You did wrong!*'

When there came no reply from the other side of the door, Tilly tutted loudly and, shaking her head angrily, she returned to the back parlour, where numerous little eyes turned to look at her, anxious and hungry.

Sensing that the children were made nervous by the raised voices between her and Joe, she promptly set about putting them at their ease. 'Oh, take no notice of grown-ups,' she declared, putting on a smile to cover her anxieties. 'They shout at nothing sometimes . . . just like you little tinkers.' Sitting herself on the standchair at the head of the table, she clapped her hands to draw their attention. When all eyes were looking at her, she bent her head, peering over her brows to ensure the children followed suit. Then, being satisfied, she quickly gave up a prayer of gratitude for the 'adequate spread of food on our table'. After which, the muffins and preserve were duly shared out, and everyone appeared to forget about the angry young man in the next room.

That is, all but little Sal and Tilly; the one hoping desperately that her mammy would soon be back to take them to their 'own place', and the other sad at heart that such a rift should ever come between her and her eldest. At the same time though, Tilly stood by her accusation that Joe had done wrong. She was made also to think on Molly – finding her way to London Town along dark and unfamiliar streets. What would she face once she got there, eh? Strangers? Hostility? Happen some'at far worse. Who knows, thought Tilly. Who knows.

Some time past midnight, Joe woke up in the throes of a terrible nightmare. Sweat was trickling down his back and the sound of a fist thumping against wood resounded in his head long after his eyes were open and his senses returned. Bang! Bang! The whole house seemed to tremble around him. Rising above the din came Tilly's voice, terrified and shocked. 'Joe! . . . What in God's name is happening? *Joe! Joe!*' Her cries became a scream.

Scrambling into his trousers, Joe raced to the bottom of the stairs. 'Quick, Mam . . . I'll fend the buggers off. *You get Molly's young 'uns away as fast as you can!*' He stared up at her with pleading eyes. 'Do as I say, Mam . . . for pity's sake, DO AS I SAY!' He knew now. It was no nightmare! Dear God above, what devil had possessed him to go to the Justice Crowther?

As she stared at her son's stricken eyes, Tilly was gripped with an awful realization. When she spoke, it was with a sinking sense of horror. 'Aw, no! Dear Lord, our Joe . . . you've never brought the authorities to the door?' The guilt on his face was her answer. 'Jesus, Mary and Joseph! *You have*. You've betrayed Molly's trust in old Tilly.' She threw her hands to her head and shook her whole body from side to side, as though fending off an attacker. 'What'll we do now? Dear God, what'll we do now?' All sense of reason fled her thoughts, as the noise outside grew more insistent. Now there were voices – angry, threatening voices, promising all kinds of terrible retribution 'if this door isn't opened straight away'!

By now the children too were out on the landing, some loudly crying, some softly whimpering. Only little Sal remained deathly silent.

On swift and silent steps, Joe bounded up the stairs. '*Please, mam!* Get the bairns out afore they break down the door!' he urged, taking Tilly by the shoulders and gently shaking her. 'I'll hold 'em off while you make your getaway. Head for the Navigation . . . tell them Joe's asking a favour. They'll give you shelter till it's safe.' At that minute, the thumping and shouting stopped and there followed a chilling silence. Tilly put her fingers to her lips, urging the children to be quiet. When gradually they did so, she murmured to Joe, 'They've gone, son. The buggers have gone after all, eh?'

'No. They haven't gone,' he told her in the softest of whispers, beginning to gather the children towards him while keeping an eye on the front door. He was mortally afraid that it might fly open at any minute. 'They'll not leave this house till they get what they've come for.' He looked at Tilly, and the warning in his eyes was like a knife through her heart.

'And what is it they've come for, our Joe?' she demanded, her condemning eyes drilling through him. 'What have you done, you bad 'un? *What is it they want?*'

Joe gave no reply, other than to shift his fearful gaze to

where Molly's three were huddled together. *It was enough!*

'Oh, you bad 'un, Joe. God forgive you,' Tilly muttered, making the sign of the cross on herself, and rushing back in the bedroom, from where she collected a shawl to cover her long nightshift. The children were not afforded such 'luxury', but nevertheless were warm and decent enough in their thick ankle-length garments. Quickly she ushered them down the stairs. 'Softly now, young 'uns. Stay close to Tilly.' Joe led the way, praying with every step that they might get away with it. In a long, silent line, they tiptoed through the back parlour. Joe had a mind to send them along the narrow ginnel that led to the brook. From there they could climb the bank and find their way along the alleys to the Navigation ale house. It would have been easier for them to go by way of the cellar but since the steps from these cellars led directly to the front of the house, he was left with no choice.

'Hurry up! For God's sake . . . get a move on.' He fed the small, trembling bodies through the back parlour door and into the scullery. Here Tilly was desperately fumbling with the bolt on the back door. 'I can't budge it,' she told him, 'it's stuck fast and my hands are that sweaty.' It was dark, too. Almost pitch black. Yet it was more than they dared do to light a candle. The only glimmer of light was the moon's soft glow as it played in through the small window panes.

Without a word Joe came forward, gently pushing Tilly to one side. When the bolt shot back, a sigh of relief filled the air. *But then came the worst*: it all happened so quickly that no one in that scullery could have prevented it. As the door swung open, they were pounced on!

Dark, fleeting figures in the moonlight, surging forward, intent on creating mayhem. In the furore that followed, both Tilly and her son fought to protect the children, who cowered together in a corner of the scullery, their sobbing pitiful to hear. Only Sal came forward, throwing herself again and again into the uproar, to be sent reeling backwards by flaying fists.

In a matter of minutes, Tilly and her son were overpowered. '*Bastards!*' Tilly spat the word out, employing the last dregs of her strength when, in one last determined effort she rammed her two fists into the chest of her attacker. His answer was to strike out a vicious hammer blow to her head. As she fell sideways, Tilly's temple cracked against the corner of the slopstone. With a strange, muffled cry, Tilly slumped to the ground. The brave fight was over, and Joe feared that, because of him, his own mother had paid with her life. Openly sobbing, he fell to his knees, collecting Tilly into his arms and begging her forgiveness.

'*Fools!*' The voice was cunning, dripping with satisfaction. 'Fools, the lot of you!' Justice Crowther stepped into the scullery where, with a quick, sure movement, he lit the candle which stood on the window ledge. In the flickering light his face became an eerie sight, the eyes narrowed to thin dark slits, his lower features embedded in a mass of thick, greying hair. As his gaze fell on them, the children clung to each other more fearfully, each struck dumb by the grotesqueness of those smiling, cruel eyes.

From the alcove in the far corner where she had been flung, Sal watched with wary eyes, afraid to move a muscle. *She had seen this man once before.* On a particular day outside Nelly's house, when she and her mammy had run away. Sal remembered how terrified her mammy had been on seeing this man. Now *she* felt that same terror. But mingled with the fear was a spiralling disbelief. Also shock and fury *Joe* had brought these men here! At first Sal couldn't bring herself to believe that he had done such a terrible thing, not even when Tilly had said so.

But if the child had any doubts before, they were dispelled in the moment when Justice Crowther laughed in Joe's face, telling him, 'I hope for your sake, Watson, that you haven't brought us here on a wild-goose chase.'

'You *lied* to me,' Joe accused, cradling Tilly's blood-soaked body, and the tears raining down his face as he glared up at the formidable, smiling features. 'You promised there'd be no violence.'

'So I did. And, if you hadn't had a change of heart like the coward you are, there would have been no need of any violence.' The smile slithered from his face. In its place came a look of malevolence. 'On your feet, man,' he instructed, glancing towards the children. 'Three of these are the urchins belonging to the woman called Molly, you say? Point them out! *Which are the three I've come for?*' He raised his cane and made a sweeping gesture over the children's heads.

'I'll tell you nothing more!' shouted Joe. 'You lying bastard . . . you've done for my mam . . . when you promised there'd be no harm come to us!' Suddenly he was on his feet and launching himself into that mountainous figure. 'I'll kill you!' he yelled, clutching his fingers round the thick, ageing neck with a cry that was terrible to hear.

In the chaos that followed, two of the men leapt

forward, and Joe was quickly prised away, eventually silenced by a heavy blow to the head. He slithered to the floor, unconscious, beside the crumpled figure of his mother. 'Damned fool! ' Caleb Crowther was seething. 'His sort never learn.' He might have had Joe run through there and then. But there were *more* important issues at stake here. What could be more important than Emma Grady's grandchildren?

The Justice glared at the children and chuckled aloud. When that fool Watson brought him news that a certain person had left her offspring in his mother's care – a certain person by the name of Molly, and whom he understood the Justice might have a warrant out for – he could not have known what a precious package he was bringing. A package so important that it could even be the means by which Emma Grady herself might be brought to heel!

Advancing on the small, trembling figures, he put on his most pleasant and cajoling voice. 'Which of you belong to the woman called *Molly*?' he asked, bending his face to them. 'There are *three* of you, I understand.' When he was greeted with big, frightened eyes and a stony silence, his manner became harsher. '*Those three will step forward!*' He waited a moment, enraged when his demands only made them huddle together all the more. Every child was in deep shock at what had taken place. Nothing he could do or say could persuade them to talk, or offer themselves up. Instead their eyes were drawn to the two lifeless figures on the floor, and they visibly trembled.

'I'm surrounded by dolts!' he declared, furiously thwacking his cane into the air. '*Take them all!*' he told the nearest man. 'If they think to get the better of me

. . . they would do well to remember how others were treated when they thought to do the very same!' He kept his steely glare on the small, terrified faces, while pointing with his stick to the pitiful figures of Tilly and her eldest. 'Get to it!' he snapped at the men, who appeared somewhat reluctant to carry out his orders. 'Damn and bugger it . . . you're being paid well enough, aren't you? *Do as I tell you!* Children such as these are no more than thieves and vagabonds in the making! *Scum! Ruffians!*'

In the face of such fury, it was only a matter of minutes before the children were bundled from the house and into the waiting carriage. By this time, their silence was broken. Cries of 'Mammy' and 'Sal . . . Sal' trailed behind the carriage as it fled away.

One by one the few neighbours who resided in Dock Street came hesitantly to their doors. Curious and afraid, they made their way to Tilly's door, now swinging back and forth in the gentle breeze. They couldn't begin to guess what had taken place there; they were afraid of what they might find. All they did know was that the children had been taken. *All of them!* Every last one, judging by the cries they'd heard. There were people in authority who could do that. People who had the right by law to commit such a crime against ordinary folk. You didn't go out of your way to pit yourself against such wicked creatures. Not unless you wanted them to turn on *you*, you didn't!

As the neighbours came in through the front door, nervous and afraid, a smaller, even more terrified creature sped through the dark, rat-ridden cellars below, then up the flight of steps on to the front pavement.

From there, her heart still beating furiously, Sal ran

along the cobbled streets, tears flowing down her face and occasionally crying out for her mammy.

After Justice Crowther and the men had taken away the others, Sal had remained pressed tight in the dark corner, desperately fighting the impulse to show herself in an effort to save her brother and sister, together with Tilly's brood. She knew instictively though that to betray her presence there would be a foolish thing to do. It had been hard, so very hard, to see the young 'uns all taken away and to be unable to do a single thing to stop it.

As she sped along the streets, Sal dared not think of Tilly, and the 'bad 'un'. In her mind's eye she could still see them lying there, and she was mortally afraid. What if her mammy had been there tonight? Oh, it didn't bear thinking about!

As she ran and ran, losing her way, then finding it again, Sal had one thought in mind. One person to whom she could turn. Even then, she was afraid. Because hadn't her own mammy told her that this one was *not* to be trusted! *Not* the friend they thought she was.

In her headlong flight Sal reminded herself of this. But she *had* to trust someone, didn't she? *She would trust Nelly!* Because, deep down, she had come to love that lady. *Nelly would help*. Nelly *must* help. There was no one else in all the world to whom Sal could turn. Tilly and Joe were badly beaten. The young 'uns had been taken. And her mammy was away to London Town, trying to find them a place to live.

Upstairs in the big house, Emma could not rest. She felt old and weary, afraid to hope in the wake of recent developments. Thoughts of the young woman called

Molly would not let her be. There were too many things still left unanswered, too much that played on her mind. The watch chain found by Nelly in this very house . . . the same piece that Emma's father had given to her shortly before he departed this world. The same piece that had been lost on a twilight morning so many years ago, when she had given birth to a girl-child, before being unjustly transported from these shores.

Something else even more disturbing had come to light since Marlow had taken Mick Darcy into his confidence. Only yesterday the young man who adored Molly had returned to Eanam Wharf, dejected and weary after scouring the country far and wide in search of her. The closest he had come to finding Molly was when he paid a seaman for 'certain information' which had taken Mick to a café beside the Liverpool docks. The proprietor – a surly creature by the name of Bill Craig – had spoken badly of Molly, calling her 'the worst kind o' trouble . . . a bad mistake that he had been glad to see the back of'. Apart from that, he would say little else, except to warn Mick 'if you've any sense at all, you'll steer clear o' that one . . . a wicked little baggage if yer ask me!' Mick's response was a sombre word of advice that left the disgruntled fellow in no doubt at all that if he should continue besmirching Molly's good character, he would find himself answering to Mick Darcy!

Since that particular encounter, there had been no word of Molly or the children. To the disheartened Mick, it was almost as though she had disappeared from the face of the earth. Disillusioned and hoping against hope that Marlow and Emma might have news of her, he had come home to Blackburn after many weeks away.

But there was no news. Even the private detective hired by Marlow Tanner had uncovered nothing of Molly's whereabouts.

Restless and afraid that she might disturb the sleeping Marlow, Emma draped a shawl about herself and went from the bedroom on soft footsteps. She still could not come to terms with it all; especially in the face of Mick Darcy's astonishing revelation that 'Molly was brought up by an old tramp . . . an eccentric old dear known as old Sal'. When Mick was questioned further by Marlow, it was discovered that the old tramp's full name was Sal Tanner – Marlow's very own *sister*.

Realizing that Molly was one and the same girl who had gone out of her way to ensure that old Sal did not suffer a pauper's grave, Marlow immediately set about moving heaven and earth to track her down. There was so much that he owed her, so much that he wanted to ask her with regards to the sister he had loved and lost. On top of which, Emma herself had a great need to speak to Molly, the question of her watch chain being paramount.

But to Emma's mind, there was something else. Something both unnerving and exciting. Some deeper instinct that would not easily be denied. A strange, insistent feeling in her bones that maybe . . . just maybe, this young woman called Molly might be *her own daughter*. The seed of her forbidden love with Marlow. The same girl-child she had given birth to, and who was pronounced stillborn, and left in the gutter as the prison-wagon drew away. Knowing how there was nothing to substantiate such a phenomenon, and in the wake of her own illness these past weeks, Emma had been careful not to voice her deep feelings to anyone. Not to Marlow, who had been deeply concerned for Emma's health of late. And not even to Nelly, who over so many long years in exile had been Emma's loyal friend and confidante. Nor could Emma bring herself to speak to the priest about her troubled soul, for she had turned her back on the Church when her only son had been so cruelly taken from her.

There was no one in whom Emma dare confide. So she tortured herself, recalling certain instances that were all pieces of a jigsaw split asunder by cruel circumstances so very long ago. The time between had been like a fast-running brook spilling into a vast ocean. Gone forever. And yet, and yet! Was it all to do with Emma's long and desperate wish that the girl-child might have survived? How could she tell whether it was all just wishful thinking born of a terrible loss which, even now, caused her great pain. How could she tell? Dear God, what was she to think?

For weeks now, Emma had been haunted by all those little encounters which only seemed to add to her confusion – the fact that old Sal never had any children of her own, and on a day not too long after Emma was transported, Sal was suddenly in possession of an infant . . . *a girl-child with the same black eyes and dark hair as Marlow himself!*

Oh if only it had been possible to discover *where* old Sal had got the infant! But until now, no one seemed to know; Sal claimed that 'the little people sent her to me'. Then there was the watch chain. Emma could not satisfy herself as to how it came to be in this house; not belonging to either staff or household, yet discovered soon after Molly's departure. And, if it *had* been in Molly's possession, then how did she acquire it? Had she stolen it? Certainly, as Nelly pointed out, Molly had stolen to survive. Had she been given it, perhaps by an admirer who was himself a thief? Or – and it was this possibility that tormented Emma – *had the piece been found by old Sal in the same spot as she had found the girl-child herself?*

If that 'spot' were none other than the cobbled street behind the prison where she and Nelly were held, Emma would be convinced that the dark-eyed Molly was her long-lost daughter. Hers *and* Marlow's!

So deep in thought was Emma that when Nelly came into the drawing-room carrying a lamp before her, Emma did not detect her presence. Instead, she remained by the casement windows, gazing out to a star-studded sky and wondering whether the heavens held the secret of all that went on below.

Placing the lamp on the mantelpiece beside the smaller lamp which Emma had brought down, Nelly took stock of her old friend. It hurt her to see how the slim shoulders were drooped, as though carrying an unbearable weight. Emma's whole countenance seemed greatly saddened. If only the boy had been spared, Nelly thought now; if only that particular source of joy had not been so heartlessly torn from her. It was true that Marlow was Emma's strength in these troubled times, and she adored him as always. But the love between a mother and her child was special, a unique and wonderful thing that could never be replaced.

Now, as she went forward, deliberately making a noise in order not to startle Emma unnecessarily, Nelly did so with a purpose. Unable to sleep herself, she had heard Emma leave her room. For a long time now Nelly had fought with her conscience. There were certain things she should confess to Emma. Things of the past that had somehow found their way into the present, and possibly had the power to affect the future.

Nelly was afraid, convinced that her long-overdue 'confession' would signal the end of Emma's affection for her. All the same, and because she loved Emma above all else, Nelly had decided that on this night she would open her heart and afterwards beg Emma's forgiveness.

'Oh, Nelly!' Emma swung round on hearing her dear friend's noisy procession across the floor. 'Couldn't you sleep either?' She came forward. When Nelly seated herself in one leather chair beside the empty fire-grate, Emma seated herself in the other. In the lamp's soft glow, Nelly was pained to see how Emma's hitherto rich, chestnut-coloured hair was now heavily streaked with grey. The bloom of youth had long left her face, but now a terrible weariness seemed to draw the lines of age so much deeper. But for all that, Emma retained a certain grace and beauty that was timeless.

'I've a good mind ter wake Marlow and tell him how yer haunting the house in the middle o' the night!' Nelly chastized, her face a picture of annoyance. 'Yer knows very well what the doctor telled yer. "Stay in yer bed," he said, "get yer strength back after being laid so low with the illness." And what d'yer do, eh?' she demandded, shaking her tousled head. 'Well . . . yer wanders about in the cold night air, that's what!'

Emma smiled at her old friend's sharp tongue. She knew that Nelly meant well. 'I couldn't sleep,' she said, 'and I was afraid I might wake Marlow. He's so exhausted . . . these past weeks haven't been easy for him.' She laughed, a gentle unhappy sound. 'We're none of us getting any younger, Nelly,' she said.

'Huh! . . The past few weeks ain't been easy fer none of us, my gal,' replied Nelly, 'what with this business o' Molly, an' you being took so poorly.' Suddenly her voice softened as she asked, 'Are yer feeling better, gal? . . . Feel stronger in yersel', d'yer, eh?' The doctor said that Emma had been struck down by 'a particularly nasty fever'. But Nelly knew better; t'weren't no matter o' the fever that had laid Emma low. It were *other* matters, much more powerful to a woman. Matters of the heart, that's what had struck Emma down: grief, and longing, and the loss of two children. Yes! *Two* children, because to Nelly's mind, Emma had *never* got over the loss of that new-born girl-child. Nelly could not ease that loss for Emma. Nothing she could say would ever ease it. Indeed, what she had to say could even make that loss *more* unendurable. Or, in the light of recent events, it might prove to be a godsend. Nelly didn't know. All she *did* know was that only days before, she had confided all to Marlow. Now, and on Marlow's insistence, she had to tell the truth of what happened on that terrible night so long ago. 'What yer been thinkin' about, Emma . . . down here on yer own, gazin' outside the window like a lost soul?'

'Life, Nelly . . . I've been thinking about life. How good it's been to me, and how bad.'

Nelly was compelled to broach the subject of Molly, because unbeknown to either of them, the very same suspicions that had been plaguing Emma had also been tormenting *her*. 'I've been doing that an' all, gal . . . y'know, thinkin' about how good life's been to me. In particular, how fortunate I was to have come across such a friend as you.' She saw that Emma was about to

intervene. 'No. Let me finish, Emma darlin'. Y'see, I
ain't never been entirely honest with you all these years.
There's some'at I want to get off me chest, like. Some'at
that yer 'ave ter know . . . an' I'm not altogether certain,
mind . . . but well . . . I've a feelin' it all might 'ave some
bearing on Molly.'

Emma's attention had been wandering, but now at the
mention of Molly's name, she grew excited, leaning
forward in her seat. 'What is it, Nelly? . . . What have
you to tell me that might relate to Molly?' she urged.

Swallowing hard, Nelly prepared to launch into an
account of how she suspected that Emma's new-born
was still alive when the prison-wagon carried them
away. But at that moment the room was filled with the
sound of bedlam. *'Nelly! Help me, Nelly! . . . Let me in,
please!'* The desperate cries were accompanied by a
series of other, more violent noises like the kicking of a
boot against the front door, together with the familiar, if
more desperate sound of the heavy iron knocker being
crashed again and again into its metal base.

'Good Lord above!' exclaimed Emma, her face ashen
as she scrambled out of the chair. 'Who on earth is that?'
Even before the last word was uttered, she was collecting the lamp from the mantelpiece and hurrying from the
room.

'Sounds like bleedin' old Nick himself,' declared Nelly,
staying close behind Emma, 'though I don't know why
the bugger might be callin' my name!' In a moment
of panic, it had crossed her mind that the sins of the past
had caught up with her.

It was no time at all before Emma and the doubting
Nelly were in the vestibule and struggling to reach the
upper bolt of the front door when Marlow – awoken by

the uproar – rushed to Emma's aid. The parlour maid and the cook stood someway behind, both unkempt and wide-eyed, with the maid squashed close to the other woman, fearful that upon the door opening some unspeakable creature might clap its eyes on her and devour her instantly. Even so, when Nelly insisted that these two return at once to their beds, they went away most reluctantly, their curiosity threatening to get the better of them. They had no sooner gone a few paces than the door was opened, and a sobbing mite fell forward into Nelly's arms. 'Gawd almighty! . . . It's little Sal . . . Molly's bairn!' Nelly clung to the small, trembling figure. 'What is it, child? Where's yer mammy? What yer doing here?'

'*Don't* badger her, Nelly.' Realizing that the child was in a state of shock and in danger of being overawed by the presence of herself and Marlow, Emma thought the best thing was to let the child recover enough to explain lucidly exactly what had brought her to this door at such a deadly hour, and in such terror.

'*No! No!*' When Nelly made an effort to help Sal into the house, she was astonished at the vehemence with which the girl fought her off. 'STOP HIM, Nelly . . . we've got to stop him! *He's killed Tilly, and he's taken the young 'uns.*' The memory of the awful scenes she had witnessed that night was too much. Sobbing loudly, the child fell to the floor, her arms doubled beneath her head and her whole body helpless in the grip of convulsive sobs.

As Nelly made to stoop and raise the child, Emma came forward, gentle in her manner and soothing little Sal with her low, soft voice. A terrible suspicion had crept into Emma's heart. A suspicion which only this small girl, *Molly's girl*, could answer. 'We will stop him, Sal,' she told her, 'but we need to know his name. *Who* killed Tilly? *Who* took the young 'uns?'

'*The man!* The man who wants to kill my mammy too!' Sal could hardly speak for the choking sobs, her vivid blue eyes raised to Emma's tender, loving face – the face of her own grandmother, although she was not yet aware of that. 'I want my mammy back,' she cried now, 'please, missus . . . I want my mammy back!'

'We'll get your mammy back, sweetheart,' Emma promised, 'but first . . . we need to know who the man is. Can you tell me his name?'

For one agonizing moment, when little Sal raised her head in response to Emma's question, it was thought that all would be revealed. She opened her mouth to speak. But the name they all waited to hear was lost in a whisper as the exhausted child sank away in a dead faint.

Tenderly Marlow carried the small, limp figure up the stairs, where it was put carefully to bed, and the doctor urgently summoned. 'Later, when she's rested,' he told the anxious Emma, 'we will know who "the man" is.' The intimate smile he gave her was a curious yet reassuring one. It came to Emma in that moment how Marlow also might have been secretly mulling over all the events that had taken place regarding Molly. Events that were deeply woven into his own life, and into the life and death of old Sal, the beloved tramp.

One thing Emma believed was that Marlow could not be agonizing over whether Molly was his own daughter. Because Emma had never confided the truth in him, and so he knew nothing of her either conceiving or giving birth to his girl-child. That was the way that Emma had wanted it, for it would have served no real purpose for

Marlow to know, except to cause him heartache.

Unbeknown to Emma, however, Marlow *did* know of the girl-child born to Emma all those years ago! And because of it, he also wondered just how deeply Molly's life was linked with his and Emma's. Since Nelly had recently confided in him, he had been driven that much harder to find Molly, because in his heart he wanted to believe that she was his daughter. *He prayed that it was so*.

Because Nelly had begged to be the one who would tell Emma of the possibility that her girl-child might have survived that night, Marlow had kept his own counsel. Now though, in the light of Molly's own child being here, under this very roof and in need of help from them, he felt that Emma should be told all there was to know. Not even one moment should be lost.

Marlow ushered both Nelly and Emma downstairs to the drawing-room. 'There is much for you to know, Emma,' he told her, the light of love as strong in his dark eyes as it was when they had first met: he just a boy, she a young and gently blossoming girl. The feelings that had stirred between them then were still as young, still as wonderful in both their hearts.

What he had to tell Emma now seemed to Marlow like a blessing from the Good Lord, in compensation for having taken their son. Nothing was certain, though. When all was revealed, it might be that Molly was *not* their own flesh and blood after all. But even before Nelly had unburdened her heart to him, Marlow had been deeply disturbed by something he could not understand – a certain feeling about the infant that his dear sister had found and raised as her own. No, nothing was certain. But there was always hope. And that hope would bind him and Emma closer still.

With lighter heart, Marlow followed Nelly and his beloved wife into the drawing-room. Between the three of them, they would find whatever truths there were. In all of his distress following Emma's illness and during the search for Molly, Marlow, like Nelly, had derived much comfort from their faith. It would have given Marlow so much joy to know that Emma's own faith had returned. Perhaps one day soon, he thought, when the pain of losing their son was not so unbearable.

How much sooner that would be if, by the grace of God, their first-born was returned to them. Was it too much to hope for, Marlow asked himself now as he closed the drawing-room door.

It was some time later when the messenger came: an ill-mannered lout of dubious character bearing news that struck both fear and joy into the hearts of all present. There was nothing delivered in writing, but the fellow was obviously well rehearsed. 'I've been sent by a certain gent,' he addressed Emma, 'a certain gent whose name I'm not at liberty to disclose, yer understand, but what I've to tell yer is this . . . the gent is in possession of a number o' brats. I'm to tell yer that *three* of 'em are yer own grandchildren.' When the colour drained from Emma's face, he seemed momentarily surprised. 'That's right, lady . . . *yer own grandchildren* . . . an' I was to make quite certain that yer understood that. The brats belong to a young woman by the name o' Molly . . . your daughter.'

'What proof d'you have of all this, you disgusting ruffian?' demanded Nelly. Emma seemed lost for words.

'Aha! . . . the gent said yer might ask such a thing. In the event I was to disclose certain information.'

'Out with it then!' Emma had recovered, and her tongue lashed him sharply.

The fellow went on in hurried voice, not caring much for the turn of atmosphere. He remembered all the Justice had told him concerning the origins of the one called Molly. 'Old Sal Tanner found the infant near the jail where Emma Grady was kept afore being despatched on the ocean voyage,' he revealed, adding that the information 'came straight from the mouth of the old salt who wet-nursed the abandoned girl-child'.

All the while he was speaking, Emma had her hand clutched to her heart, for his every word only served to confirm what she suspected – that she and Marlow were indeed Molly's parents. If there had been any vestige of doubt remaining, it vanished when the fellow stretched out his arm and opened his fist. There, nestling amongst the callouses of his thick, grubby fingers was a tiny, delicate timepiece. 'I'm to deliver this,' said the fellow, 'with the information that the young woman in question wore it round her neck even as a child. *T'weren't stolen!* It belonged to the child . . . right from the start.' Here he deliberately paused before going on in a cunning voice, 'Afore that, it belonged to your good self . . . this 'ere timepiece . . . an' the girl-child with it.'

Nelly had seen how his words were affecting Emma, Emma who had been so poorly, and she was incensed by it all. 'You blaggart!' she snapped, pushing at the fellow and threatening to tumble him out of the front door.

'No . . . leave him, Nelly.' The tears were flowing down Emma's face as she stepped up to look more closely at the piece of gold. It should have been twenty pieces of silver, she thought. Even without the fellow mentioning the name of the one who had sent him,

Emma knew it by heart. It could be none other than
Caleb Crowther. *He* was the one who had betrayed her
all those years ago. He was betraying her now. *He was an
evil man!*

With tender reverence, Emma collected the tiny piece
into her hand. 'Where are the children?' she asked, and
in such a chilling manner that the fellow stepped back a
pace. 'What does he want? . . . *Justice Crowther!*'

''*Ere!*' He was suddenly trembling, his eyes protruding with fear. 'I ain't said no name! Yer didn't get no
name from me!' He was gabbling now, the words
careering one over the other. 'Yer to cancel a certain
court case that comes up shortly! . . . Drop all charges
an' put an end to it once an' fer all. That's what the gent
said . . . *If yer wants ter clap eyes on them brats while
they're still alive, that is.*' He backed away, his message
delivered and his every nerve-ending urging him to
make a hasty retreat. '*That's it!* That's it . . . I ain't
saying another word,' he yelled, turning about and
ready to run. Suddenly he was kicking and struggling.
Pinned fast by two sturdy arms – *Mick Darcy's* arms.
'So, you're not saying another word, eh?' Mick asked
with a half-smile. 'Then we shall have to change your
mind!'

'At least the authorities will.' The rejoining voice was
Marlow's. Grim-faced and struck to the heart by what he
and Mick had overheard, he gestured to the bargee to
get the fellow inside. 'You'll talk all right,' he promised
the shivering fellow. 'When the authorities arrive, you'll
have *plenty* to talk about.'

As Mick manhandled the unfortunate messenger into
the library, Emma voiced her fears to the outraged
Marlow. 'The children, Marlow . . . if we don't send this

man back to my uncle, I'm desperately afraid that he will harm the children.'

Reaching down to kiss her greying head, Marlow gently assured her, 'He won't do that, sweetheart. He's a bad sort, a coward of the worst order. But he won't murder children . . . he thinks too much of his own precious neck to risk it on the gallows.'

Nelly felt the need to intervene. 'That's as maybe!' she declared angrily. 'But that's where the bugger will end up! *Stretched on the gallows* like any common criminal!' Loudly tutting, she went in a great fury towards the library. She had a thing or two to say to that grubby fellow, and it wouldn't wait.

Marlow explained how he had gone to Eanam Wharf where he had alerted Mick Darcy of the developments. From there, Mick had taken him to Dock Street where Tilly Watson lived. And no, it wasn't true that the Justice had killed Tilly, although she had been brutally knocked about.

'It's a bad business, Emma,' Marlow said, 'but our priority is to get Molly and the children back safe. The rest is a matter for the authorities.' He clung to her, saying softly, 'God willing, we'll have our daughter and grandchildren safe soon. Very soon.'

Chapter Twelve

Agnes Crowther stood with one hand on the ornate mantelpiece: a tall, regal figure in a blue taffeta gown, her aged features as chalk-white as the pearls about her wrinkled neck, a look of horror on her face. 'What is it you want with my husband?' she demanded curtly. Though thinly disguised, there was undeniably a trace of nervousness in her voice. Her manner, however, remained haughty.

The officer felt the need to be cautious. 'As my colleague explained, ma'am . . . we have reason to suspect that Justice Crowther might be able to assist with our inquiries.' The stocky officer with the drooping moustache and heavy eyelids made no secret of his delight at the reason for being at Breckleton House. His smile was infuriating to Agnes Crowther.

'Then you are fools!' she retorted now. 'How dare you suggest that a respected and eminent figure such as the Justice could possibly know *anything* with regard to a woman being "viciously attacked"? And it is absurd to think he could ever be involved in the "abduction of children".' Her indignation was amazing to behold, especially since she had already suspected that her 'respected and eminent' husband was up to no good. 'My advice to you both is to go away and find the real culprit. I don't mind telling you that, on his return, Justice

Crowther will have a great deal to say concerning your visit here.'

'I can assure you, ma'am . . . we're only doing our job,' explained the thinner of the two. 'Of course we're sorry if our visit has caused you distress. But we really do need to talk with the Justice.' He put on his trilby and seemed to make a little bow. 'And you have no idea of his whereabouts at present?'

'None whatsoever.'

'But should he return, you will inform us?'

'I will inform *my husband* of your visit. Oh, you may depend on it!' Agnes Crowther swept angrily across the library. Swinging open the door, she assured them in a cutting voice, 'And when he discovers *the reason* for your desire to talk with him . . . the "distress" will *not* be mine. It will be yours! Good day to you.'

On the two men leaving the house, Agnes Crowther hurried to the window in the great hall. From a discreet distance she watched them walk from the front door to the waiting carriage. She stepped back a pace when they half-turned towards the house, seemingly immersed in deep discussion. Then, when eventually they climbed into the carriage and were taken at some speed towards the road, she continued to stare after them, her face a study in confusion. Her fears were heightened when she realized that an officer was being left behind to stand guard outside the gates.

'Father will have their heads for this!' Martha Crowther had been sitting in the library throughout, stunned into silence by the conversation between the two officers and her mother. Now, as she led the way back to the library, her eyes were narrowed with anger, and her uneven nostrils grew to twice their size as she sucked in great helpings of air. '*How dare they?*' she said in an explosive voice. When her tantrum drew no response from the woman behind, Martha Crowther deliberately slowed her footsteps and turned her ungainly brown head to ask, 'What will you do, mother . . . ? Will you tell him?' Of late, her father's temper had been unbearably short. The thought of his reaction to this tiresome episode made her visibly tremble.

'Of course he must be told,' Agnes informed her. Martha's state of anxiety had not gone unnoticed, though; to Agnes Crowther's mind her foolish daughter had created her own deplorable situation, by constantly refusing to be a 'proper' wife to Silas Trent. Time and again he had begged her to join him in Australia, where he had taken on Emma Grady's already prosperous trading company, and expanded it even more. The man had worked hard and, as far as Agnes Crowther was concerned, he deserved the same support and loyalty from his wife as he got from his son, Edward. Martha, however, gave him neither support *nor* loyalty. And for too long now she had withheld all form of affection from him. Was it surprising, therefore, that her unfortunate husband had sought solace in the arms of the woman who worked alongside him? In Rita Hughes he had found a loyal colleague and, according to Martha's peevish innuendoes, a generous lover. There was no doubt that the marriage was over. Agnes Crowther, for one, was not surprised.

The conversation of mother and daughter was interrupted by a soft tap on the door. '*Come!*' Agnes Crowther called with some irritation. She was at once on her guard when she saw that it was the maid. Amy had been with them a long time, but she was far too curious about matters that did not concern her. 'Yes, what is it?' There were other, more pressing matters on her mind than domestic trivialities.

'It's Cook, m'lady.' Amy made an odd little curtsy, inclining her head to one side in the way she did when nervous. At this moment in time she did look exceedingly nervous and – because of the fact that she had come to the library earlier and overheard the riveting conversation that had taken place there – Amy was also acutely embarrassed. At the same time, she bubbled inwardly with excitement. Amy was very partial to a snippet of gossip, and here was a deal *more* than a snippet. What she had learned through a chink in the door was the most astonishing, the most awful and the most delicious revelations it had ever been her unpleasant lot to bear. She hadn't told Cook yet, because the last time she imparted a bit of juicy gossip to Cook all she got for her trouble was a belt round the ear. But she *would* tell her soon, because if she didn't, she would just burst.

'Yes, yes . . . what about Cook?'

'I'm to inquire, m'lady . . . whether dinner is to be served now. Or should we wait the master's return?'

Agnes Crowther appeared to give the matter small thought, but then she instructed, 'Tell Cook we will *not* be waiting the master's return. She may serve dinner as usual.'

'Very well, ma'am.' With another curious little curtsy, Amy left the room.

The lamps were burning long into the evening at Breckleton House.

Upstairs in the drawing-room, Agnes Crowther sat in

the deep comfortable armchair by the window, a look of disbelief and shock in her eyes as she gazed out to the two figures bathed in moonlight and discreetly positioned by the big gates. Earlier there had been only one man on duty, but a second officer had remained behind after yet another visit by the authorities. During this particular visit it had been revealed to Agnes Crowther that 'a certain man who had delivered a blackmail threat to the Tanner home' had been taken into custody. After lengthy interrogation he had reluctantly put forward a statement that incriminated Justice Crowther, and which also appeared to substantiate certain earlier allegations made by a Mrs Tilly Watson and her son, Joe. The charges were serious: the Justice was urgently wanted for questioning.

Cook sat in the upright, uncomfortable standchair, her chubby arms stretched out across the table, and a letter clutched tightly in her fist; a very old and condemning letter, written by a woman hanged many years before.

Cook had been stunned by the news regarding her employer, most of which had reached her ears via the parlour maid. Although it was all a most unexpected and shocking revelation, Cook was not altogether surprised by it. There was no doubt whatsoever in her mind that Justice Crowther was a bad, bad man; a tyrant of the worst order, if this letter were anything to go by. A heartless fiend who did not stop even at *murder!*

Cook shuddered. In her hand she held a statement that was far more damaging to Justice Crowther than any statement the authorities had in their possession. It was not to do with the abduction of children or the battering of a woman – though they were obscene enough crimes. No! This letter accused him of other things. Things beyond the imagination of normal, civilized beings. Things that made a body's blood run cold.

The letter pointed this 'respectable eminent man' out as the same creature who possibly *murdered both of Emma Grady's parents!* Her mother, following a secret affair with Caleb Crowther, and her father, when it seemed he might change his will to remove power over Emma from that evil man.

'What to do . . . ? Burn the blessed thing, or show it to the world?' Cook murmured, her breath fanning the candle-light and sending the shadows scurrying about; the ensuing gyrating shapes on the wall held her mesmerized for a moment. They look like him, she thought – dark and furtive, shifting this way and that.

Only a few months before, Cook would have suffered no dilemma where the letter was concerned. It had always been her 'insurance' against poverty and home-lessness in her old age. She had kept the letter hidden away, and would not have hesitated to use it for black-mail against the Justice if he had ever carried out his threat to put her 'on the streets'. Fortunately she had not been made to resort to such shameful means, mainly because of kindly intervention by Agnes Crowther her-self. Only recently that same lady had confided to Cook, 'I may shortly be leaving this house and taking up residence in a smaller property of my own. I would very much like to retain you, in my new home'. Of course, Cook had been both eager and delighted at the sugges-tion, especially as there was a 'possibility' that Amy also might be 'taken care of'.

Her thoughts driven to the past, Cook was made to

think on the young, innocent girl that was Miss Emma.
How unspeakably cruel Justice Crowther had been in
deliberately keeping father and daughter apart and how
devastated she had been at the death of her father. Soon
after, he had married Miss Emma off to an unsuitable
man. Then, when she was accused of murder, he had
turned his back on her, afterwards ransacking her inheritance and building his own prosperity on it.

'But your sins have come home to roost, ain't they,
m'lud,' Cook said now, looking accusingly towards the
stairs that led from the kitchen to the upper hall. On
her homecoming from Australia, Emma had put into
motion a series of events to right the injustice towards
her. These events were now set to culminate in a trial
that would have the whole of Lancashire agog. There
was no doubt in everyone's mind that the outcome
of that trial would serve as the Justice Crowther's
downfall. And there wasn't a single person – with
perhaps the exception of his daughter Martha and
his grandson Edward – who would wish it to be otherwise.

'Yet you're a crafty fox, Justice,' Cook said softly,
'and though the cards is set against you, it wouldn't
surprise me at all if, somehow, you was to wiggle out of
it.' The possibility was appalling to her. 'We *all* have to
pay for our sins . . . and the likes of you should be made
to pay twice over, because you've been blessed with the
best that life can offer. *And you're still hungry for more!*'
The one thing that turned Cook's stomach was the
thought of Justice Crowther outwitting Miss Emma yet
again. Oh, it was true that Miss Emma was now a rich
and powerful lady when at the time she was ill-used by
her uncle she had been little more than a child, but the

man had some powerful and influential allies. He was a Justice, after all.

Suddenly Cook's mind was made up! She *would* make the letter known! Her first instinct was to show it immediately to Miss Emma, but then she recalled that Miss Emma was reputed to be not fully recovered from her illness. Mr Tanner than? No! There was no doubt in Cook's mind that he would likely strangle the Justice, and be hanged for it. The authorities? Well, yes . . . but they had an uncanny way of dragging an innocent body into the proceedings in a way that terrified a simple soul such as Cook.

At the point when the agitated woman was in her deepest thoughts, the bell on the wall behind her loudly jangled. 'Mercy above!' she gasped, clutching her two chubby hands to her breast and rising from the chair. 'It's a wonder I ain't struck dead!' With a bright red face and pounding heart she looked up to see who on earth could be summoning her at this late hour. 'It's the drawing-room,' she observed with interest, 'it can't be the master, because he's not back yet, I think. And it can't be his spoilt daughter Martha . . . because Amy took a glass of hot milk to her room some two hours ago, together with a headache powder to "soothe my aching head". No! That one would be out to the world and snoring like a good 'un,' Cook decided with a measure of indignation. That left only one other person to be ringing the bell. *Agnes Crowther*. 'What in heaven's name could she be wanting at this time of night?' Cook wondered, at the same time ramming the letter into her pocket, then straightening her pinnie and patting her grey curls into place. 'There's no peace for the wicked,' she told herself, mounting the steps as fast as her thick old legs would allow.

In the drawing-room, Cook found the mistress in a strange mood. 'I wasn't certain whether you had all gone to bed,' Agnes Crowther explained, being mindful of the fact that she had already informed Amy there would be no further need of her that evening.

'That's all right, ma'am,' Cook said, waiting her instructions, 'I wasn't ready for bed . . . had too many things on my mind, d'you see?'

'All the same, I would not have disturbed you at this late hour if it were not absolutely necessary,' Agnes Crowther said, thinking how Cook was not the only one to have 'too many things on my mind'. Looking away from Cook, she raised the long, slender fingers of her left hand to her temple, gently massaging the area with a look of discomfort on her face. 'I have the *most dreadful* headache.'

'I'll fetch you a powder at once, ma'am.' Cook put her hand on the door knob. 'Will there be anything else, ma'am?' She suddenly thought of the letter. Her heart beat furiously at the idea of revealing it to the mistress. She wanted to, oh so much, but she was half-afraid of what Agnes Crowther's reaction would be.

But then the anxious woman was afforded a golden opportunity when, in answer to her question, the lady of the house peered at her most intently, as though secretly debating some inner thought. Presently she said, 'You have been with us a very long time . . . you must know us all so well.' She smiled, but it was a sad, lonely smile. 'Of course, you recall the day when my brother Thadius Grady came to live at Breckleton House.' She appeared not to be directly talking to Cook now. Instead she seemed to be rambling, lost in thought. 'My brother . . . so trusting . . . so desperate that his adored daughter should be well taken care of.' Here she gave a small, cynical laugh. 'Like Breckleton House itself, Thadius was in a state of decline when he came here to live. Yet, because of his kindness and generosity, the house was restored to its former glory. And how did we manage to repay him?' Her head was lowered as though in shame as, with broken voice, she went on, 'By denying him the comfort of Emma by his side when he needed her most . . . cried out for her! And after his death, by betraying his most heartfelt wish . . . that Emma should be well taken care of.'

There followed a long, painfully drawn-out silence during which Cook remained silent and motionless. She was deeply shocked at the manner in which Agnes Crowther had uttered such shameful and private thoughts in her presence. Such a thing had never occurred in this household all the years Cook had been retained there. Yet, in some strange, instinctive way, in that moment it seemed so very natural. With tingling astonishment, Cook suddenly realized that the mistress had been drinking. There, on the table beside her, was a half-empty sherry decanter and a partly filled glass. So that was it! They did say that the drink loosened a body's tongue.

'I was not altogether innocent in the proceedings regarding Emma. I am not proud of that fact . . . and I have since lived to regret it.'

'I'll go and fetch the powder, ma'am.' Cook was suddenly afraid of hearing things she had no right to know – or perhaps of having the contents of that letter confirmed. She would have made a discreet exit there and then. But suddenly she was confronted by Agnes Crowther's direct question and it frustrated her intention.

'Have you seen the two officers guarding this house?'

'Yes, ma'am.'

'Do you know *why* they're watching the house?' She did not wait for Cook's answer. 'I'll tell you why . . . ! They're waiting for your master . . . *the Justice.*'

'I'll fetch the powder, ma'am.' It was all too much for Cook. She felt totally out of place, and convinced that, on the morrow, when the mistress realized the extent of what she had confided to *a servant*, no less, Cook would be sent packing forthwith.

'No . . . ! I want you to stay. You've seen it all, I know. You've seen everything over the years. You're no fool, I'm well aware of that. What do you *really* know, I wonder . . . ? Do you know that your master is accused of attacking a woman? Do you know that they say he is wanted in connection with abducting children?' She swayed on her feet.

'*What* do you know? All these years . . . what do you really know?'

At this point Cook remembered the letter in her pocket. She remembered also the awful possibility that Justice Crowther might yet outsmart Emma in this forthcoming court case. *That must not happen!* Without a word, she took the letter from her pinnie pocket and held it out to Agnes Crowther, who, being cautioned by the serious look in the other woman's eyes, took it hesitantly and went across to the lamp where she might read it more easily. Cook chose that moment to leave quietly, hoping that her departure would not be a permanent one, once the contents of that terrible letter were made known to Agnes Crowther.

* * *

Cook had waited in the kitchen for over an hour, bone-tired and preparing herself for the moment when Agnes Crowther would come bursting through the door. *But it never happened*. Eventually, unable to stay awake any longer, she laid her head back into the curve of the easy chair by the empty fire-grate, and dozed off into a troubled sleep.

She was not aware that, incensed and deeply shocked by what she had read, Agnes Crowther took·it upon herself to rouse the groom and instruct him to quickly make the carriage ready. From the gate – where they were briefly questioned by the two men on duty – the flustered driver was told by Agnes Crowther to 'make haste to Park Street. *To the Tanner residence.*'

It was some two hours after Agnes Crowther's speedy departure that all hell was let loose. 'WAKE UP . . . ! *For Gawd's sake, Cook, wake up!*' Amy's cry was desperate as she shook the older woman back and forth in the chair, the tears running down her face, the look of a wild thing about her.

'Lord love and save us!' shouted Cook on being so rudely awakened, convinced that Agnes Crowther had ordered her execution. 'Whatever's the matter . . . ? Are we all to be murdered in our beds or what?' She scrambled frantically to get from the chair.

'Happen we will . . . if we don't get to a safe place smartish!' Amy told her. ''Cause there's a madman loose upstairs. *A bloody madman!*' Her two eyes stuck out like hat pins as she clutched the long shawl over her nightshift and made ready to escape.

Normally Amy would have received a severe scolding from Cook for using 'untoward language', but the moment was interrupted by an officer of the law, who repeated Amy's instruction that they should leave the house as quickly as possible.

As Cook was unceremoniously propelled from the house by a trembling, terrified Amy, she asked, 'What in God's name is going on?'

Amy replied in a fearful voice, '*It's the Justice*. He's locked himself in his room upstairs, and he's daring the officers to come and get him.'

'Good Lord!' exclaimed Cook, adding, 'Where's the mistress . . . and her daughter?'

'It seems the mistress went out on an urgent errand some time ago.' Amy hesitated to say more.

'Well? Are you deaf, girl?' Cook demanded, having recovered enough of her authority to put the parlour maid in her place. '*What about Mrs Trent?* I asked.'

Amy made a faint-hearted gesture with her tousled head, to indicate the upper reaches of the house. 'Martha Trent's in there . . . with her mad father,' she said in a low, irreverent voice. 'But I don't expect she'll ever again see the light o'day.'

'What are you talking about, you foolish creature?' Cook felt an awful panic rising in her.

'The Justice has threatened to kill her an' all, if the authorities move in. He will too! *He's got a shotgun!*'

Dawn was already lighting the sky when Agnes Crowther returned home, her conscience easier than it had been for many a long year. The information which she had carried in that letter had been badly received by Emma, outlining as it did certain suspicions that Caleb Crowther was directly responsible for the death of her father, Thadius, and that of her mother also. However, in view of the fact that Agnes Crowther had delivered the letter herself, condemning though it was, and because Emma's aunt held nothing back of her shame in the part she had played when Emma was imprisoned and desperate for help, there was a deal of forgiveness in Emma's heart for her father's sister. The letter itself was handed to the officer on duty at the Tanner residence.

Now, as the brougham travelled along the lane which led to Breckleton House, the driver was alerted by another carriage, manned and guarded by officers of the law, and stationed in the drive leading up to the big house. This observation was quickly reported to Agnes Crowther, who on leaning from her window as the carriage drew nearer was astonished to see how the house itself appeared to be under siege.

'Sorry, m'lady . . . you can't go no further, I'm afraid,' the officer at the gate told her. Being one of the men who had questioned her on leaving the house earlier, he recognized her at once and explained the situation, adding with genuine sympathy, 'I'm very sorry, ma'am.'

At that point, a loud shot rang out and the officer sped away to investigate. Defiant and afraid for Martha's life, Agnes Crowther clambered from the carriage and hurried after him. 'My daughter's in there!' she called. 'You must let me go to her.'

'*Stay back!*' The officer grabbed her by the arm and thrust her behind the shelter of an old oak tree. 'There's no question of *anyone* going in there just yet. The fellow's beyond all reason . . . firing at random. Every effort will be made to get your daughter out,' he promised, 'but we have to choose the right moment to move in.'

346

Before he could go on, there came another volley of shots. 'Stay where you are, ma'am. I'll send someone to escort you back to your carriage. It's too dangerous for you to remain here.' He went cautiously forward, staying low and occasionally slipping out of sight. Agnes Crowther followed at a discreet distance.

As she came closer to the big house, all manner of things careered through Agnes Crowther's mind. Suddenly she felt the years lying heavy on her shoulders. She felt old. She *was* old, and now it didn't seem to matter any more. Nothing did, *except Martha*. Martha, peevish, spoilt and with no thought for anyone but herself. That was not entirely true, because she adored her son, Edward, and she had always loved her father to the point of obsession, the same father who had callously rejected her from the day she was born. Agnes's heart went out to her now.

As she moved forward on slow, secret footsteps, nearer and nearer to the rear of the house, Agnes Crowther was made to reflect on other things of the past. That letter had planted so many distasteful seeds in her mind. It had opened up so many questions that had lain dormant all these years: questions regarding her husband's faithfulness during the early period of their marriage. She was under no illusion with regard to his infidelities these past years, but now that was not the issue any more.

Casting her mind back, Agnes Crowther remembered her brother's wife, Mary . . . unusually lovely, vibrant and captivating. She recalled how enchanted Caleb was in that young woman's presence, and how she herself had suffered agonies of suspicion and jealousy when the two of them were together. How she loved Caleb in those days; he was so tall and handsome, so virile and overpowering. Strange, she thought now, how a love so deep and trusting could turn to cold indifference – even hatred – over the passage of time.

The letter had intimated that Caleb had murdered Mary following an affair, when Emma was but an infant. A terrible thought had entered Agnes Crowther's mind. Was *Caleb* Emma's real father? Could it also be true that he had suffocated the life out of Thadius, before that poor suffering man could change his will? *She had to know!*

'Jesus Christ! . . . There's a woman in there!' Agnes Crowther could be seen through the open doorway. With determination she mounted the stairs and pressed on, beyond restraining hands, beyond help.

Unafraid, she pushed open the bedroom door, her heart soaring when she saw that Martha was safe – the unfortunate creature was trussed into a chair, her unattractive face contorted with pain, and a faint cowardly whimpering emanating from her lips. When she heard her mother's voice, thick with emotion and authority, issuing the instruction, '*Let her go!*' Martha was at once silent. And more fearful than before. She knew at last how much her father loathed her – had *always* loathed her. She knew much more than that. Here in this room she had been her father's confessor. She knew his deepest secrets – and his madness.

Caleb Crowther swung round, his eyes wild and excited, the barrel of the gun aimed at his wife's throat. The chuckle started as a rattling sound deep in his chest. In a moment he was roaring with laughter – frightening, insane laughter that sent a chill down the spines of all who heard it. Outside, huddled together in a carriage and waiting to be transported to an even safer distance, Cook and Amy heard it also. 'God love and save us,' whispered Cook, hurriedly making the sign of the cross, 'it's the devil himself!'

As soon as the laughter had started, so it ended. The ensuing silence was more than the officer in charge could bear. '*I'm going in!*' he said in sombre voice. 'The rest of you stay here . . . there's no point in risking *all* our necks. Keep alert, mind!' he warned. 'He's a devious devil.'

No sooner had the officer gone a dozen steps than a shot rang out, causing everyone to dive for cover. The echo had barely died down when there followed a short burst of laughter, then a second shot.

For what seemed an endless moment, the startled birds overhead ceased their dawn chorus. A deathly hush prevailed.

On cautious footsteps the men inched their way forward, dreading what might await them. At any minute each one feared the shot that would mow him down. However, they had no choice. Two shots had been fired in that room, yet there were three people there. If the third was alive, it was their duty to get her – or him – out alive.

As they silently entered the house, there wasn't a man there who did not offer up a prayer for his own safety.

Chapter Thirteen

'Well now, sure *there's* a song to light up some lucky fella's life, eh?' The good-humoured Irishman came into the hotel bedroom, jauntily flinging his carpet bag on to the bed and appreciatively eyeing the slim, uniformed figure that emerged from the bathroom.

'Oh, I'm sorry, sir,' Molly said, obviously embarrassed at being overheard humming a merry tune as she went about her duties. 'I was just changing the towels . . . I've finished now.' She crushed the soiled towels to her breast and would have hurried by him if he hadn't called out, 'Won't you tell me what wonderful thing has happened to put such a jolly melody in your heart, eh?' There was a twinkle in his eye and a certain unsteadiness about him that told Molly he also had been doing some celebrating.

Molly warmed to his friendly manner. 'Nothing more "wonderful" than landing a proper job,' she said, smiling at him, 'and soon . . . I hope to bring my children to live with me.' Molly's smile was radiant, bathing her whole face with loveliness. Her dark eyes sparkled like black gems.

'Kids, eh . . . ? And where's your ol' fella?' His gaze was suddenly intense.

Molly was on her guard now. She thought the man was too interested. 'Excuse me, sir,' she apologized, 'but I've a deal of work that won't wait.'

'Aw, go on with you . . . there's never been work that won't wait.' He sauntered towards her.

It was when Molly put her hand to the door knob with the intention of making a hurried exit that there came a slight tap on the door, after which it was swung open to reveal a matronly figure with stiff, disapproving features, and a deep scowl on her face as she glowered at Molly. 'Go to my office,' she said, before instantly addressing the man. 'I do apologize. Staff have strict instructions *never* to intrude on a guest's privacy.'

'No, you've got it all wrong, darling. The little girlie was only doing her job.'

'That's perfectly all right, sir.'

'Hey, I hope she's not in any trouble on account of me?'

'Please don't concern yourself.' The proprietor's wife feared that a distasteful scene might be brewing. Checking first to see that Molly had reluctantly started her way down to the office, she leaned into the room, saying in a lowered voice, 'You should consider yourself very fortunate, sir. Lately there has been a spate of stealing.' She deliberately glanced after Molly's retreating figure. 'I'm thankful to say that we have tracked the culprit down.' Her intimation left the fellow in no doubt as to who 'the culprit' was.

'You don't say?' He was momentarily shocked, but mindful of the fact that only last night an innocent-looking whore had stripped his pockets bare. 'It just goes to show, eh?' he chuckled. 'My old ma was right when she warned me never to trust a pretty face.' Molly's dark, smiling eyes came into his mind. 'There's no need for the police, surely?'

'Don't worry, sir. It's our policy not to involve the police if it's at all avoidable,' she assured him, before closing the door.

Even before the proprietor's wife came into sight of the office, she could hear Molly vehemently protesting her innocence. She quickened her step, fearful that the fracas might be overheard. As it was, the entire episode had cast a shameful slur on their 'respectable' hotel. Thieving from the guests' bedrooms! Such a thing would damage trade badly if it were to get out. Thank goodness they had managed to nip it in the bud. It *was* that wretched young woman, however much she might deny it. There had been no such incidents prior to her arrival. What a fool her husband was to take the creature on without previous experience or references of any kind.

Storming into the office where her husband showed signs of believing Molly's protests, the woman slammed shut the door. 'I'll thank you to keep your voice down!' she warned Molly.

'But I'm innocent, I tell you!'

'*You're a thief . . . that's what you are.*'

'Now, now, let's keep calm,' the flustered proprietor intervened. 'This needs to be discussed quietly and sensibly.'

'Don't you give me that,' his wife rounded on him viciously. 'It was *you* who took her on. It speaks for itself . . . the thieving only started when she was put to work as a chambermaid.'

'It weren't only me who started then,' Molly reminded her. 'What about *Vera*?' Normally Molly would never point the finger at anyone, but she was desperate. She needed this job, and the big cellar room that went with it. The proprietor had already promised that, if she worked well, the children could live down there with her 'so long as they keep quiet and don't become a nuisance'. She knew it was an arrangement that his wife had never agreed to. But the promise was made and Molly had skivvied her fingers to the bone to keep him to it. Besides which, she was innocent of the thieving. It hadn't escaped her notice that the other new chambermaid – who also happened to be a relative of this surly woman – had a full purse lately, and money to spare. 'Have you questioned *her*?' Molly wanted to know.

'How dare you suggest that my sister's daughter is a thief!'

'Well, *I'm* no thief neither. I won't be sacked for something I didn't do.'

The woman laughed at Molly's defiance. 'Oh, you *won't*, won't you?' A particularly nasty smile came over her face. 'In that case, we should send for the authorities . . . don't you agree?'

Her words were met by a thick silence. Molly knew she was bluffing, but she dared not take the chance. What if they did come? What if they found out who she was, and where she'd come from? What about the children? She might be delivered into the hands of Justice Crowther! Dear God! *The very thought filled her with terror*. She'd be hanged for the murder of that café owner, Bill Craig. Hanged, as sure as day follows night. No, she couldn't risk it. *Daren't* risk it.

'Well?' The woman's voice was a sneer.

'I'll not leave without my dues though.' Molly brazened it out, knowing that she had lost the argument.

'Your "dues", eh?' snorted the woman. 'You won't get a brass farthing!'

'The lass is entitled to her dues.' The proprietor surprised them both by stepping forward and taking a sum of money from his pocket. This he handed to Molly saying, 'We'll not keep back what you've sweated for.' He cast a cursory glance at his wife, 'Because then *we'd* be the "thieves", wouldn't we, eh?' He pressed the money into Molly's hand. 'Best go quietly, eh, gal?' he suggested kindly. And that was just what Molly did.

As she pounded the streets of London, desperately searching for a new place of work and a home where she could bring the children, how different it might have been if only Molly had known that the best thing that could have happened was for the hotel proprietor's wife to call the authorities as she had threatened.

Molly's belief that the authorities were searching for her was very true, because even at that moment there were a number of people scouring the streets of London for Emma Tanner's daughter, including the frustrated private detective hired by Marlow. There was another also. The man who was never far from Molly's mind; the man she loved but, for so many reasons, had sent away. Mick Darcy was her strength and her comfort during the dark, lonely hours. He was also a great source of pain and unhappiness, for she was convinced that he was lost to her for ever. How it would have gladdened her heart to know that, even now, he was not far away, searching for her, determined that he would not go home without the woman he adored.

Chapter Fourteen

It was early in the month of June, in the year of our Lord 1887. The evening was hot and uncomfortably humid. During the day, the streets had been alive with people strolling about in their summer outfits; the women bedecked in pretty bright colours with the hems of their skirts swirling about the tops of their buttoned shoes, and looking very summery in their frilly hats and fancy waistcoats. The men too looked dapper and handsome in their stiff white collars with neat little dickie-bows, and bright, becoming boaters.

From early light there could be heard the cries of the many vendors who sold their wares in the streets: the muffin-man, the flower-seller, the costermonger, and even a man with a small cage alive with birds, strapped to his middle. But now it was evening, and the night creatures were stirring.

'Lonely are yer, darlin'? D'yer fancy a bit o' company, eh? I'm a fair enough fella . . . willing to pay, o' course.' The fat man doffed his hat and leered at Molly through cunning eyes. 'What d'yer say?'

Weary and disheartened by the many refusals of work and lodgings, Molly turned away from Piccadilly Circus, quickening her footsteps towards Hyde Park. The night was coming in fast, and she had a mind to find a quiet corner where she could hide herself away from prying eyes. Last night she had huddled in some dark alley. It had been a fearsome place, haunted by scavenging vermin and frequented by lovers who giggled and coupled, blissfully unaware of her presence. One poor fellow had been brought there for a beating, and a particularly nasty vagabond had warned Molly to 'stay off my patch'! Fearful that she might be robbed of the wages given to her the day before by the hotel proprietor, Molly had barely slept a wink.

All day Molly had trudged the streets, knocking on any door where she thought she might find work. But so far she had not been successful. Tomorrow, she thought, tomorrow I'll find work. Suddenly her courage threatened to desert her, and she felt close to tears. Every minute of every day, she kept certain memories warm in her heart: memories of happier days, of the children, and of Mick. Engulfed by these wonderful memories, she was tempted to make her way home. Home to Blackburn, to Tilly and the children. But then she was cruelly reminded that she *had* no home.

A well of gratitude for Tilly rose in Molly's tired heart. The children would be well looked after; she knew that. All the same, she wanted them with her. There had not been a single minute when she hadn't missed them, every one. She thought of little Sal, and her heart ached. Two other faces filled her mind, those of Peggy and of Tom. It was almost more than she could bear. She had been away for a fortnight now and, after believing that it was only a matter of days before she could collect the children and bring them to London where they could begin a new life, all her hopes were cruelly shattered yet again.

'Tea, is it?' The grinning woman wiped the table and

stared at Molly as she settled herself in an upright chair by the door. It occurred to her that here was a streetwalker, looking to pick up a client. But then she saw how proud were Molly's lovely features, even in spite of her poor, unkempt appearance.

'Yes please . . . and a muffin.' Molly had suddenly felt hungry, which wasn't surprising considering that in order to preserve her meagre savings, she had denied herself food all day. Besides which, she was loath to leave the busy, lamplit streets. A terrible feeling of loneliness had settled on her. For some strange reason, she felt restless and deeply disturbed, filled with a terrible sense of impending doom. The night was sultry, but Molly was cold.

'All right, are you dearie?' asked the woman, setting a mug of steaming tea before her. When Molly nodded and smiled back, she went on, 'We ain't got no muffins left. But if you look along the counter there, you'll see there's all manner o' pies . . . apple tarts and barm-cakes. Now then, you just tell me what takes your fancy, dearie.'

Inching forward in her chair, Molly let her dark eyes rove over the mouth-watering delicacies, her hunger like a sharp pain inside her. Her glance went from the barm-cakes to the apple pie. Then to the newspaper pages that lined the shelf beneath. The headline of a particular report blazed from the page.

CHILDREN ABDUCTED
JUSTICE OF THE PEACE
WANTED FOR QUESTIONING

Ashen-faced, Molly came closer. Her sense of horror was realized when she read:

The distinguished Justice of the Peace, Caleb
Crowther, now retired, is wanted for questioning
by the authorities.

In the early hours of yesterday morning there
was a break-in at the home of Mrs Tilly Watson of
Dock Street, Blackburn, Lancs . . .

At that point the words disappeared beneath the folded
paper. Half-crazed with fear, Molly tore at the shelf,
spilling plates and pastries as she frantically tugged to
loosen the paper. Oblivious to the loud protests and
screams from the woman behind, Molly read on:

Mrs Watson herself was brutally attacked, and a
number of children were forcibly removed from
the premises. No charges have yet been made.

The newspaper was dated some two weeks previous.
'Hey! What the bloody hell d'yer think yer playing
at . . . ! POLICE! HELP! POLICE!' The woman had
been both astonished and terrified at Molly's puzzling
behaviour. When, wide-eyed with shock, Molly pushed
past her to run on to the streets, she yelled and shouted,
threatening to heap all manner of punishment on Molly's
head. But Molly couldn't hear her. All she could think of
was that he had got her children. THE JUSTICE HAD
GOT HER CHILDREN! Dazed and shocked to the
very core, she was aware of only one thing: she had to get
home. She must get home . . . *must* get home!

Having carefully avoided the many horse-drawn carriages that thundered along the busy roads to converge
on Piccadilly Circus, Mick Darcy leaned against a lamp

post, where he drew out his pipe and proceeded to light it. He was foot-sore and exhausted by the many miles he had covered these past weeks.

Mick had searched high and low, delving into every nook and cranny, questioning more people than he could ever hope to remember. But Molly was nowhere to be found. Dear God in Heaven, he thought now, where else am I to look? Even the detective hired by the Tanners had fared no better than himself. But then London was a big place, bustling with people and covering many square miles. All the same, he felt as though he had covered every available inch. Certainly he had followed up on what Tilly had told him, inquiring at all the big hotels. Molly had been to none of them, 'as far as we can recall'.

On the far side of the busy road, the uproar was so loud that it drew Mick's attention. For a moment, he took little notice – there were always people shouting and yelling, competing with the costermongers and fighting amongst themselves. He began to turn away, to bring his mind back to his Molly. But then, as though the image in his mind had suddenly materialized, *there she was*! Her black hair more unkempt than the last time he had seen her, and her figure painfully thin, but it was Molly right enough! His heart leapt inside him. There was something wrong. She was being chased. Molly was in trouble. '*MOLLY!*' His desperate cry cut above the noise. For a split second she half-turned. 'Molly . . . Stay where you are!' he yelled, running forward along the pavement and frantically seeking an opening where he might dash across the road to her.

Afraid that she had not seen him, Mick yelled again and again, 'Molly! Stay there!' Several times he made to run across the road, but was driven back by the many rushing carriages. Suddenly Molly was running in his direction, two men and a woman in pursuit. Mick could not be sure whether or not she had heard him. '*Molly! Molly!*'

When the horse and carriage careered alongside the kerb, the spin of a wheel catching Molly and flinging her across the pavement, Mick was momentarily paralysed. Then he surged forward, her name on his lips and a fervent prayer in his heart. 'Dear God . . . don't let her be dead. *Don't* let her be dead.'

Molly was not dead, although when Mick gathered her into his arms she at first appeared lifeless. After a moment, when he sobbed her name over and over, his warm tears spilling on to her still, white face, she opened her eyes to murmur his name. 'Mick . . . oh, Mick.' Then a look of terror darkened her face as she struggled in his tight embrace. 'My babies! He's *got* my babies!' The tears rolled down her face and her voice broke into sobs.

'No, sweetheart. Your "babies" are safe.' He would have added, 'with Emma . . . their grandmother, your *mother*', but Molly knew nothing of that. Not yet. He gently assured her that they were out of harm's way, and so, thank God, was she. When Molly tearfully confessed how the authorities would hang her and make her children orphans because she had murdered a café owner by the name of Bill Craig, Mick softly laughed. The relief flooded her lovely face when he explained how the man was not 'murdered' because he himself had lately spoken to Bill Craig in the flesh.

'Take me home, please, Mick,' Molly begged, her features contorted with pain and her arms clinging to this man whom she loved so much.

'Oh, Molly . . . my sweet darling,' he murmured, his heart heavy with love. He wanted nothing more in this world than to take his Molly 'home'. To take her and keep her, and love her forever.

Seeing that the young woman would live – and some feeling cheated because of it – the crowd began melting away. Only one man lingered a while longer: a man attired in evening suit and with an air of prosperity about him, a man with brown eyes and a serious look on his attractive face. In the dark, in the background, he remained unobserved, although he was in a position to see both Molly and Mick clearly. For one uncertain moment it seemed that he might make himself known. But then he abruptly turned away and climbed into the waiting carriage.

Now, as he smiled at the redhead waiting there, her slim shoulders wrapped in fur and her long fingers bright with diamonds, the seriousness of the previous moment swiftly left him. 'Drive on!' he urged the man up front.

'*Was* it an accident?' his companion asked, her pink-painted nails stroking the vivid scar down her cheek as was her habit.

Taking hold of her fingers, he put them to his mouth and began playfully biting them. 'Don't worry your pretty head about such things,' he told her with a twinkling grin. 'Just concentrate on me, darling. Because, now that the Justice has gone to his maker, *I* intend to be the only man in your life. And I won't complain if you should blackmail me to your heart's desire!' He laughed aloud. 'So long as it's me *body* you're after . . . and not my money!'

'*That'll* be the day, when you've got money of your own,' she chuckled. 'No wonder they call you Jack-the-Lad.'

The sound of their raucous laughter echoed behind them. There was a moment when his face peered from the back window to see Mick gently raise Molly from the pavement. His arms about her were strong and sure. She clung to him, and they looked so right together.

Turning to his vulgar, teasing companion, Jack kissed her full on her scarlet mouth, his fingers reaching inside her silken blouse. They laughed and drew closer. Suddenly he felt as though a mountain of responsibility had fallen from his shoulders.

Lapsing into a short, troubled silence, he realized that Molly would never willingly give herself up to any man while she believed herself to be wed to another. Suddenly he was filled with guilt. He should have told Molly long ago how their 'marriage' had been a carefully arranged sham. He was not one to be shackled by any woman, even one as captivating as Molly, and he knew she would not sleep with him unless it was with a ring on her finger. He had cheated her. Now, he must right that wrong. Somehow he must get word to her that she was a free woman. No doubt she would curse him for the rogue he was, but he hoped she would forgive him. He believed she would, for Molly was never vindictive. He chuckled aloud.

'What's taken your fancy then?' inquired his companion with a giggle.

'Nothing for you to worry about,' he replied, hugging her tighter. Nothing for either of them to worry about, he mused, wiping his mouth along her neck. He had his woman. Molly had her man. All was right with the world.

Chapter Fifteen

'How can I ever thank you, Miss Nelly?' Cook's round face was squeezed into a most uncomfortable expression as she tried to suppress her tears of joy. 'If you hadn't come forward with such a generous offer . . . well, I daren't think what might have happened to me and Amy.' She glanced at her smaller companion, who was seated demurely beside her on the couch, seemingly overawed by all that had happened. '*Amy!*' Even in her delight, Cook had not lost that air of authority with which she had kept the hapless little maid in check all these years. 'What have you got to say to this kind and benevolent lady who's saved us from the workhouse?' Her frown deepened when she saw Amy look gormlessly about. 'Amy! I asked . . . what have you to *say?*'

'I don't know what to say . . . I really and truly don't.' She raised her eyes and Nelly saw that they were swimming with tears. 'I was so afraid, you understand . . . I never wanted to go in no workhouse!'

Deeply moved, Nelly leaned forward in her chair and patted Amy's trembling hand. 'Don't you worry yourself, my gal!' she declared firmly. 'There ain't nobody gonna put you in no workhouse . . . nor Cook neither. You've got Nelly's word on that.' She pursed her lips into a circle of perfect wrinkles, waiting until Amy had finished loudly blowing her nose in a linen square. 'Right then, you two,' she said smartly, rising from the chair, 'take yersel's off ter Blackpool an' get that there tea-rooms open, while the summer's on us. There'll be many a thirsty tripper just waiting fer such a dandy little place, I'll be bound. What's more . . . you'll happen get a visit from the Tanner family afore long.' A beam of delight spread across her homely face as she went on, '*All* on us! Mr and Mrs Tanner with their daughter Molly and her fella, Mick Darcy. And the chillder o' course. Oh, without a doubt, the darlin' chillder.' She stared at the two women with a look of incredulity. 'Did yer know that them poor chillder ain't never paddled in the sea?' she demanded. 'Oho! We shall soon mend *that*. What! Me an' Emma's looking forward to it like no-body's business.' She clutched her chubby belly and chuckled aloud. 'So, get yersel's off like I said . . . 'cause ye'd best have that there tea-rooms open afore we get there!'

'We'll do our best . . . seeing as it's thanks to you that we've got the opportunity of our own little business.' Cook positively beamed as she, too, got to her feet, indicating for Amy to do the same.

'Well, it ain't no gift, is it, eh?' Nelly reminded her. 'I'll be looking for the monthly payments on the loan, soon as ever yer get the first customer through the door. *And* I'll be expecting a handsome bonus on my share of the takings.' Nelly prided herself on the fact that she had actually put some of her savings into a business venture. Huh! T'weren't only *Emma* as had a good business head, she told herself. She had told Emma the very same, and what more could that darling woman do than agree with her!

'Oh, you won't be sorry, I promise you,' Cook assured

her. 'Me and Amy . . . we'll have the busiest tea-rooms in the whole of Blackpool.'

'I should think so, too!' Nelly was eager to see the women gone now. She had other, more important matters on her mind. 'Go on then. Off yer go.' She stepped towards the door, leaving Cook and Amy with no choice but to follow her.

In the outer vestibule, Cook hesitated, before venturing seriously, 'I hope you don't mind me saying, but I'm so glad that things turned out right for Mrs Tanner, what with finding her daughter and her grandchildren. It fair broke my old heart to see the way she was betrayed.' Her eyes misted over, and she made a strange, coughing sound. 'Emma . . . I mean Mrs Tanner . . . well, she were always a very lovely, amiable girl.'

Suddenly Nelly felt ashamed. 'O' course! *You* knew Emma long afore I did.'

Cook nodded. 'Her father was a good man.' Her voice cracked with anger. 'And to think how he met such a terrible end.'

'There are some things best not talked about,' warned Nelly in a sombre voice.

Cook was at once repentant. 'No, no, of course not. All the same . . .'

'Good day to you.' Nelly began closing the door.

'Good day. And thank you again.'

Long after the two women had disappeared down the lane, Nelly gently propelled herself back and forth in the rocking-chair. Cook's departing words echoed in her troubled mind. What a wicked, wicked fellow the Justice had been. Not content with shooting himself and his unfortunate wife, he had put his hapless daughter Martha through such a devastating experience that she might never recover from it; not even with her son's tender care, nor with her husband on his way from Australia at this very minute. Although to Nelly's mind – and from what Cook herself had been given to understand by hearsay – that particular marriage was long dead and gone. It would be to her son Edward that Martha would turn for strength and comfort. No doubt Silas would return to the arms of his Australian comforter.

What the Justice had confessed to his own daughter were crimes of the most evil and sadistic nature. Into her unwilling ears he had poured out the most vile and corrupt secrets, which he had carried in his black heart these many long years – the illicit love affair with Mary Grady, even while his *own wife* was heavy with child. The fact that he had pressed a pillow into Thadius's face and suffocated the life out of him while the wretched man lay weak and helpless. How he had later abused that same man's trust, and prematurely married Emma off. Then when she was unjustly accused of murder, he had shamelessly blackmailed a fellow Justice in order to engineer Emma's transportation from these shores, so that he could take over her inheritance. An inheritance which had provided him with the means to gamble and keep the company of whores.

From his own lips, Caleb Crowther had proudly related all this to his daughter, actually *boasting* of adultery against her mother, Agnes; treachery, fraud and, most damning of all, the heinous deed of *murder*. Word by word, he had shattered every illusion that his daughter held of him. He also admitted with great relish how he had set Martha against her own husband, Silas. 'You're a dim-witted fool!' he had laughed. There had been so much more that he had told the gullible creature. Things that had cut her to the heart. Awful, soul-destroying things that she would not forget in the whole of her lifetime. Things that she could never bring herself to reveal, not to any living person. And certainly not to Emma. *Especially* not to Emma.

Rocking thoughtfully in her chair, Nelly reflected on Martha's state of mind when she had related the things her father had confessed to her. The ordeal was written in every line of that woman's face, thought Nelly now, as she realized how the dreadful experience appeared to have changed Martha somehow; made her softer and more understanding of others. Oh, but wouldn't it change anybody? First, to be taken hostage by your own father, and trussed up at gunpoint. Then, to be an unwilling and horrified confessor to his many sins. And finally, to witness the murder of her own mother before her disbelieving eyes, before her father turned the gun on his own miserable person.

Nelly visibly shivered. What a monster was Caleb Crowther. *Why*, in the name of all that was decent, could he not have spared his daughter such punishment? Dear God. It didn't bear thinking about. Suddenly Nelly brought the rocking-chair to a halt. *There was something not quite right.* Something with regard to Martha, and the telling of what had taken place in that room. Some furtive and secret look in Martha's brown speckly eyes. Something that had suggested to Nelly at the time that Martha was not revealing the full truth of what had been done, or said, in the final, desperate moments of her parents' lives.

Nelly began her rocking again; slow, methodical movements that seemed to suit her deep, thoughtful mood. 'You were keeping some'at back, Martha, my gal!' she muttered. 'What were it, eh? What could be so fearful that yer chose ter keep it in yer own broken heart? Surely to God . . . it couldn't be more terrible than the things yer disclosed to us all, could it? COULD IT?'

Distressed by her own imaginings, Nelly thrust the puzzling matter of Martha from her mind. Her thoughts flew to other, happier events. Like Marlow's pride and Emma's great joy at having found Molly and her brood. Now they not only had the daughter lost to them many years ago, but they had also been blessed with two adorable granddaughters, and a lovable, rascally grandson, whose crippled leg would receive the very best medical attention that money could buy.

Closing her eyes, Nelly cast her mind back over the long, eventful years, to when she and Emma had first come across each other in that rat-infested prison cell. So many years. So much had happened since that fateful day, when the two of them were little more than children; afraid and friendless, not knowing what the future held, or whether they might never see another day. 'Oh, but we did, didn't we, Emma, gal?' Nelly chuckled. 'We ain't so easy put down, are we, eh?' She blessed the day when she and Emma were flung together, because it had brought her the very best friend any woman could have. Suddenly Nelly's heart was filled with love for that darling woman who had suffered so much in her life, and yet had emerged all the stronger for it. 'Bless yer, Emma,' she said softly, the tears rolling down her lined face, 'bless yer yeart, Emma darling.' She clambered from the chair and went to the sideboard. From here she took out a bottle of gin which she quickly opened and, with her feet doing a little jig, she tipped it to her mouth and gulped down a sizeable measure. Afterwards, returning to the rocking-chair with the bottle clutched to her lap, she closed her eyes and fell into a delightful slumber.

The last impression on Nelly's mind was that of Marlow and the children, who had all been ecstatic when Mick Darcy had returned with Molly that very morning. All six of them had gone to the church to reunite Molly with her mother. Too emotional to be patient, Emma had made her way there as soon as the news had come through that Molly had been found and would shortly be brought home.

The priest gazed on Emma from a discreet place at the back of the church, his face wreathed in smiles as she knelt at the altar, her eyes raised to the crucifix, and her lips murmuring a prayer of heartfelt thanks for her new-found grandchildren, and for Molly's safe return.

Silently the priest moved away, having already given his own prayer of gratitude and being overjoyed at the news that Molly was being returned from London this very morning. It was a miracle that Emma's grand-children were also safely recovered from a derelict warehouse along Bank Top. These were wondrous tidings. As was Emma's return to the Church – which she had so bitterly denounced on the tragic death of her son.

Seeing a group of people approaching, and at once recognizing Marlow, he hurried forward, eager to make the acquaintance of the new additions to the Tanner family.

* * *

Emma sensed that there was someone behind her. Suddenly, even in the heat of a blazing June morning, her every limb was trembling. When at last she was compelled to turn round, her heart almost stopped. '*Molly*,' she whispered, the name warm and loving on her lips. As she gazed at her daughter, the slim figure wrapped in a tattered shawl, her hair so rich and black, and those dark, beseeching eyes intent on her, Emma could not stem her tears. Through a bitter-sweet mist she continued to gaze on this girl, *this young woman*, who was her own flesh and blood – hers and Marlow's. Dear God above!

So many images rampaged through Emma's mind, the strongest and most painful being that of a cobbled street outside a prison. And of a girl-child, newborn and abandoned to the gutter. 'Oh, Molly! Can I really believe you're home with me now?' she cried brokenly. Through her tears, Emma saw that Molly also was crying. Taking a hesitant step forward, she stretched out her arms, unable to speak for the strength of emotion that overwhelmed her. Without a word, Molly fell into her mother's loving embrace. Together, in a silence that bound them like no words could, the two of them went at a gentle pace to where Marlow, Mick and the children had waited, and had witnessed the tender scene with full hearts. There was so much to talk about. So many memories to relive, and so many more to make.

Now, as the children surged forward to take their place with their mammy and their grandmother, Marlow took out his handkerchief and surreptitiously dabbed at his eyes. His voice was shaking as he told Mick, 'I'm a fortunate man, Mick Darcy . . . a very fortunate man.'

'No more than meself,' Mick replied, 'for I have the love of my Molly at long last.'

Emma stole a moment to go to her father's resting-place. Here, she whispered of her love for him, telling him with glad heart, 'It's all over, Papa. We must forget the heartaches now, and learn to live again with hope for the future.' She paused for a moment, remembering the man her father was. He had always been her strength. Her example. 'I love you,' she murmured, momentarily closing her eyes and bathing her mind with fond memories of him. How he would have loved Molly and the children, she thought. And now he could rest in peace because at long last, her life was fulfilled. Over the coming years she would tell his granddaughter and great-grandchildren all about him. Thadius Grady was a special man, a man they could be proud of.

The horse-drawn ensemble travelled slowly down the winding lane that passed the churchyard. From the carriage, Martha saw how proudly Marlow stood beside his grandchildren, and how occasionally he glanced lovingly towards Molly, who was safely enfolded in Mick's strong embrace.

In the foreground was Emma, bent over her father's tombstone, her handsome face so peaceful, so very proud. Fleetingly Emma saw Martha, and her smile was warm and genuine. Emma bore no grudges. She believed that Martha had suffered enough. They had *all* suffered enough.

Martha, too, was of the same mind. She returned Emma's smile, and settled back in the seat beside her son Edward, the awful truth kept hidden in her heart.

What her father had told her must remain her secret forever.

Martha realized with shame how, many years ago, she would have enjoyed inflicting a degree of pain on Emma. But not now. Not after all that had happened. The resentment was all a long time ago – to do with hate and love and passion.

Emma must never be told that Thadius Grady was not her real father. Nor that she was begot from an illicit affair between her mother and Caleb Crowther. Most damning of all, that it was Thadius himself who had murdered Emma's mother in a fit of insane jealousy, when she took a bargee for a lover. The bargee was Bill Royston. This unfortunate fellow had met his sorry end at the hands of Caleb Crowther. Later, both Caleb and Thadius had remained silent when that man's own wife, Eve Royston, was hanged for the murder in which she had played no part.

Thadius Grady and Caleb Crowther were cowards of the worst kind: each bound to protect the other. Emma, Molly and her children, were innocent pawns. Vagabonds on the road of life. Now though, because of hope and love, and the kinder hand of fate, they were vagabonds no more!

The very next evening the house on Park Street rang with laughter. Passers-by smiled knowingly. The story of Emma and Marlow's reunion with their daughter and grandchildren had been told far and wide. It was good that all had come right for Emma Grady. She was a fine woman who had known great heartache. Now it was only right that she should also know great joy.

'I do love you so, Emma.' Marlow had gently drawn

her from the table, where she had been helping Tilly Watson, Nelly and Molly to supervise the children's party. It was a noisy, happy affair. With Molly's three youngsters and Tilly's brood, the exasperated Nelly had earlier been heard to remark loudly, 'By! The whole bleedin' house is shakin' on its foundations!'

'Oh, Marlow, I'm so happy . . . so very happy.' Emma's grey eyes were awash with tears as she lifted her gaze to his.

Taking Emma's hand in his own, Marlow raised it to his lips, brushing it with a kiss and telling her, 'We have our family now, Emma, and so very much to look forward to.'

'Our family,' Emma repeated thoughtfully. She found untold comfort in those words. She pressed into the arm that lovingly encircled her. 'And oh, Marlow . . . aren't they all wonderful?' Emma was smiling now, softly laughing as she looked across to where Sal was causing mayhem by indignantly insisting that the other children should 'take proper turns at the jelly dish.' Nelly was red-faced from trying to keep 'order', and Tilly's brood were all complaining to their mam that 'Sal's being bossy again'.

Laughing aloud, Marlow told Emma, 'Our eldest granddaughter is going to be as cantankerous as her namesake. With my sister Sal . . . *nobody* could ever get a word in edgeways.'

At the far side of the room, Molly was helpless with laughter. In that moment, her dark eyes glanced towards Emma. A well of love rose between them, subduing them for an instant. The two of them had talked deep into the night and on into the dawn. There had been many tears, of both joy and regrets, yet through it all had emerged a bond so strong that nothing would ever weaken it.

'It's a glorious evening, me beauty,' Mick Darcy murmured in Molly's ear.

'That it is, Mick Darcy,' she replied in a teasing manner, her black eyes dancing mischievously. She thought of Jack-the-Lad, and of the hastily scribbled note telling her the two of them were never wed. But it was in the past now. 'I wonder if a certain fella would take a lass for a stroll in the garden?' she asked. She slipped her small hand into his and smiled up at him.

'If you mean *this* certain fella . . . he would follow the lass concerned to the far corners of the earth.' He bent his head to kiss the top of her unruly hair. 'I'd be a proud man to stroll with you in the gardens, sweetheart,' he said softly, 'on this night . . . and on every night for the rest of our lives.'

A moment later, Emma watched Molly and her man go quietly from the room. Her heart was full. The good Lord had answered her prayers.

Now, as Marlow's arm slid round her shoulders, Emma glanced up at him, at those familiar dark eyes that held a lifetime of love. For the rest of her days she would remember this day above all others.

Bad Boy Jack

Josephine Cox

Deserted by the two women in his life, Robert Sullivan is left to raise three-year-old Nancy and her seven-year-old brother Jack. Unable to cope, Robert is driven to abandon his children to those who he believes can provide them with a better life. However, he quickly has a change of heart and decides to go back for them. But on the way there, he is involved in a horrific accident.

Unbeknownst to him, Jack and Nancy are placed in the brutal regime of the Galloway Children's Home, where Jack's fierce devotion to his sister and fiery temper land him in more trouble. Clinging together, the two children find themselves at the mercy of the corrupt Clive Ennington, who splits them up and sells Nancy off to the highest bidder.

When Robert begins to recover in hospital he is determined to find and reunite his family. But he soon begins to realise the terrible consequences of his own cowardly actions.

Praise for Josephine Cox's writing:

'Cox's talent as a storyteller never lets you escape' *Daily Mail*

'Driven and passionate' *The Sunday Times*

Bad Boy Jack is also available in an audio edition.

0 7472 6640 9

headline

Jinnie

Josephine Cox

Jinnie is the child from a one-night liaison between Louise Hunter's husband, Ben, and Louise's sister, Susan. When Ben takes his own life, and Susan deserts her newborn child, Louise puts aside her own heartache and adopts little Jinnie as her own. Louise's solace down the years is little Jinnie, and their close relationship. But what will happen when Jinnie finds out the truth? And then, one day, a letter arrives from Susan, saying she intends to get Jinnie back.

There are others whose lives are badly affected by the tragic events of the past: Adam, who witnessed his mother's murder, and his sister, Hannah, inwardly traumatised by what she too saw that night. And their beloved grandmother, who longs to keep them safe, but knows in her heart that the day will soon come when she must take them back to the place where it all happened. It seems Fate is already taking a hand.

Jinnie is the heart-rending new novel from the number one bestselling author of *The Woman Who Left*; both novels follow the dramatic and compelling fortunes of the Hunter family.

'Cox's talent as a storyteller never lets you escape the spell' *Daily Mail*

'Driven and passionate' *The Sunday Times*

0 7472 6639 5

headline

The Woman Who Left

Josephine Cox

Riddled with guilt, she was far from being sleepy. Because even when he held her as close as any man could hold his woman, her mind was filled with thoughts of another man.

Louise and Ben Hunter have a happy, loving marriage, marred only by their unfulfilled longing for a child. Living and working with Ben's father, Ronnie, they quietly accept their uneventful but contented lives. But when Ronnie dies, their whole world changes.

News of his father's passing brings Ben's lazy brother, Jacob, back on the scene, in the mistaken belief that he stands to inherit Ronnie's small fortune. Added to which he means to have his brother's wife; though just as she did years before, Louise warns him off. Jacob, however, is not so easily dismissed.

When he realises it is Ben who will inherit everything, Jacob is beside himself with rage, and commits a terrible deed, one that threatens to destroy everything his brother and Louise hold dear – their home and their family, their friends, their marriage and even their very lives . . .

Praise for Josephine Cox's writing:

'Cox's talent as a storyteller never lets you escape the spell' *Daily Mail*

'Impossible to resist' *Woman's Realm*

'Driven and passionate' *The Sunday Times*

0 7472 6634 4

headline

Now you can buy any of these other bestselling books by **Josephine Cox** from your bookshop or *direct from the publisher*.

FREE P&P AND UK DELIVERY
(Overseas and Ireland £3.50 per book)

Bad Boy Jack	£6.99
Jinnie	£6.99
The Woman Who Left	£5.99
Let it Shine	£5.99
Looking Back	£5.99
Rainbow Days	£5.99
Somewhere, Someday	£5.99
The Gilded Cage	£5.99
Tomorrow the World	£6.99
Love Me or Leave Me	£6.99
Miss You Forever	£6.99
Cradle of Thorns	£6.99
A Time for Us	£6.99
The Devil You Know	£6.99
Living a Lie	£6.99
A Little Badness	£6.99
More Than Riches	£6.99
Born to Serve	£6.99

TO ORDER SIMPLY CALL THIS NUMBER

01235 400 414

or visit our website: www.madaboutbooks.com

Prices and availability subject to change without notice.